MICKEY ZUCKER REICHERT

THE BOOKS OF BARAKHAI

The Beasts Of Barakhai

The Lost Dragons Of Barakhai

DAW BOOKS, INC.

DONALD A. WOLLHEIM, FOUNDER

375 Hudson Street, New York, NY 10014

ELIZABETH R. WOLLHEIM
SHEILA E. GILBERT
PUBLISHERS

http://www.dawbooks.com

DAW TRADEMARK REGISTERED
U.S. PAT. AND TM. OFF. AND FOREIGN COUNTRIES
—MARCA REGISTRADA
HECHO EN U.S.A.

PRINTED IN THE U.S.A.

The Beasts
Of Barakhai

To Mikey Gilbert:

You told us you were sick,
and some of us never took
you seriously enough—
but, damn it, did you have to prove it?

Every moment of every day, you are sorely missed.

Acknowledgments

I would like to thank the following people:
Mark Moore, Jackie Moore, Koby Moore, Sheila Gilbert,
Jonathan Matson, Jo Fletcher, Sandra Zucker, Jennifer
Wingert, the PenDragons, my billion or so science
professors, and Picasso (who made endless hours of lonely
keyboard-time more interesting).

Chapter 1

RACKS of plastic hutches lined the walls of the biology laboratory at Algary campus, each with a test-tube water bottle jutting from its mesh screen lid. Surrounded by wood-topped metal stools, six fused desks/cabinets filled the center of the room, a chaotic jumble of notepads, pens, pipettes, and goggles cluttering their faux wood surfaces. Stomach growling, Benton Collins ladled fresh wood chips into the pan of an empty cage while its usual occupant, a fat white rat, nosed at the corners of the cardboard box that temporarily held it.

The odor of the cleaner churned Collins' hunger into nausea. He flung strands of dark brown hair from his eyes with a gloved hand, smearing wet food mush across his forehead, then immediately berated himself with sarcasm for the habitual gesture. *Smart move. Good thing I wore gloves to protect me from this slop.*

As the sweet aroma of cedar replaced the chemical smells, Collins' gut rumbled again. He had skipped breakfast and lunch, the expectation of a Thanksgiving feast holding hunger at bay. He had promised his girlfriend to do whatever he could to make it to her family's home by 2:00 P.M., to meet her parents for the first time. Collins doubted his skinny, bespectacled self would make much of an impression on an old-money family like the Johnsons, especially reeking of rat and with green-gray smudges of food stick goo across his face. He glanced at his watch. *3:30 P.M.*

And he still had an entire row of cages to clean, as well as Professor Demarkietto's notes to review, before he could call it a day. The drive alone would take an hour.

Feeling more like a punching bag than a graduate student, Collins filled the water bottle, placed a few fresh sticks of food in the cage, then hefted the cardboard box. He poured the rat back into its cage. It scuttled about, hurling chips, then hunkered down with a food stick clenched between its front paws. Collins clipped the lid back in place and replaced the cage on its rack. He peeled off the gloves with a snap of latex and tossed them into the trash can. Using a damp paper towel only little finer than sandpaper, he scrubbed the grime from his forehead, then washed his hands and drank from his cupped palms. The water sat like lead in his otherwise empty belly. After drying his face and hands, he wadded the paper towels together and launched them, like a basketball, into the can.

Only then, did Collins take a deep breath, close his eyes, and reach for the telephone. Fumbling through the papers for his own organizer, he opened his eyes and leafed to the last page for the home number of Marlys Johnson's parents. He punched it in.

Marlys answered on the first ring. "Hello?" Her tone hardened. "Benton, that better be you."

Seized with a sudden urge to hang up without speaking, Collins forced a laugh. "If I'd been Publishers' Clearinghouse, wouldn't you have felt dumb?"

Dead silence.

Collins cringed. He pictured her: long red hair permed and styled for the holiday, the green eyes that could as easily scald as melt him, the slender legs that seemed to climb to her small-breasted chest. In his mind's eye, he imagined a glare that would send tougher men skittering for cover.

The distant sound of laughter wafted across the receiver, followed by song. The background noise brought Collins back to his childhood, when his parents lived together and his Uncle Harry and Aunt Meg spent every Thanksgiving with them. Harry loved to tell jokes but butchered the punchlines. Meg would try to correct them, laughing so hard that she usually only succeeded in making them hopelessly obtuse. The interaction between the husband and wife always seemed so much funnier than the joke, even correctly told. Collins had spent last Thanksgiving with his mother and her new boyfriend, a paunchy, socially inept engineer with three visiting children he could not control. This year, the two were spending Thanksgiving in Vegas on their honeymoon. Collins' father was touring Europe with his quirky girlfriend, Aviva. Harry and Meg had not invited him.

"You'd better be calling from a cell phone." Marlys' frigid voice jarred Collins back to the present.

Collins sighed, hands sliding instinctively to the cell phone, pager, and multitool at his belt. "I'm still at the lab."

"Why?" Her tone implied no explanation short of nuclear catastrophe would suffice.

Collins knew better, but he could not resist another joke. "The rats invited me for dinner. I couldn't resist . . . food sticks."

"That's not funny."

"I'm sorry."

"Am I a joke to you?"

"Of course not." Collins rolled his eyes to the whitewashed ceiling, wishing he had not attempted humor. "I'd be there if I could, Marlys. You know that. But the power system's been touch and go with all the grain harvests. Lab loses electricity long enough, crash go some of the experiments. Including Dundee's two-million-dollar grant."

"You're not working for Dundee," Marlys reminded. "Why can't her grad student handle it?"

Collins sat on one of the stools, propping his sneaker-clad feet on another. "Marly, come on. You know Dave's parents live in Florida."

"Don't call me Marly—"

"Once they all found out my family wasn't available for the holiday—"

"It's Mar*lys*, Benton, not Marly. And why do you let people take advantage of you?"

Collins gave the expected reply, though he had tired of it. "Just call me Ben. And it's not a matter of taking advantage. It's—"

"Demarkietto's a slave driver."

Though true, it was not what Collins had been about to say. "Well, yes, but—"

"Why don't you just tell him to go fuck himself?"

"Marlys!" Collins had never heard her use that word before.

"You have a right to a holiday, too."

Collins hated to remind Marlys of his shortcomings, especially when she had her mother to disparage him. "A lot of candidates applied for lab positions this year. I was lucky to get one."

Marlys refused to concede. "No, Demarkietto's the lucky one. Lucky he could get *any* grad assistant after Carrie Quinton."

Collins had also heard the rumors, that the beautiful postdoctoral genetics student had disappeared without a trace in an effort to escape Professor Demarkietto's demands. "I need the money, Marlys. I'm already three payments behind on student loans. And I need the recommendation. Whatever you or Carrie Quinton thinks of ol' D-Mark, he's well-respected in the scientific community."

Something white caught the edge of Collins' vision.

"Benton, my parents are starting to think you're unreliable."

Distracted, Collins returned to wit. "So is student loan services."

"Benton!"

A white rat scurried from behind the desks, scrambling through the gap in the partially opened door.

"Damn it!"

"Benton! Did you just swear at me?"

"Big problem." Wondering whose ten-year, million-dollar experiment he had just ruined, Collins said, "I'll call you back." Without waiting for a reply, he started to replace the receiver.

Marlys' small voice chased him. "Don't you dare—" Then the earpiece clicked down, cutting off whatever threat Marlys had uttered. Uncertain whether or not he would ever see his girlfriend again, Collins bashed the door open with his shoulder.

The panel shot wide, and the impact bruised his arm even through his emerald-green Algary sweatshirt. Collins caught sight of the rat squeezing beneath the door of one of the unused classrooms provided by grant money. He had once overheard some of the professors discussing the perks of earning such a room, then using it for storage, a badge of honor for bringing in a large endowment. Collins groaned, doubting he could find the escapee amid years of a scientist's accumulated crap.

For a moment, Collins froze, paralyzed by despair. If an experimental animal came up missing on his watch, he would lose his job for certain; and those who graded him might no longer feel so kindly disposed. His thesis might become less valuable than the paper on which he printed it. He would never get a job. His student loans would plunge him into poverty. He had lost his parents to the pursuit of their own happiness, and he had no siblings with whom to commiserate. He had probably just lost his girlfriend; worse, he was not sure he even cared. Suddenly, the idea of becoming a second Carrie Quinton, of disappearing without a trace, seemed the best of all his lousy options.

Collins shook his head, tossing hair the color of bittersweet chocolate; it had gone too long since its last cutting. Driven only by a deeply rooted sense of responsibility, he pulled open the door. Light funneled in from a dusty window that made the room seem full of smoke. Mathematical equations, complicated and incomprehensible, scrawled white across a blackboard. Piled boxes, desks, and chairs crafted strange shadows across the tiled floor. On an open stretch, someone had sketched out a pentagram in purple chalk. A chill spiraled through Collins, and the urge to flee gripped him like ice. He calmed himself with logic. Roleplaying gamers abounded on Algary campus, and they often sought out hidden rooms and alcoves for atmosphere. In his college days, he had played some *Dungeons and Dragons* on the roof of Domm Hall.

Collins flicked the light switch. It clicked, but nothing changed. The bulb had, apparently, burned out. He debated leaving the door open to channel in a bit more light, but it seemed prudent to block the only exit. *Rat in a dark storage room. Kind of makes the old needle in a haystack seem like simple hide-and-seek.* He closed the door, pulled his sweatshirt off over his head, and stuffed it under the crack. Satisfied the rat could not squeeze out, he sat on the cold floor, half-naked. *What now? A radioactive, rabid cockroach bites off my three chest hairs?* He glanced around for a cup or empty box to hold the creature until he could transfer it to its cage but found nothing suitable. Accustomed to handling, the rat would likely prove tractable enough to carry in his hands.

Hunger churned through Collins' gut again. Even the rubbery turkey slices Algary's cafeteria served up on holidays seemed like a treat, garnished with ketchup from a can as big as his torso. They would serve it up with some weirdly spiced institutional stuffing, a canned blob of cranberries, and something that vaguely resembled cheese. The denouement: cardboard pie colored some fruity color, as vivid and unrealistic as Froot Loops. The whole situation suddenly seemed hysterically funny. Shaking his head, he laughed until his ribs ached.

A flash of white ran right past Collins' left sneaker.

"Hey!" Instantly sobered, Collins leaped to his feet and gave chase. The rat skittered between a row of boxes and disappeared beneath a pile of desks. "Hey," he repeated, diving after the retreating tail.

Collins slammed against stacked cartons; they exploded into a wild avalanche. Not bothering to assess the damage, he kept his gaze locked on the rat. His foot came down on something hard, and his ankle twisted. Pain consumed his leg. Afraid to lose the rat, he bulled through it, plunging into the darkness beyond the stack of desks.

The world went suddenly black. Collins blinked several times, seeking a bare trickle of light leaching between boxes or around the irregular shapes that defined the desks. Worried about losing his target, he continued forward blindly, sweeping the space ahead with his hands to protect his head. An occasional squeak or blur of white movement kept him going far longer than seemed possible in such a small room. He got the distinct impression he was chasing his own tail instead of the rat's, caught in a wild spiral of madness constructed from nothing more substantial than stress. Focusing on this current problem kept him from dwelling on the anger his parents aroused, the advantage his preceptor had taken of a miserable situation, his inability to appease the one person he professed to love. His world narrowed to the excitement of the chase.

At length, Benton Collins realized that the passage of time had become more than just a perception. His stomach gnawed at its own lining; dinnertime surely had come and gone. His memory of the telephone call seemed distant, indistinct. His back ached from stooping and his knees from crawling. He reached above his head, his groping fingers meeting nothing of substance. Cautiously, he rose and discovered he could stand without having to stoop. The room remained utterly black.

Collins glanced at his left wrist. The hands of his watch glowed eerily in the darkness: *7:18*. Shocked, he studied the arrangement of hands and hash marks. He could not believe he had been slithering around after a rat for over three hours. The thought seemed lunacy. If true, he should have crashed into a wall or door, should have stumbled over boxes, should have caught glimpses of light through the window. But his world remained dark, and he felt none of the stored items he had seen before while scurrying beneath the desks. *I'm not in the same room. Can't be.*

Vision straining, Collins took careful steps forward, waving his arms in front of him to head off a collision. At length, the fingers of his left hand scraped an irregular wall. He pawed along it for a light switch, feeling damp and craggy stone. *What the hell?* He shook his head, scarcely daring to believe it. *I'm lost in some dark, secret corner of Daubert Labs. But how did I get here?* He sucked in a calming breath, then let it out slowly through his nose. *Must have accidentally crawled through a vent or tunnel or something. No wonder the gamers like it here.*

A sharp squeak startled Collins from his thoughts. He glanced around for the creature, more from habit than true interest anymore. His heart pounded, and a shiver racked him. Rationally, he knew he could not remain lost in a campus building for longer than the four-day holiday, yet disorientation pressed him toward panic. Suddenly, his location seemed the most important piece of information in the world.

Pressing both hands to the wall, Collins chose a direction and followed it to a corner. At some point, he reasoned, he would have to find a door into a hallway. From there, he would surely come upon a part of the laboratory he knew.

A lump formed in Collins' throat. His heart hammered against his ribs, and his thoughts refused to coalesce. His elbow grazed something hard at his belt, and this finally triggered coherent thought. *Pager. Got my cell phone, too.*

And other stuff. He fingered the odd assortment of objects in his pockets, identifying keys, calculator, and the lighter he used for bunsen burners and alcohol lamps before ending the silly game. Relief triggered a nervous laugh. *What's wrong with me?* He tugged the phone from its plastic holder, lengthened the antennae, and pressed the lower left button. It came on with a beep, the display revealing the word "on." The indicator showed no signal strength whatsoever. *Weird. Charged it last night.* Collins lowered the phone with a shrug of resignation. *Who would I call anyway?* He considered the situation. *Hello, Dr. Demarkietto? I took a wrong turn, and I'm lost in the lab. Please send Lewis and Clark.* He jabbed the phone back into its holder. His ego preferred no one ever found out about his little adventure.

Collins continued his march along the wall, surprised by its irregularity, as well as his steady footing. He kept expecting to stumble over cartons or furniture, but he continued to walk unimpeded. Then, finally, he discovered a depression in the wall, its surface more like poorly sanded wood than stone. He groped for a doorknob but found none. Confused, he shoved it. To his surprise, it budged. Encouraged, he threw all of his weight against it. The wood panel gave beneath the effort, the hinges twisted free, and it collapsed forward. Momentum dragged Collins along with it.

Collins hit the floor before he realized he was falling, his face slamming into the door. Pain jarred through his nose and chest, and his glasses tumbled. He rolled onto wet mulch that clung to his bare torso and realized he could see now, though blurrily. He lay in a crudely constructed room with a large, paneless window. He fished around for his glasses; his hand came up empty. He saw dust, shattered stone, and moss but no sign of his glasses. Drawn to the window, he abandoned his search to look through it, out onto a plain filled with smeary weeds and wild-flowers beneath sky the color of slate. Beyond it lay the shadow of a vast forest. Stunned more by the sight than the fall, Collins spoke aloud. "Where am I?" It looked like nowhere he remembered on Algary campus. Panic returning, he shouted. "Where the living hell am I?"

No answer came. Collins turned and drifted toward the fallen door. His gaze played over an uneven dirt floor, the piled dust displaying his every movement in bold relief: the starburst pattern from the gusts generated by the falling door, every treaded footprint, but no glasses. Collins dropped to all fours, searching diligently around and beneath the fallen door. He found only mud, stone, and moss. Hunger snaked through his gut with a long, loud growl. *Great. What else can go wrong?*

Collins abandoned his glasses for the more driving need for food. He could never remember feeling so unremittingly, miserably starved. He knew he should turn around, should attempt to retrace his steps; but the thought of wandering aimlessly in silent darkness for another three hours or longer, weathering the growing agony in his gut, seemed impossible beyond reckoning. He studied the room. Four stone-and-mortar walls rimed with moss enclosed him, the only exits the doorway into darkness and the window. He cast one last look around for his glasses, but they had disappeared as completely as the familiar rooms and hallways of Daubert Laboratories.

Collins dropped to his buttocks, stunned. Nothing made sense. In a matter of three dark hours, the world had changed in a way no logic could explain. He felt desperately confused, unable to find so much as a thread of logic despite his science background. Either he had plunged into madness or he had clambered into a parallel dimension, much like Dorothy and her Oz. *Only,* Collins reminded himself, *that was fiction.* In the real world, people did not follow white rabbits down holes to Wonderland. Or, in his case, white lab rats.

Only one thing seemed wholly, unutterably certain: he was hungry. Perhaps if he satisfied that single, desperate need, everything else would fall into some sort of proper, or even improper, order.

In a daze, Collins swung his legs over the window ledge and jumped. He regretted the action immediately. Without his glasses, his depth perception had failed him; and he found himself airborne, surging toward the slope of a massive hill that supported the decaying structure. He hit the ground, right shoulder leading. His teeth snapped shut, pinching his tongue, and he tasted blood. A hot bolt of lightning burst through his head. Pain lurched through his arm and chest. Then, the world swirled around him in alternating patterns of green and silver as he spilled in savage circles down the side of the hill.

Pollen tickled Collins' nostrils. Stems crackled beneath him, stabbing his naked chest, sides, and back. The odor of broken greenery joined the mingled perfumes of the flowers. He wrapped his face in his palms and let gravity take him where it would, sneezing, wincing, and huffling as he went. At last, he glided to a gentle stop. Weeds and wildflowers filled his vision, and his head spun, still several cycles behind his body.

Collins lay on his back. An edge of sun peeked over a horizon he could only assume was the east, throwing broad bands of pink and baby blue through the gray plain of sky. Pale-petaled flowers swayed, intermittently blocking his vision, interspersed with woody stems that he hoped would prove edible and harmless. *Sunrise.* He blinked, the scene senseless. *I couldn't have crawled around that long.*

An interminable, aching groan issued from his stomach.

Collins sat up. *Now what?* He studied the building he had abandoned on the hill, a crumbling ruin of a stone fortress that defied modern construction. If it connected to Algary campus in any fashion, he could not see how. Later, he would explore it for some underground tunnel or well-hidden passage. Food had to come first.

Movement rattled the grasses.

Collins held his breath. He had not gone camping since Boy Scouts, and the image of Jimmy Tarses dumping a copperhead out of his boot remained vivid. No one had teased Jimmy for his high-pitched screams. The rest of them had been equally startled; from that time on, no boy put on any gear without checking it thoroughly first. Now, Collins' skin prickled at the thought. His heart resumed its wild pounding, and he rose cautiously. For all he knew, rattlesnakes might be cavorting all around him.

The rustling recurred, closer.

Collins watched a column of weeds dance, then stop. Hand dropping to the multitool he always kept on his belt, he forced himself to step toward it.

At that moment, the thing sat up on its haunches, peering at him through the grasses. Its nose twitched, its ears rose above the wildflowers, and it examined Collins through enormous black eyes. Collins took one more step, squinting, and finally got a good look at a fat, brown rabbit. It seemed remarkably unafraid, studying him, whiskered nose bobbing.

Never seen a human before? Collins guessed. *Or maybe someone's pet?* He cringed. If he caught the thing, he would have to eat it. If he ever found an owner, he would apologize and replace it; but he had no way of knowing when, or if, his next meal would come. Until he found Algary campus, he would have to make do.

"Here, bunny, bunny." Collins kept his motions fluid and nonthreatening. He held out a hand to it.

The rabbit remained still a moment longer, head cocked. Then, it dropped to all fours and stretched its nose toward Collins' hand.

Collins held totally still, allowing the animal to sniff at his fingers.

The rabbit glided toward him, outstretched front legs followed by a more solid hop of the back ones.

Prepared for it to scratch frantically or bite, Collins reached out and hauled the animal into his arms. Recalling kittens from his childhood, he scooped one arm under its legs, pinning its clawed feet, and used the other to clamp it against him. "Gotcha." The fur felt thick and soft against his chest.

The rabbit made small noises in its throat. Its coat mingled brown-and-gray agouti-striped hair in tufts.

Okay, Alice. You've caught the rabbit. Collins looked at the animal, hating himself for what had to come next. He wished he could keep it as a companion in this bizarre and, thus far, lonely world. *What happens now? The Queen of Hearts shrieks, "Off with his head?"* Though it seemed madness, he spoke to the creature. "You're not one of those magical talking animals, are you?"

The rabbit seemed to take no notice of Collins. It lay in his arms, surprisingly dense, its nose continuously wobbling.

"Because, if you are, you'd better tell me now." Collins carefully shifted the rabbit's weight to free his right hand. Opening the clasp on the belt case of his multitool, he unsnapped it and pulled out the tool. He worked free the knife blade, then looked at the rabbit again. "No? Sorry, bunny. It's over." The words came easier than the deed. Collins hesitated, cringing. He had pithed rats and frogs before, but the idea of slaughtering someone's sweet-tempered pet seemed an evil beyond his tolerance.

Collins closed his eyes. The pain in his gut intensified, an aching exhortation. Opening his eyes to slits, he pressed the blade against the top of its head, just behind the ears. In one swift motion, he drove the point deep into its brain.

The rabbit squealed, a high, haunting call that sent a stab of dread through Collins. Then, it went limp in his arms.

Collins shivered; the lingering horror of the noise weighed heavily on his conscience. He set the rabbit on the ground, his knife beside it. Never having hunted, he did not know the proper way to skin and gut; but he believed his anatomy classes would help. *First, a fire.* Collins pulled up a circle of grass and flowers, picked the driest for kindling, and walked in widening circles in search of twigs. At length, he gathered a handy pile and started the fire with his lighter.

Settling by the glow and crackle of the flames, Collins drew rabbit and knife into his lap and started skinning.

Chapter 2

BENTON Collins had heard rabbit meat described as tough, greaseless, and stringy; but experience clashed pleasantly with the report. He savored its rich, gamy flavor and streaming juices that sizzled in the fire. Succulent as a steak, it satisfied his empty stomach. He had teased out the organs carefully, yet guiltily suspected he had wasted quite a bit of edible meat with the skin. In the future, he hoped he would learn to rescue every scrap; his life, as well as more rabbits', might depend on it. He prepared to sink his teeth into the last leg.

A horse whinnied, sharp and sudden as a whipcrack.

Collins sprang to his feet, whirling toward the sound. Distant figures emerged patternlessly from the forest. He squinted, managing to make out a single, light-colored horse, its rider, and three or four milling people. His spirits soared. "Hey!" he shouted, waving the drumstick. "Over here!"

Their movement stopped. Without his glasses, Collins could not tell if they turned toward him.

"Here!" Collins called louder, waving the remainder of his food frantically. "Over here." *Human contact, thank God. I'm saved.* He realized his story would sound positively ludicrous, unless others had come to this place through Daubert Laboratories before him. Perhaps some of the gamers did so regularly. Even if no one had, he doubted he would sound insane enough for them to have him institutionalized.

Assuming, of course, this parallel dimension is even at the same tech level as ours.

Two dogs shot ahead of the people, barking wildly. They bounded into the weeds, leaping like porpoises through the tall grasses toward Collins.

Collins laughed as they approached, the horse cantering after them. A thought struck with chilling abruptness. *What if they're hostile? What if they're members of some primitive warrior tribe that hates everyone?* He discovered eerie parallels in his undergraduate history and sociology classes. People tended to fear differences, to revile what they did not understand. *Oh, come on, Ben. There's no such thing as other worlds. This is twenty-first-century America, for Christ's sake. What's wrong with me?*

Copper highlights glimmered from the horse's sleek golden coat, and its black mane and tail trailed it like streamers. Its rider appeared broad and well-muscled, apparently male, wearing what looked like a thigh-length rust-colored long-sleeved T-shirt with matching bicycle pants and leather riding boots.

The dogs arrived first, sneezing and waggling their tails, snuffling every part of Collins. One resembled a beagle, medium-sized and tricolored. The other towered over its companion, uniform brown except for black on its muzzle. Its ears stuck up in sharp triangles, and its tail curved over its back in a broad, stiff loop. Collins smiled at them, alternately petting each. He offered the last of his dinner to the beagle.

Delicately, the dog sniffed at the meat, whined softly, and retreated. Surprised, Collins held the drumstick out to the other dog. He had never met a large dog that did not gobble down proffered meat in an instant; yet this one also refused, pacing backward and forward nervously. It appeared to Collins as if it wanted the food but dared not take it. Realization seeped slowly into his thoughts. *Probably trained to only accept treats from their trainer.*

The horse skidded to a stop at his makeshift camp, trampling grasses and flowers beneath prancing hooves. Now, Collins could see the crude stitching and deep staining of the man's clothing and the deep saffron of his cuffs and collar. Widely spaced brown eyes studied Collins from coarse, weathered features, and he bore a headful of tangled sandy curls. He reeked of sweat. A sheathed sword dangled from his left hip. The fine-boned mare rolled a blue eye that contrasted strikingly with its buckskin coat and wind-whipped mane and tail. It bore no saddle and only a rope for a bridle, yet it clearly obeyed its rider.

Collins could not help staring back. He could no longer doubt that he had transported through time or discovered a world with no connection to his own. Seeking saliva in a mouth gone painfully dry, Collins broke the silence with a compliment. "Well trained dogs you got there. Wouldn't take fresh meat from a stranger." He brandished the rabbit leg.

The rider leaned forward, gaze sweeping the crafted clearing. Suddenly, he jerked back. He shouted something indecipherable to his slower-moving friends, who quickened their paces.

Collins glanced to his right, trying to figure out what had provoked his new companion. He saw only crushed and broken weeds, his multitool, and the remains of the rabbit. *The multitool,* he guessed. *Probably never seen anything like it.* He continued speaking, trying to radiate trust. "Well trained horse, too. Don't know many people who could ride without—"

Collins broke off as the other four people caught up, panting, with the leader. Though dressed the same, including the swords, they otherwise seemed as different as possible. Two were blonds, both male, one fair and the other dark as cola. One of the brunets was a pale and lanky man with a Roman nose, the other a sinewy, brown-skinned woman with her hair tied in a rough bun. Collins loosed a pent-up breath. At least, they seemed unlikely to comprise a homogeneous group that would hate him simply for his appearance. "Hello," he said.

The people ignored his greeting. The one Collins assumed was the leader dismounted. He and the ample-nosed brunet stood on either side of Collins, examining him intently. The blonds approached the remains of his dinner. A sword rasped from its sheath.

Collins recoiled; but its wielder, the darkest man, kept his back to Collins and the others. He shuffled through the bones, skin, and organs, speaking rapidly in a language Collins could not identify. It sounded like nothing he had ever heard before, even from the international graduate students who shared his campus apartment building.

Abruptly, all of the humans spun toward Collins. Several started speaking at once, their tones frenzied and their gestures savage. The horse's eyes rolled white, and it danced sideways.

The sandy-haired leader stabbed the air with his hand and spoke over the others. Silence followed, but the glare on every face seemed unmistakable.

Collins back-stepped warily, abruptly terrified. His eyes jerked wide, his nostrils flared, and his heart rate doubled in an instant. Drained of thought, he whirled to run and nearly impaled himself on the woman's sword. He stopped short. The metallic rasp of drawing weapons echoed through the clearing. He froze. Then, slowly, he raised his hands in an innocent gesture of surrender. "I mean you no harm. Friend." He hooked a finger toward his naked chest. "Ben. My name is Ben. Ben."

Collins felt motion at his flank. He spun. Something heavy crashed against the side of his head. Pain shocked through his skull with an explosion of white light. The impact flung him to the ground. He ducked behind his hands, protecting his aching head. Five swords leveled at his vitals held him in place.

The leader gave a command.

The lighter blond sheathed his sword. He shouldered off his backpack and rooted inside it. A moment later, he pulled out a braided mass of rope, which he carried to Collins.

Collins bit his lip but otherwise remained perfectly still. His head felt on fire, and he did not know what might antagonize them to finish him off.

The sandy-haired giant motioned at Collins and said something uninterpretable.

Collins shrank further against the ground, head pounding. "I–I don't know what you're saying," he squeaked.

The brunet man exchanged a few words with the leader. Then, he hooked a boot beneath Collins' shoulder and flipped him prone.

Collins did not fight the motion, though it sparked flashes of light through his brain. Behind him, someone seized his hands and roped them together. As the knots tightened, they bit into his wrists. The blonds rifled his pockets, removing everything: loose change, calculator, keys, mechanical pencil, lighter, notes, wallet, the remote keyless entry to Marlys' car. They unfastened his belt, taking it along with his pager and cellular phone. They added his watch and the multitool to their haul. Craning his neck, Collins peered around the nearest of the strangers to watch others scoop the remains of his meal into a sack. Another stomped out his fire. When it seemed every trace of Collins' presence had disappeared into one sack or another, the four men seized him by the arms and knees, hefting him awkwardly onto the horse.

Collins did not fight, recalling the words of his neuroanatomy professor: "In movies, you see heroes bashing guys in the head all the time to knock them out. Truth is, the difference between causing a brain bruise and a deadly hemorrhage is incalculable. Guy goes out longer than a minute or two, it's a murder charge for the hero." If he could help it, Collins would not give these strangers another reason to strike him.

The horse snorted, humping its back. At a warning from the commander, it settled back on its hooves, prancing nervously sideways. The leader spoke soothingly to it, stroking its nose. The mare calmed, docilely allowing them to tie the sacks in place behind Collins. Two people on each side, the sandy-haired man leading the mare, they headed toward the forest.

Every step of the horse jarred through Collins' spine, and he suspected the animal deliberately made the ride as bumpy as possible. It stumbled over invisible stones, losing the delicate grace that had previously characterized its movements. The rope shifted with his slightest motion, grinding into his flesh until he worried it might sever his wrists.

Soon, the forest swallowed the group. Collins found himself in a shade as cozy as an early spring day. Most of the trees closely resembled those he knew: maple, oak, and locust. Others he did not recognize, including one with starshaped emerald leaves so bright they seemed like polished holographs. His escorts spoke rarely to one another, though he caught them staring at him with evident hostility on occasion. He wondered what about him bothered them so much and, given their wildly different appearances, how they even knew he did not belong among them. The answer came almost immediately. *Duh, genius. Perhaps my complete inability to communicate with them?*

The self-deprecation did little to elevate Collins' spirits. His mind drifted to his telephone call with Marlys. In his current situation, the whole thing seemed foolish. *When I get back, I'll take all the blame. Buy her flowers. Treat her like a queen. She'll forgive me.* The words "if I get back" interspersed themselves into the thought, quite against his will. Apologizing for something not his fault seemed trivial compared to the possibility that these men and woman might be hauling him to eternal imprisonment or death.

Not death, Collins tried to assure himself. *They could have killed me easily enough in the field.* He felt like a suspect whose life now lay in the hands of lawyers and judges. During his first year of college, he had dabbled in radical liberalism. He still recalled trying to convince his father of the "truth" of the prison system. He pictured James Collins in his favorite La-Z-Boy, setting down his newspaper to debate with his son. Gray-flecked, army-short black hair receded from his freckled forehead, and he carried about twenty-five extra pounds, all of it in his gut.

"Prison just hardens criminals, makes them better and crueler criminals."

James had grunted at that. "Not our job to soften em, Ben. In prison, at least they're not hurting anyone innocent."

Collins had hardly dared to believe his father could not understand at all. Until his teens, he had always looked up to this man. "But when they get out, Dad, they're worse."

James had given his son a deeply searching look. "Worse than if we let 'em get away with their crimes?" He opened the newspaper again. "I don't think so." He lowered the paper to his knees. "Or are you suggesting executing them all as the alternative?"

The words had shocked Collins. "Dad, the death penalty's barbaric. You know that. And it's not a deterrent."

James had raised the paper again, turning the page with a loud rustle. "It's the ultimate deterrent."

"No." Collins had delved eagerly into the argument. This time, he had clear facts on his side. "No, Dad. It's not. The studies show—"

James' voice became muffled by the newspaper. "I don't need studies to tell me that once a guy's dead he can't hurt anyone any longer. Nothing more deterring than that."

At the time, Collins had given his father up as a lost cause who might never see the light. Now, with his stomach skittishly churning the rabbit meat, his thoughts flying in strange directions, his wrists and back aching, he realized he had discovered that terrifying limbo that precedes a fate wholly determined by strangers. The loss of control alone felt like torture. He could not speak for others, but the terrified wonder would deter him from ever committing a crime. If he ever had the chance.

Again, Collins attempted to steer his thoughts from the depressing possibilities. He concentrated on the scenery. They traveled a dirt path through towering trees whose shade and shed leaves discouraged undergrowth. The branches held vast bounties of leaves in myriad variations of green. Though not as colorful as the bursts of amber, scarlet, and orange that had characterized the autumn foliage in Algary a scant month before, it seemed even more beautiful. The plants seemed to glow with health and, despite mud and dust, looked remarkably clean. The sun streamed through gaps in the highest branches, lending a shimmering glow to the star-shaped leaves and dancing tiny rainbows through clinging droplets of water. In other circumstances, Collins would have enjoyed stretching out beneath the canopy, reveling in birdsong, gaze filled with nature's radiance. Now, distracted by the agonies jolting through his spine and threatening to dismember his hands, and by the uncertainty of whether or not he even had a future, he could only look in mute alarm. He wondered how much more beautiful it might appear with his glasses.

It occurred to Collins suddenly that he should have etched the route they had thus far taken into his memory. If they released him, or he managed to escape, he would have to find his way back to this place. In fact, he would need to keep his wits about him from this point on if he hoped to survive this world intact. *If it's not already too late.* He shook that thought aside. It could only lead to hopeless despair.

The idea proved easier to concoct than to implement. The pathways branched and looped, and Collins lost track of turns that came naturally to his captors. The intensity of his headache muddled his thinking; twice, he found himself drifting into a strange, conscious oblivion. The other pains remained a constant, intermittently overwhelming diversion.

Then, just as Collins began to believe he'd been captured by nomads, the forest opened to pastures and fields. A low wall of corn blocked their way, and the people led the horse around its squared edge. As they rounded the corner, he saw a vast green pasture grazed by several goats, horses, and pigs. Younglings frolicked around them, the different animals intermingling freely in their games. A cow stood by itself, chewing its cud, its round abdomen looking ready to pop out a calf at any moment. Beyond the animals stretched more fields of unidentifiable shoots and, farther, a huddle of buildings that made up a small and primitive town.

Collins took heart at the sight of the animals. A society that accepted people of all appearances as equals seemed likely to prove reasonably broad-minded. For reasons he could only attribute to childhood cartoon watching, the peaceful coexistence of the animals added to the image of tolerance that might prove so important to his fate. The "good guys" always loved a wide variety of animals as well as their fellow men.

The horse trumpeted out a whinny that shook its entire frame. Caught off guard, Collins lost his balance. He toppled from its withers. Instinctively, he went to catch himself with his hands. The rope burned as it shifted across his wrists, and he slammed the ground with his already bruised shoulder. Pain shocked through him. He lay still, eyes closed, teeth gritted. The hands that shoved him back into position disappeared in a dizzying rush of spots that scored his vision. He fell against the horse's slimy neck, panting against pain. *I can't believe this is happening to me.*

The ride continued as a blur of motion and distant voices. Collins remained dimly aware of being carried into a large building and thrust into a cell. The door crashed shut with a metallic ring. He lay on his belly, face pressed against cold stone, and allowed nothingness to overtake him.

Benton Collins awoke in the same position he had lost consciousness. He opened his eyes to a mortared stone wall that smelled damp and as musty as an old book. He struggled to sit, automatically tossing one hand out for balance. He winced against the anticipated pain that movement had caused the last time he performed it, only to find that his arm moved freely. Using his hands, he managed to sit up easily. He examined his wrists. The ropes had scraped them raw, and clear fluid oozed from several places. His head no longer hurt. Dirt splattered his chest and abdomen in smeared patches, glazed with a fine coating of dust. His jeans were damp with horse sweat and grime speckled with short golden hairs.

Collins glanced around his prison, approximately four yards square with bars on three sides. The one across from the only stone wall opened onto a hallway, while the other two separated his cell from the ones on either side. He saw no other captives, which seemed like a good sign. Apparently, they did not confine people on a frequent and arbitrary basis. Once they realized he meant them no harm, they would surely release him.

Two bowls lay on the floor in the front left corner. One held water so clear Collins could see every blemish on the inner surface of the crockery. The other contained what appeared to be salad, dotted with lifesaver-sized and -shaped objects of black and brown. The rabbit sat heavily in his gut, and even the thought of food made him queasy. He wondered how long it would take for anyone to miss him. None of the professors intended to return until Sunday. His parents would assume he had gone to the Johnsons, and Marlys would likely believe he was just being rude. He amended the thought. *Not rude. Passive/aggressive.* A psychology student, she always had a long word, often in unpronounceable Latin, to describe even the most normal aspects of human behavior.

Taking his cue from prisoner movies, Collins examined the bars and lock of his cell. Though pitted in places, they all seemed more than solid enough to withstand any barehanded assault he could muster. He paced the cell a couple of times, expending nervous energy. Finally, with a sigh of resignation, he sat with his back against the stone wall, his legs stretched in front of him and his throbbing wrists in his lap.

Soon after Collins took his position, two men appeared

at his cell. They wore the same rust-and-gold uniforms as the ones who had captured him, but he recognized neither. One looked about six feet tall, with a shock of red hair, pale skin, and wide features. The other stood shorter but outweighed the first by nearly half again as much, most of it muscle. He had hair a shade lighter than Collins' dark brown, and he wore it in a braid. His skin matched his hair almost perfectly. Each carried a sword and what looked like a billy club in a wide belt.

Collins approached, glad for a chance to attempt explanation, though it seemed futile. "Hello," he said in his friendliest voice.

Both men turned.

"My name is Ben." Collins jabbed a finger toward his chest. "Ben."

The men watched him, saying nothing.

"I–I mean no . . . harm." Collins assumed a bright smile, placing his hands casually between the bars on a horizontal support. "I just want to go home." He stabbed a thumb toward the back of the cell. "Home. Understand?"

The men gave no sign that they did. Abruptly, one freed his club, slamming it down on Collins' fingers.

Pain shocked through Collins' hand, and he jerked away instinctively. "Ow, damn it! Why did you—"

The two men were laughing. They glanced at Collins, exchanged a few words, then broke into hearty chuckles again.

Collins withdrew to the back of his cell and slumped against the stone wall. He nursed his left hand in his right. Nothing seemed broken, and the pain dulled swiftly. The agony in his spirit took longer. Tears stung his eyes for the first time in more years than he could remember. *Can't escape. Can't communicate.* He sobbed. *I'm going to die here.*

Apparently having sated their curiosity, and their cruelty, the guards left. A few hours later, others replaced them. These, too, came to study their charge, the first a rangy, middle-aged man, the other a woman of about his age, twenty-three, with silky black hair and a golden tan. They also wore the standard uniform, including the swords and batons.

The thought of repeating the previous encounter repulsed Collins, yet he knew he had to try. He rose, slowly and carefully, edging toward the bars. This time, he stopped beyond reach of their weapons. "Hello," he said miserably.

The man said something to the woman, who nodded. She watched Collins' every movement through intent blue eyes. She sported high cheekbones, spare lips, and a generous nose. Though not classically beautiful, she had a refinement to her movements and features symmetrical enough to make her reasonably attractive. Though slender, she had a sinewy physique that revealed strength.

It seemed a hopeless question, but Collins asked anyway. "Do you speak any English?"

They did not reply.

"Eng-lish," Collins repeated.

The guards exchanged glances. The male ran a hand through the brown-and-white stubble of his hair and shrugged. He said something in their strange language.

The woman replied, equally incomprehensibly.

"Hurt." Collins hit his left arm with his right hand. He shook his head vigorously. "No hurt." He peeled his right hand away, dropped it to his side, and patted it with his left.

The two watched his every movement.

Collins continued, "Friends." He hugged himself fondly. "Friends?"

"Frinz?" the woman repeated in a questioning tone.

The man put things together more quickly. A frown scored his features, and his crow's-feet sprang to vivid relief around his eyes. "No friends."

Encouraged by their clear attention, Collins explained again. He slapped his left arm again, then looked surprised. "Hurt." He shook his head. "No HURT." He plucked loose his right hand and patted it again, followed by a self-hug. "Friends. Yes." He bobbed his head eagerly.

The man glared. "No friends." He jabbed a finger at Collins. "No no no friends." He turned his back. "Yes, *aguryo*."

Clearly, the guard had understood his pantomime. And rejected it. Heaving a deep sigh, Collins slunk to the back of his cell, dropped to the floor, and buried his head. "Friends," he whispered. "Friends . . . yes."

Hopeless terror kept Benton Collins awake far into the night. Despair gave way to rocky acceptance, then to desperate worry. He paced the confines of his cell like a zoo tiger, afraid to try to sleep. When he went still, thoughts crowded him, horrible considerations of what his future held. Suddenly, all the things he had cursed earlier that day seemed insignificant. So his parents had chosen their lovers over their son. He was grown now, and they had a right to lives of their own. It only made sense for the other lab assistants and professors to go home over Thanksgiving, since he had nowhere to go. His student loans—only money. None of it mattered one iota if he never found his way back to Algary.

In the wee morning hours, the female guard reappeared. She stood quietly in front of Collins' cell, studying him. The lantern light kindled glimmers in her pale eyes, but she otherwise blended into the dark obscurity of the prison.

Collins stopped his pacing to look at her. With little hope, he tried one more time, touching a hand to his chest. "Ben. That's me. Ben Collins."

"Falima," she replied.

"Falima," Collins repeated. "Pretty. Is that your name?"

"Yes. My name is Falima."

He had not expected a reply; so, when he got one, it stunned him to wide-eyed silence.

"Why?" Falima added.

Collins found his tongue. "You–you *do* speak English," he said, holding accusation from his voice.

"English," she repeated, rolling the word in her mouth as if to taste it. "Is that what I am speaking?"

"Yes." Collins approached the bars but did not touch them. "And quite well, I might add."

"You *might* add?"

Knowing idioms, slang, and expressions often confused newcomers to a language, Collins amended. "Well, I *did* add, I guess. Do all your people speak English?"

"No." Falima considered her own answer briefly, apparently recognizing the word from their previous encounter. Her eyes narrowed, and she studied him further. "No friends." She spoke the last two words with a heavy accent that had not tainted her previous conversation.

Collins' heart rate quickened. He had finally found someone with whom he could communicate, and he seemed to be failing miserably. "Why 'no friends?'" he asked with genuine concern.

Falima pronounced each word with slow and bitter force. "You ... are ... evil."

"Me?" The question was startled from Collins. "Evil?"

"Yes."

"Why would you say such a thing?"

"Murderer," she hissed. "Cannibal."

Collins blinked ponderously, certain Falima had chosen the wrong word. "Cannibal? What are you talking about?" A moment later, he wished he had reacted as strongly to the claim of murder. To his knowledge, he did not have a violent bone in his body.

Apparently misunderstanding, Falima defined the word. "One who eats its own kind. Cannibal. You."

"I've never eaten a person in my life." Seeing the opportunity, he added. "And I've never killed anyone, either."

Using her thumb and middle finger, Falima pulled back her locks, black as ink, thick, and shiningly soft. They fell instantly back to the sides of her head. "You killed Joetha, Ben Collins." The blue eyes filled with ice. "Then you ate her. We found the remains in your possession, some in your very hands."

"What?" The suggestion seemed nonsense. "I didn't have—" Realization struck with the force of a speeding truck. "Are you talking about the rabbit?"

"Joetha," Falima corrected.

Stunned, Collins stuttered. "I couldn't—I mean I didn't—know ..." He trailed off. It seemed impossible that he had discovered a society so tolerant of differences that its citizens considered animals on a par with humans. *Why not? There are people in our world who do.* He recalled incidents of loonies breaking into laboratories, murdering humans to "rescue" laboratory animals that swiftly perished in the wild. "I–I didn't know. You have to believe me."

"I have to?"

"Because it's true. In my world, animals are considered ..." Collins chose his words with care. "... our charges, not ... our equals."

The blue eyes narrowed, as if Falima found his explanation impossible to fathom. "What is your switch-form?"

The compound word made no sense to Collins. "My what?"

"Your switch-form. Your switch-form?"

The repetition did not help. "I don't understand."

Falima spoke louder and with awkward sluggishness. "YOUR . . . SWITCH . . . -FORM."

Baffled, Collins regarded Falima blankly, then came back with the same volume and tone, "I . . . HAVE . . . NO . . . CLUE . . . WHAT . . . YOU'RE . . . TALKING . . . ABOUT."

Falima tilted her head. Her lips pursed, and she squinted. Clearly, she thought him a moron. "What are you when you are not a man?"

"Not a man?" Collins shook his head. ". . . well, I used to be a boy." He could not help adding, "My girlfriend thinks I still am."

Falima rolled her eyes. "So, you are hiding it. A carnivore of some sort, no doubt. Or a bear, maybe. They are always the ones that fall off their oaths."

Collins threw up his hands in surrender. "I honestly have no idea what you're getting at." He put the scattered details together. "Are you saying that sometimes you're something other than a woman?"

Falima's hands clamped to her hips. "You rode me here."

"I did?" Collins' eyes widened at the realization. "You're . . . you're . . . a horse?" The words sounded twice as ridiculous coming from his own mouth. *One of us is entirely crazy.* He studied Falima more fully, now noticing the minutiae that seemed too clear for coincidence: the large blue eyes, glossy black hair, and golden skin tone. As impossible as it seemed, he believed. Once Collins' mind made that leap, worse had to follow. "Oh, my God!"

"Yes, my switch-form is a horse. What's wrong with that?"

"That rabbit was . . . was—"

"A sweet old woman." Falima's eyes narrowed again. "And you *ate* her."

Collins' stomach churned. Bile climbed up his throat. "Oh, my God. My God!" Though nauseated, he felt certain he could not vomit and desperately wished he could. "Holy shit. My God. My God!" Nothing more coherent seemed possible. "I—" His voice emerged hoarser than he expected.

"I . . . didn't know. Where I come from, people are just people. Animals are . . . animals. All the time. Always."

Rage rekindled in Falima's pale eyes, and she regarded Collins like some loathsome insect. "In Barakhai, you are a murderer and a cannibal. And you will be hanged mid-morning."

Stunned dumb, Collins could only stare as Falima turned her back on him and strode swiftly beyond sight.

Chapter 3

Benton Collins sprawled on the floor of his cell, the stone warming to his body. His eyes lay open; he felt incapable of closing them. The irregular plank ceiling became indelibly etched on his vision: the watermark in the shape of a bottle, the knothole like an ever-staring eye, the spidery crack that emitted a steady patter of water droplets. *You will be hanged midmorning.* The words cycled through his mind, always in Falima's voice, a death knell he had no way to escape. "I didn't know," he said to no one. "How could I possibly know?"

Collins scraped his fingers along the damp stone in mindless circles, his back aching and his wrists throbbing with every heartbeat. *This can't be happening. People changing into animals? It can't be real.* He forced his eyes shut, hoping that, when he opened them, he would awaken from this nightmare. The darkness behind his lids was filled with shadows.

Beyond his control, Collins' eyes glided open to confront the same water spot, the knothole, and the crack. The water plopped steadily against stone.

Collins awakened with no realization of having slept. Only the diffuse glow illuminating the prison revealed that morning had come. Distant voices wafted to him, unintelligible and intermingled with the occasional clink of metal. He sprang to his feet, the movement inciting a sharp pain through his back and right shoulder. The hard floor had stiffened him during the night.

Four men entered Collins' field of vision. They all wore the familiar rust and gold, swords, and batons. They also carried a rope.

Terror seized every part of Collins. He flattened against the back wall of his cell.

The men spoke to one another in their odd language, then gestured Collins forward.

Collins did not move. "There's been . . . a mistake," he wheezed through a throat gone painfully dry. "I didn't know. I . . . didn't . . . know." Enough time had passed that the rabbit no longer filled his belly, a constant reminder of a heinous crime. Yet he found it impossible to eat.

The guards exchanged more words. Then, one stepped forward and unlocked the cage. Two of the men entered, one carrying the rope. The door clanged shut behind them.

Collins measured the two with his gaze. Both stood shorter than his five-foot-eleven frame, and only one outweighed his one hundred fifty-five pounds. However, both moved with a wary dexterity that threatened experience and strength. It seemed as foolish to fight as to go willingly. The first would gain him bruises in addition to his sentence, but the latter would mean he had done nothing to avert his fate. Either way, he had nothing to lose but more pain. He was going to die. *I'm going to die.* Despite the time he had invested in it, the thought seemed beyond comprehension.

The man without the rope, the heavier one, drew a loop in the air with his finger, an obvious gesture to turn.

Collins only blinked, pretending not to understand. It seemed safer than insolence.

The men conversed a moment, then nodded. They lunged for Collins simultaneously. He leaped backward, crashing against the wall with enough force to send pain lurching through his spine and breath huffing from his lungs. A moment later, they had him prone, arms pulled behind him. The ropes tightened around his wrists again, reawakening the previous day's agony. He screamed.

The guards shouted over Collins. The two hauled him to his feet, the door opened, and they all escorted him through the prison hallway. They went through another door, attended by two women in the standard uniform, then emerged into sunshine so bright it seared Collins' eyes. He shut them, allowing the men to guide him blindly, stumblingly forward. Gradually, the sounds of a crowd grew around him, mingled conversations interspersed with an occasional call and sometimes pierced by a bark or whinny. He opened his eyes to slits, seeing a blur of faces, streets, and cottages in a glaze of brilliant sunlight. Then, he caught sight of the gallows towering over the rest, and he forced his eyes fully open despite the pain.

Collins now saw that he walked through a village of mud-and-thatch cottages, shops, and mills. The gathering consisted of a teeming mass of people, as varied in appearance as Americans, except they all wore simple homespun: grizzled elders and slouching adolescents, adults of every age, some clutching children's hands or babies in their arms. The shadow of the gallows loomed over them. Collins pinned his attention on the vast wooden monstrosity. A rope dangled from its uppermost pole, over a high, warped platform with massive, metal hinges. Clearly, the rope went around the victim's throat, then the platform was dropped, suspending him, by his neck, just above the level of the crowd. *Him.* Collins shivered. *Him is me.* He would feel his spine snapping, a moment of excruciating pain followed by absolute and permanent nothingness. *Permanent.* The enormity of death filled his mind with a terror beyond panic, the realization that the world would go on without him in it, that his time on this earth would end, not in years, but in minutes.

Collins reared backward, against his captors, screaming in mindless hysteria. Their grips tightened painfully, nails gouging his arms, then his legs. He felt himself lifted into the air. He squirmed, desperate, howling, aware only of the complete and monstrous need to break free. Though Collins recognized forward motion, the significance of it refused to penetrate the thought-shattering horror that drove his fight.

It all came home moments later.

The noose tickled, then hugged Collins' neck, and he went utterly still. *It's going to happen. It's really going to happen. I'm going to die.* A hopeless rationality filled him, a strange relief from the previous panic. *And I'm not going down in the history books as the hero who faced his end bravely.* His mind slid to a story he had read in junior high, about a man hanged from a bridge who hallucinated a grand escape in the moments before death. He wondered if it really happened that way and realized that no one could possibly know. He would, but he could do nothing with the information. *If only I'd gone to the Johnsons'. If only I hadn't followed that rat. If only I hadn't eaten that rabbit.* Regrets followed, the inability to apologize for small misdeeds, to say good-bye. He thought of all the things he would never get to do: hold a job, marry, coddle his children. *Visit Disney World.*

A man said something Collins could not understand.

Collins laughed hysterically, screwing his eyes shut. Then, the floor fell out under his feet, and he felt himself plunging. He tightened the muscles of his neck and face, bracing for the final impact.

The fall seemed to last forever. Then, a jolt shocked through his groin. Agony cramped his stomach, and he tumbled forward. His nose struck something hard and hairy, driving more pain through him. The crowd roared. Collins forced his lids open. Immediately, wiry hair slashed his eyes, and he shut them again. He felt forward movement, gaining momentum. The noose lay heavy on the back of his neck. He dared a shuddering breath, and air glided silkily, surprisingly easily, into his lungs.

The crowd continued shouting, sounding like they were in an open air sports stadium. Collins sat, splay-legged, on something warm and furry that carried him at a rocking sprint away from the gallows. He remembered the name of the hanging story: "An Occurrence at Owl Creek Bridge," though the significance of knowing it eluded him. Pitching his torso back, without the use of his still-tied arms, he wrenched open his eyes again. His breaths came in pants, due to shock, not pressure.

Farm fields flashed past Collins, and forest loomed ahead. Behind, he heard yelling. The noose remained around his neck, trailing a length of rope. He sat astride a horse, its black mane whipping into his face, one golden ear forward, the other flicked backward. A set of saddlebags lay slung across its withers. *Falima?* he wondered, doubting the possibility. She had seemed so hostile toward him the previous night. He eased more steadily onto the horse's back, not caring who or what had caught him, only glad that he had at least a little longer to live.

The horse lunged around the trees, racing between trunks with a speed that quailed Collins. He wished for the use of his hands. Weight shifts and knee pressure seemed woefully inadequate to keep him astride as the animal kept up its breakneck pace on narrow deer trails through dense tangles of forest. Then, as if in answer to his wish, the ropes loosened on his wrists. He fingered them, his exploration rewarded by frayed areas where it had, apparently, broken. He twisted it blindly over fingers, hands, and wrists, hampered by a warm, sticky liquid. Then, the rope fell away, freeing his hands. He pulled the noose from his neck, rubbed his bleeding wrists, and seized handfuls of mane.

The horse loosed a low nicker and slowed, slogging through denser brush and between more tightly packed trunks. Something buzzed past, irritatingly close to Collins' ear. He swatted at it, missed, and turned his attention to the terrain. The horse wallowed through tangles of brush, forcing Collins to flatten against its neck or side to avoid braining himself on leaning deadfalls and shed branches caught in the crotches of other trees. Time and again, he jerked a leg onto the horse's back to rescue it from being crushed.

Collins had done some riding with his high school girlfriend and realized he could steer the animal better than it could randomly pick its way along the trail. Taking up the rope intended to kill him, he fashioned it into a raw bridle, essentially a loop with reins. Gliding up the horse's neck, he flicked the coil around its nose.

The horse made a sound deep in its throat but otherwise seemed to take no notice of the rudely fashioned tack. As panic receded, Collins considered his situation. He rode on a horse that might, at other times, be human, possibly even Falima. The animals he had thus far seen acted exactly like the creatures they resembled in his own world, except for the too-friendly rabbit. *Joetha,* he corrected, cringing. Apparently, while in "switch-form," they lost their human memories and fully became animals. He wondered if all humans here had an animal-form, whether he might acquire one if he remained here too long, and how much control they had over the change.

Collins steered the buckskin around a thick, low-hanging branch. It ignored his gentle pull, so he increased the pressure, then drove his opposite heel into its flank.

The ears jerked backward. The horse reared with a sharp squeal, then followed Collins' instruction. The horse's reaction flashed guilt through him. Perhaps the horse did retain at least some of its human understanding. Suddenly he remembered the dogs' unwillingness to share his feast in the field. *They must have some crossover between human and animal time. Otherwise, the dogs would never know they could not eat meat.*

Collins had acted from impulse, accustomed to steering horses with reins and heel strikes. The horses back home had always taken these techniques in stride, a standard and accepted form of communication. Apparently, people here had a different way of making contact with their horses. He had tried talking to the rabbit and had received no response or indication that it understood. In the field, the guards had used a rope on Falima's horse-form, so she had to have some experience with being led. Nevertheless, he resolved not to kick her any more.

Something buzzed past Collins' head again. This time, he caught a glimpse of what appeared to be a large bumblebee or horsefly zipping past him. *Human, too?* he wondered, then dismissed the thought. No world could support even a hundredth as many people as bugs.

Collins turned his attention back to the horse. "Hello," he tried. "Are you Falima?"

The animal gave no indication it understood, though one ear did rise from its previous position, plastered angrily against its head.

The ride continued for hours, the horse ignoring every attempt by Collins to end it. Pulling back on the rope only made it raise and shake its head. Verbal explanations and, later, exhortations were met with nothing more than a few flicks of its ears. When he tensed to leap from its back, it quickened its pace dangerously, tossing him back into his seat. Eventually, Collins gave up, settling into the most comfortable position his sore thighs could find, flicking off the rope, and allowing the animal to take him where it would.

Finally, deep in some clearly unexplored part of the forest, the horse stopped. It dropped its head to graze at weeds poking around deadfalls and fallen clumps of leaves, then shook its entire body. The sudden movement caught Collins off guard; a grab at the flying mane barely rescued him from a fall. He slid down the horse's side, dislodging the saddlebags and clinging only by his hands. Mane hairs bit into his fingers.

The horse responded with an abrupt toss of its head that tore his grip free, as well as several strands from its mane. Collins dropped to the ground, rolling, hands protecting his head from a chance movement of the animal's hooves. It placidly returned to grazing, paying him no attention at all. The saddlebags lay on the ground.

Carefully, gaze fixed on the animal, Collins eased the saddlebags to him. Made of some natural fiber, the saddlebags yielded easily to his grip, much lighter and flimsier than the leather bags he had used in high school. Its well-crafted shape and metal weights sewn into the central areas kept it in place despite the lack of a pommel. He unlatched one of the two buckles and peered at a bulge of fabric. Hoping for something to replace the sweatshirt he had left to block the door crack in Daubert Labs, he pulled free several pieces. He unfolded a brown dress wrapped around a braided rope halter and lead, followed by a royal blue tunic that looked child-sized. Three knives thumped to the dirt, then a canteen and a stoppered crock. He worked the stopper free and peered inside, discovering a moving mass of what appeared to be enormous bugs. Startled, he dropped the crock. Three black beetles rolled to the ground, bearing a striking resemblance to the round objects he had seen on his salad in the prison cell. One opened its wings, then lifted soundlessly from the ground. The other two followed a moment later, and Collins recorked the crockery.

Collins discovered several more articles of clothing, in varying sizes, including a green tunic and cloak as well as a pair of brown britches that looked as if they might fit him. He pulled the tunic over his head, leaving the lacings undone. It felt odd, the fabric rough against his chest; and it was strangely tight in some places and loose in others. At least it kept him warm. The other pack contained more clothing, another canteen, a parcel of white paste resembling Play Doh, his cell phone and watch, and three pairs of wood-and-rope sandals. He also found a few hard rolls, wrinkled apples, and a wrapped packet of something that looked and smelled like the curds he had tasted on a field trip to the cheese factory in sixth grade.

Collins clipped his cell phone in place and stretched his watch back onto his wrist. It read six o'clock, which was clearly wrong. The sun lay directly overhead. He reset it for noon. Then, needing to relieve himself, he struggled into the weeds. Even as he walked, he realized the ludicrousness of his action. It hardly mattered where he chose to urinate in the depths of a forest. Only the horse would see him, yet he felt odd doing it in front of her, in case she was an intelligent alter ego of Falima. He walked just out of sight to perform his business, then studied the scene around him.

Trees and brush stretched in every direction as far as Collins could see. The intertwined branches emitted sunlight in patches, checkering the forest floor in patterns of gray and gold. In this area, oaks grew predominantly, their distinctive serrated leaves closely resembling the ones in Collins' world. Deep layers of rotting brown leaves lay like foam beneath his feet. He took a long breath of air, savoring the clean dampness. A whiff of smoke entered with it, and he froze. He was an escaped murderer now; he had to assume he'd be pursued.

Whirling, Collins ran back to the horse. A root hooked his foot, sending him sprawling. He skidded through leaf mold and muck, coming to a stop near the saddlebags. Beyond the horse, a campfire burned a cheery, crackling dance. In front of it sat a middle-aged man with skin like milk. From beneath a broad-brimmed hat, white-blond hair fell to his shoulders; and his eyebrows and lashes became invisible in the sunlight. He wore black linens that resembled some of the clothing from the saddlebags. Collins stared, reviving his genetics lessons. Albinism accompanied certain syndromes, including some that dangerously weakened the immune system. But, he recalled, most albinos simply inherited a recessive gene from both parents that left them without melanin.

Shocked by the thought, Collins pushed it from his mind. He could not understand why he remained so calm when, likely, the other was hunting him. Caught, he would certainly be executed immediately. He whirled to run.

"Come!" the albino said in English. "No run." He repeated, more emphatically. "No *run.*"

Curiosity warred with common sense. Collins turned carefully. "You speak English?"

"Little," the man responded. "No hurt." He rose and gestured toward the fire, seeming frustrated with his own limited ability to communicate. "Help you. Bringed here." He shook his head in irritation. "Come."

Still uncertain, Collins took a step toward the other man. A crock rested in the center of the fire, bubbling lazily.

"Me . . . Zylas," the albino said, looking up. Pale blue eyes met Collins' brown ones. "Zylas." He pointed at himself. "Understand?"

Collins nodded vigorously. Then, realizing the action might not mean the same thing here, verbalized his answer. "Understand. I'm Ben. Benton Collins, actually; but you can call me Ben." The horse moved nearer the fire and whinnied.

Zylas reached up and patted it reassuringly.

"Is that . . ." Collins started, wondering if the question might be improper. "Is that Falima's switch-form?"

"Falima." Zylas patted the horse again. "Yes, Falima."

Collins made an intuitive leap. "And you're . . . you're that rat." Hoping he had not offended the man, he softened the question. "Or aren't you?"

"Rat, yes," Zylas returned. "Me rat." His pidgin English clashed with Falima's fluency. Collins found himself wishing for her human form, even if she did seem to intensely dislike him.

"Did you . . . rescue me?"

Zylas nodded, glancing at the cooking food. "Chew rope off neck. Chew rope off hand." He stirred the contents of the crock with a stick. "Falima catched."

"Yes." Collins glided nearer. "Falima caught me. Thanks. Thank you. Both of you." He reached out to pet Falima, but her ears jerked flat to her head, and it seemed safer to remove his hand. "I don't think she likes me."

Zylas grinned. "She'll . . . come around."

It sounded funny to hear someone who barely knew the language using idioms. Collins guessed Zylas had learned English by example rather than textbooks. "I—I truly didn't know about the animal . . . transformation thing. Honest. I would never have eaten—"

Zylas waved Collins silent. "I know. Haven't talked into

Falima . . . yet. I been there." He made a throwaway gesture. "She no been."

Collins filled in the missing words. "You've been to my world."

"Yes." Zylas wrinkled his nose.

Hope soared, and Collins smiled. "So you can get me home from here."

A light flickered in Zylas' soft eyes, and he shrugged. "Try."

"All right," Collins said carefully. "Try." He reminded Zylas of the obvious, "Because, if you don't, I'm dead."

"Yes." Zylas went back to stirring.

Expecting something a bit stronger, Collins chewed his lower lip. "I really appreciate your saving me."

"Mmmm."

"And your taking me back to the . . . the way back to my world."

"All right."

Collins glanced at the crock, recognizing it as the same one from which he had poured the beetles. "Um, are those . . . um . . . bugs you're cooking?"

Zylas followed the direction of Collins' gaze. "*Fraharas*." He translated. "Bugs, yes. Big, hard-shell bugs." He added, as if it might matter, "They clean."

Collins had not eaten since the rabbit. Terror had kept hunger at bay, but now he realized he would like a bite. *Not bugs.* "Is that what you eat?"

Zylas bobbed his head. "Bug. Fruit. Vegetable." He said the latter with an extra syllable and an improper emphasis, so it emerged like vejah*tah*bull. "Fish. Milk. Cheese. Egg— but not with baby in." He tossed the parcel of curds. "These better?"

"Much, thank you." Collins popped one into his mouth. It squeaked as he chewed it, but it tasted at least as good as any cheese in his world. He ate three more pieces before speaking again. "Do all people here become animals?"

"Not *opernes*." He considered the translation. "King . . . and . . . such like . . ."

"Royalty?" Collins tried.

"Royalty." Zylas rolled his eyes as if tasting the word, then bobbed his head. "Royalty. Others all yes."

"And all animals?"

"Become person."

"All?" Collins put more cheese into his mouth, talking as he chewed.

"All."

Collins found the contradiction. "But you said you eat fish."

Zylas scooped a liquid spoonful of beetles from the crock and slurped it into his mouth. "Fish not animal."

Collins' gut churned, and he looked away to keep himself from vomiting. The logic seemed maddeningly circular. All animals became humans, but "animal" was, apparently, defined by the ability to transform to human form. "Anything else living not considered animal?"

The beetles crunched in Zylas' mouth. "Bug. Plant. Fish." He shrugged. "That all." He eased the crock fully from the fire.

Falima wandered off for better grazing, still well within earshot.

"And when you're an animal." Collins downed more cheese, keeping his gaze averted. "Do you remember and understand . . . people stuff?"

"Stuff?"

Collins tried to explain. "Speech, hands, manners."

Zylas scooped and ate more beetles. "Some." He clearly fought for words. "Depend on want. Age. Ex . . . ex . . ." The word would not come.

"Experience," Collins supplied.

"Experience," Zylas repeated. "Experience."

"So the more times you become a rat . . ." Collins trailed off.

"Better . . . overlap."

"Between human and animal forms?" Collins supplied

"Right."

Collins ate more cheese, then asserted. "I think I'd spend half my childhood in switch-form, or even more. Get the hang of it as soon as possible." Feeling Zylas' intent gaze upon him, Collins met the pallid eyes.

"No choice."

"What?"

Zylas used wild hand gestures to punctuate his words, as if this might aid the translation. "Spend half time people, half animal. Change at time, same time, always. No choice."

"Every day?"

"Every day," Zylas confirmed.

Collins tried to understand. "So, half the day you're a rat and half a guy?"

Zylas nodded.

"Do you get to choose which half at least?"

"No choice," Zylas replied again. "No choice at all."

A million more questions occurred to Collins as they rode Falima, for hours, through the woodlands; but he remained silent as Zylas had requested. Sunlight sliced intermittently through breaks in the forest canopy, alternately covered by clouds and branches. Although Collins did not recognize the pathways they took, he had little choice but to trust his new companion. The rat/man had rescued him from execution and did appear to diligently check their route. At irregular intervals, he slid down from his position behind Collins to scout. Some things, Collins could figure out for himself. For example, clearly each person had an individual change time. Otherwise, Falima would have become human at noon, as Zylas had.

Brush rustled. Zylas reached around Collins to lay a pale hand on the left side of Falima's neck. Instantly, she swerved to the right, then went still.

Collins turned to look at his companion. The other man shook his head, gestured at Collins to remain in place, and made a motion near his mouth that Collins took as a plea for quiet. Worried about unseen dangers, he felt his heart rate quicken.

A squirrel appeared on the trail, an acorn clutched between its paws. It gnawed at the nut, flicking its tail in jerky bursts, then continued on its way.

Falima glided back onto the path. Collins smiled at Zylas' paranoia, which seemed oddly stronger than his own. Then he remembered. *That squirrel could be the local police.* As they continued on their way, Collins had to ask, "That squirrel. Was that someone you know?"

"No." Zylas replied into Collins' ear. "*Durithrin.*"

Collins shook his head at the unfamiliar word. "What?"

"*Durithrin,*" Zylas repeated, the word no more comprehensible the second time. "A . . . a . . ." He sighed. "Not . . . city . . . people."

Collins nodded, letting Zylas off the hook, though he still did not really understand. He guessed it was a concept his world did not need, something that applied only to human/beast interfaces.

Collins missed the signal that brought Falima to a stop. Zylas dismounted and disappeared into the brush. Collins remained in place, finger combing the horse's mane and laying the strands in their proper position. Falima stood stock-still, giving no sign she noticed his ministrations. Shortly, Zylas returned. "The ruins." He pointed ahead. "Not far." He flung a hand from Collins to himself, then jabbed it toward the ground.

Taking it as a signal to dismount, Collins slid to the ground. The movement revealed a tightness through the muscles of his thighs and buttocks that would likely become an ache by morning. His wrists had stopped bleeding, but they still dribbled clear fluid and throbbed with every beat of his heart. Both shoulders felt bruised. He looked at his watch. If correct, they had ridden for more than two hours.

Zylas talked softly to Falima and stroked her nose. The horse pawed the ground and snorted. A large insect buzzed past Collins' face.

"Ready?"

Collins looked up, only then realizing Zylas had addressed him. The blue-white eyes lay unsettlingly upon him.

Collins' gaze shifted unconsciously to Falima.

"She not come," Zylas explained, stepping around Collins and heading in the direction he had scouted. "No need."

Collins continued to study the horse, who had lowered her head to graze and seemed to take no notice of the humans' conversation. He hardly knew her; yet, for reasons he could not explain, he would miss her. "Tell her I said 'good-bye.'"

"I will," Zylas assured without looking back.

Collins turned and followed the rat/man through the brush, excitement building with every step. Soon, he would return to the mundane world of troubles that no longer seemed so significant. Staring death in the face, he might not have found courage, but he had found new perspective. Nothing less would ever seem formidable again.

The forest broke gradually to the familiar field of wildflowers and weeds. On the hill, the broken fortress looked positively welcoming. Collins raced toward it.

"Wait." Zylas charged after his impetuous companion. "Wait!" He dove on Collins.

Abruptly driven to the ground, breath dashed from his lungs, Collins twisted to glare at Zylas. "What the hell did you do that for?"

Zylas' answer was an inclination of his head.

Collins followed his companion's gesture. Just ahead, a ragged line of arrows scored the ground. They had not been there when he had started his run.

"Damn." The expletive left Collins' mouth without intention.

Zylas seized Collins' hand and wriggled back toward the forest.

"Damn," Collins repeated, following. "Guards?"

"Would guess," Zylas returned.

More attuned, Collins heard the second round of bowstrings singing, the rattle and thunk of the arrows landing. He lunged for the forest, Zylas at his side.

There, beyond range of the bowmen, they stopped to study the ruins. Collins saw only the stone building, sunlight flashing from chips of quartz in the crumbling construction. "How did you know?"

"Didn't." Zylas also studied the ruins. "Sense. Smell . . . guess."

Sensed and smelled. It seemed logical to Collins that some of the animal instincts would permeate into the human phase as well. *Thank God.* Now relatively safe, he started to shake, terrified in a way he had not felt when the arrows directly menaced him. *I almost died. Again.* He looked at Zylas, skin white as paper and hair the nearly colorless blond most men loved and many women sought in a bottle. As they retreated back to Falima, he tried to lighten a mood wound as tensely as a spring. "Got any friends who change into rhinoceroses?"

Zylas blinked. "What?"

"Never mind." *A dinosaur or an army tank might do it.*

Falima made a soft, snorting nicker, then pawed the ground.

Zylas spoke to her gently in his own language. He turned his attention back to Collins. "We go." He leaped onto Falima's back, sliding toward her hindquarters to make room for Collins.

Collins' heart felt as if it were sinking into his toes. "Go? But . . ." *But . . . what? What do I expect him to do?* Clearly, approaching directly and in broad daylight could lead only to their deaths. Apparently, at midnight, Zylas would resume his rat form. Then, he could slip past the bowmen. *And do what? Give them all bubonic plague?* He stifled a hysterical chuckle. With a sigh of resignation, he clambered onto a rock and, from there, to Falima. The horse took off, going back the way they had come.

Chapter 4

BENTON Collins mulled the situation over as they rode silently into a deeper part of the forest. Trees glided past in a silken green blur, and Zylas' scouting became a remote background to Collins' thoughts. The fluid motion of the horse also lost significance, though the growing aches in thighs, buttocks, and groin gradually grew too prominent to ignore. His watch read almost 5:55 when they finally stopped in a clearing surrounded by scraggly junipers and scrub pines. Clouds raked across the sky, a gray accompaniment to Collins' dispirited mood. He dismounted beside Zylas. Falima lowered her head and snorted. Zylas stripped off the pack and tossed it to the ground. He unhitched the lead rope/halter from her head and let it fall.

"Now what?" Collins asked, kicking a deadfall at one edge of the camp site. Bark flew amid a spray of rotted wood. A large black beetle with angry-looking pincers scrambled from the carnage.

"Dinner?" Zylas suggested, catching the bug with a swift grab.

"Dinner," Collins repeated. He shook his head and turned to sit on the deadfall. The scream of leg muscles changed his mind in mid-movement, and he struggled back to a stand. Pain made him irritable. "I just lost my appetite." He wrinkled his nose at the beetle kicking madly in Zylas' grip and attempting to twist its pincers to meet the restraining fingers. "Besides, I'm more worried about my neck than my stomach."

Zylas stepped closer, gazing at Collins' throat. "Hurt neck? Sorry. Me tried get rope not with—"

Collins interrupted. "That's not what I meant. I ... if ... I have to get out of this ... this place. My life—"

Zylas frowned and threw his hands in the air. Before he could speak, Collins caught an unexpected movement out of the corner of his eye. He whirled toward it. A naked woman stood where the horse had once grazed. Black hair fell in a satin cascade that formed soft curls around ample breasts. Though not thin, the body looked toned and well-muscled, the curves delicate and in exquisite proportion. Pale eyes made a radiant contrast to the golden/tan skin. She said something Collins did not understand, then snatched the beetle from Zylas, crushed it, and tossed it into her mouth.

Revulsion broke the spell. Flushed from the roots of his hair to his chin, Collins averted his gaze.

The beetle crunched between Falima's teeth, then she said something else to Zylas. He knelt beside the pack, pulled out the linen dress, a pair of something that looked like shorts, and two of the wood-and-cloth sandals. He tossed them to Falima.

Collins heard the rustle of fabric. He focused fanatically on the other man. "Are you always ... like that ... when you change?"

"Like what?" Zylas looked from Falima to Collins.

Falima said something simultaneous with Collins', "Like ... bare. Nude. Naked."

Zylas stuffed clothing back into the pack. "Have to be, you think?"

Collins nodded, swallowing hard. It only made sense. He dared a peek at Falima, who returned a hard glare. She spoke to Zylas again, and he made a throwaway gesture as well as answering with words. Falima stomped a foot, horse-like.

"What's wrong?" Collins asked.

Zylas looked at Falima first, urging her to answer. When she did not, Zylas tried. "She have thing ... mine. Not—"

Apparently even more frustrated with Zylas' broken rendition of English than Collins, Falima interrupted. "The reason I cannot give you your translation stone back is because some *moron*..." She glanced pointedly at Collins, then back to Zylas. "... kicked me and made me swallow it."

Collins' face reddened again. "I'm sorry. I didn't mean—"

"It all right," Zylas soothed. "Now both can talk and understand Ben."

Falima tossed her head, ruffling her hair so that it fell over her shoulders in inky stripes. "You, barely. Me, I have no interest in speaking to him at all." She turned her back.

Not wishing to engage in another war, Collins ignored the woman for his more cooperative companion. "This stone?"

"Magic," Zylas explained with a word. "Let know all tongue."

Collins accepted the revelation without further questioning. It seemed no more outlandish than humans turning into animals and back, which he had already witnessed. "Remember when I asked about a friend rhino?"

"Rhino*saurus*," Zylas corrected.

"You don't have any in... this place? Whatever it's called."

"Barakhai." Zylas sat on the deadfall, examining the hole where he had found the beetle. "Mean 'whole world' our tongue."

"Barra-KIGH." Collins tried to pronounce it correctly, uncertain of the spelling and doubting his companions could illuminate it. It was a lot easier to learn to speak a language than to read it, especially in rat form and on the sly.

"Durithrin Forest be exact."

Durithrin. Collins recognized the word from their previous conversation, applied to a squirrel.

Still ignoring them, Falima pulled food from the pack and stuffed cheese curds in her mouth. Collins glanced at her.

"Very hungry," Zylas apologized for Falima's manners. "Ride most of day. Not time graze."

Falima made a wordless noise around her food.

Collins put aside the issue of how someone who spent half her life as an herbivore and half as an omnivore managed to digest anything but grass. Barakhai clearly followed different natural laws and logic than his biology, chemistry, and physics textbooks. Returning to his original point, Collins cautiously sat beside the albino, this time ignoring his aching muscles. "What about lions? Eagles? Bulls?" He added one he had already seen here. "Big dogs?"

"Know dog," Zylas admitted. "Bull?" His eyes crinkled. "That mean . . . lie?"

Only the shit. Collins dodged the slang to explain as simply as possible, "Man cows. They have horns, and they're big."

"*Pepsa,*" Falima said around another mouthful.

Zylas bobbed his head. "*Pepsa.* Bull. Yes. Why?"

Collins waved away another large, flying insect. The answer seemed so obvious, he could scarcely believe the question. "Don't you people fight?"

"Fight?" Zylas repeated, looking at Falima.

"*Augin telishornil bahk.*" Falima drank from the waterskin. It seemed like a lot of sounds to explain a one-syllable word.

"Fight." Zylas cocked his head to the heavens. "No."

"No?" The answer was nonsensical, especially after the barrage of arrows that had nearly killed them. "They were fighting." He jabbed a hand in the general direction of the crumbling fort.

Zylas followed the gesture with his gaze, eyes shadowed by his hat.

"Different. They *solen ak opernes.*"

This time, Falima translated without entreaty. "Royal guards."

Collins considered the foreign phrase. "*Solen ak opernes.*" He remembered now that Zylas had used *opernes* before to refer to royalty. "*Solen ak opernes.*" He quit practicing the foreign phrase. He had no reason to learn their language; he would have to escape as soon as possible . . . and never return. "No one else fights?" he asked dubiously. It seemed beyond possibility. "Ever?"

Falima laid out apples, hard rolls, and cheese, then started peering under rocks and rolling logs.

"Sometime," Zylas admitted, loosening a strand of white hair sweat-plastered to his temple. "Not . . . as group. Not like . . . like . . . king cop."

"*Solen ak opernes,*" Collins supplied.

Zylas smiled. "Language go wrong direction."

Collins laughed. He had once watched an exchange between a teacher and an English as a Second Language student via interpreter. At one point, the teacher had used a Spanish phrase that the translator dutifully recited for the Peruvian student—in English. Now, Collins broke bark from his seat with his heel.

Falima rushed in to gather the revealed bugs, placing them in the crock.

Collins wondered how hungry he would have to get to share that meal. "If we could marshal some strong animals, they wouldn't necessarily have to have formal combat training—"

Falima straightened suddenly. "You self-centered bastard!"

The outburst, in perfect English, startled Collins; and he nearly fell off the log.

"Falima," Zylas warned.

But nothing would silence Falima until she spoke her piece. "Is it not enough that we will probably die for saving a cold-blooded cannibal? Do you want more innocents to sacrifice their lives for you?"

Collins found himself unable to reply, though regret filled his stomach like lead, and the bare thought of eating now made him ill.

"Falima," Zylas said again, a clear plea to quiet her. He added more in their own language.

"I do not care," Falima replied, still in clear English. "He is a fool and a clod. We should have let him hang."

Zylas said more, punctuated by broad hand gestures that displayed the anger his tone did not.

Collins tried to defuse the situation. "I'm sorry. I really am. I am very grateful that you saved my life. I didn't mean to suggest others should die to help me." He tried to catch Falima's eyes. "I don't want anyone to get hurt."

Falima dodged his gaze. "What sort of dimwit finds himself in a strange place and immediately kills and eats someone?"

"I'm sorry," Collins practically pleaded. He needed Falima and Zylas to help him negotiate Barakhai, but he also desperately wanted a friend. The idea of being alone in a foreign world with rules beyond his understanding overwhelmed him. Nevertheless, he chose to gently defend himself. "If you came to my world starving, wouldn't you start eating every bug you saw?"

Falima hesitated, clearly seeing the trap. "You were starving?"

"Yes." Collins refused to allow her to sidetrack him. Though no third world orphan, he had gone twenty-seven hours on nothing but water. "Would you eat the bugs?"

"Maybe," Falima said, then clenched her jaw. "Why? Is that murder where you come from?"

The urge to reply affirmatively became a burning compulsion. It would make his point swiftly and efficiently, but Collins never lied well. "No. But it's disgusting. You wouldn't get hung—"

"Hanged," Falima corrected.

Collins blinked, barely daring to believe a person who could only speak his language because of a magical device thought it possible, even necessary, to correct his grammar. "It's hanged? Not hung? Really?"

"Trust me."

Collins returned to his point. "You wouldn't get hanged." It still sounded wrong. "But you might get locked up." He did not bother to differentiate between prison and a mental unit. It would only weaken his point, and at least he had not directly lied.

Another large, flying thing zipped past Collins' head. He smacked it out of the air. "No wonder you can eat the bugs here." It flew in an awkward arc, then crashed into the dirt. "They're as big as—"

Falima's sharp intake of breath cut off Collins' words before he could make a fatal faux pas. Zylas scrambled to check on the fallen creature, Collins presumed to augment dinner.

Zylas scooped it up but did not add it to the crock. Instead, he cradled it in his hand, massaging it with a gentle finger.

Dread crept through Collins' chest in icy prickles. *What have I done this time?* Leaping to his feet, he raced Falima to the thing in Zylas' hands. A tiny hummingbird lay there, its colors vivid against the chalky whiteness of the rat/man's palms. Its body was deep emerald, the wings a lacy lighter green. A patch of pink decorated its throat. The long, thin beak was black. "I'm sorry," Collins gasped out, gagging. "I thought it was a horsefly. I swear I did. I–I . . . is it . . ." He shuddered at the idea.

". . . dead?"

"Just stunned." Zylas held up his hand, and the bird's wings became a blur. It zipped into the air and disappeared, to Collins' relief.

"He is a menace," Falima grumbled under her breath.

"Honest mistake," Zylas replied.

Collins suspected both of the English comments had been directed at him, though they addressed one another. To his surprise, he appreciated them talking around him rather than in their own language. At least, he felt included. "I'm sorry," he said again. "I'm really sorry." He wondered if he had just destroyed their security or enhanced it. If he alone noticed the hummingbird, and it had been spying, then he might have averted capture. More likely, he had whacked some innocent bystander who would now find him less a curiosity and more a danger to discuss with guards and friends. Collins dropped to the ground and buried his face in his hands. The new lines of thought this bizarre world inspired left him with millions of possibilities and little direction. "Perhaps . . . perhaps, the guards at the ruins might get tired of waiting for me and give up?"

Falima's amused snort shattered that last hope. Even Zylas loosed a laugh. "Not likely. Even best time, guard . . . zealous." The last word seemed a difficult one for a tyro to choose, and Collins suspected its similarity to the rat/man's name made it easier for him to learn. "They know you comed from there. Want you." He shrugged. "Not go till get you."

"They know?" Collins felt his features grow tightly knit. "How?" There seemed only one logical explanation. "Have others come from my world?"

Zylas glanced at Falima, who shook her head with a grimace. They exchanged more dialogue than Collins thought necessary. Either they had or they had not. If space aliens had visited his town, he could not imagine anyone not knowing.

Finally Zylas addressed Collins again. "No."

The answer seemed too simple for the time it had taken to gather it. "No?"

"Not that either of us knows of," Falima clarified. "The royals might have more information."

Collins doubted it. If others had come, it seemed likely the so-called royals would have kept him from entering Barakhai in the first place.

Apparently thinking along the same lines, Zylas added, "If other come, royal not know from where till you."

Or else I would have found the ruins better guarded. Collins nodded to indicate he understood, then stumbled over an odd thought. "Do your people come to our world often?" He had studied some strange animals, like the platypus, that seemed otherworldly. Perhaps it explained the disappearance of the dinosaurs; somehow they all got zapped to another dimension.

Falima continued gathering bugs. "Zylas is the only one I know of who has gone. And I only just found that out because of you."

Zylas looked at his sandals. "Know one other. Not think more."

"Let us eat." Falima held out the crock, now half-full with crawling insects.

Collins' stomach lurched.

Falima poured water into the crock, replaced the lid, and set it near the food. "Hurry up. Gather kindling."

Immediately, Collins obeyed, glad to find some small way to start repaying his rescuers. He brought back armfuls of dry twigs, choosing wider ones with each pass. The first gray stirrings of dusk settled over the forest, bringing a chilly breeze that stirred the leaves into rattling dances overhead. Oncoming darkness dimmed the trees to skeletal hulks swarmed with fluttering leaves like dark, limp hands. As Collins dropped his third load, he found his two companions squatting in front of a well-arranged tower of kindling with a pile of leaves beneath it. He hunkered down between them. "Be a lot easier if you'd brought my lighter."

"Not need." Zylas reached into his tunic pocket.

Before Collins could marvel over Zylas even knowing what he meant, the albino's hand emerged wrapped around a translucent purple Zippo. Expertly, he flicked the wheel with a callused thumb. A tiny flame appeared, and he used it to ignite the leaves.

Zylas sat back. "Brought own."

Collins dropped to his haunches. "You . . . you have lighters?" It seemed impossible. If Barakhai had that technology, he should see so much more; and it made no sense that they would have an otherworld brand name version even so. Then realization clicked. "You must have got it in my world."

Zylas watched the sprouting flames, brushing aside his cloak and replacing the lighter blindly. "Work hard drag back."

"I'll bet." Collins pictured a rat scooting the Zippo across a dark, dirty floor for hours. He bit back a smile. Zylas probably would not appreciate the humor, and he doubted Falima would either. Reminded of his own devices, Collins expressed gratitude that had gone too long unspoken. He now understood that Zylas must have packed the saddle-bags. "By the way, thanks for getting my watch back." He held up his wrist. "And the phone, too." He patted the Motorola StarTAC clipped to his waistband.

"You welcome." Zylas fanned the growing flames with his hat as they danced onto the wood. "Not able get all. Pick good?"

Collins measured his response. No matter how misguided, good deeds deserved praise, not condemnation. "Fine."

Apparently reading the hesitation, Zylas looked up, snowy hair plastered to his head in the shape of his missing hat. "Truth, please."

"Honestly," Collins returned carefully. "I do appreciate your help."

"But . . ." Zylas added, replacing his headgear.

"But," Collins continued dutifully. "Time doesn't make a whole lot of difference." He gestured at his watch, then pulled the cellular phone from its holster. He pressed the button and got no response. "Without a charger, it's not much use." He chuckled. "Even if it worked, who could I call?"

Zylas grinned crookedly. "Do better next time."

"Next time. Right." Collins studied the creases at the corners of Zylas' mouth and realized his companion was kidding. He laughed. "Next time."

Even Falima managed a smile, though she turned away as if afraid the men might see it. "Why do we not start eating? The main course will come soon enough."

Hungry, Collins nodded. He had eaten only cheese curds since daybreak and not nearly enough of those. They sat

and ate most of the apples, hard rolls, and cheese curds in
their possession while the bugs bubbled merrily over the
coals. They shared the water in the canteens. It tasted dusty
and stale, but it slaked Collins' thirst. By the time Falima
pulled the hot crockery from the fire, he felt satisfied, not
the least bit interested in the boiled mass of recently crawling pests.

Suddenly, Falima stiffened, a handful of dead bugs halfway to her mouth.

"What?" Zylas said.

Falima tipped her head. "Listen."

Collins strained his own hearing. Wind rattled through
the leaves, and branches swished softly. Crickets screeched
and hummed in a rising and falling chorus. Farther away, a
hound bayed.

"Dogs!" Zylas sprang to his feet, kicking dirt over the
fire.

Falima stuffed the insects in her mouth, then started
shoving loose possessions, willy-nilly, into the pack.

Caught up in his companions' urgency, Collins looked
about for stray objects, finding only the lead rope/halter he
had used to guide Falima. Snatching it up, he set to using a
branch to erase all signs of the camp. "I presume dogs mean—"

"Pursuit," Falima interrupted.

Zylas qualified as he scattered the partially burned kindling. "All horse and all dog is guard."

Falima draped the saddlebags over Collins' shoulders
and seized the halter from his hand. "Go! Go! Due north. I
will find you. Hide in the . . . the sixth oak."

"But—" Collins started.

"Come." Zylas grabbed his arm and ran. Dragged two
steps, Collins stumbled, caught his balance, then charged
after the albino.

"What about Falima?"

"She make smell-trail. Catch up." Zylas' pull became insistent. "Come."

Scarcely daring to believe Falima would risk her life for
his, nor that Zylas would allow it, Collins did as Zylas bade.
"Why the sixth oak?"

"Random," Zylas replied, still running. "Far enough for
safe. She find us."

Collins looked back. Falima dragged the crude rope halter through the dirt, then disappeared among the trees in the opposite direction.

"Up! Up!" Zylas shoved Collins into a fat trunk. He crashed against it hard enough to drive the breath from his lungs. White petals showered down over him, silky on his skin, filling hair, mouth, eyes. Amid gasping in air thickened by the cloying perfume of flowers, spitting out petals, and regaining his vision, he managed to seize a low limb. Zylas scrambled over him, quick and agile as a monkey. The albino clambered higher, dislodging more flowers in a gentle rain over Collins, who hauled himself into the sheltering branches. The tree reminded him of a densely blooming tulip poplar or catalpa, but more thickly flowered with fatter, longer petals and indigo centers.

Realization came with shocking abruptness. "This isn't an oak."

Zylas silenced Collins with a hiss.

Collins glanced down. The ground lay barely five feet beneath him. "But Falima won't be able to find—"

Zylas' cloth-covered sandal tapped Collins' cheek in warning. "Hush. Better hiding. Thick and smell."

Collins reached for a higher branch and hauled himself deeper into a suffocating wall of leaves and petals. Zylas' reasoning made sense. The dogs would have a more difficult time catching their scent amid flowers that also concealed them from sight. Yet, he could not help worrying about their other companion. It seemed unlikely Falima could find them either. He tried to think of something he might not have considered; but, even focused on the differences between Barakhai and home, he found nothing. He did not believe horses had an unusually well-developed sense of smell, certainly not keener than hounds.

The barking grew louder, closer, then more insistent. At Zylas' steadying touch, Collins realized he was fidgeting. Adrenaline was driving him to run or pace, foolish urges in their current situation. He looked up. Zylas had climbed even higher. He had had to stretch his toes as far as possible to reach Collins at all. Cautiously, Collins raised a hand to grab an overhead branch. Rapid rustling through the brush stopped him in mid-movement. Below, Falima pressed through a clump of reedy stalks. Something louder slammed the weeds behind her, snuffling.

Falima! Though driven to shout, Collins held his tongue. He swung to a lower branch, then caught the woman's shoulder as she passed.

Falima hissed and spun. Her fist slammed Collins' ear. Fire slashed through his head, and he lost his grip, plummeting to the ground. Pain jarred through his left elbow and hip.

"Oh, sorry," Falima whispered, finally recognizing Collins. She grasped a lower branch and swung herself into the tree.

A hound burst through the foliage.

Collins froze.

The dog skidded to a stop. Young and gangly, it sported long legs, floppy ears, and a tail too long for its body. Patches of brown and white were interspersed randomly over its face and body. Head raised, it opened its mouth.

"No." Collins sprang for the dog, snapping its muzzle closed with one hand and scooping it up under its legs with the other. He could hear its companions baying in the distance, but no others followed it through the brush. Yet.

Clutching the half-grown dog, Collins ran for the tree. It struggled in his grip, making climbing all but impossible. He braced its weight against the lowest branch. Still holding its mouth, he managed to gain a toehold and drag self and dog amid the flowers.

"What are you doing?" Falima asked incredulously.

"Keeping it quiet." Collins loosed the dog's snout. Immediately, it howled. Collins swore and clamped his hand back over its muzzle, stifling the noise. It struggled wildly, clawing at him and trying to duck its head through his grip. Collins clung tighter to the dog, his balance on the tree branch swaying dangerously.

Falima steadied Collins. "You've got to get up higher."

Though true, it seemed impossible. "Here." He thrust the dog's backside at Falima. "Help me."

Muttering something uninterpretable, Falima placed the bulk of the dog's weight on a higher limb. Collins kept one hand wrapped solidly around its muzzle and attempted to climb with the other. Bark scraped a line of skin from his forearm, and the movement unleashed a storm of leaves and petals.

"Easy," Zylas cautioned.

Collins managed to work his way to a reasonably hidden branch. With Falima's help, he steadied the dog in his lap, fingers stiffening on its muzzle. It managed an occasional whine, but he stifled the barks and bays that might bring the hunters. *If they find us, we're dead.* Nevertheless, it never occurred to him to harm the pup.

The barking grew louder, then fainter, occasionally mingled with human voices. Collins' breathing turned erratic as he fought not to contemplate the situation. If he did, he might panic, just as he had at the gallows. That image quickened his breathing to pants, and he shoved it aside. He thought instead of grade school autumns, playing tag with friends among the maples and dogwoods.

Over time, the surrounding odor of flowers became more stench than fragrance. The dog's weight seemed to treble; Collins' legs fell asleep beneath it. He passed the hours until full nightfall mentally singing every song he could remember, mostly childhood nursery rhymes, lullabies, and those from his high school musical, *Anything Goes.*

A whistle cut through the night sounds that had risen so gradually, Collins had not realized he was straining his hearing over them. The dog resumed its struggle with a vengeance, pained whines escaping Collins' hold. An explosion of petals and leaves cascaded to the ground. The branch shook violently. Collins fought for his hold, Falima assisting. Finally, the dog ceased its kicking and lay, hopelessly snared, in the tree.

Apparently, the whistle called the dogs home, because the sounds of movement, the barking, and the voices disappeared. For a long time, the three humans and the dog remained silently in the tree. Then, finally, Zylas spoke. "Let's go."

Painstakingly, Collins eased the dog from his lap. It dropped to the ground and immediately loosed a fusillade of barks.

Collins leaped from the branch, jarring a wave of buzzing pain up his legs. The dog whirled, teeth bared, and growled a warning that Collins dared not heed. He dove for it, bearing it to the ground, then grabbed its mouth again. His cramped fingers responded sluggishly, and the dog managed to slash his left hand before he subdued it.

A pair of legs eased into Collins' view. He looked up at

a fine-boned stranger dressed in brown and green. He could barely judge height from this angle, but the other seemed small, almost frail. Short, brown hair hung in shaggy disarray, and dark eyes studied Collins with a heated glare.

Collins froze, arms winched around the dog. *Caught.* There was no way he could overpower a dog and a man simultaneously, no matter how slight they were. He cringed, turning the newcomer a pleading look, hoping for some miracle to keep the other from shouting. He found no mercy in the keen brown eyes and lowered his head. "It's over," he whispered. *And I'm going to die.*

Chapter 5

HURL the dog at the man and run! Any action hero would pull it off, but the more rational portion of Collins' mind dismissed the idea immediately. Jackie Chan could outmaneuver a dog; Benton Collins would be lucky to manage two running steps before the animal's teeth sank into his buttocks and the man's shouts brought armed companions to finish what the dog started.

Time seemed to move in slow motion. The stalemate dragged into that strange eternity mortal danger sometimes creates. The aroma of the tree flowers condensed into a cloying cloud, like the worst humidity Collins had ever encountered. His lungs felt thick with pollen.

Displaying none of Collins' caution, Falima and Zylas swung down beside him. A chaos of petals and sticks wound through the woman's thick, black hair. She addressed the newcomer in their musical tongue, and he responded in turn. Zylas placed a hand on the dog, and it resumed its struggles.

Clutching the dog's muzzle tightly, Collins braced himself against its sharp-nailed paws. Attention fully on the animal, he addressed his companions. "What did he say?"

Zylas helped support the dog's floundering weight. His first word eluded Collins, but the rest came through clearly, ". . . still angry you hit." He paused. "Falima not helping." He glared at her.

As the dog again sank into quiet despair, Collins glanced

at the rat/man and tried to fathom his initial utterance. "Yah-linn?" It sounded Chinese to him.

Zylas enunciated, "Ialin. Ee-AH-lin. Other . . . friend."

Falima and the newcomer continued to converse.

"Friend?" Relief flooded Collins, followed by understanding. "He must be . . . the hummingbird?"

Zylas considered, then smiled and nodded. "Ialin. Hummingbird. Yes."

Only then did Collins finally put everything together. He had assumed "Ialin" the Barakhain word for "friend," but it was, apparently, the hummingbird's name. "Ialin," he repeated, then slurred it as Zylas had the first time so it sounded more like, "Yahlin." Collins glanced at Falima, only to find Ialin's gaze pinned on him. *Duh, Ben. You said his name. Twice.* Cheeks heating, he addressed the other man. "Hello and welcome."

Ialin's scowl remained, unchanged.

Falima said something in their tongue, Ialin replied in a sulky growl, then Zylas spoke in turn. The conversation proceeded, growing more heated. At length, even Zylas punctuated his statements with choppy hand gestures and rising volume.

Collins sat, drawing the dog securely into his lap. This time, it barely fought, settling itself in the hollow between his legs. Helplessly studying his companions' exchange, watching it ignite into clear argument, he found himself fondling one of the dog's silky ears. In careful increments, he eased his grip on its muzzle until he no longer pinned it closed. The dog loosed a ferocious howl so suddenly it seemed as if the sound had remained clamped inside, just waiting for him to release it. Collins wrapped his fingers around the slender snout again, choking off another whirlwind round of barking.

All sound disappeared in that moment. Then, leaves rustled in the breeze, and petals floated in a gentle wash. Collins realized what was missing. In addition to birdsong and the dog's cry, his companions' discussion had abruptly ended. He glanced over to find three pairs of eyes directly and unwaveringly upon him.

Collins' face flared red, and he forced a sheepish grin. "Sorry about that." Aware that treating a human the way he had the dog practically defined assault and kidnapping, Collins attempted to mitigate his crimes, at least to his companions. "I'd let it go, but . . ."

Zylas nodded, expression serious. "Cannot." He stroked his chin, clearly pondering. Then, shaking his head, dislodging a storm of petals from the wide brim of his hat, he unraveled a ropy, green vine from a nearby trunk. Carrying it to where Collins sat, he expertly bound the dog's mouth shut. Zylas turned his gaze to Falima. "Know this dog?"

Collins eased away his hand.

The hound's nose crinkled menacingly and it jerked its head, but the vine held.

Falima responded in their language, and Zylas raised a warning hand. "You have stone. Not waste."

Falima glowered.

Zylas' look turned pleading, weary.

"I'd rather Ialin understood than . . . him."

Collins ignored the loathing in Falima's voice and supplied, "Ben."

Falima grumbled something that sounded suspiciously like a snarly teen's "whatever." She switched to English, "We had best move on."

Zylas studied the skeletal shapes of trees against the growing darkness, the crescent moon overhead. "Quickly. I have to sleep soon."

Falima pushed through the trees, Ialin following. The hummingbird/man moved with a flitty grace, individual movements quick and jerky, yet the whole merging into a smooth and agile pattern. Only Zylas remained, frowning at the problem that remained in Collins' lap. Collins elucidated, "He can't bark if we let him go, but he also can't eat or drink if he doesn't find his way home quickly."

"Still think like your world." Zylas grinned. "When he switch . . ."

Collins imagined trying to tie a man's mouth closed and shared Zylas' amusement. ". . . the vine will fall off."

"Right."

Collins rose, dumping the dog from his lap. "Shoo. Go home." Other thoughts dispelled his smile. "But won't he go back and tell everyone who we are and where?"

Zylas' smile also wilted. "Falima say he . . . he . . ." he fumbled for the right word, then supplied one questioningly, "little?"

"Young?" Collins tried, remembering how he, too, had assessed it as a partially grown pup.

Zylas nodded. "Like . . . teenager."

The dog watched them, tail waving uncertainly.

"Probable very dog. Very very dog. Not . . . not retain . . . ?" He looked to Collins to confirm the appropriateness of his word choice.

Collins made an encouraging gesture.

". . . what see in switch-form, not same."

Collins nodded to indicate he understood despite the poorly phrased explanation. Zylas seemed to be struggling more than usual, a sure sign of stress. "Is it possible he might . . . retain . . . some of what happened here after he resumes human form?"

"Not impossible," Zylas admitted.

Collins trusted the decision to his companion, glad the dog made it easier by remaining with them unfettered. Its soft brown gaze rolled from one man to the other, and its tail beat a careful rhythm.

Zylas sighed, air hissing through his lips. His face lapsed into creases that seemed to age him ten years. Beneath the shadow of his hat, his pale eyes radiated troubles, and the white-blond hair hung in limp, tangled strings. "Too tired to make wise choice." He ripped another stout vine from the tree and looped it around the dog's neck. "Keep with us now. Talk. Think." He headed in the direction their companions had taken. The dog balked.

Collins went, too, encouraging the animal by tapping his leg and calling, "Come on, boy. Come on," in a happy tone.

Tail whipping vigorously, the dog followed.

Camp consisted of downing the last of their cold rations, tossing their bodies on layers of moldering leaves, and drifting into sleep. Zylas dropped off almost at once. Falima and Ialin chattered in their incomprehensible language, occasionally glancing furtively in his direction. Though exhausted, Collins found sleep more elusive. He knelt by the tethered dog who no longer required the muzzle tie and had eaten his share of the remaining foodstuffs.

Collins ran a hand along the animal's spine. It quivered at his touch, then lowered its head with a contented sigh. Collins continued to stroke the fur, stopping now and then for a pat or a scratch. The dog sprawled on its side, moaning with contentment. Its tail thudded against the ground, and it wriggled as if to keep every part in contact with Collins' hand. He could scarcely believe it the same beast that had inflicted the gash across his hand.

Thinking of it brought back the pain that desperation and need had made him disregard. Collins examined the wound. Clotted blood filled the creases, making it appear to encompass the entire back of his hand. He spit on a finger, rubbing and scraping until he revealed a superficial, two-inch laceration. He had gotten lucky. He doubted a doctor back home would even bother to stitch it.

The dog whined, sniffing at Collins' hand. It licked the wound.

"Yuck." Collins jerked his hand away, only then thinking of infection. It seemed unlikely this world had a sophisticated medical system, such as antibiotics. *Probably at the level of leeches and bloodletting.* The image sent a shiver through him. He had heard that dog saliva contained natural anti-infection agents, the reason why they licked their own injuries and suffered fewer infections. He wondered whether the benefits of those agents outweighed the germs inherent in any drool of a species that drank from mosquito-infested puddles, groomed itself in unsanitary places, and lapped up horse excrement like candy. *Better,* he decided, *to clean this wound myself.*

Collins glanced at Zylas. The albino slumbered comfortably, the stress lines smoothed from his brow. Collins' watch now read nearly 11:00 P.M. Assuming this place had days the same length as his own, Collins realized Zylas would become a rat again in about an hour. A flash of heat passed through him, followed by a hysterical shiver. Without Zylas' calm reason, he doubted the group would stay together. Apparently, Falima and Ialin hated him, perhaps enough to turn him in to the guards. *They'll hang me.* He wondered if he had now compounded the crime enough for a worse fate, though what fate could be worse than death he didn't even want to imagine. He slumped to the ground, abruptly incapable of anything. Hopelessness overpowered him, a dense blanket that forced his thoughts to a tedious slog. Escape lay only a day's travel away, yet it was beyond his ability to navigate. He still did not know the way. Once there, he would have to battle his way through armed warriors, with only a rat for assistance. *A rat.* A wave of despair buffeted the last of his reason. Twelve hours utterly alone. Twelve hours dodging a hunt he scarcely understood in an unfathomable world. Twelve hours without a friend.

Tears stung Collins' eyes, then rolled down cheeks still flushed with distress. He had so many questions, and he needed those answers to survive Zylas' rat-time. It seemed safest to lay low, to mark time until he had a trustworthy companion to plan with again. He wondered how the people of Barakhai stood the change, interrupting half their lives daily, putting relationships and experiences on hold just as they started to build. Romance seemed impossible without careful coordination of the switching times—if such could even be arranged. He shook his head, the tears flowing faster. He knew so little to be suddenly thrown, friendless, back into an inexplicable world beneath a sentence of death. He had never felt so completely, so desperately, alone.

Leaves rustled. Something warm brushed Collins' cheek. He looked up into the dog's fuzzy face, and it licked tears from his face again. It whined, sharing his discomfort. Collins managed a smile. Even amid all of Barakhai's strangeness, a dog was a dog after all. He placed an arm around the furry body, and it lay down against him with a contented sigh, sharing its warmth.

Falima spoke from startlingly close. "Dogs are good judges of character." She added snidely, "Usually."

Collins tried to surreptitiously wipe away the tears. He did not look at Falima, not wanting her to know about his lapse. "Maybe *you're* the one who misjudged me."

A lengthy pause ensued. "Maybe," she finally admitted, grudgingly.

"About Joetha . . ." Though Collins hated to raise the subject, he knew he would have to resolve the issue before Falima could ever consent to like him. "I truly didn't—"

"I know," Falima interrupted.

"You do?" Collins could not keep surprise from his voice.

"I . . . think I do. It is hard seeing things . . . that way." Falima added insightfully, "Through the eyes of a foreigner."

"Yes." Collins wholeheartedly agreed.

Another long silence followed. Collins thought Falima must have left as quietly as she had come. So when she spoke, he jumped, turning his tear-streaked face to her. "What were you doing to the dog?" She simulated stroking with her hands, then crouched beside him.

Collins blinked the last of the tears from his eyes. "You mean when I was petting and scratching?"

"Yes."

The answer now seemed wholly obvious, but she seemed to expect one, so Collins reiterated. "Uh, I was, uh, petting. And ... uh ... scratching."

"Yes." The word emerged in an emotionless monotone that revealed nothing.

Sorrow gave way to sudden terror. "I always ... I mean I never thought ... it's just ..." Collins gathered his thoughts. "Did I do something terrible? Again?"

"No," Falima reassured. "Not terrible. It is just ... well, stroking someone. That is kind of ... personal, do you not think?"

Collins patted the animal snuggled against him, and the dog's tail thumped the ground. He tried to consider the beast as a human, and a strange thought eased into his mind. "Is this a boy dog or a girl dog?"

"Male." The response held a hint of question.

Collins' mind returned to the summer of his freshman year of college, just before his parents' divorce. His best friend from high school, Bill Dusumter, had taken leave from the army at the same time. They had agreed to meet at Bobcat Den Park. When Collins arrived at the picnic grounds, he found several of the old gang sitting around talking. He waved to Diana Hostetler, with whom he had exchanged jokes and shared a love for the trombone. Dusumter had dated her for a time, their breakup messy; and Collins had avoided pressing for a relationship for fear of losing their friendship. She looked the same as he remembered: dark, shoulder-length hair that shimmered in the sunlight; eyes starkly blue in contrast; high-pitched, freckled cheeks; and a broad, wry mouth. Katie Tonn and Dave Hansen had become a couple, attending Cornell University together. Dusumter claimed to have lost his virginity with Tonn, but none of the three seemed to hold any ill will. Several other friends from high school played a lively game of frisbee. But Collins' gaze fixed on Bill Dusumter, his tomcat best buddy, and the stranger at his side.

Both wore the standard military haircut, matching brown hair buzzed to half-inch prickles. Both were skinny, with lean angular faces; and they both smelled of cigarettes. They wore Levis and T-shirts, Dusumter's red with the name of a local bar and the newcomer's plain black.

Collins' brain worked overtime, trying to divine the relationship between the two. Before he could speak, Dusumter gestured him over, a delighted grin on his face. "Ben. Buddy. How's it hanging?"

Still deep in thought, Collins had to force a smile and missed the opportunity for a snappy comeback. "It's hanging fine. Army treating you okay?"

"Great!" Dusumter gestured toward his companion. "This is Gene." He winked conspiratorially. "You're going to be seeing a lot more of Gene around here."

"Oh." Something seemed wrong, and Collins could not put his uneasiness into words. "Is Gene . . . moving here?"

"Yup."

"Ah." Collins gazed into his friend's eyes and read more there, something exciting and interesting that he would not reveal until asked. Collins felt too dense to find the proper question, whatever it might prove to be.

Dusumter retook his seat. As he did so, he placed a hand squarely on Gene's thigh.

Collins' breath caught in his throat. A million thoughts swirled through his mind in an instant. *Bill's gay?* The thought bothered him deeply, and that troubled him. *I'm for gay rights. I have gay friends. Am I just a hypocrite?* Collins wanted to cry. Few things upset him more than people who preached values to others while cheating on their spouses, fanatics who sabotaged animal experiments then eagerly popped medications born of that research, fiends who labeled women who suffered through an abortion to save their own lives as murderers then encouraged their daughters to destroy the fetus of a man they did not like. *It's easy to cling strongly to morality when it doesn't affect you.* Collins analyzed his discomfort, delving to its source. *I don't have a problem with Bill being gay. It just came completely out of the blue, so opposite from the Bill I knew. I can and will deal with this. It's my problem, not his.*

Collins exchanged pleasantries with his old friend, then headed off to see some of the others. He had taken fewer than half a dozen steps, prepared to step around their scattered purses and backpacks, when Dusumter came up beside him. Grinning, he asked, "So, what do you think of Gene?"

Still shocked, Collins did not know what to say. He barely knew the newcomer, who had not yet spoken a word. "Um," he mumbled. "Seems nice." Unable to meet Dusumter's sparkling brown gaze, he glanced at the backpacks.

"Don't tell anyone else; I wanted you to be the first to know ..."

Collins braced himself, wishing he had had time to prepare, seeking the most supportive words he could muster in his own panicked moments of shock.

"... Gene and I are getting married."

Married? Collins whirled to face his friend. Even as he moved, his eyes registered a name on one of the backpacks: "JEAN." *Jean, Gene.* It all came together in that moment. *Just because Bill's fiancée is too skinny to have boobs doesn't mean she's not a woman!* Relief flooded him, not because Dusumter was not gay; that truly did not matter. Collins' solace came from the realization that he did know the man who had been his best friend, that he had not missed signs of misery or need, had not been kept from a significant secret for lack of trust or closeness. "Congratulations." He caught Dusumter into an embrace, not the least bit self-conscious.

Dusumter's familiar voice hissed into his ear. "Way to keep a secret, buddy."

Now, in an alien world with a dog who was also a man curled against him, Collins smiled at the memory. As weird as the situation had become, it seemed marginally preferable to having made what might have seemed like a sexual advance on some strange woman who, properly and without insult, could be better called a bitch.

Oblivious to Collins' train of thought, Falima continued. "A *young* male, of course."

Great, so now I'm a child molester. Collins cringed. *That makes it much better.*

Attuned to Collins' discomfort, Falima continued, "It is all right, really. He is probably the closest thing to a dog of your world that you will find here. He clearly enjoys the attention, and he probably will not remember much of it in human form."

Collins studied the dog's brown-and-white patches.

"So go ahead and stroke him. If it makes him uncomfortable, he will let you know."

Yeah. Collins glanced at his wound. *Next time, he'll bite my hand clean off.* Tentatively, he petted the dog's back. It sighed and snuggled more closely to him.

Falima smiled. "Actually, I like it when people stroke my nose."

Collins gave Falima a strange look.

"In switch-form, of course." Falima's cheeks turned scarlet, to Collins' surprise. She seemed too strong to let anything embarrass her. "And a scratch behind my ears now and then feels wonderful. Especially when the flies are biting." Her features lapsed back into their tough demeanor. "But I do not like being kicked. In any form."

"I'm sorry," Collins said, meaning it. "It's just that's how we steer in—"

"—your world," Falima finished.

"Yes. In my world. The only world I knew existed until yesterday. I'm very sorry I kicked you. It won't happen again."

A strained silence followed, into which Collins wanted to insert something clever that might finally bridge the gap between them. Instead, a question came to mind. He wanted to know why discussing her petting spots shamed her more than switching to human form buck naked. Wisely, he put aside that train of thought for a safer one. "I guess it's just us till Zylas becomes a man again."

Ialin strolled to them, crunching something between his teeth and carrying handfuls of leaves and stems. He turned Collins a withering, imperious look, then focused on Falima. He remained standing, the only position that allowed the tiny man to tower over his seated companions. He spoke in the language of Barakhai.

Falima's reply took much longer as she, apparently, filled him in on the conversation to date.

With the memory of Bill and Jean Dusumter in his mind, Collins studied Ialin. The hummingbird/man, too, could pass for a slight, curveless woman. For an instant, the thought that he might have made the same mistake twice swept through Collins, banished by the memory of Zylas' use of the pronoun "he" to refer to the hummingbird's human form. *Of course, Zylas' English is rather primitive.*

Falima addressed Collins again. "Zylas will not desert us just because he is in switch-form."

The dog stretched its legs, pressing its back against Collins, groaned, and dropped back off to sleep.

Collins nodded, certain Falima spoke the truth. "I just meant we won't have a way to talk to him until he's . . . until he's human."

"I will." Falima patted her tummy and tossed her black hair, highlights of scarlet, purple, and green shifting through her tresses.

"You will?" Hope rose in a wild rush. "You can . . . you can . . ." Collins barely dared to believe. ". . . talk to each other in animal form?"

Falima held a brief exchange with Ialin that left the man snickering before replying, "Not usually. But Zylas is older. He has good, solid *overlap* between his forms; I know of no one with more. And I still have his translation stone." Her blue gaze hardened. "Thanks to you."

Collins stroked the dog's side, and its tail thumped in gratitude. In addition to a near-flawless grasp of English, Falima had clearly mastered sarcasm. "I'm sorry." He wondered how many times he would have to apologize before Falima would forgive him, hoping she would not prove as difficult to appease as Marlys. *Maybe it's a woman thing.*

Apparently mistaking Collins' attention to the dog for an unspoken question, Falima said, "No, I cannot talk to him. He has little or no *overlap*. He might not even have reached coming-of-age yet."

"Coming-of-age?" Collins repeated. That brought to mind David Fein's bar mitzvah, expanding lip disks, and quests to kill wild boars and leopards.

Ialin made a grunted comment to which Falima responded before switching back to English. "When a child is born, he assumes the same switch-form and at the same times as his mother. He has no *overlap* at all. On his thirteenth birthday, he gets a party. His switch time melds with his personality, *overlap* begins, and, if he is a *Random,* he transmutes."

Collins put up a hand to stay Falima. "Hold it. I was with you up until the thirteenth birthday party. *Randoms.* Transmuting." He shook his head. "What are you talking about?"

Falima eased to a cross-legged sitting position. She spoke painfully slowly, as if to an idiot. "At thirteen, all right?"

Collins did not grace the question with so much as a nod. If he did, he felt certain she would drag a simple explanation into next week.

"A child becomes a man or woman. He gets a switch time . . ." Falima glanced at Collins to see if he still followed her description.

Collins bobbed his head. He knew about switch times from Zylas. "Does some person assign each teen a switching time? Or is it random?"

Falima conversed with Ialin before answering. "Neither. It seems to have more to do with the . . ." She used Collins' word, ". . . teen's personality. It just happens, and it seems to suit the person. *Overlap* between human and animal form begins. *Regulars* tend to learn control faster than *Randoms,* but they also spend more time in animal form."

Collins frowned, shaking his head. "You've lost me again." He considered the problem. "Maybe if you explain what you mean by *Regulars* and *Randoms.*" He looked up at the sky. The moon had risen higher, a crescent that scarcely grazed the darkness. Stars spread across the darkness, remarkably similar to the spring pattern of his own world.

"*Regulars* occur when animals of like type mate, whether in human or animal form. A man who becomes a bull, for example, marries a woman whose switch-form is a cow." Falima studied Collins' reaction, and he gave her what he hoped was an encouraging look. This made sense to him. "Since animals can only mate within their type, and they tend not to worry about or understand human conventions when it comes to marriage, *Regulars* outnumber *Randoms* by about three hundred to one."

Collins reasoned, "So a *Random* would come of a union between two humans with different types of switch-forms."

"Right." Apparently impressed by his reasoning, Falima passed it on to Ialin.

Ialin came back with something that sounded gruff, almost warning.

Beaming, Collins struggled to continue. Falima's opinion

of him mattered more than he could explain. "Until thirteen, *Randoms* become the animal of their mother. Then, they become . . ." He did not know how to proceed. Logic dictated that boys might follow the father and girls the mother, but the opposite could prove equally true. *What am I doing seeking logic in magic?* Sticking with what the name implied, he tried, ". . . something random?"

"Exactly," Falima crowed. "Though maybe not totally random. It probably has something to do with the physical or emotional makeup of the person. Or maybe the animal-type influences those things. It would be hard to ever know for sure."

"Which are you?"

Falima's open excitement disappeared. Her features lapsed into a mask, and her movements looked calculatedly casual. "What?"

"Which are you?" Collins repeated carefully. "*Regular* or *Random*?"

"All horses are guards," Falima said in a not-quite-indifferent tone. "Senior to dogs. Ours is a respected position, nearly always bred on purpose."

"And you?" Collins pressed.

Falima blinked, now clearly annoyed. "You heard me. You may assume me a *Regular*."

It was not a direct answer, but Collins accepted it. Though he had clearly stepped into dangerous territory, he could not keep himself from asking. "And Zylas?" He glanced toward his companion as he spoke, only to find a set of empty clothing. "He's changed!"

"A few moments ago," Falima confirmed.

Collins studied the britches. He rose with a caution designed not to disturb the dog, drawing nearer to where Zylas had fallen asleep until he found the rat-sized lump stirring regularly beneath linen. "Is he a *Random* or a *Regular?*"

"*Random,*" Falima said with a wide yawn. "Do you think we breed rats on purpose?"

Collins thought of the lab. *We do.* "And Ialin?"

This time, Falima dodged the question. "I'm getting tired. We really should sleep." Without awaiting a reply from Collins, she headed away to curl up on a pile of leaves. Ialin went with her.

Put off by Falima's sudden detachment, Collins lay back down beside the dog. Its warmth soothed him, even as he worried for the propriety of his action. At least he could explain it away as a means to keep watch over an animal that might sneak off and report them to the authorities. He wondered about the information Falima had given him and why discussion of the origins of self and friends made her so uncomfortable. He vowed not to press the question the next day. To do so might lose him what little trust of hers he had managed to gain or leave him in the bleak loneliness he had dreaded only an hour ago.

With these thoughts buzzing through his mind, it surprised Collins how swiftly he found sleep.

Chapter 6

BENTON Collins awakened to a sweet but unrecognizable aroma that sent his stomach into a ferocious growl. It reminded him of his mother's freshly baked cinnamon rolls, yet was different in a way he could not quite define. He opened his eyes to a subdued fire surrounding a crock blackened by charcoal. Ialin and Falima spoke in hushed tones, their shadows flickering through the brush at their backs. The sun had not yet penetrated the dense cover of leaves and branches. The two chatted like old friends. Though Collins could not understand a word of it, he noticed that neither wore the tense expression of hostile distrust that had become so familiar to him.

The dog rolled its head to look at Collins. It wagged its tail in greeting, tip stirring the leaves. Ialin and Falima took no notice, so Collins continued to study them in the scarlet-and-amber strobe of the fire. Her golden skin looked beautifully exotic. She had braided her mane of black hair away from her face, though a few strands lay damply against her cheeks. Apparently, she had washed and combed it out earlier that morning. Though lost beneath an overlarge cloak, the curves of her naked body remained vividly in Collins' memory. His mind's eyes conjured the generous breasts, the fine curves, and the well-toned body with an ease that made him flush. He felt himself responding to the image, which abruptly heightened his embarrassment. He tried to quell desire by turning his attention to his other companion.

Ialin rose and walked to the fire, movements odd though never awkward. The words that came to Collins' mind in description: flitty, quick, birdlike fit best, though he found none of them quite adequate. The man reminded him most of Jean, who had become a dependable, almost supernaturally daring, friend over the years. Though small to the point of scrawny, she never hesitated to face off with the largest man. They had once stopped to examine a snake on the road. None of the men in the car would touch it, but Jean had picked it up without a second thought. And, upon discovering that she held a rattlesnake, she had attempted to keep it for a pet. On two occasions, he had watched women leaving a public restroom that Jean had just entered whispering angrily about the man who had dared to walk boldly into their haven.

There was something equally androgynous about the hummingbird/man, and Collins wondered if it had anything to do with the fact that bird gender was difficult to read at a glance. *Or is it?* When he thought about it more carefully, he realized that in many species of birds, like peacocks, blue jays, and chickens, the male and female looked phenomenally different, far more so than, say, horses. Or rats.

Collins shook his head, tired of trying to find rhyme and reason in a world that either had none or, at least, none that he could logically and rationally fathom without the assistance of those who lived it daily. At that moment, he found Ialin returning his gaze with steady yellow-brown eyes. The man said something to Falima, and she looked at Collins as well. For a while, they all simply stared, saying nothing. Finally, Falima's face broke into a cautious, weary half-smile. "Good, you are awake. Come join us."

Collins gave back a genuine grin, glad Falima had actually welcomed him, though it hardly mattered. Soon enough, he would return to his own world and these people would fade into the blurred uncertainty between reality and dream. He had read enough fantasy as a child to know that others, and maybe eventually he, would dismiss whatever adventures he had in this world as the product of distraught imagination. *Assuming I make it out of here alive.* He stood, rearranging his jeans to cover his dwindling excitement. He could taste his morning breath but could think of no way to remedy the problem. He ran a hand through his hair, dislodging wilted petals, twigs, and curled leaves. His appearance and hygiene, he knew, should not bother him; but it did. *At least I probably look better without my glasses.* He squinted, surprised at how easily he found himself getting along without them. He could see better than he remembered, and it sent his mind into another round of unusual thought. *Do I not need them as much as I believe? Am I simply getting used to not having them? Or is it just another part of the magic of Barakhai?*

Using a stick, Ialin eased the crock from the fire.

The dog rolled to its feet, yawned, and stretched. Its tongue uncurled, and the mouth spread wide to reveal rows of surprisingly blunt teeth. Then, finished, it followed Collins to his companions near the fire.

Falima glanced upward, though interwoven branches blocked the sky. "I was about to wake you. I wanted you up before my switch."

"Your switch?" Collins rolled a panic-stricken gaze to Ialin. *Please. Don't leave me alone with . . . him.* He did not voice the concern. He had grown accustomed to Falima's animosity, had even managed to crack it somewhat. The idea of spending time with only Ialin chilled him, colored by his experiences with Jean. He liked Jean, but she also liked him. With Ialin, he could imagine that rattlesnake "accidentally" winding up in his bed. The analogy did not carry well, since any snake here would also be human and, presumably, barred by law and convention from harming others.

"It is coming soon." Falima used an edge of her cloak to ease the crock toward her. Ialin said something to which Falima replied. This time, she deigned to translate. "He wants me to wait until it cools. But I do not get *gahiri* often and do not eat it in switch-form."

"*Gahiri?*" Collins repeated, surprised to hear a Barakhain word during an English rendition. She had never mixed the two before. Then, he realized the word probably had no equivalent in his language.

Using a stick, Falima ladled a gloppy brown mixture onto a leaf as dark as spinach. It steamed in her hand as she offered it to Collins.

Collins hesitated. Then, worried it might burn her palm if she held it too long, he accepted it. It warmed his grip, its aroma a cross between pecan and currant pie, with a bit of baking potato.

Without seeing if Collins ate it, Falima made similar packets for Ialin and herself. They ate them like tacos, one hand folding the contents together, the other perched below to catch any runoff. He took a delicate bite of just the filling. It burned his tongue, and it took an effort of will not to spit it out. Instead, he swirled it around his mouth, never letting it settle in one place long enough to singe until it grew cool enough to swallow without hurting his throat. Only then, he allowed himself to assess the flavor, sweetly spicy with a subtle crunch he hoped had nothing to do with insects. It tasted sinfully good, like doughnuts for breakfast. He blew on it carefully before daring another bite. This time, he took a chunk of leaf along with the filling; and, to his surprise, it only enhanced the flavor. "Delicious," he said around a heated mouthful.

"The best," Falima agreed. "Most of the ingredients are quite common, but you have to get the *vilegro* seed at the right time. When you can even find it. It is valuable, too, so we can sell what we do not eat. A worthy find, Ialin had. That is the advantage of a small flying switch-form with a good sense for finding sweet things."

Falima's description sparked an idea. "Perhaps," Collins started thoughtfully. "Perhaps Ialin could distract the guards, fly around their . . ."

Before Collins could stop her, Falima translated. Ialin's reply was accompanied by a spark of anger.

Falima laughed. "Ialin suggests we distract you instead so the guards can catch you easier."

Collins brows rose, and the look he gave Falima was similar to Ialin's own.

All mirth disappeared. "He was only kidding," she said defensively. She and Ialin feigned sudden, inordinate interest in their *gahiri*.

Collins reached for his own half-eaten breakfast, only to find a large white rat devouring it. Startled, he skittered backward, then realized who had stolen his food. "Zylas!"

Falima laughed again, and even Ialin could not suppress a snicker. Zylas turned Collins as innocent a look as a rat could muster, then returned to eating.

Falima made three more *gahiri*, handing one to each of her human companions and eating the third. Abandoning his booty, Zylas crawled up Falima's arm to her shoulder, placed both paws on her ear, and squeaked emphatically.

Falima listened for a long time, nodding occasionally with her mouth full of food. She replied in their regular language, stuffed the rest of the *gahiri* into her mouth, then rose. Placing her hand inside her bodice, she plucked a cherry-sized piece of rose quartz from between her breasts and thrust it toward Zylas. The rat took the stone between his teeth, skittered from his perch, and dropped it on the ground near his food. Placing one paw on the rock, he commenced eating.

Collins looked at Falima. "What was that about?"

In response, Falima only shrugged.

"She can't understand you." Zylas' squeaks now formed high-pitched English words. "She passed the translation stone, and now I have it."

Knowing Falima had swallowed the stone, Collins did not want "pass" defined. "And you understand me?"

"Yes. But the others do not."

Torn between relief that he would not have to make conversation with two people who disliked him and worry that he might have to find other ways to make himself understood, Collins nodded his comprehension. If he could only communicate with one of his companions, he preferred it to be Zylas, even if he was a rat.

Collins glanced at his watch. It read a few minutes till 6:00 A.M. "So, what do we do now?"

Falima rose, brushed crumbs from her shift and cloak, and spoke a few words to Ialin, who nodded. She headed into the woods. The dog trotted after her, tail waving like a flag. With a few crisp words and a jab toward the men, she ordered it back. It obeyed, tail low, only the tip still twitching.

"Come here, boy!" Collins used a happy tone, and the dog bounded to him, tail again whipping broadly. He petted it, and it wiggled and circled in excitement. Zylas grabbed up the translation stone in his teeth and scuttled out of the way of the prancing paws. "Falima is switching?" Collins guessed.

Zylas' reply was barely audible. "Yeth." He dodged between the dog's feet to reach Collins and started clawing his way up Collins' jeans. The denim bunched under his claws and weight, dragging them down.

Worried Zylas might pants him, Collins bent, offering a hand to the rat. "Where are you trying to go?"

" 'our thoulder, ith 'ou peathe."

Thinking he understood, Collins hoisted Zylas to his left shoulder.

The rat scrabbled off, settling into the hollow between Collins' neck and shoulder. He spat out the stone and clapped it in place with a paw. "Can you hear me better now?"

It suddenly occurred to Collins that Zylas' speech had gone from halting and uncertain to grindingly clear since he had become rat. Though Collins knew it had to do with the magical stone rather than the transformation, the irony made him laugh.

Zylas' claws sank into Collins' flesh. "What's so funny?"

Collins went still, and the nails loosened. Resolved not to laugh or stumble again, to spare himself a gouging, he dismissed the thought. "Nothing important. So," he repeated his earlier, unanswered question. "What do we do now? Try the ruins again? Hope the guards have gone?"

"They're not gone," Zylas replied emphatically. His whiskers tickled Collins' ear.

"You're sure?"

"I'm sure." Not a bit of hesitation entered Zylas' reply.

Collins frowned. "So we have to get past them."

"Can't." The grim certainty remained in Zylas' voice.

"So you're saying it's impossible?"

Zylas did not waver. "Yes."

It went against every self-esteem-building encouragement Collins had received since infancy. "But nothing is really impossible."

"For us," Zylas said, "this is."

Collins opened his mouth, but remembrance of Falima's tirade choked off his words. *Is it not enough that we will probably die for saving a cold-blooded cannibal? Do you want more innocents to sacrifice their lives for you?* He did not want to die, did not want any of his companions to lose their lives, either, especially not for him. "All right." He tried to keep disappointment from his tone, without success.

Zylas clearly read beyond the words. "The guards will not allow us near the ruins. They will patrol now." He shook his head. "You cannot escape through that portal."

That portal. Fresh hope flared. "Could we ... could we maybe ... find another portal?" Collins looked up, remembering his companions for the first time since he had asked about Falima's transformation. The buckskin grazed placidly at a patch of weeds, her golden coat glimmering in the patch of sunlight penetrating the forest canopy. Ialin was stuffing Falima's garments into the pack, and the dog lay curled on the ground at his feet.

Zylas paced a circle on Collins' shoulder, clearly vexed. His gaze played over the party as well, lingering longest on the dog. "I don't know of any other portals ..."

Anticipating a "but," Collins remained silent.

"... I know someone who might ..." Zylas went suddenly still. "But ..." He fell into a long hush.

When Collins' patience ran out, he pressed. "But?"

Zylas skittered down Collins' side, stone in mouth, then leaped to the ground. He darted to Falima's lowered head, dropped the crystal, stepped on it, and commenced squeaking loudly.

The horse pranced backward, trumpeting out a whinny, then another.

Slower now, more thoughtfully, Zylas approached Ialin. Their conversation lasted no longer than the previous one. Finally, he returned to Collins.

Wanting to forgo more scratches, Collins crouched, anticipating Zylas' need. He scooped up the rat and replaced it on his shoulder. "So?"

Zylas spat out the translation stone. "Falima only has a partial overlap, so she's difficult to converse with in this form. Ialin ... well, Ialin will come around." He made an abrupt motion, as if shaking water from his coat. "Come on."

Having no idea what direction Zylas meant, Collins raised his brows. "Where are we going?"

"We're going," Zylas said thoughtfully, "to visit a good friend of mine."

They rode Falima, Ialin leading from the ground, Collins astride, Zylas sitting in the V formed by his legs. The dog trotted obediently at the horse's heels, apparently used to walking in that particular position. A gentle rain pattered on the leaves overhead, occasional droplets winding through the foliage to land as cold pinpricks against Collins' skin. He did not pressure his companions. Quite literally, they held his life in their hands. *Or rather,* Collins corrected, *in their claws, talons, and hooves.*

Zylas explained as they rode, "Vernon's a good guy. A longtime friend. You and Falima will be safe with him while Ialin and I go . . . elsewhere."

"Elsewhere?"

"To see someone older. Wiser." Zylas shook his pointy-nosed head. "That's all I can tell you."

"Can't I go?"

"No." Even for a rat, Zylas sounded emphatic.

Feeling like a sulky child, Collins grumbled. "Why not?"

"Too dangerous."

Collins looked at the dog who still followed them, tail waving. "For me? Or the elder?"

"Both."

"Oh." Collins considered that answer for several moments in a silence broken only by the swish and crackle of branches, the song of the drizzle on the canopy. "How so?"

"Vernon's a good guy," Zylas repeated, and Collins knew he would get no reply to his previous question. "A longtime friend."

Collins dropped the subject. They rode onward, brushing through wet foliage that left streaks of water across his tunic, jeans, and sneakers. Zylas wandered the length of Falima, pausing to guide her with whispered commands in her ear or to exchange a conversation with Ialin. Collins' watch read ten minutes to nine when Zylas called a halt. He spoke soothingly to Falima; and she slowed, snorting and pawing divots from the ground. Ialin stopped, patting her neck reassuringly. Collins slid from her back. He offered his hands to Zylas, who clambered aboard, little feet warm against Collins' palms. Images of his guinea pig rose to mind, its brown-and-white fur soft as down, its enormous black eyes studying him, and its loud "week, week, week," when it heard his mother making salad. He had named the animal George, which had become Georgie-girl several years later, when he learned how to differentiate gender.

Zylas leaped to Collins' shoulder. Falima dipped her head, nosing for grass amid tiny trees and mulch. Ialin turned his back, perhaps surveying the forest, more likely relieving himself. Three hours bouncing around on horse-back had given Collins a similar urge. Working around the rough material of a tunic now as soiled as his jeans, he urinated on a mushy pile of leaves.

"He's getting smaller." Zylas' sudden voice in his ear startled Collins, who jumped. Then, he sounded out the words and grew even more alarmed.

"Wha–what?" Collins stammered, stashing his manhood safely behind his zipper.

"Ialin," Zylas explained. "He's getting smaller. Switching."

Collins whirled to see, finding only an empty pile of clothing which the puppy snuffled eagerly.

Zylas continued, "You'll have to pack his things."

Collins nodded dully, now the only human. With a shock, he realized nearly twenty-four hours had passed since his aborted hanging. Then, too, all his companions had taken animal form, working together to rescue him from death. Approaching the shed clothing, he bent. Zylas scampered down his arm to the ground. Collins gathered the crudely sewn garments, approached Falima, and stuffed them into her saddlebags. He turned to find the pup crouched with its front legs extended, bottom high, and tail wagging cautiously as it urged Zylas to play. Realization glided into his mind. When Ialin appeared as a human, the dog was already in switch-form. Now, Ialin had become a bird again, but the dog remained a dog. "Zylas?"

The rat disengaged from the dog and approached.

"Shouldn't our . . . um . . . unexpected companion have become human by now?"

Zylas twisted his head to look over one shoulder at the puppy. "Not necessarily. *Regulars* spend more time in animal form than *Randoms*." He turned back to Collins. "If he just entered switch-form when he found us, I could even change before he does."

"Really," Collins said thoughtfully.

"We need to get going again." Zylas headed toward Falima. "I only stopped to give Ialin some dignity during his switch."

Collins trotted after his companion.

Zylas stopped by the grazing horse. "A boost, please? I can climb, but it makes her nervous."

Glad to help, Collins hefted Zylas to Falima's back, then mounted himself. Falima's head rose with obvious reluctance. Zylas clambered along her mane and thrust his muzzle into her ear. Falima snorted but resumed her walk through the forest.

Collins recalled that he had set his watch for noon about the time Zylas had become human, and Zylas had switched to rat form around midnight. Falima had turned into a horse at six in the morning and a human at six at night. Ialin changed at nine. That understanding brought a realization: Falima had lied. Aware his companions could and had exchanged information he could not understand, he prodded with utmost caution. "*Regulars,* like the pup, spend more time in animal form?"

Zylas returned to his steadiest position, planted between Collins' thighs. "That's right. And, on average, gain overlap at a younger age."

"Overlap meaning shared understanding and memory between forms."

"Right."

"Hmmm."

"What?"

Collins studied the white rat, suddenly feeling insane. If any of his colleagues had caught him talking to a laboratory animal like this, they would deem him certifiable. *Thirty-six hours in Barakhai, less than a day with animal companions, and it already feels natural to converse with a rat.* "It's just that you seem to have an exceptional amount of overlap."

"I do. Nearly perfect, in fact."

"Why is that?"

Zylas turned a circle, then settled against Collins. "First, I'm older than the others. I apparently have a natural talent for it. And I practice. A lot."

"Practice?" It seemed ludicrous. *Practice what?*

"Rats don't eat much, and any old garbage serves me fine in this form. I pay attention. I have no job. I'm not married. No . . . children." The last word emerged in a pained squeak, and he paused. He turned away for a moment, curling his hairless pink tail around his legs, then regained his composure and continued without missing a beat. "I've concentrated most of my life on enhancing my overlap, with good success." He added, "And it doesn't hurt that I spent my childhood in a similar enough form that I could use most of that training at adolescence rather than starting over. More like a *Regular* without the disadvantages."

Collins recalled that, until coming-of-age, children had the same switch-form as their mothers. "So your original switch-form . . . ?"

Zylas obliged. "A mouse. My father was a blue jay."

Collins laughed, earning a glare from Zylas.

"What's funny?"

Collins did not lie. "It's an odd combination."

The rat's mouth stretched into a grimace that Collins interpreted as a weary grin. "Not in human form." He anticipated a question Collins had not even thought to ask. "And, yes, they were both albino."

Startled into silence, Collins took several moments to craft a coherent question. "Is . . . is . . . it common in . . . in your world?"

"Albinism?"

"Yes."

"No."

"No?"

"I only know of two others." Zylas licked at his fur. "I think that's what brought my parents together. Something in common other than the usual shared switch-form."

"Hmmm." The white mouse came easily to Collins' imagination, the jay with more difficulty, though he had actually seen one at Algary's science museum. He glanced at the passing scenery, mostly leaves and needles, trying to appear casual. The rain had stopped, but droplets still plopped irregularly from higher branches. "What about Falima's parents?"

Zylas continued cleaning himself. "A milk goat and a squirrel, I believe."

A Random. Collins had suspected as much from the start. When he learned *Regulars* kept switch-form longer, it had seemed nearly certain. He wondered why Falima had tried to deceive him. "And Ialin?"

"Owl and shrew."

That combination did not surprise Collins at all. It seemed to fit the hostile, flighty young man. "So, you're all *Randoms?*"

Zylas stopped grooming. "Who told you about *Randoms?*"

"Falima."

Zylas shuddered his fur back into place. "Yes. We're all *Randoms*. Except the pup. Once she came of age as a horse, Falima got fostered to guards."

That seemed odd, though no more so than most of the other things Collins had learned here. "Why?"

"All horses are guards."

"Oh." Collins asked the logical follow-up. "And all rats?"

"We're *vermin*."

It sounded shocking from the mouth of a human rat. "Well, yes, but . . . I meant what job do rats do?"

"*Vermin* were always discouraged from breeding, especially as *Regulars*. The only ones left come out of *Random* unions."

"So your . . . mouse . . . mother . . . ?"

"Also a *Random*, yes. My father, too." Though Zylas did not seem uncomfortable discussing these matters, as Falima had, he did change the subject. "So, tell me about your world. I've seen many things that confuse me. Like why do you keep your white rats in cages while the brown ones run free?"

Chapter 7

BY the time they reached Vernon's ramshackle cabin in the woods, Collins suspected he had raised more questions than he'd satisfied, which seemed only fair. He felt the same way about Barakhai. Falima grazed the clearing. Zylas pulled clothing over his pale human body. The dog romped around all of them, alternately begging pets from Collins and exploring every inch of their new surroundings. Collins did not see Ialin but suspected the hummingbird buzzed nearby, more cautious since being mistaken for an insect and clouted across the forest.

Within moments, the door banged open and a man, apparently Vernon, appeared, britches hastily tied over thick legs, still pulling a coarse linen shirt over his broad, brown shoulders. Though Collins had seen dark-skinned people in this world before, Vernon was the first who closely resembled an African-American in his own world. He sported close-cropped curls, full lips, and shrewd eyes nearly as dark as the pupils. Tall, well-muscled, and bull-necked, he made a startling contrast to the slight albino, who disappeared into his welcoming embrace.

Zylas and Vernon exchanged words briefly. Then, Vernon's gaze shifted across Collins to settle alternately on Falima and the wagging-tailed dog. He shook his head and addressed Zylas with a challenging tone.

Collins recognized "Falima" in a reply otherwise gibberish to him.

Vernon nodded thoughtfully as he laced his shirt. He turned his attention fully on the dog and grunted something.

Zylas merely shrugged.

Collins looked at Falima. By the time he glanced back, Zylas was heading toward him.

"It's settled," Zylas explained, drawing his hat down to shade his forehead. "You and Falima remain here with Vernon. Ialin and I should be back tomorrow."

Collins' gaze rolled to the dog. "What about him?"

Zylas did not bother to follow Collins' gesture. "The dog stays with you. Do what you must to keep us safe."

Collins froze, hoping those words did not mean what he thought they did. He would not murder again, especially a child. He opened his mouth to say so, only to find Zylas watching him with distinct discomfort.

The rat/man held out his hand, fingers clenched to a bloodless fist. Collins watched each finger winch open, finally revealing the rose quartz stone. "You'll need this."

Collins stared at the translation stone. It made sense that he should carry it, as the others could all understand one another, at least in human form. Without reaching for it, he looked at Zylas.

The rat/man's lips pursed to lines as white as his flesh, and he dodged Collins' gaze. His fingers quivered, as if he battled the urge to close them safely around the stone again.

"This is hard for you, isn't it?"

Zylas nodded. "I've rarely let anyone use it, and then only in my presence." He glanced at the stone, and it held his stare. "It's unique and irreplaceable." He finally managed to tear his gaze free, to turn a worried look toward Collins. "It's also illegal."

Collins' brow furrowed. "Illegal?"

"Magic of any kind. The royals hate it."

The words shocked Collins. Shunning such a powerful tool seemed as absurd as locking away the secrets that science revealed. Yet, he realized, his world had done just that for many years now known as the Dark Ages. Despite himself, he found some logic in the realization that technology had brought the atomic bomb as well as computers, pollution along with transportation, thalidomide in addition to penicillin. With the good came the bad, and common sense could dictate none as easily as both. "But, you're all magic—"

"Except the royals," Zylas reminded. "They don't switch forms."

"Right." Collins recalled his companion telling him that, though it seemed ages ago. "Well . . ." Running out of things to say, he reached for the translation stone. ". . . I'll take good care of it. I promise." It seemed ridiculous to vow to protect a rock when he could not keep his own life safe, but he knew Zylas needed the words. "One way or another, no matter what happens, I'll get it back to you."

"Thank you." The lines dropped from Zylas' face, and he managed a slight smile. "I'm sure you will."

Collins took the stone, oddly warmed by Zylas' trust. He wondered if he could ever win it from his other companions.

Zylas made a broad wave toward Vernon, who returned it with a grudging movement of his hand that looked more dismissive than friendly. Ialin zipped out of nowhere to hover at Zylas' left shoulder, then the two headed into the woods. Collins watched them until they disappeared among the trees. When he finally turned back, he saw Vernon leading Falima toward the cottage, the dog trotting at her hooves.

Certain Vernon's cottage would lack indoor plumbing, Collins thought it best to relieve himself before getting to know Zylas' friend. He dropped the rose quartz into a pocket of his jeans. As he walked to a secluded spot, he allowed his thoughts free rein. His limbs felt heavy, world-weary, and uncertain. He went through the motions of preparing to urinate, thoughts caught up in the realization that he had stumbled into something quite impossible. It amazed him how quickly he accepted companions who spent half or more of their lives as animals, his own transformation from mild-mannered graduate student to hunted fugitive under sentence of death, his need to find some magical doorway back to the world he had once thought alone in the universe. It seemed unbelievable that people spent their lives searching for creatures from other planets when a whole other world existed through a storage room in Daubert Labs.

Collins' urine pattered against dried weeds.

A distant, high-pitched sound touched Collins' hearing suddenly, and he froze. For a moment he heard nothing but the wind rustling through branches and his own urine splattering against dried weeds. A howling bark wafted over those sounds, sharp as a knife cut and followed by another.

Startled, Collins jerked, wetting his left shoe. Staccato words soft as whispers came to him. "This way, this way." "No, over here." "Smell . . . smell target." "Smell." "Smell." "Smell." "Here!" Then a loud, trumpeting voice sounded over the rest, "Hate wood-ground. Go home!"

Uncertainty held Collins in place. Only then, he realized he had wormed a hand into his pocket and clamped it over the worn-smooth rose quartz. *Oh, my God! It's translating barks and whinnies.* A worse understanding penetrated. *They've come for us.* Whirling, he sprinted toward the cabin, securing his fly as he ran.

Vernon met Collins at the door. "Come," he said in rough English. "Hide you."

Collins careened inside. The cottage had no windows. Thatch poked through the mud plastered between the logs. A crooked table surrounded by crudely fashioned chairs took up most of the space. Straw piled on a wooden frame filled one corner and, beside it, stood a chest of drawers. Near that, a trapdoor broke the otherwise solid floor.

Vernon thrust the dog at Collins with a force that sent man and animal staggering. He fell to one knee, arms, chest, and face filled with fur, managing to catch his balance, though awkwardly. Vernon shoved aside the dresser to reveal what seemed to be plain wall until he caught at something Collins had not noticed. Lashed logs that appeared as part of the structure glided open on unseen hinges, and Vernon gestured frantically at the darkness beyond it.

Still holding the dog, Collins dragged himself into the hidden room. Almost immediately, his nose slammed against solid wall, and wood slivered into his right cheek. He barely managed to turn before Vernon smashed the panel closed, and Collins heard the grind of the dresser moving back into position. Worried its claws might make scrabbling noises, Collins continued supporting the dog, one hand wrapped around its muzzle, the other grasping the translation stone.

For several moments that seemed more like hours, Collins stood in the silent darkness. Gradually, his heart rate returned to normal, and worse thoughts descended upon him. *What if they find us? What if they take Vernon away? What if we're walled in here to die?* The tomblike hush of his hiding place seemed to crush in on him, airless and boring, and he stifled an abrupt urge to pound on the door in a mindless frenzy. If the guards caught him, death went from "what if" to stark and graphic certainty.

Shortly, Collins heard footsteps clomping down nearby stairs and realized several people had passed through the trapdoor he had seen, likely into a root cellar. He had heard nothing of whatever exchange occurred in the cottage, but here their voices wafted to him in muffled bursts.

"Why is it that every time we're hunting fugitives, the trail always ends here?" The voice contained clear exasperation.

Vernon's reply sounded gruff. "Why is it that every time you're hunting fugitives, you chase them toward me? I'd thank you to stop. Puts me in danger. Would you like it if I started sending thieves and killers to your—"

The dog shifted, and Collins tightened his hold. If he could hear the men, likely they would hear any noise from him also.

"Cut the crap, Vernon." A loud, irritable voice joined the others. "What did you do with them?"

Vernon's answer dripped sarcasm. "I ate them."

The dog went limp in Collins' arms. The sudden dead weight made it seem twice as heavy, and it took all his strength to lower it soundlessly to the ground. *What the . . . ?*

The first speaker huffed out a laugh. "You're a mouse, Vern. You can barely eat a *hallowin* seed before you fill up."

Worried he might have strangled the dog in an overzealous attempt to keep it quiet, Collins continued to bolster some of its weight. It felt liquid in his arms, all fur and limbs, and he fought for orientation. He no longer had its mouth, which put them at serious risk. He groped for it, swearing silently, overwhelmed by heat. All of the oxygen seemed to drain from the room. His heart rate trebled.

"I'll have you know I can eat three *hallowin* seeds before I fill up."

"Not funny," came the gruff voice again. "This guy we're

hunting actually did eat someone. Cannibal. Try and hide him here, he'll probably eat you, too."

"Cannibal?" Vernon sounded shocked. "You're right. That's not funny."

Collins thought his heart might pound out of his throat. The dog became even harder to support, squirming into positions he could not fathom in the darkness. He no longer felt fur beneath his grasp, and that proved the final clue. *God, no. He's switching.* He gripped harder, now seeking a human shape among the movement. *Not now, dog. Please, not now.* He held his breath, awaiting the scream that revealed them.

"I . . . didn't know. I'll do whatever I can to help."

Collins could no longer concentrate on the conversation. He found a human ear beneath a wild mop of hair and lowered his mouth to it. "Please don't make a sound. I'll explain everything."

To Collins' surprise and relief, the boy obeyed. Now he turned his attention back to the speakers, but the voices and footsteps faded away. Vernon's revulsion had sounded sincere, concerned enough to reveal Collins to the guards. His chest clutched and ached. *He doesn't know me, has no loyalty to me.* He cringed, prepared for the worst.

The conversation grew uninterpretable, and Collins realized he had dropped the rose quartz in his struggle to maintain control of the dog. He pressed himself breathlessly to the wall, helpless, waiting for the guards to find him, for the dog/boy to shout, for Vernon to surrender him. Then, the voices faded away. Footsteps slammed up the steps, then disappeared.

More time passed, immeasurable in the sightless, soundless prison. Then, Collins heard the creak of the moving dresser. The door sprang open, and the dull interior of Vernon's cabin blinded him. "Thank you," he gasped out in English. The boy tumbled onto the floor, blinking repeatedly and glancing wildly around the room.

Vernon assisted the boy to his table, talking softly, while Collins fumbled around the hiding space until he found the quartz. He closed his hand firmly around it before shutting the panel. Now that he knew of the false wall's existence, he could see the faint outline of its crack and the indentation that allowed Vernon to pull it open. He shoved the dresser back in place.

Vernon approached Collins, enormous hands outspread. "Hi. Think him . . ." He gestured at the boy, who Collins saw for the first time. Blond hair fell around a heart-shaped, beige face, and brown eyes studied Collins with awed curiosity. Skinny, with long arms and legs, he could pass for a young American teenager if not for his completely unselfconscious nakedness. ". . . think you . . ." Vernon struggled for the word, his English not even as competent as Zylas' pidgin speech.

The boy dropped from his chair to his knees on the floor, head bowed. "Your Majesty."

Collins understood. "*Opernes?*" he supplied. It seemed absurd, and he wondered what about his humble self might give such a noble impression. *My clothes?* The simple homespun his companions had provided clashed with his battered jeans and grimy Nike knockoffs. *My watch?* It seemed more likely until he realized that the boy had made his assumption as a dog. *My scent?* "Why does he think . . . ?"

Vernon's features opened in surprise. "You—you speak . . ." He recovered swiftly, warning in his undertone. "Why does he . . . ? Don't you mean *how?* How does he know you're royal, don't you, Your Majesty?" His lips formed sounds that did not match his words at all, like a badly dubbed movie. Collins had not gained that impression from Falima when she had carried the stone, and he guessed it rendered the speaker immune from that effect.

Clearly, Vernon expected him to play along. Though he did not understand why, Collins would not disappoint a man who had just saved his life. "Yes, of course." He turned to the boy. "How *did* you know?"

Apparently released by Collins' direct questioning, the boy clambered back into his chair. "Only royals don't switch." He studied Collins through liquid eyes, as though the answer should have been obvious.

It should have. Collins tried to cover. "I just didn't know one so young could determine that in switch-form."

"And retain it," Vernon added, almost hastily. "You must have good overlap."

The boy beamed, then blushed. "Not really. Not yet."

For Zylas' sake, Collins did not glance at the translation stone, though he could not help clutching it like a treasure. He could understand Zylas' reluctance to lend it; at the moment, he would not trade it for the Hope Diamond. As he and Vernon took the seats on either side of the boy, he could not help wondering if it proved as useful to Zylas. Nothing required him to visit Collins' world; and, as far as he could tell, all citizens of Barakhai spoke the same language, at least in human form. *But there's more than a little advantage to learning how to communicate with animals, especially here.* He wondered if that explained Zylas' near-perfect overlap.

Unlike Collins, Vernon did not become too lost in thought to remember his manners. "I'm Vernon." He made an arching motion over the boy's head to Collins. "Benton-Collins." He slurred it into one word.

"Just Ben's fine," Collins said before Vernon could stop him. "And what's your name?"

"Korfius, Your Majesty." The boy stifled a yawn.

"How old are you?" Collins asked.

"Twelve," Korfius replied. His posture improved abruptly as he added, "Almost a man."

Barely a kid. Collins kept the thought to himself. "What do you remember ..." He glanced at Vernon for help. "... from ... switch time?"

Vernon nodded his approval of the query, so Collins turned his attention back to Korfius.

"Not much, Your Majesty," Korfius' face reddened again. "I knew I was with royalty. And a horse-guard." His eyes crinkled. "Though I don't know why or how." He looked askance at Collins, who pretended not to see. The less Korfius knew, the safer he remained.

Apparently thinking along the same lines, Vernon rose and gestured at the pallet. "Why don't you get some sleep, Korfius?"

Collins winced, anticipating an explosion. No near-teen he knew would agree to nap like a child.

But the boy only nodded before glancing hesitantly at Collins. "Is that all right, Your Majesty?"

Struck dumb, Collins could only imitate Vernon's gesture. "You sleep, Korfius. I'll be fine. Vernon and I have work to take care of."

Korfius bowed. "Thank you, Your Majesty." Still naked, he headed toward the pallet.

"I've got clothes in the drawers." Vernon walked to the door. "Something in there should fit you."

Collins doubted it. Anything that covered Vernon's enormous form would fit Korfius about as well as a circus tent. "Sleep well." He followed Vernon outside and closed the door. As it clicked in place, he hurriedly tried to explain. "About that cannibal thing—"

Vernon interrupted, leading Collins among a stand of poplar at the outskirts of the woods. "So, what did you eat?"

"Well—"

"Let me guess. A pig?"

"No, but—"

"A cow?"

"No."

"A chicken?"

"No." Turning the details of murder into a game embarrassed Collins. "You don't—"

Vernon whirled suddenly toward Collins. "Give me a hint."

Collins stammered, "I—it was . . . a—a rabbit named Joetha."

Vernon came to an abrupt halt, and terror ground through Collins. "It seems," the hermit started coolly, "that you don't know what 'a hint' means." Apparently to show he meant no malice, he turned Collins a broad grin.

"You don't hate me?"

"Nope."

"But . . . but . . . I ate . . ."

Vernon resumed his walk. "I presume you ate her before you knew about switch-forms?"

The bare thought that Vernon might even consider otherwise twisted Collins' gut. "Yes! I–I wouldn't—"

"Of course, you wouldn't. Who would?"

Outside of a few lunatic serial killers, Collins could think of no one.

Vernon continued, "If you're kind and decent, and I believe most people are, you wouldn't kill someone on purpose. I'm not going to condemn an accident, even if it did result in death."

Collins went speechless with gratitude. He felt tears welling in his eyes.

Vernon politely studied the trees, then chose a deadfall and sat. Shadows dappled his skin, making him appear even darker. "Zylas gave you his stone, didn't he?"

Relieved he would not have to keep a secret from Vernon, Collins nodded.

"He must really like you. And trust you. He's rarely even let me hold it, and we've been friends for thirty years."

"Thirty years." Collins wiped the moisture from his eyes and looked over his companion. The stocky man appeared too young for such a long friendship. "How old are you?"

"Thirty-five."

Collins made a wordless noise that Vernon took for encouragement.

"Our switch time overlaps perfectly. And his mother and I—both mice."

"Yes." Collins intensified his scrutiny, gaze flickering over the broad neck, solid musculature, and whaleboned figure of his newest companion. "So I heard. Hard to believe."

Vernon's eyes narrowed curiously. "Why?"

The answer seemed so obvious to Collins, he found himself simplifying to the level of Tarzan. "Mouse small. You . . . big."

Vernon stretched, sinews rippling. "Sometimes it works out that way. Especially *Randoms*." He smiled. "Would it surprise you to find out my father was a bear?"

"Your mother must have been an amoeba."

Vernon halted in mid-stretch. "What?"

"Never mind." Then, feeling the need to explain at least somewhat, Collins finished, "I'm just thinking a bear would have to combine with something really really tiny to make a mouse."

"Mama was a skunk."

Collins' head jerked toward Vernon before he could hide his surprise. "A skunk?"

Vernon's dark eyes hardened. "Yeah, I'm half *downcaste*. What about it?"

Surprised by the sudden hostility, Collins raised his hands in a gesture of surrender. "Nothing about it. I don't even know what *downcaste* means, at least not the way you're using it."

The softness returned gradually to Vernon's face, then he managed a short laugh. "Of course, you don't. I'm sorry."

Collins nodded.

"The *downcaste* are necessary animals relegated to the

most distasteful tasks. Creatures the civilized animals wouldn't lower themselves to associate with because they have some undesirable characteristic or habit that makes them . . . repulsive to the *urbanists*."

"Like skunks?" Collins asked carefully, not certain he truly understood. He saw nothing essential about skunks. A friend who lived on a small acreage talked about regularly trapping and killing them because more than ninety percent carried rabies in that area.

"Garbage handlers," Vernon explained. "Vultures and hyenas take care of the dead, the only ones allowed by law to eat meat. Goats and pigeons manage the sewage." He wrinkled his nose, unable to keep even his prejudice wholly in check. "They prefer the company of *urbanists* and eat anything."

"*Urbanists?*" Collins prompted.

"Creatures who live in cities." Vernon drew a leg to his chest. "Cows, horses, dogs, cats, and such. Some birds."

Recalling an earlier conversation with Zylas, Collins added, "*Durithrin.* They also form a social group?"

"The *wildones* include creatures who prefer the woods to others' company."

Collins realized the stone sometimes translated even those words that worked better in the other language, such as replacing *durithrin* with *wildones.* He supposed *urbanists* and *downcaste* had Barakhain equivalents that would have given him less clue to their meaning. "Deer, squirrels, bears, songbirds . . . ?"

". . . wolves, alligators, wildcats." Vernon shivered. "Once one of those gets a taste for meat, there's no choice but hanging. They *will* kill again."

That explained the severity of Collins' punishment, the lack of a trial, and the intensity of the hunt. *Not like in my world where serial killers are rare and always crazy.* He displayed his new understanding. "*Urbanists, wildones,* and *downcaste.* Your social classes in order of . . ." He searched for words Vernon might not find insulting. ". . . perceived importance."

"Don't forget royals at the top: all human all the time. *Workers* before *wildones.* And, at the very bottom, *vermin.*"

With a start, Collins realized that had to include Vernon and Zylas. He swallowed hard, pressing any emotion from his voice. "Define *vermin.*"

"Those forbidden to breed with their own kind." Vernon shrugged. "Who wants more mice, rats, snakes, and the like?"

"But you and Zylas—"

"*Randoms.* We weren't made what we are on purpose."

Uncomfortable with the subject, Collins pressed on. "And *workers?*"

Vernon drew up his other leg. "Those who don't quite fit with the *urbanists* but have a high, useful skill to market. Like beavers, who build. Porcupines, the tailors. Moles and weasels, miners, though some would debate whether they go with the *workers* or the *downcaste.*"

Collins glanced around the forest, seeing the trees gently bowing in the breeze, the sun glazing every leaf and branch with gold. It seemed impossibly peaceful, hiding the moment when hounds and hunters once again crashed through them, seeking him. He could imagine other specialized creatures: songbird musicians, shrew crop-weeders, bear beekeepers, but he did not question. Closer matters needed discussion, and a realization required voicing. "So you're the other one who's visited my world."

"Several times," Vernon admitted. "With Zylas."

"Why?"

"Why," Vernon repeated, running his fingers through tight curls, straightening them momentarily before they sprang back in place. "Why not?"

Collins suspected that was all the answer he was going to get. "Where's Falima?"

"Hidden." Vernon lowered his legs. "Underground. Too big for your hiding place."

"Agreed." Now, Collins pulled his own feet onto the deadfall, turning to fully face Vernon. "Underground bunkers. Hidden crawl spaces." He spread his fingers. "Why?"

"Because," Vernon said with caution. "Sometimes, good folks need hiding."

It answered nothing. But, for the moment, Collins thought it best not to press.

Chapter 8

BENTON Collins learned more about his newest companion as they headed into the woods surrounding Vernon's cottage. Despite his first thirteen years as a garbage scavenger, Vernon had inherited his father bear's sweet tooth. In addition to visiting another world with Zylas, he had trusted the albino in many situations where common sense suggested he do otherwise. Not the least of these involved treating a horse-guard and a dog-guard to secrets that could get him in as much trouble as Collins and make it impossible for him to help other needy folk in the future.

Known as a reclusive *vermin,* Vernon had few friends or visitors, except when fugitives needed hiding. Luckily, this was not often, so he spent most of his time as he preferred, alone or with Zylas or the handful of *durithrin/wildones* he found worthy of his company. This included Ialin, whom he assured Collins was pleasant and honorable, if flighty, company under most circumstances.

Collins' mind still struggled against the full picture. At times, Barakhai seemed surreal and distant, at other times too vivid and terrifying. He had discovered a place where dream met savage reality, where nightmare fused inseparably with an existence too obviously genuine to deny. He wanted to get to know his strange companions, at least two of whom already felt like friends. At the same time, he could not find a new portal home too soon. "What are we going to do with Korfius?"

Vernon stopped in what seemed like a random location, studying the trees, shrubbery, and weeds with a wary anxiety. At length, his shoulders fell, his arms uncoiled, and his fingers opened from clenched fists. He turned to face Collins. "I don't know."

Collins studied the site intently, wondering what detail had reassured Vernon. "What are we looking at?"

"Falima." Vernon gestured at scattered leaves piled not-quite-casually in a circle of trees. "Undisturbed. They didn't find her." He headed back toward his cabin.

Collins hated the idea of leaving Falima alone in some underground bunker, but he saw no good alternative. He heard nothing to suggest the location upset her, no thudding hooves against planking, no frantic whinnies. By now, she had probably found a comfortable position to sleep, and disturbing her might prove more foolhardy and dangerous than leaving her in the quiet darkness. He stumbled after the black man. "Korfius?" he repeated.

Vernon shrugged, reminding Collins he had already answered the question.

"What did Zylas say about him?"

Vernon did not look back as the cottage came into view. The thatched roof sagged at the center, and clear gaps had worn through some of the cracks between boards. Wood lay in a neat stack that obliterated the western wall, the one concealing Collins' hiding place. "Zylas called it 'necessary abduction.' Said the boy hadn't changed yet, but ought to soon. Asked if I could help you come up with a story that might convince him not to betray you to the other guards."

Collins considered. "What did you come up with?"

Now, Vernon did turn. "Me? Nothing. I didn't think anything would convince that boy to cooperate. Figured we'd wind up having to do something . . . desperate."

Collins sucked in a quick breath, his mind substituting "murder," though consideration made that doubtful. Little more than strangers to him, these people had already risked their lives and futures for him. Surely, they would not add a capital crime to the lesser ones they had committed for him.

Apparently oblivious to Collins' consternation, Vernon continued, "But the boy made it easy for you, didn't he?"

"How so?" Collins' voice emerged hoarser than he expected.

"Figured you for royalty." Vernon flashed a broad-lipped smile. "That should give you lots of possibilities."

Collins did not share Vernon's confidence. "Except I don't know how to act like royalty."

Vernon laughed, a deep full-throated sound. "Doesn't matter, really. We common folk don't know how royalty acts anyway. We don't intermingle."

It seemed impossible. "Never?"

Vernon dipped his head. "Pretty much. The town leaders take audience now and again, to get their instructions, convey new laws, handle disputes and disasters. Stuff like that." He started walking again. "And we sometimes see a royal guard or messenger, though they're not full-time humans like blood royalty. Only rarely do actual royals choose to walk among us."

"So my strangeness . . ."

". . . could pass for normal royal behavior, as far as a twelve-year-old boy could guess. And he wouldn't know any royal by appearance alone."

"What about my complete inability to speak the language? Don't you think that'll cue him in?"

Vernon stopped at his door to regard Collins again. "Not a problem currently." His gaze dropped to Collins' fist where the translation stone nestled against his fingers. "Probably not later either. All but the most distant of the *downcaste* speaks the language of the *urbanists*. But the *wildones,* the *downcaste,* and the *workers* have languages of their own. And some of the more reclusive species have a tongue based on their animal-speak. Zylas and I sometimes use your language when we want to keep things private. It seems likely the royals would have a private language as well. It wouldn't surprise anyone to find out some royals don't even bother to learn the most common speech of *switchers*." He seized the latch, still looking at Collins. "Ready?"

"Yes," Collins said, though he was not. He doubted he ever would be, however, so now seemed as good as any time.

The door swung open noiselessly to reveal Korfius sitting at the table. His head jerked toward the suddenly open door, he fumbled with something, then chewed vigorously. Crumbs speckled the table, the floor, and the laces at the neck of a shirt that fit him more like a dress.

"Hello, Korfius," Vernon boomed. "Up already?"

Korfius replied with a muffled, "Couldn't sleep."

"What did you say?" Vernon winked conspiratorially at Collins, who grinned. Korfius looked like a toddler caught with a hand in the cookie jar. As glad to have another friend as to discover a wink meant the same thing here as at home, Collins played along.

Korfius swallowed, then cleared his throat. "Couldn't sleep." He looked up to reveal bits of food clinging to his face and a telltale smear of honey on his right cheek.

"Hungry?" Vernon suggested.

Korfius flushed, wiping his mouth with the back of a sleeve. He glanced at the table, realizing he was caught. "Very. I couldn't wait. I'm sorry I took without asking."

Not wishing to embarrass the boy further, Collins added, "I could do with some food, too."

Korfius sprang from his chair. "At once, Your Majesty." He scurried toward the trapdoor and nearly reached it before skidding to a horrified stop. He looked askance at Vernon, who laughed.

"My home is your home," Vernon said, still chuckling, "apparently." He made a broad gesture. "Bring up the best you can find."

Without further encouragement, Korfius lifted the hatch and slid into the parlor. His footfalls echoed on the wooden stairs, growing gradually softer.

Collins oriented as he watched the boy disappear. Clearly, the guards had looked for him and Korfius in the larder, and he had heard their voices as they descended the stairs. He tried to fathom why he had heard them there but not inside the cabin.

As if reading Collins' mind, Vernon explained. "It's not normal to have hiding places, so sound travels oddly. You can hear and be heard by anyone on the parlor stairs but no other place as far as I know. If you have to hide again, though, I'd suggest you stay silent, just in case."

Collins shivered at the thought of cramming himself into that tight, seemingly airless space again. Nevertheless, he found it preferable to hanging. "You can count on it."

"You'd never believe how many times those fools have searched the dresser, leaving me a mess of clothes to pick up." Vernon gestured at the irregularly stained, off-center chest of drawers. Clearly handmade, it occupied most of the eastern wall. "I stash all kinds of clothing in there; people give what they can. Those who can't give wash or patch. You find anything your size, feel free to change. Dirties'll get washed and go to someone else. Or you can get them back next time you drop in."

"I do appreciate your help and your kindness." Collins continued to study the dresser, seeking some indication of the secret area he knew took up most of the space behind it. "And I hope I don't offend you when I say that I hope I never have to receive it again."

Vernon turned, brows raised and mouth crinkled with amusement. "You're welcome. And, yes, I understand."

Korfius' bare feet clomped up the stairs. He appeared through the opening hugging a variety of flasks and crockery. Straw-colored hair lay in snarled disarray. Streaks of dirt decorated otherwise cherubic cheeks, like war paint, the right still bearing a dab of honey. His gray robe had a tattered hem that dragged on the planking, and its V-neck, even laced, revealed most of his hairless chest. Awkwardly, he dropped his finds on the table. A covered mug rolled across the surface until Korfius caught it and righted it. "I found lots of stuff, Your Majesty, though not what you're used to of course; but it will have to— "

"All right." Vernon interrupted the boy's excited patter. "Let's see what we have here." He lifted and replaced lids, occasionally sniffing the contents. "Black bread, honey, assorted insects, nut paste, roundfruit, roasted beetles, watered wine, mulled fruit juice." He looked up. "Any of that suit you, Your Majesty?"

A clumsy silence followed before Collins remembered they addressed him. "Oh. Oh, yes. Honey bread. Maybe some of that nut paste. Fruit and fruit juice, please."

Vernon started doling out the fare, placing each share directly on the table. "No beetles, sire? They're the best thing I have, a real delicacy. The big kind with lots of substance and a gratifying crunch."

Korfius peered eagerly into one of the crocks. "Real good ones, Your Majesty. Look!"

"That's all right." Collins did not care to see. "I'm not much of a . . . um . . . bug-eater." He took his seat at the table while Vernon plopped a golden, viscous fluid, spotted with bits of honeycomb onto a thick slice of dark bread and pushed it in front of his guest. The sweet odor of the honey sent a rumble through Collins' stomach. Instinctively, he thought back to his last satisfying meal and realized, with a guilty start, that it was when he had eaten the rabbit. *Joetha.* The queasy feeling settled back into his gut, though the bread continued to tempt him. Vernon slapped a handful of semi-solid brownish glop interspersed with chunks onto the table beside the bread. Oil formed a ring around the edges. Though unappetizing looking, it smelled vaguely similar to peanut butter, which tweaked Collins' hunger again. Two wrinkled balls, stored fruit, rolled across the table toward him, followed by a mug of dull orangish-pink liquid, dense with pulp.

Korfius claimed the chair to Collins' right, clambering onto his knees. "I've had some bread and honey, thank you. I'd just like some of those beetles and a bit of wine, please."

Vernon slopped down a half-dozen insects the size of Collins' first thumb joint. Their black legs curled against their abdomens, and their wings shimmered a pearly aqua, burned to dull black in places. A dribble of saliva escaped Korfius' mouth, but he waited patiently for his host and his fellow guest.

Vernon served himself a bit of everything, then relaxed into his chair. Collins suddenly felt all eyes on him. Apparently, as the presumed royal, he was supposed to take the first bite. Needing cues as to how best to eat the other food, he went for the bread first, taking a healthy bite. It had the consistency of a kitchen sponge, and a hint of mold marred the otherwise pleasant flavor. The honey tasted as fresh and sweet as any he had ever had, though he would have preferred to have strained out all of the comb.

The others started eating, too, Korfius with doglike gusto. "So," the boy said around a mouthful of beetle. "How did I wind up here?" He swallowed. "And when can I go home?"

Vernon's gaze flicked to Collins, and he chewed vigorously.

Collins finished the bite of bread, then set the rest down. He cleared his throat. "Well . . ." If they waited until Korfius became a dog again before releasing him, they probably had half a day before he could report back to the guards. *Unless, as a dog, he can communicate fully with the other dogs.* His ignorance foiled him, yet he could not leave Vernon to handle a problem that he had created. He already depended too much on his companions' charity. "It's difficult. I'm on a top secret royal mission, and I don't know if I can trust you."

"Top secret?" Korfius repeated, features screwed into a knot as he crunched another beetle. Obviously, the term meant little to him, and the translation stone did not leave room for quibbling. Likely, it had portrayed the words "top" and "secret" rather than the compound concept. "Of course you can trust me. Why wouldn't you trust me?"

To emphasize the gravity, Collins thrust all his food aside. "When you're on a mission this secret, you can't trust anyone."

Korfius swallowed, his own food forgotten for the moment, too. "Not anyone?"

"Not . . . anyone."

"Why?"

"Because," Collins leaned toward the boy. "It's so important and so very very secret. If the wrong person found out, if someone told them, thinking he could trust them, or if they merely overheard it, it could destroy the mission."

Korfius swallowed again, harder. "What is the mission?"

"If I told you, I'd have to kill you."

Korfius' features opened, and his jaw fell. Even Vernon turned his head to give Collins a warning stare.

Collins dropped his voice to an urgent whisper. "It's that secret. And that vital."

When the two continued to gape, Collins continued, "The lives of thousands rest in my hands. I can't betray that sacred and dire trust. And I can't let anyone else do it either." He lowered his own gaze to his hands. "I've already said as much as I dare about it."

Korfius bobbed his head, clenching his hands on the edge of the table, knuckles bloodless. "Before I switched, before the hunt. The guards in human form said . . . they said . . ." He looked at Vernon, who waved encouragingly. "A man with your description ate someone."

Collins' thoughts raced. He knew Korfius must have switched to dog form shortly before Collins captured him and that he would understand little of the subsequent details. He should have figured the boy might have known the intention of the hunt. The guards had caught Collins in the process of committing the crime; he could hardly deny it. That would put his credibility, already thin, in hopeless jeopardy.

"Did you . . . did you . . ." Korfius clamped his attention on Collins. ". . . kill . . . and eat . . . that rabbit?"

Collins calmly ladled nut paste into his mouth, stalling. He chewed, maintaining the air of casual innocence, swallowed, took a sip of fruit juice to clear his mouth, then spoke in the most matter-of-fact tone he could muster. "Had to."

Korfius blinked.

"She threatened to tell others about me, about the mission. I hate killing more than anything in the world. But . . ." Collins gave Korfius a look of dangerous sincerity. "In the wrong hands, that information would doom the mission. One life seemed a small price to pay to save thousands."

"I–I," Korfius stammered, voice dropping to a whisper. "I wouldn't tell anyone."

Collins hissed back, "I'm counting on that."

As if he'd suddenly discovered his food, Korfius went back to stuffing beetles into his mouth.

Collins glanced over to Vernon's half-grin.

"Who can't know?" Korfius said between crunches. "Whose hands are the wrong hands?"

"*No one* must know. Where I am, who I'm with, what I'm doing." Collins added conspiratorially, "You're the only one besides my friends who even knows I'm royal."

Vernon wiped his mouth with an edge of his tunic. "Korfius, here's what I suggest you tell the other guards and your parents."

Korfius sat up, attentive.

"You fell or got hit or something. You're not sure, but it made you sleep for many hours. When you woke up, you wandered around confused for a long time. Finally, I found you. Fed you. Took you home. Got it?"

Korfius' mouth pinched. "But that would be a lie."

"Yes," Vernon said simply.

Believing the boy needed more, Collins added, "A necessary lie. One that will help save the lives of thousands. Do you understand?"

"Sort of," Korfius replied, swallowing a mouthful. "Not really. Not the details."

"Can't give you those," Collins said apologetically, then hardened his tone. "If you don't agree, you leave me no choice but to . . ." He trailed off with clear significance.

Korfius hugged himself. When he finally spoke, he used a small voice. "I want to help save lives."

Vernon made a noise of approval, deep in his throat. "So you won't tell anyone about His Majesty or his companions?"

"I won't," Korfius promised.

"Good boy." Vernon returned to his food, and the others followed suit.

For several moments, they ate in silence, then Collins rose and yawned. "My turn for a nap?" he suggested.

Vernon also stood. He walked to the chest of drawers, pulled open the top one, and removed a clay pot. "Let me show you to the well. You can wash up and change."

It seemed more logical to wash after the nap, so Collins suspected the older man wanted to talk with him alone. "Great," he said, waving at Korfius. "See you soon."

Korfius eyed the beetle jar.

Though Vernon headed for the door, he did not miss the gesture. "Have as much food as you want," he called over his shoulder to the boy as he exited the cottage, Collins behind him.

The sun slanted toward the western horizon, and Collins' watch read ten minutes until four. Vernon strolled toward the back of the cottage, waiting only until they had clearly passed Korfius' hearing range before asking, "That was brilliant. Where did you come up with all that stuff? About missions and thousands and lives and . . . ?" He showed Collins an expression that bordered on awe.

Collins did not have the heart to tell his companion it came from the meanest B-grade spy movies he had seen in high school. Choosing an air of mystery over idiocy, he reverted to the same understated melodrama that Vernon had laid on him when he asked about the bolt-holes. Cocking his brows, he put on a tight-lipped grin. And left the answer to Vernon's imagination.

Collins awakened to the slam of a closing door and the pound of footsteps on floorboards. For an instant, his mind returned him to the dark enclosure behind Vernon's dresser,

desperately clutching a frightened and morphing dog/boy
who might give them away in an instant. His lids snapped
open to candlelight that held evening grayness at bay in a
circle. He lay on the pallet. Korfius sat in the chair Collins
had vacated hours earlier, his yellow hair mostly flopped
over his right ear, his small hands clasped together on the
tabletop. Vernon and Falima stood on the threshold, the man
carrying the aroma of cool evening wind and the woman
wholly naked. For the second time, Collins caught a glimpse
of that wonderful body: the generous, sinewy curves, the pert
breasts, and the black triangle between muscular thighs.

Falima glanced at Collins, and her golden skin turned a
prickly red. She hid behind Vernon, her discomfort an obvious change from the unself-conscious dignity with which
she had carried herself a day ago.

Sensing Falima's uneasiness, Vernon removed his cloak
and tossed it over her bare shoulders. She drew it tightly
around her while he crossed to the dresser and began sifting
through clothing. At length, he pitched out a simple dress of
coarse weave, dyed a sallow blue. Falima turned her back to
pull it over her head, giving Collins a full view of her round,
firm buttocks—every bit as pleasurable as what she hid. The
fabric fell into place, disguising the exquisite angles beneath
a shapeless blob of material. Only then, she returned the
cloak to Vernon.

Collins waited until Falima had dressed before sitting up
and rubbing grit from the corners of his eyes. His mother
had called them "sleepy seeds," but Marlys had broken him
of the habit. She felt it best not to refer to bodily fluids,
whether liquid or dry, at all. Even earwax made her ill, and
a used Q-tip accidentally left on a bathroom ledge sent her
into a frenzy. *Marlys.* Collins grimaced. He knew she would
not appreciate him staring, or even worse enjoying the sight
of, another woman's naked body, no matter how amusing or
dire the circumstances.

Vernon and Korfius seemed to take no notice of the process, though the older man prodded the washbasin they had
filled earlier that now perched on top of the dresser and
waved at the clean pile of clothing beside it. "Your turn," he
said in heavily accented English, then winked at Collins.

You bastard. Collins glanced in the indicated direction,
then sat. He thrust a hand in his pocket and wrapped his

fingers around the translation stone. He withdrew his hand, clutching the quartz to his palm as he removed the travel-stained tunic to reveal his ribby, nearly hairless chest. "Happy?"

Korfius glanced over.

Vernon smiled.

"Not yet," Falima said, mouth widening into a grin.

Now it was Collins' turn to blush. Seeking a distraction, he rose and strode to the basin. He splashed water over his face, abdomen, and armpits, then ran the fingers of his free hand through his hair. Grit rasped against his nails, and twigs pattered to the ground. Without a heavy stream of water and a lot of shampoo, it seemed hopeless. He looked at his companions.

Korfius had lowered his head to his arm, but the other two still watched Collins intently.

All right, I can do this. Collins thought of his two deli-cious sessions of Falima-watching. *It's only fair.* He reached for his fly, thinking back to his experiences in the locker room. For size, he fell squarely into the average category, and his slender figure only enhanced what he had. He turned around, freed the metal button and unzipped. His pants slid to his ankles. He stepped out of them, then his underwear, baring his backside for his companions.

Collins felt more self-conscious now than the time his six-year-old cousin, Brittany, had pulled the bathroom door wide open during her sister's wedding reception, while he performed inside. He splashed water over his legs and privates, his back to Falima, hoping she had the decency to look elsewhere as he had done for her.

Collins snatched up the fresh gray britches that Vernon had laid out for him, the fabric rough and scratchy against his hand.

"Turn around," Falima teased.

Collins winced.

"There's nothing to be embarrassed about, Your Majesty." Vernon restored the title and the charade of respect, even as they stripped Collins of all physical dignity. "Those of us who switch see one another naked all the time. There's a lot of . . . normal variation."

Let's get this over with. The longer Collins put it off, he knew, the more Falima would expect when she finally saw him. *And so what? What does it matter what she thinks of . . . that?* Even in his thoughts, he had to use a euphemism, and it intensified the scarlet circles of his cheeks. *It's not like there could ever be anything between us.* Yet, somehow, it did matter. Whether or not they ever came together, he wanted her to like him, to want him, as much as he wanted her. *This is ridiculous. As if a guy like me could ever attract a hotty like her.* Screwing up his courage, he turned, only then realizing that Falima was accustomed to seeing stallions.

Nervously, Collins watched Falima's face as the smile wilted and her pale eyes widened. She back-stepped, gasping.

Collins could not have imagined a more unnerving reaction. "Very funny."

"Wha—what . . . ?" Falima stammered, not sounding the least bit amused. "What happened?"

"It . . . I . . ." Collins floundered with the britches, and it seemed to take inordinately long to find the leg holes. "Sometimes . . . they're all . . ."

Vernon smoothly stepped in to assist. "The cutting," he explained. "The foreskin. We don't do that here."

Collins tied the britches in place, the excess color draining from his face. He dropped the rose quartz into a pocket to speak the word in English that he knew must not translate. "Circumcision." He took up the stone again, so as not to miss anything. "It's a . . . a . . ."

"Royal thing?" Vernon suggested.

"Exactly." Collins appreciated the reminder. In the horror of the situation, they had all apparently forgotten his cover. Otherwise, Vernon would have said "*switchers* don't do that" rather than "we don't do that here." Collins explained, "Keeps it cleaner." *I can't believe I'm discussing the details of my penis in mixed company.* He tried to drop the subject. "So, any place to get a real bath around here?"

"Doesn't it hurt?" Korfius piped in, rising to join the others.

"What?" Vernon inquired.

"That." Korfius jabbed a finger toward Collins' now-covered groin. "Doesn't it hurt to . . . to . . . cut it like that." He added, belatedly, "Your majesty."

Though unnecessary, Collins followed the direction of

Korfius' motion naturally. "Oh, that. I don't know. It's done when you're just a couple days old."

"Does it still work, Your Majesty?"

"Work?" All of the blushing returned to Collins' face in an instant. "Of course it works. All the . . . all the . . ." He glanced at Falima, then wished he had not. It only intensified the embarrassment. ". . . functions work. It's just . . . well . . . cleaner, I guess." Again, he tried to redirect the conversation. "Please stop with the 'Your Majesty,' though. No one's supposed to know who I am, remember?" He placed a finger to his lips. "Top secret."

"Top secret." Korfius repeated vigorously. His expression wilted from open and eager to wrinkled disappointment in an instant. "Will I ever get to tell my friends I met a royal?"

Falima placed an arm around the boy. "I've kept the secret a year now. Think you can last half that long?"

Korfius nodded. "Longer even."

"Good boy." Falima tousled the boy's hair.

Collins used the distraction to finish dressing quickly, glad they finally seemed to have moved beyond his genitalia. Now that they had all seen him, he felt like a great weight had lifted from him.

"My turn to nap," Vernon announced suddenly. "Got to get my human sleep time in before the switch."

Collins glanced at his watch. It now read 6:45 P.M., which meant Vernon had a little over five hours before the change; since, according to Vernon, he and Zylas switched at exactly the same time. Collins resisted the urge to ask for an explanation about sleeping. It seemed only right that they would need to do so in both forms.

Collins relished and dreaded the chance to spend some time alone with Falima, to finally explain, one-on-one, his mistake with Joetha. He could get her to understand that she and Ialin had misjudged him, that one error made in good faith, did not make him a monster. For reasons he could not rationalize or elucidate, he needed her to like him. Now, one of his companions slept, but they still had to contend with Korfius. By the time the dog/boy switched, Vernon might already have awakened. *I can't catch a break.*

Korfius and Collins took seats at the table while Vernon stretched out on the pallet. Falima searched the top drawer, then the middle, finally emerging triumphantly with an un-wearable rag. She set to work, dusting the surface of the dresser.

Vernon tucked his arms behind his head. "What are you doing?"

"Cleaning." Falima continued without a pause. "For what looks like the first time in years."

"Really," Collins said, trying to save their host's face as well as display the manners his mother had taught him. "I hadn't noticed." Now that Falima had drawn his attention, he saw cobwebs looped and hammocked along the ceiling, walls, and especially the corners. Dust peppered the floors, and food stained the wooden table.

"Of course, you hadn't noticed." Falima redoubled her efforts. "Filth is invisible to males."

The words struck staggeringly close to home. Collins recalled the times his father would pass his room as adequately straightened and let him watch television. His mother would poke in her head, shaking it and rolling her eyes.

"Not invisible." Vernon rolled to his side. "Just tolerable."

Collins rose. "Toss me a rag. I'll help." Sitting had become the most boring pastime in the universe. Though he had never considered himself much of a watcher, he missed television, movies, the internet, video games. It seemed so natural to flick on an electric light rather than search out dust bunnies in the dim flicker of a tiny flame. He suspected even finding a book here would prove nearly impossible. He would rather grade freshmen papers than sit twiddling his thumbs while Falima worked. "What do you people do with your free time?"

"Free time?" Falima repeated as she rummaged through the chest of drawers. "What do you mean by that?"

"Try the bottom," Vernon suggested. "Older stuff there."

Falima slammed the middle drawer shut and opened the bottom one. In a moment, she pulled out the torn remnants of a sleeve. "Here." She tossed it to Collins, who caught it in his right hand.

"Thanks." Collins returned to his question. "You know, free time. Like now. When you have nothing in particular that needs doing."

Falima tossed Collins' dirty clothes on the floor near the door. "I don't know, really. It almost never happens." She scrubbed at the dresser top. "I used to spend all night patrolling or guarding the prison. During the day, I was carrying someone or something. When I wasn't doing either of those, I was sleeping or eating."

"Or searching for food," Vernon said. "Or fixing things that broke."

Korfius added his piece, "Or helping someone find something he lost. Or picking up the slack from someone who's sick or something."

"This situation." Falima made a grand gesture. "This waiting for someone, unable to go outside because someone else is hunting you—"

"Very unnatural," Vernon finished.

"Never happens." Falima dunked her rag into the washbasin and resumed working. "Normally."

Collins thought of all the things his new friends knew nothing about, did not even have the experience to miss: washing machines, dishwashers, music on demand, refrigerators and freezers, vacuum cleaners, cars, ovens, plastic raincoats. The list seemed endless, and he wondered when he had stopped appreciating any of it. No wonder Zylas and Vernon left Barakhai when they could. He suspected they had visited his world more times than they admitted; to have learned even as little as they had managed seemed miraculous. "Zylas brought a lighter back," Collins remembered.

Vernon's deep rumble of laughter surprised Collins. He had not realized he had spoken aloud. "You should have seen him struggle. Entertained me for an entire day. Still makes me laugh."

Falima looked up from her work. "Why didn't he just wait for the switch?"

Vernon propped up his head on one hand, rolling his gaze toward Korfius in a pointed gesture. Though Falima had asked the question, he answered in broken English. "Only can go as animal. Not switch there."

Intrigued by the answer, Collins wrapped the cloth around his hand and casually released the translation stone. "You can't switch? Or choose not to?"

"Can't."

"Interesting." Collins surmised that they had to obey the physical laws of his world once there. *The Law of Conservation of Mass and Energy, perhaps?* He hoped that did not mean he would become a shapeshifter while here, though the thought of soaring like an eagle, swinging through trees like a monkey, or running as wild and free as a cheetah intrigued him. *With my luck, I'd probably turn into some plodding old tortoise.*

Collins set to flicking at cobwebs with his rag while Korfius watched him from the table. The boy did not seem to miss working at all, enjoying the opportunity to spend the entire day sitting, sleeping, and talking. *And why shouldn't he?* Collins refused to begrudge the seeming laziness. *He probably doesn't get the chance to do absolutely nothing as often as once per year.*

Though he would have preferred listening to Nirvana or Matchbox 20 slamming from a CD in the background, Collins enjoyed the slowed pace as well. For the first time since entering this odd and backward world, he felt almost safe.

Chapter 9

AN hour and a half later, Vernon snored musically on the pallet, Korfius lay, in dog form, with his head on Collins' foot, and the cabin practically sparkled. Falima tossed herself into a chair across from Collins, regarding him in silence.

Feeling the need to speak first, but not wanting to launch into contentious subjects immediately, Collins simply said, "He's a good man, Vernon."

A forelock of black hair fell over Falima's forehead, between the strikingly blue eyes. Her long lashes swept downward, then up again. "Yes."

"Zylas, too."

"Yes."

"And Ialin . . . ?"

"Yes," Falima repeated, as if Collins had spoken the third name in the same tone as the others rather than in question.

Collins smiled. "What do I have to do to get you to use more than one syllable?"

Falima tapped her balled hands on the tabletop. "Try asking a question where the answer isn't obvious." She also smiled, apparently to show she meant no malice.

"All right." Collins leaned toward her and addressed his mood. "Are we really safe here?"

Falima's grin broadened. "Yes."

As Falima returned to her ubiquitous monosyllable, Collins groaned. "All right, then. Let's put this in the form of an essay." He cleared his throat. "Do you believe we're really safe from Barakhain guards here? Why or why not?"

Though Falima could not have understood the reference, she laughed. It was a surprisingly loud sound, full of joie de vivre and mirth, nothing like the dainty bell-like twitters Marlys loosed when she deigned to enjoy one of his jokes. "As safe as we can be for the moment, I guess. Vernon has a web throughout the *durithrin* community. If the guards remained in or returned to the area, they would tell him."

That explained why Vernon spoke so freely in the forest as well as in his cabin.

Korfius smacked his jowls a few times, then sighed deeply.

Collins jerked his attention to the dog. "Do you think *he* understands any of this?"

"No."

"You're sure?"

"Yes."

Collins forced his attention from the dog to Falima. "Positive?"

"Yes."

Realizing he had cornered Falima into monosyllables yet again, Collins placed the onus on her. "How can you be so sure?"

Falima slouched. The candle struck red-and-purple highlights in hair otherwise dark as shadow. "Horses are senior guards, dogs junior. I spent my last twelve years working over dogs. He's too young for much overlap, even if he had put most of his effort into it. But he's clearly . . ." The last word, though apparently enunciated, did not translate.

Collins placed the rose quartz on the table, deliberately removing his hand. "Clearly what?"

"*Lesariat*," Falima repeated dutifully. She inclined her head toward the translation stone, and Collins placed his palm squarely over it. "Zylas *really* trusts you."

"He honors me more than I deserve."

Falima did not argue that point. "I knew him almost ten years before he let me use it." She turned Collins a telling look. "Now, thanks to you, it'll probably be another ten before he lets me touch it again. If ever."

Collins felt his cheeks warm. "Sorry." He directed the

conversation back to its previous point. "What is this *lesar . . . lesar . . . rat*?"

"*Lesariat.*" This time, the stone allowed the foreign word through without attempting translation. "It's a . . . a . . . state of mind . . . of being." Falima sighed, struggling. "The *masuniat* find their animal form an inconvenient interruption. Most don't bother to seek balance or overlap. They live from human time to human time. Some leave themselves notes to allow them to take up exactly where they left off. It's more common in *Randoms*. The *Regular masuniat* often take herbs at coming-of-age to shorten switch time."

Worried about getting hopelessly lost, Collins tried to clarify. "All right. So the *masuniat* try to spend less time as animals and more time as humans."

"Right. The *Regular masuniat*," Falima reminded. "The more successful the herbs, the more like *Randoms* they become, at least in terms of switch time. Fulfillment would mean they spend exactly half their time human, like *Randoms*."

"And you?" Collins looked pointedly at Falima, who lowered her head.

"You know, don't you?"

"Yeah, and I'm not quite sure why you lied to me." Worried that he'd never understand Korfius, he reluctantly dropped the matter. "But first, *lesariat*."

"Getting to that," Falima promised. "The herbs have side effects that limit their use. They can cause bellyaches, rashes, vomiting. Even coma or death. They also lessen overlap. So it's a balancing act."

"I'd say so." Collins could think of nothing short of cancer that would make him take anything so toxic.

"The *winariat* accept the change as a natural part of life. They tend to have the best overlap, though that partially depends on philosophy. Some truly believe it more innate to act as animal as possible in switch-form and as human as possible in human form."

Collins saw the direction Falima appeared to be taking. "So the *lesariat* must prefer . . . their animal form?"

"Exactly." Falima beamed at him. "Most have no interest at all in overlap, or they even reverse it. They may bring more habits from their switch-form to their human form. And they take herbs to lengthen their animal time."

Things started to come together. "So Korfius drools. And looks for food all the time."

Falima chuckled. "Exactly. It also helps that I smell the *lesariat* herb on him."

Collins had completely missed that. "What does it smell like?"

"It's . . . distinctive." Falima's lips twisted, then returned to normal. She shook her head. "Ever try to describe a smell?"

Collins bobbed his head and opened his hands in concession. Without a comparison, it could become almost impossible, like taste. For the first time, he realized why so many meats got compared to chicken. It seemed simpler to whiff at their companion sometime after the switch. He studied Falima. The candlelight sparked from her golden skin, revealing smears of grime. Her pale eyes watched him back, striking in their color and depth. Though a bit large, her nose suited her, and the curtain of jet black hair gave her an air of foreign mystery. Though not classically beautiful, she drew his gaze in a way he could not quite explain. He could enjoy staring at that face every morning over the breakfast table, even rumpled, coarsened, and travel weary, for eternity.

Falima broke the spell. "Is it normal where you come from to gawk?"

As usual, Collins groped for humor; but the words that left his mouth surprised even him. "Only when there's something this pretty to gawk at."

"Me?" Falima asked incredulously.

"Of course not," Collins said facetiously. "I meant the gorgeous woman standing behind you."

Falima tensed as if to glance around, then relaxed. "Thank you. But there's no need to lie. I know I'm not . . . attractive."

Stunned, Collins turned defensive. "Of course you're attractive. Where I come from, men would fight over you."

"They would?"

"Yes."

"In human form? Or horse?"

"Human," Collins replied, then added, "In horse form, the girls would fight over you."

Falima blinked several times, obviously confused. "The girls? Why?"

Collins considered briefly. "Because, where I come from, it's almost like a law. Pretty much all girls love horses at some point in their lives. Sometimes forever." He leaned toward Falima. "That's not to say boys and men don't like horses, too. Just not so . . . almost universally."

"Love to . . ." Falima fidgeted, looking at her hands, ". . . eat them?"

"Horses?" Collins shook his head vigorously. "Yuck, never. We don't eat horses where I come from." He had heard people in other countries did, but he saw no reason to get technical.

"But you eat animals."

"Not horses." Collins crinkled his face and shook his head again. He caught sight of Korfius at the corner of his vision. "Or dogs. Or mice, hummingbirds, rats . . ." The latter made him think of the television show *Survivor,* but he did not voice it. There seemed no reason to complicate matters more than already necessary.

"What do you eat?"

Collins spoke slowly, watching Falima's reaction as he spoke each word. "Cows."

Falima winced but continued looking at him encouragingly.

"Pigs, chickens, turkey, and fish."

"Fish aren't animals."

"They are where I come from."

"Oh."

An uncomfortable pause followed.

"What else?" Falima finally said.

"That takes care of about 99.9% of all the meat eaten in the United States." Collins knew he had to mention rabbits for her to believe him. "The rest is what we call game, which you would call *durithrin* or *wildones*. Rabbits, deer, ducks, geese. A few people do bear, squirrel, turtles, possum, snakes, stuff like that. But most people wouldn't consider those animals savory or, in many cases, even edible." He recalled the time one of the international students had brought a tomato-based stew to a potluck that everyone ate with relish, until a rumor circulated that the meat they had sucked down with gusto moments before was actually cat. The ladle never again dipped into that bowl.

"Not horses."

"Not horses." Collins confirmed.

Falima fell silent again, fingers clasping and unclasping on the tabletop.

"This is really creepy for you, isn't it?"

"Not—not really. I mean, I knew—" Falima finally met Collins' gaze. "It's just that sometimes, when you look at me—" A flush crept up her neck. "You look so ... so ... hungry."

"Hungry?"

"Right after I change back." Falima rolled her stare to her hands, pinning one with the other. "I don't notice when I'm in switch-form. "It's like you want to ... to devour me."

Now Collins understood and appreciated that Falima did not meet his eyes. *I do. Just not the way you're thinking.* "That's not hunger, Falima. That's ..." Words failed him completely.

Now, Falima looked directly at him.

"Well ..." The word came, but Collins hesitated to use it. "... lust."

Falima's expression did not change for several moments, then her brows fell in clear confusion. "What?"

This time, Collins looked away, index finger tracing a stain on the tabletop. "I'm sorry. I do know it's rude to stare at your body, but it's so ... so beautiful." *And I don't get to see naked women very often.* He had seen Marlys, of course, but only twice. Most men of his time would consider her the prettier of the two: slight, red-haired, high-cheeked, full-lipped and well versed in enhancement with makeup. Yet, for reasons he could not yet elucidate, Falima seemed much more exciting.

Falima's mouth clamped to a severe line. "That's the second time you've called me beautiful."

"You are."

"I'm not."

It was an unwinnable argument, so Collins sidestepped it. "You are to me. Why don't you think so?"

Falima studied Collins, as if trying to read the intention behind an obvious scheme. "I'm a *Random*. I'm muscled like a horse, without a woman's proper softness. My colors match my switch-form better than my human form, which is manifested at night."

Collins felt a grin edging onto his lips and stopped it. "None of those things matter to me."

"They don't?"

"Why would they?"

Falima had no ready answer. "Because ... because—"

"Because nothing." Collins took Falima's hands and allowed the smile to glide across his face. "You know what I see?"

Falima shook her head.

"I see an athletic woman with eyes like sparkling sapphires." Collins suppressed a wince at his own triteness and wished he had paid more attention in the poetry class he had taken to fulfill his English credits. "A perfect tan. Hair midnight black and as sleek and wild as the sea. Beautiful." He pinned the smile in place. "And a creamy buckskin horse any breeder might envy."

"You do?"

"I do."

"Thank you."

Collins' grin slipped. "No need for thanks. I was simply describing what I see."

"But your words make me feel good."

"I'm glad."

They smiled at one another, and joy suffused Collins. His heart skipped, then quickened. Excitement tingled through his chest in a way he could not recall since his first crush on Betty Lou Finnegan in junior high and, prior to that, not since childhood.

Korfius yipped, breaking the mood. His legs twitched rhythmically, kicking Collins' shin.

Collins slid his feet free, rolling the dog onto his back. Korfius awakened briefly, whacked his tail on the boards, and resumed snoring.

Collins hated to even raise the issue when things were going better than he could ever have imagined, but it needed saying. "About Joetha." An image of his own grandmother came to his mind: her gray-and-white hair falling in curls to just above her shoulders, her small stout form smelling of peppers and cookies, the welcoming smile she had always given him, surrounded by the familiar wrinkles that had come to define unconditional love. She had died two years ago, of natural causes, and he missed her. He forced himself to contemplate some savage serial murderer stabbing her to death, cannibalizing the body. The picture proved too much. Horror dragged through him like a hot knife, and he dropped his head, sobbing, into his hands.

Collins did not hear Falima move, but her warm body enfolded him and her hands stroked his hair like a child's. She rocked him gently as he wept, his tears plastering the rude fabric of her dress against her solid curves. "I'm sorry," he gasped out. "I'm sorry." He wanted to say more, but grief would not allow it. *I killed someone's mother, someone's grandmother. I killed her, and I callously ate her.*

Collins did not know how long he cried into Falima's arms. But, when he finally regained control, his face bore the indentations of every thick fiber. She looked as if she had spilled a glass of water down her bodice, rumpled and pinch-faced.

"It's all right," she finally said.

"It's not." Collins shook his head. "It never will be."

Falima could not deny those words. Collins would have to learn to live with the guilt or go insane.

"A bad thing happened." Falima lowered herself to her haunches. "But the cause was mistake, not malice. Zylas has forgiven you, and so have I. At some point, you have to forgive yourself."

"Joetha's family—"

"—can never forgive you, of course." Falima asked cautiously, "Can you live with that?"

Collins had been about to say "—will suffer," so Falima's question caught him off-guard. He considered. "Yes," he realized to his own surprise. "I can."

Falima rose and returned to her chair. "Then it's settled. We don't need to speak of this again."

Collins liked the way she had phrased it, assuaging his shame but leaving the subject open if he ever felt the emotional need to talk about it. It was a talent he had not known she possessed, and it only made her more desirable.

Collins awakened with a start that left him disoriented to place and time, yet burdened with a decisive thought that usurped all other need for understanding. My friends: Zylas,

Falima, Vernon, even Ialin, are good people, better than I
could ever be. He tried to imagine himself risking his life
and freedom for a murderer on death row, but the image
refused to form. He would not do so, even if he knew the
man innocent, let alone guilty only from ignorance. He
would, of course, come forward to testify; but he would not
hazard electrocution by cutting power lines to the electric
chair.

Collins opened his eyes. He lay on the pallet in Vernon's
cottage, straw poking him through the threadbare blanket,
a bundled tunic serving as a makeshift pillow. Falima curled
on the floor, snagging the four hours of sleep she required
in human form. He would have preferred to give her the
more comfortable sleeping place, but maintaining the illusion of his royalty took precedence until they left Korfius in
Vernon's care. He saw no sign of Korfius or their host.

As Collins rolled to his right side to face the wall, he
found his feet pinned in place. He jerked at the covers, dislodging the dog, who groaned and clambered from the pallet. Freed, Collins finished his intended movement and
snuggled back into the straw. He could understand Zylas'
assistance. The rat/man might feel responsible for leading
Collins into Barakhai and, therefore, the subsequent crime.
Vernon clearly made a career out of helping the needy, so
perhaps he got some personal satisfaction from hiding Collins. Falima's and Ialin's motivations escaped him completely. *No wonder they're hostile. Zylas must have talked
them into it, perhaps against their better judgment.*

Knowing he needed his sleep, Collins forced these
thoughts from his mind. He could speculate about their motivations all day and never come near the truth. It was an
exercise in futility that he could better solve by simply asking. *Hard enough understanding people of my own world.*
Collins pushed his mind to less intrusive thoughts and,
eventually, found sleep again.

The next time Benton Collins awakened, he heard low
voices. He sat up, the blanket tumbling to his ankles. Zylas
leaned across the table, talking softly to Vernon. They made
an odd pair, one slight and white as cream, the other power-
fully muscled and dark as untouched coffee. Though taught
to revile eavesdropping, he strained to overhear. His

companions had left him out of conversations about his own welfare so many times that he somehow felt owed the knowledge.

Korfius floundered from beneath the blanket that now covered his head. He flopped to the floor, the cloth fumbling after him in an awkward twist.

The men at the table looked toward them. Zylas said something louder, accompanied by a friendly wave.

Only then, Collins realized his moments of straining could have gained him nothing. Without touching the stone, he could not understand a word of the Barakhain they exchanged. He thrust his hand into the pocket that held the rose quartz, withdrawing it. "You're back," he finally said.

"I am," Zylas admitted. His gaze wandered to the translation stone, and his grin widened. "Thanks for taking such good care of my rock."

Collins returned the grin. "It was nothing," he said honestly. "I really appreciate your leaving it. I couldn't have done anything without it."

Zylas nodded. Collins certainly did not have to explain the merits of the magic to its longtime owner.

"So," Collins pressed for the important news immediately. "Is there another portal?"

Zylas glanced at Vernon, who shrugged, then gave his head a slight shake. The rat/man's attention returned to Collins. "Not . . . yet. But . . ."

Collins waited for his companion to continue. When he did not, Collins made an impatient gesture. "But . . . ?"

Zylas pursed his lips, then spoke quickly, as if he had to force the words out before he changed his mind. "The elder wishes to meet with you."

Uncertain how to react, Collins asked cautiously, "He does? Why?"

Zylas opened his mouth, then closed it without speaking. He gave Vernon another meaningful look, but the black man turned away, arms folded across his chest. Clearly on his own now, Zylas said lamely, "It's not a simple matter. The elder . . . can explain it better."

"All . . . right." Collins looked from companion to companion, but neither returned his stare. "What do I need to know before I agree to this?"

Silence.

Irritated with his companions' behavior, Collins demanded, "You said my going would be dangerous to the elder and to myself. Don't I have a right to know why before I'm smack dab in the middle of that danger?"

Vernon said gruffly, "It's not you we're worried about."

Zylas placed a hand on Vernon's shoulder, an obvious plea to let him handle it. "It'll become clear, but Vernon's right. So long as you don't do anything foolish or mean . . ."

Like eat some innocent woman? Collins thought bitterly.

". . . you're perfectly safe. The elder . . ." Zylas flicked strands of dirty white-blond hair from his eyes. ". . . has more at stake. We just want to protect—"

Vernon jumped in again. "—the elder."

"Right," Zylas confirmed.

Korfius thrust his nose into Collins' hand. He patted the dog absently, still focused on his oddly behaving friends. "I'm not going to hurt anyone, if that's what you're jazzed up about." Collins wondered how that translated, but Zylas and Vernon showed no sign of confusion. "I didn't mean to kill Joetha," he said for what seemed like the thousandth time. "It was an awful thing for which I'll feel eternally guilty, but can't we ever—"

Zylas and Vernon made broad motions to silence Collins. "We know that," the albino assured. "We don't have to talk about that anymore."

Vernon stood, nostrils flaring in clear distress. "It's just that you come with . . . certain dangers."

Understanding dawned, dispelling the irritation. "You mean the guards chasing me."

Zylas vigorously nodded confirmation, but Vernon did not let the matter drop. "We don't know you well enough to be sure—"

"Vernon," Zylas warned, but it did not stop his friend.

"—you can keep your mouth shut."

Collins felt the prickle of returning irritation but forced it away. Vernon had a reasonable point. "I owe you all my life at least two times over. I'm not going to give away any secret."

Zylas rolled his gaze to Vernon, who did not seem satisfied. "Can you bind that as a vow?"

Collins blinked, tightening his grip on the translation stone, which didn't seem to be fully functioning. "What?"

Vernon rephrased his question. "Do you have some sanctified words, some gesture, that binds important promises beyond breaking?"

Now Collins understood. *Nothing in my world is so sacred someone can't and won't abandon it.* That answer, he knew, would not satisfy Vernon. He would not break his word because he considered himself an honorable and moral person. Nevertheless, a white lie seemed worth it to appease Vernon. "We have both." He cleared his throat, assuming the most serious expression he could. "I swear to God . . ." It did not sound like enough, so he added, "with sugar on top, that I will . . ." He looked at Vernon questioningly.

Catching the intention of the pause, Vernon supplied the next words, ". . . not divulge the name, location, or even the existence of the elder to anyone ever, no matter what good reason I think I may have for doing so."

"Uh." Collins had no trouble agreeing to the terms, but he could not recall all the words Vernon had used. "I will not . . . uh . . . divulge . . . uh . . . the elder forever no matter what." *Mouthful of mostly long words to express the obvious. He'd have made a good lawyer.* Collins spit on his right hand. "Now we shake on it."

"Shake on . . . it?" Vernon studied Collins' fingers dubiously.

Collins took Vernon's enormous paw of a hand into his own, flicked it vigorously, then released it. He wiped his palm on his britches, and Vernon did the same.

"Done?" the larger man asked.

"Done," Collins agreed.

Vernon muttered something of which the stone translated only, "Weird."

Unable to miss the irony, Collins hid a smile.

Chapter 10

ZYLAS and Collins set off immediately, with the sun still high in the sky. They rode Falima, and Collins caught occasional glimpses of Ialin zipping to Zylas and hovering near his ear. The hummingbird always gave Collins a wide berth, which pleased him as well. The wind carried streamers of Zylas' unnaturally white hair into Collins' face at intervals so irregular he forgot to protect against it. Accustomed to wearing glasses, he rarely reacted in time to rescue his eyes, and the strands whipped across them, stinging, until he wondered if he had permanent red lines across the whites. Adding a buzzing, insectlike bird to the aggravation might have driven him over the edge, from sullen irritation to rage.

Zylas carried the translation stone again, which seemed to make no difference as his other two companions would remain in their animal forms for about five more hours and the rat/man had settled into a nearly unbreakable silence. He led them on a circuitous route that confused Collins utterly. At times, he thought he recognized landmarks they had passed a half hour earlier. They might be traveling in an endless loop for all he knew, and he could not help recalling the Winnie-the-Pooh tale in which the silly old bear and his friend, Piglet, track themselves in a circle, worried that, at each pass, another two creatures have joined the ones they were following. Despite the warmth and humor of this childhood remembrance, Collins found his discomfort growing.

The weather seemed hell-bent on displaying all the happy grandeur Collins' mood lacked. The sun beamed through the trees in golden bands. A breeze danced around the trunks, keeping the temperature hovering at what felt like a comfortable seventy degrees. Crystal-blue sky stretched from horizon to horizon, dotted with a few fluffy clouds that gleamed whitely in the broad expanse of azure.

The ground grew rockier. Falima stumbled. Abruptly jarred sideways, Collins found himself on the ground before he realized he was falling. Pain shot through his left shoulder. Dull aching pounded through his thighs and buttocks, a reminder that he had spent more time riding the last two days than in all the rest of his life combined. He looked up to a hovering hummingbird and a still-mounted Zylas peering down at him, arm extended. "Are you all right?"

"Just fricking fine." Collins had no idea whether the almost-swear word would translate as the real thing or into a somewhat-acceptable substitution like the one he had provided. He clambered painfully to his feet, ignoring Zylas' gesture. "Mind if I just walk for a while?"

"Not at all." Zylas peered into the distance. "In fact, we'll take to the mountains soon. Probably better if we all walk."

Ialin disappeared.

Collins massaged his aching shoulder.

"Only kept us mounted this far to make as small a scent trail as possible. Ialin's seen guards out there, though they don't seem to have located us."

"What about Vernon and Korfius?" Collins asked, worried.

Zylas dismounted, clutching Falima's lead. "No reason to think they're not safe. They've got their stories, and we just have to hope no one convinces Korfius to rat us out."

Collins laughed at the play on words, which seemed to baffle Zylas.

"What's funny?"

Collins saw no harm in explaining, this time. "Rat us out. You're a rat."

Zylas continued to stare.

"Just seemed funny," Collins mumbled, withdrawing back toward his irritability.

"Is that how it translates?"

"Yeah."

Now, Zylas chuckled. "It's not the word I used. We don't have a lot of animal-based slang."

Collins nodded. "Makes sense."

"Ready to continue?"

No, Collins thought but said, "Yes."

They headed into rocky hills that soon became forested mountains. The trail continued to spiral, double back, and loop. For a time, Collins tried to trace the route. When that became impossible, he attempted conversation. "So now will you tell me about this elder?"

Zylas looked up with clear reluctance. "You'll meet soon enough."

Foiled again, Collins bit his lower lip. "How soon is soon enough?"

"Tomorrow evening."

"Tomorrow!" Collins complained, recalling that Zylas and Ialin had made the trip and returned in about twenty-four hours.

Zylas' eyes widened. "Did you want to take longer?"

"Shorter."

"We could arrive a little earlier," Zylas said slowly. "If you won't be uncomfortable with Falima and Ialin in switch-form."

Collins considered. He might perform better with Falima communicative. She seemed to have warmed up to him in Vernon's cabin. Ialin, he thought, might do him better as a speechless bird. "Perhaps somewhere between the two?"

Zylas tossed his tangled hair. "Of course, there's the elder's switch time to consider, too." He rubbed his forehead. "While you sleep, I'll meet with the elder and talk about that."

Surprised to have his opinion considered at all, Collins merely said, "All right." He had not thought about the details such coordination might require, but he should have. He had learned enough under dire enough circumstances. *I should be thinking all the time.* It bothered him to consider that he was, perhaps, not as smart as he believed. He had always done well in school, earning A's and B's with relative ease and not just in rote subjects. Yet he worried that his ability to anticipate and react to life situations might not prove as competent. *What happens when I get out in the real world where life doesn't consist solely of classes and tests?*

The thought now seemed ludicrous. *Assuming I survive Barakhai and ever make it back to the "real" world.*

Zylas led Falima up the slope. "Speaking of sleep, we work best when we get half in each form. Thought we could take a break: eat, nap."

Though Collins had slept a solid eight hours, he suffered from hunger, thirst, and physical exhaustion. He supposed he could learn to coordinate his sleep with Zylas', in three- or four-hour blocks rather than all at once. "Sounds good to me."

Despite his suggestion, Zylas continued hauling Falima up the mountainside. "There's a cave not too far. I'd rather hole up on higher ground. Safer."

Collins followed, now aware of his growling tummy, his dry mouth, and the soreness of his legs. He wished Zylas had waited until they'd arrived at the cave to mention food and rest.

Half an hour later, Zylas waved Collins into the rock crevice he had referred to as a cave. A curtain of vines hung over the entrance, swarmed with round pink flowers; and grass softened the floor. Collins touched a wall slimy with algae and moss and immediately jerked back his hand. Warm and moist, the interior seemed stifling after the dry, cool wind that had accompanied them through the day. Falima remained outside, grazing, but Ialin swept onto a ledge and perched. Zylas went outside nearly as soon as he entered, then returned moments later dragging the pack that had rested on Falima's withers. As Collins hurried over to help, Zylas let it flop onto the floor.

"I appreciate that Vernon doesn't want us to starve, but I would have packed a bit lighter."

At the moment, Collins would have carried the pack the rest of the way if it meant a steady supply of Vernon's peanut-buttery nut paste. He helped Zylas unpack enough food to satisfy them both: bread and nut paste, bugs and fruit, roots and berries. They ate well, then settled down to sleep on the grassy carpet.

Collins dreamed of a violent earthquake rocking him in wild, insistent motions. "What? Where?" He leaped to his feet. "Huh?" The world came into abrupt focus, despite his

missing glasses. Falima stood beside him, still clutching the
arm she had been shaking. Zylas stood near the pack, smiling slightly from beneath his hat brim as he watched the
exchange. "Bit jumpy, are you?"

Still slightly disoriented, Collins glanced at his watch.
"What time is it?" It read 6:15. Falima would have changed
fifteen minutes ago, which would have just given her time
to dress and wolf down some food before awakening him.
He yawned.

Though Collins had found his own answer, Zylas gave
him another. "Early evening. You're a good sleeper."

Collins yawned again. "Most grad students are." He
stretched, the pain in his thighs and buttocks even more
pronounced. He was glad Falima had taken human form
and they would have to walk for a while. "Now, if I could
just get some coffee."

Zylas laughed. "Don't have that here. But you're welcome to eat dirt. Tastes about the same to me."

"Let me guess. Not a coffee fan?" Collins sprang forward
and hefted the pack before his older and smaller companion could do so. It settled awkwardly across his neck, obviously constructed to balance across a horse's unsaddled
withers without sliding. Now, he had to agree with Zylas;
fewer supplies would suit his shoulders better. "It's an acquired taste."

"Apparently." Zylas did not fight Collins for the pack.
"But why bother to acquire it?"

"For the caffeine." Collins trailed his companions
through the viny curtain and into sunlight that, though
muted by evening, still burned his unadjusted eyes. "Helps
you wake up."

Zylas headed back up the slope. "Why not just take caffeine?"

Why not, indeed? Collins recalled a professor once telling the class that, in the name of avoiding hypocrisy, No-
Doz was his morning beverage. It seemed more like an
admission of drug addiction than the heroically honest
statement the professor had clearly intended. "I actually
like the taste of coffee." *Now.* When he first started drinking
it, he had diluted it more than halfway with milk. Gradually,
the proportion had decreased until he had come to take it
with only a splash of nondairy creamer.

"All . . . right," Zylas said slowly. "If you say so."

"It's good." Collins hopped after Falima, who had darted up the hill with a dexterity her horse form could never have matched. "Really. Coffee has a great—" Struck by the ridiculousness of the argument, Collins laughed. *Why am I defending coffee to a man who eats bugs and calls them a delicacy?* "—flavor," he finished. "When it's made right." It seemed rude to leave Falima out of the conversation. Not wanting to lose the ground he had gained with her the previous day, he asked, "So how are things with you, Falima?"

At the sound of her name, Falima turned and shrugged.

"She can't understand you," Zylas reminded.

Oh, yeah. Disappointment flashed through Collins, gradually replaced by guarded relief. As much as he wanted to chat with her, at least, this way, he could not ruin their friendship by saying something stupid.

They continued through softly contoured mountains carpeted with weeds, wildflowers, and evergreen forests. Now, Zylas' diversions became clearer to Collins, as they meandered down and sideways as often as upward, and he often forgot that they traveled through mountains at all. Occasionally, the vegetation gave way to barren rock faces, especially where the walk grew steeper. These proved a minor challenge that would bore a real climber, though Collins found himself guarding every step. A fall seemed unlikely, but it might result in serious injury; and he had taken more than a few missteps in his life on flat, solid ground.

The weather remained clear. That, and a comfortable sleep, vastly improved Collins' mood. He could almost imagine himself on a youth group hike, scurrying up Mount Chockorua with a backpack, a canteen, and a bunch of rowdy boys. The fear of becoming trapped in a world that condemned him as a vicious murderer receded behind a wash of reckless hope.

Collins met Falima's gaze on several occasions, exchanging short nervous smiles whenever they did so. The strange and silent flirtation passed time otherwise measured only by the slow downward creep of the sun. At length, it touched the far horizon, pitching up broad bands of color that blurred and mingled at the edges, cleared to vivid extremes, then dulled into the next. Bold spikes of pink interrupted the pattern at intervals, radiating in majestic lines.

Collins paused on a crest, staring. Evening breezes chilled the sweat spangling his forehead, and he could not tear his gaze from the beauty of the vast panorama stretching out in front of him. He had never seen anything so grand. The few clear sunsets of his camping days he had viewed through forests of skeletal branches that blotted the grandeur with shadows. City lights blunted the epic, almost violent, hues that now paraded before his eyes. In recent years, he had forgotten to look, his evenings gobbled up by essays and lab work, indoor dinners and rented movies.

"What's the matter?"

Zylas' now-familiar voice startled Collins. He jumped, slammed his foot down on a loose stone, twisted his ankle, and toppled. Before the rat/man could move to assist, Collins lay on the ground. His ankle throbbed, but he still managed to say, "What's the matter? The matter is some guy who calls himself a friend scaring me and dumping me on my face."

Zylas drew back, feigning affront. "I never touched you. You dumped yourself on your own face."

"With incredible grace, I might add." Collins rose gingerly and found he could already put most of his weight on his leg. He was not badly hurt. "Don't sell me short, now. I'm excellent at dumping myself on my face."

Zylas agreed, "A real professional." He offered a hand, though Collins had already stood.

"Mind telling Falima it was your fault? She already thinks I'm a clod."

Zylas glanced toward his flank. "I'd do that, but she does have ... um ... eyes."

Collins looked around Zylas, only then noticing Falima nearby. She had probably witnessed the entire exchange. He tried to remember which parts of the conversation he had spoken. She could not understand him, but Zylas could come across plainly to both of them. Much like listening to one end of a telephone conversation, she could surely infer much merely from what Zylas had said. *But why the hell do I care what she thinks?* Collins could not explain it; but, somehow, he did. He looked back at the horizon, but the sky's exquisite light show had dulled toward flat black and the first stars had appeared. He rounded on Zylas. "If you must know, I was enjoying that gorgeous sunset. You made me miss the last of it."

Zylas turned his attention westward, with the air of a man so accustomed to seeing radiance, he no longer notices it.

Of course, Collins surmised. *They get sunsets like that every day.* In that moment, he grew less fascinated by the life of a models' photographer. It seemed impossible that staring at beautiful women for a living gradually sapped it of all thrill, yet surely it must. *Does a man ever tire of looking at an attractive wife?* An answer popped swiftly into Collins' mind, though he had never intended to address his own unspoken question. *I don't stare at Marlys the way I used to, and she's only grown more lovely.* In fact, it surprised him to discover that, of all the things he missed most, she barely made the list. *If absence makes the heart grow fonder, then either I don't have a heart or she was never really there.*

Falima followed the direction of Zylas' stare to the now-blunted sunset. She said something, the slight up-tick at the end Collins' only hint that she had asked a question.

Zylas responded in their lilting language, leaving her nodding thoughtfully.

The albino turned his attention back to Collins. "Ready?"

"To go on?" Collins guessed. "Sure."

Zylas adjusted his breeks. "To meet the elder."

Collins blinked. "Tonight? But I thought . . ."

Zylas shrugged. "You requested; I asked." He held out a hand, and the hummingbird alighted, tiny talons gripping his index finger. "Ialin says we've lost the guards. The elder thinks we've muddled the trail enough."

Though he had suspected it, Collins barely dared to believe Zylas had dragged out their journey so much that they could chop off an entire day and not even notice it. "Definitely. I'm ready." Finally, he would find out how to get home. *Home to professors furious that I ruined all their experiments.* He doubted anyone could believe his reason for not taking care of the animals. Each rat had enough water to last several days, and they could go without eating for weeks, if necessary. He wondered if he could get back to Daubert Laboratories before vacation ended; if he cleaned all the cages thoroughly, supplied fresh food sticks and water, no one would know he had gone. The deceit bothered him. It might change the results of some of the analyses, but it seemed preferable to him sacrificing the future he had gone into hock for. A bad relationship, a sundered family, student loans—these all seemed minor inconveniences compared to remaining always a jump ahead of a local constabulary fixated on executing him.

As Zylas headed across a ridge swarming with leafy vines, Collins finally found the argument that might have gotten him to the elder sooner. "You know, Zylas." He tried to keep his voice casual. "I'm the only one taking care of those rats back at the lab for four days."

Zylas continued walking, a stiffening of his back the only clue that he had heard the pronouncement. At length, he spoke. "Are they . . . are they going to . . ." It took a real effort to squeeze out the last word. ". . . die?"

Well, yes. After an experiment, they all die. Collins kept that realization to himself, suddenly wishing he had not raised the topic at all. It seemed cruel to leave Zylas believing he had had a hand in the deaths of a roomful of creatures he considered kin. Initially planning to use the information to help speed things along, Collins suddenly found himself in the position of comforter. "I don't think so. I gave them enough water for at least three days. They might get a bit hungry before the others get back, but they should survive all right." *Great. That accomplished a lot.*

Zylas' movements became jerky, agitated. Falima glided up and gently placed an arm across his shoulders, speaking calmly.

Collins slammed the heel of his palm against his forehead. *Blew that one big time.* He tried to simultaneously rescue his point and Zylas, though the two goals seemed entirely at odds. "They certainly won't die. Certainly not. But the sooner I get back, the sooner I can attend to them. Clean cages, feed. You know, make them comfortable."

Zylas and Falima made a sudden turn, disappearing behind a crag.

Collins jogged to catch up, then slammed into his companions who had come to a halt just beyond the angle. Driven forward a step, Zylas whirled, while Falima just shook her head and continued studying the cliff wall in front of her. Ialin buzzed into flight.

"Sorry," Collins muttered, then realized the ivy-covered stone in front of him had a central area darker than the surrounding stone. He stared, trying to visually carve clear the outline of the cave mouth that he guessed lay there. "We're here?"

"Yes." Zylas placed a hand on Collins' arm and ushered him forward. "Please, be polite." His tone fairly pleaded, and Collins found it impossible to take offense from the implication. "Respectful. Not . . ." He trailed off, looking more nervous than Collins had ever seen him.

"Not rude?" Collins supplied, with just a hint of indignation.

Zylas finally glanced directly into Collins' face and smiled. "I'm sorry I'm treating you like a child. It's just that . . . well . . . sometimes your people . . . don't handle elders . . . um . . ."

Collins thought he understood. Americans did tend to value youth and vigor more than wisdom. "With appropriate esteem?"

Zylas let out a pent-up breath. "Right."

Falima spoke through gritted teeth, and Zylas translated. "She says that would be a big mistake here."

"I understand." Though tired of reassurances, Collins said and did nothing more. The more impatience he showed, the longer the likely delay. It made sense that the people here showed a deference bordering on awe toward their elders. Given their lifestyle, they likely had few who lasted all that long.

A gravelly voice emerged from the cave scarcely louder than the whisper of windblown vines against stone. "Zylas, Falima, Ialin, please come in. And bring your guest."

No longer able to delay, Zylas executed a bow the elder surely could not see. "At once, Lady Prinivere." He tugged at Collins' arm.

Lady? Collins had to adjust his entire image as he trotted into the cave at Zylas' side. Ialin fluttered ahead, and Falima followed them.

The darkness seemed to swallow them, and Collins blinked several times, seeking some small source of light on which to focus his vision. Afraid to move for fear of knocking into people or furniture, he turned in place to catch the lingering grayness at the opening.

"Forgive me," a sweet but ancient voice said. "I forget that others need this." A ball of light appeared, pulled apart like a chain of glowsticks, then diffused into a pale, sourceless glow. Collins saw a round face as brown as a berry and cast into extensive, deep wrinkles. Dressed only in a loin-cloth, the old woman left most of her withered flesh exposed. Her breasts hung so low they covered her slender abdomen. A thick, untidy mop of snowy hair sprouted from her freckled scalp, hanging to just below her ears. Though recessed into hollows, her eyes looked remarkably clear, green as a cat's with the same slitted pupils and full of an ancient wisdom that the wateriness of age could not diminish. Her small nose seemed little more than a pair of slitty nostrils in a sea of pleats. Collins studied her in unbelieving fascination, certain he had never seen anyone quite this old. He barely noticed the furnishings, which consisted entirely of two large chests.

The elder smiled. "I am Prinivere."

Wanting to introduce himself before Zylas could do so, to avoid forever becoming an amalgamation of his full name, Collins found his tongue. "Ben," he said. Despite himself, he added, "Just Ben." He caught himself at once. *Great. Now she's going to call me Justben.* It sounded uncomfortably close to Dustbin, though still better than Bentoncollins or, worse, the Benton Zachary Collins his mother used whenever he got into trouble.

But Prinivere made no such mistake. "A pleasure to meet you, Ben."

"Thank you," Collins said politely, only then blurting a sudden realization. "You speak English."

Unobtrusively, Zylas stepped on Collins' foot.

"I speak all languages," Prinivere explained. She folded her legs, sitting on the floor with surprising grace for one so frail in appearance. "Come join me, Ben."

Without hesitation, Collins dropped to his haunches, then sat in front of the old woman. "Thank you," he said again. Though perhaps not the most suitable response, they were the politest words he knew.

"You're welcome." Prinivere studied Collins in silence then. Her eyes looked tired but very alive, a discomforting contrast to a body that seemed long past its time.

Collins sat very still, feeling like a piece of steak at the meat counter. The long silence that followed made him even more restless. Wondering if it were his job to break it, he looked at Zylas.

The albino shook his head stiffly.

Like a hunter with prey, the movement caught Prinivere's attention. "Who has the stone?"

Zylas crouched beside Collins. "I do, Lady."

The stabbing gaze went fully to the rat/man now, to Collins' relief. "Don't you think it would serve better in his hands?"

Zylas swallowed hard but remained adamant. "I can't afford to lose it. I was hoping . . . can't you . . . ?"

Prinivere leaned forward, and her breasts drooped into her lap. Collins found himself noting this matter-of-factly, the way he might view a fat, shirtless man's stomach overflowing his pants at a sporting event. There was knowledge and venerability but nothing sexual about this primordial creature. "Maybe. After I've slept, switched." She shook her head. "I think I might be able to."

Able to what? Collins wondered, but he did not ask. He looked up, only to find the sharp, green eyes back on him.

"So," she said. "What do you think of Barakhai?"

At home, it might have seemed a casual question, a polite query intended to illicit a stock response. Now, Collins sensed a much deeper quality that forced him to think in a way he had not since his companions had freed him from hanging. Driven by desperation, by terror, by need, he had not bothered to contemplate the world and its wonders per se. "I think," he started, and his voice seemed to thunder into an intense and critical silence, "it's a world with some simple beauty mine hasn't known for some time." Though the others nodded, Collins doubted they understood what he meant. "Clear sunsets, fresh air, water you can drink from its source and not worry about pollution and . . . germs." He did not know for certain about the latter. Obviously, the inhabitants drank the water all the time, apparently with no harmful effects; but dogs lapped up muddy, worm-riddled puddles in his world, too. Perhaps the water here teemed with Giardia, amoeba, and other microbes that the animal part of them could tolerate; or they simply survived as long as they could with masses of intestinal parasites writhing inside them. So far, he had drunk the water without getting ill. Only time would tell for certain whether the better part of wisdom would have been to boil it first.

Only quiet consideration filled the hush after Collins' description, so he felt obliged to continue. "I've met some wonderful people." He made a gesture that encompassed Falima and Zylas. Though he did not intentionally leave out Ialin, he made no particular effort to include the hummingbird either. He sucked air through pursed lips, thinking. "I suppose I might find the rest of the people worth meeting, too, under other circumstances. I can hardly blame the guards for the way they treated me. I had just . . ." A lump filled his throat suddenly, blocking the words he intended to speak. As he tried to force them out, his eyes brimmed with tears, and he dropped the attempt.

No one came to Collins' rescue, though he thought he caught a subtle nod between Prinivere and Zylas.

Casually, Collins wiped his eyes on the back of his sleeve and changed the subject. "Lady, I don't know exactly what my companions told you, but I came to see you to find out if you knew of any portals to my world other than the one I came through."

"I know," Prinivere said, her voice a dull rasp.

Ialin settled on a shriveled shoulder. Falima lowered herself to one of the chests, listening on the fringes. As usual, she could understand only half the conversation, at most. Collins wondered whether the old woman actually used fluent English or some device translated her words into whatever language necessary for comprehension by every listener. He only knew he used English exclusively and carried nothing to make it sound like anything else.

"You know?" Collins needed clarification, but before he could voice it, Prinivere continued.

"I know the reason you came to me. Your companions told me."

Good. Collins nodded.

"There are no other portals."

Stunned by bad news so unceremoniously and abruptly delivered, Collins froze, speechless. Zylas should have told him that days ago and rescued him from this ridiculous charade. The Barakhains could have kept their beloved elder safe, unmet and unknown, and they would not have wasted time taking some inane, meandering path to her. Gradually, the full implications seeped into a mind already plagued with desperation. They had no choice but to return to the place where Collins had started and find a way past a contingent of archers.

"But—" Prinivere said. That one word seemed to float, alone in a vast vacuum of hope. It felt to Collins like hours passed before she continued, though she never paused. "—I might be able to create a new portal."

Still unmoving, Collins lost his breath. "Create . . . one?" He forced the words out, then gasped in a clumsy breath accompanied by saliva. He choked, coughing so vigorously that Falima leaped to her feet and patted his back helpfully.

Wanting to hear what Prinivere had to say, Collins waved Falima off and tried to control his seizing diaphragm.

But Prinivere did not go on. Turning her attention to Zylas, she engaged the albino in conversation while Collins lost the battle to his cough.

For several moments, Collins struggled, throat raw and full. Finally, the spasms died to a tickle, and he regained control of speech. "Sorry." His voice sounded hoarse and unrecognizable. "Did you say you could create a portal?"

Prinivere spun back to face Collins. "I said I might be able to, yes."

"So . . ." Collins kept his sentence slow to avoid the need to cough again. ". . . you're . . . a sorceress?"

Prinivere's recessed eyes narrowed, so they seemed to disappear into the wrinkles. "Sorceress." She ran the word over her tongue, then shook her head. "Not sure what you mean."

Collins sought synonyms. "A witch." He watched Prinivere's face for clues to her disposition to see if the word had the same negative connotations here as back home. "A magician. A wizard. A person who uses magic."

"No such thing," Zylas grunted. "People, magic." He shook his head. "Don't go together."

Collins suppressed an urge to laugh. *If people turning into animals isn't magic, what is?* He kept the thought to himself. It seemed the populace had little control over the transformation. "*You* have magic," he reminded.

"I carry a magical item," Zylas admitted, though he glanced around as he did so, as if afraid someone outside their group might overhear. "That doesn't make me a user of magic."

In strict terms, of course, it did; but Collins decided it was better not to make an issue of such a thing. "If not by magic, how do you make a portal?" Collins wondered if he might have the means to do it himself.

"Making a portal does require magic." Zylas confused the issue still further. "That's why we need the lady's help."

"But she's not a sorceress."

"No," Prinivere patted her hair into place.

"So you have some sort of portal-making item."

"No such thing." Zylas said.

Clear as mud. Collins sighed and took the chest seat Falima had vacated. "I don't get it."

"You will," Zylas promised with all the believability of a politician a week before an election. "You will."

An undertone in the albino's voice made Collins wonder if he wanted to.

Chapter 11

PRINIVERE wandered to the farthest corner of the cave to sleep while Collins discussed matters fervently with the one companion who did understand him and insisted on translating for the one who did not. Twilight faded from the opening and the cave so gradually that, even in a darkness that might have seemed solid under other circumstances, Collins found himself able to differentiate between the gray silhouettes of his companions.

"Let's talk about those rats back at the lab." Though redirected several times, Zylas always returned to the matter Collins now fervently wished he had never raised.

Collins sighed, certain he would have to change his major. After this day, he might never find the courage to euthanize another experimental animal. *That, or fill my home with pet rats, mice, guinea pigs, and monkeys.* He imagined the look of horror twisting his landlady's meaty features; she screamed at the sight of a large spider. "They'll be fine," Collins insisted with a finality he hoped would satisfy his companion—this time. "They've got plenty of water till my preceptor gets back." *Is that today?* "At most they'll go a day without food, and their cages will stink a bit."

Zylas' expression remained taut.

Collins laid an arm across the albino's shoulders. "Look, man. There's nothing we can do about it, is there? The whole school's getting back tomorrow. Believe me when I say every biology professor at Algary will head straight for the lab." *Where they'll see the crappy job I did and flunk me on the spot.* More concerned for his future than the temporary comfort of a bunch of laboratory rats, Collins again sought a topic switch. "So what's the big secret about Prinivere anyway? I mean, besides the fact that she's a woman when you had me believing she was a man."

Zylas shrugged off Collins' arm. "*Lady* Prinivere," he corrected in a bristly voice. "And I don't recall ever calling the lady a man."

"Not directly." Collins admitted. "But you did refer to her only as 'the elder.' Never even used a pronoun as far as I remember. Didn't correct me when I called her 'him'."

"That's you assuming, not deception." Zylas paced to Falima and joined her on the chest.

Depends on what the definition of "is" is. Collins shook off the presidential comparison. "You can claim you didn't lie. But not correcting an assumption you knew was false *is* deception." He straddled the opposite chest, facing Zylas directly. "Are you going to tell me it's different in your world?"

Zylas conceded with a sigh. "I'm sorry. Vernon thought that, if we never made it to the lady, any information you had that the guards might get would be . . . misleading. He's a smart man, and it seemed safest at the time."

Falima poked Zylas' back, and he turned to translate.

A sensation of being watched spiraled through Collins suddenly, and he shivered, glancing toward the cave mouth. "You've managed to deflect my question again, I notice. What exactly—" The hair on the nape of his neck prickled. A realization of intense and imminent danger grasped his gut like an icy hand. His heart raced into wild pounding, and words caught like a sticky lump in his throat. Panic sent him lurching to his feet, and he skittered to the cave mouth before logic trickled between otherwise ravaged thoughts. *What the hell?*

Pressed against the stone wall, Collins glanced back into the cave. Zylas and Falima had also risen, their backs to him. Though they had not run, they did seem agitated. A dinosaurlike creature took up most of the back of the cave: long-necked and -legged, covered in greenish-black scales that seemed to glow. Plates jutted from the neck, back, and tail, which ended in a ragged scar. "Dr–dragon?" Collins stammered out the only English word that might suit this massive animal. Though he knew it must be Prinivere's switch-form, he could not force himself to reenter the cave.

Ideas rushed back into Collins' mind. Memory came first, of a girl he had dated in college. A fan of aliens, angels, and conspiracy theories, she had once brought him a book that "conclusively proved" the existence of dragons. For the purposes of domestic harmony, he had read it, a pseudoscientific account filled with blurry photographs, anecdotal sightings, and misconceptions a freshmen science student should see through. He had tried to argue the biological impossibility of a heavy, four-legged creature with wings. If dragons did exist, he had asserted, they would look like pteranodons. Wings had served as the forelimbs of every flying animal throughout history.

Now, Collins stared upon a creature that defied every biological tenet. Big as a school bus, it had to weigh tons. Strong hind legs ended in massive, four-clawed feet. The forelimbs had three toes, each with talons that closely resembled curved knives. Leathery appendages near the shoulders clearly represented folded wings. It bore little resemblance to the serpents of the Chinese New Year's parades, its body blocky and its snout more like that of a Doberman. It bore none of the decorative finery, no streamers, beards, or spinners. The ears stuck up, shaped and proportioned like a horse's, jet black in color. Eyes like emeralds lay recessed deeply into its sockets.

A voice entered Collins' head, seeming to bypass his hearing. *I won't hurt you. Come.*

Collins pawed at his ears, willing them to work properly; his life might depend on it. The reassurance, apparently the dragon's, did not soothe. He found himself incapable of taking a step closer to a creature that could shred him, crush him, or bite him in half without breaking a sweat.

Zylas took several nervous steps, bowed to the dragon, then hurried to Collins. "You're insulting Lady Prinivere," he hissed.

In response, Collins pressed his back more tightly to the wall. Vines tickled his arms, and stone jabbed his spine. He tried to explain, "She's a . . . she's a . . . a dragon."

"Yes."

"We . . . we . . . don't have . . . dragons . . . in my world."

"Neither do we."

The ludicrousness of that statement finally broke the spell. Collins turned his head slowly toward Zylas to grant him a judgmental stare. "I beg to differ."

Zylas took one of Collins' hands in both of his. "Except Lady Prinivere, of course. She's the last."

Collins looked at the hand clamped between Zylas' and hoped the albino did not plan to try to drag him back into the cave. He wiped his other sweating palm on his britches and tried to screw up his courage.

"The others were killed off centuries ago."

"By knights, no doubt." Collins resorted to his usual haven, humor, to orient his failing rationality.

Zylas tugged gently at Collins. "Huh?"

"Never mind." It seemed worse than senseless to try to explain legends at a time when reality had gone beyond them.

"It's all right. Really. Come meet her."

Collins looked at the dragon, still hesitating. Falima faced the dragon, clearly engaged in conversation, arms waving at intervals. If Prinivere responded, she did so without opening her mouth. "She could eat us all in the same bite."

"Eat us?" Zylas rolled his eyes. "She's constrained by the same laws as the rest of us. Can't eat any meat, remember?"

"Who could stop her?" Collins muttered, but he did take a step forward. Prinivere posed no more threat to him than the guardsmen, and she might hold the only key to his escape. He managed another step.

Zylas released Collins' hand. Falima turned, impassively watching her friends approach. As he drew closer, Collins noticed details he had missed on first inspection. The glow that outlined the dragon seemed as feeble and tattered as a dying star. Most of the claws looked jagged, broken beyond repair. Scars marred her scaly hide in several locations, the worst a mottled, irregular patch in the right chest area. She moved with a slowness that suggested long-standing fatigue. Her dragon form had clearly aged along with her human one.

Actually, it's my human form that aged along with the dragon form. The words whispered into Collins' brain, unspoken.

Collins jumped, heart racing again.

Yes, I read minds. That's how I know every language.

Collins had not yet recovered enough to ask the question she had already answered. Remembering that he needed her, he forced calm. *If she predicts my future thoughts, too, why bother to communicate at all?* "Wouldn't it be easier if you just told me how this whole conversation's going to come out?"

Prinivere exhaled a loud snort that Collins interpreted as a laugh. *I don't usually anticipate. It's just, after a few centuries, you figure out what any human would ask. Never met one yet who didn't wonder how I get into his or her head.*

Collins glanced at his regular companions. Zylas and Falima sat on one of the chests, whispering back and forth. He wondered how much of the conversation they could hear.

All of it, Prinivere said before Collins could formulate the thought into words. *But Falima doesn't understand your side of it, and Zylas has to guess the thoughts I'm responding to.*

Zylas looked up and waved to Collins, apparently to confirm Prinivere's explanation.

Though he knew the question impolite, Collins had to know. "So how old are you anyway?"

"—my lady," Zylas added, teeth clenched in warning.

It's fine, Zylas. Prinivere swung her long neck toward the rat/man. *In his world, they rarely use titles. He means no disrespect.* She swiveled her head back to Collins. *I'm one thousand seven hundred thirty-six years old.*

Collins blinked, for the first time glad his mind went blank. "One *thousand?*"

Seven hundred thirty-six.

"Ah," Collins said, pinching his arm. The mild pain did not reassure him. It seemed equally possible that he had just dreamed it, too.

Zylas cut in, voice soft, words uninterpretable to Collins. If Prinivere responded, he heard none of it.

Finally, the dragon addressed Collins directly. *Come here. I'm going to attempt some magic.*

Hoping she meant the portal, Collins obeyed. He tried to look composed, but his steps turned more mincing the nearer he came to the dragon and he found himself trembling. Falima cleared her throat, and Collins dropped to a startled crouch, glancing wildly toward her. Ialin stood in human form between his other two companions.

Falima made an impatient gesture toward Prinivere.

Collins followed the movement to its natural conclusion. He did not know how long it had taken him to move as far as he had. It had seemed only seconds, but Ialin had had time to switch and fully dress. Collins closed his eyes, hoping that would allow him to walk blindly into a dragon, yet its massive presence still pressed vividly against his memory. Opening his lids, he forced himself to step up to Prinivere.

She gave off a not-unpleasant odor that Collins had never smelled before. It might come from something she ate, some nearby plant or fungus, even from something trapped between her claws. But, for Collins, the musky allspice aroma would forever define dragon smell.

One foot stretched toward Collins, slowly, nonthreateningly, and settled firmly on his head. At first, he felt nothing but the presence of that huge appendage, a claw dangling across his left cheek and ear and another tangling in his hair. Then, gradually, he recognized something indefinable flowing into him, like electric current without the jolt. The foot grew heavier over time, and he found himself expending increasing amounts of energy to remain standing. Finally, the strange feeling ended, replaced entirely by the full weight of a massive foot crushing him toward the ground.

Zylas, Falima, and Ialin dashed forward, hefting the dragon's claw and shoving Collins from beneath it. The foot flopped to the cave floor, and the dragon sank to the ground. Pain ached through Collins' neck and shoulders. As he massaged them, rolling his head, he noticed the dragon was lying still, unmoving. "Is she all right?"

Zylas rushed to Prinivere's side.

Falima responded. "She's very old. Even a simple spell like that one leaves her drained."

Collins nodded, still studying the dragon. Then, realization struck, and he jerked his attention to Falima. "Hey, I understood you. I know what you said, and—"

Ialin rolled his eyes.

Not wanting to look the fool again, Collins considered. "That must be what the magic she did was all about."

"Lucky guess," Ialin grumbled.

"She's sleeping," Zylas announced. "We'll have to stay and keep her safe until she's strong again."

It seemed only fair. Prinivere had exhausted herself for him, and he owed her at least that much. Nevertheless, Collins could not stay the icy seep of disappointment overtaking him. "The portal," he said to no one in particular, now far enough beyond shock and confusion to realize that Prinivere would only have assumed he needed to communicate with the people of Barakhai if she knew she could not get him home soon.

Collins anticipated a verbal onslaught from Ialin about how he should feel grateful for what the dragon sacrificed for him, but it did not come. The hummingbird/man stood in silence, letting Zylas answer.

The albino patted one of the chests, then sat. Collins came over, taking the place beside the one person he trusted completely in this world.

Zylas stared at the ceiling for several moments, collecting his thoughts before beginning. "I'm as *masuniat* as they come . . ." He paused.

Collins remembered *masuniat* as the word for people more entrenched in their human than animal forms. He nodded his understanding.

". . . I don't know a thing about magic except what the lady has told me. But—" Zylas glanced around at his companions' expectant faces. "As I understand it, the spell she just threw is a particularly simple one. She's old, even for a dragon; that and simple healings are the extent of her magic nowadays." He turned the tender look of a grandson upon the sleeping creature. "I wouldn't dare ask her to do even the spell she just cast again. Next time, it might kill her."

"She made your translation stone," Collins suggested.

Zylas shook his head. "She has made translation stones, but not mine and not in the last few decades. Making spells portable, casting onto rocks and crystals, takes a lot more energy than just throwing a bit of magic at someone." He displayed the piece of quartz. "And I told you mine's unique. Centuries old and very special. A family heirloom."

Ialin balanced, cross-legged, on the other chest, listening. Falima sat beside Collins, opposite Zylas. Attempting to anticipate Zylas' point, Collins considered whether or not creating a portal would require an item. He clung to the memory of Prinivere stating that she might have the power to make one.

"We already know Lady Prinivere does not have the strength to magic another stone."

Collins could not hold back the significant query any longer. "A portal?"

Zylas bit his lip and met Collins' gaze, clearly measuring his reaction. "Or make a portal."

Collins felt horse-kicked. "But she said—"

Zylas raised a forestalling hand. "There is a crystal, already made, that can enhance her magic."

Though reborn, Collins' hope remained guarded. It seemed that every time something started going his way, something worse intervened. "Don't tell me. It's in the possession of an eight-headed hydra."

"No."

"A werewolf?"

"What?"

"A giant; the minotaur; Medusa; titans; the bogeyman; a fire-breathing, man-eating demon vampire unicorn." Having exhausted his repertoire of monsters, Collins fell silent, hands folded across his lap. Anything they mentioned now had to sound puny in comparison.

All three regarded him with open-mouthed curiosity.

"So." Collins broke the silence. "From who or what do we have to get this crystal thingy?"

"Um," Zylas said, licking his lips. "We think the king has it."

"And there's no 'we' to it," Ialin added sulkily.

Surprised he had actually gotten things close to right, Collins brought up the matter he had expected to come to light first. "Couldn't we just ask someone with younger magic for help?"

Zylas smiled weakly. "Lady Prinivere has the youngest magic we know of."

Shocked, Collins leaned backward. "You mean you know someone *older?*"

Ialin slapped his own forehead. "You numbskull! She's the only one with magic any of us knows. She's the last dragon. Ipso facto, the last user of magic."

Surprised to hear Latin from his alien friends, Collins let

the insult pass. He wondered what Ialin might possibly have said in Barakhain that the magic would translate into "ipso facto" rather than "therefore." Collins went for funny. "So, in your quaint lovable way, you're trying to tell me that only dragons have magic."

"Exactly." Ialin ignored the sarcasm.

"And Lady Prinivere is the last dragon. And as far as practically anyone knows, she doesn't even exist."

"Right," Zylas confirmed.

That left an enormous gap in Collins' understanding. "Then why would magic be illegal?" He patted Zylas' pocket to indicate the translation stone. "Wouldn't people just assume it doesn't exist?"

This time, Falima answered. "Because of item magic, rare stuff left behind from the days when dragons were commonplace."

"Centuries ago," Collins remembered. "Does the king know about Lady Prinivere?"

"No," they all chorused with a suddenness and expressions that revealed such a thing would prove catastrophic. Zylas added, "What a horrible thought."

Certain they meant that the king would have Prinivere executed, Collins continued his questioning. "Does he know this crystal thingy is magical?"

Still wide-eyed and pursed-lipped, the others fell into an uncomfortable hush before Zylas answered. "We don't know."

Collins tried to put everything together. "So, if I fetch this crystal and bring it back, Prinivere can make a portal for me?"

Nods circumnavigated the room.

Finally, something Ialin had said sank in. "What did you mean, 'there's no "we" to it?' That I have to get this thing all by myself?"

Ialin flicked his head in a birdlike fashion. "You're not as stupid as I thought."

Collins smiled. "Thanks. That's the nicest thing you've said to or about me so far." He looked accusingly at Zylas. "Let's face it. A magic amplifier doesn't just help me. Long after I'm gone, you can use it to make and do all kinds of things. Why wouldn't you guys help me get it?"

Falima developed an inordinate interest in her feet. Ialin

yawned, leaving only Zylas to answer. "We don't really know what this crystal can do. It's possible it only works one time." He glanced at the others for help, but Falima headed across the cave to check on Prinivere and Ialin got caught up in a luxurious stretch. "But mainly, it's because the royal chambers can only be accessed by stable people."

Still in half-stretch, Ialin clarified. "Meaning people without a switch-form." His tone suggested that he did not believe Collins fit the other definition of "stable."

"We *switchers* would get caught for sure," Falima added from across the room. "And killed. But you . . ."

. . . *are already condemned to die?* Collins believed he had uncovered the real reason, one his companions would never say aloud.

". . . won't set off the security. If you did get caught, you could pass yourself off as minor nobility come to learn, to valet, or to assist," Falima finished.

"Sure. Except I know nothing about any of those things." Collins could not stop himself from arguing, though it would do him no good. If he wanted to go home, he had to get this crystal. He might die in the attempt, but remaining in Barakhai without the support of his friends also would result in his swift demise. He might just as well charge the archers guarding the other portal and get it over with swiftly.

Ialin addressed the spoken thought. "You don't have to know much about nobility. Just the fact that you don't switch should keep you safe there. Who would suspect you're not of this world?"

Collins refused to put too much faith in that explanation. "Perhaps the royal archers guarding the portal?"

Ialin interjected, almost too quickly. "From what I heard while spying, they just know there's something magical there that bears watching. They're not going to let anyone near it."

Collins tried to logically consider what the authorities in his world would do with something similar. "Until someone explores it thoroughly?"

"More likely, wall it up so no one can use it or get hurt by it. Seek a way to destroy it."

Collins looked to Zylas, who shrugged and nodded. Though he knew American politicians and scientists would feel compelled to explore any anomaly until they gleaned every possible detail, he could understand where a civilization still in its more primitive stages might prefer avoidance to investigation. *Especially a place where magic and dragons are, or at least were, real.* So far, the only ones who believed he had come from another world were people who had traveled there and their closest companions. Apparently, the authorities had not figured out the purpose of the portal, though likely their study and discovery of it came as a direct result of the crime he had committed nearby.

The idea of breaking into a heavily guarded castle seemed impossible, yet Collins saw no better alternative. The archers at the first portal had shown their clear intent to kill anyone who approached it. Also, traveling back toward the town that had condemned him as a murderer and a cannibal seemed like sure suicide. Depending on the communication between areas, the royals might know nothing of his crime. If the crystal had properties beyond helping Prinivere make him a portal, so much the better. He owed his companions at least that much for risking themselves to save the life of a stranger. *A stranger,* Collins reminded himself, *who has yet to show a suitable amount of gratitude.* "Of course, I'll fetch that crystal," Collins promised aloud. "And I hope it works a lot more than one time. I appreciate your helping me. You guys deserve it and more." Collins smiled at another thought. "In fact, after I'm home, I'll see what I can find for you. Things like Zylas' lighter that make life a bit easier."

No real breeze blew through Prinivere's cave, but a tangible rush of relief followed Collins' pronouncement.

Returning from her visit to the sleeping dragon, Falima turned to practical considerations. "Of course, we'll get you to the castle. And describe as much of the layout as we know."

"Of course." Now that he had so valiantly volunteered, Collins refused to consider details. So long as the break-in remained abstract, he could bask in his friends' adulation and convince himself he would soon get home.

Zylas became a rat at midnight, his white fur easy to spot even in the dense gloom of a cave at night. He crawled off to sleep with the dragon, while Falima and Ialin discussed keeping watches. Since they made no effort to include him in their conversation, Collins stretched out on the floor near the entrance and tried to sleep.

The hard floor bit into his back and shoulders, no matter how frequently he shifted his position. The possible challenges that awaited him, alone and in strange surroundings, kept intruding on thoughts he desperately tried to keep dull and commonplace. The sheep he counted mutated to dragons. The map of his childhood home became an Escheresque maze-castle filled with weapons and monsters. Conjugating high school Spanish verbs became so simple, it could not hold his attention. He considered the reason; he had always struggled with them in the past and should only have gotten rustier over time. *It's the dragon's spell.* Understanding dawned with a suddenness that brought him fully awake again. *If this thing's long-lasting and crosses worlds, I've got a brilliant career as a translator.*

Oddly, that thought soothed him where others had not. Now he had work to fall back on should his professors blackball him from science forever. Even if he managed to talk his way out of their wrath, having wasted millions of dollars in grants, translation could earn him the spare cash he needed to handle his student loans. *If it lasts,* he reminded himself before excitement ran away with him. *I should be so lucky.* It occurred to Collins that he had to survive Barakhai first, which brought him back to the circle of worry that had, thus far, held sleep at bay. With a sigh, Collins began the battle again.

Chapter 12

A SHAKE awakened Benton Collins from a dream, heart pounding, wildly aware. He sprang to his feet to face Falima, who retreated in a scramble.

The cave mouth remained dark. Ialin sat on a chest with his chin in his hands, a grin of amusement on his homely, androgynous features. The dragon shimmered slightly in the darkness, still sleeping. He saw no sign of Zylas.

"What's wrong?" Collins asked.

"Nothing's wrong," Falima replied in a sheepish tone. "I just thought you'd want to get up before I change."

"Oh." Collins glanced at his watch. It read 5:30 A.M. The fatigue that should have greeted him upon first awakening seeped in on him now, accompanied by a multitude of pains spread across every part of his body. *Why?* he wondered, stretching out his throbbing arms. He glanced at the wound the dog had inflicted, but it had scabbed completely, leaving no redness and only slight bruising. It bothered him less than the twinges coming from what seemed like every other part of him, especially his back.

Gradually, Collins' mind caught up to his instantly alert body. *Of course I hurt. I slept with nothing but clothes between me and an irregular stone floor, I fell off a horse, and I rode for hours.* He rubbed an aching hip and continued a conversation that had stagnated while he considered. "Good idea. You've only got a half hour of human time left." He could not help glancing at Ialin, with whom he would share three more hours as a man. They would have to converse, he felt certain, since he could talk to no one else. *Or can I?* "Zylas' stone lets him understand animal speech as well."

Falima had anticipated the question. "His stone is unique. Most, and the spell, only work for human languages; though the lady said you might get some basic idea of an animal's mood." She studied him, brows rising in increments. "If that's necessary." It seemed more question than statement.

Collins shrugged, disappointed. "It can't hurt." Not wanting to look stupid, he added. "Though, when a horse draws its ears back and raises a hind foot, or a bird screeches and lashes out with its beak, or a dog growls, I can get a pretty good notion of their bent toward me."

Ialin chimed in, "Those are pretty obvious signs." He added with heat, "Of course, when a man slaps me halfway to Carterton, I get a pretty good idea of his bent toward me, too."

"That's not fair," Collins protested. "I thought you were a bug."

"Joetha, too, apparently."

Assaulted by irritation, Collins dismissed the comment with a sharp wave. "Can't we ever get past that?"

"Past it?" Ialin's voice went crisp with angry incredulity. "You killed and ate someone. How do you get past that?"

Collins did not know, but he had managed. Zylas, Falima, Vernon, Prinivere, and even Korfius had managed as well. He emphasized every word, and they emerged in clear snarls, "It . . . was . . . an . . . accident."

"Ialin," Falima said, in the same warning tone Zylas used to use when she verbally assaulted Collins.

At that moment, the rat skidded into their midst, squeaking savagely. He dropped the translation stone to the floor and planted a paw on it. "Cool it, guys. She's awake."

While Collins still marveled at how flawlessly the two translation devices merged even into slang, the others hurried or scrambled to the dragon's side.

Prinivere stretched her long, scaly neck, peering at the three in front of her with ancient eyes. *I'm fine,* she broadcast, with no more sincerity than the claim usually held in America. Even without physical words, her weakness came to him clearly. *A few more hours and I should have the strength to fly. I appreciate your watching over me.*

"We appreciate the magic, my lady," Zylas squeaked, right front paw on the crystal.

The dragon reached out an enormous claw and seemed to enclose Zylas in it.

Fear clutched at Collins, though he knew she meant him no harm.

When Prinivere removed her claw, she left Zylas as he had been, except for a tousle of fur between his pink velvet ears. "Near-perfect overlap. I'm impressed, Zylas."

"Couldn't have done it without you and this magic," Zylas threw back the compliment, jiggling the translation stone with his paw.

"And constant practice," Falima added. "Don't go getting too humble, even in the lady's presence."

Zylas twitched his pointed nose at Falima, who excused herself and headed for the cave mouth.

Knowing she had gone to switch, Collins walked toward the group to give Falima more privacy. As they passed one another, Falima whispered, "Ialin will come around."

Collins bit his lip to keep from laughing. They were precisely the words Zylas had used about her and Ialin at various times. It hardly mattered, then or now. He only had to get along with the hummingbird long enough to steal the magic-enhancing crystal and get himself through the new portal.

Prinivere recovered more slowly than even she seemed to expect, though her loyal attendants, a horse and a rat, showed no signs of impatience. Ialin set to describing the layout of the palace to Collins in a straight, matter-of-fact manner that precluded gibes or personal affronts. Apparently, the keep had two irregular lines of curtain walls: the outer with six mural towers and two gatehouses, the inner with gatehouses directly in line with those of the outer wall, but smaller. Both walls had full-length, crenellated parapets. Between the walls lay a grassy outer courtyard, grazed by herbivore servants and horse-guards while in their switch-forms. In addition to the keep, the inner courtyard contained a stables/guard barracks, gardens, kennel barracks, and a pond.

Head overflowing with sketched diagrams and verbal descriptions, Collins sat back on his haunches. "How do you know all this?"

Ialin gave him that well-rehearsed stare that proclaimed Collins the dumbest man alive. "We're a hummingbird and a rat. How do you think we know?"

The three hours until Zylas' return to man form passed more swiftly than Collins expected as he tried to cram the information Ialin gave him into every nook and cranny in his brain. Comparing the situation to the night before finals helped, but the unfamiliar castle terms required defining, making the whole even more complicated. Collins could not help remembering why he had chosen a formulaic, theoretical, and logical field rather than one based mainly on memorization. He gained new respect for historians and geographers.

Falima grazed outside throughout the lesson. At nine, Ialin returned to bird form, and Collins heaved a grateful sigh. Anticipating three hours of blessed relief and silence, he drew the travel pack to him in search of breakfast. Crouched in front of one of the chests, he placed each item on its lid: first a hunk of brown bread, the jar of nut paste, and a wrinkled applelike fruit. He rummaged for a stick to spread the paste, wishing he had his multitool. It had served him well in many unexpected situations, from using the pliers to straighten a damaged cage clasp to cutting open the otherwise impenetrable plastic packaging that entombed so many small electronics.

Collins discarded the thought of using his companions' utility knives on food. *No telling what's on those blades.* Instead, he went to the cave mouth to find a suitable stick.

At Collins' sudden appearance, Falima raised her head and nickered. Remembering an earlier conversation, he strode over and scratched her between the ears. She closed her eyes and lowered her head, half-chewed stems jutting from her mouth. The sun beamed down from a cloudless sky, igniting red highlights in her tangled black forelock. Collins finger-combed it back in place with one hand, while the other continued to scratch.

Collins' stomach rumbled, and he abandoned his ministrations with a final pat. "Pretty girl," he cooed, feeling like an idiot and wondering how much of the encounter Falima would remember in human form. Locating a thick twig near his feet, he picked it up and returned to the cave.

Prinivere lumbered outside. Collins froze, fear twitching through him despite his knowledge and his efforts to keep the emotion at bay. He stepped aside, shoving his shaking hands into his pockets to hide them. The stick jabbed his thigh through the fabric, and he loosed a grunt of pain.

I'm going to find food, Prinivere announced, though whether at him or everyone, Collins could not tell. *Be back by the time Zylas changes.*

Collins nodded his reply, though the dragon had already swept past him. He had no idea what something so large might eat in the vegetable family to sustain herself. Though some of the largest dinosaurs had been herbivores, the paleontologists surmised that they had had to eat constantly to keep themselves alive. So far, he had not seen the dragon consume anything.

Carrying his spreading stick, Collins returned to his food, only to find Zylas nibbling at the bread. He stopped short. "You know, in my world, finding a rat eating your food might just be the grossest thing imaginable."

"Great," Zylas squeaked, his paw on the translation stone and his mouth leaking crumbs. "More for me."

"Ah," Collins reached for the nut paste. "But I'm a biology student. I could eat a block of Swiss in a pathology laboratory over the smell of formaldehyde while mice used the holes for a maze." The medical student from whom he had stolen the quote had added a nearby dissected cadaver and that, if hungry enough, he would devour the animals with the cheese. Under the circumstances, Collins felt it best to leave those parts out.

Despite his bold words, Collins got himself a fresh piece of bread on which to spread the paste. He doubted Zylas could carry any of the rat-borne illnesses of his world without infecting himself in human form, but he saw no need to take chances. "So what, exactly, does a dragon eat?"

Zylas finished a mouthful of bread. "A whole lot."

"No doubt." Collins dipped the stick into the jar and slapped a glob onto his bread. "A whole lot of what?"

"People," Zylas said without hesitation.

Collins jerked his attention to the rat, hand still on the bread. "What?"

"I'm kidding," Zylas said. "Of course, she eats the same things everyone else eats. Plants, fish, bugs."

"Oh." Collins swallowed hard. "That's not funny."

"Sorry."

"In fact, it was downright insensitive."

"I'm sorry," Zylas repeated. "I have *near* perfect overlap. Apparently, my rat sense of humor isn't as careful as my man sense of humor."

The guilt of his crime revived, Collins discovered a lump in his throat that made eating a chore. He pulled a bladder from the pack and sucked a mouthful of a sweet-and-sour fruit juice that contained a hint of alcohol. Expecting water, he nearly choked on the contents. "What the hell is this?"

Zylas jumped from the chest to Collins' lap, then skittered up his arm. He stuck his entire, furry head through the opening, then retreated with golden droplets clinging to his whiskers. He returned to his place, and the translating stone, before speaking. "It's a mix, one of Vernon's special recipes. Don't you like it?"

Collins had not given a thought to his opinion of the unexpected taste. Now, he considered, savoring the after-taste on his tongue. If he had to guess the ingredients, he would have said grape juice, apple juice, some lemon, a dash of something exotic, like guava or mango, and a touch of dry wine. "Actually, I do. I just wasn't expecting it." He turned his thoughts back to Prinivere. "She'd have to eat an ocean of fish, I'd guess."

Zylas bobbed his head, splashing the golden droplets. "She usually does most of her eating in her human form, but I'd guess she had to 'refuel' from the spell."

Refuel. Collins liked the translation, though it could not have been the actual word Zylas had used. His respect for magic grew tenfold in an instant.

"Are you ready to learn the interior of the keep?"

Collins groaned. "Can't we wait till you're . . . human?" He had looked forward to three hours of eating and quiet or, at most, gentle conversation with Zylas alone.

"Once the lady fully regains her strength, we need to move on." Zylas eyed the pack. "Could you get me one of those beetles, please?"

Collins shoved a piece of bread in his mouth. He opened the pack, rummaging for the bug jar.

"It's best you have the general layout down by then. We can review and discuss strategy en route."

Collins found the covered crock and pulled it out. He opened the lid, watching the horde of grape-sized insects crawl over one another, then placed it on the chest beside Zylas. He chewed and swallowed. "Are you sure this is really the easiest way?"

Zylas placed his nose into the crock, then withdrew suddenly, sneezing. "You mean sneaking into an unsuspecting castle and removing a small object?"

"Yes."

"As opposed to taking on a phalanx of archers ordered to kill?"

When Zylas put it that way, it seemed clear. "Well . . ."

"Near a town that found you guilty of murder and sentenced you to a hanging they damn well know they didn't manage to complete."

"All right. I get it."

Zylas again stuck his face into the beetle crock. His squeaks echoed through the confines. "Of course, if you'd rather stay here with us forever . . ."

It was not an option. Even if his days were not numbered by how long it took the guards to catch up to him, Collins doubted he could live without the conveniences to which he had become accustomed: electric lights, refrigerators, modern medicine, pizza. He sighed at the thought. How much simpler his life could become if he did stay, but it would become so much better with a portal that allowed him to bring back the occasional Tylenol or Twinkie. Finally, he stated what he knew was true all along. "I can't possibly stay."

Zylas withdrew. "Would you mind getting one of those out for me, please. Every time I try, I get the whole bunch of them glomming onto my face."

Collins reached into the crock and pinched out a single beetle. Gingerly, Zylas took it from Collins' grip with his teeth, whiskers tickling.

Collins replaced the lid. "You going to want more?"

Beetle clamped between his teeth, Zylas silently shook his head.

Collins returned the jar to the pack, smiling at how normal it now seemed to feed bugs to a talking rat. Only a couple of days ago, he would have considered it absolutely understandable to find himself locked in some loony bin for even imagining such behavior.

While Zylas ripped into the beetle, Collins studied the bland interior of the cave. The dark, irregular walls surrounded a comfortable area, with nothing but the two chests to break the monotony. "What's in the boxes?" he asked, surprised he had not wondered sooner.

Zylas abandoned the partially eaten beetle to answer. "Personal things, I'd venture. Clothes maybe, though the lady rarely wears any. Food, certainly. Baubles."

"Baubles?"

"Things friends and intimates have given her through the ages."

"Her hoard?" Collins suggested.

Now, it was Zylas' turn to question. "Hoard?"

"Money," Collins explained. "Silver and gold trinkets. Gems. Jewelry." He came by the information through his brief stint of role-playing. "It's generally believed in my world that dragons like shiny things and objects of value."

Zylas abandoned his repast, red eyes positively glowing with excitement. "So you once had dragons in your world, too?"

The rat/man looked so happy, Collins hated to disappoint him, but he would not lie. "Only in myth and fairy tale, I'm afraid."

The light died in Zylas' eyes, and he returned to eating.

"Sixty million years before people, we did have dinosaurs. Those were giant lizards, some of which bore a resemblance to dragons."

"Really?" Zylas spoke around a mouthful of bug. "Did they use magic?"

"Most had brains about the size of your lunch." Collins addressed the question more directly, "It seems highly unlikely."

Zylas made a wordless noise.

Collins returned to his point, "Anyway, in the stories, dragons keep hoards of shiny treasure which they guard fiercely."

"It has to be shiny?"

"Apparently." The details of legend seemed unimportant to Collins.

Zylas shook out his fur. "Well, that's not like dragons here. At least, it's not like the one I know. She doesn't have much interest in . . . material things, except as they pertain to causes."

"That's good to know." Collins could not see a long-term use for the knowledge. "If I ever write a story or start role-playing again, I'll keep that in mind."

Zylas finished the beetle, licked his paws, then cleaned his face with them.

Collins returned the leftover rations to the pack. Zylas waited only until he shoved it aside to ask, "Ready?"

"For what?" Collins asked cautiously.

"To learn the inside of the castle."

"No," Collins said, settling down on his buttocks. He doubted his answer mattered, however.

True to Collins' hunch, Zylas began. "The lowest floor contains the storerooms and dungeons . . ."

The lesson droned on for hours while Falima continued to graze outside and Ialin made occasional buzzing appearances. Benton Collins got his first break when Prinivere appeared at the entrance. The green-gray scales looked ruffled, the leathern wings droopy, the ancient eyes dull. She dragged wearily back into the cave, finding her sleeping corner, and flopped to the ground. Zylas abandoned his lesson in the middle of a sentence and rushed to the dragon's side. Ialin fluttered in after her, hovering at her eye level.

Savoring a few moments alone, Collins sighed and remained in place, unable to hear their exchange. His head whirled with information: kitchens and workshops on the ground floor, above underground storage rooms, food cellars, and the dungeons. The second story held the library and great dining hall, the third the servants' quarters. Every floor had what Collins understood to be a primitive bathroom, translated as "garderobe." Apparently, both dragon spell and translation stone considered it an English word, though he had never heard it before. He imagined it had not entered common American parlance; though, with their known penchant for fart, belch, and bathroom humor, it would have worked well there. Zylas described it rather like a park potty: a thigh-high platform with a hole in it. The rat/man seemed to think it might prove a suitable portal for entry, escape, or for secreting the magical crystal. Though not averse to tossing the stone down the hole, Collins would rather eat bugs than retrieve it afterward. And using it as an exit was not even a remote possibility.

Zylas knew nothing about the two uppermost floors because of their warding against *switchers,* but he surmised they held the private quarters of the royals. The roof was crenellated, with crossbowmen and ballistae protecting it, and the winding stairwell proceeded a story higher, to a trapdoor that opened onto the top of a guard tower. Heavy ironbound oak doors opened onto each floor and the roof in both directions, though the four to the two upper stories did not admit *switchers.* Apparently, if a commoner so much as touched it, the door would sound an alarm and latch up tight.

Unable to put any logical explanation to such a system, Collins had to assume magic. *Unless other portals exist, and folks from civilizations more advanced than ours have come.* He shoved the thought aside. *Zylas would know that. Hard enough accepting magic. Do I have to put some* Planet of the Apes *twist on this?* Collins had once read that "advanced science is virtually indistinguishable from magic." The average man on the street could not explain how a toaster or a microwave worked, and a significant portion of the population considered the simple running of electricity through wires a miracle too technical for understanding. He himself found the concept of fax transmission fascinating and incomprehensible. *The source doesn't matter. I just need to know how it works on the macro level.*

Shortly, Zylas returned, translation stone clutched in his jaws. He scurried up Collins' arm to his shoulder and spit out the quartz to speak directly into the man's ear. "She says she just needs a short nap. Then she should be strong enough to return home."

"Home?"

"A different cave," Zylas explained. "She has several residences. Safer." He pawed the rose quartz into a more secure position. "Better you know as few as possible, too."

Collins nodded agreement, then glanced at his watch. It read a couple of minutes until noon. "You'd better get off me. A full-grown man would definitely put a strain on my rotator cuff."

"Don't worry. I'm going." The last syllable was muffled by the translation stone, and Zylas scrambled to the floor. He settled himself by the pack to wait.

Knowing his companion would emerge from his switch-form naked, Collins politely turned his back. Experience told him it was unnecessary. Accustomed to the change from birth, the Barakhains apparently did not view nudity as a vulnerable state the way full-time humans did. But the gesture made Collins feel more comfortable and respectful, and his discussion with Falima made it clear that embarrassment could be reawakened by the wrong stare.

Stealing the few moments during which the change distracted his companion, Collins left the cave. Clouds pulled like lace across the sun, dimming it to caramel. Falima whinnied a soft greeting. Flies settled in a line along her spine, and the skin of her legs wriggled to dislodge others. Scraggly mountain grasses drooped from her lips, growing shorter as she chewed.

Collins clambered up an enormous rock near the cave mouth and looked out over the crags. Tree-loaded mountains stretched as far as he could see, sunlight glazing their needles and leaves. Peaks and boulders thrust between wide patches of greenery. Absently, he stroked Falima's back, dislodging the flies into angrily buzzing chaos. She swished her tail, black hairs like wires stinging across his bare arm. He shifted to a crouch to avoid another lashing and massaged the fur behind her ears. Her head sank, eyes closed, as she enjoyed his caress.

Collins shut his own eyes, imagining himself running his hand through the soft, black curtain of Falima's human hair. The strands glided through his fingers like silk while he massaged the tension from her upper back. He could see himself sliding his hands to her breasts, her turning her head to meet his kiss.

"Ben!" Zylas' voice shattered the guilty pleasure of Collins' reverie.

Startled, Collins jerked, lost his footing on a smear of slime, and plummeted from the back of the rock. The landing jarred through his ankles, and he slapped his hands on the rock to protect his face.

With a surprised whinny, Falima sidled away, eyeing Collins with wary caution.

Collins waited for the pain to fade before peering over the granite at Zylas in man form. "What did you do that for?"

Zylas studied Collins blandly from the shadow of his hat. "I presume my transgression was . . . um . . . speaking your name?"

Collins stepped around the rock, brushing dirt from his tunic. "The transgression part was sneaking up on us." He glanced at Falima who shifted from hoof to hoof, still watching him with suspicion. "On me."

"You were facing me," Zylas defended. "I thought you saw me."

"I had my eyes closed."

"Ah, my fault." Zylas smiled, clearly meaning none of it. "Falima was right. You are jumpy."

That being self-evident, Collins did not deny it. "Wouldn't you be, too, if you had to do what I'm going to have to do?"

"Maybe." Zylas continued to pin Collins with his gaze. "But you'll do better calm."

Easy to say. Collins grunted.

"Trust me."

Believing Zylas' description of the inside of the castle was firsthand, Collins did not argue. At least Zylas had had rat form to hide behind. Sneaking became much easier for someone the size of Collins' fist. "What did you want?"

Zylas made a gesture Collins could not fathom. "We need to finish your lesson."

Collins groaned. "Can't we take a little break?"

Zylas tensed, glancing around at the sun glimmering from chips of quartz in the rocks, the brilliant blue of the sky, and the sparse, delicate clouds. "I suppose so. I just want . . ." He stared off into the distance, stiff and still. ". . . you . . . to succeed."

"Why?" Collins spoke softly, afraid to frighten Zylas away from the truth. It seemed too important to the albino to solely hinge on Collins' survival.

The left corner of Zylas' mouth twitched. "Because I . . . like you. I want you to make it home safely."

"That's it?"

"That's it."

Collins did not believe the answer, though he knew of no reason for Zylas to lie. Experience suggested the rat/man wanted the stone for whatever magic remained in it after Prinivere created the portal. His own cynicism conjured a frown. *He rescued me from hanging. He's risked his neck for me several times since. Shouldn't he get something for his effort?*

The thought was less comforting than Collins expected. Nameless dread edged through the soothing world he had built with friendships, trust, and the understanding that a way existed for him to go home. He was missing something that his companions found too obvious to tell him, something he did not even know enough about to ask, something that might determine whether or not he survived the world of Barakhai. A breeze dragged a strand of mouse-brown hair into Collins' eye and sent a wild shiver through him. He only hoped the omission would not prove a fatal one.

Chapter 13

WITH Zylas pacing like a maniac, Benton Collins found it impossible to enjoy his break, despite the beauty of the day and Falima's soft nose and fur. Jorge Martinez, his lab partner during freshman year, had been fond of the expression "fake it till you make it." For half an hour, Collins tried to follow that advice, ignoring his agitated companion to focus on the calm animal that was his other one. But, over time, Zylas' frenzy became contagious. Falima pranced dangerously, forcing Collins to give her some space. With a sigh, he headed back into the cave, Zylas following. "Respite finished?"

"Sadly, yes." Collins searched for his memories of the castle's description. He glanced toward the chests; but, deciding he would rather have a backrest than height, chose a seat on the floor near the exit instead. He wriggled backward until his spine touched stone. "What do you want to talk about?"

Zylas removed his hat and pulled white hair away from his face, holding it behind his head. "First, I want to hear your version of the castle, make sure you've got the details. Then we can start discussing strategy."

Collins nodded, simultaneously lauding and cursing Zylas' thoroughness. The constant need to concentrate made him dizzy, but he knew his life might well depend on careful attention to details. He drew a verbal picture of the castle walls and grounds, the moat, the tents and outbuildings in

the courtyards, the location of every door and portcullis. As
he did so, he tried to put a visual image to his narration, a
more difficult process than he expected. Most people
learned better from pictures than words, but he had always
found his memory worked the opposite way. It made him
better at standardized tests, where every concept was re-
duced to text; but it meant he had to work harder than his
peers in the hands-on world of the laboratory.

Collins shifted his focus to wards and guards, then
switched to the interior. There, he faltered, requiring Zylas'
assistance to recall which room lay where, who or what he
might encounter there, and the best routes to the upper levels which most likely housed the magical crystal. Frustrated,
Collins tried to sidetrack Zylas for a few moments. "How
do you know so damn much about this place?"

"Been there," Zylas said, barely an explanation.

Collins guessed, "Did you work there? A servant,
maybe?"

"Vermin? Invited into the castle?" Zylas laughed with a
mirth so genuine, Collins could not help joining him.

Ialin zipped into the cave, buzzing frantic circles around
Zylas. The laughter broke off abruptly. Zylas sprang to his
feet, expression tense, edgy, with a touch of fear.

"What?" Collins also rose, but Zylas waved him back
and silent. The albino crept toward the cave mouth, head
cocked.

Suddenly, a hound bayed, the sound close.

Collins jumped, heart hammering.

Zylas charged from the cave toward Falima. "Get the
lady out!"

Out? Out where? Uncertain whether Zylas intended the
command for him or for Ialin, Collins ran toward the dragon.
Before he reached her, a brown-and-white dog bounded into
the cave, barking madly. Toenails scrabbled against stone as
it attempted to stop. Instead, it skidded, long legs buckling,
ears flopping. It bashed into a chest, which sent the dog car-
oming practically into the dragon's lap. Prinivere jerked
awake, wings unfolding, a hiss escaping her massive mouth
between rows of pointed teeth. Whatever she actually ate,
nature clearly intended her to be a carnivore.

The dog let out a squeak of surprise, followed by a string
of desperate whimpers. It scuttled backward, bashing into

Collins' legs, then rolled its eyes to him in terror and hope. Thrown to a crouch, Collins met the dog's gaze and recognized him instantly. "Korfius!" He dropped to his knees.

Still loosing panting whines, the dog crawled onto Collins' legs.

"Zylas, it's Korfius." Collins petted the dog all over, as it tried to fit its entire body onto him.

Zylas hauled Falima into the cave. "I don't see or hear any more dogs. He's either way ahead of a pack or alone." He glanced wildly around the cave. "When's his change time?"

Collins glanced at his watch, which read nearly 1:00. He recalled how Korfius had switched forms in his arms while hiding in Vernon's false wall. "I'd say just about now."

"Now?" Zylas leaped to Collins' side with an abruptness that sent Falima into a half-rear. "We've got to get him out before—" He grabbed the dog by the nape of the neck, and Korfius let out a startled yelp.

Zylas pulled, dragging the dog from Collins' lap. Korfius' dark eyes implored Collins. He planted his feet against stone, and Zylas struggled to move him. "Help me here, would you?"

Collins stood, uncertain exactly what to do. Korfius threw his head back and forth, trying to break free of Zylas' grip, which tightened as he surely worried about getting bitten. Korfius' form blurred.

Zylas cursed.

Falima whinnied tensely, then bolted from the cave.

Zylas let out a string of curses, which translated strangely as everything from bodily functions, to disasters, mythical creatures, and filth. He let go.

Korfius writhed as his forelegs became arms, features grew or disappeared, fur receded. Soon, a naked boy on all fours replaced the dog form, stammering a single word, "Dr–dr–dr–dr–dragon. It's a dragon." He looked directly at Collins. "I saw a dragon." He whipped his head to Zylas. "A real dragon." Finally, he turned his attention to Prinivere. "Dragon." He rose with slow, careful movements and drifted toward her as if in a daze. "Excuse me, but are you really a dragon?"

I am, young man, Prinivere returned. *My name is Prinivere.*

Zylas paced, wringing his hands.

Unself-consciously naked, Korfius bowed. "Deeply honored to meet you, Lady Prinivere. I'm Korfius."

So I gathered. The dragon settled back down. Only then, Collins noticed the black hole behind her, apparently the escape Zylas had wanted him to use. He wondered why he had not seen it before and decided the dragon had fully stolen his attention. Most of the time, her enormous, sleeping form had blocked it.

Falima trumpeted out a neigh.

"Now what?" Zylas muttered, rushing to the entrance just as a savagely panting Vernon threw himself inside.

"I'm . . . sorry," the black man gasped out. "I . . . tried to . . . stop . . . him, but . . ." He paused for several beats to concentrate on breathing. ". . . he's quick."

"Got one hell of a nose, too." Zylas held out a hand to assist his friend, but Vernon chose to remain on the ground for the moment.

Korfius drew himself up proudly. "Best sniffer in my brigade."

Collins remembered how Korfius had found them in the flowering tree when the other hounds had not. He nodded. "No doubt."

"A dragon." Korfius seemed incapable of getting past that word. He turned stiffly to Collins. "Your Majesty, you keep interesting company." He bowed. "And I am at your service."

Collins glanced at Zylas, who nodded with wary encouragement. "Korfius, I've already told you the best way to serve me."

"I know, Sire—"

"Just Ben," Collins reminded.

"I know . . ." Korfius clearly struggled mightily, but managed to blurt out, "Ben. But I want to help, to be a part of this." His wide-eyed gaze fell on the dragon again, though he did not say the word this time. "A guard superior, a royal, and a . . . a dragon." The reverent tone gained strength with each naming. "I'm staying with you. Seeing this through. You might need me!"

Once more, Collins glanced at Zylas for support. He wished the other man would say something. After all, Zylas was more likely to have the necessary knowledge to handle this situation; but Collins also knew that maintaining the illusion of his royalty required him to speak. "What I don't need is a couple of worried parents sending an entire guard force after me." It seemed almost moot, as they already tracked him on a murder charge. "Nor do I need to add a kidnapping rap."

"Parents?" Korfius laughed. "Don't worry about my parents. They're extremely *lesariat*. I'm from a litter of seven . . ."

Collins took his cue from Zylas, whose eyes went round as coins and whose lips glided open in clear surprise.

". . . and as far as they're concerned, they're finished raising me. I'm on my own."

Though it seemed easier with his parents out of the equation, Collins could not imagine any mother not worrying about her missing child. *Put it in animal terms,* he reminded himself. *Once the puppies hit somewhere between six and ten weeks, the parents often don't even recognize them.* Cynically, he wondered if whoever was in charge of the city would prove more diligent about his "best sniffer" then the parents were over their missing septuplet. Zylas' reaction made it clear that multiple births were not the norm, despite the time spent as animals. From the way Korfius stated it, Collins guessed that the ones more anchored in animal form had a higher likelihood of more than one offspring at a time. "Well, then," Collins said, surprised by his own words. "Perhaps I *could* use your help."

Zylas' jaw, already dangling from the litter comment, now positively fell. "Um . . . Ben. Could I speak to you for a moment?"

Though tempted to say "no," which would leave Zylas completely defenseless, Collins excused himself from Korfius, telling the boy to put some clothes on, and then followed his pale companion to the cave mouth.

Zylas barely waited until they got beyond hearing range. "What the hell are you doing?"

Collins wondered if the concept of hell as he knew it actually existed in this world, then shrugged off the thought. None of his companions seemed overly religious, and he saw no need to create a possible rift. "What do you mean?"

Zylas kept his voice at a bare hiss, though he clearly would have preferred to yell. "I mean, you just invited a kid along."

"What did you want me to do?" Collins finally realized what his subconscious had much earlier. "Send him back to whatever that town was that's hunting us knowing all about your precious lady?"

Zylas swallowed hard.

"Well?"

"That," Zylas said thoughtfully, "can't happen." A look of sharp terror took over his features, so intense that Collins felt fear prickling up his spine as well.

Collins fell silent, uncertain whether he wished to encourage Zylas any longer.

"What are we going to do?"

You're asking me? Collins raised his brows, throwing the question right back to his uncomfortable companion.

"They'll hunt her down and kill her."

Collins continued to study Zylas. The other option, killing a child to keep her secret, seemed even more heinous. "Zylas," he started carefully, not at all certain where he planned to go from there.

"You're right," Zylas interrupted. "We have to keep him with us. And quiet." He stomped a foot. "Damn! Why did he have to . . ." He trailed off with a noise of frustration.

"I'm sure Vernon did everything he could."

"Yeah. I trust —" Zylas' nostrils flared. "We've got to get out of here." He looked past Collins. "If one dog could follow our scent, others could."

Collins was not convinced of that.

"Or, they might just follow *his* scent."

That seemed much more likely. "Can Prinivere travel?"

"She should be able to make it to another of her . . ." Zylas ended lamely, ". . . places now." Apparently seized by another thought, he added, "In fact, she should go now, before she switches."

About eighteen hours had passed since Collins had seen Prinivere in human form. Somehow, he doubted she had to take any drugs to keep her dragon-time longer. Given that she could use all her higher functions as a dragon, plus magic and a vastly extended life-span, he suspected she considered it her more advanced form.

Zylas headed back toward Prinivere. "My lady," he said as he moved. "Forgive the abruptness of our departure, but I think it best if we all go as soon as possible." He put a subtle emphasis on the word "all" which Collins took to mean he wanted her to know that she should take off also.

He's just a boy, Prinivere sent, Collins presumed to him and Zylas, at least, and certainly not to Korfius who still stared at her with undisguised awe. *Don't do anything rash.*

"I won't," Zylas promised. "Unless it becomes absolutely necessary. But we can't risk . . ." He glanced at Korfius, as if to read how much of the one-sided conversation he might fathom, ". . . you. And I don't know many . . ." he hedged, as if seeking a code word, then brightened. Casually, he removed the rose quartz stone from his pocket and set it on an irregularity in the rocky wall. He switched to broken English, surely aware only Collins and Prinivere could understand him. ". . . child can't hold secret. Will . . ." He struggled, then touched the stone. ". . . caution." He removed his fingers and returned to English. "But if it comes to a decision—your life or his—I have no choice, my lady."

I'm old, she reminded.

"But got at least as many years left as he." Zylas inclined his head toward Korfius. "And need—" He struggled again; but, this time, did not resort to the translation stone. "—other life depend—" He glanced at Collins and fell silent, then scooped up his stone and returned it to his pocket. "Let's go," he growled in clear frustration.

Collins remained silent throughout the exchange, quietly putting the details together. Clearly, Korfius' finding them threw Zylas into a terrible dilemma. He had to keep Korfius quiet about Prinivere, not just for the duration of Collins' time here, but forever. Collins did not envy him that position; he could not kill a regular dog, let alone one who became a boy at intervals. Yet, Zylas had a loyalty to Prinivere that transcended Collins' understanding.

Collins and Zylas packed their gear in a tense hush punctuated only by occasional sighs from the rat/man. Collins did not press, certain his companion would speak in his own time. He did not have the words to comfort, so the best he could do was to listen.

Korfius seemed to share none of Zylas' consternation, chattering at the dragon with an exuberance Collins could not ever remember having. Apparently, the dragon answered him privately and with infinite patience, because

Korfius kept bouncing and talking, often not waiting long enough for Prinivere to possibly have addressed the question before zipping off another. Shortly, they had everything, and Zylas signaled for everyone to go.

Korfius obediently bounded from the cave, Zylas and Collins behind him and Ialin hovering anxiously. Falima made no complaint as Zylas lashed the pack to her back then assisted Korfius astride, still talking.

"I can't believe I'm helping a royal and a dragon. A real dragon. I can't believe there really even is a *real dragon* to help. A real, live dragon."

Zylas looked as tense as a depressed spring.

Collins placed a hand on Korfius' calf. "Listen, little buddy."

Korfius turned him a happy look.

"Remember how I told you this was secret?"

"Yes, I . . ." Korfius turned thoughtful, features screwed up in apparent pain. "Oh. Does that mean . . . ?"

"Yes," Collins said firmly, though the boy had never completed the question. "You can't tell anyone about Lady Prinivere."

"Ever?" The word seemed driven from his lips.

"Ever." Collins confirmed in a voice he hoped brooked no further questioning.

"Not even—"

To emphasize the point, Collins did not let Korfius finish. "Not even."

"But I didn't get to—"

"Doesn't matter. Not anyone. Ever." Collins dusted his hands to show the matter had ended, with no further discussion necessary or desirable. "It's as simple as that."

"Oh," Korfius said barely audibly. He hunched, disappointment clear from his stance as well as his features. "Well. At least, I'll get to help?" His tone suggested defeat, and he clearly expected Collins to burst his one last bubble.

"Of course, you can help," Collins said cheerfully, though he had no idea how. Knowing he would likely have to give Korfius a "busy" job, he added, "There are no small roles in the service of good and justice." He rather liked the sound of his own words and wondered whether he had just created them, as he believed, or if his subconscious had revived it from some long-ago comic book.

"I can't believe I met a . . ." This time, Korfius caught himself before he said, "dragon."

Collins made a "zip your lip" motion.

Though he could not understand the reference, Korfius apparently got the implication. He mimicked the gesture and fell silent.

As they headed off in a new direction, Collins glanced around. "Where's Vernon?"

Zylas continued to look worriedly between Collins and Korfius. "He'll get the lady off safely, then head back home." He held Collins' gaze. "We need him there."

Uncertain whether Zylas meant in general or for some reason related to their current mission, Collins did not press. Zylas clearly wanted to speak as little as possible about such matters in the boy's presence.

For the first few hours, they traveled in relative quiet. Then, Korfius drifted off to sleep, body sprawled across the pack, arms dangling on either side of Falima's neck. Collins paused to redistribute the boy's weight, to tuck limp hands beneath the weighted center, and to smooth hair from his eyes. Korfius mumbled something unintelligible but did not fully awaken. Collins now found himself able to continue without worrying constantly over the child's safety.

Finally, Collins went to Falima's head, where Zylas used the lead rope to haul her generally westward. "You know, between his only spending seven hours a day as a boy and the need to get sleep in both forms, he might just as well be a full-time dog.

"*Lesariat,*" Zylas reminded in a grunt. "That's the whole idea."

Suddenly, Collins found the answer to a question he had asked himself earlier. *Of course their civilization has stagnated for longer than a century. When you spend half or more of your life in animal form, it has to take all your time just to do the things necessary for survival. Who has time for innovation?*

Zylas glanced at the boy, apparently to ascertain that he slept. "Let's get back to planning."

Collins nodded, surprised to find himself eager. The more he understood, the better his chances for success. The several hours of walking had proved just the break he needed. "Let's start with the moat."

*   *   *

Another day of travel brought them down from the mountains to a road that hugged the base and a broad expanse of forest. Collins realized they could have avoided the crags and steppes simply by following the path, which most people surely did. He did not begrudge the course they had taken. Though longer, even without the looping detours Zylas had taken to foil pursuit, it only made sense for Prinivere to live where few humans dared or bothered to go. *On my world, she'd probably hide out on Everest.* He amended, *Or, perhaps, the tenth, eleventh, or twelfth highest mountain might not have quite as many determined climbers.*

They entered the forest just in time. Clouds that had stalked and threatened through the night broke open to release a splattering downpour. Rain roared against the canopy, occasionally rolling through to soak them with icy pinpoints or sudden streams of runoff. It continued into the evening, adding jagged bursts of lightning and rolling booms of thunder to the symphony of nature's pique. They ate from a pack growing welcomely lighter, and Collins appreciated that his companions found the insects the most desirable of their fare. By now, none of those remained, and they feasted on the foods he liked best: dried fruit, nut paste, and bread.

With Korfius in dog form, Collins' companions discussed the upcoming castle break in freely. Caught up in the plans, Collins listened and joined in eagerly. Though the approach changed several times, the idea that he might not succeed never entered the conversations. Heartened by his companions' confidence, Collins found himself just as certain that he would prevail. The crystal would make it back to Prinivere, she would open the portal, and he would return home to face the consequences of his absence—gladly. He only wished he could take his new friends with him. The image this conjured made him laugh. *Wouldn't that be interesting?* He curled up to sleep, dreaming of castle spires and a talking plesiosaur entrenched in a moat of blood.

Early the following morning, Ialin raced back to Collins and his friends: a rat, a horse, and a dog. "It's just ahead."

"The castle?"

"Yes, the castle." Impatience touched Ialin's tone, his

small, thin body in constant motion. "Up ahead. Come look."

As Collins went to do so, the other man added, "Carefully, now."

Collins obediently moved slowly in the indicated direction, trying to avoid crackling leaves and snapping twigs.

Ialin pranced an anxious circle around him. "Come on."

Collins stopped, studying the little man. "I can be quick or careful, not both. Choose."

Ialin sighed. "Careful." He flitted ahead, still clearly fretful, though he no longer rushed the only other companion in human form. He paused to peer through a gap in the foliage.

Collins counted Ialin shifting from foot to foot seven times in the few seconds it took him to come up beside the hummingbird/man. He wondered if the speeding metabolism required by a quick and tiny bird extended to his human form and made the world seem to move that much slower. He glanced through the gap, vision obscured in serrated chaos by overhanging leaves. Not far ahead, the forest opened to a vast plain of grass grazed by sheep, cows, and goats in a myriad array of colors. Chickens and ducks waddled through the herd, scooping up the bugs dislodged by shambling hooves.

Beyond the animals, a ring of brackish water surrounded a high stone wall with teethlike turrets and circular platforms. An even taller wall peeked over the first, visible only as jagged shadows. Above it all rose the castle, looking very much like the pictures Collins remembered from the postcards of friends who had chosen world travel over higher education. Each corner held a square-shaped tower that loomed over the turreted, rectangular roof. Every part was constructed of mortared stone blocks. It looked exactly as Ialin had described it, yet it defied all of Collins' expectations. The grandeur held him spellbound, struck by the work that must have gone into its construction, the eerie aura of power that accompanied a living fossil. The pictures his friends had sent were of crumbling ruins that barely compared with the reality of a functioning, real-time castle. "Wow," he said.

Ialin loosed a sound, half-snort and half-giggle. "Zylas said you were a people of few words, but I never realized just how few."

Collins tried to explain, gaze locked on the castle of Barakhai. "It's amazing. I've never seen anything like it."

Ialin withdrew, and Collins followed. "Where does *your* king live?"

As Collins returned to his animal companions, he tried to explain, "We don't have a king. We have a president who's elected—"

Ialin made a gesture to indicate he did not understand.

"We pick him."

"Who's we?" Ialin asked suspiciously, sliding the pack from Falima's withers. He eased it to the ground.

"We." Collins made a broad gesture to indicate everyone. "The people. All of us." It was not true in the strictest sense, as the 2000 presidential election could attest, but Collins had no intention of explaining the electoral college to a man struggling with the meaning of "vote."

Ialin dragged the pack deeper into the forest. "Regular people picked your leader?"

In rat form, Zylas galloped after Ialin. Korfius thrust his damp, icy nose into Collins' palm.

"Pick," Collins corrected the tense and scratched behind Korfius' ears. His family had always had a dog and at least one cat. His current lifestyle did not lend itself to pets, but he hoped to get one of each as soon as he graduated. "Every four years, we decide on a new one."

"And everyone agrees?"

At the same time, Zylas squeaked, "How do you keep one from taking over? From declaring himself leader for life?"

More worried about getting safely into and out of the castle, Collins found himself unwilling to get into a long discussion about American democracy. "There are whole enormous textbooks written on those very topics. It's not my field of study, but the system's worked reasonably well for at least the last two hundred years." He rushed to add, "Now, if we can get back to the matter at hand."

Zylas scurried up Collins' arm to his shoulder. "Ah, so now you're the one who only wants to talk about the castle."

"Yeah," Collins admitted, still stroking the dog. "Guess I'm a natural crammer." At the confused look on Ialin's face, he explained. "I tend to avoid things I don't want to do until a deadline looms. Then, I dive into it to the exclusion of everything else."

Ialin shrugged and began setting up the camp. "How odd."

"Not where I come from. Not for students, anyway."

Zylas spoke directly into Collins' ear. "I find I tend to remember things longer and better if I learn them slowly over time. And repetitively."

Collins flushed. "Well, yeah. I didn't say cramming was a smart thing." Realizing they had veered off the topic again, he redirected the conversation. "Any recent ideas on how I'm going to get into this castle?"

At first, Collins thought Ialin turned to look at him. Then, he realized the smaller man's gaze did not directly meet his own. He was, instead, consulting the rat on Collins' shoulder. "As a matter of fact," the man in human form started, "we have one."

Interested in what they might have discussed on the sly, Collins tipped his head toward Zylas to indicate his interest.

"Well," Ialin started, sitting on the only blanket he had, thus far, laid out. "Town guards sometimes come for brief training with the king's warriors. From what I understand, it keeps the king informed about the goings-on in his holdings and gets some elite training for the guards."

"Yeah?" Collins encouraged, not yet sure how this could apply to him.

"They usually come in pairs," Ialin continued. "So if we send you in riding Falima, no one should question it. Usually, a guard wouldn't let anyone but a royal or another guard sit on them."

Collins considered. "Falima let *me* ride her."

With a wave of his paw, Zylas dismissed that argument. "After she went 'renegade' by saving you, all bets were off."

That seeming self-evident, Collins shook his head. "No, I mean before the rescue. She carried me to the . . . the dungeon." He swallowed, fighting a forming image. A swirl of the desperate parade of emotions that had struck him there returned to haunt him.

"Because the other guards told her to do it, I presume," Ialin growled. "And I'll also wager it wasn't a comfortable ride."

Remembering, Collins winced. "You'd win that bet."

"Anyway," Ialin said, returning to the subject, "if you rode in on Falima, no one would think to question that you're both guards."

Collins still saw a gap in the logic. "Unless word of Falima turning . . ." He used Zylas' word, or at least the one the translation spell and stone turned it into, ". . . 'renegade' has reached this far."

Ialin wiped his mouth with the back of his sleeve. "Oh, we have to assume that."

"We'll disguise her," Zylas explained, whiskers tickling Collins' ear.

Collins' mind conjured images of a horse wearing a huge plastic nose, mustache, and glasses combination. The usual methods of disguise: clothes, haircut, contact lenses, perhaps a fake scar or two would not work here. They could not even sneak into the relative safety of careful cross-dressing. "As a horse? Or a woman?"

Ialin gave Collins another one of his judgmental stares. "We'll do the horse part. She'll have to handle the woman herself. We'll send the pack, so you can put anything she'll need in there."

Collins looked doubtfully from the grazing horse to the pack near Ialin's feet. "Won't I have to know something about the town I'm supposed to represent?"

"Not as much as you think," Zylas said.

Apparently missing Zylas' words, spoken low and directly into Collins' ear, Ialin said, "Just a bit."

Sensing Collins' tension, Korfius whined, butting the now-stilled hand.

Absently, Collins continued his ministrations while his two older companions outlined their plan.

Chapter 14

COLLINS' watch read 5:00 P.M. when he rode Falima across the well-cropped grassy field that separated the outer curtain wall from the forest. He tucked the watch into his pocket, wishing he could have left it behind with Zylas. Pulling out impossible technology at the wrong time might give him away, but he relied upon it to determine a proper and consistent pretend switch time, to keep track of Falima, and to have a clear idea of how long the whole process was taking him. The black fur beneath him was disorienting after several days of riding a golden buckskin. Having never heard of bleach, his companions found it impossible to lighten Falima's coloring, so had chosen to make her body the same coarse ebony as her mane, tail, and points. Apparently, jet black was one of the most common horse colors in Barakhai and should not attract undue attention.

At switch time, Falima would make herself scarce. The dye might carry over into her human form, though probably not with much consistency. Apparently, some items in the pack would allow her to touch up blotches or to change her appearance in other believable fashions. Collins hoped he would recognize her, though it did not matter. His escape plan and hers did not hinge upon one another.

Sheep looked up as they passed, baaing noisy greetings. The goats proved more curious, approaching them to sniff, bleat at, and chew the cloth shoes his companions had provided in place of his Nike look-alikes. The horse's ears went flat backward, and she emitted occasional warning squeals that sent the goats scattering, though they always returned. The cows paid them no attention at all.

As they crossed the plain, Collins got a clear view of the outer wall, and he steered Falima toward the attached roofed structure that clearly represented the gatehouse. A massive construct of plank and rope pressed against the stone wall, apparently the drawbridge. Collins pulled up in front of the gatehouse, at the edge of the moat. Insects skittered over the surface of the water, leaving star-shaped wakes. Far beneath them, fish glided through the transparent pond, apparently accustomed to having no place to hide.

The gatehouse consisted of two of the round towers that interrupted the wall at regular intervals, with a straight stretch of stone no wider than the drawbridge between them. On the roof of each tower stood two guards dressed in white-chested aqua tunics, the top portion decorated with designs that looked like thinly stretched clover to Collins. Black belts held their uniforms in place and supported long, thin swords in wooden sheaths. All four watched Collins' approach with obvious interest, though they raised no weapons. One called down in a strong, female voice, "Who's there?"

Collins had initially assumed they were all men, so the speaker caught him off guard.

When he did not answer immediately, the woman's partner boomed out, "You were asked a question, good sir. Are you deaf or rude?"

Collins dismounted and bowed, hoping they would attribute any violated protocol to his foreignness. "Just tired, sir. I am Benton." It seemed ironic that he would use the full name he had so many times asked others to shorten. He had often wished his parents had named him Benjamin, like every other "Ben" he had ever met. His current friends had assured him that Benton fit this world much better than Ben; and, by using his real name, he would not forget it, as he might a pseudonym, in the heat of a chaotic moment. If he accidentally did call himself "Ben," it would follow naturally as a proper shortening or interrupted utterance. "And this . . ." He made a flourishing motion toward Falima, "is Marlys." It was another alias he would remember, though he knew it made things harder for his companion. He dared not use anything approaching her real name, as it might trigger suspicion. "We've traveled a long way under less than ideal circumstances."

"From where?" the woman asked, and the others leaned forward for the answer. Now, Collins was able to get a good look at all of them. Mail peeked from beneath their collars and sleeves, and helmets pinned down their hair. Their faces ranged from the male partner's dark brown to the woman's café au lait to the paler khaki of the guards in the other tower. Wisps of sable hair escaped onto one man's forehead, but the others kept their locks bunched beneath arming caps and metal helmets.

Collins used the town name Ialin had given him, "Epronville. We've come to do our shift for the king."

"Where are your colors?" one of the pale men asked.

Anticipating the question, Collins had a ready answer. "Bandits. That was part of our less than ideal circumstances."

The woman's partner snorted. "Bandits robbing guardsmen. You're right. You do need a shift here. Some competent training."

Collins feigned affront. "Do you think we don't feel foolish enough? You have to rub our noses in it?" He wondered how the slang would translate. "Perhaps you'd like to bring the whole guard force out here to point fingers and laugh at us?" He simulated the guards, jabbing a digit toward Falima. "Ha ha ha, simple rube guards can't even keep *themselves* safe from bandits." He dropped his hand. "And, by the way, don't bother to mention we faced off six of them."

The dark man made a gesture of surrender. "Take it easy. I meant no disrespect." The tight-lipped smirk he tried to hide told otherwise. He turned and disappeared from the tower.

Keeping his own expression neutral, Collins congratulated himself on his acting. He had managed to divert the guards from the issue of the missing colors. The fact that it made him look weak did not bother him at all.

The fourth guard reappeared at his position. Then, a ratcheting, clanking noise ground through Collins' hearing. The drawbridge edged downward, adding a squeal of massive, rusty hinges to the din.

"You'd best move back," the woman instructed. "Or you might get crushed."

Collins led Falima away from the moat, hoping his failure to exercise the proper caution would pass for small town ignorance rather than a complete lack of knowledge about castles. He knew Barakhai had only one such fortress, that the dwellings of the outlying superiors consisted only of mansions with the barest of defenses. When he considered their system, it seemed miraculous that they managed even that much. At most, the people had only eight hours a day to accomplish any work along with such necessities as eating and general personal care.

Suspended by two sturdy chains, the drawbridge dropped across the moat with a thud that shook the ground. Falima loosed a low nicker, prancing several more paces backward.

"Easy, girl." Collins rubbed her neck soothingly, feeling the warm sweat that slicked her fur. He glanced surreptitiously at his palm, worried the moisture might disturb the dye. Though caked with dirt and foamy horse sweat, his hand remained free of black smudges. He breathed a sigh of relief.

Gripping the lead rope more tightly, Collins drew Falima to the drawbridge. She eyed the board warily. Collins stepped up first, hoping that would ease her concerns. One front hoof rose, then settled on the wood. The other followed. She took a step forward, hoof clomping on the board. Another carried her directly over the moat, and a hollow sound rang through the drawbridge. With a snort and whinny that left Collins' ears ringing, she stumbled back to solid ground.

Afraid the horse's lurching might toss him into the water, Collins skittered after her. "Falima, honey, it's all right," he whispered. "It's all right. You need to come."

Falima trumpeted out another whinny.

"Not much overlap," one of the guards guessed.

"Some." Collins remembered what Zylas had told him. "But she's still pretty young."

One of the guardsmen took pity on the weary travelers. "First time across is always difficult. Just keep trying. If necessary, I'll get someone in switch-form to show her across."

"Thank you." Collins did not try to lead Falima again but just stood at her head murmuring reassurances and stroking behind her ears. He knew horses would go almost anywhere if they saw another horse safely make the journey ahead of them. A friend had once told him she trained colts to cross streams and puddles by having them shadow a staid old trail horse. "Ready, Marlys?" he finally said out loud, suddenly wishing he had chosen another name. It seemed to stick in his mouth, desperately out of place. It reminded him of how he and his elementary school friends had become so used to Michelangelo referring to a mutant ninja turtle, they giggled wildly when it came up on an art museum field trip.

One hand grasping the rope at the base of Falima's chin, the other clutching the cheekpiece, he urged her forward with him. He did not know how people encouraged horses in Barakhai; but, back home, the position gave him unprecedented control over an animal large enough to crush him. He remembered a favorite saying of an old girlfriend, "He who has the horse's head has the horse." It applied to leading horses, grooming and immunizing, as well as reining, but he could not help getting a *The Godfather*-like image of the amputated head resting in someone's bed.

With Collins close and urgent, Falima raised a foreleg high, then placed it on the drawbridge.

"Good girl," Collins encouraged. "Good, good girl."

Falima took another step, the thunk of its touch sending a quiver through her. This time, she did not attempt to withdraw, but took another hesitant step onto the surface.

"Come on, honey. You can do it." Collins reverted to a pet name, which allowed him avoid the whole "Marlys" issue. He hoped Zylas and Ialin had called it right when they claimed Falima understood enough in horse form to get the gist of the plan. He kept imagining her becoming human surrounded by king's guards with no memory of how she got there and, in a wild blithering panic, giving them all away. Surely, they had talked to her before the change, while he slept. *Surely nothing.* So many of his friends' motives appeared bizarre or inscrutable, it seemed senseless to even speculate.

Collins continued to cluck encouragingly as Falima took more steps onto the drawbridge. Head bowed nearly to her knees, she studied the surface and her own hooves as she moved, her steps never growing confident. At least, she continued forward. In fact, her pace quickened as she clearly attempted to get past the portion of ground that felt and sounded unstable to a horse's ears.

When they came to the part of the drawbridge on the far side of the moat, Falima's demeanor returned to normal. She clopped through the opened double doors and into the gatehouse with little more than a glance.

The woman guard and one of the men from the other tower met them in the span. Doors shaped like cathedral windows opened onto the towers, while a heavy set of iron-bound oak doors blocked further entry in the direction of the castle.

The man raised his right hand in greeting. "I'm Mabix. Welcome to Opernes Castle, home of King Terrin and Queen Althea, high rulers of Barakhai."

Zylas had prepared Collins with the names, though the albino had warned him to stay alert for changes. The royals did not discuss coups and ascensions with the regular folk as a rule, though the information eventually reached even the lowliest *outcaste*.

King Terrin and Queen Althea. King Terrin and Queen Althea. Collins worked to fix the titles in his mind, only then realizing he had completely forgotten the name of the man in front of him. For a moment, he teetered on the decision of whether to let it pass and fake it or ask for a repeat. Then, deciding it best to look the fool now rather than later, he pressed. "Thank you, kind sir, but I'm afraid I didn't quite catch your name."

"Mabix," he repeated without offense. "This is Lyra."

The female guard dipped ever so slightly to acknowledge the introduction. Though a motion of respect, it fell short of an actual curtsy which, Collins presumed, she reserved for royalty. "Lyra," Collins repeated. "Mabix."

"Now," Mabix said, getting down to business. "If we could just see your writ."

Collins fought a grin. Other than a utility knife, the saddest bit of rations, and a ragged change of clothes, the presumably forged paper was the only thing his friends had given him.

"Or," Lyra added with just the barest hint of suspicion, "did the bandits get that, too?"

"Over my dead body," Collins said, hoping it sounded as

emphatic in Barakhain as English. He thrust a hand into his tunic and emerged with the crumpled paper covered with flowery scribbles. The spell that allowed him to speak fluently apparently did not extend to the written word. *With my luck, it's probably really gibberish.* A sudden thought rose. *Or worse, calls the king a pickle-nosed bastard.*

Mabix examined the paper, Lyra looking over his shoulder. They both nodded. Now, Collins got a good look at their uniforms, the patterned white ending just below their breastbones. Joined by impressively straight stitching for a world without machines, the aqua material fell just past the knee. Mail showed at the collar and arms, while high boots of stiffened cloth covered their legs. They wore bowl-shaped metal helmets.

Once they had the writ, the two relaxed visibly, which left Collins wondering where Zylas had gotten it. Because his friends had initially rescued him in animal form and they switched naked, he had seen all their personal belongings in the saddlebags he found tied to Falima that first day. Vernon had packed them much fuller; but, if the mouse/man had stuck in such a thing, it meant they had known how he would infiltrate the castle ever since they left the cabin. He wondered why they had not discussed it with him sooner. *They also didn't let me know the gender of an elder who turned out to be a dragon until I saw her with my own eyes. Why does this surprise me?*

Lyra and Mabix pulled closed the massive doors through which their guests had entered. As they banged shut, a ratcheting sound echoed through the small enclosed room, the drawbridge lifting. Other than a bit of diffused sunlight filtering through cracks in the wooden construction, the room went dark. Falima danced, whinnying her discomfort. Collins patted her, whispering nonsense in a steady patter while Lyra and Mabix slid the bolt on the door behind them and pushed the panels open. Light rushed in, accompanied by the sweet odor of young plants and the mingled sounds of answering neighs, whines, barks, and human voices.

Falima squealed out another whinny, the shrill sound reverberating painfully in the still mostly enclosed area. She charged for the outside, and Collins let her go. Peering beyond her, he saw an emerald stretch of well-grazed grasses crisscrossed by pathways. Several horses, a few mules, and a

goat placidly ate, though the nearest ones looked up as
Falima joined them. She snorted, nostrils widened as if to
suck in all the unfamiliar smells, then lowered her head to
graze.

Collins glanced around as the guards ushered him into
the outer courtyard. Now, he could see the towers that
looked round from the outside had flat backs that turned
them into semicircles. Behind the wall-wide crenels and
merlons lay battlement walkways paced by guards in the
same uniforms as his new companions. Small buildings lay
pressed against the wall, their construction wooden except
for the stone backings they borrowed from the wall itself.
Shingles or thatch topped them. Directly ahead, Collins saw
another double-towered gatehouse, larger than the one
they had just exited. Another crenellated wall ringed the
still distant castle.

Lyra rushed ahead to the second gatehouse. Mabix
looked at Falima. "She can stay here if she wants."

Collins considered. He liked the idea of her only needing
to escape one wall should he fail at his mission. "That's up
to her," he said casually. "She's due to change shortly and
should be quite capable of making the decision by herself."
He removed the rope halter and placed it in the pack, de-
bating whether or not to remove the whole thing and carry
it himself. Not wishing to burden himself when Falima remained clearly untroubled by it, he left it in place.

"So what's the news from Epronville?"

"From—?" Collins stopped himself from saying *where?*
"—Epronville?" He laughed to cover his mistake. "Never
much happening there." He could have kicked himself. He
felt trapped by the easiest, most casual and obvious question in the universe, one he had even anticipated. Larger
concerns and the need for haste had made him forget the
problem he had initially raised. Now, his ignorance undid
him, leaving him unable to even fabricate a credible answer.
He had little idea of the size of Barakhai, let alone its various towns and cities, could not guess how intimately they
intertwined, and what might serve as news. In some cul-
tures, information about who had married whom or which
babies had survived the winter was welcome knowledge as
far as a man could travel. "At least compared with here."

Uncertain whether his last comment had helped or only

dug him deeper, he switched to a different tactic. "No matter what I say, Marlys will contradict me." Those were the first words since he arrived at the castle that rang surprisingly true. "I'm always wrong."

Mabix chuckled. "Sounds like you two are married."

"Marlys and me?" Collins was as struck by the next words that escaped his mouth as Mabix was amused by them. "What a horrible thought."

Now Mabix laughed openly. "Often that which a man protests the most will or should come to pass." He winked, and Collins was again struck by the similarity of that gesture to his own culture. "At least according to women."

Lyra returned, the gatehouse doors now open ahead. "What was that?"

Mabix shook his head. "Nothing you need to hear."

Lyra sighed, speaking in a tone that implied confidentiality, though Mabix could surely hear her. "Something between men, no doubt. I'm tired of that."

For the first time, it occurred to Collins that he ought to see as many female guards as male since, presumably, the horses gave birth to as many fillies as colts. He made a mental note to ask Falima about it later, though he managed to devise a possible answer from his own experience. Likely, the women spent more of their human time house-and child-keeping. Or, perhaps, the women did more of the routine guard chores that did not involve the possibility of direct combat. The less industrial and enlightened a society, in general, the less it could afford to emancipate its women without endangering its survival.

Lyra led them through the second gatehouse and into the courtyard that surrounded the castle. Here, he saw less grass, though a few horses did graze around the scattered buildings. Gardens took up most of the space, paths winding between them. A vast variety of vegetables flourished in crooked rows, and Collins saw none of the tended panoramas of flowers he expected from his visits to the arboretum. Each and every patch grew edibles of some type, from herbs to roots, fruit trees to vines. He did find some attractive blue flowers, but these grew in a planned line, obviously the source of some delectable seed. *Perhaps vilegro.* Collins remembered the name of the plant Falima had turned into a sweet treat called *gahiri.* Here, too, buildings cropped out from the wall, kennels, guardhouses, and stables in remark-able abundance.

All of that flashed across Collins' sight in the instants before his attention became riveted upon the castle. Like some massive university, it stood grandly, towering over its walls and gardens. Sun rays skipped across its surface, ignit-ing glimmering lines of quartz and mica. The four square towers at the corners stood like sentinels, their tops crenel-lated with antlike figures of guards pacing atop them. A stone-cut stairway led into the open door.

Falima clomped through the gatehouse to pull up beside Collins. While he studied the structure, she grazed with an aloofness indicative of indifference.

Mabix spoke, "Magnificent, isn't it?"

Only then, sound returned to Collins' world, and he heard the background noises of giggling children, conversa-tion, and animal sounds of a myriad types. In response, he only nodded.

Lyra drew up. "So, what's the news from Epronville?"

"Fine," Collins murmured, still staring.

Mabix laughed. "You'll get more from her when she switches, I'd warrant. This one seems due for some sleep." He jerked a thumb toward Collins, which finally seized his attention.

"Sleep's fine." Collins yawned broadly, remembering Zy-las' advice. "But I'd rather some food. I switch soon, too, and I'd like to grab a bite of something substantial before I'm committed to grass."

Mabix and Lyra nodded vigorously. "I'm with you on that one," the woman muttered. He had clearly struck a chord.

"That's where the dogs have the advantage." Lyra headed toward one of the barracks. "Though I don't know many who'd admit it so freely."

Collins supported the confession for the purposes of cre-ating camaraderie with those who believed themselves his peers. "Right now, I'm so hungry I could eat a ..." He doubted the spell would translate as "horse," but he dared not take that chance. ". . . tree."

Mabix completed what was, apparently, a common say-ing, ". . . two shrubs, three beehives, and a garden."

"That, too," Collins added, to his companions' amusement. He found himself liking them and hoped his theft would not reflect badly on them or cost them their jobs.

The man inclined his head toward one of the buildings. Reminded of their purpose, he and Lyra started walking. Collins and Falima followed.

They stopped in front of one of the guardhouses, animals noting their passage with curious looks. Collins felt like he had entered a dim, creepy house where the eyes of pictures seemed to fix on anyone who passed. "Bring your pack," Mabix said. "I'll show you to your quarters." Without waiting for Collins to obey, he shoved open the door and entered. "Hope you two don't mind sharing."

Collins tried to sound matter-of-fact. "Not at all." He supposed it made sense to part-time animals that they house men and women in the same barracks, even the same rooms. He wondered how many accidental marriages and out-of-wedlock births this created in buildings at least half full of stallions. He undid all the clasps, clips, and ties with Lyra's assistance, shouldered the pack, and trotted after Mabix.

The door opened onto a common room strewn with clothes, bits of food, and half-finished games of chess and dice. Crude, mismatched furniture, mostly constructed from crates and barrels, interrupted the vast chaos. If not for the lanterns instead of overhead lights and the lack of a television, it could have passed for the recreation room of most men's dormitories. Smaller doors led off in several directions. Crossing the room, Mabix knocked on one of the doors before opening it.

Through the portal, Collins saw a square, windowless room the size of a large bathroom. Three rolled up pallets leaned in one corner, a pile of chamber pots in the other. A chair crafted from a quarter-cut barrel stood pushed against a wall. A cushion affixed to a circular piece of wood lay on the floor beside it, apparently the seat.

Mabix squeezed past Lyra and Collins in the doorway, picked up the cushion, and pointed into the seat. "You can store your gear here."

Where? Collins followed Mabix and examined the chair. He saw a hole where his backside would usually go, creating a good-sized hollow that ended with a thick wooden bottom. Clearly, it served as a neat storage area as well as a piece of furniture once the cushion was balanced on top of the opening. About to say something about the cleverness of its inventor, Collins held his tongue instead. For all he knew, everyone had these in their homes.

Mabix noticed Collins studying the arrangement. "Convenient, huh?"

"Very." Collins let a bit of his respect seep into his tone.

Lyra added, "Craftsman who came up with that design won himself a permanent place on the king's staff.

Mabix bobbed his head. "A *Random,* too. On the king's staff. Can you believe it?"

"Wow," Collins replied, holding back a storm of questions he could never ask his *Random* companions. He swung the pack to the floor, feeling trapped. He had to leave it so Falima would have clothes and access to the makeup, but he hated to risk losing it. Suddenly, he realized he had no reason to hide that piece of information. "You know, I think I'd better put it back on . . ." He caught himself about to say *Falima.* ". . . on Marlys. She gets cold easily and likes to dress as soon as possible." He had originally planned to say she felt uncomfortable naked among strangers but liked what came out of his mouth better. *How do you like that? I can think on my feet.* A less wholesome thought followed, *Or am I just becoming a better liar?* Winning over Korfius and Vernon had certainly given him plenty of practice.

Collins looked at the pack, as if noticing it for the first time. "She's due to switch pretty soon." He wondered if he had just made a crucial blunder. As partners, they ought to know one another's habits well enough that he would never have removed the pack in the first place.

But, if Lyra or Mabix thought the same way, neither revealed it. They headed back outside without another word or anything Collins would consider knowing glances. Falima grazed placidly among a small group of horses and one mule. As he reattached the pack, Collins found himself wondering about the long-earred animal. In his world, they came from breeding a donkey with a horse and were always sterile. He wondered how that applied here and how it affected the creature's human form.

Stop it! Collins blamed nervousness for his thoughts taking off in a trained but unhelpful direction. *Focus!* Casually, he poked a hand into his pocket, seized his watch, and glanced surreptitiously at it around folds of fabric. It now read 5:50 P.M., only ten minutes before Falima's switch. He needed to draw the guards away from her so she could have the privacy necessary to affect her disguise. "Now, about that tree I plan to eat . . ."

Mabix laughed, taking the hint. "I'll walk you to the dining hall. It's getting on toward dinner anyway, so you'll have a chance to meet a good bunch of the guards and staff."

Lyra made a throwaway gesture, and Mabix nodded. "She needs to return to her post." He took Collins' elbow, steering him toward the castle as Lyra headed back toward the gatehouses. "I'll have to get back myself, as soon as I've got you settled in. Can you do all right on your own?"

Still stuck on the realization that he would share the dining hall with a crowd, Collins forced a nod. "I'll do fine." He hoped he spoke truth. He was hungry, but he would have to feign starvation. So long as he had his mouth full, he would not have to answer questions. He only hoped dinner would not consist of a plateful of bugs as large as puppies. His mind conjured images of enormous beetles, crisply browned, legs stretched upward with turkey caps on all six drumsticks.

Mabix stopped suddenly, halfway down the courtyard path to the castle. "Didn't you say your partner would switch soon?"

The query put Collins on his guard, though it seemed foolish to lie. "Yes. Yes, I did."

"Won't she want to join us for dinner?"

Collins thought it best to leave Falima alone, at least for the change. "No," he said, fighting down an edge of terror. "No, she . . . she doesn't like to eat right after. The combination of rich food piled on a bellyful of grass." He wrinkled his features. "Bothers her."

"Interesting," Mabix said with the air of one who has found himself in the same situation many times but never had a similar experience. "But maybe it's different for us daytime humans. That's never bothered me."

"Me either," Collins agreed. "But it bothers her."

Mabix accepted that explanation, and Collins hoped he would not have to make up many more. The more implausibilities he forced them to consider, the more suspicious they would likely become. Though he enjoyed having a reasonably kindred soul, he was just as happy that Mabix would have to leave. Spreading his stories farther apart might make them harder to penetrate.

Mabix led Collins up the castle stairs, muddy with shoe and boot tracks, to the open door. Voices wafted through, a disharmonious hum of myriad conversations. Suspended by chains, a wooden cross-hatching hung overhead like the sword of Damocles. Collins' new knowledge of languages allowed him to give it a name, a raised portcullis. He had seen them before, in every swashbuckling movie that required a castle. Always, the heroes, from the Three Musketeers to Robin Hood dived beneath the closing grate at the last possible second, while guards' swords rattled futilely on the portcullis behind them. The very object meant to trap them saved them instead.

The door opened onto a spiral staircase that wound clockwise upward and also went downward. Cold funneled from the lower areas where Collins knew the dungeons and storerooms lay. Mabix took him up, past one landing with a set of doors opening on either side. Collins knew the right one led to the kitchens, the left to workshops. The noises grew louder as they continued their ascent, and Mabix stopped at the next set of doors. He opened the right one, revealing a vast dining hall, its grandeur surpassing Zylas' description. At the far end of the room, a smaller table stood on a dais. At it sat ten people in splendid silks and satins, their robes trimmed with gold lacework or embroidery. The women wore nappy dresses and capes, the men fine tunics and sashes, doublets, and robes.

Three massive tables stretched between the door and the occupants of the dais, filled with people whose dress, demeanor, and appearance spanned a gamut that would once have seemed to Collins beyond possibility. Dogs of varying shapes and sizes wound freely around the diners or hovered beneath the tables. Tapestries and banners hung from every wall, their colors a rainbow mix of pattern and picture. Above them, cathedral-cut open windows revealed a balcony blocked by waist-high handrails. Men and women in matching aqua-and-white plaid looked down over the diners, clutching oddly shaped instruments and conferring with one another.

"Impressive, isn't it?"

Mabix's description jarred Collins from his daze. He made no apology for staring. He was supposed to be an awestruck bumpkin. "Wow." It finally occurred to him to evaluate the food he had trapped himself into eating with gusto. He could not see what occupied the gold and silver platters of the head table, but the regular folk scooped a gloppy substance, with hands and spoons, from what appeared to be stale slices of bread that served as plates. Servants wove between the tables, refilling goblets, and plopping down fresh bowls of stew for the guests to ladle onto their bread plates.

"That's King Terrin at the head table," Mabix said, gesturing toward the central figure, a burly man with wheaten ringlets and a full beard." In order, that's the constable, the pantler, an adviser, the butler, the queen's steward, the prince, the queen, the king again, a princess, another princess, the king's steward, another adviser, the children's steward, the ewerer, and one more adviser."

The list came too fast for Collins to follow, but that did not matter. He did not intend to remain here long enough to care who he had seen and met.

"Find a seat on one of the benches at any trestle table. Whoever's next to you can help you with the proper procedures."

Collins nodded. "Thanks." He suspected he could teach them a thing or two about manners. Unlike those at the head table, the commoners lacked forks. They all used spoons and fingers, even in the communal bowls holding the only course. They shared goblets as well. Though he had no intention of eating a bite of what he imagined was a worm stew drenched in spider guts, he did take a seat for the sake of appearances. He chose the place between a demure woman in a stained white apron and a thin man animatedly engaged in conversation with the guard on his other side.

Mabix stepped around to a cluster of uniformed guards sitting at the center table. He chatted with them briefly, then they turned toward Collins. Pinned by their stares, he froze, abruptly afraid; but Mabix's cheerful wave dispelled his tension almost as soon as it arose. *Of course, he would have to tell someone about Falima's and my arrival.*

A boy rushed in to place a slice of bread in front of

Collins. Dark and stiff with blue-green mold along one edge of crust, it did nothing to stimulate his appetite. The same boy laid out a spoon beside it.

"Thank you," Collins said.

Blushing, the boy bowed, then hurried to assist another diner.

Mabix trotted from the room, back onto the staircase, then disappeared.

The musicians launched into an upbeat song, and the conversations died to a hum. Harp, lute, and fiddle braided into a sweet harmony filled with riffs and runs. Collins looked at the bread plate, then at the woman beside him. "Excuse me," he whispered. "Where would I find a rest room?"

Silently, the woman lifted a hand to point beyond the royal diners. Only then, Collins noticed a door in the far wall that surely led to one of the garderobes Zylas had described. She hissed back, "If you don't want to walk past the royals, there's another one in the library. Just go out the main door, across the landing, and through the cross door. The only other exit from the library is the garderobe."

"Thank you." Collins rose and headed back the way he had come. Once in the staircase, he crossed to the library door. He had his hand on the ring before he remembered his interest in the rest room was only diversionary. *What better time for exploring than when most of the staff and royals are gathered in the dining room?*

Quickly, Collins scurried up the stairs. He reached the next landing, heart pounding, and paused to regroup. A tall window overlooked the castle grounds, a ledge jutting from it. He perched on it, glancing down at the courtyards. Horses sprawled, bathing in the sunshine while others quietly grazed. A gardener pulled weeds, feeding them to a spotted goat as he worked. A pair of dogs frolicked with a young colt, barking at its heels. It charged them, as if to crush them beneath its hooves, then turned aside at the last moment, leaving the dogs to whirl and charge after it again. Collins tore his gaze from the scene to turn his attention inward. The doors on either side should open onto the servants' sleeping chambers, which meant he had one more floor till he came to the first warded area. He resumed his climb.

The next landing also held a window overlooking a

slightly different view of the courtyards. A calico cat curled on the ledge, the resemblance to Collins' first pet uncanny. Like Fluffy, this cat had one black ear and one white, its body covered with blotches on a chalky background, tail and paws darkly tipped. The memory brought a smile to his lips. "Here, kitty, kitty," he said softly. "Here, girl." The scientist in him came out to wonder whether the same rules of genetics applied here. He knew cats carried color genes on their X-chromosomes and, at most, two different hues on each X. Since males only had one X and females two, and calicos had three colors by definition, all calicoes were either female or the uncommon XXY, a usually sterile male mutation.

The cat lifted its head.

Collins approached gently, fingers extended. The cat sniffed curiously. He lowered his hand to its back, making a broad stroke. The cat arched, a purr rumbling from it. It jammed its head into his cupped hand.

Smiling, Collins stroked the entire length of the cat, enjoying the soft rush of fur beneath his palm. He missed having a cat terribly. Studies showed that petting an animal naturally lowered blood pressure and relieved stress. He could scarcely recall a time when he needed a natural tranquilizer more. He scratched around the animal's ears, ruffling its fur into a mane. Its purr deepened to a roar.

Only then did Collins realize what he was doing. *Oh, my God, I'm stroking a human woman!* He cursed his lack of caution. Caught up in his memory of Fluffy, he had completely forgotten that no creature here was what it seemed. He withdrew his hands, and the purr died immediately. The cat bounded down from its perch with a thud that made him cringe, then twined itself against and through his legs.

Collins back-stepped. "That's it for now, kitty. I've got work to do." Reaching for the door ring, he pushed it open. Every cat he had ever owned had to run through any newly opened door no matter where it led, but this one did not attempt to enter the royal bedchambers. Warded against *switchers,* it would not allow her entry. Seeing no movement inside, Collins headed in, pulling the door shut behind him. His heart rate quickened again, and any stress-easing that petting the cat might have achieved disappeared. His pulse pounded in his temples, and sweat slicked his back. He had just reached the point of no return. No logical explanation could cover him now.

Much smaller than the great dining hall, the room contained a curtained bed with a shelved frame, a chest, a stool, and a chandelier with a dozen white candles. A massive tapestry depicting a hunt covered most of one wall. Collins dredged up the description of the crystal: a smooth oblong rock the size of a peach with five, smooth edges of different sizes, milky blue in color. The room held few enough furnishings that it would not take long to search.

Collins walked first to the bed, suddenly struck by something that had gotten only his passing notice when he had glanced at it. *A hunting scene?* It seemed an impossible thing for a society that considered the killing of animals murder. He jerked his attention back to the tapestry. It was clearly old, a museum piece faded nearly beyond recognition. Washed to shades of gray, its figures blurred into the background. Yet Collins had managed to take away a solid impression, and he struggled now to find the details that had previously caught his eye. Men on horseback raised spears, while a pack of dogs harried some huge, indiscernible animal.

You don't have time for this, Collins reminded himself. Tearing his gaze from the tapestry, he opened one of the drawers. Stacks of neatly folded tunics in a variety of colors met his gaze. He felt under and between them for a hard lump, glad for its size. Anything smaller might require him to rifle the room, which would definitely cast suspicion. If possible, he wanted to get the stone without anyone noticing it, or him, missing.

Drawer by drawer, Collins checked through the king's clothing, intensely aware of every passing second. He had no more than an hour to search before he either had to furtively withdraw or find a hiding place and hope he had a chance to look again, perhaps at another meal. A better thought came to him. *While they're sleeping.* He shoved the last drawer shut and cast his gaze around the room again. It seemed worth losing a few minutes of trying to find the magical stone in order to locate a haven. The drawer-base meant no room beneath the bed, and its position flat against one corner gave him no space to squeeze beyond the curtains. Even if the chest did not surely contain something, it would prove a tight squeeze even for his skinny frame. Two other doors led out of the king's chamber.

Footsteps thundered on the staircase, growing louder. *They're coming.* Terror scattered Collins' wits, and he bolted for the far doors in a desperate scramble. Seizing one at random, he shoved it opened and hurled himself through. He skidded across a polished clay floor. His shoulder slammed into a low shelf. He sprang to his feet, braining himself on an overhanging lip. He bit off a scream, teeth sinking into his tongue. Dizziness washed over him in a blaze of black-and-gray spots. He caught a blurry glimpse of what he had hit, a wooden board atop a bench with a hole cut into the wood. *Bathroom.* He whirled to face four men with drawn swords.

Collins' skin seemed to turn to ice. His head throbbed, and he tasted blood. He retreated, raising his hands to indicate surrender. Wood pressed into the backs of his calves, and he stopped, forced into a sitting position on the bench. "I won't fight. Don't hurt me." His vision cleared enough to reveal faces familiar from the dining hall, including the goldenrod hair and beard of Barakhai's king.

Chapter 15

COLLINS froze, pressed against the garderobe, with three swords hovering in front of him. His mind raced. He braced himself for the rush of panic that had assailed him just before his near-hanging, but his thoughts remained strikingly clear. The world seemed to move in slow motion, while he mulled the situation. *If I go with them, they'll execute me. If I fight, they'll kill me.* There appeared no choice at all, but memory assisted him. Falima had claimed only the king's guards could use weapons, which meant, in most situations, they only had to raise them in a threatening manner. Since they had come through the door, these three had to be royalty, even less likely to possess true combat knowledge.

Based on this train of thought, Collins took a chance. Hands up, features displaying honest terror, he begged. "Please, don't hurt me."

The men edged closer. As they did, Collins dove beneath the raised swords. His shoulder crashed against the king's legs, staggering the Barakhain and sending pain screaming through Collins' arm.

"Are you all right?" The men instinctively went to the aid of their king.

Collins rolled to his feet, then made a crouched sprint back into the king's bedchamber.

Terrin bellowed. "Get him!"

Collins cleared the room in three running strides, then

wrenched the stairwell door open and hurled himself through it. Only then he realized he had just tossed himself into a mass of armed palace guards. "Shit!"

"Get him!"

Collins flailed wildly, arms connecting with flesh in several directions. His vision filled with a chaotic forest of arms, legs, and swords. A fist slammed his cheek, and cold steel sliced his hip. Pain clipped through the site, and he howled, balance lost. He felt himself falling, control utterly beyond his grasp. He tumbled, stone steps slamming bruises across his back, his face, his limbs. He grabbed for support, fingers opening and closing like fish mouths, capturing nothing.

"The portcullis!" someone yelled, the sound a dull echo amid the shouts of the guards.

A clanking reverberation joined the other crisscrossing sounds in the tubular stairwell. Collins caught his fingers in cloth. He jerked to a stop, clinging desperately to this anchor, chest and belly splayed across several stairs. Then, the stabilizing object whipped suddenly upward, breaking his grip. Before Collins' dizzy mind could register that he had been clasped to someone's leg, it swung back. A heel struck him in the eye, stealing vision and sending bolts of white light flashing through his brain. He tumbled, fully out of control again.

Collins had so many wounds, it all numbed to a single overwhelming agony that encompassed his entire frame and made coherent thought impossible. He registered only the savage plunge and the rumble of voices dulled by a steady ringing. He forced both eyes opened. Ahead, he saw the falling portcullis, with barely a body length remaining between it and the floor. *I'm a Musketeer.* On all fours, he launched himself for the opening.

It disappeared as he arrived. His face found delicious freedom an instant before the heavy wooden portal slammed into his skull. Vision shattered, hearing crushed by buzzing, limbs too heavy to lift, he lay in place fighting a losing battle with unconsciousness. His neuroanatomy professor's words cycled through his mind: *The difference between causing a brain bruise and a deadly hemorrhage is incalculable. Guy goes out longer than a minute or two, it's a murder charge for hero. A murder charge for hero . . . a murder charge for hero . . .*

Hands seized Collins' britches and tunic, hauling him back to the landing. *Got to stay conscious.* The movement proved too much. He closed his eyes, and darkness descended upon him.

Collins awakened to a limbo that dissolved in a fierce rush of pain. His breath emerged in agonized grunts, and he dared not move for fear of worsening any of them. Tears dribbled from his eyes. His mind seemed to work, though hopelessly overwhelmed by a throbbing headache and distracted by his myriad other wounds. "Oh, God," he managed to huff out. "Oh, God."

Collins opened his eyes, but they refused to focus. He blinked several times, catching a blurry impression of metal bars, a stone floor, someone standing nearby. The presence of another human might mean imminent danger, but Collins found himself unable to care. At the moment, they could slowly dismember him and he would consider it a favor. The cold of the stone floor seeped through his clothes, offering some relief from the bruises on his chest, arms, legs, and abdomen. His lids became heavy, and he let them drift closed. Once he did, sleep overtook him again.

Collins did not know how long he drifted in and out of consciousness, but he knew he had awakened on several brief occasions. His dreams had seemed more surreal than usual, taking him from home to school to Barakhai in moments that defied logic or consistency. He thought he remembered someone sewing the gash in his hip, the pain flowing into the mass that had come to define his current existence. Now, when he opened his eyes, the world came into instant focus. Prone on the damp, stone floor, he felt stiff as well as physically anguished. Enclosed by three stone block walls and one barred gate, he saw no other cells. Shackles and collars hung from chains, apparently the usual method of separating, controlling, or punishing prisoners. Collins shivered, certain he could not tolerate that kind of treatment in his current condition. *As opposed to what? Hanging?*

Having visually explored his quarters, Collins glanced beyond them. Two guards sat in the space between his cell and the door to the stairwell, watching him. Both men, they wore matching uniforms that differed from the ones of the tower guards. They had mail but no helmets, and the white portion of their tunics carried no design. A slight blond with swarthy skin and dark brown eyes, the one on the left followed Collins' every motion. The other, a dark brunet kept his sword drawn and in his lap. Though he had no reason to know, Collins guessed them to be dog-guards. A station below, they likely would wear simpler uniforms.

"Hello," Collins tried.

The guards studied him blankly, without replying.

Collins attempted to move. He hurt in every part, but he bulled through the pain to gather his limbs beneath him. They all seemed to function, at least, and he did not believe he had broken anything. *A small miracle.* He ran his fingers over his hip, through the tear in his britches, and touched a line of knots that confirmed his waking realization. Someone had tended the sword cut, stitching it in whatever clumsy, dirty fashion they did those things here. If it did not fester, it would scar badly. The irony raised a grimace. *So my executed corpse has a boo-boo.* He shook his head at his own stupidity. *Like it really matters.*

Only then did it occur to Collins to worry about Falima. He drew some solace from his solitude. Zylas' floor plan did not include two dungeons, so they should have brought her here if they'd captured her. *Unless they executed her.* He shoved that thought aside. *They'd have far more reason to execute me, and I'm still here.* He wished he could leave things at that, believing Falima safe and well; but reality intruded. He could imagine that treason might carry a stronger and swifter sentence even than murder. Or, as a trained warrior, she might have fought in a more directed and lethal manner than he had managed.

"Hello," Collins said again, not certain where to direct the conversation. He desperately wanted to know Falima's fate, but he did not want to place her into danger by mentioning her if the king and his guards had not yet made the connection between them.

The guards continued to study Collins in silence.

Collins eased himself into a sitting position, grimacing and grunting with every movement. Using the wall for back support, he regarded the guards with the same intensity as they did him.

The quiet stalemate continued for several minutes before

a knock at the wooden door sent both guards leaping to attention. Wishing he could still move that fast, Collins remained in place.

The door winched open cautiously, and a helmeted head poked through it. "Jiviss?"

"Here, sir," the blond said with a salute from around the door.

The newcomer glanced at Collins. "Has he changed?"

"No, sir," Jiviss said.

Collins disagreed. He had awakened and even managed to sit.

"The king wants to see him. In the upper quarters."

Jiviss shrugged, hiding the motion behind the door.

"Shackles?" the brunet said, his voice unexpectedly hoarse.

Jiviss returned to his scrutiny of Collins. "I hardly think they're necessary. In fact, someone's going to have to carry him, I'd warrant."

The newcomer frowned. "He fights, I'll deliver his bloody pieces to the king myself."

Tired of being discussed in the third person, Collins promised, "I won't fight." Realizing he would say the exact same thing if he did plan to fight, he added. "I can't fight. Just breathing hurts." He sucked in a deep lungful of air, sending agony shooting through his ribs, and reassessed the possibility that he might have broken something.

"He's not going anywhere." Jiviss seemed convinced that Collins' anguish was no act. He added emphatically, "And he is, apparently, royalty."

That caught Collins by surprise, though he swiftly realized it should not have. They had captured him in an area magically prohibited to *switchers*, and he guessed they had kept him in the dungeon long enough to ascertain that he had no switch-form. Even though the king did not know him, what else could they assume?

The helmeted man's demeanor softened. "You're right, of course." He addressed Collins directly. "Sir, you need to come with me. The king wishes to speak with you. No one will harm you if you come freely." He stepped fully into the area, revealing the aqua-and-stretched-clover pattern against white that Collins had first come to associate with royal guards.

Using one of the hanging chains for support, Collins clambered to legs that felt like rubber. *I'm sure he does want to speak with me. I've got to be a real puzzle.* "I'll come freely." He realized he had not done anything terrible yet. The king might forgive a relative's unauthorized presence in his room, especially when he found nothing missing. Collins felt certain his encounter in the stairwell had hurt no one so much as himself. As long as nobody made the connection between him and the man who had cannibalized a rabbit/woman, he might bluff his way out of serious punishment. He only wished he had the knowledge to convincingly fake it and wondered how much of his ignorance he could blame on the head injury. *It's not over yet. I still have a chance.*

The horse-guard took a ring of iron keys and shoved one into the lock. It clicked, and he stepped back. "Come."

Collins limped toward the entrance. Every muscle felt strained or bruised, and he tried to find a gait that caused the least amount of pain. Finally, he reached the exit. The horse-guard moved aside, drawing the door with him, and Collins exited into the guards' area. He waited there for them to cue him.

The horse-guard opened the wooden door. The brunet went into the stairwell first, then the helmeted man gestured for Collins to follow. He did so, and the two men settled into place behind him.

Clinging to the wall and scattered torch brackets in lieu of absent handrails, Collins made slow progress up the seemingly endless flights of stairs. He appreciated that the clockwise spiral kept the bracing wall always at his stronger right hand, though he knew the masons had never had him in mind for their construction. Likely, it had more to do with defense. Invaders running up the steps would have their sword arms hampered while defenders coming down would gain the advantage.

At last, the procession stopped, and the brunet knocked on the door opposite the king's bedchamber. It opened immediately to reveal a woman close to Collins' age. He recognized her from the dais table in the dining hall, introduced as one of the king's advisers. She wore a blue velvet dress with colorful embroidery and lace trim that complemented a slender but curvaceous figure. A hammered gold chain around her neck dipped into her bodice. Dark blonde curls fell to just past her shoulders, and strikingly pale eyes made her high cheeks and full lips seem rosier. She was the most beautiful woman he had seen since his arrival in Barakhai, perhaps in his life.

"Bring him in," she said, her voice a lilting alto. "Then wait outside, please."

"I'll see myself in." Collins hobbled into the room, while the guards settled in behind him and closed the door. Two cathedral windows lit the room, tapered from the inside to the out so that by the time they opened, they had narrowed to slits. The lowest part of the windows began at twice his own height from the floor. A cloth-covered table in one corner held a candle in a silver holder, a pitcher, and two goblets. Three padded chairs took up most of the center of the room.

The woman gestured at the chairs, and Collins took one gratefully. "Would you like a drink?"

"Yes," Collins said without bothering to ask about the contents of the pitcher. He had consumed nothing for at least fifteen hours. Thus far, pain had kept his mind from his belly, but he hoped his internal organs would resume functioning soon.

The woman crossed the room to the pitcher and filled both goblets.

It occurred to Collins that they might have poisoned the drink, but only briefly. They had had plenty of time to kill him if they had chosen to do so. In a spy movie, it would contain truth serum, but he seriously doubted anyone in this world had the wherewithal to create sodium pentothal. "Thank you."

She carried over both goblets, handed one to Collins, and sat in the middle chair.

"Thank you," Collins repeated, sniffing the pinkish liquid. It smelled faintly of alcohol and more strongly of fruit. "What is it?"

"Watered wine. Or more aptly, wined water. You'll find it's a bit safer to drink than straight city water."

Collins stared. This woman did not talk like any Barakhain he had met before.

She set her goblet on the floor beside her chair, rummaged through a pocket in her dress, and pulled something out. "You look like you could use some of these, too." She opened her fist to reveal a flat metal pillbox with *Advil* emblazoned on the side.

Collins' eyes widened, and understanding struck like lightning. "You're ... you're ... Carrie Quinton."

"Yes."

"Demarkietto's previous assistant."

The woman smiled. "How is ol' D-Mark anyway?"

The use of the professor's nickname dispelled all doubt. "Oh, my God." Collins chugged down his drink, too thirsty to set it aside. "Oh, my God. How ... how ..." He meant to ask about her arrival and subsequent life, but he only managed to finish with, "... are you?"

Quinton laughed. "Well enough for a woman trapped in a godless, primitive, louse-infested world ..."

"... that considers bugs a delicacy," Collins could not help adding.

"Actually, those aren't bad, once you get used to them. Aside from fish, milk, and eggs, they're the only source of protein."

Collins grimaced. "I think I'd stick with the fish, milk, and eggs, thank you very much."

Quinton rattled the pill case. "Go on. Take them. You look like you owe money to two guys named Guido."

Collins imagined he had to look a fright, bruised from head to toe, coated in travel grime, scrawny even before he skipped a few meals. He accepted the case and flicked it open to reveal four enteric-coated tablets of the proper size and shape. They even had *Advil* clearly written across each one, which fully allayed his suspicions. He dumped three into his palm, put one back, then popped the two remaining into his mouth. Quinton refilled his goblet, and he drank them down with the full contents. His belly felt stretched, but the meager calories in the two drinks only aroused his hunger. "Thanks." He thought back to something Quinton had said, "Once I find what I came for, you're no longer trapped. We can go home."

Quinton met the news with none of the excitement Collins had anticipated. "Is that what Zylas told you?"

Shocked by her knowledge, Collins stammered. "Wh–what?"

"Zylas. The white rat." Quinton studied his expression. "Or did he give you another alias?"

Quinton fumbled at the chain around her neck. "This is what he sent you after, isn't it?" She dangled an irregular peach-sized hunk of bluish-hued quartz from the necklace."

Collins could not find his tongue. "How could you ...? How did ...?" He licked his lips. "What ...?"

Quinton answered one of the unspoken questions. "I was working alone in the lab, and I followed a white rat here. Sound familiar?"

"Very," Collins admitted.

Quinton dropped the stone back down between her breasts, giving Collins a casual glance at well-shaped cleavage. "What did Zylas tell *you* it was for?"

"It?" Collins probed, averting his eyes too late.

"The stone."

"Oh." Collins turned cautious, bewildered by the situation. "He said it would get me home."

"It won't."

The abrupt cold pronouncement sank Collins' hopes and raised too many quandaries. "How ... how do you know?"

Quinton smiled. "I'm still here, aren't I?"

"Yes, but," Collins started, then caught himself. He had suspected that his companions had withheld information, but he had trusted them enough to believe it nothing significant. Now, he knew they had lied outright. Zylas had claimed no one from Collins' world had come to Barakhai before him, yet he sat talking to evidence of that deceit. *Unless she's the one who's lying.* Lives might be at stake depending on what he revealed. He shoved aside rising irritation. It made no sense to get angry until he knew for certain who had betrayed him. "You're still here, indeed," Collins finished lamely.

Quinton crossed her legs. "Zylas told me he needed that stone to rescue innocent people from the king's brutal regime."

"He did?" Collins clamped his hands over his spinning head, the abrupt movement awakening a whole new round of pain. He tried to sift logic from a sea of bewilderment, to find the truth hidden amidst so many lies. He studied Quinton. "Can you prove you're who you claim to be?"

Carrie smiled. "He's good, isn't he, that rat." She reached into the folds of her dress and extracted a battered wallet. She tossed a handful of cards into Collins' lap.

Setting aside the goblet, Collins sifted through the pile. Among Visa, Hallmark Gold Crown, and PetCo P.A.L.S. cards, all in the name of Carrie A. Quinton, he found two with picture identification. A Missouri driver's license showed her with shorter hair and a crinkled, quizzical expression. The student photo ID held a more flattering picture of a smiling Carrie Quinton with permed hair and the familiar pale eyes. No doubt, this was the same woman. Collins gathered the cards and returned them.

"Convinced?"

Collins nodded.

"Bill Clinton was president when I left." Quinton stuffed the cards back into the wallet. "You'd have a new one now."

"George Bush," Collins said.

"Again?"

Collins opened his mouth to explain, but Quinton waved him off.

"Kidding. I know it's gotta be George W. And no surprise, there. They knew that years before the election, before I left. Not sure why we even bother to vote."

Collins wondered what Quinton would think if she knew about the legal and political wrangling that had resulted in that squeak-by victory, but decided not to broach the subject. They had more important things to discuss, matters of faith and survival.

Quinton continued to vocalize proofs. "Before Clinton was Bush, Reagan before him, and Jimmy Carter the smiling peanut guy was president when I was born. And you and I are the only ones in Barakhai who know the difference between a dominant and a recessive gene."

"All right." Collins made a gesture of surrender. "You're the real deal. Now tell me how you wound up here."

Quinton gathered her cards, replaced them, then shoved her wallet back into its pocket in the folds of her dress. "I told you. I followed a white rat. He gave me this." She withdrew a hunk of white quartz from another pocket and deposited it on the arm of her chair. "I assume you have one, too?"

Collins did not reply.

Quinton continued, "He convinced me to try to steal this." She inclined her head downward to indicate the crystal. "I got caught, found out the truth, joined the right side." She shrugged. "Been here since."

Collins gripped the sides of his chair, the implications sinking deeply into him. He ran a finger along the stone. "It's a translation stone?"

"The guards searched you but didn't find yours." Though not a question, it begged answering.

Collins thought fast. Just because Quinton came from his world and time did not mean he could trust her with information that might harm people who, though more alien, he had come to consider friends. She would never buy that he had learned the language so quickly, and she apparently did not know about Prinivere. Recalling Falima's early dilemma, he tried, "I . . . swallowed it."

Quinton reclaimed the stone. "You did?"

Seeing no reason to swear to a lie, Collins shrugged. "The guards didn't find it. Did they?"

Quinton studied the rock. "I just didn't know it could work that way."

"Try it," Collins suggested.

The woman's features remained pinched with doubt. "Doesn't it . . . well . . . eventually come out?"

Worried they might start collecting and examining his excrement, Collins shrugged. "Mine hasn't. Maybe it got stuck, but it hasn't come out. At least, not yet." Needing to change the subject, he questioned. "So you're saying Zylas—?"

"Maybe I will try it." Gaze still fixed on the stone, Quinton did not seem to realize she had interrupted. "As soon as I'm with someone who can't understand every word I say without it." She smiled. "You don't know how long I've waited to talk to someone in English. I mean real English. And to hear the answer in good old English, too."

"Real English?" Collins laughed. His aunt and uncle had once visited Great Britain, returning with quaint stories of loos and lifts, windscreens and tellies. "I'm not sure anyone outside the United States would call what we speak 'real English.' Not enough u's, for one thing. Slangy and sloppy for another."

Quinton smiled. "It's real enough for me." She slapped the stone down on the arm of her chair, deliberately not touching it. She stretched luxuriously, showing off a long, lithe, and very feminine figure. It seemed almost impossible that she and Falima came from the same gender and species, though, in a way, they did not. "So," she purred. "How is Zylas doing?"

Collins shrugged, too vigorously this time. The movement ached through his body. "He seemed fine, but I have nothing to compare it with."

"Too bad."

Collins' brows rose. "You don't like him, I take it."

"No," Quinton admitted, then clarified. "Oh, he's charming all right. Friendly, easy to get along with, seems like a real straight shooter, right?"

Collins recalled times when he thought the rat/man might be hiding things from him; but, for the most part, he found the description accurate. "Yeah. Are you saying it's an act?"

"You betcha. And a damn good one."

"Why do you say that?"

Quinton met Collins' gaze with directness and sincerity. "Because he's a famous troublemaker, a rebel leader with plans to destroy the natural order and the kingdom."

"What?" Laughter jarred from Collins before he could think to stop it.

"It's not funny." Quinton's horrified expression gave Collins instant control.

"I'm sorry."

"He lured me here. He lured you here." Though it seemed impossible, Quinton's gaze became even more intense. "And I was not the first."

Now, Collins could not have laughed even had he wished to. "What?"

"Don't you remember?"

Collins shook his head carefully, though it still increased the ache. "Remember what?"

"The janitor. The one who disappeared about five years before I did."

Collins tried to recall. "The papers said he ran off with a young coed. Left a shrewish wife and three in-and-out-of-trouble teenagers to make a new, secret life."

Quinton's expression remained stony. "Want me to show you his body? And the coed's, too? Her name, by the way, was Amanda."

"Not . . ." Collins gulped. ". . . necessary."

"Before that was the kid who played that weird game, what's it called?"

Collins knew who Quinton meant. "*Dungeons and Dragons.*"

"Yeah, that's it. Got too wrapped up in the game and lost track of reality."

"Wound up in a mental institution, as I recall."

Quinton finished, "Rambling about ancient ruins, magic, and *people who transform into animals.*"

"Oh . . . my God."

Quinton fell silent and pressed her hands between her knees, letting the whole scenario sink in.

"Oh, my God," Collins repeated. "Damn." His mind moved sluggishly. "So you're saying that my following Zylas was no accident?"

"Nor me." Quinton leaned forward. "He led us here on purpose."

Collins had to admit it seemed right. He remembered chasing the rat into the proper room, losing it several times, only to find it again by what seemed like impossible luck. "Why?"

"To get this." Quinton dangled and returned the blue crystal again.

"Why?" Collins repeated.

"I don't know." Quinton sighed. "No one here does, but it has to have something to do with the rebels' plan to overthrow the kingdom."

Collins slumped in his chair, his world crumbling around him. Nothing made sense. The people he had dared to trust, to whom he owed his very life, were frauds. *True, Zylas saved my life; but it was his fault I needed it saved in the first place.* Other past uncertainties clicked into place. *No wonder he shushed the others when they grumbled about my underwhelming gratitude. And why he didn't dare hold Joetha against me.*

Apparently noting his distress, Quinton softened her tone. "I'm sorry. They had me fooled, too."

"They?" Collins repeated, not wanting to believe Falima had had a hand in the deceit, although she surely must have.

"Zylas and his accomplices. Different ones than you would have met. We caught the snake and the chipmunk."

"And?"

"And what?"

Collins had to know, could not help substituting Falima,

Ialin, and Vernon for the snake and the chipmunk. "What happened to them?"

Quinton hesitated. "You can't expect traitors in a primitive society to be treated with any more leniency than in our own."

Collins filled in the detail Quinton had implied but not voiced. "They were killed."

"Painlessly. And with decorum."

Collins blinked. When he had faced execution, he had turned a dignified ceremony into a panic-stricken tussle. Decorum seemed insignificant when the end result was one's own death.

Quinton's voice seemed to come from a distance. "Are you hungry?"

Barely noticing the abrupt change of topic, Collins nodded.

Quinton rose and crossed the room. She placed a hand on the door latch, then smiled without tripping it. Instead, she turned, walked back to her seat, and scooped up the translation stone. "Oops."

Collins lowered his head into his palms, thoughts a desperately unsortable swirl. He listened to Quinton's footsteps as she crossed the room again, heard the door winch open and a soft conversation ensue.

The panel clicked shut, and she returned. She wandered behind Collins, her delicate hands settling onto his shoulders. "Where were we?" she asked.

Collins spoke into his hands. "Discussing execution."

"Ah." Quinton kneaded the knotted, aching muscles of Collins' neck, and he winced. "We'll come back to that. Am I hurting you?"

She was, but her massage also comforted, a grueling mixture of pleasure and pain. "No," Collins lied, uncertain why. "It feels good." In his most testosterone-driven, adolescent moments, he had imagined a woman this beautiful touching him, concerned for his pleasure. The reality of it seemed well worth the torment. "You want to leave, right?"

"I did."

For the moment, Collins pushed aside the change of heart that answer suggested. "Why didn't you?"

Quinton's hands smoothed the tension from Collins' coiled muscles. "Tried. Couldn't find my way back, even with the kingdom's help."

Collins twisted his head toward Quinton, wishing he had some bulk to the muscles she was working over. Most women claimed they did not like the bodybuilder look, but he had yet to meet one who preferred his bony carriage. Despite the distraction, he found a discrepancy that made her claim seem ludicrous. "The king knows exactly where that portal is. He's got a contingent of archers parked right in front of it."

"What?" Carrie's hands stilled. "That's ridiculous."

Collins swiveled halfway around in his chair. "Is it? I saw them. They shot at me. Tried to kill me."

"The king's archers?"

"Yes!"

"Dressed in white and blue-green uniforms?"

Collins considered, forcing his mind back to the scene. Everything had happened so quickly, and he had worried more for his life than anyone's clothing. "They . . . didn't have a set uniform. They just wore any—"

"Who told you those were the king's archers?"

Realization dawned. "Zylas."

"Who had reason to keep you in Barakhai?"

Collins slumped back into his seat. "He wouldn't—"

Quinton restarted her massage. "Don't you think that if the king knew the location of the portal, he would *want* you to leave, not stop you? Don't you think he would work to close it, to stem the flow of outsiders sent by the renegades?"

Things Collins had not closely considered before became suddenly vitally important: Zylas' and Falima's discussion before claiming they knew of no others from Collins' world, the surreptitious exchanges between his companions when he received Prinivere's spell, the many little things that did not quite add up and often left him wondering if he were "missing something." He remembered Falima's deceit, trying to make him believe her a *Regular* rather than a *Random.* "Does this have something to do with the *Regular/Random* thing?"

"Not exactly," Quinton said. As Collins became accustomed to her ministrations, he noticed the pain less and the enjoyment more. "Most of the renegades are *Randoms,* though I think it's only because they tend toward instability. More undesirables are *Randoms,* since no one tries to make them on purpose. Of course they tend to be more likely to have a criminal bent, to not like authority or government."

It seemed logical that the least satisfied would seek the most radical changes, but that did not justify the events of the last several days. Zylas had seduced Collins here, knowing that others he brought had died for a cause in which they held no interest, understanding, or stake. Thanks to the renegades, Collins had to live with the guilt of having not only murdered but eaten an innocent woman, with the hysterical memory of having nearly died on the gallows, and with the knowledge of having become a thief as well. Rage finally stirred. "What does he want that stone of yours for anyway?"

"We don't know." Carrie admitted. She ran a hand through Collins' hair, fussing the overlong, grimy strands into proper position. "We're waiting for the dragons to mature."

"Dragons." Collins perked up at the word. "But they told me dragons were extinct." Carrie's fingers in his hair sent a shiver of desire through him that reawakened the aches the *Advil* had relieved. *At least one part of me still works.* "Was that another lie?" Though he now intended to reveal some information about the renegades, his vow to Vernon still bound his conscience. He would not give up Prinivere without a compelling reason.

"Dragons are extinct," Quinton confirmed. "But the king confiscated two *Randoms* who transformed into dragons at coming-of-age. The law compels him to kill them, but he just couldn't bring himself to do it. He's hoping that, raised and handled properly, they won't harm anyone."

"Wow."

The pace of Quinton's speech quickened, revealing excitement. "They're young now, babies by dragon standards. I figure they're maturing about one human year for every twenty. It seems the people here grow according to their slowest maturing form, and dragons—" Apparently realizing she had taken over the conversation, Quinton laughed. "Sorry if I'm boring you. I find them absolutely fascinating."

"I'm a bio grad student, too," Collins reminded her, interest piqued. "Are they male or female?" Simple statistics suggested a fifty-fifty chance they would come up opposite genders.

"Both," Quinton blurted, then laughed and corrected. "One of each, that is, not hermaphrodites. I get to train and, eventually, breed them."

Collins stared. "The king wants *more* dragons?"

Quinton's hands dropped back to Collins' shoulders. "Not yet. But I'm working on him." She squealed. "Can you imagine? I'm thinking they're egg layers, but they're definitely warm-blooded; and I think I'm seeing rudimentary nipples. Probably the closest thing to dinosaurs we'll ever see, don't you think? Imagine what we could learn from them."

Quinton's excitement was contagious. Though intrigued, Collins found himself distracted by troubling thoughts. The people to whom he had believed he owed his very life had actually placed it into danger. Those he had trusted as friends had lied to and betrayed him, played him for a fool. He pictured Falima; her silky black mane and startlingly pale eyes no longer seemed so beautiful when he knew they housed a soul that had used him, that found him unworthy of truth or trust, that pretended to like him while manipulating him like a brainless puppet. Zylas apparently made a career out of deception. *A rat, indeed. I should have seen through it.* His blood warmed, grew hot, and seemed to boil in his veins. "I'm with you," he said evenly. "Breeding dragons, finding the portal, going home."

"Revealing the traitors?" Quinton added.

Collins squirmed. *I owe the bastard nothing.* "What do you want to know?"

Chapter 16

MOMENTS later, Benton Collins sat in a pillowed chair nearly as comfortable as his father's old La-Z-Boy in front of a table laden with food. King Terrin occupied a similar seat across from Collins, and Carrie Quinton held a place to his left and the king's right. A large slice of white bread slathered in honey took up most of Collins' plate, surrounded by an array of berries in colors that ranged from deep ebony to brilliant green with stripes of indigo. He had chosen his meal from the myriad of dishes at the table, and many of the ones he bypassed still called to him. The warm aroma of sweet spices mixed with mashed, orange roots reminded him of pumpkin pie, and he instinctively reserved that for dessert. Though he had never cared for spinach, the buttery aroma of the assorted greens beckoned, and a platter of cubed fish smothered in a spice that resembled curry lured him to try it next. The complete absence of anything insectlike thrilled him, clearly a dispensation extended by the king.

Hunger got the better of Collins' caution, and he found himself incapable of concentrating on protocol. He dove into the meal with gusto, glad his choice of bread made sorting out the crude utensils unnecessary. As he gradually went from famished to merely interested in the feast, he deferred to Quinton's manners and worried more over what the king might think of him. The man held the power of an entire world. He could promote with a word, execute with a gesture.

Collins wished he had taken the time to grill Quinton on how to handle the situation. He knew next to nothing about royalty in general and less about Barakhain royalty in particular. A poorly chosen turn of phrase, an improper glance—anything might constitute a capital crime, Collins realized. Days ago, the simple act of filling his belly had condemned him to the gallows; and, then, he had not had the arrogant and arbitrary whims of a king to consider.

King Terrin seemed nearly as uncomfortable as Collins. He shifted in his chair and examined the food choices of his companions with hawklike intensity. Collins could not help noticing the lack of servants, guards, and food tasters, which he might have attributed to a genuine show of trust if not for the fact that they now sat in the room above the one he had shared with Quinton. *Switchers* could never make it through the door.

As Collins mopped up the last crumbs and filled his plate with all the delicacies he had missed, the king cleared his throat. "I understand your name is Ben."

Collins froze with the warm bowl of mashed, cinnamony roots clutched between his hands. "Yes, sir." *Sire,* he reminded himself, but it felt too weird to say aloud. He remembered the time he had gone for jury duty, equally stymied by the requisite, "Your Honor." He had grown up calling his parents' friends, and several of his teachers, by their first names. Titles implied a hierarchy that Americans prided themselves on never having to consider. All men and women, he had heard since birth, are created equal.

The king did not seem to notice the lapse of protocol. He looked at Quinton with darting brown eyes, as if begging her to assist him with the same propriety with which Collins struggled. He cleared his throat again and stroked the stiff amber curls of his beard with thoughtful motions. "And you come from the same place as Carrie?"

"Yes, sir," Collins said again, still incapable of forming his lips around "sire." That started to bother him. Since titles held little meaning in America, he thought he should be able to speak them as easily as any name. He wondered if it had to do with the same damnable honesty that kept him from saying "I love you" without long consideration and absolute certainty or singing the "dear" in Happy Birthday to a stranger. *Didn't keep me from lying to Korfius at all.*

That reminded him of the boy, another innocent caught in Zylas' and Falima's game. He should make certain Korfius did not get punished for a forced and contrived association. He shoveled the mashed roots onto his plate, then replaced the dish, only then realizing the king had asked another question.

"I'm sorry." To demonstrate the sincerity of his apology, Collins forced out the proper title. "I'm really very sorry, Sire. I missed what you just asked."

Without a hint of offense, the king repeated, "Do you know how you got here?"

Now that he had heard the question, Collins needed it interpreted. "I'm not sure what you mean, Sire." The title came out easier the second time. "I walked here under my own power. I was following—" He glanced at Quinton, wondering just how much the king already knew. The guards had escorted him directly here, and he had waited less than ten minutes for Quinton and the king to arrive. If she had briefed him on their conversation, it had not taken long.

Quinton nodded encouragingly.

King Terrin finished the thought. "You were following a white rat."

"Yes," Collins admitted, his food forgotten for the moment. "I'm not the first, I understand."

The king bobbed his head as Quinton had done, blond curls pitching and raising. The movement released a wave of musk. "There were three before you, including Carrie. The first two came together and got killed breaking into the castle."

Terrin did not elaborate, and Collins found himself less curious about the details than he expected. He did note that the first visitor, the D & D player, apparently never even made it to the castle.

"Then Carrie came, and talking with her brought sense to the matter." The king leaned forward, as if to share something private. "That rat, that agitator . . ." His gaze became distant, and he shook his head with a suddenness that revealed intense emotion: anger or frustration. ". . . He's been a thorn in our side for years. Circumvents every law, fights order at every step, despoils every logical decree."

Collins bit his lip, struggling to see Zylas in this new

light. Though enraged that the rat/man had tricked him, he could not help liking him. "Why?"

"Why?" the king repeated, straightening. "Why, indeed." This time, he consulted Quinton with his gaze.

Quinton responded with a flourishing wave. "Because it's the job of the royals to civilize a society of animals."

Literally, Collins realized and cringed. Though he had flirted briefly with idealistic anarchy, that phase had not lasted long. His politics had grown more centrist the older he got. And, while he still considered himself a democrat, no one would mistake him for an over-the-top liberal. He now accepted the necessity of leaders to maintain order and civility.

"And, sometimes, we have to make laws that place priority on safety over freedom."

It was the very definition of governing, creating laws that restricted the rights of individuals for the good of the community. "We have those, too," Collins said, not even trying to tack on the "sire." "I understand so far."

Quinton chewed and swallowed, her bites small and delicate. "For obvious reasons, enforced vegetarianism is essential."

Collins shuddered, once again reminded of his lapse in this regard. He covered with humor, spearing a piece of fish. "Sort of a lacto-ovo-ichthy vegetarianism."

Quinton smiled around her food. "Right."

Joy accompanied the realization that he had finally found someone to whom he did not have to explain a biology-based joke. He suspected the translation magic turned his description into "milk-egg-fish vegetable-eating" for the benefit of the king.

The king glanced between his guests. "Certain types of animals cannot control their appetites for meat."

"Carnivores," Collins said to Quinton.

"Some carnivores," Quinton corrected. "Cats and dogs, for example, have civilized to an omnivorous state. Like natural omnivores: foxes, bears ..."

"... people," Collins inserted.

Quinton nodded. "... they can be taught young to avoid meat. Scavengers, like vultures and hyenas, serve as a sort of cleanup crew and can get away with eating carrion, though most people find it as disgusting as we do. Herons, egrets, and 'gators eat fish. Lots of things can live off bugs. But certain animals . . ." She trailed off with a shrug.

Collins ate the piece of fish. Soft-textured, fresh, and lightly spiced, it tasted better than anything he remembered eating in a long time. "Like, say, lions? Wolves?"

"Exactly." Quinton shook back blonde tresses that shimmered like gold in the candlelight. "They got executed into oblivion long before His Majesty came to power." Speaking of the king apparently reminded her of his presence. She jerked her attention to him, and her cheeks turned rosy. "I'm sorry, Sire. I didn't mean to take over your explanation."

The king grinned gently, swallowing a mouthful. "Continue." He made a regal gesture. "You're doing marvelously."

"Anyway," Quinton continued awkwardly. "The only way carnivores come up is through *Random* breedings. Quite rare, but their danger is significant. On average, they kill six times before they're caught, so the law calls for destroying them as soon as the switch-form manifests."

"At thirteen," Collins recalled.

"At thirteen," Quinton confirmed.

Collins considered the implications, features crinkling. "So they execute innocent kids to avoid future crimes?" He turned his attention to the king as he asked the question.

Terrin studied his hands in his lap, without meeting Collins' gaze.

Quinton rescued the king. "It's an unfortunate circumstance, a fully avoidable one. People understand the risk they take when they breed *Randomly,* and it's always a conscious choice made in human form. Animals cannot interbreed outside their species."

"I saw a mule in the courtyard."

Quinton smiled. "Always the scientist, aren't you?" She laughed, the sound light and bellish, very different from Marlys' rare twitters or Falima's uninhibited, horsy guffaws. "Me, too. Mules are considered *Regulars* since their switchform is completely predictable when a donkey and a horse mate. They're also sterile, so there are no future offspring to consider."

Collins set aside his fork. "Wouldn't it be better to at least try to train these carnivores to eat bugs and fish?"

"Tried." Quinton rubbed the base of her fork. "Never succeeded."

Collins felt as if time had receded and he had returned to his argument with his father over the death penalty. "But what if one can do it? Shouldn't you at least wait until they commit a crime before irreversibly punishing them?"

"Let them kill someone else's child?" The king sounded anguished. "Six of them on average?"

"No," Collins said, still unable to reconcile the idea of confining someone, let alone inflicting the death penalty, simply because statistics said they would probably commit a crime. If the United States worked by the same rules, the jails would be overflowing with inner city black males, the ones destined to overcome poverty, prejudice, and cultural fetters lost along with those consumed by these conditions. The great ones, like Colin Powell, like Martin Luther King, would never have the chance to change the world for the better. "But . . . but . . . what about . . . ?"

Quinton tried to anticipate his question. "Ever see a tiger in a small zoo cage?"

Collins dropped the larger point to picture the striped beasts wandering in mindless circles. "Yes. They pace. But, if they could talk, I doubt they would say they prefer death."

"The ones of this world would disagree, according to the history books. A previous king tried imprisonment, and suicides resulted. Others begged for death rather than life in a cage."

Collins' doubt must have shown on his face, because Quinton turned defensive.

"Step out of the we-know-what's-best-for-everyone American persona for a moment. Dorothy, you're not in Kansas anymore."

Surprised by Quinton's sudden switch from empathetic listener to cut-the-crap critic, Collins forced himself to think in a different way. She had a definite point, one Falima had made much earlier. He had to stop judging Barakhai by twentieth century democratic standards.

Quinton's tone softened slightly. "You have to remember, we're talking about boring, nothing-to-do dungeons here. No phones, no gyms, no TV, and no conjugal visits."

"Why not?" Collins asked. At Quinton's "no one's that dumb" look, he clarified. "I mean why no conjugal visits?"

"No birth control, either," Quinton reminded. "Does Barakhai need more vicious carnivores to further crowd its dungeons?"

Collins had to insert. "But *Randoms* are random—"

"Not completely. There's a definite genetic component to what they become." Quinton spoke to her area of expertise. "Not strictly Mendelian, I don't think, but—" Apparently realizing Collins had exploited her own interests to throw her off track, Quinton returned abruptly to her point. "How many ladybugs do you think it would take to fill up a full-grown lion, anyway? Hard enough supplying adequate protein for the innocent people. According to my studies, iron deficiency anemia is rampant here. I'm surprised they don't see more kwashiorkor, too."

Collins went quiet, picturing large-eyed, African orphans with skeletal limbs and enormous bellies caused by the severe protein malnutrition she had mentioned. In fact, Quinton had several valid points.

"Our rich society gives us a lot of leeway these people just don't have. You notice a lot of small people here? Nutritional adequacy's a constant battle in an undeveloped society, and the kids can't just pop a Flintstone's with Iron." Quinton's blue eyes seemed to drag Collins' gaze deep inside of them. "You can't coddle murderers when you can't properly feed the loyal and innocent. Capice?"

"Capice," Collins said in a small voice, turning his attention back to his meal. As he ate, he wondered how much of their exchange the king had understood and whether or not he found any of it offensive. Abruptly remembering what had brought them to this point in the conversation, Collins attempted to turn it back to his original question. "What does all this have to do with Zylas anyway?"

Quinton and King Terrin traded glances, and the king took up the explanation again. "He had a daughter."

The rest seemed obvious. "A carnivore?" Collins guessed, chest tightening and food once more forgotten. His mind formed an image of the albino standing in stunned silence while guards hauled his little girl away to die, his face a white mask that defined abject, depthless sorrow. He remembered the earlier tears when Zylas mentioned not having a family.

"Yes," King Terrin said.

Collins could not help saying, "Poor Zylas."

The king pursed his lips, head falling. Quinton's jaw tensed, and she wrested the discourse from him again. "I thought the same thing. At first. Then I discovered how many daughters and sons, mothers and fathers died because of his . . . his junta. His rabid schemes to destroy the Barakhain hierarchy, to ravage the kingdom and the royal family have resulted in so many deaths: guards, his own followers, innocent bystanders." She tried to catch Collins' gaze; but, this time, he dodged her. "Bystanders like Bill the janitor and Amanda the coed. Like me, almost. And you."

Collins swallowed hard, head ringing. The information he had gained revealed so much he had never suspected, explained so many of his former companions' nudges and lapses. *Zylas, Falima, how could you do this to me?* He felt like a lost child.

The king's voice was soothing, fatherly. "What happened to the horse, Ben?"

The horse? Collins was momentarily puzzled by the question, and then understanding hit. His nostrils flared, and his eyes widened. *He means Falima. They know! They know who I am. What I did.* "The horse?" he repeated, trying to hide his nervousness. Perhaps he had misunderstood.

"The one who saved you from the gallows," King Terrin said, without malice. "The buckskin who goes by the name of Falima."

"The gallows," Collins repeated, a tingle passing through his neck where the rope had once lain, and a shiver traversing his body. "You . . ." it emerged in a desperate squeak, ". . . know?" He added quickly, "Sire?" This did not seem like a moment to skimp on propriety.

"Of course we know," Quinton said. "And unlike the renegades, we're not going to lie to you. Didn't you think Olton would let the king know about a murderer on the loose?"

"Olton?" Collins did not know whether Quinton named the place or an informant. Though it did not matter, he focused on the detail to delay the moment when he discovered his fate. Whether they sent him back to that town or performed the execution here, he would end up just as dead. He wondered why they had not just left him to rot in his cell rather than bring him here to talk to Quinton and the king. Within a moment, he had the answer. *Because they plan to get as much information as possible from me first.* His manner grew guarded.

"Olton's the town that sentenced you," the king explained. "We'd still like to know about the horse."

Collins could not get past the matter of his future, or lack of one. "Are you going to hang me?"

The king and Carrie Quinton jerked. Simultaneously, they said, "What?"

Collins rose, scarcely daring to believe how calm they remained, how surprised they seemed that he might worry about his neck. "Are you sending me back or performing my execution here?"

"Neither." The king's leonine head swung up to follow Collins' movement. "As soon as Carrie and I figured out what you had to be, I pardoned you."

Quinton added, "Didn't you notice no one was chasing you anymore?"

"I . . ." Collins started, sinking back into his chair. "I thought we just eluded them."

Quinton's wispy brows rose nearly to her hairline. "Eluded human-smart hounds? Please."

Collins could scarcely believe it. "So I'm not going to be hung?"

"Hanged," Quinton corrected. "The past tense of 'hang' when you're killing someone is hanged. Laundry is hung."

How do you like that? Falima was *right.* "Thanks. My grammar really is more important here than whether or not I'm flung off a platform so a heavy rope around my neck *chokes me to death!*"

Quinton's lips twitched at the corners. "Sorry. Just one of those pet peeve things." She added, "If you were actually going to get hanged, I wouldn't have said that."

Collins grunted, still sarcastic. "Of course not. That might have seemed . . . well . . . tacky."

The smile became genuine. "Just so you know, if they had to drag you there, you'd be *dragged,* not drug."

With his life spared, Collins enjoyed the banter. "But a load of laundry would be drug?"

"Dragged, too," Quinton said. "It's always dragged. Drug is a noun or a verb, but the past tense of drug is drugged."

"Not drag?"

"The doctor drag her prior to surgery." Quinton laughed. "Nope, doesn't work."

Though not a part of it, the king smiled broadly at their friendly exchange.

Growing remarkably comfortable, Collins had to wonder whether or not *he* had been drugged. "Not that I'm complaining, Sire, but why did you pardon me? You didn't know me."

"Ah, but I did." King Terrin turned his gaze to Quinton. "Once we figured you for an *Otherworlder,* Carrie could innocently explain all your actions."

Collins poked at his food, considering. "I spoke a completely different language." He popped some mashed roots into his mouth, delighted by the flavor. He tasted cinnamon and allspice in a mixture halfway between sugared pumpkin and sweet potato.

"That was a big clue." Quinton pushed her plate aside. "Also, that you made no attempt to hide your crime from the guards showed you had no idea you did anything wrong."

King Terrin reached for the serving bowl of mashed roots. "You killed and ate in human form. Murder rarely happens like that and cannibalism never."

Though he craved more of the root dish, Collins put his fork down. He schooled his features. "I want you to know I'm very very sorry about what I did. I've suffered a lot of recriminations, tears, and soul-searching to deal with it, and I still have moments of heart-wrenching regret. If I had known—"

The king raised his hand. "You would not have done it. I understand."

"Thank you, Sire," Collins said, this time without difficulty. If his original companions had forgiven him this easily, they could have spared him and themselves a lot of bickering and discomfort. "I don't have the words to express how much I appreciate your understanding."

The king ladled root-mash onto his plate. "You need say nothing more."

As it sounded as much a command as a suggestion, Collins obeyed.

The king sat straighter in his chair, steam from the root-mash twining into his beard. "You have a choice, Ben. You may stay here and become another adviser."

"A generous offer, Sire," Quinton inserted, and Collins wished he had had the chance to say that first.

"Or you may show us the way to the portal so that you and Carrie, if she wishes, may return to your home."

I'm going back. Excitement trembled through Collins. *I'm going home.* "Thank you, Sire," he said, not voicing his choice because his quick decision to leave might offend the king.

Quinton clutched the front of her dress. "So you know the way to the portal?"

"I—" Collins started, then stopped with nowhere to go from that point. "I ... don't you ... I mean ..."

No one jumped in to help him.

"The way to the portal?"

Quinton's hands sank to her lap.

Collins shook his head to clear it. "Shouldn't be that hard to figure out. It's in a set of ruins on a hill not far from Olton. The guards caught me in a field close by. They should know."

The king and Quinton exchanged glances.

Quinton shook her head. "We sent guards to where you got caught. I remembered coming in through ruins, too; but the only ones they found that looked right took us nowhere."

Collins crinkled his eyes as the impossibility of the statement overtook him. "How can that be? How many ruins are there?"

"A lot." The king answered before Quinton could. "Centuries ago, the kingdom sat in that very area, sprawling for miles, with cities and towns at myriad locations. You can't go there without running into the ruins of something."

Collins' eyes slitted further. "Maybe if Carrie and I went with your guards, Sire. Taken place to place, surely we'd recognize—"

"Tried that," Quinton interrupted. "Amazing how similar a crumbling pile of stone and mortar can look to another crumbling pile of stone and mortar. Over hundreds of years, things get picked through until nothing of value remains for a landmark."

Collins shook his head, maintaining his confused

expression. "But Zylas uses the portal again and again, so there must be some way to recognize it." He considered his next utterance, not wishing to offend. "Men do have ... some advantage in the spatial relations realm."

Quinton adopted a deep, broken caveman speech. "Girls talk, men logic. Ugh." She pretended to scratch herself, ape-like. "I got a 780 on my math SAT, I'll have you know. That's about an eyelash from a perfect 800."

Glad he had not resorted to the word "superior," Collins tried to make amends. "I'm not saying women are dumb, just that their brains are wired different from men's. Not worse," he added swiftly, "just different."

"Different*ly*," Quinton said.

"Differently." Collins accepted the correction without comment, especially since it served to make his point. "Look, women have that extra X chromosome that protects them from hemophilia, color blindness, and a whole host of other deadly diseases. They live longer. They've got an advantage when it comes to verbal and nonverbal communication. Men had to get something."

"Testosterone?" Quinton suggested.

Collins knew his only hope now lay in self-deprecatory humor. "I mean *besides* the drive to kill each another."

Quinton laughed, opening the way for Collins to finish.

"And it just happens to be a better handle on how one object relates to another."

"Which is why guys never ask directions."

"Exactly." Collins grinned. "To do so would be abdicating our maleness, our one claim to ... to equality."

The king, who had quietly feasted on the roots while his guests argued the merits of gender, finally spoke. "I'm afraid I can't let you leave the castle, Ben. At least, not yet."

Collins' smile wilted. "I'm a prisoner?"

The king laid aside his fork. "Not at all. You're free to go anywhere within the fortifications. The guards will politely stop you from going farther."

Although Collins had no plans to go anywhere, the idea of a restriction bothered him. "If I'm not a prisoner, then why?"

King Terrin did not bother to consult Quinton this time. "We've been honest with you. Dangerously so. We can't risk you rejoining the renegades."

Collins weighed the king's words. The man had a point. He thought of Zylas, picturing the fair skin and soft waves of tangled, snowy hair beneath the ever present broad-brimmed hat. The pale blue eyes had always seemed so wise, so desperately earnest, a strange contrast to the inscrutable red beads he looked through in rat form. They had formed such a swift, strong friendship based on the mortal danger they had shared. Danger, Collins now knew, contrived by the very man he had seen as a savior. He thought of Falima, unable to suppress a smile. That evening in Vernon's cabin when they had finally reached an understanding, that camaraderie could not have been feigned. *And Vernon*. Collins still had difficulty reconciling the enormous man to the tiny mouse he became. Vernon had mentioned that he remained in mouse form, and Zylas a rat, whenever he visited Collins' world, even if he passed his switch time. Collins wondered if that had something to do with a difference in the physical laws in effect in each world. *Thank goodness gravity, at least, works the same.*

Realizing his thoughts had rushed off on a tangent, Collins redirected them. He knew the king wanted him to give up as many of the renegades as he could. They already knew about Zylas and Falima, so he did not need to worry about betraying them. He doubted he had any information about those two that the king did not already know. Collins saw no reason not to surrender Ialin, too. The tiny man had treated him with persistent hostility despite the trials he and his friends had deliberately caused for Collins. The realization irritated him. *At least Zylas and Falima had the decency to acknowledge their debt to me.* Which brought him to Vernon. There, Collins found a real dilemma. The mouse/man clearly dedicated his life to assisting people of many types, often without explanation or reason. Daily, he put himself in danger to help others, and he apparently did it from innate kindness rather than any expectation of reward.

I thought Zylas was a good guy, too. Collins grimaced at the realization. For reasons he could not fully explain, he believed Vernon truly had no ulterior motives. And then there was Prinivere. He realized how important knowing about her would be to the king, yet he also liked her. His vow to Vernon, though a sham, ached inside him. He had promised to keep her existence a secret, and his word meant more to him than he realized. Though the ceremony of spitting and shaking had no real significance, the fact that Vernon believed it did brought it to a whole new level. And Korfius was completely innocent. These thoughts rushed through Collins' mind faster than he expected. "I need time to sort all of this out before I make an irreversible decision."

"Understood." The king seemed unperturbed by this response. "And until then, you must see why we need to keep you here."

Collins did understand. "Yes, Sire." Politeness seemed the best policy. "And I appreciate your hospitality." Though no one had threatened or even suggested it, Collins realized they held a trump card. If he refused to cooperate, they could reinstate his death sentence. He appreciated that they made it look like his choice, though, in the end, he truly had none. On the other hand, he saw advantages to leaguing with Barakhai's royalty. Quinton's presence, alive, well, and happy showed the king rewarded loyalty. He and the geneticist had spent time alone together. Even if the king had some way of listening in on their conversation, Quinton had shown that she could switch to English simply by setting aside the stone. Surely she would have warned him of any hidden agendas or cruelties of King Terrin or his staff.

Aside from holding him at sword point and in a cell, both understandable under the circumstances, they had, thus far, shown Collins nothing but kindness. They also seemed almost brutally honest in their dealings with him. In exchange for some information about people who had lured him into mortal danger and then accepted credit and trust for rescuing him from it, he would get a pardon, a way home, a beautiful companion to corroborate his story and maybe even, through a shared experience no one else could understand, a life partner. That he could pick and choose who he exposed and no one could know that he had done so proved the icing on the cake.

Collins needed time alone to think, and the king of Barakhai happily granted that request.

Chapter 17

BENTON Collins awakened to the scattered glaze of sunlight through the slit of his window. He sat up and stretched, regretting it immediately as a wave of suffering washed through him. His bruises and strains had stiffened during the night, but time and sleep had erased the sharp edges of pain. He lay in a bed of simple construction, just a wood frame and blanket-wrapped straw, but it far exceeded the one in Vernon's cottage. The cloth had warmed to his body through the night, and the idea of leaving the snuggly cocoon formed by his coverings seemed onerous. He glanced around the room. A chest of drawers filled most of one wall, full of clean clothing he looked forward to pulling over a body too long enmeshed in the same grimy tunic and britches. They had allowed him a bath before bed, a luxury more welcome even than painkillers or sleep. A table sat in the middle of the room, a basin of fresh water on its surface and a chair at its side.

A single pounded knock echoed suddenly through the chamber.

"Who is it?" Collins called.

He received no answer; but, shortly, another knock hammered against the door.

Guessing the wood was too thick to admit voices, Collins hopped from the bed, dressed only in a long, linen sleep shirt. He pulled the wooden panel open to reveal a guard who took one look at his garb and averted her eyes. "Sir, there's a woman who wishes to see you." She gestured lower on the spiral staircase.

Collins poked his head through the opening. A short, chunky woman stood there, glancing at and around him nervously. He did not recognize her and wondered what she wanted. "All right." She stood too far away to address directly, though she surely heard him. "Tell her I'm coming as soon as I dress."

The guard continued to avoid looking at him. "Very well, sir." She withdrew.

Collins closed the door and examined his sleep shirt. It fully covered him, and he guessed it made the guard uncomfortable only because of its purpose. It reminded him of the discomfort of barging in on a woman in her bra and panties, though the same woman in a bikini on the beach seemed perfectly decent. *All of which is ridiculously moot in a place where people see one another naked all the time.* He amended the thought, *Except the royals, of course, and I'm now considered one.* He rummaged through the drawers, pulling a crisp tunic, a thin long-sleeved shirt, and britches from piles of similar ones dyed different colors.

Collins threw off the sleep shirt and tossed it on the bed, smoothing the blankets into reasonable order. Since the bedroom was on the top floor, no maids could enter to clean it. He wondered if the king also made his own bed or whether lower level royalty or children served as menial labor in these "safe" areas of the castle. He pulled on the clean clothing, fitting the shirt under the tunic and tucking his watch neatly beneath the sleeve. Now that the king knew what he was, he saw no need to hide the device; but he had no intention of trying to explain it to every curious guard and servant who noticed it. He pulled on the boots the king had given him, made of soft cloth stiffened with wooden battens.

By the time Collins exited, the guard had left; and only the strange woman remained. He excused himself to use one of the garderobes. Returning, he joined her on the spiral staircase. She fidgeted as he approached, and her hands moved into various positions before finding a haven in the pockets of her dress. She wore her chestnut hair short, and sunlight struck highlights of blonde, black, and red through the strands. She had brown eyes so pale they looked almost yellow, and they dodged Collins' with uncomfortable caution. "My name is Lattie. Could we talk outside?"

Collins nodded, glad to move from the stuffy confines of the castle to fresh air and sunshine.

"I'm sorry I woke you." Lattie led the way down the stairs, past a pair of guards who stopped chattering and watched them go. "It is late morning, and I thought—."

Collins tried to make her feel at ease. "I was up. Just hadn't bothered to dress yet." It was essentially true. He had awakened before the knock. He did not press her for her business, though curiosity pounded at him. He had only just become a welcome member of the royal entourage that night, and it seemed impossible that people in the king's employ would already seek out his advice. *Of course, now is the best time. Once they have a taste of my uncanny wisdom, they'll all know to steer clear of it.*

After passing several more guards and servants, Lattie and Collins departed the castle, through the open portcullis. The sun beamed down, too warm for the long shirt he had chosen to hide his watch. The sweet odors of grass and pollen wafted to Collins' nose, a pleasant change from the stale smells of old food, mustiness, and mildew. Horses in a variety of conformations and colors grazed the grassland, while dogs wound among them. A group of children squealed and giggled as they threw balls as much at as to one another. Gardeners weeded, joined by goats and geese who carefully plucked around the healthy plants.

Lattie stopped walking, glancing around to assure no one stood close enough to overhear. "Before we go any further, I want to apologize."

Collins' shoulders lifted in a questioning shrug. "Apologize? For what?"

Lattie looked down. Collins followed her gaze to the wood and cloth sandals on her feet. "I—I'm the one who got you . . . hurt."

Collins let his gaze stray up her thick legs, over the bulges of belly and breasts, to her round baby face. "What do you mean?"

"I reported to King Terrin when you went in his room." Lattie shuffled her feet in the dirt. "I didn't know you. I worried . . . I mean . . . the king's own room."

"It's all right." Collins reassured, needing to know. "How did you see me?"

"You . . . you . . ." Lattie's gaze fell back to her footwear. "You . . . stroked me. It felt . . . it felt very nice."

Stroked her? Collins pursed his lips as his mistake became utterly clear. *The cat on the window ledge.* "It's all right," he repeated. "You had no loyalty to me, and I'm sure the king believes you did right."

Lattie sucked in a deep breath and let it out in a slow, relieved sigh. "Thank you for your forgiveness." Her attention remained on the ground, and she continued to shuffle. "I'm going to switch-form soon, and I wondered if you would . . . if you would . . ." She seemed incapable of finishing.

Collins smiled, believing he knew the rest. "You want me to pet you some more?"

"You must think me very forward."

"Not at all." Collins wondered what the cats in his world would say if they could talk. "Where I come from, once you choose to own a cat, your lap belongs to them."

Lattie finally met his gaze, her eyes moist with horror. "Own?" she repeated.

Oops. Collins laid blame the only place he dared. "Sorry, I'm new to your language. I meant, if you live with a cat, it gets your lap whenever you make one. Cat hair becomes an accessory and a condiment. When you're not petting them, they're rubbing against you, even if that means lying on your book, marching across the table, or standing in your plate."

Lattie's eyes fairly sparkled, and she asked not quite casually, "Where are you from?"

Collins laughed. "Too far for you to go, I'm afraid. I'm not even sure I'll ever get back there." Not wanting to explain, he returned to the original topic. "Actually, I find petting animals calming, so I'd enjoy it as much as you do."

"Really?" Innocent excitement tinged the word.

"Really," Collins replied, meaning it. He still had a lot of thinking to do, and experience told him he could do so in a calmer state and more clearly with a contented cat purring in his lap.

Lattie circled Collins with a sinuous grace, her earlier nervousness lost. "I know a place. A private place, in case some of the others don't understand. It's got catnip, too."

"Catnip. Hmmm." Collins did not know what to say, as he had no particular affinity for the stuff. In fact, he would not even recognize the growing plant; despite his science background, he had only a passing interest in botany.

Caution tainted Lattie's otherwise excited demeanor. Clearly, Falima had a point about the dubious propriety of petting Barakhain animals.

Collins raised his arm, allowing his sleeve to slide back just far enough to peek at his watch, which read 10:50 A.M. So far, everyone who switched did so on an exact hour, which seemed like an uncanny coincidence until he remembered he had reset his watch by Zylas' switch time. Presumably, Lattie would transform at 11:00, and he refused to take her into his lap until that happened. So far, he had remained faithful to Marlys, though he already planned to break up with her if he ever managed to see her again. Carrie Quinton's behavior suggested he might have a chance with her, and he had no intention of ruining that opportunity to appease a cat.

Lattie led Collins toward the inner gatehouse. Guards stood in the towers, looking over the outer courtyard. The doors were open, allowing free passage between the courtyards. A man led an oxcart through the passageway, the vigorous, young beast effortlessly hauling a load of hay. A sow slept in the pile, two piglets of varying sizes nosing around her. Lattie stepped aside to let them by, then gestured Collins through the gatehouse.

Collins paused, watching the cart creak and rattle toward the castle, not wanting anyone to think he was trying to escape. At Lattie's urging, he continued, looking up as they headed into the outer courtyard. The guards remained at their posts, giving him only a passing glance. He eased out a pent-up breath, realizing that the king must consider both courtyards available to the castle staff. More horses and dogs occupied the inner areas, along with guardhouses, stables, and kennels to house them; but they moved freely between the two areas.

Lattie continued walking, leading Collins along a path through the grasslands, past mixed herds of sheep, cows, and goats, to a shaded garden filled with a mixture of flowering plants and covered by a fringed cloth canopy built against one stone wall. Tall thistles stretched into makeshift walls on either side, blocking the garden from general view and making it appear as if it had no safe entrance. Bees buzzed by on their way to and from the flowers, and butterflies flitted in colorful circles through the air.

Lattie brushed through an area that looked impenetrable. Beginning to wonder if he had made a dangerous decision, Collins followed. Thorns glided from his sleeves, rattling against his heavier britches and tunic, then parted to reveal a simple garden. Unlike the tended patches of the inner courtyard, this one grew relatively wild. Flowers of countless hues intermingled patternlessly, and vines twisted through them to overflow from the low stone frames. In the center sat a clay bowl on a stand, looking very much like a birdbath, though the canopy did not admit rainwater. Beetles and bees hovered around it, and Collins caught a sweet, unfamiliar scent beneath the already clashing perfumes of the various flowers.

Collins turned to question his companion, only to find her gone. Soft fur tickled his ankles. He rolled his gaze downward to the plump calico he had discovered in the castle stairway window. The issue of the bowl's contents would have to wait until he met with Carrie Quinton again, since his current companion would remain an uncommunicative animal for at least the next twelve hours.

Collins wandered farther into the garden until he found a carved granite bench. He sat, leaning against the smooth back. Cold seeped through his britches but could not penetrate the double layer of his shirt and tunic. The cat leaped up beside him. Before he could even find the most comfortable position, she clambered delicately into his lap, curled into every contour, and purred.

Laughing, Collins stroked the multicolored fur, immediately drawn to memories of his childhood. In those days, his parents had made a handsome, seemingly happy couple. Fluffy had had her choice of laps, preferring Mom's but accepting his when she was not available. Though third choice, Dad enjoyed his time with the cat, often devoting his full attention to stroking the silky fur, examining the ears for ticks or lice, the body for scratches.

Collins forced his thoughts to his current situation. Essentially alone in a sweet-smelling garden, caressed by spring breezes, his wounds dulled to a tolerable ache, a refreshing sleep just behind him, he felt contented and clear-headed. During the night, his thoughts had shifted and resettled. He liked the king and the beautiful woman who shared so much in common with him: a student trapped in a world where magic usurped laws that had once seemed utterly obvious and infallible. People changed into animals, stones and spells allowed otherwise impossible communication, massive dragons not only existed but cast magic and flew. Pardoned from the gallows, he no longer felt the anxious rush to return home to Demarkietto's demands, his imminent breakup with Marlys, his parents' self-indulgence. He wondered if anyone even missed him yet, aside from the inconvenience of dirty rat cages and experiments lost to unintentional neglect.

Carrie Quinton filled his mind's eye. Beautiful, graceful, intelligent, she seemed the perfect woman . . . and way out of his league. Yet he dared to hope that their shared interests and experience might bring them together. Like the veterans of Vietnam, they had become part of a world that strangers would never understand, that would likely taint their lives for eternity. That alone would have to bring them together, if not as a couple, at least as lifelong friends. Her decision to touch him, her gentle kindness, gave him hope where once he would not even have dared to consider a relationship possible.

Necessarily, Collins' thoughts went to Zylas and his crew. The king's and Quinton's explanations brought so much that had once seemed fuzzy to brilliant clarity. A million tiny details that had eluded him or that he had tossed away as unimportant now worked their way to the fore. Clearly, Zylas had deliberately brought him to Barakhai. He remembered how the white rat had kept appearing just when he had lost hope of ever finding it. Zylas had led him directly to this world; and, he now knew, others before him. All the things Collins had gratefully accepted: Zylas and Falima saving his life, returning his watch and cell phone, feeding and clothing him, protecting him from taunts and disdain, had become a sham. Zylas owed him all of that and more. One simple discovery, that Zylas had deliberately lured him here, turned the whole relationship, the whole matter, on its ear.

Lattie rubbed against Collins' hand, purr insistent. He

increased his attention, running both hands the full length of her silky body, dislodging fur to spin wildly through bars of sunlight. So many glances, so many stifled comments and other-language exchanges gained meaning. It now seemed clear that he would give up Zylas, Falima, and Ialin to the king; but other things still needed consideration. He believed Terrin would understand Korfius' decision to join them, given that it mostly hinged on loyalty to the royal line, to which he believed Collins belonged. Though Vernon likely had some understanding of the scheme, Collins liked him and hated the thought of getting him into trouble. As to Prinivere, he needed to understand more about why dragons had become extinct. Given the greatness of her age and the withering of her magic, she seemed harmless without the enhancing stone. Perhaps he could negotiate for her life as well.

The thistles to Collins' left rattled. He glanced toward them, hands stilling on the cat.

Lattie butted his hand.

The plants quivered again, the movement too broad for wind. A yip wafted to him.

The cat froze, attention now on the sound as well.

Suddenly, a dog burst through the foliage. Ears swung down beside an ebony head, followed by a long-legged black body. It launched itself at Collins.

Lattie's body swelled to twice its normal size, and she yowled a warning. Her claws sank into Collins' leg.

"Ow!" Collins sprang to his feet, dumping the cat. She scrabbled wildly, raking gouges into his already bruised thighs. The dog hurled itself into Collins' emptied lap, all legs and tongue. The cat raced into the gardens. The dog flew after her, tearing up plants and flinging dirt with every bound.

Collins charged after the animals, trying to stop them. "Hey!" he yelled. "Down, dog! Get down!" He watched helplessly as Lattie scrambled up a canopy post, the dog yapping at her heels.

"No! Bad dog!" Collins lunged for the dog's neck, but it bounced out of reach, still barking at the cat.

Lattie made it to the top, but the give of the canopy turned her motions into an awkward stagger and roll. The dog pranced around the stake for several moments, keeping just beyond Collins' reach. Then the cat lost her footing, tumbling to the center of the canopy where she thrashed desperately. The dog continued leaping and barking at the overhead lump in the fabric of the canopy. Lattie yowled in terror. Abruptly, the dog raced from the garden.

For a moment, Collins breathed a sigh of relief. Then, realizing he could not rescue Lattie from beneath the canopy and that the dog might know another way to get to her, he sprinted after the dog. Thistles jabbed his legs, ripping his right sleeve, and vines snagged his ankles. He fell on his face, rolling from the brush to the freedom of the grassy courtyard. He saw the dog running toward the stone stairway leading to the parapet. The nearest guards paced several yards away and clearly had not noticed the dog.

Collins struggled to his feet, every injury reawakened by the fall. Despite the pain, he managed a frantic sprint. The dog scrambled up the stairway. Collins reached the bottom as the animal gained the platform, then turned sharply toward the canopy. The dog's plan became clear. The canopy lay almost flush with the wall, and the dog could easily leap from the parapets to the entangled cat. Gravity would pull both struggling animals to the center where they might tear and bite each other to serious injury or death. Or the cloth could tear, spilling both animals to the hard ground. Collins quickened his pace, thundering up the stone stairs as fast as his screaming muscles would carry him.

"Hey!" someone shouted from the ground. A horse whinnied wildly. "Hey, you can't—"

Collins was not listening. He reached the parapets and turned sharply left, toward the garden and the dog, who had slowed to a lope.

"Stop," Collins yelled, trying not to look down. "No! Bad dog!"

To his relief, the dog whirled toward him.

"Bad dog!" Collins shouted again. "Leave that cat alone. Come here."

The dog obeyed, soaring toward Collins at a perilous gallop. Collins tensed to brace himself; but, at that moment, something sharp smacked into his left cheek. Thrown off-balance, he took a step to regain it. His foot came down on a soft object that screeched, then disappeared from beneath his boot. Collins staggered backward, the world spinning dizzily beneath him. The dog hurled itself into his arms, throwing him and itself out over the parapets.

Air slammed Collins, slinging his scream back into his face. He flailed wildly, panic overwhelming thought. He saw the moat rushing up to meet him, the dog twisting in midair. Then, he slammed into something much harder than water, incapacitating pain arching through his gut, agony spiking through him and overwhelming logical thought. He felt the world moving beneath him and grabbed on to keep from falling into black oblivion. His fingers winched around rope, holding him in place, and water splashed his face. A high-pitched voice sounded in one ear, over a disharmonious chorus of ringing, "Hold on, and you'll be all right. I promise."

Dazed and disoriented, Collins did as the voice told him. It reminded him of his tonsillectomy, awakening from anesthesia memoryless and suffering inexplicable pain. Then he had yelled for his mother, worsening the anguish in his throat, and he had cried for a long time afterward. "The cat," he croaked out.

"She's fine." The voice stayed with Collins, vaguely familiar, soothing, and the only thing he had on which to ground his reason. "You're fine. Lie still, and don't try to talk."

Collins closed his eyes, still clinging to the rope, and let his body go limp. He concentrated on tactile sensations, the steady movement and velvety surface beneath him. He tried to put the whole thing together. *I was in an accident. A fall. They're taking me to surgery.* Memory trickled back into his mind, and it did not fit the scenario at all. *Anesthesia dreams,* he reassured himself, but it did not ring true. He opened his eyes. The ground scrolled out beneath him: sticks, stones, grass, and dirt. He lay slumped across something hard, his legs dangling and his hands wound beneath smoothly braided ropes. *This is no hospital; I'm outside.* That discovery led to more. He smelled damp air and the distinct odor of horse. Shouts massed behind him, and birdsong wafted from in front. Finally, it all came properly into sync. *I'm lying across Falima, and she's carrying me away from the castle.*

Once Collins found the truth, it all seemed ridiculously obvious. Dyed as black as the horse, Korfius ran alongside them, and the voice in his ear could only belong to Zylas.

Ialin had deliberately flown into his face, he had stepped on Zylas, and Korfius had completed the task by knocking them both from the parapets. The audacity of the plan floored him back to speechlessness. *We could have been killed.* He dared not move for fear of rolling beneath Falima's flying hooves. He knew they could crack open his head like a melon, and he could not take any chances. If he attempted escape, he might be worth more to them dead than alive.

The trailing shouts grew distant, then disappeared. Unable to fight for the moment, pain shocking through his body with every stride, he surrendered to the unconsciousness he had fought moments earlier. Blessed darkness gradually overtook him.

Benton Collins awakened with clear thoughts and a near-total lack of pain. Both of these realizations surprised him. Moving only his eyes, he glanced around an irregular, dimly lit cavern that smelled densely of musk. It reminded him of driving down a highway after a previous motorist had run over a skunk. Though a bit unpleasant, it compared favorably with the time he and some friends went hiking and one of the black-and-white striped animals ambled from the foliage. Before anyone could stop him, Collins' dog had leaped for the creature. So close, the resulting odor had burned Collins' eyes and throat. One of his companions had vomited, and the dog ran yelping to the car, tail wedged between its hind legs.

Zylas the man appeared from one of Collins' blind spots, circling to his head. The albino crouched, pale eyes studying Collins, hair falling in a milky curtain across his left cheek, features tensely sober. "Feel better?"

Much, Collins admitted grudgingly, but only to himself. "What did you do to me?"

Zylas blinked, but otherwise remained still. "Rescued you?" Clearly, the rat/man did not know whether or not he answered the correct question.

Collins had meant what had Zylas done to take away his pain, but he saw no reason not to continue the conversation from Zylas' response. "Rescued me?" He pushed up on one elbow. "Rescued me from going home? Or from a life of castle luxury?"

Zylas attempted humor. "Both?"

It was exactly the sort of thing Collins would have tried, but this time he saw nothing funny about it. "You tricked me to Barakhai. You lied to me. You put me in dangerous situations, then pretended to rescue me." He glared. "Why am I even talking to you?"

Zylas swallowed, still answering Collins' rhetorical questions. "To find out why I did those things to you?"

Though somewhat flippant, the response satisfied Collins. "All right, I'll bite. Why did you do those things to me?"

"Do you really want to know?"

Rage warmed Collins' blood. He wanted to tell Zylas to go to hell, to leave him alone and get out of his life; but curiosity would not allow it. He did have to know. "I deserve an explanation." He added bitterly, "But why should I believe anything you say?"

Zylas' shoulders slumped, and his head fell. "I'm sorry."

Collins gave no quarter. "Sorry I caught you? Or sorry you did it?"

"Sorry . . . I involved you in this." Zylas carried the expression Collins' mother wore when he disappointed her with his behavior. It never failed to make him feel guilty.

Now, Collins shook off the snap reaction. He had every right to wallow in spite and anger. "So you admit you lied to me."

Zylas sighed. "Let's say misled. I don't think I ever actually lied." Wrinkles creased his forehead. "So you're saying the king wasn't going to execute you?"

"Would I have been strolling freely around in the outer courtyard if he was?"

"That did seem odd," Zylas conceded. "Made things a lot easier for us to . . . to . . ."

"Kidnap me?" Collins suggested.

"But I thought—"

Collins did not wait for the rest. "You thought wrong."

"The others—"

This time, Collins let Zylas finish, but he did not. Instead, he went off on a different tack.

"Ben, the king wanted you to think you had some freedom. Had you tried to escape—"

"—the guards would have stopped me," Collins finished. "I know. He told me that."

"Once the king got the information he wanted from you, he would have executed you."

"I don't believe that."

"It's true."

Collins had proof. "He didn't execute Carrie Quinton."

Zylas went utterly still.

Collins sat, raising his brows in expectation.

A genuine grin broke out on Zylas' face. "Carriequinton is alive?" He did not wait for confirmation, but leaped to his feet and ran from the cave shouting, "Carriequinton is alive! Carriequinton! She's alive!"

Collins shifted to a cross-legged position, uncertain what to make of the whole situation. Out of his company, it had seemed so easy to surrender Zylas and his friends to the king. Now that they had come together again, the idea seemed heinous. Traitor or not, Zylas was still a human being. He did not deserve to die.

Zylas returned shortly with a slight woman in tow. Beyond her, Collins saw movement. Several others hovered in the tunnel behind them. Curious, he looked the other way. Another exit across from the first stretched into a blackness that contained several shifting shadows.

"Is Carriequinton . . . all right?" Zylas asked carefully.

"She's an adviser to the king. And she seems happy."

The woman spoke next. Small and mousy, she sported black hair and fair skin. Dark eyes looked out from small sockets. "Are you certain it was Carriequinton?"

"Trust me," Collins said, reveling in the irony.

The woman nodded.

Zylas resumed his crouched position in front of Collins, while the woman sat down beside him. "You requested explanation. I will give it to you."

Collins refused to let Zylas off the hook. "How do I know you're not just telling more lies?"

Zylas pursed his lips in consideration, then brightened. "I swear to God, with sugar on top, that I will tell you only the truth from this moment forth." He spat on his right palm and offered it to Collins.

The absurdity of the moment melted away most of Collins' malice. *Caught by my own lie.* Rolling his eyes, he spat on his hand and exchanged a shake before wiping it on his britches. *In my effort to pacify Vernon, I invented a new way*

to spread diseases in this godforsaken, Lysol-lacking world.
"Talk."

Zylas cleared his throat and sank to his behind. He studied the rocky ceiling, as if deciding where to start. The onlookers shifted, their whispers barely reaching him, uninterpretable. "Over the years, the royals have taken a stronger and stronger hand in the coming-of-age of *Randoms*."

Collins nodded to indicate that he knew. "King Terrin said he had to in order to separate out those creatures likely to murder others."

"That was, ostensibly, the original reason for doing so."

"Ostensibly?" Collins remembered having trouble with the idea of executing people who mutated to carnivores simply because they might harm someone. He recalled something more personal. "He said he had to execute your daughter."

Zylas' eyes watered, but he managed to suppress actual tears. "Trinya." His voice cracked, betraying the withheld weeping.

Collins continued, speech slowing as he watched the effect of his words on Zylas. "He said that's why ... you ... cause him ... so much trouble." From the corner of his eye, he could see the woman cringing. She placed a hand on Zylas' shoulder.

Zylas could not hold back the tears any longer; they glided down his cheeks, pale dewdrops on a background of snow. "I was trouble long before ... that."

Collins said nothing more, allowing Zylas to regain his composure.

The mousy woman stroked the fine, white hair and looked anxiously at Collins through beadlike eyes.

Zylas swallowed hard, wiping his eyes with the back of one white, long-fingered hand. "... before ... he murdered Trinya and Erinal."

Collins shook his head. "Erinal?"

"His wife," the woman explained before Zylas could. "They were—"

"Seera ..." Zylas warned.

She talked over him, "—childhood friends—"

"Seera," Zylas repeated, apparently her name.

"—and obviously deeply in love. I never saw two—"

Zylas' verbal prompting did not stop her, but his dark glare did. "Ben has more important matters to worry about than my relationship with my dead wife."

At the moment, Collins did not agree. The dead wife might have much to do with a situation he was continuing to sort through, hoping to fully understand. "What happened to her?"

Seera's face went as chalky as Zylas', and she placed a hand over her mouth. She left the explanation to Zylas, who rose and paced, clearly distressed. "She wouldn't let go." He dropped his head, hair flopping into ivory disarray. "She wouldn't . . . let . . . go."

"Of Trinya," Seera explained softly.

"The king's guards couldn't . . . couldn't . . ." Zylas remained in place, clearly waiting for Seera to finish his sentence this time.

Seera complied. "They couldn't pry the two apart."

Zylas finished in a rush of hissing breath. "So they tried to cut off Erinal's . . . her hands. But they couldn't get all the way in one — " He dropped to his knees, sobbing, and Seera rubbed his upper back. "Screaming. There was blood and — "

Collins grimaced, trying not to picture the scene. But he could not banish the image of a young woman pleading desperately, grasping for her terrified child with hands dangling from half-severed wrists. "Oh, my God."

"If only I was — "

Now it was Seera's turn to caution, "Don't. You couldn't be any closer than you were. You were a hunted outlaw. They would have executed you on the spot."

"But maybe Erinal and Trinya — "

"They would still be dead. And you, too. Then where would the rest of us be?"

"They wouldn't let me staunch the bleeding." Zylas was weeping uncontrollably now. "Why wouldn't they let me staunch the bleeding?"

Even Collins could answer that. "Because they wanted you dead more than they cared whether or not she lived." Zylas' grief ached through Collins. He felt helpless as a statue while his usually unflappable friend dissolved in front of him. The anger and bitterness vanished, replaced by a pure rush of sympathy so intense it left him speechless.

For several moments, they all remained quiet, drenched

in a grief too intense to bear. Even the onlookers grew respectfully hushed and still.

Finally, Zylas spoke. "We should have known not to make a child, both of us distant descendants of Prinivere."

"Prinivere?" Collins blinked making a connection that seemed obvious but might prove absurd in this otherworld, where even the basic principles of science did not always apply. "Are you saying Trinya's switch-form was ..."

"A dragon," Seera said, barely above a whisper.

A chill spiraled through Collins. "A dragon? Is that ... common?"

Zylas looked up. "As far as any of us know, she was the only *Random* ever to become one."

"If Carrie told the truth," Collins pondered aloud, "then there are at least two." He met Zylas' bleary gaze. "Zylas, your daughter might still be alive."

Chapter 18

THE conversation that followed left both men with unexpected hope. Collins came to understand that his
companions had brought him from the castle to an area
where dogs could not track him. Like the flowering tree
where the group had hidden just before Korfius found
them, the skunk odor that pervaded the quarters of Barakhai's *downcaste* garbage workers should hide their scent
from second tier guardsmen.

After a meal and a bath, Collins felt more open to explanations. Alone in a straw-cushioned cavern with Zylas, he
listened to the rat/man with an open mind. "You see, the
less you knew, the safer you, we, and a pack of innocents
remained."

"Maybe." It was a point Collins did not know if he could
ever accept. "It might be the scientist in me, but I like to
work with as much information as possible. The less my ignorance, the more I can figure out what to do to keep myself, you, and these innocents safe."

Zylas laced his fingers, dodging Collins' gaze. "I understand that now." He finally met the probing dark eyes. "But,
at first, you didn't want to know that much."

"You mean when I thought I was going right home?"

"I guess so."

"But you knew I wasn't going right home. You should
have told me that, too."

"I didn't know what the best thing was." Zylas threw up

his hands. "It was supposed to be simple. Bring you here. Have you get the stone. Get you home."

Collins sat up straight, holding Zylas' attention now that he had finally seized it. "But you knew it wasn't that easy from the start. You brought others before me. Others who went mad. Others who *died*."

Zylas closed his eyes and nodded sadly. "But you were different. I chose you much more carefully."

The words startled Collins. "You did?"

Zylas' lids parted to reveal the familiar, pallid eyes. "I watched you for a long time. Made a well-researched, long-studied decision. Surprised?"

"Very," Collins admitted. "Why me?"

"None of us wanted more deaths, and you are our last hope."

"I was your last hope?" Collins forced himself to blink, still stunned. "How so? My world has about five billion people at last count. You could always grab another."

"No. You *are* our last hope." Zylas thrust his hand into a pocket, emerging with the translation stone. "Our last of these, my very own, this one a unique treasure because it allows communication even in animal form. I was supposed to give it to you, but I just couldn't let it go. I won't put Prinivere through that spell she cast on you again for any reason. She nearly died, and she's not getting any younger. She's still weakened from it."

The details did not fit. Collins tried to clear his head, to force order to the last vestiges of chaos. "Why didn't the people of Falima's town guess what I was, given that I wasn't the first?"

"To them you were."

"Oh?"

"You were the first to leave the ruins before I could switch to man form and explain."

"Why didn't you just talk to me as a rat? You had the stone."

"What do you think drove our first visitor mad?" Zylas blinked with slow deliberateness. "And what was your hurry to go tearing off into the unknown, anyway?"

Collins felt foolish. "I was hungry. Very very hungry."

"I left you food."

Collins ran a hand through dark brown hair that seemed

to have grown an inch since his arrival, and it felt wonderfully clean. "I–I didn't see any food."

"You didn't look."

Collins felt a warm flush of defensiveness. "You should have put it in plain sight."

"If I made it too obvious, you would have worried you had stolen it from someone else. Or that someone had laid it out for you, poisoned."

Collins doubted either of those possibilities. "I was too hungry to worry about things like that." He thought it far more likely he would have passed up the stems, roots, and insects as some science experiment rather than food. *Given how well-read I am, it took me stunningly long to realize I had entered another world.* "And how do you know what I would have worried about anyway?"

Zylas shrugged. "As you pointed out, I made mistakes in the past. But I want you to know this. You were the first one to leave the ruins prematurely and the only one who killed. The others kept searching for the way back home." The corners of his lips twitched, but he did not smile. "And I thought your need to find these might keep you there long enough." He drew Collins' glasses from another pocket.

Collins gasped, snatching the offering from Zylas' hand and planting them on his face. Instantly, the cavern leaped to bold relief. He had forgotten how sharp every crag could look. Each blade of straw became singular and distinct, its colors a gradual blend of yellow, white, and gold. He saw lines in Zylas' face he had never noticed before. "Thank you, you horrid little thief."

Zylas grinned to show he took no offense. "You're welcome, you big ugly murderer."

Though faced with a harsh joke, Collins forced a chuckle. He resisted the urge for a crueler one, though Zylas had given him the ammunition by opening his life's story. He did not want to discourage the albino rat/man from sticking with even the most difficult truths.

"You weren't supposed to kill anyone, and you weren't supposed to get arrested."

Collins nodded, realizing a grimmer truth. At that point, Zylas could have abandoned him for another champion as they had not yet met or spoken. Collins could not have given away any information anyway, since he would have been executed before he found a way to communicate. "How did you ever manage to get Falima in position?"

Zylas waved a dismissive hand, as if to proclaim the whole thing no bother. "We'd been working on her for years, carefully trying to sway her to our side. You can see the advantage to having a horse-guard as a spy."

"Yes." Collins wondered how much convincing it had taken to push her that final step knowing that it would involve turning herself into a wanted fugitive to help a man she considered a murderer and a cannibal. *No wonder she acted so hostile toward me.* He could understand why they had chosen Falima, a *Random* considered a lesser being than the other guards, at least according to her. He had to know, "You took a huge and *unnecessary* risk saving me."

"Unnecessary?" Zylas' brows rose with incredulity. "I had led you here. I couldn't just let you die."

It was not literal truth. Zylas could have let him die simply by doing nothing, though Collins knew he meant his morality would not have allowed it. "Ialin would disagree."

Zylas did not deny it. "As did Falima at one time. She came around. He will, too." From a pocket, he pulled out the folded, broad-brimmed hat he usually wore to shield his easily burned face and eyes from the sun. "Though I would spend my life for my cause, I don't expect others to do so." Anticipating some comment about those who came before Collins, he added swiftly, "usually. Besides, I had chosen you too carefully. We needed you." All humor left his features. "We still do."

Zylas looked so earnest, so pleading, Collins found it impossible to meet his gaze. He might have to refuse him. "What's so special about me?"

"You're smart and resourceful. You're willing to sacrifice for others, and you really do understand how they feel."

"Well." Collins felt his face grow hot, embarrassed by the praise he had elicited. "I try to be a good person."

"You are," Zylas said. "I knew it from watching you. Dogs obey all horse-guards and superiors, but they like people of good character."

Collins wondered if Korfius' loyalty sprang more from believing him royal, but he had to admit the boy seemed to have a deep affinity for him.

"And Prinivere supports you. That's the highest praise I know."

"Thank you," Collins said, though the previous lies left him wondering whether Zylas' tribute stemmed more from desire and need than truth. "So tell me. What, exactly, does the stone do?"

"What did the king tell you?"

Collins blinked. "Will that change what *you* tell me?"

"No," Zylas said firmly. "I just wonder . . ."

"He doesn't know."

Zylas grinned broadly. "Good."

"Nor do I," Collins reminded.

"Yes, you do." Zylas dipped his head with clear sincerity, wadding the hat in his hands. "It enhances magic, pure and simple. It would, hopefully, give our Prinivere enough power to help us. Maybe even enough to reverse this curse."

"Curse?"

Zylas stared, as if he found Collins' question the most absurd one ever uttered. "This whole spending half our lives as animals thing. You know."

Collins physically jerked backward. "You can . . . fix that?"

"Don't know yet. Prinivere needs to have the stone in hand—or should I say in claw—to analyze it."

"Wow."

"Yeah," Zylas agreed. "Now do you understand why we want it?"

"Yes," Collins said, though he shook his head. "But why don't you want the king to know? Stopping the switching helps everyone. Doesn't it?"

Zylas threw the question back to Collins. "Does it?"

Collins folded his legs and leaned against the cavern wall, considering. He wondered if his bland perspective made him miss something obvious to those whose lives cycled from human to animal on a daily basis. He supposed someone with perfect overlap might find some advantages over those who fully lost half or more of their rational time to becoming some lumbering, half-witted creature. *People like Zylas.* Collins shook his head. The very one he thought might have the least reason to change was the same one who daily risked his life for it. "All right, I give. Who would want to keep the curse going?"

"Don't you think there might be substantial power to remaining human full-time while those around you mark time for half of their existence? Hard to contemplate insurrection when you're awake and thinking a third of the day or less."

Collins suspected many of his fellow students managed to function on less. "Unless you have near-perfect overlap."

Zylas' hands stilled on the hat. "Now you know why I'm a wanted outlaw."

Collins returned to the point. "So you think the royals wouldn't want the curse removed?"

Zylas heaved a deep sigh. "I think it's time you heard the whole story." He rose to his feet. "From one who was there."

There? Uncertain, Collins followed Zylas with his gaze. Before he could question further, Zylas disappeared through the entryway.

Collins rose also, though he did not attempt to follow. The musky odor had become familiar; it filled his nose and mouth like a persistent aftertaste. He took a few steps in the direction Zylas had gone, turned on his heel and started back the way he had come. The world seemed to have turned upside down, spun around three times, then whirled completely around again. He did not know for certain who to trust anymore. His sympathies intuitively went toward Zylas, though he could not guess whether this stemmed from truly believing the albino in the right or just because he had gotten to know the man first and better than the other side. It reminded him of the movie *Butch Cassidy and the Sundance Kid,* where he could not help rooting for the criminals mostly because the story got told from their point of view. Only one thing seemed absolutely certain. He needed to get home to a world where science made sense and the studies that had taken all of his adult life and money had purpose. At the moment, he would consider selling his soul for a Big Mac, large fries, and a cup of fountain root beer.

Zylas returned shortly with a familiar old woman in tow. Prinivere seemed dangerously frail in human form, her skin a mass of paper thin wrinkles, her eyes deeply recessed, her hair thick but nearly transparent in color. She wore a light, shapeless gown that hung to her knees. She looked older than the last time Collins had seen her, only days ago.

Collins nodded and smiled in greeting. "Good afternoon, my lady."

Prinivere returned a feeble smile. "Forgive my appearance—" she started.

"You look lovely," Collins found himself saying, the words seeming foolish and yet, to his surprise, oddly true. Survival and great age had an almost inexplicable beauty all its own.

"She wore herself down healing—"

Prinivere interrupted Zylas. "No reason to talk about that, my dear."

Collins did not need the last word to realize what had happened. She had tended his wounds, which explained why he no longer suffered the pain of his falls. "Thank you, Lady Prinivere. I feel very well now, but you shouldn't exhaust yourself for my bumps and bruises."

Prinivere smiled, the wrinkles piling up at the edges of her lips. "Healing magic is not expensive." She did not give him the opportunity for a reply. They could argue the point all day and still remain at an impasse. "But I've come to tell you a story."

Collins lowered himself to the ground in front of Prinivere. He still had many questions and hoped the story would handle most of them. "Please."

With Zylas' hovering assistance, Prinivere also sank to the straw. The rat/man took a space beside her.

Without further preamble, Prinivere began. "A long, *long* time ago, when I was young, our world was much different. Humans and dragons had waged a war since long before my birth. It was not the type of war with many battles. Simply, the dragons raided the flocks of men when food grew scarce or they became too old and slow to catch the wilder creatures. And the humans found slaying a dragon a means to prove their courage or rescue their animals. More often than not, however, those clashes resulted in the death of the man."

Collins nodded, recalling how terrifying even a feeble, elderly female dragon had seemed, though he had known at the time she would not harm him.

"They had spears and swords to pit against our claws and teeth, armor to thwart our spikes and tails. But they had no way to counteract our magic."

Collins' mind conjured images of brave knights riding off to slay dragons, only to return as charred heaps of bone in the satchel of some bypasser. Feeling he should say something, Collins inserted, "You'd think the humans would sacrifice a few sheep and goats to keep the peace."

Zylas shivered, but Prinivere only bobbed her head knowingly. "Yes, you would think so. For you realize what our friend, here, could not. These animals were animals through and through. The humans themselves regularly ate their herds and flocks as well as harvested their eggs, milk, and wool."

"It sounds very much like the olden days of my own world," Collins said. "Except, of course, for the dragons." He savored a situation where, for the first time, he seemed more in tune than his companion. Suddenly, he had found an explanation for the antique hunt scene tapestry in the king's bedroom.

Prinivere continued, "There were fewer people then, and they all lived within and around a single city, ruled by a kind and intelligent king named Larashian Elrados. He made peace with the dragons. Men could no longer hunt us for sport, and the city would welcome our visits. In return, they donated a portion of their crops, hunts, and animals to the oldest and youngest of us. Favors became as common as conflicts once were. It was not unknown for a dragon to carry someone on his back or to heal an injured man. And the people would help us with thorns and burrs, with flotsam caught beneath our scales, and they educated us about the ways of their civilization. To seal the accord, the dragons presented the king with a powerful talisman, a stone that could amplify magic. Though the humans could not use its power, did not even understand it, the king recognized that it had momentous significance to the dragons and accepted it with great honor and ceremony."

Prinivere fell silent, and her gaze rolled toward the ceiling. Zylas placed a comforting arm around the frail and sagging shoulders. Collins waited in patient silence for her to continue.

"The peace and friendship lasted throughout Larashian's long and just rule and into his grandson's. Telemar, too, seemed kind and competent. So, when he requested a closer bond between our families, it seemed reasonable to consider the request. Not all of our kind believed it wise, but our elders finally agreed to allow a dragon to take human form with magic for the purposes of breeding with the king's eldest daughter." Prinivere heaved a sigh filled with ancient pain.

"Why?" Collins found himself saying without thinking. Prinivere had explained the reasons, but they did not seem substantial enough. Kingdoms in his world had sealed accords with royal marriages and even exchanges of children; but he could not see any good coming of sexually comingling intelligent species.

"Why indeed." Prinivere's voice emerged in a puff of hoarse breath. "With centuries of hindsight, I believe the king wanted to implant magic into his own line. We had tried to teach them, but people lack something in their life substance that we naturally have."

"Or the reverse."

Wholly jarred from her story, Prinivere stared. "What?"

Under the full and intense scrutiny of both of his companions, Collins suddenly wished he had kept his thoughts to himself. Now did not seem the time for an extensive discussion of inheritance. Few enough species could interbreed, and all of those had common ancestors. Chimps shared about ninety-nine percent of their genetics with humans, yet that last one percent created so many differences. It seemed impossible to imagine that dragons and humans could cross-fertilize. *Magic,* he reminded himself. *Magic.* Still feeling the stares, he explained as simply as possible. "Perhaps humans have something dragons don't, something nature uses to protect them from using magic." Worried his words might sound supremacist, he added, "Because we can't handle it or something." Uncertain whether he had dug himself out or deeper, Collins changed the subject. "Why did the dragons want to do it?"

Prinivere ran with the question, to Collins' relief. "The dragons argued several reasons: that an important ally wanted it, that it would bring our peoples closer, that it would force all humans to see us less as animals. And one must not discount simple curiosity. They made sure the king understood the risks to his daughter. She was more than willing, especially once she saw the handsome, charming, mannered man our Ardinithil became. He stayed that way only long enough to get the job done, however, though she made it clear she would have liked to marry him."

"Dragons don't marry?" Collins guessed.

"We don't call it marriage." Prinivere's green eyes swiveled downward to meet Collins' directly. "But we do pair for life." She closed her eyes in a long blink. "We did pair for life. When more than one of us lived."

Three. Collins opened his mouth but glanced at Zylas before speaking. The rat/man shook his head ever so slightly and mouthed something Collins could not comprehend. He guessed Zylas had not yet discussed the two young dragons in the king's care and had some reason to keep him from doing so as well. It seemed unfair to withhold such important information from Prinivere, but he also knew Zylas always had his ancient ancestor's best interests in mind. When the right time came, he would tell her.

Apparently oblivious, Prinivere returned to her story. "Anyway, Ardinithil could have married her—human lives span so short a time, he would have become free to pair again still in his youth. But he had no wish to return to human form, as she surely would have wanted, so he refused. The king accepted this without obvious malice, and life continued much as it had. Until . . ." Prinivere trailed off, clearly lost in bygone thought.

Collins looked at Zylas, who shrugged. They sat for several moments in silence. Then Collins ventured a guess, "Until the birth of the baby?"

As if awaiting this cue, Prinivere returned to life. "Yes. The babies."

"Twins?"

"Dragons nearly always have twins. Occasionally singles. Rarely triplets. I once heard of four babies together, but only once in several centuries."

Collins suddenly realized why this particular interbreeding bothered him so much. "Dragons have live-born young?"

Prinivere turned her head toward Zylas, as if to get more coherent explanation for Collins' strange questions. Clearly equally befuddled, Zylas raised one shoulder and tipped his head without speaking. Prinivere returned her attention to Collins. "Don't all animals have live-born young?"

"Birds lay eggs. Reptiles and amphibians, too." Collins

did not know if Barakhains categorized the same way as scientists, so he elaborated, "Turtles, alligators, snakes, frogs." He carefully omitted fish, not wishing to compare her to a creature they did not consider animal. *Dinosaurs.*

Zylas cringed, but Prinivere did not seem offended. "Dragons do not lay eggs."

"Oh." That now being obvious, Collins found nothing more to say.

"We have live-born young." Prinivere used Collins' terminology. "Like humans." She rubbed her hands together, looking uncomfortable. "Usually." She folded her fingers in an interlocking pattern, biting her lower lip. "We monitored the pregnancy with magic, and it soon became clear that the babies, both boys, were unhealthy. Usually, we magically ended such pregnancies for the good of our society, the well-being of the parents; but the king refused to give up on them. His attachment to the hybrids became an obsession that changed him, and he would allow nothing and no one to harm them.

"To our leaders' surprise, the unborn gradually regained their health; but they did so at the expense of their mother. Dragons don't sicken as humans do, which is why our healing magic works only on injuries, not diseases. It took our monitors many months to realize what was actually happening. Months passed, during which they sensed the babies growing stronger and the mother weaker before they realized the inherent and unconscious evil of the process. The babies were drawing their strength, the very essence of their survival, by draining the life of their mother."

Unlike most Barakhain science, this made sense to Collins. Undernourished women often became ill during pregnancy while the fetus, essentially a parasite, sucked whatever nutrients it could from her blood. No one he knew would consider that process evil, however.

"Once the dragons realized what was happening, they begged the king to allow them to destroy the unborn babies. He refused. For the last few months of the pregnancy, our requests went from wishful to desperate to angry. The king would hear none of it. Even risking the life of his daughter did not seem too high a price for the twins whose very existence he had facilitated for reasons that had once seemed pure and noble. We explained, we pleaded, we ranted, all to no avail. The twins whom nature intended to be stillborn thrived while the mother meant to lose them lost her own life instead."

Prinivere clambered to her feet, and Zylas scrambled to remain at her side. Her eyes seemed to blaze through their ever-present glaze of water. "The boys looked odd for humans, their eyes too long with oval-shaped pupils, their noses like ..." She placed a hand over her own slitty nostrils. "... well, rather like mine in human form. They had points to their ears, and their skin looked more like dry scales. The humans feared them, and the dragons hated them. But their grandfather adored them. He smothered them with finery and servants, bad-mouthed those who shunned the boys, doted on them to the point of fulfilling their every whim. He demanded that the dragons train the boys in the ways of magic. The dragons, who could sense darkness in their hearts, still felt the boys should die. We refused, re-creating a rift between our societies. The boys grew up deeply spoiled and also deeply embittered."

Prinivere shook herself from head to toe, the movement strangely animal. "The firstborn, Shalas, wanted only to forget what he was, to live his life as a normal human. The second, Shamayas, resented what he should have become. He would watch us flying effortlessly overhead and desperately wished he could spend half his life in dragon form, as he felt he deserved. These desires became as focused and determined as the king's love for his hybrid grandsons, so much so that each developed a single magical ability even without our training. The boys' innate evil, the strong and covetous nature of their wishes, warped them to self-defeating talents. Shalas gained the ability to make others forget, but never himself. Shamayas could turn other's lives half-animal but not his own."

Collins grimaced at the horrible irony and wished his companions would sit. The story shivered through him like a horror movie, and having the two towering over him only intensified the discomfort. "So that's how the half-animal transformations came about?"

Prinivere held up a hand, curled like a claw. "Thinking they might find the significance of the dragon's stone, the king gave it to his grandsons. Their terrible powers mightily enhanced, the boys used them in a grander fashion. The first caused the populace to forget. The second inflicted hybrid lives on them, excepting only the king, his queen, and a few others of the royal line who struck their fancy. And, inadvertently, themselves, for they still could not affect what they truly wanted. Greatly desired magics fail on those with evil hearts. In this way, the king of humans achieved ultimate power. Inflicted with the curse, his enemies and subjects could not likely mass in rebellion. He and his direct descendants would rule forever."

The ability to do such a thing went so far beyond his experience, Collins found it as difficult to accept as he once had his entrance into a world of fantasy. "What exactly did the people forget?"

"What came before." Prinivere sank back into her sitting position. Though Zylas remained standing, Collins found himself far more comfortable. "That they had prior lives, ones without the transformation curse. So stories of that time do not trickle down to those alive today. It takes someone like me, someone who was there, to tell it."

Collins realized what had to come next. "What happened to the dragons?"

"Our magic saved us from the effects of the first spell, but we could only temper the second. Suddenly, we found ourselves involuntarily human for part of every day, and that made us furious. A horde of dragons descended upon the castle. We killed the king and the half-breeds who should never have existed, but we could not reverse the evil they had inflicted without the magnifying crystal. We never found it. The crowned prince declared war against us, and the slaughter began."

Prinivere's eyes grew even more watery, and a tear dragged down her wrinkled cheek. "Armies and bounties— a man could become rich in a day simply by proving he had killed one of us. Our magic helped, but it has its limits. They wore us down, and, one by one, they killed us." As she spoke, she sank lower and lower so that she had to glance up to meet Collins' eyes. Clearly, she believed herself finished, but he had to know one more thing.

"Some of you survived."

"One," Zylas said, his voice seeming out of place after his long silence. "Only one."

"They knew our exact number." Prinivere now sounded

as feeble as she looked. "We had given them that, the means of our own extermination."

"How?" Collins asked hesitantly. He wanted to know, though it would surely force Prinivere to relive the worst of her memories. "How did you survive?"

"I—" She choked, and Collins closed his eyes, suffering stabbing pangs of guilt for even having asked. He would never have dared press Joel Goldbaum's grandfather for details of the concentration camp he had narrowly escaped.

Collins said hastily, "Never mind," but Prinivere seemed not to hear him.

"One day, my mate staggered to our cave, mortally wounded." The tears flowed freely now, thickening her voice. "All my magic couldn't save him; we both knew it. And they had trailed him to the cave. We said our good-byes. Quickly, I cleaned up those wounds that the people could see, gave him as much strength as I could, and he charged from the cave with all the vengeful agony of an aggrieved cave-mate. They killed him—twice. By the time they managed to climb to the cave, I had made myself appear dead as well. They mistook me for their first kill, crawled off to die, and him for the second. They claimed our tail tips, as the bounty required, and left us both for dead."

A heavy silence followed Prinivere's story. Collins could think of nothing better to say. "I'm sorry. Very very sorry."

Zylas crouched, forestalling the obvious question. "She dared not leave the cave often, barely kept herself alive. She waited until long after the old-age death of the crowned prince and his successor before showing even her human self. She found a good man who claimed he would love her no matter what her switch-form, but she never let him see it. She did bear him twins, then left him to raise them, checking in when she could in human form. Once they had safely grown, becoming acceptable animals at coming-of-age, she mostly disappeared from their lives, watching only from a distance."

Though it sounded harsh, Collins believed he understood the reason. "She aged much more slowly than they did, and she would soon look younger than her own children."

Zylas nodded, "And they might figure out what she was, endangering all of them. But she oversaw their descendants, including, distantly, me. My wife, too, carried Prinivere's bloodline, which explains why our daughter ..." His tone became as strained as Prinivere's.

Collins lowered a head that felt heavy with the mass of details laid upon him by people he had alternately considered friends and betrayers. He had so much to contemplate: to consider, internalize, or discard.

Zylas studied Collins. As if reading his mind, the albino said softly, "I'm going to lay one more thing on you before we leave you to your thoughts."

Collins met the pale gaze and nodded soberly.

"The king's newest law states that *Random* unions can no longer occur. Couple that with the previous edicts forbidding certain creatures from breeding as *Regulars,* and many lines will end. Where you come from, it may not seem like such a bad thing to eliminate rats and mice, snakes and opossums, and other animals you consider vermin. But to us, it's ... it's ..."

Collins filled in the word, "Genocide." He sat up straight and tall. "It's genocide, pure and simple. And it's very, *very* wrong." He could not come up with words strong enough to fit the outrage now rushing through him.

Zylas gave him a weak smile. "I'm glad you see it our way."

Chapter 19

THEY left Collins on his own for nearly an hour while the information they had given him swirled through his mind. Despite the quantity, it all came together with a strange and surprising ease. Zylas and the others had a desperate need and an honest battle that they could not fight without Prinivere's magic enhanced by the missing crystal, and the dragon's great age and frailness made time very short indeed. His education since elementary school had stressed the inherent fairness and validity of democracy. Kingdoms and dictatorships did not fit into his view of justice without the moderating influence of parliaments, congresses, and houses. America had been built by rebels; and though the system did not always work smoothly, he still strongly believed in the underlying tenets of its governmental system.

Running footsteps seized Collins' attention. Worried about security, he lurched to his feet just as Korfius came skidding into the room. He charged Collins with the exuberance of a puppy, then stopped suddenly, as if uncertain what to do next. Wheaten hair fell across his forehead in an untended tousle, and his dark eyes glimmered with excitement.

Collins caught the boy into an embrace, struck by the thinness of his limbs. For an instant, Korfius stiffened. Then, his arms cinched around Collins' waist, and he buried his face in the royal tunic.

Falima came striding in after the boy. "Korfius, you were

supposed to—" She broke off as her gaze fell on Collins, and she went utterly silent. She looked at the boy and man enwrapped together, and a smile softened her otherwise pinched features.

Korfius released Collins and took two steps backward. "You're back, Your Majesty."

Collins winced at the lie, finding it suddenly intolerable. "Look, Korfius. I'm not really—"

The boy did not let him finish. "I know. But I still think of you as my prince."

Now knowing what the king of Barakhai had decreed, what at least this portion of the populace thought of him, Collins did not take the words as a compliment.

Falima shifted nervously from foot to foot. Collins almost expected her to whicker before she finally spoke. "I'm sorry, Ben. I . . . should have trusted you sooner. Treated you better."

Collins was not sure he agreed. "I understand why you didn't."

"Still—"

"Still nothing." Collins felt embarrassed by Falima's apology. It would have taken him at least as long to force himself to associate with someone he considered a cannibal, let alone to treat him courteously. "I understand. You're a good woman in a bad situation. I know you've had to make a lot of hard choices. Giving up a life usually reserved for high-ranking *Regulars* to help a criminal stranger who seemed incompetent couldn't have been easy. I'm sorry I put you in that position." He extended his arms.

Falima moved around Korfius to take her place in Collins' embrace. He folded his grip around her, enjoying the warm softness of her. After the scrawny boy, she felt so substantial, so real. A rush of joy overpowered him momentarily, and the world narrowed to the two of them.

When Falima stepped back, Collins realized Zylas had also entered the cavern, quietly leaning against a craggy wall near the entrance. Dressed in his standard black, eyes eclipsed by his broad-brimmed hat, he wore a bold look of determination. A knife as long as a short sword hung at his waist. "May I assume from this you've forgiven one another?"

Collins' brow furrowed. "I wasn't aware we were fighting."

Zylas shrugged. "When he's out of switch-form, I'll send in Ialin, too."

Collins could not help picturing the glare of withering mistrust Ialin always wore in his presence. "I doubt you'll catch us hugging."

Zylas raised and lowered his brows, then nodded fatalistically. "Probably not." He flipped something into the air. Torchlight sheened from its surface as it spun toward Falima, and Collins recognized it as the translation stone. "I'm off."

Falima caught the stone in both hands, then gave Zylas a tortured look.

"Off where?" Collins turned toward Falima to confirm an answer he had not yet even gotten. He could hardly believe Zylas had so casually tossed over his most valued possession. The gesture carried an air of finality.

"To finish the job, of course. To get the crystal."

Collins blinked, confused. "Get the crystal? But it's—" Realization dawned. "You can't go to the castle. They'll kill you."

"Not if they don't catch me."

Collins' expression tightened into a frown. He hoped Falima would read the anxiety he felt. "You can't—"

"I can." Zylas adjusted his hat. "And I don't have a choice." His demeanor turned serious. "I'm sorry I brought you here; and the others, too. It wasn't fair to expect outsiders to risk their lives for us."

Collins started to protest, but Zylas silenced him with a gesture.

"With the first, I didn't realize the danger. Then, I convinced myself I could make changes that would keep them safe, that the significance of what I brought them to do outweighed any threat." Zylas repositioned his hat. "You've convinced me otherwise. I've always been willing to die for the cause. Others already have. Now, it's just my turn."

Collins did not agree. "Your dying isn't going to accomplish anything." It was not completely true, assuming martyrs inflamed their followers as much in Barakhai as in the only world Collins had considered real until a few days ago.

"Who says I'm going to die?" The question lacked the fortitude required to make the decision seem determined rather than insane. Zylas' earlier bold words contradicted the brave sentiment. They all knew that, alone, he would achieve little but his own demise. "Have some faith in me."

"I did, and I do," Collins insisted. "Enough to expect you not to run off alone and half-cocked on a suicide mission."

That brought a smile. "You know, when I'm not holding the translation stone, you make a lot less sense." Almost immediately, the grin wilted and disappeared. "There's something you need to know, Ben. Something I should have told you sooner."

Now seemed as good a time as any for confessions. Collins braced himself for another horrible revelation.

"I told you Vernon and I have entered your world as a mouse and as a rat. You know that, once there, we don't switch forms."

"The Law of Conservation of Mass and Energy."

"Huh?"

Collins wished he had not interrupted. "Never mind. Go on."

Zylas dutifully continued. "I've tried to go there in human form, but I can't get through."

Collins narrowed his eyes in innocent perplexity. He studied his companion. "But you're not any bigger than I am, and I fit through all right. Easily, in fact."

"From there to here."

Collins considered Zylas' words, realization accompanied by a shiver of discomfort. "Are you telling me it's a one-way door?"

Zylas lowered his face fully into the shadows of his hat. "Only for humans."

"But I'm always . . ." The significance finally penetrated. "You mean . . ." Collins trailed off, then tried again. "No one can get from Barakhai to my world in human form." He looked at Zylas for confirmation; but, if the albino gave him any, he did not see it. "The people you brought here couldn't . . ." He remembered Zylas telling him that all of the others immediately looked for a way back to the lab rather than wandering off seeking food. No wonder Zylas had not had to worry about how long it took him to switch to human form in Barakhai. Those he lured to Barakhai became trapped. *Trapped. I'm trapped here. I can't ever go back*. The enormity of that realization froze his thoughts. He could not even contemplate the unlived future he no longer had in America.

Zylas waited long enough for the full force of understanding to seep in. "That's why the royals have not managed to find the portal."

Even when Carrie Quinton tried to lead them there. Of course, she thought she went to the wrong ruins when she couldn't go anywhere from there. Collins squeezed out the words. "I'm ... trapped ... here?" He turned a bug-eyed stare onto Falima. "I'm here forever." All at once, the details of that simple statement crashed down around him. A list of "no-mores" filled his mind: *friends, family, competent medical care, telephones, clean clothes, indoor plumbing, electric lights, heat, air-conditioning, Sony Play Station, pizza ...*

"You're not trapped. Once I get the crystal ..."

... email and instant messaging, real beds, blankets, James Bond movies, CDs ...

"... Prinivere can definitely get you home. In fact, she managed to get the first guy I brought here home without it, though she hasn't had the strength for it since."

Yeah, Collins remembered. *Home to the nut house.* "She can?" His monotone delivery revealed no hope; the claim sounded suspiciously familiar. *Wait a minute.* "You're playing me again, aren't you?"

Zylas jerked. "What?"

"Telling me the only way to get what I want is to do what you want first. That's how you got me to the castle in the first place."

"But this time I'm not asking you to do anything."

"You're trying to get me to go with you."

"Only if you want to. I'm perfectly willing to go alone."

Korfius and Falima remained tensely silent throughout an exchange that could only end in stalemate.

"I'll bet," Collins mumbled, a statement clearly well-understood by Zylas, who had picked up most of his English by listening to American conversations.

"Fine," Zylas huffed. "I wouldn't have you along with me if you begged."

Falima rolled a wild gaze to Collins, who had won the argument but surely lost the war. When neither of the men spoke again, she softly added, "Shouting at one another won't get at the truth."

Collins folded his arms across his chest.

"Ben, if you don't believe Zylas, why don't the two of you go back to the ruins and try? Either you'll get what you want or you'll find yourself trapped. Then, at least, you'll know."

Zylas' stiff posture eased. "I'm willing. You?"

Collins pictured them struggling through days of woodland travel, dodging hounds and horses, only to stand frustrating inches from the doorway that should take him home. Carrie Quinton's inability to return should corroborate the claim well enough, and the details did finally seem to fit together. "Well . . ." He gave Falima a corner of the eye glance, certain a full look would make him agree to whatever she requested. ". . . you know you're still under oath. You swore to God with sugar on top. We shared spit and a handshake. If you break that promise, the powers-that-be here will strike you down." That hardly seemed a threat given Zylas' willing death mission, so he added, "And all those you care about, too."

Zylas' grin returned. "Can't have that happening. Want me to restate my vow?"

"Not necessary." Collins tried to sound matter-of-fact. "You promised not to lie to me, and you're still fully bound by that promise, you know."

"All right," Zylas agreed. His nostrils flared. "But only to you, right? I mean, I can still lie to the king's guards if I need to."

"Of course." It seemed ludicrous to talk about how Zylas could not lie to him while Collins maintained the illusionary significance of a nonsensical ritual he had only cobbled together to fool Vernon. "The first action Prinivere takes with that stone is to make me a portal?"

"First thing," Zylas agreed, holding out his hand to show he remembered he was still bound by his promise.

"And you know damned well I'm going with you." Collins tried to match Zylas' grin, though he felt anything but confident and strong. "Don't worry. I won't beg."

Falima loosed a relieved sigh. "Thank you," she whispered. "Thank you so much."

Zylas turned toward Falima, the smile that talk of the

vow had raised turning cocksure and insolent. "I told you I chose well this time."

Falima did not argue. "And thank goodness you did."

Tattered and filthy, doing his best imitation of a hunted man, Benton Collins arrived at the outer gatehouse of the king's curtain wall. Guards peered at him over the ramparts, and the drawbridge ratcheted downward before he could utter a word. No sooner had the wood slapped the ground, then a contingent of six guards scurried to greet him, their expressions screwed up in concern and anxiety, their movements as jerky and skittish as a mother hen's. "Are you all right?" one asked.

Feigning a slight limp, Collins waved them off. "Fine. Escaped. Need to see . . . Carrie. And, if possible, the king."

The guards ushered Collins into the gatehouse more with their own forward movement than any particular words or guidance. Trying to look exhausted and pained, he tottered along with them, caught up in the motion. "His Majesty insisted we take you directly to the dining hall if we found you. We're glad you returned, Sire."

Sire? Collins wondered what the king had told them, then realized the obvious. The guards would all know by now that he had entered the upper quarters; which, to them, meant he had to be properly blooded, if distant, royalty.

Collins allowed them to fuss over him, through the second gatehouse, to the palace door, and up to the dining area. Someone must have rushed ahead for, when he arrived, the head table contained the king, Carrie Quinton, and a handful of other privileged guests. Her blonde hair hung in long ringlets, framing a face of beauty more exquisite than he had remembered. His escort joined the sparse array of servants at the common tables, surely more interested in observing his welcome than in eating. Maids still fussed over some of the furniture, suggesting that a meal had recently ended.

At the sight of him, Quinton rushed out from behind the table. "Ben, Ben!" She caught him into an embrace that thrilled through him, stirring an excitement he had not anticipated. He struggled to maintain his aura of fatigued relief as his body betrayed him. The hug became awkward as he found himself fixated on which parts of his body touched hers ... and where. "You're all right. How did you ... Did they make you ... ?" She stopped speaking, withdrawing from his arms, ready to lead him to the head table. "Sit. Eat. Get your strength back, then talk." She ushered him toward the table.

Collins dragged after Quinton, surreptitiously adjusting his clothing, for once glad the linen hung loose on his narrow frame. He cursed the adolescent hormones that allowed a pretty girl to distract him from a life-or-death mission. On the other hand, he realized that, if he played this right, he could succeed at his task and win Carrie Quinton.

Quinton indicated the chair between her own and the king's. As surprised as unnerved by the honor, Collins glanced at King Terrin. The bearded face split in a welcoming grin, and he patted the indicated seat. "We're so glad you managed to get away. Did they hurt you?"

"Your Majesty," Quinton said as she sat, a hint of warning in her tone. "Please let the poor man catch his breath before you quiz him."

The smile remained in place, genuine, taking no offense at his young adviser's presumptuousness. "Of course, Carrie. You're quite right." He clapped his hands. Servants scurried to him, brandishing napkins, glasses, and bottles to fulfill the as yet unspoken command. "Bring a plate of food for our new arrival and anyone else who wishes it. Wine for me and the others."

A broad-faced redhead immediately distributed glasses, while a tall, thin man filled each one as quickly as she set them down. Others hurried toward the door.

Though Collins wanted to put off any questioning as long as possible, he thought it best to toss off a few crumbs. He addressed the king's question. "The fall off the wall hurt a lot, Sire. I was unconscious for the trip, so I'm not sure where they took me. Later, they gave me something that made me sleep and moved me again; but I woke up and managed to escape. They were chasing me." He plastered a stricken look on his face. "Did they ... did they ... did your guards manage ... to catch them?"

King Terrin shook his head. "We tried, but the rebels slunk away like the cowards they are."

Thank God. Collins tried to display the exact opposite of the relief he felt.

The king patted Collins' hand with a palm the size of a bear paw. "They won't bother you anymore; we'll see to that."

"Thank you." Genuinely thirsty, Collins picked up his wineglass in a deliberately shaky hand and downed half of the contents in a swallow. Smooth and rich with the flavor of berries, it soothed his dry throat as well as serving as a vehicle for nervousness he no longer had to wholly fake. Necessarily vague, the plan did not anticipate an immediate meal with King Terrin. He had expected a chance to corner Quinton first, to spend some time convincing her to hand over the crystal she still wore around her neck. Zylas had assured him the rebels had a few spies placed within the curtain walls who might sacrifice their cover if the situation demanded it. At Collins' request, they would use the code word "storm" so he could identify or call for them, if necessary. The albino had also warned him to try not to let the royals lead him to the upper stories where none of the rebels could assist if something went awry.

"So," Terrin asked, not-quite-casually. "Could you describe the rebels you saw?"

Collins nearly spat out his wine. He forced himself to hold it, though a trickle eased down his windpipe. He managed to swallow the rest before a racking spasm of coughs overtook him. He hacked for several moments, sucked in a long breath that sounded more like a wheeze, then lapsed into another fusillade.

Quinton sprang to her feet, patting Collins between the shoulder blades. "Are you all right?"

Collins held up a hand to indicate he did not require her assistance. *That's all I need. A chestful of Heimlich-broken ribs to expel a molecule of liquid.* "I'm fine," he rasped, wishing he sounded it. He cleared his throat, loosed a few more coughs, then regained control. "Sorry, Sire." He sounded as much hoarse as mortified. "Went down the wrong pipe."

King Terrin smiled, lightening the mood in much the same way Collins might have done in other circumstances. "I know I'm the king and people jump to my command, but you're permitted to swallow anything in your mouth before answering questions." The smile spread. "In fact, I encourage it."

Picturing people displaying their half-chewed food, Collins could not help smiling, too. "I'll keep that in mind, Sire." He found the title coming much easier than it had in the past. The king's easygoing manner comforted, and Collins wished he had a way to reason with him rather than lie. He shook off the temptation. The king had good reason to treat Collins well: not only to extract information about Zylas and the others but for scientific advice and, in the future, perhaps even trips to his own world to fetch items of use. Having little pieces of technology would make the king even more powerful than his half-animal subjects, and Terrin had reason to believe Collins might know how to get there and back. He knew the king had another side. He had suffered the royal anger and the results of a chase that had sent him tumbling down the steps, followed by a day and night in the dungeon. He believed and trusted Zylas. *God, I hope I'm not wrong.*

At that moment, a servant returned carrying a loaded plate, which he set in front of Collins along with utensils. It felt good to hold a fork again, even one as crudely made as the steel monstrosity he took into his hand. The plate contained a cooked fruit compote with sweet spices, roasted roots cut into cross sections, and a flaky fish chowder. Possibly hungry enough to even eat bugs, he devoured the food, unable to worry about manners. The king and Carrie Quinton exchanged glances that Collins believed were sympathetic. Likely, they believed the rebels had starved him. Though not true, the fare had been meager and coarse compared with what he had before him now. He could get used to food like this.

When Collins had devoured every bite, he finally turned over his attention to the king. "Please excuse me, Sire. I was . . . famished. And the food . . ." He could not think of a suitably complimentary word. "Wonderful. Better than wonderful. Delicious." *Oh, yeah. That made it clearer.* He continued babbling, "Just the best."

"Thank you," Terrin said simply.

Needing time to consider strategy, Collins took advantage of his deliberately ragged appearance. "Would you mind if I had some rest before we talk?"

The king stiffened for a moment, then regained his casual demeanor. Catching Collins' eye, he explained his discomfort, "The sooner we get after those rebels, the less time they have to hide."

"I won't take too long." Collins bluffed a yawn, stretching sleepily. "But I really need a bit of sleep to think clearly." The absurdity of his own statement struck him; he remembered cramming till morning on some of his most important tests.

The king gestured at Quinton. "Would you mind, Carrie?"

"Not at all." Quinton rose gracefully. "Come with me, Ben."

Collins' heart rate quickened, and he could scarcely believe his luck. The king had arranged the exact situation he needed, some time alone with Carrie Quinton. He rose, almost forgetting to appear tired in his excitement. The torchlight struck silver highlights through the thick, golden cascade of hair, and he could not help imagining the silky feel of it through his fingers. He followed her from the room to the spiral staircase, and she started up.

Eyes traveling to the muscular roundness of her butt, it took Collins a moment to recognize their destination. "Are we headed for . . . royal chambers."

Quinton glanced at him over her shoulder. "Of course."

Remembering Zylas' warning, Collins remained in place. "Won't we be intruding?"

Quinton laughed. "Intruding? Intruding on what? We've spoken up here before, remember?"

Collins remembered. He also recalled swords hacking at him as he tumbled down the stairs. "Of course," he said. "I just didn't want to be presumptuous." He covered with a smile. "Being rude to royalty can be fatal."

Quinton dismissed the comment with a wave. She descended a step and offered her hand. "Come on, you goof. *You're* royalty."

"I am?" Collins accepted Quinton's smooth, soft hand.

"For all intents and purposes." Quinton started back upward, Collins now walking at her side. He studied her in the light of the bracketed torches, scarcely daring to believe a woman so beautiful would allow him to keep her hand so long. Too much protestation would raise suspicions, and it did not seem so dangerous to enter the warded areas with only Carrie Quinton. "You've heard 'it's good to be the king?' Well, it's even better to be the king's adviser. Same good food, same comforts, same deferences—none of the responsibilities. They don't even expect you to be right all that often."

They reached the next landing and continued upward. Collins digested the explanation. "But don't you miss chocolate?" His own craving for something sweet tainted the question.

"They have chocolate."

"They do?"

"The royals do. I'll get you some."

Nearly distracted from his point, Collins continued as they walked. "What about fast food?"

Quinton turned him a searching look. "You mean lumps of grease doused in ketchup?"

Collins felt his cheeks grow warm. "Well, yeah. Stuff like that."

"No." Quinton winked. "But I can get the cook to fry you up some salted lard and slap it between two hunks of white bread." She clapped her free hand down on their joined grip to simulate a sandwich. "Primitive Whopper."

"Gee, thanks."

"Seriously, most of the fun of fast food is speed and not having to cook it yourself. Here, I don't ever have to cook again, or I can if I want to. I get what I want when I want it. And I still get things 'my way' if I request them."

They paused on the next landing, and Collins noticed that the stairs continued upward for at least two more stories. Thinking back, the extension had been there the last time Quinton and King Terrin had brought him here, but he had not thought to question. He could not recall Zylas' explanation; their lessons on the layout of the castle seemed like a year ago, and he had taken more than one blow to the head since then.

Hand on the door latch, Quinton waited. "You're not expecting to sleep on the roof, are you?"

Torn from his scrutiny, Collins glanced at Quinton. "What?"

"Next stop's the roof ramparts, for the lookout guards. Then the top of the tower."

Now, Collins remembered discussing the fact that some guards might climb the stairs past the royal areas to access their positions. Zylas had even mentioned the steps ending in a trapdoor that led to the top of one tower. "Oh." *Duh*.

Quinton tripped the latch and pushed the door open to reveal a large bedroom. Tapestries hung from every wall. The first depicted a forest, with deer grazing placidly among a vast variety of trees, birds and squirrels cavorting in the branches, a rabbit peering timidly around a weathered oak. Another showed a pasture full of a mixed herd of animals. Horses raced regally through the background, a cow lumbering behind them. Sheep and goats filled most of the foreground. The third wall contained a picture of a young boy herding a flock of geese, ducks, and chickens. The last held a portrait of a ginger tabby cat stretched luxuriously on a canopied bed. A real bed, looking very much like the one in the picture, took up most of the middle of the room. Tied back with golden tassels, emerald-colored curtains surrounded a mattress clotted with woolen blankets. A blue ceiling harbored a realistic arrangement of painted stars. A beautifully carved wardrobe and a matching wooden chest completed the furnishings.

While Collins admired the bedroom, Quinton borrowed a torch from the stairwell to light the ones on either side of the room. She replaced the torch, closed the door, and sat on the bed. Shoving aside the bunched blankets, she patted a spot next to her. "Welcome to my room."

Collins approached. "It's wonderful." Wanting to remind her of their similar backgrounds, and his own sense of observation, he said, "I particularly like the night sky. I see Orion, so it must be fall."

"Yup."

Collins continued to stare. "You know, the pattern's a bit different here. How'd you get it so close to ours?"

"Kept making the artist do it till he got it right." Quinton pushed the covers to the floor and tapped the mattress again. "Went from memory, but I know it's not exactly right."

Only an amateur astronomer himself, Collins could not tell her how to fix it. He walked to the bed, not certain what Quinton wanted from him.

Quinton stood, gently straightened Collins' collar, then pressed her lips against his. Her large breasts conformed to his chest, and he thought he could feel the nipples against him. Instantly excited, he returned the kiss, thrusting his tongue between her lips. *She wants me. Oh, my God, this beautiful woman wants me.*

Quinton arched her body against Collins' and whispered in his ear. "I want you." Her warm breath stirred something so primal, he groaned. His legs felt rubbery, unable to hold his weight.

Together, they sank onto her bed.

Chapter 20

BENTON Collins lay flopped across Carrie Quinton's bed, basking in the afterglow and the wonder of the whole situation. *A smart, beautiful woman wanted me.* He stared around the canopy at the painted stars ignited by the faint light the torches provided. Hours ago, he would never have believed such a thing could happen. Now, the whole world seemed to have changed.

Quinton made a sound of contentment, which sent a wave of joy thrilling through Collins. He could count the number of times he had made love, now no longer on just one hand; but he still considered himself inexperienced. He had done his best with Quinton, holding out as long as he could, but the whole session had still lasted less than fifteen minutes. It delighted him to think he had satisfied her, too.

A trickle of guilt disrupted his joy, its source uncertain. Marlys remained far from his thoughts. He had assumed their relationship was over before he had even come to Barakhai. The fact that they had not officially broken up had to do only with his inability to contact her. The true wonder was that the relationship had lasted as long as it did. Once he realized that Marlys had nothing to do with the sensation pressing against his conscience, he puzzled over it. Some frail corner of his mind told him he had found his soul mate, and it was not Carrie Quinton.

The thought seemed madness. He and Quinton had everything in common: background, interests, sexual attraction. It seemed almost as if the world had conspired to bring them together.

Quinton sat up, reaching for her clothes. "Penny for your thoughts."

Collins studied her, the torchlight just right to capture proper details and hide the flaws. Her face held a natural radiance that required no cosmetics. The curls, disheveled from their lovemaking, looked even more attractive tousled. Pale as blue-tinted pearls, her eyes remained striking. Her large breasts, perky with youth, still excited him, even with his manhood freshly spent. Even the antiquated phrasing of her question did not seem strange or nerdish. "You're beautiful," he said.

Quinton pulled on her dresslike undergarments, then the actual dress, smoothing the skirting around her hips and thighs. "I'm intelligent, too."

Collins swallowed, afraid he had just made a fatal mistake. "Well, of course. But that goes without saying." Uncertain whether he had rescued himself yet, he added, "Ol' D-Mark insists on the brightest."

"Including you?"

Choosing humor over modesty, Collins simply said. "Well, of course." Then, finding a way to use both, he added, "Though he couldn't be quite as picky after you disappeared. Everyone thought he'd driven you to run."

"So that's what happened." Quinton laughed. "At least no one's worried about me." She pulled on the gold chain with the dragon stone.

Collins' gaze latched onto the crystal, and sudden shame slapped him. He had allowed a tryst to distract him from his mission. "I'd venture to guess your mother's worried."

Quinton's lips pursed tightly. "I don't have a mother."

The words seemed nonsensical. "Everyone has a mother." Collins reached for his own clothing.

Quinton grunted. "Squeezing a child out the birth canal doesn't make a woman a mother."

Collins pulled on his loose-fitting trousers and tied them without bothering to look at his hands. "My biology training says you're wrong."

"Well my sixteen years in seven foster homes trumps your biology training."

All humor disappeared. "Oh."

"Oh."

"I didn't know." Properly chastised, Collins reached for his tunic. "I'm sorry."

"For the first two years of my life, the woman who claimed to be my mother left me crying in a crib for hours while she went out and partied." A shadow fell over Quinton's face. "They gave her four years to straighten out her life enough to get me back. Four *years.* An eternity for a kid. By the time they realized she wouldn't, I was too old for an adoptive family. In those days, they only wanted babies."

"I'm sorry," Collins repeated, wishing he had never raised the subject. It clearly hurt her. "You've done amazingly well on your own, given the circumstances you came from." Suddenly, his own problems did not seem significant at all.

"I realized she was rotten by the time I was three, but it took an army of social workers four years to figure out the same thing." Quinton finger-combed her tangled locks. "That convinced me I was smart. I always knew I'd make it through college, though without scholarships, jobs, loans, and lab assistanceships, I'd never have made it."

"You're incredible," Collins said as he put on his glasses, meaning it. "Resourceful, determined, intelligent, *and* beautiful." He smiled. "And damned good in bed."

Quinton winced. "I don't know why I told you that. Since I got off on my own at eighteen, I've never told anyone."

Her confession made Collins feel even closer than their lovemaking had. "I have a confession to make, too."

Quinton turned him a look of innocent questioning. "What?"

"I can get us home."

"You can?" Quinton's tone sounded guarded, not the pure excitement Collins expected.

Nevertheless, he continued. "All I need is the crystal." He reached out a finger and stroked the smooth stone around her neck.

Quinton did not flinch. "I don't understand."

"What's to understand?" Collins' voice gained all the excitement Quinton's lacked. "With the crystal, I can get us back to our own world."

Quinton shook her head slightly. "Ben, this *is* my world."

"This . . . ?" Collins' grin vanished. "This—don't be ridiculous. I can get us home. To Earth." Doubting they had actually left the planet, he amended, "Back to civilization."

Quinton clenched her hands in her lap.

Collins studied her in silence for several moments.

Quinton stared at her intertwined hands. "I don't want to leave"

"But, Carrie—"

"I feel more at home here than I ever did there."

Collins wanted to say something, anything, to rouse Quinton. The idea that she would like Barakhai better than home had never occurred to him. "What if you got appendicitis?"

Carrie pointed to her right hip. "Appendectomy. Age nine."

"All right. Needed your tonsils out."

Quinton's hand went to her throat. "Tonsillectomy. Age six."

Frustrated, Collins tried something that could happen more than once. "What if you broke your leg?"

Finally, Quinton looked directly at Collins. "They do have healers here, you know. They handle broken bones all the time."

Collins huffed out a sigh. "Do they handle cancer?"

"No," Quinton admitted. "But I'd rather take my chances raising the dragons until they can heal me than getting poisoned with chemotherapy and radiation."

The dragons. Collins had almost forgotten them. Once the king's adviser/geneticist raised and trained them, King Terrin might as well be invincible.

"Carrie, please. I *do* want to go home. Can't you just let me have the stone for me?"

The pallid eyes narrowed to slits, then she dropped her head wearily. "Ben, I have another confession."

Collins fell silent, not certain he wanted to hear it.

Quinton's fingers twined like snakes in her lap. "When I first brought you up here, I just wanted to get some information out of you."

Collins closed his eyes, dreading the rest.

"But I found myself really attracted to you. Then, one thing led to another, and I never did ask any questions and . . ." She broke off suddenly. "Please look at me."

Liking the turn her admission seemed to be taking, Collins obeyed.

"I want you to stay," Quinton said with raw sincerity. "King Terrin wants you to stay and advise him. You'd have a life of luxury, the life of a prince."

Collins shook his head. "I—"

Quinton seized his hand. "I do want you to stay, too. I want to sleep with you every night. I want to bear your babies. I want to be . . . a *real* mother."

My babies. This was too much for twenty-three-year-old Benton Collins. *From one session of sex to this?* Terror ground through him, and the urge to put some physical distance between them became nearly unbearable. He suspected her swift bond with him had something to do with those she'd lacked as a child, yet the understanding did him little good. He found himself hyperventilating. He needed air. *Too much too fast.* Worried about upsetting her, he reached for the crystal again. "Please, Carrie. Just let me have the stone. I'll only go to settle some things. To gather some comforts. Then I'll come back."

Water glazed Quinton's blue-white eyes.

"I will. I promise." The words came out without conscious thought. Collins could not even convince himself he would keep that vow. Spitting on his hand and sugar on top would not work for Carrie Quinton.

She spoke softly, her voice strained and hesitant. "Once we've established a life here. A baby. Things I know you won't abandon. Then, then, you can go back."

"Carrie." Collins cupped the crystal in one hand. "I can't wait that long."

Quinton jerked backward, then hissed in pain. Clearly the gold chain cut into the back of her neck.

Now that he had a hold on it, Collins closed his hand, unable to let go. "I don't want to hurt you. Just let me have it."

"No," Carrie said, then shouted. "No! Help! Help! I need help!"

Collins knew he had to escape and fast, but he would not leave without the crystal. He wrapped both hands around it and pulled.

Carrie screamed.

The door that led to the other chambers burst open.

Three men with swords charged into the room, directly at Collins.

"Shit!" Collins gave one last desperate heave that snapped the links. Momentum hurled him to the floor, the stone clamped in his hands, the broken ends of the chain whipping his fingers. His buttocks struck stone, and agony howled through his spine. Blood splashed his face, and Carrie shrieked again.

Two swords jabbed toward Collins. He recognized their wielders as men who'd been seated at the head table on his first visit to the dining hall. Now, he noticed only that they looked well-muscled and competent with their weapons.

Collins scuttled into retreat as the blades jabbed forward. His back jarred suddenly against cold stone, and he scrambled to a stand, smacking his head on something affixed to the wall. A wash of black-and-white spots swam down on him, stealing his vision. He bulled through it, only to find himself pinned to the wall by two swords at his chest.

"Be still," said a silk-clad blond who could have been, and probably was, the king's brother. "We don't want to kill you."

Menaced by swords, Collins was not sure he believed the man. The one beside him remained quiet. He stood half a head taller, skin and hair a shade darker than his companion's. He wore a beard while the other was clean-shaven, and his hairline was receding.

Collins tightened his hold on the crystal. He had come too far to give it up now, yet he saw no way out of this situation. His only advantage came if he believed Carrie Quinton's claim that the king wanted him alive. He glanced at the geneticist, who returned his look with hate-filled eyes. Her hands clutched at the back of her neck. It surprised Collins to find himself thinking clearly in a life-or-death situation after his utter panic at the gallows. If nothing else had come out of his trip to Barakhai, he had gained composure. *Fat lot of good that'll do me dead.*

Sweat dripped down Collins' forehead, out of proportion to the rest of his body. His scalp felt uncomfortably hot. "Carrie and I were just—" He flushed, finishing lamely. "—talking and ... and ... stuff." *Stuff. The new popular euphemism for sex.* Abruptly, Collins realized what he must have crashed against that now heated his head. *Torch bracket.* He needed a distraction. "Tell 'em, Carrie."

"He stole my necklace," Quinton hissed. "A traitor."

The men's heads swiveled toward her. Seizing the moment, Collins lunged for the torch with his free hand. The bracket tore a line of skin from his thumb, sending pain howling through his hand, but he managed to complete the movement. His fingers wrapped around the warmed wood, and he swung wildly for his captors.

The two men leaped backward, sparing themselves a burning but opening the way for Collins' escape. The fire flickered dangerously low, then steadied. Collins raced for the door to the stairwell.

"Guards! Guards!" the shorter man shouted.

Collins jerked the panel open, only to find the way down blocked by a seething mass of warriors. "Shit!" Clearly, the king had anticipated that Collins' allegiances might have shifted. Quinton had known from the start that she had formidable backup. "Shit!" he repeated, louder. He needed a distraction, anything to delay the mob below him. "Storm!" he shrieked the code word to any rebel in earshot. "Storm! Storm!"

When no one responded, Collins hurled his only weapon, the torch, at the horde, then thundered up the stairs. *Up is wrong. Up is wrong!* It made no sense to corner himself on a rooftop, yet he saw no other way. At least, it might delay the inevitable and place the choice of death or capture back into his own hands. The crystal bit into his palm, and another realization struck him. At least, he might get the object of contention into the right hands. Surely, he would find someone from the rebel forces in the courtyard. *At least, my death might not be completely in vain.* Though a scant comfort, it proved better than none at all.

Collins charged upward, pausing only to collect another torch from its bracket in the stairwell. A moment later, he reached the next landing, anticipating a flurry of guardsmen from the parapets. None came through the door, and Collins dimly realized that the rebels must have managed to handle those men for him. He continued to run, breaths coming in wild pants, legs pounding upward as if under their own control. Suddenly, he found a square ceiling over his head, and the steps ended at a trapdoor. Praying it would not prove too heavy, he bashed against it with his head and right shoulder.

The panel jolted upward, but the seconds of delay proved his undoing. A hand closed around his ankle, jerking him abruptly backward. Balance and momentum lost, he felt himself falling into someone's arms. Twisting, he thrust blindly with the torch. The taller royal retreated, beard aflame. He let go of Collins' leg. Collins threw the torch and launched himself through the trapdoor. He heard Quinton's scream, high-pitched and fiercely terrified, caught a momentary glimpse of her, flames leaping from her hair, before the trapdoor crashed shut behind him. Guiltily, he hoped her distress would keep the guards busy long enough for him to find a way down. He darted to a crenel and glanced into the courtyard below. Seven stories down, the goats, sheep, pigs, and chickens looked very small. "Shit!" he yelled. "Shit! Shit! SHIT!"

The expletive caught the attention of some of the animals, who looked up at him. Something buzzed in his ear, and he whirled to face a tiny bird, its wings fluttering so fast they seemed invisible. Collins could never have imagined himself so glad to see Ialin. "Here." He thrust out the crystal. "Take it."

Dutifully, the hummingbird zipped to Collins and seized the offering in a beak that seemed too small and slender to hold it. Ialin sank almost to the ground, then ponderously, inch by inch, managed to regain altitude. He sailed away.

The trapdoor thumped back open.

Collins dumped the bit of broken gold chain over the parapets, watching it twist through the air. It seemed to take forever to reach the ground. Below him, two goats struggled with a small hay cart. It was over. The rebels had won, but Benton Collins had lost. If he surrendered now, maybe they would not kill him. He thought of what he had done: double-crossed the king, burned royals, including Carrie Quinton, and delivered an artifact into the hands of a gang of thugs who planned to use it to destroy the king. *Oh, yeah. He'll let me live all right.*

The man who looked like the king's brother appeared first, guarding his head and throat as he charged through the opening. Then, Zylas' rat-head emerged over the battlements, panting around the translation stone. From the direction of his abrupt arrival, he had clearly waited on the roof ramparts, between the two towers, and had climbed the final floor of the tower from the outside. "Jump," he managed to gasp around the quartz.

Collins looked down. He could never survive a seven-story fall. The goats labored hurriedly beneath him.

"Jump," Zylas repeated, his voice a harsh wheeze. He clambered wearily onto Collins' hand, across his wrist, and into a tunic pocket. "It's our only chance."

A guard appeared beside the royal, and Collins could hear more clambering behind them. They approached him with slow caution, swords drawn. He had only two choices, and they knew it: leap to his death or surrender.

"Trust me," Zylas said.

Famous last words. Collins realized that, whatever his fate, at least Zylas was brave enough to share it. Closing his eyes, he jumped.

"Hey!" the guard yelled. "Hey!"

Air whooshed past Collins. His hair and clothing whipped around him in a savage tangle, and sheer terror scattered his wits. He screamed, utterly helpless, incapable of opening his eyes. Then, stems jabbed and shattered beneath him, slivering into his flesh like a thousand needles. *The hay wagon,* he realized before velocity carried him through the piled hay to the wooden slats of the wagon. Agony beyond thought thundered through him, and he knew no more.

Benton Collins awakened to a rush of pain that drove an involuntary groan through his lips. He opened his eyes to a whitewashed ceiling and a repetitive beeping sound that perfectly matched the rhythm of his heart. He tried to speak, but only a croak emerged from his parched lips.

A woman in a white dress with a pink stethoscope around her neck and scissors poking from her breast pocket peered at him. "Are you awake, Benton?"

Collins licked his lips and nodded weakly. "What happened?" He mouthed more than spoke the words, but apparently the nurse understood.

"You tell me."

Collins shook his head, wondering if his experiences in Barakhai were all some sort of hallucination induced by the pain drugs they had obviously given him. "Last thing I remember, I was taking care of rat experiments in Daubert Labs."

"That's where they found you this morning." The nurse turned, clattering some objects on a metal tray. "In an old storage room. Your mom's on her way. Couldn't locate your dad."

"He's in Europe with his girlfriend." Collins glanced around, still trying to sort real from imagined. "Am I going to be okay?"

The nurse returned to his bedside, smoothed his pillow, and rearranged the covers. "You broke your pelvis, your left leg, both arms, some ribs, and you've got a small skull fracture."

The list sounded terrible. "Gosh."

The nurse apparently was not finished. She picked up a spiral-bound chart from a bedside table. "Ruptured spleen, which seems to be healing on its own. Kidney contusion— you'll have some blood in the urine for a while, but that should heal. Pneumothorax."

The last word eluded Collins. Pneumo, he knew, meant air. "What?"

The nurse set the chart aside. "Lung deflated. They put a tube in your chest to reexpand it."

"Did someone beat me up?" Collins tried to smile.

The nurse shrugged. "Only logical explanation. Looks more like you took a bad fall, but that doesn't make any sense where they found you." She lowered her head, and strands of dark hair slipped from beneath her hairpinned hat. "You're lucky that professor found you when he did. Said a very persistent dog led him to you."

"A dog?" Collins swallowed. *Is it possible?* "Where is this dog?"

"In the pound," the nurse said.

"The pound?" Collins tried to sit up, but pain and wires held him down. "What if they—"

The nurse put out a hand to stay him. "Don't worry. No one's going to hurt the hero of Daubert Labs. If you don't want him, there're about thirty others in line to adopt him. I think he's getting filet mignon for every meal."

Collins had to know. "Gangly hound with floppy ears. Brown and white."

"That's the one."

"I want him."

"I'll let them know."

"He's ... my dog. Can you hand me the phone?"

The nurse gave Collins a stern look. "I said I'd call. I'll call as soon as we're done here."

"Thank you." Collins felt very sleepy, but curiosity won out over fatigue. "His name is Korfius."

"Korfius?"

Collins nodded.

"I'll tell them." She started out the door, then stopped and turned back. These are your things, if you want them. It's everything you had when they found you. I'm afraid they had to cut off your jeans." She smiled. "I don't think you would have wanted them anyway. Dirty and bloody. You must have taken off your sweatshirt before ... whatever happened. It needs washing, but it's salvageable."

Jeans? Sweatshirt? "Thank you," Collins said, accepting the plastic bag. As the nurse left, he poured out the contents: his cell phone, his watch, its face irreparably smashed, and a piece of paper torn from a scratch pad advertising a laboratory supply company. Scrawled across it in wobbly lettering were the words:

Ben—
   Thanks from all. Me okay. Fall on you. You me pillow. Ha ha. You hurt too bad for Lady. Put old clothes and bring here. They fix, we hope. Korfius stay. Not send back. He want you.

It was signed only with a tiny paw print.

Collins lay back, imagining the effort it must have taken for the rebels to drag him, in animal form, even as far as they had. Korfius was *lesariat*, he remembered. He had gotten his wish to remain a dog forever, and now Collins had gained the smartest, longest-lived pet in the world. *My world.* He smiled through the pain.

The Lost Dragons
Of Barakhai

To Sheila Gilbert
the other half of the equation.

May she inspire, assist, and torture writers
(including me)
for many many many more decades.

Acknowledgments

I would like to thank the following:
Mark Moore, the PenDragons,
Kevin & Bambi VanDyne,
Sandra & Arthur Zucker,
Jackie, Koby, and Carly,
Spoon Branch mules
and the following:

Seeker, Aisa, Gryphon, Fluffy, Tigger, Mr. Kwik, Kelka,
Haakon, Dusty, Paladin, Masai, Ace, Fawn, Cassius, Kimba,
Bucky, McKinley, Modi, Raven, Sankie, Rocky, Doodle
and several others who provided invaluable research.

Chapter 1

WILD barking awakened Benton Collins, and he sprang from his bed without thinking. The top sheet and blanket entangled his legs, sending him sprawling, heart pounding, on the floor. Whining frantically, Korfius thrust a wet nose into his face.

Collins pushed the dog away. He lived in graduate student housing, which normally did not allow pets; however, Korfius was considered a hero, for bringing the help that saved Collins' life. The Algary College staff and his neighbors politely looked the other way, treating Korfius like a seeing eye dog and not throwing him up as an example whenever their own better-concealed cats, fish, and birds got evicted.

"Quiet, Korfius," Collins demanded, sitting on the bed and extricating himself from the awkward, encumbering twist of coverings. He groped for his glasses on the standard issue dresser, clamped a hand over one wire temple piece, and put them in place on his nose one-handed. "You'll wear out your welcome barking at . . ." Collins glanced at the digital clock at his workstation. ". . . 3:16 A.M.!" He ran a hand through sleep-tousled, dark brown hair and groaned. "What the hell are you doing up at 3:16 AM?"

Korfius nuzzled Collins, then ran toward the window, planted his forepaws on the sill, and bounced back. In his excitement, he leaped on Collins' bed, over him, and back to the window again. Collins watched the gangly legs sail past, the ears flying, the tongue lolling, the short coat an uneven patchwork of brown and white. Though fourteen years old, the half-grown hound aged in human, not dog, years and had the exuberance of a six-month-old puppy. Collins had acquired Korfius in Barakhai, a world he had entered accidentally by chasing a white rat through the hallways of Daubert Laboratories. There, he had discovered people who spent half or more of their lives as various animals. The few who had come to his world remained in animal form throughout their visits, and Korfius had chosen to stay because he liked Collins and preferred being a full-time dog.

Over the last year and a half, Collins had grown as fond of Korfius as the dog had of him, though he still found their association a bit uneasy. He used leashes and collars only when absolutely necessary and shared his own food because it seemed vulgar to feed a child Puppy Chow. Dressed only in his sleeping boxers and glasses, Collins headed toward the window. A cool summer breeze chilled his torso.

Something thumped onto Collins' shoulder. He staggered backward with a savage gasp, smacking the object with the back of one hand. It felt warm and solid, furry against his skin, and it tumbled to the bed. A shiver coiled through Collins, and he whirled to look. A white rat braced itself on the disheveled pile of sheet and blanket, whiskers twitching madly.

Collins stifled a scream, then logic took over. *It can't be. Can it?*

Korfius bounded onto the bed, sending the rat flying. It scrambled onto Collins' pillow.

"Hey!" Collins said.

The rat cocked its head. "Hey, yourself. What kind of greeting is slapping me across the room?"

It IS Zylas. Glad to see his old friend again, Collins replied in kind, "The normal reaction to being attacked by a rat. What would you do if something jumped on your shoulder?"

Zylas twisted his head to look over the snowy fur on the back of his neck. "Anything small enough to alight on my shoulder would have to be an insect, so I guess I'd . . . I'd eat it."

Still grossed out by one of the Barakhains' main sources

of protein, Collins made a noise of revulsion. "You'd eat it, huh?" He pinned the rat with a searching stare. "So you got off easy." He avoided the image of dining on raw, unskinned rat meat, not wishing to arouse a more painful memory. When he had first arrived in Barakhai, he had roasted and eaten a rabbit. Only when the villagers attempted to hang him for murder and cannibalism did he discover the dual nature of its citizenry. *Every human an animal, and every animal a human.* Collins did not forget the exception to the rule. *Except fish, which they eat freely and don't consider animal.*

"Good point." Zylas paused to give Korfius a warning nip on the jowl that sent the dog into barking retreat. One hind foot slipped over the edge, and the dog flopped to the floor. "Quiet, Korfius. I'm glad to see you, too, but we can say 'hello' without the ear-shattering racket."

The dog cocked his head, tail waving, chin resting on the bed. Usually, the animals of Barakhai could not communicate much better than the ones in Collins' own world, but a crystal that Zylas always carried allowed him to speak even with other creatures.

Crystal. Where is the crystal? A million questions came to Collins' mind at once. Before he had left Barakhai, nearly dead from a beating and a fall, he had captured another crystal, one that enhanced magic, from Barakhai's king and delivered it to one of Zylas' renegades. With the help of the last dragon, the only beings who could use magic, the renegades had planned to remove the curse that forced them to cycle through an animal form each day. Collins wondered about the friends he had made in that strange Otherworld called Barakhai. Did the crystal ever reach Prinivere, that ancient, feeble dragon who was also a distant ancestor of Zylas'? Did it enhance the little bit of magic she could still manage? Clearly, she had not actually lifted the curse, or Zylas would have come to Collins in man form. Unlike Korfius, he preferred being human.

Before Collins could frame the first question, a trumpeting whinny froze him in place. He forced himself to turn toward the window, where a familiar fuzzy head peered in at them. A black forelock lay tousled over a wide, golden nose, and black ears formed excited, pricked-forward triangles. The mare tipped her head to regard them all through one shockingly blue eye.

Startled at finding a horse in the quadrangle, Collins gasped. "What the hell did you bring her for?" Despite his accusatory question, Collins found himself smiling at Falima. He had thought of her often in the year since he had last seen her. It had taken her a long time to forgive his crimes of ignorance; but, once she had, he found her a brave and loyal ally. He stroked the silky nose and scratched behind her ears. She rested her chin on the sill, sighing heavily.

"Bring her?" Zylas paced a circle on Collins' pillow. "Do you think I could stop her?"

Collins could not answer. He knew the one-way portal allowed anyone to pass from his world to theirs, but only animals could move in the opposite direction. He had no idea whether they had to be in beast shape when they approached the portal or whether the simple act of passing through it made the change for them. In Barakhai, they had essentially no control over the switch. It happened at the same time each and every day: Zylas at the equivalent of noon and midnight, Falima at 6. Presumably, Zylas could have chosen a time when he held rat form and Falima human to sneak through the portal; but that would prove difficult. While a human, Falima would have the mental and physical wherewithal to prevent Zylas' leaving without her. While a horse, she only needed to follow him. And, despite a few brief visits to Collins' world in the past, Zylas might not realize the problems inherent in bringing a full-grown horse into an urban setting. Where he came from, all horses served as guards and lived in the most civilized areas.

Unconsciously, Collins adopted the high-pitched, singsong speech pattern most adults use when speaking to babies and animals. "Can you talk in animal form now, too?"

Zylas answered for Falima. "Not yet. Overlap's not good enough."

Collins remembered that "overlap" referred to the ability to recall animal times in human form and vice versa. Zylas, he knew, had what the old dragon called near-perfect overlap.

Zylas paced the mattress, and Korfius' eyes followed his every movement. "That crystal you liberated allowed Prinivere to make more translation stones, but Falima tends to drop hers when she lapses into . . . full horsiness."

Collins yawned, suddenly remembering what time it was.

"It's great to see you guys, but it's the middle of the night, and I've got classes in the morning. Why don't we all get some sleep and . . ." The ridiculousness of his own suggestion penetrated his sleep-fogged brain before he could even get a reply. "But not in the quad. A horse . . . would be noticed." *And I'll get thrown out on my ear. This definitely breaks my lease.*

"Indeed." Zylas bowed his ratty head. "That's why we need to talk in Barakhai. Come with me, please."

"Barakhai!" Collins found himself shouting and lowered his voice. "I can't go back there." He still bore the scars of two falls: the first down the kingdom steps with soldiers and servants stabbing and beating at him, the second a desperate leap from the parapets. Collins had tossed torches at the king's most faithful, including Carrie Quinton, an adviser from his own world, and the king's brother. It seemed impossible that he would not get arrested the moment he set foot in Barakhai, sentenced to another hanging . . . or worse. *Worse? What could be worse than strangling to death?* It surprised Collins just how swiftly the answer came to his mind. The possibilities for a slow, agonizing death seemed infinite.

Zylas balanced on his back paws. "You have to, Ben. We need you."

Collins did not agree. He studied Falima, suddenly wishing he had worn more to bed. The physical therapy from his injuries, and the healthy habits it started, left him with some muscular definition to a once too-skinny chest. He had grown a few more chest hairs, bringing his total to ten; and he had honed his arms and legs so he no longer resembled a scarecrow. Collins found himself hoping Falima had noticed the positive changes that had occurred over the past year. "I'd feel a lot better if you *asked* me. This time." He made a direct and scathing reference to Zylas' previously luring him into Barakhai and danger without giving Collins the least hint of what he was about to get involved in.

Zylas' beady red eyes turned liquid. He clamped his front paws together and lowered his head. "Please?"

"No."

Zylas' pointy face jerked up.

Collins suddenly felt foolish and cruel. It seemed unreasonable to request politeness and consideration, then turn it down outright. "I'm sorry. I have a life here. In Barakhai, I'm a dead man."

Zylas stared, and his eyes turned steely. "At least . . . *you* have a life somewhere." He turned with an unratlike air of irritation and dignity. "I thought you'd just hear us out. I thought you might care, be curious. Or, that you might want a chance to talk to Korfius again."

Collins felt all of those things; but the last, strangely, seemed the most compelling reason of all. He did want to know if Korfius was satisfied with this way of life, if he could do anything to make the dog/boy more comfortable, if Korfius might not prefer his dual life in Barakhai. Collins had made a lifelong commitment to the dog, since Korfius would probably outlive him. If Zylas and Falima had come at a more decent hour, he might be able to think more clearly. "We can't talk here," Collins reasoned aloud. "You . . . maybe, okay. But a horse? No, that won't go unnoticed." Now suspicious, he wondered if Falima had come simply to force the issue. Without her, Zylas could have safely stayed and chatted.

Zylas turned a circle, clearly reading Collins' wavering. "Come with us. We can talk at the entrance, or in a safe house, if you wish. We can always send you right back."

Sensing another trap, Collins found the problem. "It's a one-way door. Once I go through, I can't get home."

"Not the same way," Zylas admitted. "But Prinivere now has enough power to send you back."

Collins still hesitated, unsure.

"She got you back last time, didn't she?"

Collins had to admit that she had. Otherwise, he would have died of his wounds in Barakhai, not recovered in Algary's Intensive Care Unit. "Pretty much in pieces."

Zylas could not argue the point and, to his credit, did not try. "You can leave whenever you want. Whenever you decide."

Collins set his jaw, considering despite his better judgment. He had finally got himself on the right track. It had taken him months to recover enough to return to school full-time. He had won back his laboratory assistanceship and found a way to make money using the translation skills Prinivere had magically bestowed upon him to allow communication with the humans of Barakhai. The doctors could not explain how a head wound could make a biology graduate student who had struggled through high school Spanish speak every language they could throw at him fluently, but the hospital appreciated his ability to bridge the gap between explanation and understanding for their non-English-speaking patients. Prinivere's spell did not extend to the written word, however, so they could not simply ask him to translate common descriptions and treatments into brochures. He had paid off most of his student loans, the semester's tuition, maintained his quarters and his dog, and still had some pocket money for campus movies, pizza, and an occasional, although all thus far unsatisfying, date.

Falima thrust her muzzle back through the window to whicker a low "come on." Zylas gave Collins a pleading look. Korfius stood by the bed, tail wagging.

Collins heaved a sigh. "If I wasn't out-of-my-mind exhausted, I'd never even consider this." He gave Zylas a steady scrutiny that he hoped looked rock hard. "I get to decide when I leave Barakhai?"

Zylas waved a paw. "You get to decide."

"Even if it's immediately?"

Collins saw no downside. He could still reconsider on the walk to the portal; and, even once there, it was not an irreversible choice. It seemed safer to discuss any matter with a horse somewhere other than the middle of campus.

"Why don't you pack a few things," Zylas said. "Just in case."

It was a reasonable suggestion, though it made Collins wary. "I can leave Barakhai any time? Even immediately?"

Zylas opened his lids wider, making his fiery eyes seem to bulge from their pink-rimmed sockets. "You're repeating yourself."

"It's called reassurance." Collins crinkled his nose. "And don't do that eye thing. It's freakish."

"Thanks." Zylas restored his features to normal. "I love it when my friends call my looks freakish."

Collins dodged the all-too-wide opening. The "eye thing" barely touched the "transforming-into-animals thing." Without another word, he scooped up his backpack from the workstation chair and dumped its contents onto the bed. Books, notebooks, and pens tumbled out, along with an assortment of pipettes, a compartmentalized container filled with plastic balls and stems for making models of molecules, and sundry other small accessories. He tossed two packs of TGI Friday's matches back inside, added a mini mag light, his new multitool, three T-shirts, four pairs of underwear, and two pairs of blue jeans. He dashed into the bathroom, Korfius trotting along at his heels. Opening the medicine chest, he snatched up a bottle of Tums and another of Tylenol, dropping them into the sink. He tossed in a bar of soap, a toothbrush, a razor, a plastic bottle of shampoo, deodorant, and toothpaste. Seizing the hand towel, he folded all of his gathered things into it, bundled it up, and headed from the room. As a last thought, he scooped up a roll of toilet paper. Dashing back to the bedroom, he unceremoniously dumped it all inside his backpack.

"All right—" Collins started, then stopped, thinking of another potentially useful item. He jerked open his desk drawer to reveal his new personal organizer, a programmable calculator, a mini tape recorder, fold-up binoculars, and his working snacks. He had gone after the binoculars but grabbed the recorder, three Snickers bars, a handful of beef jerky, and an open bag of dog biscuits, too. He was just adding these to his now bulging backpack, when a pounding knock at the door startled him. Collins' mind had already returned to the nearly inscrutable world of his companions, with its weird violations of physical law and its strict and cruel legalities and punishments. He forced his muscles to uncoil, his breathing to slow. The worst thing he faced here was expulsion or bankruptcy, a far cry from hanging.

"Hide," Collins hissed at Zylas; who, accustomed to doing just that, disappeared in an instant. Without bothering to give a similar command to Falima, he headed toward the door, just as another fusillade of knocking exploded through the room. Loud as thunder, it left no doubt about the mood of the person on the other side.

Collins pulled open the door, only then remembering he wore nothing but boxers.

Professor Terellin studied him from the hallway, and several people peeked from partially open doors on either side. The proctor of Collins' building, the gray-bearded philosophy professor usually handled problems in a calm, rational manner that left little room for discussion. Now, his hair hung in a lopsided auburn-and-white scraggle, rather than its usual neat comb over. Long-legged, slender, and distinguished, Terellin reminded Collins of John Cleese playing the barrister in *A Fish Called Wanda*. He glanced around the hallway, and the doors hurriedly shut. "May I come in?"

Collins stepped back. "Of course, Professor."

Terellin glided inside, closing the door behind him. He studied Collins in the dim light, then turned his gaze to Korfius, who lay in a stretched-out position of doggy comfort on Collins' rumpled bed. The man cleared his throat. "We ignore your dog, Mr. Collins, despite the no-pet policy, because he's a hero."

Collins nodded, well aware of that information. He had never taken great pains to hide the animal, though he did not go out of his way to flaunt the dog either. "Yes, sir. Thank you."

"But a horse, Mr. Collins?" The professor made a bland gesture toward the window. "That's going too far."

Collins' heart rate quickened, and he followed the professor's motion with his gaze. Possibilities paraded through his mind, the most compelling to deny knowing anything about Falima's presence. He discarded the urge, however. For her welfare, he could not abdicate responsibility. "Yes, Professor Terellin. I agree."

The man grunted.

"You see, we need the horse for ... physiology experiments and ..." So far, the explanation sounded plausible, and Collins struggled to keep it that way. "... and ... I ... well, I did the ordering. I certainly didn't expect them to deliver her to my home ... but ..." Collins battled through the sleepiness that dimmed his thoughts. "... well, here she is. I jumped right out of bed and started making some calls, but it's hard to get anyone to answer this time of night."

Professor Terellin's expression softened immediately. "Any luck at all?"

Collins rubbed a hand along his other naked arm, a nervous gesture. "I found a stable that'll take her." He deliberately avoided saying where in case anyone checked the story. "I just have to get her there." He gestured to his backpack. "I was just getting ready for the trip."

"And dressing?" Terellin suggested.

Collins blushed. He wore boxers to bed rather than his

usual briefs out of modesty, but it was still underwear. "Just getting to that, sir."

A bit of testiness returned to the professor's demeanor. "Well, hurry, please, Mr. Collins. I don't want to have to explain this to the board. Or to the next fifteen people who want to know why they can't keep a finch but I'll let you turn the quadrangle into a barn. What's next? Pigs?"

Collins tried a joke, though he was too nervous to make it a good one. "We've got some of the guinea variety at the lab."

"No, thank you." The philosophy professor turned on his heel. "Just get that horse out of here."

"Right away," Collins promised.

The professor glanced back over his shoulder. "Do you want me to let your department know you won't be in today?"

Collins considered, imagining the philosophy professor delivering his cockamamie story to his crusty biology preceptor. The explanations that followed would probably turn wilder, enveloping him in an inescapable twist of increasingly outrageous lies. Ultimately, he would have to come up with a logical experiment involving horses or lose his fellowship. "Thank you, sir, but I'll do it by e-mail."

"All right," Terellin said. "You just get that smelly animal out of here ASAP."

"Consider it done." This time, the professor crossed the room and exited into the hallway without looking back. When the door clicked shut, Collins sank down on the bed, feeling as tired as if he had jogged three miles. A furry muzzle jostled his hand, and he reached down to pet Korfius, only to realize the dog lay sleeping beside him. He opened his eyes to Zylas.

"You're quick with words," the rat said.

"A quick liar," Collins grumbled. "Something to write home about."

"So long as it's for the right reasons."

Collins simply shrugged. It was not the way his parents had raised him. *The same parents who pretended to love one another throughout my childhood, then divorced and forgot all about me as soon as I left home.* He realized they might not serve as stellar examples either.

Apparently sensing Collins' continued consternation,

Zylas elaborated. "So long as you don't start equating whatever you want to 'right,' you don't have a problem."

Collins looked at the albino rat, who returned his stare, whiskers twitching earnestly. *Deceive the philosophy professor, then talk philosophy with vermin.* Mobilized, he rose, throwing up his hands at the whole ludicrous idea. "I'm getting dressed."

Collins pawed through his clothing, emerging with a green pocket tee, comfortable jeans, gym socks, and a clean pair of briefs. Turning his back to the window and Falima, he removed his sleeping boxers, then pulled on his briefs and last night's jeans. He shook out the T-shirt. "This warm enough for the weather there?" He did not worry about his packed clothing. Barring a sudden attack of insanity, he would not be staying in Barakhai long.

Zylas bobbed his head. "Though you might want something with sleeves in the woods. For protection."

"For protection?" Collins knew Zylas meant from weeds, branches, and bugs, but he could not help adding, "What I really need for protection is Kevlar."

"Kevlar?" Zylas repeated.

"Never mind." Collins finished dressing, then pulled on his running shoes without bothering to untie them. He tossed the backpack across his left shoulder. "Let's go."

Zylas sprang to Collins' shoulder. Falima whinnied, and Collins cringed. He whistled sharply. "Come on, Korfius."

The dog leaped to immediate attention, then sprang from the bed to caper merrily at Collins' feet. Usually, the dog did not get to accompany him in the morning, when he attended classes. Collins reached for the knob, then froze in mid-movement. "I'd better send that e-mail. And I'll need something to lead Falima with."

"Not necessary," Zylas said in his ear. "We can ride her."

Without a saddle or bridle? Like that wouldn't raise any more suspicions. Collins snapped on the power-strip switch, then scanned the room for something ropelike while his Gateway EV70 and its accompanying paraphernalia ran through their opening sequence. "I know that. But no one's going to believe my story if I hop up on a strange horse without anything to control it and don't worry about getting bucked to China." As his gaze fell across the familiar sparse furnishings, he mentally discarded using electrical cords, rubber bands, and duct tape. His desk filled one corner of the room, most of its surface taken up by the computer with its screen, speakers, CPU, and his Hewlett-Packard LaserJet printer perched upon the familiar, black and white cow-spotted box that had contained the shipped computer. An empty coffee can held pens, pencils, and markers and his assorted hard rock tapes and CDs. On the shelf above sat the combination CD player/double tape deck/radio that played them. Beside the desk, the television offered him nothing. He considered twisting up the bedsheets or rifling the dresser to find some clothing to sacrifice to the cause.

"Falima doesn't need to be led." Zylas' whiskers tickled Collins' ear. "She'll come along."

Focused on the rope hunt, Collins jumped at Zylas' voice. "True, but it'll look really weird if a horse follows me around like a puppy."

The speakers blared out the six beats of music that indicated the computer's readiness. Collins leaned over his chair, grasped the mouse, and clicked on the internet icon. The hourglass appeared, the icon darkened, and the globe whirled in the upper right-hand corner. Finally deciding he might have some rope in the kitchen junk drawer, Collins started to head back in that direction. A roll of speaker cord caught his eye as he moved, and he grabbed it instead.

The high-pitched dialing notes rang from the speakers, followed by the intermittent static and up-and-down resonances of the connection.

"What's wrong with looking weird?" Zylas stared at the computer.

Collins seized the coated wire, then returned to the keyboard. "Nothing, if you're a total geek, I guess. Mostly, I don't want people asking a bunch of questions. If I start blathering on about other worlds and animals who turn into people, I'll wind up locked in a loony bin like that first guy you lured to Barakhai." Dropping the coil into his pocket, he tapped out a quick, vague e-mail about a family emergency, clicked off-line, and initiated shutdown. "People already think I'm too tight with my dog. Imagine what they'll think if a horse just—" Abrupt realization bombarded him. "—or if I've got a rat hanging out on my shoulder!" He patted himself down for a suitable pocket and realized that the one in his T-shirt would prove way too flimsy and small and the ones in his jeans seemed equally unsuitable, mostly for anatomical reasons. Collins found himself wishing for the loose, coarse weave of Barakhain clothing. "You'll have to go in the pack."

"Great," Zylas muttered with a discontented sigh. Nevertheless, he did as Collins bade.

Only then, Collins thought to mention, "Hey, you're talking to me without your translation stone."

The pack muffled Zylas' reply. "I am."

Collins had believed the rest of the question was implied; but, when Zylas did not go on, he asked, "How?"

"Prinivere."

The response confused Collins, but he did not press Zylas for more information now. He would have the opportunity to ask all of his questions when he no longer had to worry about getting a horse out of the quad before anyone else saw her.

When the monitor went blank, Collins flicked the power switch. Walking to the door of his apartment, he opened it and stepped into a hallway empty except for the other doors and Professor Terellin who waited with his arms folded impatiently over his chest.

"Sorry." Collins flushed. "Had to send that e-mail and pack a few things."

The professor bobbed his head without speaking.

Collins hurried down the hallway and out the back door into the quadrangle, and Korfius followed. The false dawn painted red shadows across the benches spotted randomly around the central garden. Pathways crisscrossed the courtyard, leading to a dormitory, the English building, and the Student Union. Falima still stood peering into his window.

"Horse," Collins whispered, not wanting to use her name for fear of exposing his lies.

Falima's head jerked upward, then tipped sideways as she searched for him.

"Over here, Horse."

Falima found Collins with one eye, then trumpeted out a welcoming whinny.

Cringing, Collins took out the speaker wire and unwrapped a length.

Falima ran to him with a speed that seemed unstoppable. Collins back-stepped and pressed against the building, but need not have worried. The horse came to an abrupt halt in front of him, prancing and snorting in greeting.

Collins wrapped the soft, pliable wire in a loop around Falima's neck, guiding her away from the quadrangle, around the graduate student housing building, to the main walkway through the campus. Surreptitiously, he looked for droppings and noticed none. He did not know whether doing so might insult his friends, but he could not afford to leave such an obvious telltale. He could imagine the students trying to puzzle out a huge animal flop appearing in the quadrangle in the middle of the night. At the least, they would be watching for a major prank; at the worst, it would spark the very protest about pets that Professor Terellin wanted to avoid. *I can't have a gerbil, but you let someone walk their cow?*

The cord proved as unnecessary as Zylas had claimed, but Collins continued the charade. The other professors and students already marveled at the close bond he shared with the dog who had run for help while he lay, seriously wounded, on the laboratory floor. Collins' sudden ability to speak every human language had confounded his doctors, who had plied him with CT scans and MRIs, none of which had revealed anything abnormal. *Apparently, magic doesn't show up on X-ray.* One more eccentricity would likely push him over the edge from a curiosity to an object of aversion. Students tended to tolerate diversity, so long as it had a logical and rational basis.

Collins continued through the dark toward Daubert Laboratories, willing the hulking buildings to pass by more swiftly. The walk seemed longer than usual, the sidewalk harder, the buildings less friendly. It all passed in a dim blur of light and shadow that little resembled the cheery, student-filled pathways of Algary's days and evenings. The clop of Falima's hooves echoed strangely between the buildings.

A security guard approached, gave a habitual cheery wave, then stopped short. He waited for Collins to reach him.

Though tempted to veer away, Collins kept to the concrete walkway. Anything else would appear suspicious. "Good morning," he said.

"Good morning." The stout, dour-faced guard studied the horse. "Interesting companions you have there."

"It's a horse." Collins stated the obvious, so as not to appear to be hiding anything. *As if I could stuff a horse under my shirt.* He followed the security guard's gaze with his own, only to notice a red eye peering through the inky curtain of Falima's mane. *Damn it, Zylas, I told you to stay in the pack.* Suddenly, Collins realized the man had said companion*s*, plural. *Did he see Zylas?* He tried to come up with a plausible explanation for a lab rat crawling freely over an unperturbed horse.

"And a dog," the guard added, as if in answer to Collins' concerns. His attention turned to the patchy hound, whose tail flopped back and forth like an overwound pendulum.

"The dog's mine. Name's Korfius."

The guard's gaze returned to the horse.

Glowering at Zylas, Collins answered the unspoken question. "I'm taking her to the lab." This time, he spoke the truth, though he made no attempt to avoid the implication that he intended to use her in experiments.

The guard grunted. "You wouldn't be planning some sort of practical joke, now, would you, kid?"

Collins gave the only answer anyone would, whether or not he intended such a thing. "No."

"Can I see your ID?"

Collins didn't fight, seeing no reason to prolong the encounter with argument. Preferring the guard's focus to remain on him rather than the animals, he took his wallet from his pocket and presented his graduate student identification card.

The guard took it from him. "Collins," he murmured. "Benton Collins." He handed it back to Collins. "Now why does that sound familiar?"

Collins replaced the card and his wallet. "I'm the one who got beat up in the lab a year and a half ago at Thanksgiving."

The guard snapped his fingers. "Right. We took a lot of flak for that."

Collins said nothing. Surely, the man would not blame him for being the victim of an apparent assault.

Again, the man looked at Korfius. "So this must be the critter who saved you."

"Yes," Collins said. "He is." He let his brows inch upward. "May I please go now? I'd like to get this horse set up in time to grab some breakfast."

With obvious reluctance, the guard stepped aside. Collins continued down the pathway more quickly now, hoping to make it to the portal without running into anyone else. That realization brought an ironic smile to his lips. *The portal. What's my hurry? Do I really need to rush to a place where the people in power want me dead?* The idea seemed insanity. He had never sought out as simple a thrill as bungee jumping, and he did not relish the thought of repeating his last encounter in Barakhai. *The insanity is that I've even agreed to come this far.*

The oblong shape of Daubert Laboratories came into view, and Collins loosed a pent up breath. He raced for the most obscure side entrance, the horse trotting happily along behind him. Farthest from the main rooms and experiments, it would provide fewer opportunities for chance encounters with students or professors. Only as he hurried up the concrete stairs to the peeling, green-painted door did he remember that, for this way in, he needed a key. He fumbled at his waist, hoping he had left his jumble of keys clipped to a belt loop by habit. As usual, his beeper pinched the fabric at his left hip, the keys just in front of his right. He unfastened the metal clip, found the biggest key by feel and inserted it into the lock. It snapped to the open position. He twisted the knob and shouldered the panel inward. The mingled odors of mustiness, animal dander, cleaners, and wood chips filled his nose.

Falima whickered, apparently recognizing the scent as the pathway home, and Zylas scrabbled back to Collins' shoulder. "We're here?"

"We'd better be." Collins stepped inside and held the door open for Falima and Korfius. "Otherwise, you just earned me a one-way ticket to Bellevue."

The limitations of the translation spells kicked in. "What?"

Collins shook his head. "Never mind." He closed the door behind the animals, out of habit listening for the click of its locking.

Zylas squeaked into Collins' ear, "We didn't need a key to get out."

"You wouldn't have." Collins watched Falima continue forward, hooves clattering against tile. She moved easily despite the odd sounds, which surprised him. He had spent an anxious half hour urging her across the castle draw-bridge in Barakhai and now had to guess that embedded formica had a more solid sound or feel than overair planking. "The main door's never locked. I brought us in a different way."

Korfius raised his nose, sniffing wildly, then running to Collins.

Accepting Collins' explanation, Zylas turned to something he understood. "Korfius associates the smell of this place with you."

Now that Zylas had spoken it aloud, the dog's behavior seemed obvious. "Not surprising. I practically live here." It seemed unlikely they would find anyone in the building this time of the morning, but Collins could not discount the possibility of a cleaning crew. He hurried his animal companions down the hallway to the class-turned-storage room that led to Barakhai.

Sparse light funneled in the doorway to reveal the jumbled desks, chairs, and boxes Collins remembered from his last visit to Barakhai. Then, sunlight swimming through dust motes had given the appearance of smoke; but the current hour just made it seem ghostly dark. The strange equations remained, white figures dancing across the chalkboard, and Collins could just discern the purple chalk pentagram scrawled across the tile.

Zylas scrambled to the floor. "Let's go."

Collins studied Falima doubtfully. Her solid, golden body had to weigh at least half a ton, and her head towered over his own 5'11".

Zylas followed Collins' gaze and divined his question. "She made it in; she can make it out." He flitted beneath a desk.

Collins shrugged. The rat/man had a seemingly undeniable point, but Collins knew the loophole. He could leave his world for Barakhai through the portal, but no one in human form had ever passed from there to here. If the magic could make such seemingly impossible and random distinctions, perhaps it could make the path in more difficult than the one out of Barakhai. Deciding the pain of watching a friend struggle outweighed curiosity, he followed his albino companion.

Worried about the effect of mixing technology with the

active magic of the portal, Collins did not attempt to use his mag light as they crawled through dark debris for what seemed like an hour. At first, Collins' backpack banged against the stacked furniture, and he heard an avalanche of cardboard boxes. Falima gave an occasional snort but otherwise handled the low scramble well. Soon, he heard her steady hoofbeats behind him, no longer moving at an unnatural shuffle, and he realized she could stand. Last time, he had assumed himself still amid the debris and had crawled much longer than necessary. This time, he rose, though he found himself keeping one hand hovering at the level of his forehead, guarding against the imagined junk that had last filled his vision. Barely needing to dip his head at any point, Korfius padded along beside him. Zylas continued to lead the way effortlessly, his white fur the only thing visible in the otherwise blinding gloom. Anything that could inconvenience a rat would surely thwart any of his companions.

Then, the world began to brighten. Moonlight filtered through an opening that had once held a wooden door, revealing a crumbling ruin of a stone room. Through the gap, Collins could see a world that currently resembled his own, at least in regard to time of day. Stars sprinkled the sky, with a slight grayness that hinted of coming dawn. The rat stared ahead as Collins and Korfius emerged.

"Uh-oh," Zylas said.

Collins peered through his wire-rimmed glasses at a sea of men milling outside the ruins, dressed in the familiar silver and aqua of King Terrin's guards.

Chapter 2

THROUGH the doorway of the ruins, Collins looked down on a sea of royal aqua and white. The soldiers in front stood in regimented lines, their uniforms unadorned, their mail pristine, and their heads bare. Their hair ranged from snowy-white to ebony, and their skin spanned nearly as broad a range. Most clutched spears and some carried swords through the wide black sashes that served as belts. Dogs of myriad shapes, colors, and sizes meandered through the troops or stood attentively among the men. Toward the back, the mounted soldiers wore iron helms and the white portions of their uniforms bore a spattering of stretched, blue-green clovers.

"Damn," Collins said, his awed and nervous expletive no louder than Zylas' grossly understated, "Uh-oh."

Collins added carefully, "We're in an almighty colossal shit load of trouble." He waited for his friend to contradict him, to assure him that the renegades had expected and planned for this confrontation, but Zylas gave him nothing.

The front line leveled its spears. "Halt!" a commander yelled at Collins and his friends. "No one move."

"Zylas?" Collins implored in a desperate whisper. His animal companions, he knew, had an out. They could race back through the magical portal and hope none of the guards in their horse or dog forms dared to follow. *And leave me in Weirdoland to face an army alone.* The idea seemed reprehensible, yet Collins turned to seal his fate. At least, Falima and Korfius, the woman and the child, should seize what little security they still had.

Korfius crouched, growling deep in his throat. Falima rummaged through the debris in woman form, as naked as a newborn and no more self-conscious.

Collins groaned, the irony clear even through rising dread. At their darkest hour, every companion but Korfius had been caught in his smallest, weakest form. *It's up to me.* He glanced out over the horde, at least a hundred strong. *And I'm not going to win by overpowering them.* He considered his possessions, hoping he had included some object he could use to shock and intimidate the soldiers. He dared not make a motion large enough to unsling his backpack. Instead, his hand strayed to his pocket, sifting through loose change and lint. No simple parlor trick, no random display of technology, would work here. One of the king's advisers, Carrie Quinton, came from his world; and the soldiers already knew that Collins did, too.

Before Collins could think to do anything, Falima charged past him with a bellow of fury, brandishing a stick in each hand.

"No!" Collins threw himself at the woman, missed, and rolled through the doorway toward the massed soldiers. Clearly surprised, they withdrew, and two fell beneath Falima's crazed assault. Korfius dove for another, driving him to the ground before several dogs closed in on the writhing man and dog.

"No!" Collins yelled. "Stop it." Still hoping to find something significantly exciting to astonish the warriors, he thumbed the test button on the beeper clipped to his belt and whipped the wheel toward maximum volume. Its squeal shrilled over the din.

The combatants hesitated, and all eyes jerked to Collins. *Fine, you did it. Now what?*

An enormous object blotted out the moonlight.

Instinctively, Collins ducked and swung his attention upward. A huge, shadowy figure filled the sky. Terror surged through him, and the urge to flee became an all encompassing necessity. He ran mindlessly, no longer worrying about the menace of the guards, hearing their screams and pounding footsteps meld with the more familiar screech of his beeper. Something heavy cut the air above his head. With-

out warning, a whirlwind sucked him off his feet, sending
him spiraling to the ground. He struck a stone with enough
force to drive the breath from his lungs, then found himself
tumbling down a steep, grassy hill without the barest sense
of control. The world spun past in a dizzying array of greens
and browns. Something leathery slapped his ear, pounding
pain through his head. Then a calm voice touched his mind.
Be still.

Though it violated any shred of logic, Collins tried to
obey. He felt something pierce the upper back of his T-shirt,
scraping furrows of skin from his neck. His feet left the
ground, and he dangled dangerously over rocks as the earth
disappeared below him. Soldiers scattered in all directions,
their ranks broken, their movements frenzied and random.
Collins found himself whipping violently upward through
the trees, the front of his collar chewing into his throat,
choking off his screams and most of his breathing. "Help!"
he rasped out.

Collins' rational mind gradually caught up to reality. *A
flying animal the size of a school bus has me in its claws.*
Only one creature fit that description. *Prinivere.* Collins
fought a desperate battle for sane and logical understanding. *We're safe.* He savored that thought for less than a moment, when an abrupt turn sent him flying toward a clump
of trees. The rolled cotton bit deeper into his windpipe, cutting off his oxygen supply, and branches slashed his bare
arms. He seized his collar with both hands, wrenching it
forward with all his strength. The fabric gave only slightly,
and a trickle of air wheezed into his spasming lungs. "Help,"
he managed again, his hoarse, quiet voice lost in the swirl of
wind raised by flapping, batlike wings. Then he remembered
the dragon's nonverbal communication. *You're strangling
me!* He tried to send the thought directly at her. *I'm going
to die!*

Sorry, Prinivere sent back. *Brace for a change.* Without further explanation, she wrapped a claw around Collins'
right upper arm and released her grip on his shirt.

For an instant, Collins dangled sideways, Prinivere's long
claws digging painfully into his flesh. He caught a woozy
view of the trees far below him, and sudden terror conjured
an image of him plummeting hundreds of feet to a shattered
and painful death that made strangulation seem preferable.

Then, another claw closed over his left arm, and the balance allowed for a lighter hold.

Thank you. Collins filled the sending with genuine gratitude. Now that falling no longer seemed likely, just being able to breathe felt like an extraordinary gift, coupled with the fading of the pain in his neck and arm. He could still feel the scratches, but the sharp constancy of a deeply entrenched claw had disappeared.

Finally in control of his no-longer reeling senses, Collins worried for his companions. *Falima? Zylas? Korfius?*

On my back, Prinivere responded. *All safe.*

Collins flushed, wondering why he was the only one who had panicked, forgetting Prinivere could read the intention of thoughts as well as verbatim sendings.

You weren't alone. Zylas and Falima just have more experience with me, and I grabbed Korfius before you. I figured once he ran, I'd never catch him.

The trees now seemed a million miles below Collins, swaying wildly. He tried to pretend he was riding on a skyway at an amusement park, but he could not trick his senses into trusting the security of wheels, wires, and pulleys. Prinivere did not follow the straight path the illusion required, and nothing secured him should her grip fail, should someone shoot her down with spears and arrows, should her aged strength simply give way. *It's out of my hands.* Collins screwed his eyes tightly closed. He would live or die by Prinivere's skill, and he had little choice but to trust it.

The flight spanned a heart stopping eternity, air cutting around Collins and roaring painfully through his ears, the dragon surging and gliding, wings slapping air like shaken leather blankets. At length, she spiraled downward, and Collins dared at last to open his eyes. His vision was suddenly filled with rugged mountains poking through a vast, green forest. Prinivere sent a message more concept than words, urging him to watch for limbs and other dangers. Then, they plunged into the forest. Branches tore at Collins' bare arms and tangled into his hair. Something sharp poked his jeans at the left thigh but did not penetrate the tough cotton. Prinivere made a swaying and bumpy landing onto a rocky prominence, stretched her wings, then folded them gingerly against her sides. Balanced on her hind legs, she released Collins gently to his feet.

Collins scrambled aside, worried that a weary or accidental gesture of a wing or claw might put him into harm's
way. The quick movement stole the last of his already
shaky equilibrium, and he crashed to the ground, rolling
over stones that jabbed into his back and sides. He came
up on his knees. The outcropping overlooked forest that
seemed to stretch on forever, even blanketing the lower
peaks. The ledge Prinivere had chosen sheltered only a
few scraggly weeds and twisted, low-slung saplings that
resembled bonsai trees. The world was bathed in a flat,
steely gray that usurped all color. Dull and lifeless, it reminded Collins how much, and how soon, he wanted to go
home.

Falima clambered from the dragon's scaly back. Korfius
bounded after her, tongue lolling and tail wagging.

Collins felt obligated to say something, but words failed
him. "Wow."

"Wow, indeed." Falima approached the old dragon with
obvious concern. "Are you all right?"

Prinivere's enormous, toothy mouth pulled into a grin.
Once again, Collins marveled at how much the biologically
impossible creature resembled a dinosaur: long-necked and
long-legged, covered in greenish-black scales with plates
jutting from neck, back, and tail. Scars marred a hide that
seemed to glow, and the tail ended in a ragged cut. She
walked on four legs, despite the fibrous wings that, though
massive, should not be capable of supporting a body so
huge. Black ears pricked upward, triangular like a horse's;
and her eyes sparkled like emeralds recessed deeply into
dark-rimmed sockets. Each forelimb ended in three toes
with sharp, curved talons, while the hind legs sported four
toes apiece. The short-coupled body fit well with a blocky
snout that ended in arched and slitty nostrils. *I'm fine,* she
sent, apparently to everyone. *Stop fretting over me.*

Collins doubted the dragon was responding solely to
Falima's inquiry. He had worried only for his own life, but
his companions had clearly targeted more concern toward
Prinivere's welfare.

"Never, my lady." Zylas' squeaky voice came from farther along the outcropping, though Collins had not seen
him dismount.

Collins rose and headed toward the rat. As fear ebbed,

he grew more irritated. "You could have warned me we'd be facing spears and hitching a ride on a dragon."

"Why?" Zylas paced in a semicircle, looking up at Collins through one red eye. "Would you have come to Barakhai if I had?"

"No," Collins admitted, suspicions blossoming and anger with them. It was not the first time Zylas had tricked him to Barakhai. "Are you saying you hid—"

"He's just playing with you," Falima interrupted, giving the explanation that Zylas should have. "The soldiers surprised us, too. The king must have mobilized that force quickly. I'm guessing some spy saw us going into the ruins and decided to meet us there when we came out." She did not have to mention that, had they taken less time convincing Collins to join them, the army could not have massed in wait.

"My lady," Zylas said, turning his attention back to the dragon. "They've seen you! You should not have risked yourself."

Nonsense, Zylas. I have as much to gain from this as anyone. Perhaps more.

Zylas did not argue, though the frown that scored Falima's face suggested that she wanted him to. Collins considered the point. The elderly dragon was already living on borrowed time and had little personal stake in any project. On the other hand, she had little to lose either.

Prinivere lumbered around to face the group. *We also have spies. When Aisa brought me the news, I hurried there as fast as I could.* She pronounced the new name like the continent in Collins' world.

Zylas scrambled a few feet farther. "My lady, it's best to get you under cover."

Prinivere's huge head bobbed up and down wearily. She gave no thought-spoken reply, at least not one she allowed Collins to hear, but she did move along the ledge toward the rat/man. She could convey her communication to as many or as few listeners as she wished.

A moment later, Zylas disappeared into the weeds.

Collins hesitated, Falima at his side and Korfius at his heels. "Who's Aisa?"

Prinivere headed after Zylas, and Falima strode in the dragon's wake. "Another renegade. You'll meet her soon. If she fetched Prinivere, she must be here. And Ijidan, too. He takes care of this place."

Collins watched Prinivere push through an overhang of vines, which seemed to swallow her massive form. Apparently, a cave lay beyond the entwined cascade of greenery. He could not help marveling at the hiding places the renegades managed to find. The last time, they had kept him in the underground burrows of the outcast skunks, the garbage men of Barakhai. Their musk had foiled the ability of the guard hounds to track them. This cave, well-camouflaged and perched amid dangerous mountain peaks, could only be accessed by strong-winged birds and the most surefooted of mountain goats. And, of course, Prinivere.

When Collins followed his companions into the cave, he discovered an enormous, craggy room with several storage trunks, a fire pit, and a bed of straw. Prinivere, he knew, had simple tastes that defied the role-playing game image of dragons perched upon vast hordes of gold, jewels, gemstones, and magical treasures. A squirrel hunched on one of the chests, worrying a nut clutched between its forepaws. Beside it, a blue-and-gold macaw watched them, its head low and its feathers ruffled. Despite its calm demeanor, the parrot looked flamboyantly out of place, the royal cobalt feathers of its wings, tail, and back appearing dyed and the brilliant yellows of its belly just as unnatural. A patch of ivory skin surrounding the eyes and nostrils held black stripes composed of miniature feathers all leading to a wickedly curved ebony beak.

Prinivere collapsed into the straw, clearly exhausted. Whatever magical powers the crystal Collins had stolen enhanced, it did not, apparently, increase her physical stamina. *Or does it?* Collins realized the ancient dragon could never have flown so far before, especially carrying several passengers on her back. She had never actually fought the king's guards. They appeared to have succumbed to the same frantic, not wholly irrational, fear that gripped Collins whenever he encountered Prinivere. But she had managed to fly him and his companions into the mountains, a feat she could not have managed the last time Collins had come to Barakhai.

Once again, the dragon responded to Collins' meandering thoughts. *I can use magic to boost my energy temporarily, but the spell runs its course.*

Collins appreciated the knowledge; though the realization that she could read his every intention made him feel creepy and a bit violated. *At least, she trusts me, which suggests I really am the good person I try to be. No wonder Zylas puts such implicit faith in her judgment.* Suddenly understanding Prinivere must have received that thought, too, Collins felt his cheeks warm. He tried to redirect his mind, which only made him more self-conscious.

Zylas clambered up the side of the trunk to the squirrel and parrot. He addressed them at a volume that did not allow Collins to overhear.

Korfius ran around the cave, snuffling at every corner.

Falima assumed the job of hostess. "Ben, this is Aisa." She gestured at the macaw, who bobbed her head. She raised her left claw, opening and closing it intermittently. "Hello, Ben," she squawked.

Collins had seen a scarlet macaw at a local fair perform the same welcoming wave. He cleared his throat, this time avoiding the natural urge to use his "baby talk" voice. Though the parrot's greeting had seemed childlike, she might have the present mentality of a bird, a grown woman, or anywhere in between. "Hello, Aisa."

Falima finished, "And this is Ijidan." She indicated the squirrel. "The caretaker of this cave."

Ijidan flicked his bushy tail and stopped eating.

Zylas scurried up Collins' pants, then his shirt, to settle on his shoulder. "Aisa has decent overlap and the rare ability to speak our human tongue in switch form."

Collins nodded. The development of overlap, he knew, had to do with the amount of time spent as an animal, some natural talent, and practice. He had no means to gauge Aisa's bird age, but he guessed she would prove to be mature when she took her woman shape. It made sense that a parrot might have a propensity for remembering things between forms, given that they seemed highly intelligent. He had watched a television special in which African grays verbally identified objects, placed shapes into their proper holes, and sorted toys by size and color.

"She's one of our few *Regulars*," Zylas continued, using a term Collins remembered from his last visit to Barakhai. It meant her parents were also macaws, having bred in either human or animal form. If parents who assumed different creature forms created offspring in human form, their progeny would take the animal form of the mother for the first thirteen years, then become something ostensibly random. "Both her parents were *Randoms*, though, lucky enough to find one another and commiserate."

Apparently, Falima overheard Zylas. "Made a lot easier by the fact that they were cousins."

That made sense to biology-trained Collins. At least some of the propensity of *Randoms* to assume a certain animal form seemed to have a classical multifactorial inheritance pattern, as evidenced by Zylas and his late wife, both distant descendants of Prinivere, producing a daughter who became a dragon.

Zylas continued as if Falima had not interrupted. "The big advantage being that she's not registered."

Collins' brows beetled as he considered Zylas' words. "Registered?"

"Registered," Zylas said again, as if simple repetition could work as explanation. "As a *Random*."

Collins still did not understand.

Falima took over. "Remember how we told you the king's men attend all coming-of-age ceremonies?"

Collins nodded, deliberately avoiding Zylas' stare. When the rat's daughter had turned thirteen, revealing her new animal form, royal soldiers had taken her and killed the mother who tried to stop them.

"And that it's because the law states that obligate carnivores must be summarily executed."

Collins could not forget. "The king said that, before the law, those carnivores murdered an average of six people before they got caught." He waited for his companions to correct him, to expose the king as an evil liar.

Falima only shrugged. "That may be true."

Zylas fidgeted on Collins' shoulder.

Collins tried to shift the focus of the discussion a bit. "Last I knew, the king had issued a ban on *all Random* breedings." He turned his gaze to Aisa, who remained quietly perched, listening to the conversation but adding nothing. He wondered just how much she understood. The squirrel flitted around and up the box at lightning speed, nails skittering, objects shifting and slapping back into place as he moved.

Falima confirmed, "That law just went into effect. The royals gave it enough time to assure that all the women already pregnant with *Random* offspring could safely and legally bear their children."

It surprised and irritated Collins that the king chose to mitigate his new law with reason and apparent kindness. Collins wanted to hate King Terrin, to see him as a consummate villain as unequivocally evil as Cinderella's stepmother or Osama bin Laden. But, in all his dealings with Barakhai's king, Collins had found the man likable and logical. He only disagreed with two of the king's decisions. The first was choosing to execute innocent children barely into their teens even before they committed any crime because of the misfortune of transforming into a meat eater. The second was the king's decree against *Random* unions, which seemed little more than genocide through breeding. According to Zylas and Falima, the royal family planned to do away with "undesirable" animals, such as vermin, snakes, and certain types of carnivores, all of which were already forbidden, by previous laws, from *Regular* breeding.

"Anyway," Zylas said, returning to the original point. "At coming-of-age, *Randoms* are registered in a large book. It all looks rather special and important to the child and families, but it's just an elaborate way for the royals to keep track of us."

Without warning, Ijidan made a flying leap from the box to Collins' chest. The squirrel scampered to Collins' unoccupied shoulder, then along his left arm, leaving a line of pale scratches with each skittish movement.

"What the hell?" Collins finally managed, watching the animal scamper over his clothing and flesh indiscriminately. When Ijidan held still long enough, he ran a hand along the soft, grizzled fur. "Does he have to do that?"

Aisa let out a loud squawk. "Just checking you over."

Collins jumped at the sound, heart pounding, and the sudden movement sent the squirrel scurrying over him for another pass. This time, the animal sprang back to the box when it finished.

Collins found himself missing Ialin, their previous companion, a hummingbird/man who had despised him. At least, Ialin's actions had seemed comprehensible, after a time, and his noises weren't ear shattering. "Where's Ialin?"

Falima's gaze followed Ijidan, and she smiled, apparently reading the barb beneath Collins' otherwise innocent question. "He's spying. Didn't think you'd care if you saw him again."

Collins made a wave of dismissal. In truth, he did not care, though he still thought the tiny man's mature quietness would trump anything Aisa or Ijidan had to offer. *What am I doing? This is insane.* He thought about the greeting the king's men had given them. Now they knew Collins had returned to Barakhai, and they knew about the dragon. Even with the crystal, Prinivere's magic was severely limited by her advanced age. The shabby band of renegades had lost their one other advantage: surprise. The king, on the other hand, still had money, power, an army of trained and armed guards, and Carrie Quinton.

Collins pictured the woman, a genetics postgraduate who had originally come from his own world and now served as an adviser to King Terrin. Once, Collins had slept with her, and he found himself easily picturing the smooth curves, her cascade of naturally golden hair, her long legs and large firm breasts. She had the face of a model. *Had,* he reminded himself, wincing. When he had stolen the crystal she wore as a necklace, inadvertently cutting her neck with it, she had turned on him. To escape the swords of the guards, he had thrust a torch into her face. His last glimpse of her was with her hair aflame, her screams echoing through the stairwell.

Collins shook off the memory. He had also burned the king's brother, and he knew he would die, and die horribly, if the royals caught him. *This isn't a game; home or in Barakhai, dead is forever. We escaped once by the grace of a dragon. Next time, it may not go so well.* He glanced at Prinivere, who lay still with her head on her forelegs, eyes closed. Exhaustion weighed heavily on her, but Collins had to test Zylas' promise. "I want to go home. Now."

Falima looked stricken. Zylas said nothing, but he rubbed his thin, pink ears with a paw. Prinivere opened one enormous, green eye and rolled her attention to Zylas, still perched on Collins' shoulder.

Driven by his need to know exactly where he stood, Collins demanded, "I want to go home right now."

"Please . . ." Falima started, stayed by a tired wave of the dragon's claw.

Come, Prinivere sent to Collins. *I will send you back.*

Certain his companions would use the dragon's fatigue as an excuse to delay his return, Collins stammered out, "Y—you will?"

The dragon's expression did not waver, but she did open her other eye. *Of course, I will. I would not ignore Zylas' promises. Such a thing would dishonor us both.*

Collins glided toward the dragon, shaking. Though he knew she was old, feeble, and had no intention of harming him, he still suffered from a deep instinctive fear.

Prinivere continued as he approached, *Last time, we brought you here under false pretenses and kept you with trickery. If you choose to help us this time, it must be of your own free will, because of the goodness in your own heart.*

Collins cringed. Her final pronouncement, though delivered without emotion, cut deeply. He liked his Barakhain friends, agreed with their mission, and wanted them to accomplish their worthy goal. He also knew that they needed him in order to succeed. Sighing, he lowered his head. *They're risking their lives for their own futures and those of their children. What do I have to gain from this?* It was a bitterly selfish question. *If I could save the lives of thousands of children in my own world by sacrificing myself, I would do it. Why are the children of Barakhai worth less?* Though he saw the flaw in his own question, Collins still paused. *Because it's not a sure thing. I could die, and the Barakhains could still keep their curse, their king, and all that goes with them.*

Suddenly remembering that Prinivere received all of his thoughts, Collins looked at her fiercely. She lay in place, expression impassive, eyes nonjudgmental. It was a quandary he had to face alone, but he wished someone would say something to sway him either way.

Finally, Prinivere did. *Wouldn't you like to stay until Korfius changes? So you can talk to him, I mean?*

It was as good an excuse as any to put off a difficult decision. Collins glanced around for his dog, finding him lying on the floor near the mouth of the cave chewing on a dangling vine. "Good idea," he said. Thinking back, he knew that Zylas became a man at noon, Korfius a boy two hours later, then Prinivere became a woman about an hour after that. When he had set his watch by Zylas' switch time, Korfius changed at 2:00 P.M. and Prinivere at 3:00 P.M. Because they were *Regulars*, Korfius and Prinivere spent less time in human form than the others, who split their time exactly half and half.

"In the meantime," Falima suggested carefully, rolling her gaze from Prinivere to Zylas to Collins as if waiting for one of them to silence her again, "maybe we could explain why we brought you. Then you can make an informed decision."

That sounded like a good idea to Collins. He nodded. "All right." He crossed the cave to sit on one of the chests not already occupied by a parrot or squirrel. "Go."

Zylas jumped from Collins' shoulder to the wood, displaying none of Ijidan's grace. "The lady—" he gave a nod toward the dragon to acknowledge her "—warned us that she would probably not prove strong enough to work the crystal to its full potential."

Remember, it took two healthy young males to place the curse.

Collins remembered. The half-dragon twins of an ancient princess, embittered by their lot, had cursed all but select members of the royal family to spend part of their lives in animal form. Or, in the case of the dragons, in human form. In revenge, the dragons had slain the boys, only to find themselves hunted to extinction. Only Prinivere remained, still bearing the scars of wounds the hunters had believed mortal and the missing tail that had won them their bounty.

The crystal is powerful, but my magic and vigor have dwindled too far. Zylas tells me there are two other dragons. Young ones. Prinivere's sending contained a desperate hopefulness directed at Collins. He had told Zylas about the dragons, having learned of their existence from Carrie Quinton. One was surely Zylas' daughter. The other was a *Random* claimed by the king, as was his right, for execution as a dangerous carnivore. Apparently, it was male, as Quinton had talked excitedly of breeding them.

Collins shrugged. "I didn't see them with my own eyes, but I believe the person who told me about them."

"Carriequinton," Zylas supplied.

Falima shifted restlessly from foot to foot, then dug at the cave floor with a heel. At length, she looked up and, noticing all eyes upon her, added, "She doesn't care much for you, Ben."

Collins pursed his lips. "Not surprising." He dodged Falima's gaze, hoping she did not know he had slept with Quinton. At the time, it had seemed natural, given how much they had in common and how he planned to get them both permanently back to their world having lived an intense experience that no one seemed likely to believe. "How badly did I hurt her?"

"Her face," Zylas squeaked, hiding his whiskery nose behind a paw. "Let's just say she's not beautiful any more."

Falima added, "It's a woman thing, but I think you hurt her heart, too. And not just from the pain of losing her looks. She seems to think you ... betrayed her."

Collins sucked his lips all the way into his mouth. Quinton had grown up in a series of foster homes, bitter about a drug-addicted mother, which seemed to have warped her sense of emotional attachment. After just one time in bed, she had imagined an entire life for them together. "She *really* hates me."

No one denied or confirmed the words, the ultimate affirmation.

Aisa squawked, and Collins jumped, wondering if he could ever get used to her doing that. *Not that I need to, but the others do.*

Zylas seized on the interruption. "In any case, we've searched the whole world for those dragons, without success. There seems to be only one place left to look." He lifted his head to Collins, who figured it out with ease.

"The royal quarters." It made sense that, if they needed Collins again, it would be to enter the areas of the kingdom warded against switchers.

"Right," Aisa corroborated in her parrot voice, apparently following at least part of the conversation.

Collins doubted the king would keep dragons in his bedchambers. "Maybe there aren't any dragons. Maybe Carrie gave me wrong information."

Falima perched delicately on the opposite edge of the chest. "No. There are dragons. We started searching as soon as you told us about them and, early on, found some dragon signs deep in the castle dungeons."

"We?" Collins pressed.

"Spies," Zylas detailed. "Including myself. I definitely smelled my daughter's scent, though none of us ever saw her. The king must have moved them soon after our raid, and no one managed to follow their trail, now long cold. It's almost as if—she disappeared." Mist covered his beady eyes, and Collins read pain there. Zylas would not beg or deceive this time. He clearly had taken Collins' anger to heart and trusted Collins' previous claim that, if he had only known the facts, he still would have helped and would have proved better at it.

Such consideration seemed worth rewarding. It pleased Collins that someone had listened so intently to his words and followed them to the letter. *Zylas is a real friend.* He wondered if he had ever truly known another. The rat/man clearly had practice at treating others well, never leading from the rear but placing himself in the same, or worse, danger as his followers. "So," Collins said, "all I have to do is look through the royal bedchambers again."

Apparently missing the sarcasm, Falima said brightly, "That's it."

And Zylas continued in the same upbeat vein. "If you find them, we'll figure out a way to rescue them when you get back."

"Oh," Collins said, glancing between his companions to see if they completely missed the obvious or were just better than he was at nonchalantly stating the impossible. "So I don't actually have to retrieve these dragons. Just look for them."

Falima's smile seemed genuine, filled with joy at having Collins seriously consider the mission so soon after demanding to leave. "Right."

"In the king's warded bedchamber."

"Right."

Collins blinked. "Okay. That all seems simple enough." He hardened his tone to make it clear he believed they'd all gone mad. "So long as you ignore the fact that I have to sneak onto the castle grounds, into the castle itself, and to the king's own bedchamber past a zillion guards and other royal employees all of whom . . . *want to personally inflict on me the death of a thousand tortures.* Or something worse." He threw up his hands in disgust. "Are you crazy?"

Zylas' head swung toward Prinivere, who had obviously

communicated with him alone. Then he addressed Collins. "Did I forget to mention you'd be disguised?"

Collins continued to stare in disbelief. "That was implied, but I don't think a little grease paint and a haircut are going to fool anyone this time."

Prinivere finally gave a sending to Collins. *He means disguised by magic.*

At last, Collins began to understand. "By magic?" It had nearly killed Prinivere to cast the spell that allowed Collins to understand their language, and Zylas had sworn not to let her risk herself like that again. "The crystal?" he wondered aloud.

The crystal. Prinivere confirmed. *I can make you look like one of the guards without harming myself. And another will go as your partner.*

The nonverbal sending allowed Collins to understand that, by "your partner," she meant that whoever went with him would go in the guise of the guard's partner as well. He wondered what other spells Prinivere could now do that she could not previously manage but decided not to ask. It might violate some ethical protocol, which would greatly upset Zylas, who always insisted on proper etiquette and respect for the Lady. An instant later, he remembered that Prinivere could read his thoughts. She could choose to list her new abilities or to let him know if she would tolerate a direct questioning. "Who would this partner actually be?"

Zylas piped in at once. "Me."

"You?" Collins' brows shot up. "But you can't get into the royals' chambers."

"Nor can anyone else. That's why we brought you." The rat tilted his head into a pose probably supposed to appear brave, though it merely made him look quizzical. "I can get you there and back safely."

Falima wrung her hands. Clearly, she wanted to intervene, to keep Zylas out of harm's way. However, to do so would mean putting a lesser value on Collins' life.

"Can you guarantee that?" Although he knew better, Collins dared to hope.

Zylas' head glided back to its usual position. "Well, no, but . . . no one can ever . . ."

Collins forced a grin. "I was kidding."

"Oh. Well, then." Zylas' cheeks pulled across his muzzle

into a ratty grin. It was a strange image, like a computer-animated commercial. "I'll do my best. I'm not going to run out on you."

Collins wondered if Zylas had actually used slang or if the spell simply translated it that way. *Spell or stone or both,* he reminded himself, only then recalling that he still had not pressed Zylas on the details of a question that had occurred to him way back in his own world. "So what happened to your translation stone?"

"I don't need it anymore." Zylas raised his head proudly.

Collins doubted the rat/man had suddenly learned all the languages of both worlds, along with every animal tongue. The spell Prinivere had cast on Collins interpreted only human languages, and they had told him the crystal Zylas always carried was unique. Collins jerked his gaze past the crates to where Prinivere once again rested with her eyes closed.

Zylas anticipated the question. "No, she can't cast a spell that works like my stone did. But she was able to remove the magic from its container and place it directly into me."

Collins saw the pros and cons of such a maneuver. It meant Zylas could never lose his precious artifact; but he also could not lend it out as he once had to Falima and Collins. And the magic died with him, an event that seemed inevitable given the power and reach of those who hunted him. Now in his forties, Zylas had given the royalty problems since his youth. On the other hand, the stone could no longer be taken from Zylas or lost by him, and not having to carry it left his hands and mouth free. Zylas' value to the cause became wholly clear to Collins for the first time: a wise, bold, honest, and determined man with near-perfect overlap and a means to communicate with anyone in any form. Falima's instincts were right. The renegades could not afford to lose Zylas. "I'll do it," he said, the words out of his mouth before he could consider them. "But I can't take you as my partner."

Zylas' mouth dropped open, revealing his little pink tongue, and his crimson eyes bulged with distress and affront. "Why not?"

"Because they need you." Collins made a gesture that encompassed the entire cave. From the corner of his vision, he thought he saw the sleeping dragon smile.

Zylas dismissed the argument. "We need you, too. And you don't have any stake in this. I'm best-suited for the job, and I go."

Collins could not argue. He and Zylas did work well together, though he had to correct one thing. "Oh, I do have a stake in this. I, too, have loved ones suffering by the curse and the king's decree."

Zylas' determined look went instantly blank. "You do?"

Even before he had broken up with a girlfriend with whom he had little in common, Collins had had few close friends. Aside from Korfius, his life had only grown more empty. "You, you dim-witted quadruped. I mean you." He turned his gaze to Falima. "And others, here, too."

This time an unmistakable smile stretched the old dragon's face.

Chapter 3

WHILE Prinivere slept and recovered from her excursion, Zylas reminded Collins of a castle layout he still vividly remembered. The grand structure towered five stories, topped by a crenellated rooftop fitted with ballistae and patrolled by guards. The four corner towers stretched another ten feet toward the sky, and Collins could not lose the memory of jumping from one of these, Zylas in his pocket, to a cart full of hay drawn hurriedly into place by goats secretly loyal to the renegades. The hay had barely cushioned his fall, and the cart had broken, leaving him a gashed and bloody mess with several broken bones and damaged internal organs. The basement held the dungeon, where Collins had spent a restless day and night while the castle staff waited for him to take a switch-form. The basement also reportedly contained food and wine cellars and storage rooms, though he had not seen them during his imprisonment.

The drawbridge across the moat led to two courtyards opening onto the ground floor, which held the kitchens and various workshops. Above those, the library and great dining hall were familiar to Collins. He had eaten a meal there and sneaked out, through the library, to search the uppermost floors. The third level reportedly held the servants' quarters. The guards slept in barracks, stables, and kennels in the inner courtyard. The superiors all had horse switchforms, and the subordinates turned into dogs. In fact, Zylas had coopted Falima from a city guard force, and they had captured Korfius from that same force to keep him quiet after he found them on a hunt.

At some point during Zylas' description, Collins drifted into sleep. He came awake suddenly to find himself slumped over one of the wooden chests, his arm sticky with his own drool. Now in man form, Zylas conversed in soft tones with Prinivere, his voice an indecipherable rumble and hers, as usual, wholly inaudible. At the end of the chest, Ijidan gnawed at a piece of orange fruit clutched between his paws while Korfius watched curiously from the ground. A short, heavyset woman prepared a dining table on one of the other chests. He saw no sign of Falima.

Collins rubbed the sleep seeds from his eyes, wondering how long he had slept. He still felt sluggish, though time would tell if that came of recently awakening or honest tiredness. From habit, he glanced at his watch, which read 10:42 and could not be right. For Zylas to have switched, it had to be after noon. He had missed his chance to set the time by Zylas' change, as he had done on his last visit. The modicum of light that found its way through the heavy curtain of vines told him little. "How long was I out for?" he asked with a yawn.

All of his companions glanced at him, but only Zylas answered. "Long enough to miss three people's switches."

Though self-evident and not the information Collins had wanted, he did not press for more. The spell awkwardly translated their time system into units comprehensible to him, but he doubted they measured it the same way. Hours seemed to be the same length, as all the switch times he knew about occurred on an exact o'clock so long as he set his watch by one of them. The Barakhains just seemed more naturally in tune with time and its passage, not needing artificial conveyances, perhaps because they had to gauge more accurately. It would not do, for example, for Ijidan to become a man while clinging upside down chattering from some sky-high, finger-thin branch. "Yes, I see that. I'm sorry."

"I'm not." Zylas easily forgave the lapse, though he suffered most from the rudeness. "It means you're no longer upset, you're comfortable, and you've got the rest you need for the mission."

Comfortable was hardly the word Collins would have used, though he did not contradict. With a shrug that neither acknowledged nor disputed Zylas' claim, he headed toward the albino. Middle age coarsened features that had probably once been handsome. His ever present broad-brimmed hat shielded the almost-colorless blue eyes and skin wholly lacking pigment. Thin, white hair fell to his shoulders, perfectly matching the nearly invisible eyebrows and lashes.

"Lunch time," the woman at the chest called suddenly, her voice shrill.

Collins turned to see four plates piled with objects he could not yet identify. His stomach rumbled, and he realized he had missed breakfast. Graciously, he gestured at the dragon. "My lady?"

You go ahead, please, Prinivere sent. *I'd rather wait a few hours and fill up in human form. It doesn't take as much.*

Collins had never fully understood many of the details of the change, including digestion. He did not question Prinivere but drifted toward the makeshift table and the food it held. He realized the woman tending to lunch could only be Aisa, and her appearance surprised him. He had expected someone more like Ialin: thin, androgynous, and flitty. Aisa seemed like a perfectly normal thirty-something, with swarthy skin, finely detailed features, and a calm manner that seemed almost slow. Her only exoticisms were brilliant golden hair, short-coiffed, and steel blue eyes. She gestured him to a spot, and he sat, cross-legged, in front of it. He waited until Zylas joined him, then Aisa, and finally the squirrel, who leaped to his place but did not remain there long. Throughout their lunch, he skittered to and from the table, taking a nut or a raisin, then scampering to a safe place to eat it.

Korfius dived into a similar plate on the floor, eating it clean before Collins could do more than examine his own food. He discovered a mixture of nuts, dried fruit and vegetables, and shriveled bugs like those he might find on a windowsill. He picked out what he liked, particularly avoiding the insects, then looked to Aisa for conversation. "Prinivere would rather eat in the form that more easily fills her belly, and I got used to having a rat steal my food. I know Falima prefers to eat in human form. Am I right in assuming the smaller, lighter form is usually preferred when it comes to meals?"

"Not necessarily," Zylas said around a mouthful. "Depends on what the animal form eats, personal preference." He swallowed. "Though it is her lighter form, Falima actually chooses to eat in human form as much as possible because a continuous diet of grass gets dull."

Aisa piped in. "And Zylas eats anything anytime in any form."

Zylas smiled, shoveling in another scoop of the mixture with a hand. "That's about right."

Collins crinkled his nose at the thought of what a rat might eat. "Do you prefer eating like a ... well ... like a bird?"

Aisa gave a small heave at the shoulders. "Have you ever eaten like a bird?"

"No," Collins admitted. "Is it hard?" He remembered his aunt's cockatiel working on an apple slice, its beak shaving off miniscule pieces while most of the fruit wound up on the cage floor.

Aisa took a drink. "Just constant. We eat just about our own weight in food every day." She set the mug aside. "Between flying and opening seeds, we still have trouble keeping up." She placed her free hand on the bulge of her belly. "Obviously, that's not a problem in human form. I forget and eat like a bird, then wind up heavier than I like."

Collins laughed.

Aisa looked affronted, and even Zylas gave Collins a glare.

"You know, Ialin uses so much energy and needs so much food in hummingbird form, he can starve to death in an hour."

"I'm sorry. I'm not laughing at Aisa or Ialin." Collins resumed picking through his food, separating out the bugs. "It's just that we have an expression where I come from. Eating like a bird means just pecking a few tidbits out of the plate. Eating very light." He laughed again. "Boy, do we have that backward."

Now, his companions smiled.

Zylas swallowed. "Your people wouldn't be as in tune with animals."

Korfius whined and flopped a paw on Collins' knee.

Collins scraped the tidbits he had selected from the rest of the food on his plate, then dumped the discards on the floor. Immediately, Korfius pounced upon them. "Oh, we're in tune with some animals. The ones we keep as pets."

Before Collins could take a bite of his own meal, Korfius had finished and placed his head on the man's thigh, begging more.

Collins' own words reminded him how much he looked forward to Korfius' transition, to the chance to ask the boy his preferences while in dog form. Korfius always seemed as happy as any dog, though smarter; but Collins worried that he might be missing some important need or desire. *Like being human sometimes?* He cringed at the thought of losing Korfius, though he would do whatever the dog/boy preferred . . . and like it. Absently, Collins dropped his hand to Korfius' head and scratched around and behind the floppy ears. The dog closed his eyes, in clear ecstasy.

Zylas watched the whole display as he cleaned his own plate. "I see that."

Aisa also studied Collins' every action, exploring other details. "You're not as skinny as Zylas and Falima described you, but I can see how you stay trim with Korfius around."

Collins just smiled, thinking it better not to explain that he usually did not give the lion's share of his dinner to his dog. He did not wish to risk insulting Aisa's meal preparation, as unappetizing as parts of it were to him. It made practical sense that a parrot would construct a mixed plate of seeds, pieces of fruit and vegetables, nuts, and small bugs, even in human form. "All dogs in my world eat like that."

"Ours, too," Zylas acknowledged. "But we common folk don't get to see them a lot, unless they commandeer our larders in the name of the king."

Aisa made a sound, half-snort, half-squawk, that startled Ijidan. Dropping his nut, he sprang to a chest and scuttled across it to hide, flatly pressed, against the opposite side.

Collins thought back to the meal he had taken among the servants in the king's dining hall but could not specifically recall being able to distinguish the dog guards from the horses. At the time, his need to investigate the royal bedchambers without getting caught overcame idle curiosity. The system itself seemed to preclude manners given the communal serving bowls, lack of utensils, and stale bread slices used as plates. He did recall some eating their plates, soaked with the juices of the stew, and others slipping their sopping bread-plates to the dogs beneath the tables. Collins continued to scratch Korfius' head as he considered, then dropped that line of thought. More important matters took precedence. "So, when are we going to do this sneaking-in thing?"

Zylas sat back, folding his hands across his abdomen and exploring his teeth with his tongue. "I'm thinking tomorrow, immediately after I switch. That'll give me the most time to work before I have to worry about lapsing into switch-form in an inopportune place."

Collins nodded. "I could see how that might cause a problem." He could not imagine any disguise that might allow a rat to pass for a horse. "Isn't it more important to know when the guard you're impersonating changes?"

"Same times as me. That's why I'm the best one to go with you."

Collins suspected the coincidence was none at all. Likely, they had chosen which guard to pose as based on the timing of his switch. "And my guy? The one I'm supposed to be. When does he switch?"

Zylas glanced at Aisa, and they both smiled. "Perfect switch time."

Wondering about the private joke, Collins looked from woman to man and back. "What do you mean by perfect?"

"Eight in the morning," Zylas explained, and Collins appreciated that, this time, the translating spells turned the words the rat/man actually spoke into specific "clock" times he could understand. "And six in the evening. Human by day; animal by night. People would take some pretty daunting drugs to rebalance themselves to that schedule."

Collins recognized the two extra hours the guard spent in animal form, which confirmed him as a *Regular*. A *Random* would split the time equally in half. Though Zylas' description implied that the other guard spent half his time in each form, Collins believed that one a *Regular*, too. *Random* horses, like Falima, were exceedingly rare, and *Regulars* who preferred their human form often took herbs to become more like *Randoms* in this one regard. He even remembered the Barakhain word for them: *masuniat*. The *lesariat*, like Korfius preferred their animal forms. There was also a word for those who embraced the dual nature of their lives, seeing it as right and natural, but he could not recall it. "So," Collins guessed, "we go in when they're in animal form, so no one sees two Teds or Maxes."

"Orna and Narladin," Aisa corrected the names.

Zylas simply stared at Collins, brows rising in increments.

Collins flushed, realizing his mistake. "That wouldn't look suspicious or anything—guys running around as humans when they're supposed to be Lassic or Mr. Ed."

Zylas smiled, though, no matter the translation, he could not possible get the nuances of the joke. "Horses."

"So, we have to go in while Orlon and Aladdin—"

"Or*na* and *Nar*ladin," Aisa restored the names again.

"—are in human form without raising suspicions from anyone who thinks he's seeing double."

"Essentially." Zylas left the table to sit cross-legged on the floor near Prinivere. "We'll have people keeping the real Orna and Narladin engaged and away from the castle."

Ijidan crawled cautiously across the chest, snatched a nut from Collins' plate, then ran with it. Becoming accustomed to animals in his food, Collins barely tracked the squirrel with his gaze. "So, these guys—"

Aisa interrupted again, "Man and woman."

Collins jerked his attention to the bird/woman. "What?"

"Orna is a woman," she explained.

Now Collins whipped his attention to Zylas. "You'd better be being the woman."

Zylas looked away.

"Aw, crap." Collins shook his head. "I have to be a woman?" He shook harder, sending his brown hair into disarray. "Why can't you be the woman?"

Zylas looked at Prinivere, who bowed her nose to his head. He looked back at Collins with a neutral expression, though his eyes sparkled with mirth. "Switch time," he reminded.

"We could work around that." Collins suspected they could, though it would unnecessarily complicate the matter.

Aisa let out an indignant snort. "What's wrong with being a woman?"

Collins backpedaled wildly. "Nothing at all—if you are one. But I don't know anything about being female." He threw up his hands. "Hell, if I understood women, I'd have one as a girlfriend." *Probably along with a Nobel peace prize.*

"Orna's known for being moody and somewhat stand-offish," Zylas said.

That did not further endear the part he had to play to Collins. "What's that supposed to mean?"

"It's not supposed to *mean* anything. It's supposed to serve as an excuse for why you're not wasting time and energy trying to interact with other guards and servants when you need to keep focused on a secret mission."

Good point. Collins still felt suspicious of the role, and he looked anxiously to the dragon. "Are you going to actually turn me into a woman?"

Only your face will resemble Orna's. That's as much as the spell can do. The rest you will have to . . . handle.

"Handle," Collins repeated aloud. So long as he avoided a communal bath, he saw no reason to do anything more than tape a few socks to his chest. He might not even need to do that. Athletic women tended to have boyish bodies, and his would definitely pass. "For how long will I have a woman's face?"

Prinivere fidgeted, which alarmed Collins. He had never before seen her reveal her discomfort.

"What?" he demanded, ignoring Zylas' frown. The rat/man would not like the way his companion addressed the lady.

We don't know, Prinivere admitted. *The others have lasted only until their change, but you . . .*

". . . don't change," Collins finished for her, terror creeping into his heart. His chest felt full. "You mean, I might have a girl face forever?"

Not likely, but I can't say for sure.

Clearly still irritated with Collins' discomfort, Aisa muttered, "It would be an improvement."

The illusion might not carry into your world.

The dragon's words did not soothe him. "The translation spell did."

At the worst, I can make another illusion to restore your face.

At first repulsed by the idea, Collins forced himself to consider it. If the first mask took, he had no reason to think the second would not also. She might even be able to improve upon the original, to even out his ears, to enhance the chin and cheekbones, to widen eyes that tended to squint and add more green to the hazel.

I can do all that, Prinivere sent, reading his thoughts again. *Though I don't know how long any of it might last.*

Collins realized he would have a tough enough time explaining his new look without having to worry about it wearing off at some inconvenient time. Finding himself no longer hungry, he rose. His concern about a cross gender disguise seemed suddenly ludicrous compared to the Herculean task he had accepted. His reticence had to appear inexplicable to people who daily turned into creatures whose differences from their normal state went way beyond gender. "All right," he said in a resigned tone, accepting everything in two simple words that scarcely began to cover the situation. He was about to risk his life—again—for a cause in which he had no stake but the happiness of friends that, even if the plan worked perfectly, he might never see again.

The room itself seemed to huff out a relieved sigh. Korfius came to Collins for affection that the man delivered by petting. The normalcy of the interaction allowed Collins to forget the future for a few moments. He closed his eyes, his mind carrying him back to Algary campus where he sat on his bed stroking the dog, escaping only the familiar pressures of impending exams and assignments.

Korfius loosed a contented sigh, then whined softly, rose, repositioned his body, and settled beneath Collins' hand again. Wondering if the dog's restlessness stemmed from sensing his own discomfort, Collins sucked in a deep breath through his nose then exhaled it through his mouth, trying to blow away the tension. Korfius loosed a long whine that was almost a howl, filled with entrenched and inexplicable pain. The dog disappeared from beneath Collins' hand.

Collins cycled another calming breath, then opened his eyes. Korfius huddled in a dark corner of the cave, no longer a dog but a naked, shivering boy. A mop of blond hair fell around his heart-shaped, pale face; and he hugged his long, scrawny legs with arms equally so.

Aisa headed toward the boy, but Collins scrambled to get there first. No matter how inexperienced a comforter he was, he would be preferred. By skidding in front of Aisa, he did reach Korfius first, though the parrot/woman had to stumble backward to keep from running into him.

Collins put his arm around the sobbing boy, saying nothing, allowing the child to find his voice at his own pace. At length, Korfius shifted position, burying his tear-streaked face in Collins' grimy shirt, and managed to sob out muffled words. "Why—why—we're ... back in Barakhai, aren't we?"

"Yes." Collins pulled Korfius closer, sparking a dim memory of worrying about petting him in dog form because it might seem like child molestation. Though he now held a naked boy, he did not worry about a matter that now seemed silly and trivial. Korfius needed him, and he would support his best friend as well as he could. There was nothing sexual about comforting a loved one.

"Don't you ..." Korfius wheezed out. "Don't you ... want me anymore?"

"Want you?" Collins repeated. He squeezed Korfius. "We're a team, Korfy-pup." He used the pet name that had stuck after a woman in his housing complex had coined it. "Forever."

Korfius snuggled against Collins. "Forever?"

"Forever," Collins said emphatically, though he had no idea how long "forever" might last, given the risky assignment he had just accepted. *At least until tomorrow.*

"Then why ... ?" Korfius started but never finished. He seemed to struggle with words as he never had before, presumably because he had not used any for longer than a year and a half.

"Zylas and Falima asked me to come, and I did. I wasn't going to leave my forever pal behind." Feeling guilty for every second he had forgotten Korfius' origins and had treated him as just another dog, Collins listened intently and hoped he was getting through. "Besides, I wanted to talk to you."

Korfius sniffled, and the tears stopped. He looked up at Collins. "To me?"

"To you," Collins confirmed.

"Why me?"

The answer seemed so obvious, Collins laughed but stopped the moment Korfius looked affronted. "I want to make sure you're happy living with me. That you don't need anything I'm not providing. That I'm feeding you okay."

Korfius wiped the tears from his eyes with a fist. "I like being a dog all the time. That's every *lesariat*'s dream." He rubbed at the other eye. "And I like having you as my master."

Collins cringed. With Korfius in human form, it made him feel like a slaver. "You're sure?"

"No one forced me to come to your world," Korfius reminded.

"Well, no, but . . ."

"And I could leave if I wanted to, right?"

Stunned, Collins only nodded. "I . . . never thought about that."

Korfius sat up, freeing himself from Collins' grip. The tears had completely stopped, and his words came more easily. "Sure. I know where stuff is. Just 'cause I'm a dog doesn't mean I'm dumb."

"No, it doesn't," Collins agreed, rocking back on his heels. Remembering the others, he looked around the cave. No one seemed to be paying any attention to them. Aisa and Zylas cleaned up the remains of breakfast without so much as a glance in their direction. Prinivere dozed in her corner. "Are you happy with your food?"

Korfius shrugged. "I like the stuff you eat the best," he admitted. "And that's mostly all I get from you. Some of the others give me that kibble junk. It's not as yummy, but I know it's better for me, and I've got plenty of things to just chew on. I'd like to have you with me all the time, but I know you have to go to class and stuff." His young face screwed into a sidelong knot. "I honestly think I'd miss my quiet nap if you stayed home every day."

Collins could scarcely believe that a dog who had spent part of his life as a boy could be content with the simple ways of an average American dog. It also surprised him to learn that others in his building were feeding his dog.

"In fact, I think you should go out more." Korfius managed a smile. "With a lady who really really likes dogs."

Collins laughed, feeling like a divorced father. "Likes to pet them all day long?"

"That would be nice."

Collins thought he would have a million questions—not

many people got the opportunity to talk to their dogs—yet he found himself thinking hard to come up with even one. "Do you ... understand me ... when I talk to you when you're a dog?"

Korfius bobbed his head vigorously, and the yellow locks flew. "Mostly I do. More so the last few months. Overlap gets better the more time you spend in animal form."

Collins remembered hearing that before, which explained why *Regulars* usually gained overlap faster than *Randoms. Usually,* he added to himself, thinking of Zylas' near-perfect overlap. Other factors included practice, desire, natural ability, and level of distractions. On the other hand, it seemed wrong to refer to spending life in one form as "overlap." "So," Collins tried to summarize, "you're basically happy?"

Korfius smiled. "I'm happy," he confirmed. The grin wilted. "Or was. Until you brought me back here. Now I have to deal with switching again. And don't the royals want us dead?"

Thinking of a very touchy subject, Collins lowered his voice to make certain none of the others could overhear. He hoped Prinivere's mind reading did not carry this far or, if it did, that she had her attention turned elsewhere. "Does it bother you that your food contains ... meat?"

"It does?"

Though Korfius' tone did not contain the condemnation and horror Collins expected, he still grimaced. "I'm sorry. I eat it. And all dog food and treats have it." He suspected some protein-balanced organic kibble might exist in some vegan store, but he doubted he could afford to buy it.

Korfius stretched his limbs, a few dried tears on his cheeks the only remaining sign of his sadness. "I knew some of our shared food was, but that's okay. I know it's not a bad thing in your world." He added, as if Collins might have forgotten, "Eating meat. It's okay there." He lowered his voice to a guilty whisper. "I like it."

"Me, too," Collins whispered back. He had toyed with the idea of going vegetarian on his return from Barakhai, but the hospital food had not given him much of a chance and he had found the lure of fast food irresistible. He did deliberately avoid the pet foods that contained horsemeat as an ingredient. "Our dirty little secret, all right?"

Korfius nodded.

Collins felt as if he had taken little away from a conversation he had risked death to have. "So I should just treat you like a normal dog?"

Korfius jerked back, as if affronted. "Oh, no. You should treat me like a spoiled, pampered prince of a dog. Like . . . on that show we saw."

Show? Collins did occasionally turn on his tiny television in the evenings for relaxation. He considered, remembered the *Dateline* special on people who baby their pets, and laughed. "Well, you can forget the steak every night. Their dogs don't live long enough to have to worry about cholesterol levels and heart attacks—"

"Chol-what?"

"—but I'll work on the full-sized bed of your own when I graduate and have a good job."

"No, thanks." Korfius yawned. "I'd rather sleep on yours."

"Great." Collins laid on the sarcasm, not nearly as bothered as he claimed by waking up several times a night with a dog head on his leg or belly. In winter, he appreciated the warm body beside him, and it allowed him to forget he always slept alone. Since his breakup with Marlys, he had not had a relationship serious enough to last longer than a couple of dates, and his last sexual encounter had been with Carrie Quinton. Not that he had not had the opportunity. The notoriety his mysterious brush with death had gained him, along with the improvements physical therapy had made to his skinny physique had brought him the first flirtations of his life. Since his trials in Barakhai, the college girls seemed flighty, obsessed with the insignificant: all games and looks and alcohol. None of the unattached postgrads suited him. Somewhere along the line, he had fallen prey to the romantic notion of that one perfect mate, and not one of the girls he had met in the last year came close to fulfilling it.

Collins wondered how much of that to attribute to the meltdown of his own family. His parents had divorced soon after he left the nest, and each had become thoroughly preoccupied with his or her own affairs. Collins had ended up in Barakhai the first time because he had had no family to visit over the Thanksgiving holiday. Despite all that had happened, despite his mother's dutiful visits as he recovered and his father's calls from his European vacation, Collins had found himself stuck in the laboratory again over the next year's four-day weekend. Like Korfius' l*esariat* parents, they had raised him and then purged him, and one another, from their lives. Korfius professed not to miss his parents or his seven same-age brothers and sisters, who, like him, had an overwhelming doggy side.

Oblivious to the turn of Collins' thoughts, Korfius continued, "I like tug-of-war, and you don't have to worry that it'll make me vicious, despite what Maia says." He referred to one of Collins' neighbors, a long-legged redhead who considered herself the dorm authority on animal training. "I like the big biscuits, the brown ones—not the little multicolored ones. I'm not the one who took Bernice's shoe; it got kicked under the common room couch. I like Tom, but I wish he'd quit ruffling my back fur the wrong way. Dan's got the perfect touch on ear scratching." Korfius rolled his gaze directly onto Collins. "You could learn from him. I would never poop or pee inside, so tell Nita to stop worrying. Nick smells too much like a cat not to be hiding one. And, by the way, you have huge roaches; and they're delicious."

Collins laughed. "Slow down. I don't have anything to write this down with."

Korfius continued in the same tone, as if he did not hear. "Now, if you don't mind, I need a nap." Without further ado, he paced a circle, curled into a ball, and closed his eyes.

Collins rose from his haunches and took a seat on one of the chests, trying to remember all of Korfius' revelations. He now knew that his long-lived dog was intelligent and not color-blind but, nonetheless, a dog and Korfius had no desire to become human again. It seemed strange to Collins who, if given the option of reincarnation would definitely choose to, once again, be a man. Though he might enjoy trying out an animal form for a short time, he had no desire to become one for a lifetime, quick-witted or otherwise.

Zylas came up beside Collins. "Did you find out what you wanted to know?"

Collins bobbed his head noncommittally. "I suppose."

"Not what you expected?" Zylas guessed.

Collins' wishy-washy gesture morphed into a clear shrug.

"I don't know what I expected. Korfius is happy with his life, which is all I really needed to hear."

Zylas studied Collins through his pale blue eyes. "You're not happy?"

"I'm ... happy, I guess. I just ..." Collins paused, uncertain what he wanted to say. "Talking about Korfius' life got me thinking about my own."

Zylas gestured for Collins to continue.

But Collins shook his head. "It's silly, really. My world has so much compared to yours. And yet ..." He shook his head again. "Don't mind me. I'm a fool."

Zylas slapped his forehead in mock horror. "Great. Now I've got my life depending on a fool." He looked stern. "I picked you for a reason, Ben. And it wasn't because you're a fool."

Collins laughed, his somber mood lifted by Zylas' even more serious one. "I didn't mean I'm a permanent fool. I just meant I was being foolish about this."

"Ah." Zylas' cheeks turned pink.

"But that was pretty good. Save that motivational speech for later. I might need it."

Zylas glanced at Prinivere, who was lumbering into a deeper, darker portion of the cave. "Riches come in many forms, Ben. They can buy a lot of happinesses, but they can't fill the empty places in your soul."

This time, Zylas hit the problem directly, but Collins no longer wanted to talk about it. "Did she go to ... change?"

Zylas followed the direction of Collins' stare. "Yes. Prinivere went to find privacy while she takes switch form."

Takes switch-form? Collins considered, then remembered that Prinivere had started as a dragon, then had the human-time inflicted upon her. Over the centuries, she had narrowed her switch time. By Collins' reckoning, she took human form from 3:00 to 7:00 P.M., which reminded him to set his watch the moment Prinivere revealed herself as human. "And then what?"

"We let her eat. Which might take a while." Zylas pursed his lips and looked toward the chest where they had taken lunch and now Aisa busied herself setting out a feast for Prinivere.

"Then we discuss the details of tomorrow's castle break in?"

"Right," Zylas confirmed. "Mostly how to convincingly take on the personalities of the guards we're imitating. The rest we'll have to play somewhat by ear."

Though Collins would have preferred an airtight plan, he was not dumb enough to expect one. Only so much of the kingdom was predictable, and no renegade but Collins had ever set foot in the rooms on the upper floors of the castle. His thoughts betrayed him. *No renegade but me. I'm here a few hours, and I already consider myself one of them.* Oddly, the realization seemed more comforting than shocking, and he could not find it in him to laugh. It reminded him of the night he had dreamed that his Great Aunt Irene, ten years dead, had called and requested he repair the porch of an elderly couple on a fixed income because an elephant's foot had broken through the steps. In the dream, it had all seemed natural and plausible, and he had only questioned why the couple had chosen to paint the wood olive green. He had felt useful and needed, the one his wise old aunt turned to in a crisis. He looked from Zylas to the massive space Prinivere no longer occupied, to Aisa shooing Ijidan from the feast. The squirrel chittered angrily in the parrot/woman's direction, and Collins wondered dully whether he would survive what his desire to feel wanted and appreciated had gotten him into this time.

Chapter 4

THREE hours later, Benton Collins perched on a boulder outside the hidden cave, watching the sun dip toward the horizon he considered west and wishing he had brought a compass. He wondered if magnetic north would even exist here as a concept and realized it did not matter. He could just as arbitrarily call it magnetic southeast. If it made him feel comfortable to consider the sun's passage east to west, like home, it made little sense not to do so.

Gaze fixed on brilliant blue sky, broken only by white puffs of cloud, Collins enjoyed the fresh scent of damp greenery and natural pine, untainted by the greasy odor of rotting garbage or the bitter tinge of carbon monoxide. He knew from experience that the sunsets here dwarfed anything he had seen back home, the colors vivid and alive, undiminished by artificial lights or by plane trails. Everything seemed brighter here, as if an omnipotent haze grayed every part of his world and it took seeing Barakhai to bring the realization. The cliff tops pointed sharply upward, treelined and spreading as far as he could see by eye or with the binoculars. Zylas had said they would leave for the castle from a much closer hiding place than this. Clearly, Prinivere would have to carry them there again. Even if a climb were possible, it would take weeks to get to the lowlands.

Without fondness, Collins remembered the stomach-churning flight that had brought them here. He appreciated that Prinivere had brought him to a truly safe haven where the king's men could never reach them. Nevertheless, the idea of what had to follow seemed raw agony: whizzing through the air without the body of an airplane cocooning him or even a safety harness to keep him in place against gusts or sudden movement. He had enjoyed some of the roller coasters on his senior class trip to Busch Gardens, but no one would consider him an adrenaline junkie. Still, he planned to take part in an excursion only a stuntman could relish.

"Don't you think you should give Falima some privacy for her switch time?"

The voice, so near Collins' ear, startled him. He loosed a noisy breath and skittered sideways, banging his shin against an outcropping. He glared at Zylas. "What did you do that for?"

Hunkered on a rock, cloth bundled under his arm, Zylas blinked, expression genuinely bewildered. "What did I do this time?"

Collins put a hand over his pounding heart. "Snuck up on me."

"I'm in man form. I figured you'd heard me." Zylas looked at his shoes, composed of thin wood and string. "I'll practice making more noise when I walk from now on, okay?"

Collins suspected walking lightly came naturally to an outlaw, let alone a rat, with good cause. He believed Zylas, attributing most of his startlement to his own deep concentration. "Don't go stomping around on my account." He considered. A touch would surprise him at least as much as talking, maybe even result in someone getting hurt if his mind registered it as an attack. "Maybe you could just start speaking from a little farther away."

"Deal," Zylas said. "Anyway, what about that privacy for Falima?"

Collins looked at the horse grazing placidly, black mane striping the golden fur like spilled ink. "She doesn't look too upset."

"Agreed. But remember the other time you came to Barakhai and saw her human form naked?"

An image rose in Collins' mind of Falima's magnificent, muscular curves that complimented her high cheekbones, spare lips, and even her generous nose. "Yeah," he said dreamily. Thirteen or fourteen hours ago, she had emerged, unclothed, from the portal; but he had barely noticed, more concerned about their survival. Finally, he recalled Falima's previous discomfort. Accustomed to nakedness, the denizens of Barakhai seemed not to notice one another or to feel conspicuously vulnerable in a state of undress. Collins' lustful stare, however, had bothered Falima. She had seen it as hungry.

Apparently unimpressed by Collins' answer, Zylas pressed, "And remember how you paid for it?"

Collins' cheeks turned fiery. They had made him disrobe in front of everyone, no matter his worry about how he would stack up compared to the other men, mostly stallions, in Falima's life. "Let's go inside," he suggested coolly.

Zylas laughed, dropped his bundle, and headed toward the cave.

Collins recognized the cloth as a crude dress and leggings before limping after his friend. "I should have thought about bringing her clothes." Gradually, the ache in his shin subsided, and his walk became less wobbly.

Apparently reading the guilt in Collins' tone, Zylas shrugged off the words. "You're just not used to switchers and switch-forms."

Collins did not let himself off so easily. "Actually, I was looking forward to talking to Falima. I just wasn't thinking about the . . . whole nude thing."

Zylas gestured Collins through the opening. "Ah, so you knew you were hovering. I thought you might have been doing it without thinking."

Hovering? Collins had considered his choosing to study the outdoors near Falima's switch time a coincidence; but, before he could say so, he caught sight of Prinivere.

The ancient, withered woman was sitting, eating with a vigor that belied her primeval appearance. She wore no clothing. Her skin was carved into wrinkles, loose upon her bony frame. Her breasts sagged into her lap. Fine, white hair dangled to her shoulders. Her eyes were green, contrastingly vibrant, and catlike, with slitted pupils. She had no nose to speak of, just a pair of slitlike nostrils lost in the creases beneath her eyes.

"My lady." Zylas made a short bow.

Collins pried his gaze from the dragon in human form

and copied Zylas' gesture of respect. The stark contrasts that composed this woman drew his attention like nothing else in either world. She seemed so far past death, as though she could crumble to dust at a touch, yet strangely vivid and alive. She was utterly asexual, yet the oddities of her appearance brought no feelings of revulsion. Had Collins caught his grandmother so exposed, he would have covered his eyes, to purge the image from memory; yet Prinivere gave him no such urge. Her nakedness simply was, a phenomenon of nature and without shame. Clothing the dragon matriarch of Barakhai, even in his mind, seemed insolent.

Prinivere returned a nod of acknowledgment, barely glancing up from her meal.

Aisa hummed softly as she moved with slow deliberateness around the cave, serving Prinivere and tidying up around her. Ijidan occasionally crept in to swipe a piece of the dragon's bounty. Korfius remained huddled miserably in the corner, his snores rising and falling in regular rhythm.

Zylas dragged Collins to a back corner of the cave, speaking softly. "All right. We've got less than a day to learn strategy, mannerisms, and voices, so pay attention."

"Don't I always?" Collins grinned maliciously.

Zylas dropped to a crouch. "Sure. You learn in your sleep." Without awaiting a reply, he launched into the discussion. "Here's the general plan: Orna and Narladin are off duty tomorrow. We've got moles set up to—"

Collins had to interrupt. "Moles?"

Zylas blinked in obvious confusion. "Not moles. Moles."

Collins lowered himself to the floor beside Zylas, legs curled up beside him. "Oh, that clears it right up."

Evidently catching Collins' obvious sarcasm, Zylas crinkled his brow. "We must have hit a snag in the translation magic. Are you really hearing 'moles'?"

Collins nodded, trying to unravel the mystery. The Barakhains rarely used animal slang, which brought a rush of understanding. "You mean informants? Spies?"

Zylas nodded vigorously, removing his hat in the cool shade of the cave and running it through his fingers. "Right. They have a game of dice set up and . . ." He glanced at Collins, clearly anticipating another translation problem.

Collins gave another encouraging nod. "We have dice." He doubted the ones in Barakhai resembled the hard plastic black and white ones in his childhood board games, nor the translucent rainbows, speckles, and opaque colors of the gamers' dice. Recalling the ancient term "bones" for the game, he guessed, "You must make yours from bone? Am I right?"

"Bone?" Zylas shivered. "Heavens no. That would be ... disgusting ... dishonorable to the dead."

Missed that one. Collins tried again. "Don't tell me. You use something more palatable. Like ... dung."

"Shed antlers," Zylas corrected. "Carved into cubes. They engrave figures on each side: star, moon, sun, fire, water, and lightning. They're thrown. Depending on how they land in conjunction, you win or lose." He could not help adding, "Using dung for toys? That would be wasteful."

Collins tried not to think about proper uses for excrement, but he could not quell his curiosity. "Fertilizer?"

"And fuel. It burns nicely, depending on the type."

Not wishing to get involved in a conversation over the most useful forms of poop, Collins returned to the subject at hand. "So you've got some spies to distract these guards ..."

"Orna and Narladin."

"Orna and Narladin," Collins repeated, knowing the names would have to flow properly off his tongue. "Orna and Narladin. So we can move in in their places."

"Right." Zylas dropped deeper into his crouch. "It's a good-sized game, and they'll keep it interesting. What do you think is the best time to get in the royal rooms without being seen?"

"What do *I* think?" Surprised at having his opinion considered, Collins forgot to think. "Night? When they're asleep?"

"Guards," Zylas reminded. "Everyone always expects problems at night. And don't forget about switch times."

Collins forced himself to remember the last time he had infiltrated the castle. Then, he had moved in at mealtime, while nearly everyone gathered in one place, leaving the hallways essentially empty. The royalty made a production out of meals, all meeting together at the head table, while guards and servants occupied rows of tables in the dining hall. Collins had made it into their bedrooms without incident and might well have escaped undetected had he not stopped to pet a cat who, in his nervousness, he had forgotten would also be human. "During dinner?" he suggested next. "I could excuse myself early, and you could watch for anyone who might compromise me. It shouldn't take me long to check out a few rooms. It's not like they could hide dragons in a foot locker or under the bed." He paused, considering. Scientists had once believed the largest dinosaurs hatched from eggs the size of footballs. "Or could they?"

Zylas seemed surprised by the question. "Not in one piece. Even young dragons are huge."

The answer reminded Collins that Prinivere had once surprised him with the assertion that dragons gave birth to live-born young, not eggs. He revised his expectation to compare baby dragons to mammals rather than reptiles. Though much smaller than their parents, even newborn elephants and whales would overwhelm the capacity of most furniture.

Apparently unaware of Collins' distraction, Zylas returned to the plan. "Dinnertime sounds good to me. Now all we have to do is learn to pass for the guards we're impersonating."

Collins groaned. That seemed like an impossible task. His one maternal uncle shared only his mother's maiden name, which she never used. He looked like their mother, she like their father. They even lived in different states. Nevertheless, a new employee at Collins' mother's workplace had once pegged them as siblings based only on mannerisms. He did not believe most people were quite that observant, but basic changes in his friends' demeanors or behaviors might raise some red flags. *Yeah, but would I assume imposters?* Collins shook his head. *I might accuse them of becoming pod people, but I wouldn't really believe it.* "All right," Collins said, resigned though filled with doubts as to why he had allowed himself to get talked into doing this. Again. "How do I become Orna?"

To Collins' surprise, he found the ride to the lowlands more exhilarating than frightening. To decrease their chance of being discovered, Prinivere glided low over the mountaintops and hills, skimming the tops of the trees and using her wings mostly for balance and banking. She made the occasional leathery flap with a slow solidness that barely stirred the air around them. Clinging to her back, rather than suspended from a claw, Collins settled into a sturdy crevice between back and wing muscles and enjoyed the view. The ground did not seem that far below him; he believed he could survive a fall. The wind felt like gentle fingers rushing through his dark brown hair and caressing his face. Bathed in twilight, the world seemed vibrant with magic, the greenery a vivid emerald untainted by smog or artificial light.

In rat form, Zylas planted his forepaws on Collins' knee to look out over the landscape without losing the safety of the inner crook of the American's jeans. Falima settled into another niche in Prinivere's musculature. Korfius sat between the humans, doggy head outstretched to catch the wind in his face, tongue lolling, ears flying like streamers. Aisa perched near the base of Prinivere's tail, flapping her wings and squawking every time a movement off-balanced her.

They touched down on an outcropping that jutted into dense forest. Prinivere folded her wings and lowered her head, her breathing a heavy wheeze beneath the rustle of autumn leaves in the wind. Still in place, Collins looked out over the trees. Leaves in myriad shapes and sizes clung to the branches, their green shot through with amber, shades of ginger, and brilliant slices of scarlet. He especially liked the star-shaped leaves of a gnarled tree that did not exist in his world, and he wondered if he could drive the botany professors wild by claiming to have found it on one of Algary's walkways.

With a squeak, Zylas leaped over Collins' leg and slid down Prinivere's side, a reminder for Collins to do the same. Careful not to hurt the dragon, he scooted across her scales on his buttocks, not daring to stand on her back. When they had all dismounted, Prinivere wordlessly trudged into a cave, leaving Collins, Falima, Korfius, Aisa, and Zylas outside. The animals scampered after the old dragon, leaving Collins and Falima alone, both studying the vast expanse of forest.

Falima cleared her throat. "I'm going to switch again soon and won't be back until after you and Zylas . . . go."

Collins turned to look at her. The twilight sparked a rainbow of highlights through her ebony hair, including blue and green. It brought back a long lost memory of a fifth-grade babysitter who had watched him after school while his mother worked. The sitter had a black Labrador retriever named Shelby who was very shy around adults but loved and protected the children. One day, an anxious three-year-old girl who was the sitter's only African-American charge approached a Caucasian preschooler with a deep tan. "Look," the first girl started, excitedly comparing their arms. "You're black, just like me."

"No." The second one glanced at the two arms, brow scrunched, obviously thinking deeply. Collins recalled holding his breath, wondering what a guileless preschooler might blurt out when it came to a child of a different race. "Shelby's black," she finally said. "We're brown."

And, Collins realized now with an adult biologist's perspective, the girl was right. The racial differences that seemed so important to some people came down to little more than the quantity of melanin in their skin. All humans, except albinos like Zylas, were some shade of brown. Human hair, too, varied only in the amount and intensity of its brownness, which was why so many elderly men appeared to have smeared shoe polish on their heads when they tried to recapture the "black" of their youths. Falima's long tresses, however, defied the rule: true, deep, animal in their blackness. It was only one of several exoticisms that might make her seem freakish in his world, that made her consider herself unattractive in her own. Too animal, she had once told him, too much overlap between her horse appearance and her human one.

The timing of Falima's change also made her less desirable to the men of Barakhai, as daytime humanity was considered superior. The conventions seemed arbitrary to Collins, who found her beauty nontraditional yet definitive. He enjoyed her solid, sinewy curves, though they did not resemble the gaunt perceived perfection of American models. Her unaugmented breasts, though not huge, complemented her figure; and the width of her hips and boy-roundness of her buttocks might turn away the men of his world. Collins found her attractive despite the flaws she noticed in herself, and even the unnaturally golden skin added an interesting touch to an already extraordinary appearance.

Falima's voice broke the reverie. "You've got that look again."

"The one where I stare at you and look . . . hungry?"

Falima nodded. "Yes. That one."

Collins wondered if she still worried that he wanted to eat her. He had tried to convince her that no one in his part of the world consumed horsemeat and that he never wanted to try it. "Can't help it. You're beautiful."

Falima looked away demurely. "I don't believe you, but I like when you say it."

"Believe it," Collins said, meeting and holding her gaze. Her eyes glimmered like sapphires in the dawn light, the windows to a soul equally charming. He knew he and Zylas could not leave for another six hours; Prinivere needed the albino's man-face on which to cast her illusion. He also realized that, if they planned to attend the castle's midday meal, they could not have touched down far from the palace. It was an enormous risk, but a necessary one. If they waited, Falima would have become a horse, difficult or impossible for Prinivere to carry. Everything they did had to revolve around switch times, and Collins realized again how inconvenient that became and how much power it granted full-time humans like Barakhai's royalty. *And me.*

Falima took Collins' hands. "Be careful," she whispered.

The interaction had grown too intense for Collins, who resorted, as usual, to humor. "Careful? Naah. Far more interesting to dive in there, battle-screaming, guns blasting, and go down in a blaze of glory."

Falima blinked slowly. "I—I didn't get everything you just said, but it sounds dangerous. Foolish."

Falima's hands felt warm and sturdy. Collins laughed. "To me, too." He stroked his chin in a mockery of thought. "So I guess I'll go with your way. Careful, wasn't it?"

"Be careful," Falima repeated emphatically. She leaned forward and kissed him.

Surprised, Collins could do nothing but stand there, enjoying the moist, spongy softness of her lips against his. Then, before he could move, before he could even think, she vanished into the cave, leaving him with the lingering taste of sweet clover and a smile creasing his face.

Collins sat on a rocky outcropping and looked out over the forest. The sun turned fiery, intensifying the colors of autumn. Not long ago, he would not have needed to ponder the significance of a beautiful woman's kiss. It meant good luck and, if things went awry, good-bye. He had another year and some months under his belt: his scrawny little be-spectacled self transformed to a more average height and weight, his glasses more stylish, his dark hair cut to a proper length rather than the shaggy disarray his lack of time and cash usually left it in. He dared to hope Falima's kiss meant something more.

The thought practically banished itself. *What am I thinking? If I brought her back to Algary, she'd be a full-time horse. Miserable. And what kind of a relationship could we have?* The mere contemplation of it struck Collins as silly, and he rolled his eyes at his own attempts to create an attraction where, surely, none existed. *We're friends, nothing more. And it's perfectly normal to kiss a friend about to go off on a life-threatening mission.* Finally, he headed into the cave with the others.

Korfius greeted Collins with a bark and excited prancing. He patted the dog, then, remembering the biscuits, pulled off his pack. He rummaged through it blindly, fingers gliding over toiletries and blundering into the towel. He identified shapes by feel: the mini tape recorder, the Snickers bars, his mag light. His groping fingers stopped there a moment, and he closed his eyes with a grimace of self-deprecation. Many of the conveniences he had packed relied on whatever stale batteries they contained, and he had no fresh ones. Had he planned to stay in Barakhai longer than a few hours, he might have searched for extras, though he rarely kept spares in his room. He relished the two-minute walk to the student union even on the coldest nights, and batteries tended to get lost or ruined in the junk drawer.

Finally, Collins found the dog biscuits. He worked his fingers into the hole in the plastic and emerged triumphantly with one. Anticipating the command, Korfius sat, tail waving with excitement.

Collins gave the biscuit to the dog, who accepted it with a groan of gratitude, then slid down to a comfortable position to eat it. Korfius had switched at 7:00 P.M. by Collins' watch, instead of his usual 8:00 P.M. Falima had ascribed that to the long time he had spent in dog form and his *lesariat* mindset. Collins saw it as proof that the boy preferred his dog form and found solace in the boy's happiness and desire to stay in Collins' world.

Collins glanced around the cave for Falima. The buckskin horse lay on a flat area of the cave on top of her shed clothing. She snuffled at a vein of moss lining a crack in the cave wall but made no attempt to eat it. Aisa perched on a crag, head turned backward and tucked against her wing. Zylas lay beside Prinivere, his rat form shockingly tiny beside the hulking mass of greenish black that took up most of the back of the cave. Ijidan had remained behind, his job to guard and supply the hideaway in the mountains.

Prinivere's voice touched Collins' mind. *Come get some sleep before your trip.* Though she chose a neutral word for a possible suicide mission, the emotion in her sending made her concern obvious.

Collins nodded, feeling a bit jet-lagged by the time difference. He searched for a comfortable spot, doubting he could sleep on the uneven stone floor.

Over by me, Prinivere suggested. *Use my leg as a pillow.* She raised a foreclaw, then replaced it on the ground.

Collins hesitated. It seemed almost dishonorable, as if his comfort was more important to him than Prinivere's.

It's all right. The dragon glanced at the white rat snuggled against her. *If I'd let a dirty old rat do it, why not you?*

Apparently aware of the conversation, Zylas jerked up his head. "Hey!" He sounded more amused than affronted, but Collins flinched. In Barakhai, vermin actually had the intelligence to understand their low station. The law even forbade their mating to create Regular offspring. Few wanted more rats or mice in Barakhai, and even snakes and frogs were considered vermin. Since everyone ate insects here, reptiles and amphibians did not serve the grand purpose they did in Collins' world.

"I don't think she meant any offense about you being a rat and all," Collins said with a wink and a grin to show he was joking. "She just meant you stink."

"Oh, fine," Zylas squeaked. "That's much better." He circled, seeking a more comfortable position. "At least my fur adds some warmth. I'm small enough to scratch any itch." He added mischievously, "And, by the way, compared to you I smell like roses."

Collins muttered, "Dead roses, maybe. Steeped in pickle juice and fox urine."

"What?" Zylas said, with the innocent air of one who did not hear rather than the indignant tone of one who had.

Suddenly Collins wished he had kept his mouth shut, especially as the musky, allspice aroma of the dragon covered all other smells like a deodorant. The lab rats always smelled like cedar chips, and he had never found Zylas particularly malodorous. "Nothing. Forget it."

He said, Prinivere started, and Collins cringed, shaking his head vigorously in a silent plea for her to stop, *that either one of you smells better than any royal guard. You'll have to roll in rotting skunk weed just to pass.*

Thanks. Collins concentrated on the word, certain she understood.

Now both of you get some sleep. You'll need your wits about you.

Collins' humor turned self-deprecating, *You're assuming I have any.* He snuggled against the dragon and found that her foot made an excellent pillow and she did give off body heat, which surprised him. *They're thinking dinosaurs might have been warm-blooded now, and they were egg layers. Why not a dragon?*

A lot of lives are relying on those wits of yours, Prinivere restored the significance of Collins' mission. *And believe me, you do have them, even if our world doesn't always make sense to you.*

It seemed redundant to respond to someone who could read his every thought, so Collins concentrated on sleep instead. He did not need to vocalize his appreciation for the dragon's trust, wisdom, and support. If she found goodness and reason in him, it had to be there. If she believed he had what it took to succeed, he surely must. Though she claimed only to read the superficial, she seemed capable of digging deeper into his mind and psyche than he could himself.

Despite excitement and worry, Collins drifted off to sleep.

Collins awakened to a gentle mental nudge moments before a rat dropped unceremoniously onto his chest. He opened his lids and looked cross-eyed at the small white-furred creature.

"Excellent," Zylas squeaked. "As recently as yesterday, you'd have jumped to the moon if I'd done that."

I'd have jumped to Mars this time, if Prinivere hadn't warned me. But Collins smiled and accepted the compliment. Zylas did not have to know the little secret he shared with the rat/man's lady. He glanced at his watch, which read 11:28 A.M.

Aisa perched on a boulder, in human form, watching the interaction. "If he'd jumped to the moon, you'd have fallen off somewhere in between." She turned Zylas a steepled-eyebrow look. "If you know he's a mite . . . jumpy, don't you think you should be more careful?"

Collins sat up, dumping Zylas into his lap.

"Probably," the rat admitted, clambering to Collins' thigh. "I'm just thinking it's better to accustom him to surprises. The king's guards won't tiptoe gently around him."

"True." Aisa tucked a knee between her breasts and turned her steely gaze to Collins. "But if they leap on him while he's sleeping, they deserve what they get." She shook back her thick golden locks, and they fell right back into place. He liked the style on her, flattering to dainty features that gave no hint of the huge, black beak that adorned her face in her other form. Besides the rich yellow hair that perfectly matched her chest feathers in parrot form and the pale eyes, the only remnant of her other form that Collins noticed was darkly rimmed lids. It appeared as if she applied eyeliner, a product he doubted existed in this primitive society; and it reminded him of the miniature black feathers that striped the otherwise bare skin patches on each macaw cheek.

Collins looked around for Falima, but didn't spot her. Most likely, she had left the cave to graze, dangerous but necessary. He hoped she would maintain enough overlap to hide if she saw someone approaching.

Zylas explained. "I'd like to get started as soon as possible. I figured we could get you ready now." He sprang from Collins' leg and scrabbled to a pile of clothing on the floor. "These should fit you."

Collins followed the rat, then hefted a plain gray shift, leggings, and a faded red cloak. "Great. A dress." He glared at Zylas. "If we survive this, remind me to kill you."

Zylas paced out a circle around where the clothes had lain. "Good idea. Threaten the guy your life depends on." A grin stretched the ratty lips wide.

Collins shivered. "Don't do that. Rat smiles look positively evil." He studied the rough homespun in his hands and hoped it would not itch. He turned his gaze on Aisa, waiting for her to politely excuse herself, but she did not take the hint. Remembering that the Barakhains were used to seeing one another naked twice per day, he resigned himself to the fact that he would get no privacy.

Turning his back, Collins stripped off his running shoes, his socks, then his jeans, suddenly wishing he had left on his sleeping boxers. Wondering how the Barakhains survived without underwear, he jammed a foot into the leggings, rushing to get the whole thing finished as soon as possible.

Zylas interrupted, "You might not want to wear—"

Snarling, Collins twisted to face his companions. "You'll get my underwear when you pry it off my cold, dead legs."

A shocked silence followed, while Collins returned his attention to wrestling with the leggings. The fabric felt like burlap against his flesh and pinched his toes.

Zylas cleared his throat. "I was just going to say 'you might not want to wear those backward.'"

Collins stopped fighting and looked at his feet. Now, he noticed the fabric bunching at his heels and understood why his toes felt so squashed. "Oh," he said sheepishly.

Aisa added with a hint of disdain, "Though you probably shouldn't bare yourself in front of anyone wearing your ... precious underwear either."

Collins replied quietly, "No, I guess I shouldn't."

Zylas finally took the hint. "Come on. We're making him nervous. I think he'll do better if we leave him alone for a bit."

Obligingly, Aisa hopped down from the boulder, and Collins watched her walk away. Removing the leggings, he turned them and tried again. This time, they fit much better. He pulled the shift over his head, smoothing out wrinkles with his hands, then added the cloak. He spun, feeling the breeze of the fabric billowing away from knees and thighs, and felt like an utter fool. Suddenly, going stark naked in front of strange women did not seem so bad in comparison.

You look lovely.

Prinivere's assessment startled Collins, who had considered himself alone when Aisa and Zylas left. "Thanks, I think."

Zylas skittered up to the dragon's shoulder to examine his companion. "Good. Except Orna buttons her cloak."

Collins looked down his front, only then noticing the three cloth buttons on his chest. He fastened the lowest one, then the one above it, and finally the last.

Zylas shook his head, his little pink ears quivering. "Undo the first one."

Collins' hand drifted to the upper button.

"No, the first one. On the bottom."

Collins shifted his hand obediently, though the gesture felt as strange as his new clothing. He usually left the top button or two open when he deigned to wear a dress shirt, but he had never heard of anyone leaving the bottom one undone. He unclasped the button, and Zylas nodded approvingly. "Now you look like Orna."

Collins tossed back the cloak. "I feel like Little Red Riding Hood."

"Who?"

"Forget it."

Zylas leaned toward Collins, still studying him. "I'm just saying that's how Orna wears it."

"It?" Collins repeated. "You mean this exact cloak?"

"One of her favorites," Zylas proclaimed proudly. "Swiped it yesterday."

"You did?" Collins could not believe Zylas had slipped away without him knowing.

"Not me, personally," Zylas admitted. "One of ours, though."

Collins nodded, appreciating the renegades' competence. His life might rely on it.

My turn, Prinivere announced. *Come here, Ben.*

Though it went against every survival instinct, Collins approached the dragon. The dim light from the cave mouth seemed to swathe her in a gently glowing blanket. Ancient scars marred the green-black scales, some small as splinters, others large as craters. She reached a claw toward him, nails chipped and broken.

Collins lowered his head, but the dragon's massive foot closed over his face. The lowest toe tilted his chin upward, and he met the slitted green gaze with trepidation. He felt as if he were falling deep into those vibrant eyes, spiraling into a dense morass of age and wisdom, from outer weakness to inner strength. His face prickled and grew icy cold. It felt like his features were withering and melting like putty beneath the confines of her scaled, wrinkled claw. Then, within a few moments, she removed her toes from his face and turned her head toward Zylas, still perched on her shoulder. *How's that look?*

Zylas examined Collins, twisting his furry head from one side to the other. He smiled that frightening, ratty smile. "Perfect."

Collins' face felt numb and tingly, though he dared not touch it for fear of damaging the magic.

It's all right, Prinivere sent. *You can touch it, but it won't feel any different to you. It's an illusion.*

Cautiously, Collins ran a finger down his nose. It did seem the same, though the pressure on his face gave his flesh that pins and needle sensation he got when trying to bring feeling back into his hand after it had "gone to sleep."

Apparently having heard the same words as Collins, Zylas nodded. "Best not to touch it much, though. You'll have a tendency to look as if you're poking through your face or in your eye, and we don't know if too much handling might shorten the spell."

Collins lowered his hands, simultaneously curious and trepidatious, wanting to know what he looked like yet not sure he could stand the sight of his face. "So . . . I'm Orna."

"You look like Orna," Zylas confirmed, picking his way down Prinivere's foreleg. "And it's almost my turn."

Collins glanced at his arm, only then remembering he had left his watch and glasses with his regular clothing. They would definitely reveal the deception. Instead, he retreated to the corner that held his backpack, willing himself into character. He was a twenty-seven-year-old female guard with an attitude, gruff yet taciturn, and more than capable of speaking her mind to the detriment of those around her. Though entirely unlike him, he appreciated the role. This way, he could mostly keep his mouth shut. Under his breath, he practiced the voice Zylas had taught him and hoped he did it well enough to pass, should speaking become necessary.

While waiting for Zylas' switch, Collins opened his backpack and examined the contents for anything that might prove useful without revealing who he was. Unless he developed a headache or heartburn, he saw no need to risk discovery of the medicines. He would have loved a bath with soap and shampoo, a liberal application of deodorant, and a good toothbrushing; but those scents might attract undue attention. The illusion made a close razor shave unnecessary on his face, and he knew the Barakhain women left their legs and armpits natural. He was not a hairy man. He slipped his multitool into a shift pocket. It might come in handy, and he believed he could keep it safely hidden. He balanced the lump with his mag light and one of the packs of matches in the opposite pocket, then ran his hands along his clothing. He could feel the items, but they did not leave obvious bulges. No one ought to be touching him, and an accidental brush would not reveal the nature of the objects he carried. It seemed safe enough.

By the time Collins had made his selections, Zylas was pulling a tan tunic over matching leggings. The outfit looked strange on the albino, who usually preferred black. As he adjusted his perception, however, Collins realized the new color suited his friend better. It made his ultra-pale skin seem less stark in comparison. Zylas added a leaf-green cloak to the outfit, which brought images of forests and Merry Men to Collins' mind. Had Zylas added his usual broad-brimmed hat, he might have passed for the taxman-thieving Robin Hood himself.

Noticing Collins' regard, Zylas bowed regally. "You approve?"

Collins shrugged. "It's ... different." Caught staring, he now regarded Zylas from every angle, pacing around him with a thoughtful glower. "Suits you."

Zylas grimaced, his small, well-formed nose pulling upward to immerse his sky-blue eyes into a squint. "I'm supposed to be a royal guard, so I'll take that as a dire insult."

Collins threw up his hands in mock surrender. "I'll remember that the next time I decide to give you a compliment."

"See that you do." Zylas approached Prinivere, who had remained silent throughout the exchange. "Ready, my lady?"

The dragon's old head bobbed. As usual, she conserved motion, though she did not seem wiped out by the spell she had cast on Collins. On his last visit, the magic she had cast to allow him to communicate had left her nearly comatose through the following day. Collins felt a warm flush of pride at the realization that he had, apparently, accomplished something by stealing the crystal from the castle.

Zylas approached. The dragon raised her massive foreleg and clamped her weathered claw over his face. This time, Collins could not actually feel the magic, but he smelled ozone, heard an erratic hum, and saw random sparks and flashes emanating from the contact. The process fascinated him, drawing and holding his gaze until he doubted he could pull it away even should he wish to do so.

"What do you think, ma'am?" Aisa's voice, even as softly as she spoke, startled Collins, though he managed not to show it outwardly. His heart thudded faster in his chest, and he silently caught his breath.

"Are you talking to me?"

"Who else?"

Collins glanced around the cave, at the damp, mossy walls and the craggy floor empty except for his own backpack and a few scattered satchels. "Prinivere. Falima. Someone you might refer to as 'ma'am.'"

Aisa raised her shoulders, studying the magical activity in front of them. "You'd better get used to it."

Jarred to the remembrance that he was masquerading as a woman, Collins knew Aisa was right. He smoothed his shift with his hands and drew the cloak more tightly around him, trying to make the gestures look feminine and casual. "Thanks for the reminder. I guess I'd better." It occurred to him that women often played the part of older boys and young men in stage productions, such as *Peter Pan*. He would simply reverse the tradition. He strutted toward the entrance, swinging his hips. "How'd I do?"

Aisa's gaze followed Collins, and she loosed a snickering snort. "Way too much." She shook her head with unspoken disdain. "Just stick with your normal movements, all right? Orna's not a particularly womanly woman, not what one could describe as dainty or . . ." She pinned her gaze on Collins' hips. ". . . grotesquely over-the-top flirtatious."

Thank God. Collins hopped back up beside Aisa just as Prinivere released what used to be Zylas' face. His forehead had become broad, his eyes dark and widely set, his ears low and partially hidden by a fringe of thick, sandy hair without a hint of wave or curl. Though fair, his skin seemed positively swarthy compared to his milky hands.

Prinivere clearly addressed Aisa, though Collins, and presumably Zylas, heard the question, too. *What do you think?*

Aisa stepped between Zylas and Prinivere. Her right thumb and forefinger pinched her nose, the other three fingers curled around her pursed mouth. At length, she released her face to touch Zylas'. "A bit broader here." She brushed a fingertip along the bridge of Zylas' new nose. "And a touch of red to the hair."

Prinivere reached for Zylas, and a few more sparks flew from the contact. A moment later, she had made the changes.

Aisa nodded her approval. "Perfect."

Zylas explained. "Most birds have a good eye for small details. Aisa's great at that."

"Thank you." Aisa stepped back, still examining Zylas. She nodded again. "Yes, perfect." Her stare fell, and she stiffened. "Almost perfect." She crossed the cave, grabbed a satchel, and returned. Dropping it to the ground, she opened it to reveal jars of varying colors, slim sticks, and a slate. She opened three of the pigments and began mixing colors on the slate with a stick. Glancing between her work and Zylas, Aisa messed with the mixture several times, adding a bit of this or that until she finally seemed satisfied. "Remove your cloak."

Zylas did so, and Aisa painted his arms and hands with the mixed pigments. As she worked, she glanced back and forth from her work to Zylas' face, occasionally pausing to add some color to the mix.

Collins appreciated her intensity and her eye. She seemed a definite asset, and he wondered why Zylas had not chosen her the first time they had met rather than the hostile and flitty hummingbird, Ialin.

The answer came sooner than Collins expected. Even as Aisa worked on him, Zylas twisted his head to his companion. "Ialin will meet up with us."

Surprised that Zylas seemed to have read his mind, Collins started, "How did you . . . ?" Figuring it out, he turned his attention to the dragon. "You told him, didn't you?"

Prinivere rolled her gaze to the ceiling and gave no reply.

Zylas seemed to take no notice of their exchange. "It's important that we have someone who can let the others know if we need anything or something goes awry."

Still a bit leery of the hummingbird/man, Collins looked longingly at Aisa. It seemed impossible that, just a day ago, he had wanted Ialin back. "Can't she do it?"

Zylas closed one eye and squinted along his nose at Collins. "Uh . . . no, Ben. We need someone who can . . . um . . . fly."

"But she can . . . ," Collins started, then understood. ". . . but not until evening. Ialin's a bird during the day." *9:00 A.M. to 9:00 P.M.* He had gotten better at remembering that every human was an animal and every animal a human, except for fish; but he still had trouble with the inviolate sanctity of each individual's switch-time. That seemed the key to its inconvenience. If people could choose when they took each form, he wondered if they might not actually consider it an advantage rather than a curse.

Apparently reading Collins' discomfort, Zylas added, "He's just going to keep a lookout. For safety reasons. If he's doing his job right, you won't even see him."

Collins flipped his hands palms up in acceptance. In his most desperate situation atop the castle parapets, menaced by guards in one direction and facing a seven-story fall in the other, he had passed the crystal gladly to Ialin. The hummingbird/man had come through for the renegades repeatedly. Whatever his personal feelings about Collins, Ialin seemed to have the morality to keep him secure. In case of trouble, however, Collins had no doubt who the small, androgynous man would rescue last.

"Ready?" Zylas said.

Before Collins could reply, Aisa did. "Not yet. I need you to remove your leggings."

"What for?" Collins and Zylas said, almost simultaneously.

Aisa sat back on her haunches, stick in hand. "I need to do your legs."

Zylas' and Collins' gazes fell to the leggings.

"They're covered," Zylas reminded.

Aisa stirred the pigments on the slate. "Just do it. You never know."

Zylas complied, grumbling, "You just want to see me naked."

"I've seen you many times." Aisa kept her attention on

the circular glide of the stick through color. "Believe me, it's nothing special."

"Thanks." Zylas removed the leggings. "Is this some sort of conspiracy, or is threatening and insulting me right before I risk my life supposed to make me more competent?"

Aisa applied pigment to Zylas' legs. "I'm only kidding. I'm just worried because your coloring alone could give you away."

Seized by a sudden nervousness, Collins headed for the opening. Excitement edged with terror thrilled through his chest. After the attacks on the Pentagon and World Trade Center, a wave of patriotism had made him consider joining one branch or another of the military. But, by the time his physical therapy ended, he had disabused himself of the notion, at least until he finished graduate school. Now, he found himself preparing to enter a war in which he had no real personal stake without the benefit boot camp or other training. It seemed crazy that he had not enlisted in the National Guard but instead joined the ragged renegade force of Barakhai.

Collins looked out over the forest one more time. Sunlight sheened from the treetops, lancing through rare holes in the upper foliage. He could see a glimmer of gold between the trees that he believed represented Falima. Seized by a sudden urge to tell her good-bye, he headed out the opening.

Zylas caught his arm. "Whoa, boy. Don't forget this." He thrust a sword belt, dragging a heavy wooden sheath and blade, into Collins' hand.

Collins stared at the weapon dangling from his fist. "What's this for?"

"We're off duty elite guards, remember?"

"Off duty," Collins repeated. "Yeah."

"They often carry swords."

"Oh." Collins examined the buckle, a crude arrangement of metal that appeared to stab through the cloth. He wrapped the length around his waist. When he tried to pull the sword free, it wouldn't budge, and his efforts sent him staggering around like a drunkard.

Collins found every eye abruptly on him. He stopped trying to draw the sword and stared back. "What?" he demanded.

Zylas stifled a laugh, turning it into a quiet snort. "Maybe it's a fashion statement where you come from, like backward hats. But, here, castle guards don't wear their sword belts inside out."

Collins fingered the buckle, freeing it from the fabric. "Where I come from, we don't have castles, guards, or swords." It was not exactly true. "Except in museums." He unwound the belt, refastened it the reverse way, then experimented with pulling the sword out. It felt heavy and awkward in his hand, worse at his side. "You know I'm not going to be able to actually *use* this thing."

Zylas fastened a similar belt around his own waist. "I'm betting that, if you need to, you will."

Collins had to agree. With his life at stake, he believed he could kill someone. "Sure I will. Just not very well."

Zylas reached up, as if to touch his face, then dropped his hand to his side. "It's too late to teach you."

"I know how to shoot if that's any consolation." Collins had gone on a few hunting trips in high school, though he had never had the heart to actually aim at anything living. Luckily, his friends had mostly arranged them as an excuse to get away from their parents, party, and bang away at a few targets.

Zylas took Collins' arm and led him into the forest. "None whatsoever. We're not imitating bowmen."

Collins went with his friend, lips twitching into a smile. He wondered what Zylas would think if he knew the truth: Collins had never held a bow in his life.

Chapter 5

A DISGUISED Benton Collins and Zylas approached the castle of the king of Barakhai about an hour after Zylas' change to human form. The forest opened to a grassland grazed by solid, patchy, and speckled cows in a myriad of whites and off-whites, tans and dark browns, blacks and agoutis. Goats ranged between them, their colors displaying a similar spectrum, grazing and prancing, pausing to rear, sidle, and slam their horns together at intervals. Those, too, ran the gamut, from broad and squat to long, tapering corkscrews, hoary pink to ebony. Chickens and ducks ran crazily between them, chasing insects dislodged by the larger animals' hooves.

Though unchanged, Opernes Castle captured Collins' full attention with all the intensity and violence of his first glimpse a year and a half ago. Four square corner towers thrust toward the heavens, the turreted, rectangular roof supported between them. They seemed higher than the last time, and he shuddered to think that he had once jumped from one of those towers nearly to his death. The jagged shadows of the inner courtyard wall peeked over the outer wall he and Zylas would have to face first. It consisted of defensible block work, interrupted at regular intervals by semicircular towers with the round sides facing outward. A still, crystalline moat ringed the entire structure.

On opposite sides of the wall, a peak-roofed structure supported by two of the towers formed a gatehouse. Collins and Zylas walked toward one of these, trying to look casual. Despite his attempts, Collins' heart beat a frantic, whirlwind cadence, and he fought a war against nerves that tried to drive his hands to a million ordinary tasks: finger-combing his hair, rubbing his eyes, stroking his chin. He contented himself with smoothing his unfamiliar clothing, allowing that small task to occupy hands that seemed determined to reveal him.

A figure on the left tower gestured broadly at them, and Zylas returned a crisp wave. Others shifted on towers and parapets while they drew closer. Then, apparently recognizing them, the guards lowered the drawbridge on sturdy chains. The plank came down with a squeal of rusted hinges, and the lip struck the ground beyond the water with a dull but massive thud. Zylas kept his pace stolid and even, and Collins tried to match it. The urge to run across and inside burned only a bit less brightly than the one that drove him to turn and bolt in terror. Strolling casually through enemy gates barely came in a distant third.

Strangers in the familiar uniforms of King Terrin's horse guards peered down at them. One spoke in a gravely voice, "Orna." He nodded. "Narladin." Another nod. "What were you two up to?" His tone held a hint of teasing singsong.

"None of your business," Collins growled before he could think of something better to say.

Zylas added with a crooked smile. "It is our day off. She has a point."

"A point, indeed," added a woman peering over the right tower. "She's a regular spear."

Everyone laughed heartily, except for Collins who did not think the joke merited more than a gruff chuckle. He guessed translation weakened it and supposed it probably had a sexual connotation in Barakhain. His sophomore roommate's girlfriend had been fond of saying that men saw a penis in anything with more length than width—and they turned anything wider than it was long ninety degrees. Nevertheless, it seemed appropriate for him to sidestep the mirth, being the butt of the joke and known for having little sense of humor. Grunting, he waved the others off and headed across the drawbridge without waiting for Zylas.

The other man's footfalls scurried after him. As he drew

closer, Zylas whispered. "Tread a bit more lightly. For all her crustiness, Orna's still a woman."

Collins eased his step, trying to make it appear as if he had stomped off in mild offense. As they reached the half-way point on the drawbridge, the double oak doors into the gatehouse flew open, revealing the smaller side doors that opened onto the towers and the enormous oak ones that led to the outer courtyard. They marched inside, and the bigger doors slammed closed behind them with a loud finality that made Collins stiffen, though he managed to resist the urge to whirl and face them. He glanced at Zylas, who stood in easy silence and stared at the second set of doors like a passenger on an elevator. The world plunged into a darkness that seemed nearly total, at first. Then, Collins discovered the many small cracks in the wood and stone construction that admitted small squiggles of light. A ratcheting sound echoed eerily through the confines, the sound of the drawbridge rising. Then silence entombed them.

Muffled voices wafted to them as an eternity seemed to pass in the dull prison of the otherwise empty gatehouse. Collins lowered his head and fought welling panic. He tried to convince himself that discomfort was expanding time tenfold or more, but it still seemed way too long.

"Something's wrong," Zylas whispered, deliberately using English.

A surge of terror jarred bile into Collins' throat. He swallowed hard and forced himself to think around the fear.

The right-hand tower door banged open, and a blond head appeared. "You two are having altogether too much fun alone in the dark. Would you finish up, please, so we can all go back to our jobs." The speaker wore the standard elite guard uniform: tunic white above the breastbone, patterned with stretched aqua clovers, then finishing with the blue-green fabric to just past his knees. He wore a bowl-shaped helmet, and mail showed at his collar and arms. His boots were stiffened cloth.

Now it was Zylas' turn to freeze, clearly uncertain what was expected of them. Although he had surely passed through these gates before, he could only have done so in rat form, perhaps hidden on one of the rebel spies. Collins' mind raced back to the last time he had stood in this position. Then, calming Falima in edgy horse form had taken priority. He recalled that two guards had met them here, having descended from the towers. He tried to remember their names, without success; but a light dawned. He and Zylas were guards and expected to perform whatever duties those others had in the past.

Wishing he had not fought so hard to resist the movement, Collins turned. Though closed, the doors still required securing. Feigning casualness, he stepped toward them, seized the bolt, and tried not to look burdened as he wrestled the massive piece of wood into place on its iron mountings.

Rather than assist, which might have looked cued, Zylas approached the opposite doors to wait for the bolt on the opposite side to lift. With an air of nonchalant patience, he waited for Collins to finish maneuvering, then eased open the doors on his side. The massive set of doors to the courtyard creaked open, and light once again flooded the gatehouse.

"Thanks," the blond grunted, withdrawing back into the tower with a shake of his head and a muttered, incomprehensible comment.

"That close one," Zylas whispered, again choosing English, though it turned his speech pidgin. "Very close one."

"True." Collins concentrated on using English also, less practiced at deliberately dodging the translation spells. He recognized the limitations of the rebels' intelligence work. Small details would lose out to more significant information and events, and clearly no one had posed as a castle guard before. "Let's not compound that by standing here talking about it."

Nodding, Zylas headed into the outer courtyard, Collins at his heels. A jewel-green pasture stretched ahead of them, spotted with gardens and striped with pathways. Wooden buildings jutted from the crenellated wall behind them, and others pressed against the one separating the outer courtyard from the inner. Scattered horses, a mule, and several goats grazed, the latter plucking the less delectable thorns and broad-leafed plants from amid the fuzzy expanse of tender grasses. Gardens interrupted the span at intervals, well-tended beds of vegetables, tubers, and flowers.

Collins took in the scene at a glance, trying not to stare. Last time, he had come masquerading as a city guard from one of Barakhai's territories. Studying the castle scenery in wonder had fit the part. This time, it did not.

Now aware that they should handle gates and latchings, Collins and Zylas breezed through the second gatehouse with only a few grunted greetings. The inner courtyard was as he remembered: less grass, more gardens and orchards, stables, kennels, and barracks with pathways linking all of them. Catwalks rimmed the inner walls, hidden behind the toothlike pattern of crenels and merlons. The guards pacing them gave up an occasional wave, though they seemed not to expect a response as they paced their way in proper step around the periphery.

As before, the castle caught Collins' eye, though not with the same stunning intensity. It blossomed from the center, sun rays gleaming from the construction as if to illuminate it in some glimmering heavenly glow. The four, square towers pointed, straight as spears, to the sky; and the rectangle between them seemed as staid and steady as eternity. The photographs of ancient European castles that Collins' friends had brought home from various vacations told otherwise, crumbling ruins with only a hint at their previous grandeur. That train of thought brought back images of the World Trade Center towers collapsing like giant-squashed anthills. They, too, had seemed as solid as the ages.

Collins walked with Zylas along a cobbled path to the stone-cut stairway leading into the open door of Opernes Castle. He saw the animals grazing the pasture, a random-seeming mixture of horses, sheep, and cows. He saw the goose, goat, and human gardeners weaving delicately through the crooked rows of crops. He saw dogs romping across walkways, grassways, and tended plots, playing rowdy games of tag or barking wildly at larger animals who chose not to join their play. Yet all of that registered only peripherally on his mind. Collins' gaze was riveted on the portcullis that hung open over the entrance, and memory descended upon him. He remembered his desperate dive beneath the falling cross-hatching of metal and wood, the moment of excruciating pain that had exploded through his head, followed by a nothingness that ended in a locked cell in the dungeon.

The anxiety Collins had struggled against since the mission began gripped him then, dragging him into a morass of fear and doubt. *We couldn't even figure out how to get through a gatehouse without arousing suspicions. How are we going to make it in the castle?* His hands trembled, and he trapped them in his cloak pockets to hide their revealing display. He took some solace from the fact that Zylas seemed not to notice; if the man right next to him did not, hopefully others would not either.

As before, the door opened on a spiral staircase that wound upward and downward. From memory, Collins climbed, passing the first landing and its two doors to stop at the second level. There, he paused in front of the right one, drawing a deep breath in preparation. He could hear voices floating freely from behind it, a steady hum punctuated by loud bursts at irregular intervals. He reached for the latch.

At that moment, the door jerked open, and a guard in elite uniform nearly ran into them. Collins back-stepped and found himself staring at familiar female features, a guard he had met on his last journey here. To his delight, he remembered her name. "Lyra," he said on the pent up breath racing from his lungs.

The guard nodded briskly. "Orna." She added, "Narladin." She headed past them, then turned suddenly.

Collins' heart skipped a beat.

"It's *harling* stew," she warned. "I know how much you despise that."

Uncertain which of them she addressed, Collins rolled his eyes and nodded knowingly.

"Thanks for the warning," Zylas said in his Narladin voice.

Lyra continued down the staircase, soon lost from sight.

"*Harling?*" Collins repeated, letting the door swing closed rather than entering.

"Don't worry," Zylas said soothingly. "It's a type of fish, not a bug."

"Good." Collins again steeled himself to enter. "But do I hate it? Or do you?"

"Don't know," Zylas admitted, reaching for the door ring. "We'll have to fake it."

It seemed like an important detail to Collins; but, as the door swung open, this time at Zylas' hand, he found himself preoccupied with more important things. As before, the king and his retinue occupied a dais at the farthest end of a dining hall that had changed little in the year and a half since Collins' last incursion. *If, in fact, time passes at the same rate here as at home.* King Terrin looked the same, his crown nestled among wheaten ringlets and a full beard. Shrewd brown eyes looked out from a middle-aged face that seemed wise and weathered. At his right hand sat a scar-faced, homely man dressed in a satin robe trimmed with golden embroidery. It took Collins a moment to recognize him, a man who had once appeared to be, and probably was, the king's brother. The scars that swirled and puckered his skin had almost certainly come from his brush with a fiery torch in Collins' own hand.

Hot pinpoints of guilt settled into Collins' chest, quickly banished by the memory of swords flying at him. If the man and his companions had not attacked, Collins would not have had to defend himself in such a reckless manner. They had tried to kill him, would have if not for a hay wagon well-placed by Zylas' friends, the renegades returning his broken body to Algary, and the miracle of modern medicine. Collins had only done what a desperate man had to do in self-defense. The king's brother was lucky to be alive at all.

To the king's left sat a slender woman whose silver-fringed blue silk dress hugged spectacular curves. Gauzy veils covered her face, stirring in the breeze of the open door. Small, white-gloved hands, clutching a spoon, disappeared beneath the fabric at intervals, carrying food to an unseen mouth. Others less familiar and unnamed sat amid the privileged, including the queen, stewards, princesses, a butler, and an adviser. Three trestle tables stretched from the doorway nearly to the perpendicular dais, packed with on and off duty guards as well as servants. A wide variety of dogs wound beneath the tables, accepting offered tidbits or foodstuffs that fell on the floor. Banners and tapestries hung from the walls, and minstrels in white-and-aqua plaid looked down on the diners from a balcony blocked by waist-high handrails and cathedral-cut windows.

Collins absorbed all of this in the moments it took Zylas to usher him from the door to a seat at one of the long tables. "That's Carriequinton," Zylas whispered as they sat between a plump maid and a uniformed low-tier guardsman whose attention seemed focused on a dog just behind his place at the bench. Collins chose the seat closest to the maid, not wishing to attempt small talk with someone who, though an inferior, could get him into huge trouble if Collins flubbed his alter ego's role.

"What is . . . ?" Collins glanced around the room, taking inordinately long to spot the obvious. Finally, his attention settled on the veiled woman, and he responded with "Oh," and then quickly looked away.

"Oh," Zylas repeated.

"How bad is it?" Collins kept his voice below the regular murmur of the diners.

"Bad enough she keeps it covered."

That being self-evident, Collins only nodded. He turned his attention to the food, then wished he had not. Communal bowls held a brownish-gray soup filled with unidentifiable lumps. A servant whisked up behind them, dropping a stale slice of brown bread in front of each of them.

Zylas watched his neighbor glop a handful of the slightly steaming concoction from the serving bowl onto his makeshift plate. "*Harling* stew?" he said, as if guessing.

"Yup," the dog guard replied, glancing across Zylas to Collins and back. "Guess your partner won't be eating much."

Oh, thank God, it's Orna who hates it. Though the stew smelled surprisingly appetizing, the idea of sharing food that had had a dozen filthy hands dunked into it made Collins' stomach lurch in protest. These primitives probably did not even know to wash their hands after wiping their butts. *It's a wonder they haven't all sickened and died.* Collins wondered if the switch protected them, allowing their human forms to drink from the same worm-infested mud puddles as their animal forms. *Or maybe early exposure to every germ in creation makes their immune systems stronger than the bacteria-phobic, antiseptic-loving people of my world.* He banished the thought, seizing the moment. "Not eating much, huh? I wouldn't pollute my mouth with a bite of this swill." With that, he shot up from his seat and stormed from the room, leaving Zylas to apologize for and explain his rude behavior.

Once through the door, Collins forced himself to appear casual. He yawned and stretched on the landing, studying the area as he did so. He could hear voices below him, but the winding staircase hid the speakers from view. *They can't see me either. Yet.* Without waiting another moment, he quietly padded up the stairs to the third landing.

A boy of about ten, dressed in servants' aqua linen and sporting a bowl haircut, exited from one of the doors that Collins knew led to the servants' sleeping chambers. The boy stiffened at the sight of him, and Collins froze. His mind raced, seeking words to explain his presence in some innocent and logical fashion.

The boy bowed, head low and hands trembling.

Realizing it would look far more suspicious for an elite guard to stammer out excuses to a young servant, Collins steeled himself and tried to look haughty. "Carry on," he said, gesturing regally for the boy to descend.

The boy did so in a relieved scramble.

Collins continued upward, hyperalert, heart pounding. The last time he had come here, the innocent stroking of a calico cat had given him away. Now, he worried that a chance encounter on a servants' landing might do the same. *Stop it, Ben. It's all right. Guards go up here all the time to get to the upper palisade and towers.* Unlike the cat, the boy had not seen him enter a restricted area, yet he could not help feeling desperately afraid. *You're a guard,* he reminded himself. *And a woman, can't forget that. An elite woman guard of Castle Opernes.*

Collins hurried up the stairs and paused on the next landing, avoiding the huge arched window opening onto the courtyard below. Last time, the cat had perched on its ledge, looking irresistibly like his childhood pet. Now, he saw no humans or animals of any kind. Forcing out a breath held too long, Collins reached for the door ring.

Warded against switchers, the door would never have yielded to the touch of any of the renegades, and they would have triggered a magical alarm had they made the attempt. But it opened easily, and mercifully silently, for Collins. The magic baffled him; he had given up worrying about its operation. All that mattered was that it worked for him. Cautiously, he peeked into a room he had searched once before, though far more thoroughly than it required now. He did not need to open drawers, chests, and cupboards to find something as large as a dragon. The hunt for the crystal had seemed like impossible folly. This struck him as far more reasonable: a glance into each room, and he could leave with no one the wiser.

Despite these reassurances, Collins glanced nervously around the room before daring to enter and shut the door behind him. It looked much the same as it had on his last inspection. A curtained bed took up most of the middle of the room, its frame more like a squat dresser with multiple drawers and shelves. A chest pressed up against the foot of the bed; and, overhead, a wrought iron chandelier held a dozen unlit candles. A massive tapestry, faded and irreparably dusty, depicted a hunt scene from a past when animals and humans had existed independently, a past only Prinivere was old enough to remember. Blurry mounted men harried a huge animal with spears. Last time, Collins could not discern the object of the hunt. This time, armed with a greater knowledge of Barakhai's history, he made out the frayed outline of a dragon.

The woven picture bombarded Collins with the terrible images of Prinivere's story. Once, Collins knew, dragons and humans had made peace sealed by a crossbreeding that was agreed to reluctantly on the dragons' part. A dragon ensorcelled to man shape and the king's daughter created a set of male twins. Though nature intended the miscarriage of those boys, the fetuses kept themselves alive, with magic, at the expense of their mother's life. The dragons saw evil in a phenomenon the humans viewed only as unfortunate tragedy. Shunned by their father's side, feared and despised by most of their mother's, the boys grew up bitter, robbed of the magical training they saw as their legacy. Ultimately, the intensity and focus of their resentment had resulted in the Curse, twisted by the inherent wrongness of their very conception. One wanted to forget and the other to spend half his life in the dragon form he believed his birthright. Each got his wish for everyone but himself. One caused the populace to become ignorant of its own past, and the other made all but the royal family half-time animals. Too late, the dragons destroyed the twins, provoking the war that had, ultimately, resulted in their extinction.

Reminded of his purpose, Collins headed for the other two doors he knew led from this room. The one he had exited through before led into a garderobe or primitive bathroom. The memory of diving into that room to escape four swordsmen and bashing his head on the overhanging lip of the seat remained painfully vivid, and he shivered. No one could have squeezed even one dragon into such a small space, so he ignored that door and discarded the remembrance. He had never passed through the other door, but he guessed it opened onto another bedroom, solely on his own instincts. Zylas' descriptions of the upper two floors necessarily ended at the landings.

Collins put an ear against the door, hearing nothing. The gesture seemed futile. Danger would more likely come at him through the door he had entered from the landing, since the only outside access to this room would have to be a window. Steeling his muscles nearly to the point of pain, Collins tripped the latch and shoved.

A rush of flowery perfume struck Collins' nose. His gaze played over the furniture, registering nothing but the absence of any movement. Reassured, he stepped inside, not quite ready to shut the door behind him. Pushed against the far wall, the bed in this room sported gauzy, flowered curtains. They fluttered in a slight breeze that managed to ooze through the slits the cathedral windows gradually tapered into as they approached the interior. Collins suspected he had found the queen's chamber. Like the previous one, it had drawers and shelves built into the frame of the bed, obviating the need for dressers. Pretty knickknacks in the shape of tiny bottles, birds, and horses decorated the open surfaces. A large chest held a gold-handled brush, comb, and hand mirror.

Seeing no dragons, Collins withdrew back into the first room. Leaving that one, too, he found himself back on the landing, facing the opposite door. *One down. Three to go.* Sucking in a deep breath, he opened the door onto another familiar room. Here, he had met with Carrie Quinton to discuss the renegades and the kingdom. She had revealed Zylas' deceit: bringing both of them to Barakhai with lies and trickery, and Collins had come dangerously close to defecting.

Apparently a private sitting room or library, this room held a shelf of books, three padded chairs, and a table. An eight-armed candelabrum rested in the middle of the table on a lacy oval of cloth, a pitcher beside it. Two windows like the ones in the queen's bedchamber lit the room, revealing no dragons but two other doors. Choosing the left one at random, Collins opened it onto a garderobe. Shutting that door, he selected the other and found a third bedroom, less orderly than the first two. Two beds lay flush against opposite far corners. The first had neatly tied curtains and matching linens of blue and gold, as vivid as Aisa's plumage. The second was trimmed in rainbow hues, rumpled, and covered with a pile of stuffed animals. Balls, blocks, and dolls lay scattered across a dog-shaped rug in the room's center. Spanning the entire far wall except for where the beds stood, an ornately carved dresser held two sets of grooming supplies. Silver-handled and matched, the first sat in an orderly line on an embroidered square. The set near the unmade bed lay in wild disarray, the brush dangling between the dresser top and wall, the mirror facedown on the floor, and the comb tossed sideways on the bare wood. Between these, a large bowl held two toppled pitchers and a layer of brackish water.

Knowing he had found the princesses' room, Collins took some solace in the realization that even royal children had to share. An only child, he had not had to endure that discomfort, a fact that had endeared him to his friends and eased the pain of having no siblings. Retreating from the room, he closed the door, then escaped back to the landing.

Half done. The realization brought a smile to Collins' lips. For the first time, he allowed himself to believe he might actually succeed. *It's going to work. It's really going to work.* Collins headed up the stairs, this time not surprised to find no one on the landing. Thus far, his luck appeared to be holding.

Collins had gone through both of the fifth-floor doors in the past. The left one, he knew, led to the guestroom where he had spent a peaceful night as the king's visitor while they very nearly swayed him to their side. One door from that room opened onto another garderobe. Two others led to the shared bedchambers of the king's male relatives. The right door from the landing led to Carrie Quinton's bedroom.

Collins' blood ran cold at the thought of entering that room again, so he turned his attention to the other one. In no time at all, he had established that the guest and male royal quarters had no dragons in them. Forced to confront Quinton's room, he sucked in a deep, calming breath, re-

leasing it slowly from his pursed lips. Memories descended
upon him again, of the exquisite hour they had spent alone
together here. He could picture her beautiful, high-cheeked
face looking up at him, the baby blue eyes filled with desire,
the dark blonde curls falling around the sweet curve of her
neck. It had been an hour of perfection floating free from
the day of terror surrounding it. The most stunningly attractive woman in the world had given herself to scrawny,
average-looking Benton Collins. In moments, though, that
joy had shattered into pain. She had fashioned a vast future
for them in Barakhai. He had tried to convince her to hand
over the crystal she wore as a necklace and escape back to
their own world. When she refused, he had tried to steal it,
and she had called in a mass of hidden protectors. Images
rolled through Collins' mind in an instant, bittersweet, rife
with an excitement that spanned both ecstasy and terror.

Steeling himself, Collins tripped the latch, and the door
swung open to reveal the bedchamber of the Otherworld
adviser to the king. Unlike the rest of the castle, this room
had changed a lot. The tapestries full of cavorting animals,
cheerful forests, and happy people had been replaced with
more somber images. Only one remained the same, an
enormous portrait of a ginger tabby cat luxuriating on a bed
similar to the one that took up most of the rest of the room.
One depicted sad-eyed children plucking flowers in a deso-
late field, another a dull still life of stunted vegetables and
flowers. The last was the most animated, but also the creep-
iest. Carnivores dominated the otherwise muted colors. In
the foreground, a sable wolf crouched menacingly in front
of a roaring tiger, and a lion flew toward a rearing leopard
or jaguar. In the background, a mass of surging claws, teeth,
fur, and feathers blended into a bloody, riotous war of color.
Once painted to resemble a night sky in their own world,
Quinton's ceiling now held only flat, blue paint. Curtains lay
draped around the bed, missing the golden tassels that had
tied them back. A new chandelier hung in the center of the
ceiling, and the wall brackets that had once held the torches
he had used as weapons were gone. Only the carved wardrobe and matching chest remained unchanged.

A shiver racked Collins as he crossed the room to peek
into the garderobe and the royal women's quarters, where
he found no dragons. He closed those doors and prepared

to leave; but, once again, the wardrobe grabbed his attention. It seemed unlikely that he might find the dragons there, yet foolish not to check every possible place while he was here. One unturned stone meant eternal doubt that could only be quenched by another foray here. Catching the clasps, he wrenched open both doors.

A figure inside sent Collins leaping backward with a gasp, heart galloping dangerously fast. He glanced wildly around him, awaiting the inevitable scream. When it did not come, he dared to peek into the wardrobe again. His own eyes looked back at him from behind the dangling clothing. *A mirror.* Warped and scratched, it reflected Collins in imperfect detail, yet he could still make out the familiar features and the distinctly unfamiliar garb. He looked silly in a dress. Then, he remembered the purpose for it, and terror froze him. He focused in on his face as ice streamed through his veins. *That's my face, not Orna's. The spell has worn off!* Stock-still, he tried to think of a solution to his dilemma, without success. A myriad of options ran through his mind, all immediately discarded. He could not remake the features himself, and he had no time to return to Prinivere, even should he make it from the castle alive. He certainly could not stay here.

Zylas! Thoughts of his companion spurred Collins to action. *If his wears off, he's dead.* Desperate to capture the leader of the renegades, the king would spare no man to do so, would show no mercy once he did. *I've got to get Zylas out of here.* Snatching up one of many veils hanging in the closet, Collins sprinted from room to landing, pausing only to shut the door.

To Collins' relief, he met no one in the stairwell. He charged downward, feet thundering on the steps, pulling the veil over his face as he ran. Momentarily blinded, he misgauged the uneven stairs. His foot slammed on wood higher than he expected, and he stumbled. The sole of his cloth shoe skidded down the edge of several stairs, and he scrabbled wildly for balance. For an instant, he hovered between recovery and collapse, arms pitching, body weight hopelessly committed. A flash of heat surged through him, then he regained his equilibrium and continued his headlong rush. He still had not encountered anyone else as he adjusted the veil in front of the dining room door.

Only then, logic finally caught up with Collins, worming through the panic. Most likely, the magic of the warded doors had stripped his face of Prinivere's magic, which meant Zylas still looked like Narladin. Hidden behind the veil, he would have to quietly inform his companion of the problem, and they could both slip safely beyond the castle walls.

At that moment, a dog-guard burst through the dining hall door, dancing sideways with a surprised gasp to keep from colliding with Collins. Several heads jerked toward the pair in the entryway, as the guard eased around Collins with a gruff epithet. Revealed, Collins caught the door, scanning the interior for Zylas. On first inspection, he did not find the albino. He adjusted his search for the man of Prinivere's illusion and, this time, found him sitting among the guards and servants. Zylas stared at Collins with the same incredulity as some of the others, but his strange features contained a trace of fear.

Forcing himself to keep his composure, Collins glided across the room to Zylas, trying to give his movements a bit of femininity.

Zylas met Collins halfway, then hissed into his ear, "What the hell are you doing?"

"The spell's worn off. It's worn off!" Collins struggled to keep his voice at a whisper. "We've got to get out of here."

Zylas peeked beneath the veil. "What are you talking about, you moron?" He spoke directly into Collins' face. "You look fine."

Quinton's voice wafted over the gentle music. "Hey! That's mine. How did you get my—?"

Zylas whipped off Collins' veil. The breeze of its movement chilled his exposed cheeks, and a shiver spiraled through him. He shielded his face with his hands. "What are you doing?"

A serving dish crashed to the floor, splashing stew and hunks of bread over the nearest diners. Instead of attending to the mess, the servant who had carried it rounded on Zylas and Collins, arms flailing. "It cost me a week's wages to get you that food. I don't care if you did come all the way to pick it up yourselves. You're still paying."

Confused and growing frantic again, Collins backed away. "Wh'what?"

Zylas tried to salvage the situation. He took Collins'

arm, dropping the veil. "Sorry. Day off. Too much to drink."
He addressed the servant. "You'll get your money, don't
worry."

But the servant stopped gesticulating, arms falling to his
sides. He studied the pair in front of him with eyes dropping
to wary slits. "There's no way you could have got here so
fast. You were in the middle of a dice game when I — "

King Terrin sprang to his feet. "Seize them!"

The scrape of shifting chair legs filled the room.

Zylas took slow backward steps, voice strained. "Easy
now, friends. I can explain everything."

The room surged toward them like a tide. Past reasoning,
Collins whirled and ran. He slammed into a burly man. His
head snapped backward, and pain shot through his tongue.
He staggered into a sea of arms. Callused hands grasped his
wrists, scratching and pinching flesh. His first instinct, to surrender to them, passed swiftly. The whole situation overwhelmed him. He had seen his own face, yet Zylas assured
him the disguise remained intact. And, somehow, the king
had seen through it all.

Zylas' acting voice sputtered over the shouts. "Stop, you
fools. It's me! Narladin. What are you doing?" His sword
rasped from its sheath, and Collins suddenly remembered
his own.

If they catch us, they'll kill us. Energized by the realization, Collins clamped his teeth onto one of the restraining
hands. The man jerked back with a curse, releasing Collins'
right wrist. He swung wildly into the crowd, connecting with
a meaty thud that sent pain searing through his fist and
down his arm. "Let go of me!" he howled, lashing a kick
toward one's face. The guard retreated, sparing his mouth,
but several others moved in to take his place. Collins
twisted, making a bold leap for the door.

Hands gripped his left wrist and ankle jarring him up
short, kindling a fire through his knee. He crashed to the
ground. Fists pounded into the back of his head, smashing
his chin against the floor, and someone relieved him of his
sword. *My fault,* he realized. *All my fault.* He caught a dizzy,
sideways view of a now-silent, disarmed Zylas being carried
through the door by three guards. "No. Nooo!" He lunged
again but, this time, gained no ground at all. A half-dozen

guards held his limbs or pinned him to the floor. "I didn't do anything—"

The hands slammed into the back of his head again, this time driving his face to the tiled floor. Pain exploded through his head. His entire body went limp, beyond his control. Urine warmed his thighs, then merciful oblivion descended upon him.

Benton Collins groaned awake, the agony in his head momentarily overwhelming all other pain. Nausea roiled through his gut, but he managed to keep from vomiting with an effort that hardly seemed worth the result. Acid burned his throat, and as he became more aware of his body, pain screamed through his left knee, his nose, and his arm. He tasted blood. He scraped his tongue against his teeth, discovering a sharp bite on the right underside toward the front. *I don't believe it. I don't frickin' believe it.* He clearly had passed out for longer than a minute or two, which meant he had suffered a concussion, at the very least, perhaps even a brain hemorrhage. He knew he might die in this accursed place, but it seemed unfair. Somehow, he had expected his brave words to carry him, for poetic justice to see his mission safely done. He opened his eyes.

Light flooded in, accentuating Collins' splitting headache. He groaned again, narrowing his gaze to a slit that admitted only a pair of curious dark eyes looking back at him. Startled by the sight, he wrenched his eyes fully open again. A man crouched in front of him, on the opposite side of heavy, iron bars. He held his head tipped sideways to meet Collins' gaze, his expression quizzical. A huge nose disrupted an otherwise softly contoured face, and wispy brown hair scarcely covered his jutting ears. He wore a sword at his left hip, a key ring at his right. "Who are you?" the other man asked.

For a moment, Collins did not understand the question. Panic crowded his thoughts. *Do I have amnesia?* He dismissed the thought at once. He knew his identity. It was not a question of who, but of where. Afraid to move his head, he rolled his eyes, trying to see around his prison, which consisted of three windowless stone walls, a granite floor, and the barred gate. Dangling collars and shackles, and a dented dingy chamber pot, completed the image. "I'm in hell," he whispered.

"Opernes Castle," the stranger corrected, looking perfectly comfortable low to the ground. "Now, who are you?"

Collins shook his head. The charade was clearly over.

"And don't say Orna," the guard cautioned. "We know you're a man."

Collins' hand went instinctively to his privates; if they had looked, they might have meddled. A quick touch revealed no pain. Everything seemed intact, even his underwear; though they had confiscated his sword, its belt, the cloak, and the objects he had carried in his pockets. "I'm not telling you anything." He tried to keep his tone defiant, though fear shuddered through him. Zylas might have trained to withstand torture, but Collins would probably fold like a warm candle.

The guard only shrugged, rising. His position had made him seem small; but, now, Collins could see the man stood probably no more than an inch to either side of his own five feet eleven inches. "Your choice. We'll just wait for your switch, if you wish."

That'll be a long wait.

The guard lowered his head. "But you should know, the king prefers cooperation."

Doesn't everyone? Collins kept the snide observation to himself. The less he said, the better. *Or is it?* Terror fluttered through his chest as he realized delay and time were not on his side. When he did not change within twelve hours, they would know he did not belong in Barakhai. If anyone had recognized him at the portal, before Prinivere had rescued him, they would know his identity as surely as if he had switched. More importantly, Zylas would switch, and they would know the white rat instantly. Collins could only hope the king's guards had not already discovered the toner Aisa had applied to hide the pallor of Zylas' albino skin. "Where's . . . my companion?"

"Who's your companion?" the guard asked, his attempt to speak casually an obvious sham.

What am I, a moron? Realizing Zylas had called him just that before the charade fell apart, Collins tried to play the game safely. "My companion. The man who came with me."

"In another room." The guard straightened his silks,

aqua and white, without the stretched clover pattern of the elite force. This man, at other times, was a dog. "You didn't think we'd keep you together to conspire, did you?"

Clearly rhetorical, the question did not warrant an answer, so Collins did not give one.

"King promised to go easy on the one who talks first, gives up the other."

Having seen his share of cop shows, Collins wasn't about to fall for that ploy, especially since he knew Zylas would never let the burden of punishment fall on an innocent companion. On the other hand, he could not see silence working to their advantage. Time would reveal Zylas and, ultimately, himself. His thoughts raced in myriad directions, every one a dead end. With his heart pounding an aching drumbeat in his head, he found it nearly impossible to think clearly. *Maybe Falima and the others will rescue us.* Collins knew he could not pin all of his hopes on such a thing. The renegades would first have to get word that the mission had failed, then find a way to break into the king's dungeon, all before Zylas' midnight change. He could not count on that happening any more than he could that Zylas would escape and rescue him, too. He had to find his own way out. "All right," he started carefully, "I'll talk. But only to Carrie Quinton."

The dog guard crooked an eyebrow, clearly trying to figure out Collins' angle. The request had to seem stunningly bizarre. "Why?"

Collins stared back. "Carrie Quinton," he insisted, keeping any hint of insolence from his voice. Antagonism would not get him what he wanted. "I'll talk to her and *no one else.*"

The guard bobbed his head, rubbing his chin with his fingers. "Very well. I'll see if she's willing." He headed toward the door Collins knew led to the upper staircase, jabbed one of the keys into the lock, and twisted. It gave with an echoing click. The guard eased open the door and slipped through, then the bolt rang home behind him.

Collins sagged, letting the coldness of the floor numb his wounds. He worried about the blow to his head; nothing else seemed worse than a bruise or strain, a nagging background cacophony with the sole purpose of slurring his thoughts. Still incapable of finding a good solution to his dilemma, he focused his hopes on the desperate gambit he had taken. Carrie Quinton hated him. Of all the people in this strange world, she would most like to watch him slowly tortured to death. Yet she alone could fully understand the position in which fate had placed him. The best and the worst of his hopes lay with her.

An eternity seemed to pass while Collins waited, alternately concerned about and glad of the delay. It gave him time to think and to brood, to nurse his wounds and to suffer them, to hope and to worry. He dozed a bit, his anxieties peppering his dreams. Then, when all seemed lost, two new guards appeared, with Quinton in tow. She wore a simple dress that hid her deliciously proportioned curves, and a veil covered features Collins had once found singularly beautiful.

"Alone," Collins said, his voice a hoarse whisper.

They all knew what he meant. The guards looked askance at Carrie Quinton, who hesitated before returning a decisive nod. "Stay just outside. I'll call you if I need you."

The guards gave her a look of fierce concern, then pinned Collins with a pair of savage glares. Without a word, they left the room, closing the door behind them.

Quinton did not waste a second. "Who are you?"

Collins swallowed hard, and all of his rehearsed words left his mind in an instant. He would have to play this carefully and by ear. "Someone . . ." he started, his voice maddeningly unsteady. ". . . from your world."

"Yes," she said, her stance revealing the sternness her hidden features could not. "The flashlight was a dead giveaway."

My mag light. Collins closed his eyes. *Gone already, along with my multitool and matches.* It was the second multitool he had had confiscated by Barakhains, and he darkly wondered if he could supply the entire royal family.

Quinton's tone gained spite. "It's *you*, isn't it?"

Many humorous replies came to Collins' mind, but he forced himself to discard them. No matter how self-deprecating, jokes would only antagonize Quinton. He knew exactly what she meant. "I'm sorry." He lowered his head, his tone sincere. "I am so very sorry, Carrie. Please believe me; it was an accident. I never would . . . I never could . . . I . . . I never . . . meant to hurt you."

Quinton's entire body stiffened. For an instant, Collins thought she would leap on him in a mindless frenzy of hatred. Instead, she wound her hands in the fabric of the veil and yanked it from her face.

Scar tissue marred the once classically beautiful features, leaving lines, ridges, and swirls of odd-looking, hairless flesh. Her sculpted nose listed to the right between keen blue eyes with their irregular lashes and gleam of deep anger. Her ridged brow reminded him of a *Star Trek* Klingon, and her silken blonde tresses started farther back on her head, leaving a jagged and receded hairline. Though sickened by the sight, Collins would not allow himself to look away. He sank to the floor in a gesture of abject apology. "I'm so sorry." *I caused all that.* Moisture blurred his vision, wholly unfeigned. "I am so, so very sorry."

"Why?" Quinton asked, emotion choking her words. Whether she suffered from a rage too intense to speak clearly or anger mixed with deep sorrow, Collins could not tell. But he did understand that she wanted to know the reason he had caused her such agony, not why he now chose to beg her forgiveness.

"You were talking marriage. Kids." Tears glided onto Collins' cheeks. They had slept together one time, and she had used it as the basis of an entire future. "I was twenty-three. A boy. I . . . got scared."

"Of me?"

Collins shook his head. "Of commitment, not you. You're smart, beautiful. Perfect."

Quinton turned away. "Not anymore."

"You are," Collins forced out, "to me."

Quinton whirled, scarred features bunched, a raw primal rage flashing in her eyes. "I'm ugly, Benton Collins. Ugly." She stepped menacingly toward him. "And it's because of you."

"Yes," Collins admitted. "It is because of me. And I want to make it right."

Quinton crouched in front of the bars, lowering herself nearly to Collins' level. All trace of humanity disappeared from her eyes, leaving a depthless madness that scared him more than anything in his life. "I've thought about this for a long time, and I know exactly what to do."

Collins froze, allowing her to speak her piece.

"We'll start with a leisurely castration. No anesthesia, dull dirty knife, and you get to watch."

Collins shivered.

"We'll slather you with dung and let you suffer the slow festering of your wounds."

Not allowing himself to focus on the image, Collins fell into the nervous humor he had managed to previously avoid. "Sounds like you've got this whole thing planned out pretty well."

Quinton rose, towering over him. "I had plenty of time to work on it while they cleansed my wounds and changed oozing bandages."

An apology now seemed totally inadequate. "You've got me, and you can do what you want with me. But it doesn't cost you anything to hear me out."

Quinton said nothing, which Collins took as an invitation for him to continue. "Korfius and I came back to check on you."

"Korfius?" she repeated thoughtfully, and Collins hoped that meant she believed the dog was his captured companion. The Barakhains had far less reason to harm him than Zylas.

"You have to believe me. If I'd known how badly I hurt you, we would have come back sooner."

Quinton stared.

"I had a long recovery myself. I fell off a castle tower, broke a bunch of stuff, had some internal injuries. So, it couldn't have been a lot sooner, but—"

Collins waited for Quinton to say something, anything. When she did not, he continued, "I couldn't get you off my mind. I realized . . . I . . . love you." It was a lie, and Collins felt as if the words were sticking to his tongue. He had always had difficulty saying things he did not mean.

"You did?" Quinton finally managed.

"I do," Collins said, for some reason finding those words much easier to speak. "I still do."

Quinton turned away. "No one could ever love this face."

"Someone who loves you only for your appearance is not worth having. Looks fade over time." Though true, Collins could not help feeling hypocritically shallow. He had pursued Quinton as much for her flawless features and figure as the many things he had believed they had in common: a science background, their time in Barakhai.

And Quinton was not buying it. "What a trite and easy thing to say."

Collins walked a fine line and knew it. He needed her to trust him, but if he insisted too much, his insincerity would become transparent. She had seemed a bit crazy to him before their confrontation, and the destruction of her most powerful attribute could only have further unbalanced her. "Look, I came here because I missed you. Then, the king's men attacked me, and I found out how bad off I had left you. I didn't know how to handle that. I thought if Korfius and I could sneak in here, I could find out the truth. My mistake was trying to let you know who I am without alerting anyone else."

"The veil thing?" she guessed with clear puzzlement. "That was supposed to—"

Collins tried to look embarrassed. "Okay. Not my best work. But I knew the kingdom wouldn't forgive me, and I thought you might."

Quinton frowned, shaking her head.

"I mean I hoped you would, stupid as that sounds. I still love you."

"Do you?" She sounded more cynical than hopeful.

"And I know how to fix the damage I did."

That got Quinton's attention. "You're not talking about skin grafts, are you? Because they can't—"

"No. I'm talking about magic." Collins made a gesture that outlined his own face. "Like this. A real fix. Complete and total."

Quinton gritted her teeth, her face puckering into fierce lines. "Don't toy with me, Ben. I'd sooner see you suffer an excruciating, drawn-out death than look at you."

Collins believed it. "Look at me, Carrie. Look at my face. This isn't clown makeup." He rubbed his cheeks until they blanched, then turned scarlet from friction. "If they can do this for me, imagine how much easier to just restore what was already there. Or even better." Catching his mistake a moment too late, he added quickly, "As if that was possible—how do you improve on perfection?"

Quinton dropped to her haunches, her movements still

hauntingly graceful. She had maintained the figure of a Hollywood dancer, pure beauty if one could overlook the twisted, furrowed scars of a once-handsome face. *And her clingy, intense, and desperate personality.* Collins could scarcely believe he had once found Carrie Quinton so stunningly attractive, and that thought made him feel even more small-minded. He had seen her as the permanent answer to an otherwise lonely existence: pretty, smart, with the shared experience of Barakhai from a vantage point no one else could understand. *Was I really seeing all of that, or just a pretty face, a pair of large breasts, and gorgeous curves?* He had discovered the volcanic flaws seething just below her superficial beauty, yet that had not stopped him from wanting to sleep with her again. *Sleep with, not marry.* Collins realized that, until she got some serious mental counseling, Quinton's looks were all she had had, and now melted into a puddle of fleshy scars. *Poor Carrie.*

Several moments passed in silence while Quinton considered the situation and Collins waited for an answer. Finally, she said, "I assume there's a price for this fix?"

Collins had no problem bartering away Prinivere's abilities. The renegades owed him this much. "Only freedom for me and my companion."

"Oh, is that all?" Quinton spoke with clear and evident sarcasm. "I'm sure the king won't mind letting his prisoners go just to help me."

Quinton could not bluff Collins, who already knew how seriously King Terrin took the counsel of his adviser from a high-tech world. "He'll listen to you."

"Maybe."

"He'll listen to you," Collins insisted. "Especially if you tell him you're going to personally meet the one with the power to change people's faces." He worried about revealing Prinivere, especially since he had once promised he never would; yet he saw no real harm in it. The renegades would see to it that no one followed him and Quinton. The dragon had already shown herself to the king's troops once, and he knew she would accept risk to rescue Zylas and, he hoped, himself.

Quinton rose with slow thoughtfulness. "I . . . could do it," she finally said, the words anything but a guarantee.

Collins could not afford to let it go at that. "And will you?"

"I ... will." Quinton continued to study Collins. "With conditions. You take me to whoever can fix me. Korfius stays."

Though relieved Quinton had taken the bait, Collins tried to appear circumspect. "Korfius?"

"Sorry. Your partner. He stays."

Collins attempted to control his response, but he couldn't conceal the horror he felt over this proposal. "No!"

"As collateral. To assure you take me to the right place and don't try to hold me prisoner."

Collins could understand why she might need such reassurance, but he could not afford to agree to it. "Release both of us or no deal."

Quinton ran her fingers lightly over her ruined cheeks, shuddering as she did so. "I can't agree to that."

"How do I know you'll release my friend, then?"

"How do I know you won't just kill me?" Quinton shrugged. "One of us will always have an edge. That's what brought us to negotiation in the first place. Since we captured you first, I think it's only fair that we have it."

Collins did not agree but saw no benefit to arguing the point. She did have the upper hand. "Maybe you could keep me instead. Is that enough of an edge?" The words came out before Collins could consider them, and he appreciated and cursed his own courage. Zylas would do a better job of leading Quinton to Prinivere, keeping both safe, and rescuing him afterward. Collins just did not know whether or not he would survive long with his identity revealed. *Longer than Zylas would.* Though Collins dreaded the thought of staying, he hoped Quinton would accept his sacrifice.

"Very noble of you."

"Thanks ..."

"But no."

Hope died before Collins could even savor it. "No?"

"You take me; your friend stays."

"But—"

Quinton cut him off with a wave. "That's it."

Collins knew no argument would change her mind on the matter. If he became too insistent, she might figure out the true identity of the man she now believed was Korfius. "All ... right," he finally said. "But, since you get the advantage, I get one more condition."

Quinton's brows beetled, a look that might once have made her look sensuously angry. Now, it made her features appear even more homely. "What?"

Collins minced his words. To speak them directly would expose his claim to have come to see her as a lie. "You'll . . . talk to me. See if we're still . . . compatible." He gauged her expression as he spoke, pleased to find a glow coming to her ruined cheeks. "Tell me if and why you still want to stay in Barakhai and what's happened with your dragons."

Quinton stiffened. "My dragons?" she said, honing in on exactly the words Collins had tried to soften.

Damn. Collins nodded. "They're what was keeping you in Barakhai the last time we talked, remember? You're a geneticist." He reminded her of his own interest. "I'm a biologist. You were raising them, studying them, wanting to breed them eventually."

"Right." Quinton seemed to look through Collins, then her attention returned to him and she met his dark gaze with her icy blue stare. "And when I get my face back you'll . . . want me again?" The hardness left her eyes, replaced by a desire that seemed more grasping than sexual.

Collins approached her, winding his arms through the bars. He could not understand how the self-esteem of a woman as competent and beautiful as Carrie Quinton had been could hinge upon the interest of an undistinguished, plain-looking man like himself. *Is it real, or is she bluffing as much as I am?* "Come here."

Warily, the woman approached, allowing Collins to wrap his arms around her, to draw her face near his. He forced himself to keep his eyes open, to look upon the fleshy carnage he had wrought. "It's not your face I'm in love with." *Nor any part of you*, he added to himself, the only way he managed to force out such a heinous lie. His lips found hers, and he kissed her with all the passion he could muster. To his surprise, his young body responded even to this feigned ardor. "It doesn't matter to me if you never get restored. Looks don't matter," he repeated, "to a man in love."

Benton Collins hoped his own conscience would forgive him.

Chapter 6

THOUGH every second dragged like an hour, Benton Collins found himself outside with Carrie Quinton extraordinarily quickly. He could scarcely believe any bureaucracy could act so swiftly, yet they moved with a brisk and obedient efficiency that would startle any governing body of his world. Even so, the guards clearly disliked their duties. Each one gave Collins a narrow-eyed glare, and some whispered chilling threats against him and the partner he left behind should he fail to return Quinton in at least as good shape as he took her from them.

The day seemed too cheerful for the somberness of Collins' thoughts. The setting sun glared into his eyes and ignited chips of quartz like diamonds in the walls of the palace. The stretches of open pasture resembled a soft, emerald sea, and the animals that grazed it watched them with clear contentment. Only the horses gave them shrill, grating greetings, their ears flattened and their hooves grinding up clods of dirt. Several dogs followed them to the drawbridge, some snarling softly behind bared teeth; but none crossed the moat. At length, Collins found himself alone with Quinton and suddenly missed the animals and their hostility. At least, he did not have to carry on a dishonest conversation with them, heaping lie upon lie and hoping to remember all of them.

Quinton mirrored Collins' discomfort. A wary frown pinched her lips, and she glanced around them in every direction, as if expecting hordes of renegades to surround them at any moment. As she swung her head back and forth, the last rays of sunlight shimmered from hair as yellow and soft as corn silk. A bit behind her, ignoring the bald scars, Collins could almost imagine her as he had first seen her: a young coed with dancing blue eyes, skin like cream, high-cheeked and full-lipped, with the body of an angel. Yet, he knew, madness tainted a beauty that, like the old sayings warned, lay only skin deep. She had seemed nice enough, but her upbringing had left her with a clingy desperate need for love. He did not want to betray her again, but, at some point, he would have to do so.

Quinton spun suddenly toward Collins, her face hidden by a fluttering, translucent veil. "You have to lead."

Collins hesitated, uncertain where to take her. Likely, Prinivere had moved since he had last seen her. She did not tend to stay in any one place long, and she had a massive network of renegade helpers to keep her safe. He knew the *durithrin* or *wildones*, the creatures of the forest, reported to a kindhearted mouse/man named Vernon, who remained staunchly loyal to the dragon. Surely, some shrew, vole, or sparrow would observe and report them. He only hoped they would send help, rather than simply watch to see what they did and where they chose to go. Time, for Zylas, was running out.

The grassland turned to forest. They remained on the cleared pathway; and, as they slipped between the trees, Quinton took Collins' hand. Her palm felt small and smooth, her fingers clammy against his. The reason for her amiable gesture escaped him, and he muddled through a thousand explanations in an instant. *Is she holding on to slow any escape I might attempt? To keep her balance on uneven terrain? Is she really trying for reconciliation or playing into my own con? Or is this all just a part of her insanity?*

Collins gripped Quinton's hand firmly, protectively. She seemed small and helpless; though he knew her tall, slender figure hid a ticking time bomb. Though not physically powerful, she was clever and emotionally volatile, with the force of a king and a kingdom behind her. He wished he could love her enough to marry her. She deserved someone who could look past her injuries and bond with her soul, a mate who would forever find her the object of his desire. Although she apparently believed otherwise, that man was not Benton Collins, and he doubted even the right man would look beyond ruined features he had never seen at their best. Instinctively, Collins knew he belonged with someone else, and he was beginning to believe he might know who.

As it grew darker, Quinton took out a mag light, probably the one confiscated from Collins himself. Turning it on, she passed it to him to light their way.

"So," Quinton said suddenly, her voice startling in the otherwise silent woods. Her tone still contained a trace of hostile mistrust. "Who is this secret person who can fix my face?"

"You'll just have to wait until you meet . . ." Not wanting to reveal gender, he finished lamely, ". . . it."

Quinton pounced on the impropriety. "It?"

"I'm not giving anything away."

"No, you're not." Quinton's fingers tightened around his. "You're taking me to . . . it   anyway. What does it hurt to tell me now?"

Collins glanced through the trees, uncertain where to veer from the well-worn path. He wondered if the king's guards followed them stealthily through the underbrush and whether the renegades would notice and prepare for an ambush. He had escaped the only way he could conceive of and had not fully considered the danger he might inflict upon others. "It's not my right to give away anything. It's up to . . . it . . . to decide when and where to reveal . . . itself."

Quinton punched Collins in the shoulder with her free hand. Though clearly intended to seem playful, the gesture felt forced. "You're phenomenally weird, Ben Collins."

Talk about the pot calling the kettle black, Collins thought, but said only, "Thanks."

A sudden squawk shattered Collins' hearing and sent him skittering for cover, dragging Quinton with him. Collins aimed the mag light toward the source of the sound. A blue and gold macaw that clambered beak over claw from a nearby trunk, dropped cautiously to the ground, then trotted toward them with a rolling gait.

Collins watched, trying not to laugh. "Aisa?"

"Who else?" the parrot said. She glided to his shoulder, a thousand times more graceful in the air than on the ground. "Where ya goin'?"

"I'm not sure," Collins admitted, swiveling his neck to look at her and finding one steel-blue eye boring into his. "I need to take Carrie to . . . the . . . elder."

Aisa squawked again, the sound ringing through Collins' ear long after it finished. He imagined owning such a bird as a pet might guarantee eventual deafness. "Who?" She fluffed up her feathers, tossing out a spray of dandrufflike dust.

"The elder," Collins repeated, using the term Vernon and Zylas had chosen when they had conversed about Prinivere for the first time in front of him, before he knew the details and they felt they could trust him.

Aisa scratched her head with one claw, loosing more parrot dust. "Who?" she repeated.

"Who? Who?" Quinton emitted a tight laugh, and Collins hoped that meant she was beginning to trust him. "Is that a parrot or an owl?"

Aisa made an affronted squeak. "I'm a blue and gold macaw."

"Yes," Collins said soothingly, "You're a blue and gold macaw, Aisa. A parrot. But I need to find . . ." Though he hated to give away anything, it seemed preferable to standing here trying to explain things to a bird with only partial overlap. ". . . the lady."

Quinton smiled with wicked triumph. "Ah, so we're a couple of X chromosomes closer to the truth."

Aisa cocked her head toward Quinton, fixing an eye on the woman.

Collins ran a gentle finger along Aisa's head, and her attention rotated back to him. Quinton carried a magical stone the renegades had given her on her arrival in Barakhai, when they had expected her to remain on their side. It translated for her, the way Prinivere's spell did for Collins; but he doubted the genetics concept came through clearly.

"Scratch backward. Feels best. Gets the itchy stuff off the new feathers."

Collins obeyed, carefully watching for the bird's reactions. He did not want to take a chance on losing a finger to a hard, black beak built for cracking nuts. He explored the hard, plastic-like prickles of new feather sheaths against his fingertips, and the bird lowered her head, twisting sideways, to enjoy the full effects of his grooming.

"Can you lead us to the lady?" Collins asked as he stroked.

"Oh, yes." The bird slurred, though whether in response to his ministrations or his inquiry, he did not know. Her head flicked toward Quinton in a not-so-subtle gesture, though she did not seem to have the words to ask the obvious question.

Collins doubted the bird could understand the subtleties of the situation in her current form. "She'll have to go with us."

Aisa flapped and screeched, clambering up and down Collins' arm twice before shooting between the trees.

Quinton watched her disappear among the branches, targeting the parrot's path with the mag light. "Walk this way?" she guessed.

Collins perverted the old Groucho Marx joke. "If I could walk that way, I wouldn't need a helicopter." He headed in the direction the macaw had taken, following the glimpses he got of the brilliant sapphire and amber feathers amidst the duller browns and greens of the forest.

Quinton laughed out some of the horrible tension that had existed between them since their reuniting. She took Collins' arm in both her hands as they walked. "I like a man with a sense of humor, even if he is wearing a dress and tights."

She's flirting with me. Collins could scarcely believe it, and that raised suspicion. *Is she playing me? Or just crazy.* He ran with the change, reinforcing it with more humor. He pretended to ash a cigar, still imitating Groucho, "And I like a woman who feeds me straight lines, especially if she's wearing a tight dress." He appreciated her softening attitude toward him but worried that it might abruptly degenerate into the same expectation of a lifetime relationship as it had before. *Not that I could wholly blame her. I started it this time with desperate talk of love and marriage.*

They found Aisa a short distance ahead, perched on a low branch. "Hello," she said in her gravely bird voice, flapped once, then took off again into the forest.

And so it went, the bird leading Collins and Quinton between the trees, the woman seeming to lose more of her inhibitions as anticipation overcame mistrust and anger, and Collins exhausting his repertoire of one-liners. Occasionally, they lost Aisa, but she always returned to lead them deeper between the packed trunks, intertwining bushes, and scraggly overgrowth.

Collins tried to avoid the plants he recognized as skin irritants, but those became too numerous to do much more than work to keep bare skin away from them. He hoped they would find a lake or clear stream near Prinivere's current cave so he could wash the oils from his face, hands, and hair; and that she would have brought his backpack so he could change his clothes. Despite his flippancy, he felt distinctly uncomfortable in woman's face and garb, especially speckled with bruises and smeared with poison ivy. He worried about Quinton's instability and changing moods; she seemed capable of flipping from love to hate, from kindness to cruelty in an instant. At least, he counted on Aisa's meandering route to confuse Quinton and any pursuers as much as it did him. He could not have found his way back should his life depend on it, which, he realized suddenly, it very well might.

At length, they came to a rocky cliff amidst all the plants. Aisa alighted on a shelf, flapped, and screeched out, "Wait here."

Collins found a large stone and sat. Something sharp poked his behind, and he leaped back to his feet almost immediately. He looked down, only to find his leggings and the lower half of his shift covered with burrs.

"What's wrong?" Quinton followed Collins' gaze. "Ouch."

Collins looked at her linen boots and dress, similarly decorated. "I guess we have something to do while we wait."

Quinton looked at her own clothes and groaned. "Why don't we start with the ones stabbing me in the butt?"

Walking behind his companion, Collins began prying out the pointy seeds with his thumb and first finger. He found long ones with a single barb in the tip and round ones, like puffer fish, with points in every direction. The former slid out easily with a single sharp tug. The latter tended to cling and to jab painfully into his fingertips with even a light pull.

When one of those became wedged under his nail, Collins jerked back with a curse. "Ouch, damn it!"

Quinton twisted her head around toward him but did not inquire about his welfare.

Collins cautiously closed his teeth around the burr clinging to his finger, ripping it free but leaving the barbs deeply embedded. "I don't mind the little spears. But the caltrops really hurt."

"Spears? Caltrops?" Quinton shook her head with a sigh. "Leave it to a guy to weaponize even the most banal and benign."

"Benign, hell." Collins sucked on his sore finger. "Real caltrops may hurt more, but at least they don't leave shrapnel."

Quinton worked on the front of her clothing. "I think of them more as sewing needles and porcupines."

Collins nodded. The description seemed at least as apt. "You've got to admire their survival skills. I bet we spread their seeds over a mile."

"Just what we need. More spears and caltrops."

Collins looked at the ground, where trampled leaves and brush hid the burrs they had managed to dislodge. "You gather them up and throw them away. I'm not touching those things any more than I have to."

"Me, either." Quinton walked around Collins. "I guess it's only fair I get your back, too."

"Thanks." Collins hauled out as many burrs as he could from the front while Quinton attended his back. Believing he finally had her trust, he tried, "So, where are those little dragons anyway?"

Quinton jabbed him with a burr before removing it.

"Ow!"

"You know the deal. Healing first."

Collins could understand her reticence. "Yes, but — "

"And they may be young, but they're hardly 'little.' "

A man appeared. Thin, draped in an overlarge tunic and hose, with brown hair and a dark mustache, he wordlessly ushered the pair inside.

As Collins shut off the mag light, Quinton reached out and took it back from him.

It occurred to Collins suddenly that, if Aisa had held parrot form for at least the last hour, and that they had needed to use the mag light for even longer than that it had to be later than 10:00 P.M. *Less than two hours to rescue Zylas.* A wave of panic flashed through him, and all of the humor of the last few minutes seemed wasted.

A voice entered Collins' mind. *What's happening? Why did you bring her here?*

Collins stiffened in surprise, then realized Prinivere hid not far from where he stood. He stifled the urge to look around for her. His searching might attract Quinton's attention, and he would not reveal the old dragon without permission. He concentrated on his thoughts, trying to give Prinivere a quick and dirty image of all that had transpired. *If you fix her face, she'll release Zylas and tell us where to find the dragons.* He recalled that Prinivere had once healed him after the king's guards had injured him and he had fallen down the stone stairs. She had managed it before she even had the enhancing crystal, stating that healing spells took less energy than most.

Fix her face? Prinivere seemed stunned by the revelation. *Ben, I can't do that.*

I ruined it. It seems only fair—

Prinivere broke in before he could finish the focused thought. *I don't mean I won't. I mean I can't. I'm not capable of doing such a thing.*

Shocked, Collins did not consider his words carefully. *Are you kidding me? Of course you are! You made me look like this.* He caught himself reaching toward his face and stopped his hands in mid-movement.

Apparently finished glancing around the craggy, empty room, Quinton jostled Collins' arm. "Why are we just standing here? What happens next?"

Startled from his mental conversation, it took Collins a moment to find his tongue. "We ... we ..." He licked his lips, summoning saliva in a mouth gone uncomfortably dry. "We—"

Prinivere continued the previous conversation, *Yours is illusion, not healing. It's temporary.*

"We," Quinton prompted, seizing Collins' forearm. "We what?"

If I could heal old wounds, Ben, don't you think I'd start with my own?

Collins remembered the ugly lines and puckers that marred the dragon's murky green scales, the ragged tail tip. The wounds she had healed for him had been fresh bruises, abrasions, and cuts.

Quinton's grip tightened, painful in its persistence.

Caught in the middle, Collins froze, mind dangerously blank.

At that moment, a dog raced from the dark depths of the cave, barking a welcome that rang through the confined space. Collins recognized the voice, then the gangly form, an instant before it struck him full in the chest. Bowled over, he toppled, dragging Quinton down with him, Korfius lapping at his face.

Collins shoved the dog aside, thrusting a protective arm in front of his face. "Stop it! Down, Korfius." He used the opening to clamber to his feet, then offered Quinton a hand as the hound capered and pranced around him.

Quinton accepted Collins' hand but sprang to her feet without allowing him to carry more than a modicum of her weight. She struggled to readjust the veil.

"Korfius, no!" Collins put his most demanding tone into his voice. "Korfi—" Only then, his mistake struck him, and he looked at a brow-furrowed Quinton.

She voiced his worst fear. "So that's not Korfius in the dungeon."

Collins tried not to sound defensive "I never said it was."

"You implied it." A dangerous edge entered Quinton's tone.

"No." Collins would not allow himself to be bullied. He had made too many errors. "You assumed it."

"So, who is your partner in crime?"

Collins knew his answer, no matter how evasive or vague, would still give Quinton a clue. The more defensive he seemed, the more important the identity would grow until it became obvious. He shrugged, then smiled, trying to appear nonchalant and hoping Quinton would see it all as part of the continuing game. "You know the deal. Healing first." He squeezed Quinton's hand, still caught in his.

"That wasn't even part of the deal," she reminded.

"Exactly." Collins saw that as making *his* point.

"I thought you loved me."

"I do." Even though he had not spoken the actual words this time, Collins' response still stuck in his mouth, a chore to verbalize. "But my coconspirator might not." He took her into his arms, surprised to find himself aroused by her again despite his discomfort and dislike. She was still a beautifully contoured woman, soft and delicate against him.

He hoped Prinivere saw through the necessary deceit, then realized she would also read his lust. Cheeks warming, he forced his thoughts away from his penis. "If I betrayed the trust of a friend, even to you, could you ever trust me again?" Now, Collins realized, he had placed Quinton in a vulnerable position. If she pressed much further, she compromised the integrity of both of them.

Quinton pursed her lips. "I trusted the social workers who told me my mother could stop drugging and drinking and get her act together."

"You were four," Collins reminded. "And you didn't. After a year or so, you stopped believing them. Because they had violated your trust." He whispered directly into her ear. "I'm not going to do that." He meant that he would not reveal his jailed companion's identity; but, even as the words left his mouth, he realized she would take them a different way. She would see it as a promise never to betray her, a vow he had no intention of keeping. Eventually, she would learn that he did not love her, that he never had. *What have I done?* He refused to surrender to guilty contemplation. Zylas' safety had to take priority over Carrie Quinton's feelings, no matter how hard her past life or how deeply her hatreds festered.

Korfius' nails gouged Collins' leg.

"Ow!" Collins ripped from Quinton's embrace to turn his wrath on the dog. "Stop that! Bad dog."

Korfius lowered his head, ears flipped backward, and whined softly.

Thoughts of betrayal gave Collins an idea. *Lady, can you hear me?*

Certainly, Prinivere returned. *I just didn't want to interrupt.* She added soothingly, *You're handling a tricky situation as well as an honest man can.*

Though clearly meant as a compliment, the words fueled Collins' shame. *If you can still call me an honest man, you must have no idea what I'm thinking right now.*

You want me to illusion her face to look as if I've healed it. As eerily as always, Prinivere had again accurately read his mind. *But I can't do that.*

Frustration flooded Collins, along with a hint of relief. He had no other ideas, but he did not want to toy with Quinton any more than he already had. *Why not?*

Because I never saw her before the accident. I'd need to have studied her face to get it right, and . . . Prinivere's worried tirade ground to a halt as another idea formed in Collins' head. *But you have a solution to that, don't you?*

Collins felt Quinton's warm presence beside him, simultaneously desirable and revolting. Korfius lay obediently at his heels, and he remembered the man who had led them into the cave who stood silently by the entrance. Aisa flew inside the cave behind them and settled on a rocky prominence. *It's called a photograph,* he explained. *An image of a person recorded at a certain point in time. Like a portrait, only instantaneously and exactly detailed.* The first time they met, Quinton had shown him the contents of her wallet to prove her identity, including her driver's license and student photo ID. She had no need to continue to carry it in Barakhai, but she might do it from habit or for a sense of security, the same way Collins had instinctively fastened his keys to his belt loop before heading to the portal.

Prinivere asked no further questions. Either she trusted Collins or gleaned enough from his thoughts to fully understand the concept. *If both of you concentrate on what she looked like, I should be able to put together a reasonably accurate likeness. But that photograph-thing would be better.*

Collins addressed Quinton. "Would you happen to still have your wallet on you? The lady needs a picture."

Quinton glanced around the cave, surely seeking "the lady"; but, without some clue from Collins, she did not know where to look. He trusted the renegades to have hidden Prinivere reasonably well. The woman patted her left hip. "Strangely enough, I do have my wallet. I almost always do." Her lips framed a crooked smile of embarrassment. "I arrived here unexpectedly. And—"

Prinivere filled in a detail Collins had never considered. *She stopped herself from saying that she entered a third "world" as accidentally as this one.*

Collins' eyes widened. Catching himself reacting to a nonverbal communication, he covered by rubbing his eyes. Once Quinton realized he had brought her into the presence of a mind reader without warning, all cooperation would end. *A third world? Where?*

That's all I could get. I only hear surface thoughts, and she's a particularly hard read.

Quinton finished, "—and I always worried I might step into some room or cave and find myself back . . ."

Collins naturally finished with "home," so Quinton's words caught him by surprise.

". . . where we came from." She turned a sheepish smile on him. "Silly, huh?"

So, Barakhai is home now. And Algary is "that place we came from." Collins said the necessary words. "Not silly at all. I'd probably do the same, if I had brought a wallet with me." He shrugged. "After losing everything on my last visit, I knew better than to bring it this time." Collins could not let Prinivere's revelation go. *A third world? Really? How many are there?*

Only two that I know of. Despite the significance of their conversation, Prinivere redirected Collins to what currently mattered, *Take that wallet thing, and let's get going on this.*

Deep in thought, Collins obeyed.

While Collins hurriedly changed into clean underwear, jeans, a T-shirt, socks, shoes, and his glasses, the unfamiliar man rigged a curtain across the back of the cave, with two slits that admitted the dragon's claws. It seemed safer to Collins to blindfold Carrie Quinton, but the magic required Prinivere to access all parts of the woman's face, including her eyes. He would also have preferred the task done while Prinivere held woman form, but they did not have time to quibble. Once she completed the process, he would count himself lucky to save Zylas before his switch.

As magic flowed from dragon to woman, and the harsh scars of Quinton's face faded to her normal, soft contours, Collins paced wildly. He knew the woman had mastered biology and would recognize that those claws belonged to nothing in their own world. Quinton had worked with the young dragons and would notice how the claws seemed more birdlike than mammalian, their size and shape, the lack of anything resembling paw pads. Others might wonder, but Quinton would know a dragon had healed her and might report that fact to the king.

Stop worrying. They already know we have a dragon. He took momentary satisfaction from the image of Prinivere plunging down on the soldiers at the portal entrance, their disciplined ranks exploding into screaming chaos. As terrifying as he had found the situation, they must have found it doubly so, since they had no reason to believe the creatures still existed. He could liken it to warriors on a battlefield suddenly menaced by a pterodactyl, but that would not catch the full scope of these men's experience. At least the men of the twenty-first century had seen 747s and *Jurassic Park* movies.

Korfius trotted at Collins' side, invigorated by the constant movement of the master who would not be comforted. The only one who might have the right words to calm him was too engrossed in the process to speak them. Aisa watched with uncharacteristic quietness, letting out only an occasional soft grunt, her head feathers ruffled like a hatchling's.

Collins glanced at his wrist repeatedly, each time remembering that he had not taken the time to riffle through his pack for his watch. Now, he felt lost without it, at the mercy of circumstances and a nonsensical world that violated many of the tenets he relied on as facts. His mind edged back to the day an avowed Catholic coworker had argued with his father, a balding, conservative man of few words. "After all," the Catholic had argued haughtily, "evolution is only a theory." James Collins had ended the conversation with a gruff: "So's gravity, but I wouldn't go jumping out any windows." Now, huge men morphed into tiny mice, four-legged dragons bore wings that could support their massive weight, and animals shared a digestive system with their human alter egos. Gravity seemed like the only scientific principle Benton Collins could still count on.

"How's that?" Aisa said suddenly, and Collins jumped at the coarse sound. He whipped his attention toward the blue and gold macaw who stood with her head cocked, one eye fixed on Quinton, the pupil widening and contracting in an instant. The reek of ozone filled the air.

Collins guessed the question actually came from Prinivere, though she must have thought it wiser to direct her mental communication solely at Aisa. If the dragon had a physical voice, Collins had never heard it. He peered around the women to look. Quinton's features closely resembled those he remembered, minus a year or two of age. "Beautiful. Perfect." He smiled encouragingly.

Quinton pulled a small mirror from her pocket and examined Prinivere's handiwork from every angle. She made a few suggestions regarding cheek apples and eyebrow widths that made little sense to Collins but sent the dragon's claws diligently back to work on her face. The odor thickened, and a bright series of sparks rose from the contact.

Collins' pacing grew more frantic as he worried about the time. Once the kingdom realized who it had imprisoned, even Carrie Quinton might not be able to talk them into releasing Zylas.

Again, Quinton examined her face and again found faults that seemed meaningless and miniscule to Collins. He could not understand why the woman could not just appreciate the second chance at normalcy that Prinivere's magic granted her, why she had to pick and poke at every detail.

During one of Quinton's surveys, Prinivere explained. *She sees this as her only salvation and doesn't want to regret anything about it.* The dragon gave Collins an intangible smile. *Let her be as fussy as she needs to. We don't get many second chances in life.*

Collins nodded in understanding, though he barely did. Time constraints weighed heavily on his soul, and hardly noticeable details seemed all the more ludicrous since he knew it was all a temporary illusion. Only then, he recalled his own changed features and wondered how difficult Quinton had found it to take the hand, arm, and embrace of a man who was currently a dead ringer for a female guard. *Maybe that's why she could do it. My changed appearance allowed her to put aside that I'm the one she hates most in all the worlds.*

I'm concerned about time, too, Prinivere sent to the earlier parts of Collins' thoughts. *But to rush her would arouse suspicions we can't afford.*

Collins had to agree, though he did not like it. He needed not only to convince Quinton of the dragon's ability to permanently heal her, he needed to act as if he believed it, too.

Before Collins could reply, Prinivere directed her attention back to Quinton, erasing lines and blemishes invisible to Collins' eyes. He sighed deeply and resumed his pacing.

At length, Quinton finally seemed satisfied. She studied her face in the mirror from every angle, reaching to touch her cheek with an expression of perfect awe.

Remembering Zylas' warning about touching, Collins caught Quinton's hand. "Don't mess with it." Needing a reason besides exposing the illusion, he added, "It has to . . . to set." Collins hoped that did not sound suspicious or stupid.

Quinton lowered her hand and smiled.

Collins found himself staring into a face so gorgeous it left him speechless. The first time he had looked upon Carrie Quinton, he had believed her the most beautiful woman he had ever seen. Now, his jaw sagged open as he looked upon features brought to smooth, unwavering perfection.

Wow? Prinivere supplied.

"Wow," Collins forced out. "You're . . . you're . . . absolutely . . ."

Now it was Quinton's turn to supply him with words. "Hot?"

Collins continued to stare. "Hotter than hot. You're drop-dead stunning."

The grin broadened. "Apparently so."

Collins shook free of his trance. "Let's go."

Quinton's smile disappeared. "That's it? You're pretty, let's go?"

Careful, Prinivere sent.

Worried about what the old dragon might have read, Collins jerked his attention to her. *What? Is she thinking something . . . dangerous?*

Prinivere's thoughts seemed slowed, vexed. *I only get what's on the surface,* she reminded. *And that's tied up with excitement, curiosity, seeking a perfection that goes way beyond matching what she had. Deep down, that girl's a volcano.*

Quinton concerned Collins as well, a boiling wellspring of hatred, mistrust, and need veiled with a thin veneer. *I'll be careful. But we have to go now. It's got to be close to midnight.*

Dangerously close, Prinivere admitted. *Go and Godspeed.*

Collins had never understood that expression, and it troubled him doubly now. He had never heard any person in Barakhai mention a deity; and, for the first time, he wondered if they even had religion. Given the inherently magical nature of nearly all the people here, seeking divine explanations for the lesser mysteries of the universe seemed unnecessary. Though no more eerie than many of the other oddities of this place, the lack of a formal system of beliefs gave Collins goose bumps; he had never been anywhere where religion did not play a major role in society. He wondered what Prinivere had actually said and why the spell had translated it into "Godspeed" rather than "good luck" or something equally banal. Now, however, did not seem the time for an explanation. Clutching Quinton's hand more firmly, Collins steered her toward the cave mouth. "Now can we save my companion, sweetheart?"

"Of course," Quinton studied her reflection in the hand mirror, lips taut as she clearly battled the urge to touch it. Her fingers twitched in his, and her free hand fluttered near her face as if to brush away a few errant strands of hair.

The young dragons, Prinivere reminded him. *Where are they?*

Though Collins hated to leap directly into all parts of Quinton's promise so soon after honoring his own, he knew it safer to hear the information in front of others. That way, if something happened to him, the renegades could still rescue the young ones. Also, Prinivere would know if Quinton described some place that did not exist, and he could threaten to take back her new features while still in the presence of the one who had crafted them. *An illusionary place.* Collins grimaced. *To go with her illusionary face.* "So—where are the dragons?"

Quinton sighed, clearly unhappy with Collins' decision to ply her for information before taking sufficient time to adore her. "They're dead."

Collins stiffened, every muscle frozen in terror.

She's lying.

Collins did not take the time to delicately rephrase Prinivere's discovery. "You're lying."

Quinton jammed her hands onto her hips, her new features twisting in affronted anger. Somehow, she managed to make flawless features turn ugly. "How dare you!"

Collins could not afford to give ground, nor waste time. "I dare because you promised me the truth." He put his face nearly against hers and tried to look deeply wounded.

"They're dead. Why won't you believe me?" Quinton sounded so sincere, Collins would have believed her had he not had Prinivere to tell him the truth.

Collins sighed deeply, lowered his head, then shook it sadly. He made a throwaway gesture at the curtain. "I'm sorry I wasted your time. Put back the old face."

"Wait!" Quinton squeaked. She glanced around the cave, from the man waiting quietly in the darkness at its mouth, to Aisa, to the faceless claws poking through the curtain. "I promised to tell you. Not the whole world."

Collins saw no reason to argue. So long as Quinton told him within range of Prinivere's mind reading, she would hear, too. "Whisper it." He tipped his head toward her.

"You're the only one who knows this, and you have to promise not to tell a soul."

"I promise." Collins nodded, saved by a technicality. Prinivere would learn it from Quinton, and no similar vow bound the old dragon to silence.

Quinton placed her mouth over Collins' ear. "Cavern. South of Pashtir, west of the Uraffs, north of the Kastarnin Sea."

The directions sounded impossibly vague to Collins. *Do you know where that is?*

I know. A hint of discomfort entered Prinivere's sending, but she did not elaborate. *Now go save Zylas.*

"Oh." Collins did not have to feign confusion. He had heard of none of the places Quinton had named. Shrugging, he hauled her toward the exit, Korfius eagerly following.

Quinton lost her grip on the mirror, bobbled it, then caught it before it hit the stony ground. She returned it to her dress. "Whoa, Ben. What's the hurry?"

"The hurry is a locked up friend. Once we free him . . ." Collins pressed his body against Quinton's. "I'll be able to give you my *full* attention." He raised and lowered his brows in an exaggerated motion, emphasizing the innuendo.

Quinton snorted. "I'm gorgeous again, remember? I can do a hell of a lot better than you."

Though not wholly certain Quinton was joking, Collins bantered. "You think so? How are you going to do better than the best?"

"The best? You?"

Collins continued to steer Quinton toward the exit, trying to figure out how to rid himself of the dog. "Best in Barakhai, anyway. I've got the highest education. A driver's license." He added with a scratch. "No fleas."

"No fleas? How endearing. And I've got my own driver's license—not worth the plastic it's printed on here."

"Oh, yeah? Well, I'd venture to guess, I'm the only one with a Snickers bar."

Quinton whirlcd. "Oooh, really? You've got candy?" Her eyes narrowed in sudden suspicion. "That's not just another name for your ... manhood, is it?"

Despite his urgency, Collins huffed out a laugh. "No. I have real candy, and a few other luxuries from home." He hissed in her ear, "But my ... manhood is pretty sweet, too."

Quinton slapped him, harder than flirtation demanded, then ran from the cave.

Rubbing his cheek, Collins stopped at the opening. "Stay, Korfius."

The hound ignored him, tail waving, waiting for his master to move.

I don't think it'll hurt to take him with you.

Collins had never considered doing such a thing, accustomed to leaving the dog in his room while he attended classes. The overeager animal seemed worse than useless in a dangerous situation. *You don't think he'll be in any danger?*

No more than with me. He really misses you, and he can run for help if you get in trouble.

Collins doubted Korfius would know how to bring help. He seemed more the type of dog who would dote on thieves and murderers, so long as they were human or carried biscuits. Nevertheless, Collins considered the possibility the dog might help him in a violent situation, and he could not deny that Korfius *had* brought people to save him when he returned to Daubert Labs badly injured. Besides, Collins would not gainsay Prinivere. Without argument, he followed Quinton into the night.

Korfius bounced after them, tail waving.

Moonlight sheened from Quinton's tresses, glinting like metallic gold. Her step turned light and happy, and she consulted her mirror often, though she had to hold it nearly to her nose to see. Collins did not attempt to distract her, though he felt a fiery pang of guilt every time a smile of recognition stretched her lips. The higher joy buoyed her, the lower she would crash when the illusion decayed, leaving the scarred, withered cheeks and bald spots in its place. For Zylas' sake, he had no choice but to continue the charade. The life of a friend had to take precedence over the happiness of a self-sworn enemy.

The cloud cover unraveled, revealing a nearly full moon that obviated the need for the mag light. Nevertheless, the walk back felt twice as long as the one to Prinivere, though Collins had not known her location at the time nor had the full visual clarity his glasses provided now. Every pause Quinton took to stare at her reflection felt like an eternity, an intolerable delay from rescuing Zylas before his change overtook him; yet Collins could not find a way to rush her without admitting to his friend's identity or seeming utterly insensitive to the needs of a woman he claimed to love. *Love,* he considered, uncertain of its meaning. He had believed his parents the very definition until their divorce and personal quests for new companionship left him feeling orphaned. Love certainly did not describe the feelings he had for Carrie Quinton. If his last relationship, with Marlys Johnson, had taught him nothing else, it was that devotion without respect, without trust, was meaningless. Quinton's attitude did not evoke admiration, and he doubted she thought all that much of his abilities either.

The castle came into view, and sudden anxiety overtook Collins. He had many bad memories of that place and only a few good ones. "Come on," Quinton pulled playfully at his arm. Korfius barked.

Collins eased free of her grip and patted the dog. "I'll wait here. After you've let my friend loose and had a chance to explain me, I'll meet up with you again."

Quinton gave Collins a pouting, doubtful look. "It'll be all right."

"I don't think so." If the guards grabbed Collins, he would find himself in a worse situation than when he had started: not only would he and Zylas both be prisoners but Korfius as well. "I think I'm better here, thank you."

Quinton plastered herself against Collins. Even through the fabric of her dress, he could make out the gentle contours; and they excited him wildly. "Are you sure?"

Collins kept his voice steady, willing it not to crack. He could feel the imprint of a nipple on his arm. "I'm sure. We can do . . . that . . . after."

"Assuming my offer still stands," she teased.

Collins could not afford to give in to desire. He nodded,

squirming free of her embrace. "I think it will." It took a monumental effort of will to add the necessary confidence to the claim. He barely considered his looks ordinary, even when not illusioned into those of an unpleasant woman. He knew an intelligent beauty like Quinton, until the burns, could have had anyone she wanted. "I really think it will."

A flash resembling anger passed through Quinton's eyes, then disappeared. If Collins had interpreted correctly, though, she gave no sign of it in her tone, which remained upbeat. "I think you're being silly, but what can I say?"

"Better silly than sorry, right?"

"If you say so." Quinton turned on her heel and strode toward the castle, jiggling her hips and well-shaped buttocks as she moved.

Collins watched her walk quickly across a grazing field still dotted with animals despite the late hour. Korfius wormed his head under Collins' sagging left hand and sat.

A voice emerged from a nearby copse of weeds. "I hate her."

Korfius barked madly at the newcomer. Equally surprised, Collins whirled to face Falima. The deeply tanned, black-haired woman melded easily with the darkness; and her blue eyes, several shades darker than Quinton's, narrowed menacingly.

Korfius' wild greeting dropped to a soft whine, and his tail waved into a blur of recognition. He ran to her, crashing through the weeds to lie at her feet.

Collins desperately hoped Falima had not seen the flirting between him and Quinton. "How . . . how long . . . were you there?"

"Long enough to see her try to trick you back into captivity." Falima fumed, still watching after Quinton's retreating form. "I've been waiting for you since I left switch-form. I assume Aisa got you back to the lady by the new look of Carriequinton's face."

Collins continued to watch Quinton until she disappeared into the outer courtyard, then turned his full attention on Falima. "Is Zylas all right?"

Falima ran a hand through her tousled black mane. "I don't know. Last report was just after Ialin switched."

Collins nodded his understanding. He now remembered that the hummingbird became human at around 9:00 P.M., which made him the perfect partner for Aisa. They changed at exactly opposite times, with no human intersection, which would make it harder to share information, especially when Ialin took bird form and Aisa woman. However, at all times, one of them could fly.

"Then, Vernon went in after his change, which was a pretty critical time."

Collins' chest clutched. Vernon's and Zylas' switch times perfectly corresponded, which had allowed them to become the best of friends. *So it's after midnight. We're too late. They know!*

Falima seemed oblivious to Collins' alarm. "Of course, without Zylas, we'll need the lady to communicate with Vernon."

King Terrin knows he has Zylas!

"We worked out some basic signals, but his overlap's not perfect and the code doesn't cover much."

Collins felt himself trembling, and not only from the cold night air. "Maybe I . . . should have gone with Carrie."

Korfius whined and slunk back to Collins, who patted the dog comfortingly.

Falima frowned, shook her head. Though not the classically beautiful model type that Quinton typified, she had a more honest, exotic attractiveness that Collins preferred. "If she deals fairly, she'll release Zylas with or without you. If not, she would still have Zylas. And you, too."

Collins nodded. He had come to the same conclusion, but a stifling guilt crept over him now. He could not help reliving the moment in the keep when he had seen his reflection in the mirror and believed his disguise had fallen. His panic had caused their capture. If he had kept his cool, they might have escaped unscathed. If not for him, Zylas would be relaxing now in the safety of some cave, regaling the renegades with modest tales of their adventure, teasing Collins about his oddly uncanny ability to play a girl. Unlike his illusion, Quinton's had held up under the reflected scrutiny of her hand mirror, which meant either his imagination had run amok or the mirror in Quinton's closet held some secret he had no means to understand at the present time.

Brush rattled, then a slight, androgynous man skittered into the clearing. Though short, his coffee-colored hair fell in shaggy disarray around finely chiseled, angular features. His small, delicate form belied a personality that Collins knew could become stolid and dangerously hostile.

Falima seized the man's arm. "Ialin, what's wrong?"

Ialin glanced from the clearing, to his companions, to the castle and back, never still. "Run. Run now. Guards . . . they've come to kill you."

Collins had followed Ialin's glance to the castle. When he returned his attention to the hummingbird/man, he found the dark gaze directly on him. "Me?" he blurted without thinking. For some reason, he had believed the comment addressed to Falima.

In response, Ialin rolled his eyes.

Though Collins knew it only made him look even less intelligent to Ialin, he had to question. "How do you know they're planning to kill me? Maybe they just want to take me to the castle, like Carrie asked."

"Maybe," Ialin said, hopping from foot to foot. Collins had recently read that fidgeting burned a significant number of calories. Knowing that, it seemed a wonder Ialin managed to weigh anything at all. Ialin's lids narrowed to slits. "If you don't mind them carrying you there by spears stabbed through your neck, heart, gut, and groin."

Collins could not keep his mind from conjuring the image of his impaled body held triumphantly overhead by four guards splattered with his dripping blood. He grimaced, banishing the mental image. "That doesn't sound like a welcoming party," he admitted. "But are you sure?"

"He's sure." Falima grabbed Collins' wrist and jerked him back the way he had come. "We need to get out of here. Fast."

Off-balanced by the unexpected maneuver, Collins staggered after his companions. "What about Vernon?"

Falima quickened her pace, half-dragging Collins behind her. "He'll be fine. Come on."

Collins gathered his legs and kept pace with his long-legged companion and their flitty friend. Korfius bounded along beside him, tugging at his pants, apparently believing the whole situation a game. In that moment, Collins suddenly understood Korfius' preference to remain a dog full-time, the world simplified to solid blacks and whites, purged of anything gray.

Shortly, Collins realized they took a different route than the one he and Quinton had used. "Where are we going?" he huffed out as he ran.

The Barakhains exchanged glances but did not answer. They continued to plow through the brush and trees, dodging copses, leaping brambles, and treading lightly on the piled leaves. The more carefully Collins tried to place his steps, the more mold he plowed up with every step. He soon gave up and abandoned the effort, concentrating more on forward movement and not losing the companions who seemed to know where they were going. *Or maybe they're counting on me to let them know if they go the wrong way.* The thought became an obsession. Though silence seemed safer, he addressed Falima. "I can take you where I last saw . . . the lady."

Before Falima could answer, Ialin snapped. "She's not there anymore. That Carriequinton bitch gave away her position to the guards, too. Even if we hadn't warned ahead, the lady's smart enough to move."

As the forest scrolled past Collins, branches battering his face at irregular intervals, he took slight solace in the realization that the twigs hit the illusion of Orna first, though they still hurt. He imagined Ialin had not actually used "bitch," given the dearth of Barakhain animal slang, but something similarly derogatory. *Move, all right. But where?* This time, he did not speak the words aloud. Either his companions knew and would drag him there or they would head for a safe hiding place and let the dragon find them. The renegades excelled at hide-and-seek despite the royal family's dog and horse advantage. They had played it with great success since long before Collins' arrival, and his constant questioning could only make their jobs more difficult. Benton Collins closed his mouth. And ran.

Soon, the route grew more difficult, sending him scrambling through a blackberry net that seemed more cave than copse. On hands and knees, or sometimes on his belly, he crawled and slithered through the mess of vines, ignoring the thorns that stabbed his sides and tore bits of flesh from his ears. At last, his companions took to the treetops, swinging like monkeys through the vines. Forced to carry Korfius, tired from his previous trip, Collins found himself hardpressed to follow, even when Falima backed up to help him with the dog. At one point, exhausted and dripping sweat, he paused to use the high vantage to look out over the forest for pursuit. Though he saw none, it didn't really reassure him. The guards had expected to find him waiting and willing, a sitting target. When they discovered him missing, they would have had to assemble dogs and horses, a task that might not have taken long, but would have widened the renegades lead considerably. He only hoped their tactics would fool the tracking animals.

Finally, Ialin swung to the ground, prancing in anxious circles while Falima and Collins eased Korfius down. The dog planted his paws on the dirt, broad-based and rocksteady while the man and woman skittered down after him.

"We need to move," Ialin reminded.

Falima made a wordless gesture to indicate that he should continue to lead rather than discussing the matter.

Ialin darted deeper into the woods.

Back on sturdy footing, Collins found himself capable of focusing on things other than just trying to follow and keep up with his companions. The clean foliage odors of the trees and brambles mingled with a shifting taint of rotting evergreen and mold. An occasional whiff of musk carried to him as they, or the breezes, moved, though whether from a skunk, fox, or weasel he could not tell. The world became a quilt of patchy greens: ranging from a deep olive to brilliant aqua and emerald. Stalk browns muted from the usual invisible dull support to a vivid color contrast as beautiful as any of the geometric panoramas formed by flowers, shoots, and leaves.

Cold points of water stung Collins' face. He jerked backward, only then noticing a thin stream meandering through the forest. His friends waded through it, the dog romping amid a wild spray of water.

Ialin growled through gritted teeth. "Korfius, no! It doesn't do us any good to hide our scent in water, if you're splashing it all over the banks."

Korfius whined. His head and tail drooped, and each step became a concentrated, deliberate movement, as if mimicking a gaited horse.

Apparently satisfied, Ialin went back to leading their scraggly band through the water. Though hating the idea, Collins placed a foot into the stream. Icy water rushed into his forty dollar Nike rip-off, chilling his ankle through his sock. He followed Falima who glanced curiously back at him at intervals. Her wood and cloth sandals surely afforded no protection against the cold, but at least they did not act like sponges. As Collins' toes grew number, his feet began to feel like boulders, sucking up as much of the stream as possible and driving his running shoes deep into the mucky silt.

Ialin plunged a hand into the water, then removed it, grinning and clutching a fish. "Got one." He took a bite from the wriggling tail.

It was all Collins could do not to throw up. Grimly, he turned his attention directly on Falima and concentrated on the soaked and grimy mass his socks had become inside his shoes. Suddenly, he thought of the mouse again. "Are you sure Vernon's all right?"

"He's Aisa's charge." Ialin spoke around a mouthful of some fish part Collins did not want to recognize. He had eaten sushi and liked it well enough, but he wondered how the Barakhain got around all the tiny bones. "You're mine."

"Aisa's?" Collins had last seen the parrot in the company of Prinivere, though he supposed she could easily have followed Carrie Quinton and himself without their knowledge. The renegades had surprised him so many times, he had begun to believe they used him for sneaking-up-on practice. He discarded the thought, suspecting that spending half their lives as animals and a chronic need to dodge danger simply made them more cautious than the average man on the American streets. *At least before September 11th.*

"Aisa's," Ialin repeated, though Collins' thoughts had gone way past the original question. "We thought it logical to give the inexperienced man to the man and the mouse to the bird big enough to carry him. But silly us. What do we know about strategy?"

Already tired of Ialin's hostility, Collins defended himself. "I wasn't questioning your perfectly perfect plan, Mister Perfection. I just didn't know Aisa had made it back here, yet. Is that all right with you?"

Ialin glanced at Collins over his shoulder, his lips bowed into a smile. "I suppose 'Mister Perfection' can live with that explanation." He went back to leading, and Falima turned to wink at Collins.

Collins shrugged. Ordinarily, self-doubt and politeness would have kept him from such a tirade; but his filthy, water-saturated, boulderlike shoes worried at his patience and mood. He understood the need for diversionary tactics, but it seemed more logical to get to Prinivere as swiftly as possible. Once they climbed on her back, she could fly anywhere and no dog could ever pick up the scent from there. Collins did not voice his opinion, however, as he harbored no wish for Ialin to belittle him in front of Falima again. He did not care what the hummingbird/man thought of him, but Falima's opinion mattered deeply.

At length, Ialin hopped from the stream to a rock, then to another farther away, and finally to the stony ledge of a hill tucked into a tangle of forest. Falima performed the same maneuver, then Korfius bounded after them. Collins leaped heavily to the first stone, throwing out his arms for balance. Water squirted from his running shoe, spilling in rivulets down the gray face. He jumped to the next rock, his shoes sloshing.

Ialin said nothing, though his head waggled disapprovingly at Collins' gracelessness. Ordinarily, Collins could make those jumps with ease, but the loads of water he carried like cement blocks turned the task into a monumental undertaking. If he ever came back to this magical world, he vowed, he would wear waterproof boots. Eventually, he straggled to the ledge, hoping they had reached the end of their journey.

Ialin wandered around the hill, then disappeared.

Falima took Collins' hand to lead him into the cave opening he had, once again, not previously noticed. Korfius wriggled between them and rushed into the cave, the humans following. This one was smaller than the previous ones had been, its edges worn smooth, with moss and tiny plants lining every crack. Prinivere took up most of the space, and Collins saw no supplies, such as the usual chests. He wondered how many safe houses the renegades had and how they communicated where to find Prinivere, their gear, and one another.

A lot, Prinivere sent. *We've practiced a long time and have a lot of spies.*

Collins drew up his left foot and removed his shoe, pouring several ounces of water onto the dirt floor. It disappeared quickly, soaking into the soil, leaving him with a slimy sock that had once been white. Hopping on his squishy right running shoe, he removed the sock, tossed it to the ground, and started on the other shoe.

"My lady." Ialin made a swift, slight bow. "As soon as Carriequinton got back to the castle, she sent a contingent of guards out to kill him." He gestured at Collins, who continued to hop around the cave, now on his bare left foot.

Prinivere lowered her scaly head. *I know. Aisa brought the news. I sent her to check on the caverns, see if Carrie lied about them, too.*

Collins paused to dump the water from his muddy right shoe.

The dragon's massive head swung toward Collins. *Aisa's gone to check where Carrie said they hid the dragon kits.*

Ialin gave Prinivere an earnest look as Falima came up beside Collins and put a hand on his shoulder to steady him while he removed his other sock. Collins guessed the hummingbird/man addressed the dragon in thought, perhaps to warn her not to say too much in the presence of one he still did not wholly trust.

Prinivere returned with a communication they could all hear. *He needs to know, Ialin. He's the only one who can get inside.*

Collins froze in mid-motion, the grubby, sodden sock dangling from his hand. "Are you saying I've got to sneak into the royal chambers? Again?" He touched his face with his free hand. "How many times can we pull that off?"

You don't have to go back there.

Ialin added, "And your face is back to normal, by the way."

Falima squeezed Collins' shoulder. "Dirt-streaked and tired, but normal."

Good. Collins wondered how long Quinton's illusion would last and how much worse she could do to him when it failed. Though her double cross had caught him by surprise, he could not wholly condemn it. After all, he had deceived her, too. In fact, he found her betrayal a bit of a relief, easing some of the guilt of his own.

Though Collins now stood squarely on bare feet, Falima still held his shoulder as she asked, "Did Aisa get Vernon out safely?"

He's with me, Prinivere confirmed. *From what I can*

get, the royals have identified Zylas. Then, Carrie Quinton ordered Ben killed and locked up Zylas.

Collins wriggled feet becoming dangerously cold and wondered where they had left his backpack. "Locked him up? He was already locked up." He glanced directly at Falima, then at Ialin from the corner of his eye, wondering if he had missed something. The woman nodded agreement, and even Ialin seemed interested in the answer.

In a rat-sized cage.

Falima gasped; and, this time, Collins knew he had failed to consider something important. He kept his mouth shut, hoping it would come out in context, but he could not help wondering, *What? Is he a claustrophobic rat?*

At noon . . . Prinivere started, then left Collins to finish.

"He turns into a human and . . . and what happens?"

Ialin said gruffly, "If the iron's sturdy enough, it crushes him dead."

Something wet splashed Collins' cheek, and he glanced at Falima. Spidery red lines wound through her eyes, the lids half-closed in pain.

"Not Zylas." Collins put a comforting arm around Falima, and she folded against him. Though well-muscled, she felt strangely small and helpless to Collins, who could never have imagined her surrendering to despair. He wondered if her relationship with the albino went deeper than he had known, despite the vast difference in their ages, surprised to suffer a flare of jealousy. He could no longer deny his feelings for her. He drew himself up, willing a determination he did not feel. "So we have to rescue him before noon tomorrow." He shrugged, as if it were the simplest matter in the world. "We can do that."

Ialin nodded, though the gesture seemed more habitual than reassuring. He had clearly weathered a lot for this cause, and it never seemed to end.

You still have the right to go home whenever you wish. You don't have to risk yourself for this.

Though cautiously sent and clearly intended out of fairness, Prinivere's reminder irritated Collins. He turned on the dragon with a tone that surely baffled his companions, who had not received the message. "I'm not going anywhere till I know Zylas is safe. I got him into this mess—"

Falima interrupted, "No, he got himself into it. He insisted on going, and—"

"It was my fault." Collins' voice cracked, and he felt tears building. "I got us caught. I did something very very stupid."

Ialin's head rose and swiveled toward Collins. His expression still presented an image of sorrow, but his eyes gained the stormy darkness that had become so familiar to Collins. Even Falima stiffened.

"There's a mirror in Carrie's room. It reflected me as me—the real me, not the illusion. I thought the disguise had worn off. I . . . thought my cover . . . gone, and I panicked. I didn't think things through clearly and . . ." Collins swallowed hard, and the tears dribbled down his cheeks. "I'm sorry." Now, he could almost feel Prinivere scanning his mind for details.

A mirror that sees through illusions is magical.

"Clearly." Ialin scratched his head, rearranging the disarray of his hair into further chaos. "But why would Carrie-quinton have such a thing?"

Prinivere squinted, and her eyes disappeared amidst the scaly folds of her aged face. *Seeing through illusions may not be its primary power. Any magical mirror would cut through to the truth.*

Falima removed her hand from Collins, using the back to wipe tears from her cheeks. "So what's the real purpose of this thing likely to be?"

Collins appreciated that the conversation had gone from his blunder to the significance of the mirror. "If I had to guess, I'd bet it shows her face the way it used to look."

Very likely. Though Prinivere agreed with Collins' assessment, she still appeared pensive, eyes lost amid the wrinkles. *Though that, too, might simply be a function of it being magical. It might not have anything to do with its intended purpose when it got magicked.*

Ialin made a thoughtful noise. "So, if it has another power, Carrie might not even know about it."

Now Collins frowned. As a scientist, he would examine and experiment with that mirror until he discovered its every secret. He doubted Quinton would have done less. "In any case, is it more likely to give away that her facial repairs are illusion? Or to show her her original face before the scars?"

I . . . don't know, the dragon admitted. *This is a distinctly unusual circumstance. If I had it here to examine . . .*

Stepping out of Collins' embrace, Falima continued to mop up tears with her sleeve. She had seen Quinton's repaired features and had, apparently, figured out the rest by context. "Carriequinton obviously never planned to cooperate with us anyway, so it hardly matters when she realizes we tricked her."

We? Collins appreciated that Falima accepted his deceit as a group decision. It made him feel like an integral part of the renegade operation, though he suspected her word choice had more to do with the fact that Prinivere had decided to assist in the duplicity. In college, he had supported liberal causes with the unambiguous moral certainty only a neophyte to the big bad world could muster. As his personal burdens grew heavier, he had become essentially apolitical. He wondered what his friends and family would think if they knew he had deliberately embroiled himself in the sticky and perilously deadly affairs of another world.

Prinivere opened her enormous green eyes and rolled her gaze toward Falima. *I'm not so certain she never intended to cooperate. She did trust Ben enough to come with him alone. And she did eventually tell us where to find the dragons.*

Collins shook his head, having difficulty making sense of the matter. "Why would she tell me, then try to have me killed?"

Falima and Ialin remained silent, without the necessary information to participate fully in the conversation.

Prinivere paced out a cautious circle and lay back down in a new position. *She whispered the directions in your ear, remember? Then you left right away, without the chance to tell anyone else. Once you died, you couldn't pass it on. Or, if you lived, she figured you'd forget all those unfamiliar names before you could pass them along.*

Collins realized he already had.

Even if you remembered, she knew it wouldn't do us any good.

Collins recalled the earlier, unfinished conversation. "Because this place is warded *against* switchers?" A light dawned. *That's got to be the place Carrie considered a "third world."*

Right.

"Why?"

Prinivere glanced at Ialin, who sighed, shrugged, then nodded wearily. Not long ago, he had cautioned the dragon not to tell Collins about this place at all and now she had passed him the job. "Because it's basically a dungeon, and a long-ago king worried that people might either try to release prisoners or blunder in and get themselves killed. The warding works both ways, so it also kept the prisoners from escaping."

Collins paused to consider the words before asking any questions. The more he figured out on his own, the less Ialin would judge him. He knew the king had never warded his dungeon in a similar way, if for no other reason than that it would also exclude guards. However, the current king had nothing to do with the magic that kept switchers from the royal bedchambers either. In fact, he had written decrees banning the possession or use of magic by anyone in the kingdom, which suggested he might not know about Quinton's mirror and explained why she kept it hidden in the wardrobe. He guessed some ancient king had wanted prisoners housed farther from the castle while later ones preferred to keep enemies close and had moved the lockup to the basement. Collins tried a different tack, "Perhaps that king wanted to keep the more violent criminals as far as possible from his home and family."

Ialin's nostrils flared, and the corners of his mouth bent slightly upward. He did not seem disappointed with the direction of Collins' questioning. Yet.

Prinivere provided some assistance without giving Collins the answer. Perhaps she sensed the blow that might cause to his self-esteem. *And the most violent prisoners would be . . .*

. . . meat eaters? Collins guessed, then cringed at the understanding that answer brought. "It's the lockup for the *Randoms* who take the form of obligate carnivores?" He cursed himself for answering too quickly. "No, that's not right. King Terrin has them executed."

"King Terrin," Falima said, "and several kings before him. But long ago, rulers tried imprisoning them." She glanced at Ialin, as if willing him to go easier on Collins. "Without much success."

Collins remembered something the current king had told him. "I did know that. The king said most of the carnivores preferred execution." He narrowed his eyes. "But locking them up occurred generations ago. Even if they got to live out their natural lives in prison, wouldn't they all be long dead by now?"

Ialin shifted from foot to foot. "Unless they bred."

Prinivere added the finishing touch. *A long-ago king who didn't believe in executions had an "inescapable" catacomb engineered to house the most recidivist and wicked criminals. After one trickster still got out, he hired dragons to ring it with magic. Some of his successors continued to use it. After the Curse, the wards operated mainly to prevent switchers from entering or, more importantly, leaving and to imprison cannibals.*

After nearly getting hanged for ignorantly eating a rabbit, Collins preferred the term "carnivore." It all made sense now. Likely, the earlier criminals were all male, and the king had expected them to destroy one another or starve. At best, they would die of old age without bothering the honest citizens of Barakhai. Once the worst crime became uncontrollable cannibalism while in animal form, the proportion of men to women would presumably become equal. Thirteen-year-olds not yet used to their new forms would find themselves ripped from loving, protective families and thrust into a lawless world filled with uncivilized people and man-eating carnivores, never to see their loved ones again. He shivered at the implications. The wild animals would instinctively produce more of their own. Rape seemed inevitable, and some would deliberately pair off in human form, creating *Random* offspring that might find themselves the only rabbits or zebras in a den of lions, tigers, and wolves. No telling what kind of horrors might lurk in such a hellhole.

Then, the realization hit home. Suddenly Collins found his eyes so widely rounded they hurt. "I'm supposed to go . . . I mean, you expect me to face that . . . alone?" Suddenly, sneaking into a castle and rescuing a caged rat from dozens of guards did not seem so hard.

Eyes still enormous, Benton Collins glanced around the room, scarcely daring to believe his companions could even consider such a task possible. Each looked back at him with such desperate hope that it tugged at his heart. *Maybe if I had an army, a couple of bazookas, and a whole fleet of warplanes.* He shook his head in dumbfounded disbelief. "I want to help. I'll do everything I can. But . . . I just don't think . . ." He continued to glance around at his companions, who remained stoically silent. ". . . it's possible to . . ." The tears puddled in Falima's eyes again, and it cut Collins to the heart. "But I will help with Zylas."

They did not need Collins for that mission.

"But I'm not sure you'd want me. I don't have any experience. I might mess up again, and—"

Prinivere spoke first, with a mental communication that did not disrupt the uncomfortably heavy silence of his companions. *I could send you home and bring you back for . . . those things you think you need.*

Collins sighed, not wanting to explain modern weaponry, even to one as intelligent and intuitive as Prinivere. "Armies, bazookas, warplanes. I don't actually have access to those things, although . . ." He could barely believe he was considering this. ". . . I could probably scrounge up a gun." *Get around the three-day waiting period in the wake of September 11th? Fat chance.* Unlike the renegades, he had no sources for illegal goods. *Wait, isn't it just handguns that require a permit?* Having never purchased such a thing before, he had no idea of the details. He had gone target shooting with his friends a few times but had always borrowed one of their rifles. No one in his family that he knew of had ever owned a gun of any kind. "I suppose I could look into it." It was a flimsy dodge at best. A single shot was unlikely to stop a charging lion, and anything could get him while he reloaded. He did not even know if he would find the dragons tame enough to follow him once, or if, he found them. "How about if we save Zylas first, then worry about how to get the dragons from the catacombs?"

Each of the renegades nodded and, for the moment, Collins found himself free of an impossible burden. It was a temporary reprieve at best.

And Collins knew it.

Chapter 7

PRINIVERE lumbered forward, revealing a shadowy cavern containing several sacks as well as Benton Collins' overstuffed and battered backpack. Korfius trotted over to sniff at the contents, but Collins got there first. He could scarcely wait to paw through his things again. First, he wanted his watch. Then he would look for anything else he had brought to this backward world that might aid in rescuing Zylas. He could no longer recall everything he had packed.

Collins jerked out the rolled up T-shirts first. Uncomfortable in the wet, grimy clothing he had worn through the swamp, he tugged off his shirt without worrying about propriety—more concerned about not smearing slime across his torso. He pulled on a clean, black pocket tee and his only other pair of jeans. He added a pair of dry socks. Though he needed a bath, he felt much more comfortable in clothing steeped in the familiar essence of Era Ultra. He still worried that the perfumy aroma of deodorant might give him away, but he could not resist brushing his teeth.

Around Collins, his companions plotted with a solemn thoroughness that revealed their desperation. He missed much of the conversation; Prinivere did not always generalize her sendings, and Vernon could communicate only with her. From what Collins could gather as he sorted through his possessions, Ialin planned to impersonate a particular merchant with a macaw switch-form. Aisa would play his wife. They would have to disguise Falima as a mule, since all

Barakhain horses worked only as guards for established governmental entities. Vernon would remain a mouse until Zylas' return to man form and could hide in any pocket or crevice.

Collins found his watch buried with his keys and beeper under his clothing. He flipped it around to look at the face. To his surprise, it read almost 5:00 A.M. He had not realized how much time he had spent traveling back and forth from the castle to Prinivere's various hiding places, and he now understood why even his frantic excitement floundered through hovering exhaustion. He strapped the watch to his wrist. Falima, he knew, would switch next, which explained why she was the only one the renegades planned to disguise in a form different than the one she currently held. It also meant they had to wait until 6:00 A.M. just to start working on her. That still left them a solid five hours to free Zylas, but any delay seemed intolerable.

Collins separated out a handful of Tums and Tylenol. Concern for Zylas kept him wide awake despite the wee morning hours. The constant state of alert stress had not yet touched off a headache or a boil of stomach acid, but he wouldn't be surprised if it did soon. He could feel the early prickles of beard on his face, but it was not yet enough to bother with shaving. He put the matches in his pocket. He could not think of a use for the mini tape recorder and fold-up binoculars, but he believed the jerky, Snickers bars, and dog biscuits might prove useful when he faced off with Barakhai's carnivores. *When?* Collins groaned at the realization. He had already started planning for something he had just dismissed as impossible. His friends would talk him into doing it, he felt sure; and Prinivere's attempts to remain neutral, to leave the decision wholly to his conscience, would only make him more certain to agree. He wondered how this group of Otherworld creatures had come to know him better than he knew himself.

Believing Prinivere entirely ensconced in three other minds, Collins did not expect an answer; but he got one. *Because you're an easy read, Ben. A good man with a good heart.*

Warmed by the compliment, Collins flushed, biscuits clutched in his fist. "I—I didn't know you were listening in on me."

I have to. Once again, you're our only hope.

... to free the dragons, Collins finished, turning his gaze, as well as his attention, to Prinivere.

Yes. As if feeling his eyes upon her, Prinivere lurched around to face Collins. *But also to rescue Zylas.*

Collins nodded, then realized he did not understand. So far, the plan Ialin and the others had outlined left no place for him.

The king will be expecting us to attempt a rescue.

Collins' mouth set in a grim line, and he passed the dog biscuits from hand to hand. He wondered why he had not seen it before. King Terrin could have executed Zylas immediately or tortured him for information. Instead, he had given the renegades a limited amount of time to come to his aid. There could be only one logical reason for such a strategy. King Terrin knows we'll come and even when, within the space of half a day. He wants to catch more renegades, ones who'll be easier to intimidate and question than Zylas.

Collins had no experience with reading dragon expressions, and that unnerved him. When she gave no reply, he continued thinking his part of the silent conversation to her.

We can't let anyone go.

What choice do we have, Benton Collins?

We .., Collins started and stopped. We could ... He shook his head to clear it and only realized Korfius had approached when one of the biscuits jerked in his hand. He watched the dog gently ease it free of his grip. There was no prudent way to finish the sentence. They could either attempt a rescue or leave Zylas to die. Suggesting they could risk lesser figures in the movement seemed judgmental and cowardly at the same time. What do we do?

We, Prinivere measured the word so that it referred only to herself and Collins. *We free the young dragons.*

After—

Prinivere's raised claw stayed him. *Once the dragons are with me, we can use magic to save Zylas and anyone else captured in the meantime. If their rescue attempt fails ... we'll still have you.*

Collins barely felt Korfius tug the second biscuit from his hands. His mind went utterly blank.

Prinivere did not press. In the background, Collins could hear the discussion growing more heated. Switch times and switch-forms did not match, and they debated the pros and cons of representing themselves as a new group rather than trying to pass for a known entity.

Finally, Collins managed to think, *I'm the ace in the hole?* He rolled his eyes. *God help this mission.*

You can do it, Prinivere's faith came across as unwavering, to Collins' chagrin. It seemed far more likely that all of them would die.

Prinivere sent Collins nothing more, and the gaps in the other conversation told him she had turned her attention back to them. As promised, she left the decision to him, though she had burdened him with understanding. He would rather have remained ignorant. He wished he had something more than raw guesses to bet on, some knowledge of the future that could guide him to the course most likely to bring all of them out alive. Prinivere had a definite point. At some point, Collins would have to make the decision about whether or not to enter the lair of the carnivores. Serial plans depended on the success of the first one, while simultaneous ones did not. Rescuing Zylas did not require Collins, since no one had to enter the royal chambers. Freeing the dragons depended entirely on him.

If they don't get to Zylas in time, if Fallma gets hurt or killed, I'll blame myself forever for not going with them. Collins bit his lip at the thought of his friends dying because of his decision. Frantic worry assailed him, making concentration even more difficult. It astounded him how swiftly these people had become his closest companions, how Barakhai had become every bit as real as the world he had once considered unique in the universe. *But if I'm the reason the plan fails, I'll suffer worse.* He looked at the objects around him. None of them could help with freeing Zylas. If he still had his multitool, he might feel otherwise; but that had vanished at the castle.

His fear of death receded beneath the horror of living with the knowledge that he had let his friends die rather than assist them. Collins knew he could not leave until he saw as many as possible to safety. "Prinivere?" he called.

The dragon swung her enormous head back to him. Huge, emerald cat's eyes steadied, gleaming with anxiety but demanding nothing.

"When you said 'we' would free the dragons, you

meant—?" Collins had no words to finish the question disguised as casual statement.

As always, Prinivere went straight to the heart. *I'm a switcher. I can't directly accompany you. But—*

The last words seemed to hover tangibly in the air.

Collins waited, scarcely daring to breathe.

I can stand at the entrance. My roar—

This time, Prinivere did not have to finish. "Scares everyone. It should scare the carnivores away, and—" This time, Collins broke off. Though strong and terrifying, her roar did not carry far. "Couldn't you turn me into something . . . mean? Something even a carnivore wouldn't mess with?"

Like a dragon?

Collins' desperate idea had not gotten that specific, but he felt a small glimmer of hope. "That would do."

Prinivere's eyes gleamed, and the edges of her enormous mouth twitched. *If I could do that, the Curse would no longer matter. I could just zap everyone into whatever shape he preferred.*

Collins was thinking more along the lines of an illusion.

Prinivere did not wait for him to form the words. *I'm limited to human faces. I could make you unusually ugly . . .*

"Not necessary." Collins saw no purpose to that. With his luck, an illusion like the one she described would remain stuck in place forever. He looked at his scattered belongings, gaze skipping from clothes, to toiletries to the bits of technology. "I've got it!" He snatched up the tape recorder.

Prinivere's head cocked sideways, like a dog trying to make sense of lilting English. She verbalized the details his thoughts supplied her. *It's like that thing you called a photograph. Only sound.*

Collins had never thought of it that way. He scrambled to a crouch. "Right. It captures a sound and allows me to replay it. A few roars into this should keep me safe for a while, as long as I can rewind." Now that he knew he would not have to change into period clothes, he stuffed the jerky and several biscuits into his front jeans pockets. He put the candy bars into his shirt pocket and crammed the fold-up binoculars into the back pockets of his pants. Looping the recorder strap through his belt, he pushed the machine into its own strap, affixing it. "I'm ready."

Prinivere snorted out a noise that sounded like laughter.

Every head swayed toward her, and all conversation ceased. Clearly, she did not do that often.

Collins flushed at the attention. He had gone from abject refusal to leaping almost blindly into the task in moments, without much external convincing. He had spent some time in consideration, but the thing that had finally pushed him over the edge was the realization that he had the ability to come up with solutions for a problem that had once seemed insurmountable.

Prinivere detailed her own timetable. *I'll need to use the illusion magic on Ialin to get him to pass for the merchant. Aisa's fine as she is, and I don't have any spells to turn a horse into a mule.*

Ialin nodded grimly, tucking a small hand into his filthy, well-worn tunic. "We'll handle that. But I might need some help whipping up a cart and wares, and I'll need some richer clothes." He glanced at Prinivere. "Vernon?"

Prinivere remained silent for several moments as she sorted out a conversation with a mouse who had reasonable, but imperfect, overlap.

While he waited, Collins swiped the deodorant across his armpits and sorted the Tylenol and Tums, half of each into the two bottles. One he returned to the pack, and the other he forced into the biscuit pocket. By the time he finished, he was no longer anticipating Prinivere's reply, so her sudden presence in his mind startled him.

*Vernon always has clothes, but he's having trouble grasping the concept of what a merchant might wear. We can fake product. I have a few spells that could help there. . . . *

Ialin's and Prinivere's conversation turned private, leaving Collins alone with his thoughts. Too much consideration would lose the current surge of motivation. The conditions the dragon had described in the caverns could lead to any number of possibilities, from a dangerously lawless society to one that had consumed itself in a matter of a few scant years. As a scientist, he had learned to examine all the possibilities. In Barakhai, he worried that approach might paralyze him into total inactivity. At least, he could count on Prinivere's spell from his last visit to help him master any language they might have constructed during the centuries of isolation. Collins would have the technological advantage; he doubted any king would have provided deadly prisoners with anything they could learn to use as weapons.

Collins did think of more items he might find useful. He emptied his pockets back into his backpack, atop the spare clothing and toiletries. The Snickers had softened from his body heat, and was malleable in his grip. He chose his pocketed items more carefully: the pack of matches in his T-shirt, the tape recorder still looped onto his belt, the beef jerky and a few dog biscuits at his hips.

"Nervous?" Aisa squawked suddenly.

Collins jumped, nearly braining himself on an overhang. He studied the parrot, who returned the favor, head cocked. She balanced on a prominence, two toes on each scaly foot stretching forward and two backward. Speckles of dirt and parrot dandruff stippled her otherwise brilliant plumage. "Apparently," he finally managed with a smile.

"I would be, too," Aisa admitted. She straightened her head. "You should probably take some torches." She hunkered down, measuring distances before launching herself from the stone. Once in the air, she went from clunky to graceful, gliding effortlessly around the craggy interior to land on a box near where Collins had found his pack. "In here."

"Thanks." Collins dropped his pack and headed toward her.

Korfius looked up from where he lay, straight-legged and sideways, on the ground. His tail whacked the dirt, but he did not bother to rise.

Collins hefted the lid of the trunk to reveal a stack of wood wrapped at one end in oily rags. He took a half dozen, adding them to the load in his pack.

Aisa settled on the lip of the open lid. "You're up to this task?"

Collins did not know how to answer. "I hope so."

"Zylas depends on us. On you."

Collins wondered why the parrot/woman felt a need for this awkward conversation. "I've already said I'd do it. You don't have to convince me."

Aisa shifted from one bird foot to the other. "I know."

An uncomfortable silence ensued, and Collins suddenly wished he had not sounded so accusatory. The last time he had come to Barakhai, the renegades had brought him here by subterfuge and won his allegiance with half-truths. He wished they would stop trying so hard to ascertain that he made all his own decisions, free from coercion. All choices involved at least a little duress, and he was not at all sure that, if his mission failed, he wanted full responsibility for his own death. Or worse, for Zylas'.

Aisa broke the hush. "I just want to make sure you don't commit yourself to something dangerous in ignorance."

"In this case, a certain amount of ignorance is unavoidable." Collins strapped up his pack and hefted it, testing its weight. He had to balance bringing anything he might find a use for against making a burden that might slow him in a life-or-death run for safety. He realized he could always drop it should speed became the determining factor. *Can't outrun most predators anyway.* He looked at Aisa again, still gripping the lid with first one claw, then the other. It suddenly occurred to him that she was not talking to reassure him, but herself. She had a dangerous mission ahead of her as well. "But I'm definitely going forward with it. If you, Ialin, and Falima can't rescue Zylas, I will."

Where Aisa's enormous black beak met the wrinkly white skin, it pulled taut, a birdie smile that compressed the fine, tiny feathers that formed the black stripes around her eyes. "I'm new to the special operations team."

Despite his own concerns, Collins had to suppress a grin. Those words sounded hilarious from the mouth of a parrot, even though he knew she had surely chosen others. The translation spell did a remarkable job with slang and jargon.

Aisa did not seem to notice Collins' lapse. "I didn't expect to get thrown into something so big so quickly. Our spies are good, but they can't know everything, everyone. Plans go awry; sometimes informants get caught. There are gaps . . ." She shook her head, dislodging a feather. "I don't know if I can fake through those well enough, especially in bird form. More nervous, worse overlap."

Collins could hear the difference discomfort made in her speech even as she explained it. Some of his fellow graduate students deliberately procrastinated before a major project, claiming they performed better under pressure. Clearly, stress had the opposite effect on Aisa. He tried to put her at ease. "From what I've seen so far, you're smart and capable. Don't lose your head, and you'll do fine." He could scarcely believe he found himself in the position of senior operative. Scrawny and bookish, he had never harbored any illusions about becoming a James Bond or a Walker, Texas Ranger. With his straight B average, he was not even destined to become one of those genius scientists the evil-doers kidnapped to force them to help with some nefarious plot. He stroked her just behind the nostrils. "If I can do this, you can, too."

Aisa closed her eyes, clearly enjoying the touch as much as the pep talk.

Falima approached at that moment, and Collins watched her every fluid movement. There was nothing delicate about this woman, from her broad face to her chunkily muscled limbs, yet she still managed to carry herself with remarkable grace. She paced deliberately, yet every step seemed light and buoyant. Though built more for function than appearance, her unadorned dress swirled around well-proportioned curves. She would fill a size ten better than a model's two, but she needed that extra space for voluptuous breasts and sculpted hips that made her waist disappear. In his world, her naturally golden skin might make sun worshipers jealous or some doctor worry over jaundice. He loved the shape of her face, the imperfect set of her features, and the long hair, as black as ebony.

As Collins' fingers stilled on her face, Aisa opened her eyes. Without a word, she spread her wings and glided back to Ialin and Prinivere.

"I just came to say . . ." Falima lowered her head and kicked at a stone on the ground. "I mean we may not . . ." She looked to Collins to finish her point, but he could not. He truly did not know what she was trying to say.

Falima heaved a heavy sigh, then finally met Collins' gaze. Her eyes looked as untouched and beautiful as a blue-tiled pool before the swimming season, but depthless and bright. The black forelock that fell around them made an exotically stunning contrast. She was to Collins the loveliest creature on any world, and he realized without a hint of doubt that he loved her. "We're both going on . . . very difficult missions . . . and . . ."

Collins placed a hand on her shoulder and felt a sharp thrill of desire. It was not the first time his young body had responded to such casual contact with a woman, but it felt more honest, more innocent and real. "We're both going to succeed."

Falima did not seem as certain. "Just in case. I wanted to say—"

"Don't say 'good-bye.' " It sounded corny, and Collins tried to remember from what movie the line came. He could not even recall what the hero had told his girl to say instead; "farewell," perhaps. "We'll see each other again."

Collins' optimism was not contagious. Though Falima did not directly contradict him, her expression remained pained and uncertain. She passed the stone between her feet, and Collins found himself idly thinking that she would make a good soccer player.

Collins placed his other hand on her other shoulder. "Falima, both of these missions have to succeed, or it's all over. Our cause is just."

Falima pursed her lips, then spoke slowly. "If need and good and justice alone were enough, nothing bad would ever happen."

"This time," Collins said, "those things will prevail. You have to believe that." She did not have to, and he was not even certain that he did. But going into danger with the right attitude could spell the difference between triumph and failure. "Falima," he started, not sure where he intended to go until the words slipped from his mouth. "I love you."

Falima finally managed a weak smile. "I know."

It was not the answer Collins wanted. "Oh."

"And I love you, too."

Collins appreciated the addition, but suspected she had not finished. "Like a brother?" he suggested.

Falima stared, those bluer than blue eyes growing wide. "You *do* have some strange customs in your world. In Barakhai, it's considered anathema to court one's own children, parents, or siblings."

Collins grinned, too gripped with joy to care about the misunderstanding. *She loves me. She really loves me.* His hands slid around her back, and he winched her into a tight embrace. She raised her worried face to his, and their lips met in an uncertain kiss that warmed to passion. It all seemed so drearily ironic. He would undertake this mission for her and her cause, yet it might well separate them for eternity. The fact that she could only come to his world as a horse, that even here she spent half her life as an animal, seemed trivial compared to the tasks that awaited them both. They would have to see what changes success brought to figure out how, or even if, they could remain together.

Falima broke the embrace. "You'd best let go if you don't want to find yourself hugging a horse."

"Not such a bad thing." Collins enjoyed the sweet musk of her equine aroma, mingled with plant smells and loam. "I happen to know you like scratches behind the ears."

Falima shook back her hair. "Well, yes, but it's best I change outside. I don't want to step on anything. Would you please gather my clothes when I'm done."

Collins nodded, watching her walk to the cave mouth. He knew from experience that switching happened quickly and painlessly, nothing like the old werewolf movies where a creepy half-human thing writhed and howled with madness. In fact, when he arrived at the cave mouth, he found the horse silhouetted against the sunrise, her clothing in a heap near her hooves.

Collins wadded up Falima's clothes, clutching them to his abdomen. They smelled like her, a mixture of her natural body scents, damp, and dried grasses. It tickled his nose, a pleasure he had never noticed in the scoured, perfumed, disinfected, and deodorized world of the early twenty-first century. He had read about pheromones in animals and the studies that suggested people responded to them as well. Reveling in his girlfriend's dirty laundry, he had to admit they were probably right.

Are you ready? Prinivere's sudden presence startled Collins from thoughts that turned his ears scarlet. He had forgotten that she could read minds.

Ready? Collins squeaked in his mind. *Ready for what?* He shook his head to clear it. "Ready to record your roar, my lady." He patted the mini tape recorder at his belt, thoughts still lost in the cloud of his exchange with Falima.

Ialin headed outside, presumably to work on Falima's disguise. His own features had changed dramatically, but Collins did not have a chance to study them in the moments it took the little man to flit past. Aisa sailed out behind him.

I wondered when you two were finally going to get together.

The flush spread from Collins' hot ears across his cheeks.

"How long have you known?" He forced himself to look at the dragon, into eyes like green flame.

I've lived long enough to see some things coming before they happen.

Collins continued to stare into those fire and moonlight eyes. "That's a nonanswer."

Perhaps, Prinivere said. *But the answer doesn't come down to one moment in time. I've seen the early signs and wondered if they might come together.* She lowered her head, and her lips pulled back from wicked-looking teeth. *I'm glad they did.*

Collins resented that he might have had more time with Falima before circumstances separated them, possibly forever. "Why didn't you say something?"

Because my saying something might have changed what happened, even how you felt. You might have seen it as my way of keeping you here, and you would never have faced your true feelings. And it makes no sense to encourage something that might not have a chance. You're not just from different backgrounds, you're from different worlds.

Collins had to agree. *Half the time, from different species.*

Prinivere's shoulders heaved slightly. She had made her point. *So—are you ready?*

Though uncertain, Collins nodded and checked the buttons. The first time he came into Prinivere's presence, the urge to flee seized him. He wondered if hearing her roar might send him scurrying from the cave.

Prinivere answered with an unsettling suggestion. *You might want to cover your ears.*

Trusting Prinivere to warn the others, Collins pressed the record and play buttons, then plastered his hands over his ears. The roar shattered through his defenses, chilling him to the marrow, and he fought the scream building in his own throat. Terror, not reason, rooted him in place. If it hadn't, nothing short of a harness could have kept him from running.

As the echoes of the sound died away, Collins could hear Falima whinnying wildly in the distance. Heart slamming, rationality returning in a slow trickle, he hit the stop button. "Is Falima . . . all right?"

Fine. Prinivere did not elaborate. *Are you?*

Collins did not answer, not only because he wasn't sure, but because Prinivere could read his state of mind better than he could.

Do you want another?

No! Collins forced himself to say, "Yes, please." He had originally planned to try to fill the tape, not knowing how much effort he could expend rewinding and replaying. With less than six hours to work and the unpleasantness of Prinivere's first vocalization, he would settle for two. He pressed the buttons and thought hard, *Go!* Almost in afterthought, he clamped both palms over his ears. This time, he prepared his mind as well, thinking in a cycle. *It's just Prinivere. She won't hurt me. It's just ...*

The second roar exploded through his mind, scattering his thoughts and stiffening every muscle. He bit his lip, grabbing for the stabilizing anchor of his chant. *It's just Prinivere.* The discomfort lessened gradually. This time, when Collins uncovered his ears, he came immediately back to himself. He hit the stop button.

Let's hear, Prinivere suggested.

Collins guessed she spoke from curiosity. She wanted to see for herself how the technology worked. He needed to test the recording, to make certain it had not failed and that it displayed the necessary clarity to keep the carnivores at bay. "All right," he said cautiously, pressing the rewind button. The tape hissed for a moment, then the button clicked up. "But please be ready to stop me if I charge off into the ozone." Collins pushed in "play." A half-second of silence was broken by a full-throated roar that could put a chorus of lions to shame. Collins' heart skipped a beat, and he tensed every muscle, but he did not have to fight instinct to remain in place. He thumbed down the volume just as the second roar exploded through the speaker.

Amazing!

"Yes," Collins agreed.

Prinivere dipped her head. *Is that what I sound like?*

Collins smiled. *Some things are the same everywhere.* It was the first question nearly everyone in his own world asked after hearing a recording of his or her voice. "Yup." He realized he was not being entirely forthright. "Well, I didn't get the full effect of the real thing, since I covered my ears. It seems the same, and everything I've ever recorded comes out exactly like the original." He frowned. "Your recorded roar, even without my hands covering my ears, doesn't scare me as much as the real thing. I'm not sure if that's because I'm getting used to it or if it's just scarier coming directly from a dragon's mouth."

The carnivores won't know I'm not standing right there.

Collins nodded. They would have no knowledge of whatever technology had come to Barakhai since their imprisonment, let alone the much more advanced level of his own world.

Prinivere lumbered toward Collins and the cave exit. *Ialin has a couple of things for you. Then I think we should head out.*

Collins turned as the dragon walked past him, noting the ancient parchmentlike skin, the swampy gray-green of her scales, the myriad scars. Even the triangular plates that ridged her back looked tired, some flopped over at the tips like the ears of a scraggly mutt. He wondered how closely related her DNA might be to that of the dinosaurs.

Korfius trotted happily after her.

The dog could not come with him, Collins knew, given the prison wards against switchers. Korfius could not join the other team either since all dogs were guards.

Prinivere gave Collins the answer to the question he was on the verge of asking. *I'll bring Korfius with us to the caverns. He won't be able to follow you in, so I'll take him back with me. I'll keep him safe until you return.*

"Thanks." Though Collins appreciated the economy of speech Prinivere's mind reading allowed, it still bothered him. He imagined he now knew how a stutterer must feel when a well-meaning but impatient acquaintance insisted on finishing his sentences for him. Collins wished he had some way to ensure a modicum of privacy.

I can stop it, if it makes you feel uncomfortable.

Prinivere's pronouncement caught Collins by surprise as he followed her from the cave. "You can stop reading minds?"

Well, no. But I can stop responding to thoughts until you've spoken them aloud.

Collins considered, then shook his head. "Actually, I prefer things as they are." Without the occasional reminder, he tended to forget about Prinivere's skill until he had already become focused on something embarrassing. The ability went so far beyond the logic of his own world that he found it almost impossible to continually bear in mind. Even as the thought came to him, he knew he had just informed Prinivere of his reasons as well. *And again.* He laughed at the hopeless cycle. He had discovered a few things about her skill. She could read only surface ideas and emotions, and she could only focus on one or two at a time, especially when engaged in conversation. The more the views were steeped in duplicity, the harder she found it to interpret them. Capturing others' thoughts and feelings had often seemed as much a curse as a skill in science fiction novels and movies, yet Prinivere seemed to handle it deftly enough. Of course, she had had thousands of years to adapt, and it did come naturally to her species.

Prinivere let Collins know she still followed his train of thought. *It's as natural as breathing to a dragon. Learning to deal with spending part of my life as a human was much more difficult to handle.*

Collins believed that but did not dwell on the image. He headed toward Ialin who worked over an edgy, whickering Falima with bursts of quick movement.

Ialin gave Collins only a glance. In that instant, he could see the coarser, older features Prinivere had given Ialin. His dark brown eyes had turned hazel, and the shaggy mop of short, brown hair now fell around a bulbous nose and broad cheeks that looked beefy on his slender frame. "Are you done scaring the crap out of Falima?"

Collins approached the horse with slow gliding movements intended to soothe her. Her eyes rolled backward, and her ears lay pressed against the back of her head. The ground below her was pocked with the scars her prancing hooves had left. "Easy, girl. Good girl." He reached out a hand.

Falima jerked back her nose and rose into a half-rear, whinnying shrilly.

"Easy, girl." Collins held his ground, hand still extended.

Falima nuzzled Collins' fingers. Encouraged, he ran a gentle hand across her muzzle, then scratched behind her ears. His fingers glided over a furry lump, and Vernon scuttled into Falima's mane with an indignant squeak.

"Sorry," Collins murmured, keeping the apology to Vernon at the same volume and timbre as his words to Falima. He continued to look at the horse as he spoke.

Falima calmed, nuzzling his shirt.

Collins looked at Ialin, who watched the exchange, shifting from foot to foot. "Will that do?"

"Nicely," Ialin said gruffly, holding out a sword to Collins. "I have to admit, you have a way with her that I don't."

Collins resisted talking about his new relationship with the human form of Falima. "It's all a matter of slow, unthreatening movement. Predators and other dangers come swiftly and suddenly."

"Predators?" Ialin snorted. "What fear would any horse of Barakhai have of predators?"

Prinivere came to Collins' aid, to his relief and surprise. On his last visit, Ialin had freely baited him, and Falima had often joined in against him. *Remember, animals and humans were not always one here. Instinct ingrains deeply and often doesn't dislodge even long after it's no longer needed.*

Collins nodded his agreement, then added, "Plus, all horses, including Falima, are trained as guards. It's usually best to approach them slowly and unthreateningly as well."

Ialin grunted, the closest he would come to agreeing with Collins. His fidgeting continued. "If you haven't noticed, I don't do slow and steady well. I'm more of a quick and busy mover."

It was gross understatement. If Collins had not known Ialin turned into a hummingbird, he would have had no trouble guessing it. Not all of Barakhai's inhabitants proved so easy to read, however. Collins would never have believed Vernon's enormous, dark-skinned human form could possibly compress down to a tiny gray mouse. In fact, many Barakhains did not share so much as hair or eye color with their switch-forms, and bearing little resemblance to the animal they became was one way of assessing attractiveness. Falima believed herself homely because her golden skin and black hair matched the buckskin coloring of her horse form and her well-muscled human limbs seemed "horsey."

Ialin tapped the sheathed blade against Collins' arm. "Are you going to take this?"

Collins looked at the sword. Cloth blackened by dirt and age hung from the cracked wooden sheath, and only a spiral of bright metal showed where rope or string had once wrapped the grip.

Guessing at the reason for Collins' hesitation, Ialin said, "I have another. It's not the only one."

Nodding, Collins took the sword, and Ialin pulled a short knife from his belt.

"Take this, too."

Believing he might have more use for that, Collins shifted the sword from both hands to one. He wrapped his fingers around a hilt that had absorbed the morning chill and felt like ice in his grip. Gingerly, he took the knife in his other hand.

Prinivere lowered herself fully to the ground. *Hop aboard.*

After several unsuccessful attempts to place the sword comfortably and securely through his belt, Collins secured it through his pack instead. The knife worked better against his hip, though it had no sheath and he was more afraid of accidentally stabbing himself than someone else. "Thank you." He headed for Prinivere. "Good luck, Ialin. Good luck, Aisa."

"Good luck," they called back.

Collins swung onto Prinivere's back, and Korfius scrambled up beside him. The reality of the task set in at that moment. *I'm actually doing this.* The coolness of the knife blade seeped through his jeans. Once again, the world had changed and would never, ever, be the same again.

Chapter 8

ENTON Collins clung to Prinivere's back as she skimmed over the forests, dodging the open areas that revealed Barakhai's occasional towns and cities. The wind whipped his seal-brown hair into a tangle, and the banking movements sent his already squeamish stomach lurching. Only the realization that it would mortify Zylas kept him from vomiting on the dragon's verdant scales. Trees zipped past in a blur of green and brown, while sun and sky seemed to shift position every time the dragon wove, yawed, or banked. Collins tried closing his eyes and concentrating on his many questions, few of which he was likely to find answers for, but he soon found that seeing and feeling the aerial stunts helped his equilibrium more than feeling them alone did. In clear contrast, Korfius seemed to enjoy the ride with the exuberance of most dogs on car rides. He kept his face turned into the wind, ears plastered inside out, jowls flapping.

Prinivere could not describe the layout of the caverns, given their warding against switchers. She knew a stream flowed through them, providing fresh water for any remaining inhabitants. People occasionally threw foodstuffs, blankets, or other useful items upstream, out of sympathy or from the belief that some ancestor confined there might have spawned them cousins. Even Barakhai's royals were known to order that cadavers be flung into the water when a famine, illness, or a mass execution overwhelmed the vultures, crows, and hyenas who served as Barakhai's gruesome cleanup brigades, the only ones allowed by law to consume meat.

Prinivere did not even know for certain whether or not the little dragons would be capable of reading or projecting thoughts. The ability came to dragons early, but the parents taught and honed it. Without guidance, they might not learn it at all. Conversely, Collins realized, the youngsters might have discovered the strange form of communication by using it to speak to one another. When Collins spoke the thought aloud, however, Prinivere shook her hoary head.

For a human, twenty years makes an adult but, to us, that's barely toddlerhood.

Collins wondered which form would dominate. He knew Korfius aged in "people years," his dog form lagging to correspond with the human stages of maturity.

This time, Prinivere did not wait for Collins to verbalize his question. *I got the longevity and maturation rate of a dragon, but I don't know if that came of it being my first form or the longest lived one. As far as I know, everyone else's life spans a normal human lifetime.*

Collins kneaded his hands in frustration. "So, if you had to guess?"

Prinivere dipped leftward. *This is a unique situation; I've got nothing to compare it with.* Apparently knowing that would not appease Collins, she elaborated. *It seems unlikely that their human forms could have reverted back to infancy, but we can't entirely rule that out. As humans, they might stay at the same maturity level until their dragon forms catch up. It's possible their dragon selves might have gained some understanding from at least those first thirteen years before their birth forms became Random.* She paused, forest unscrolling beneath them. *I'm not even sure which to hope for. If the dragon form takes precedence, they'll have a stronger bent toward magic and live far longer, but it may take decades before they gain the maturity to assist in lifting the Curse.* She did not need to add that those were decades she, as a greatly aged dragon, might not share.

Collins mulled the possibilities as they zipped through a pristine landscape mostly untouched by human progress. He wondered whether their human forms could actually regress. It seemed terribly unlikely given that time, at least,

seemed to follow physical laws. Though it would also involve a time glitch, he found it less difficult to believe that
their dragon forms might have matured more quickly, making them the equivalent of young teens. Maybe their switch-
forms simply aged at different rates, making them twenty or
so in their human forms and infantile when dragons, or the
forms meshed in some odd manner in-between. Carrie
Quinton would, of course, know; and Collins ruefully
wished he had asked her. He could not recall her ever mentioning them having a human form. She discussed them like
animals, talking about breeding them as if they had no humanity to consider. Now, he could scarcely believe the
thought of questioning her about their exact nature had
never before entered his mind.

As usual, Prinivere intervened in Collins' thoughts. *It
didn't seem necessary to know such a thing. And we had
other details to worry about.* She added one more thought
that relieved him, *And I happen to know you figured you
could always turn to us for those sorts of specifics.*

Prinivere was right, as always, but it did not console Collins very much to realize it. He glanced at Korfius who sat
nestled in a hollow between Prinivere's left wing and torso,
head up and tongue lolling in the breeze.

Collins turned to more practical concerns. He would not
have time to draw more than a crude map in the caverns,
even if he had had a pencil and paper with which to do it.
Leaving a food trail had obvious disadvantages that went
way beyond Hansel and Gretel. He had no rope or string to
mark his way back to the entrance. He would have to rely
on his memory and as many stones as he could carry into
the cave along with his gear, or some other method that
came to him in the next few minutes.

One more question occurred to Collins as Prinivere spiraled into a descent among a spattering of low hills covered
with a multicolored carpet of wildflowers. "The dragons are
switchers, too, right?"

Right, Prinivere sent back, concentrating more on her
landing than on divining the intention of Collins' question.

Obligingly, Collins continued, "So how did someone get
them through the magical barrier and into the caverns in
the first place?"

Prinivere landed on rocky ground with a hop and a

bounce, then walked a few steps to keep her passengers settled. *That's an excellent question, Ben. One I hadn't considered.*

Collins scrambled from her back, only to be met by Korfius, who had leaped to the ground more swiftly. The dog trotted to his side, tail waving hopefully. Collins stirred his fingers through the dark fur on the top of Korfius' head with his fingertips, surprised by Prinivere's confession. He expected the ancient dragon to know everything and had hoped she had an equally excellent answer.

Clearly, the kings of the past had a way to get prisoners inside, some sort of one-way portal, since no one has ever escaped or entered without the express will of the royals. A crystal, perhaps, imbued with magic. I'd have thought such a thing destroyed, though, when King Terrin's father tried to purge the world of everything magical.

"Tried." Collins pounced on the operative word. The realization enhanced his understanding of why Zylas had so fiercely guarded his translation stone and Prinivere's life, why the crystal he had rescued meant so much to them. Collins could see why the Barakhain royalty might take special pains to see to the demise of an item that allowed switchers through long-placed magical barriers, since it would also grant commoners access to the rulers' quarters. "Apparently, that one-way portal is another magic item he missed destroying."

Apparently. Things imbued with enough magic protect themselves, and it would not have been used for its proper purpose in at least a hundred years. Prinivere stretched her neck to delineate a specific hill. *There's a natural entrance to the caverns here.*

This time, Collins had no difficulty seeing the cave mouth amid a tangle of vines and blue-green clover. Idly, he wondered whether practice had improved his vision or if it had more to do with the diligence with which the renegades camouflaged their hiding places. This cave's cover grew spontaneously, without tweaking from outlaws who could not afford discovery. As Prinivere had mentioned, a stream wound through the hills and into the entrance, a spare trickle that burbled against its bed of rocks and fallen foliage.

Prinivere dipped her muzzle into the water and drank.

Taking her cue, Collins knelt at the bank and dipped his hands into the stream. Icy water as clear as fresh-cleaned glass spilled through his fingers. After decades of warnings about Giardia, amoeba, and other invisible pathogens teeming even in the water of the highest, untouched mountains, Collins had to force himself to drink. It was not his first natural water; he had shared his companions' rations on both trips to Barakhai. Rationally, he knew their stored water came directly from unchlorinated rivers, brooks, and streams like this one, but deceiving himself proved easier when his sustenance came from a man-made vessel.

Collins lowered his mouth to his hands and sipped at the remaining dregs of water. It carried no taste at all, not even of the bracken that raced downstream into the caverns. As a budding scientist, he knew the human eye could not discern even the most lethal pathogens in the world, but he found assurance in the clarity and lack of taste of Barakhai's water. Uncertain when he would get his next chance to drink without having to watch his back, he sucked down several handfuls of water, feeling like a young gazelle at a communal drinking hole. Cheetahs and leopards also knew the scent of water.

Ready?

Though pointless and unnecessary, Collins appreciated the question. Prinivere knew exactly how unprepared he felt, how he felt incapable of truly steeling for any mission this important and peppered with so many unknowns. He resisted the urge to say, "Ready as I'll ever be." Prinivere might never have heard the phrase spoken, but his thoughts would betray its triteness. She understood he felt hopelessly ill-equipped and unready, emotionally as well as physically, yet she had already given him all the appropriate pep talks. From the moment he stepped into the cave, Benton Collins was on his own.

Not quite. Once again, Prinivere read his mind. *Don't forget my roar.*

In the flurry of more recent concerns, Collins had let that slip his mind. He smiled at the reminder. Had Prinivere not mentioned it, he might have got caught running in terror from the sound along with any inhabitants within hearing.

Collins tried one last desperate measure. "Can you keep in touch with me? With your mind-talking thing, I mean?"

Prinivere made a huge movement Collins interpreted as a shrug. *I can try. But it's not likely to penetrate the magic. And I can't stay here long either. Like us, the king has many spies, but he pays well for their loyalty. Also, I'm the only one who can bridge the gap between thoughts in human and animal forms. The others may need me, too.*

Certain he would catch no easy breaks, Collins had anticipated the answer. "I'm ready," he announced.

Cover your ears. Prinivere trudged to the cave mouth.

Collins obeyed and cycled the reminder of Prinivere's harmlessness through his mind. This time, the roar barely stiffened him, though it echoed eerily through the caverns. He loosened his grip and shrugged his backpack onto both shoulders. Though accustomed to stylishly carrying it on one, Collins found practicality and ease more compelling than image here. He marched boldly toward the cave.

Good luck. All our hopes go with you.

Collins did not bother with a reply. He scooped up a large sandstone, then stepped into the mouth of the cave. It opened onto a cavern the size of his apartment, dimly lit by sunlight funneling through the opening. Craggy outcroppings shadowed corners that might hide any number of man-eating beasts. Stalactites jutted from the ceiling like pointed teeth, and Collins felt as if he had just stepped into the jaws of the largest carnivore of all.

Korfius barked wildly.

Glad for the excuse, Collins exited the cave. He stepped back into daylight that seemed extraordinarily bright. For inexplicable reasons, he expected to find himself in some new and strange location, utterly alone; but the scene looked exactly as it had mere moments earlier. Prinivere's neck glided toward him, and Korfius jumped up on him, knocking him to the ground and covering him with doggy kisses.

Prinivere remained silent, avoiding the obvious question. No flimsy excuse could work against a mind reader. She knew Collins had faced no clear danger.

Collins extricated himself from the dog and clambered to his feet. The silence bothered him, so he asked the obvious, in reverse, "Why did I do that?" He anticipated something profound from Prinivere, about how only he could answer that, so her actual words surprised him.

You forgot to say 'good-bye' to your dog?

Collins liked Prinivere's answer better than the one that came to him: *Because I'm an infernal coward.* He knelt, this time preserving his equilibrium despite the attention from the overeager puppy. He caught the fuzzy face between his hands and squeezed it like a seldom-seen aunt might at a family reunion. "Korfius, I just want you to know I love you. And, no matter what anyone else says, you're the best dog a guy could ever have."

Korfius cocked his head to one side and whined.

Collins hugged the mongrel close, kissing the warm fur of his neck. "Now," he whispered in Korfius' floppy ear, "go with Prinivere."

Korfius whimpered again.

Without further words, Collins headed back into the cave. Again, the dimness swallowed him, and he waited for his eyes to fully adjust. The rocky prominences and concavities of the entryway formed a mad chaos of hiding places, and Collins imagined a deadly man-eater behind every one. Since they became people at intervals, these carnivores would have none of the wariness of humans shown by the wild, gun-hunted creatures of his own world. Seized by the sudden urge to leave one more time, to reassure Korfius and request one last roar from Prinivere, he glanced at his watch. It was after eight o'clock. Shocked, he looked again, staring. He had less than four hours to find the dragons, rescue them, and use them, if possible, to save Zylas. That motivated him. Pausing to scrape a huge "1" on the cave wall with the piece of sandstone still clutched in his fist, he hurried around the walls, seeking breaks.

A third of the way around the cavern, Collins found what he sought. A slitlike hole opened onto darkness. Deciding on his marking strategy, he put another "1" at this exit. If he marked all the doors, he would know where he had been and where each fit in the pattern of his search. It seemed wisest to number by caves rather than openings. That way, he would know if he had returned to a place he had already explored.

Loath to leave the light, Collins looked for other ways out. Unless he marked all of them, he ran the risk of performing double searches or of getting himself lost in familiar territory. Amid the stones and crags, he discovered only one other exit from the cavern, a wider, jagged hole that would admit him far more easily than the other. Collins could fit through either without much effort, but he thought it best to stick with the wider openings, more likely routes for dragons. He tried not to think about the fact that these would also attract larger carnivores of other varieties. Neither opening from this cavern could wholly stop even a creature as large as a tiger, but the slit might compress the big cat's whiskers enough to deter it. Chalking another "1" at the side of the opening, Collins walked into the deeper cavern.

As Collins passed through one crude "room" to the next, his shoe sank into something soft and squishy. Warmth trickled around his shoe, and the explanation wafted to his nose. *Dung.* From the feel of it under his sole, it seemed fresh. The deeply buried hope that the carnivores might have hunted one another to extinction instantly evaporated. Prinivere's roar might have chased them from the front caverns, but he had no idea how long the effect would last or how far they might have run. Fingers shaking, he seized the recorder at his belt and fumbled with the play button. The silence erupted into another roar, a pale shadow of the first one yet terrifying enough. Ahead of Collins, nails scrabbled against stone, clearly retreating.

Collins slid off his pack, then groped through it for a torch just as the second recorded roar broke the stillness. Taking one of the rag-wrapped sticks in hand, he fumbled the matches. Silence descended around him, broken only by the hiss of the recorder, now playing blank tape. He lit the torch, jammed the rest of the matches back into his shirt pocket, and clutched the torch between his knees. Hands free, he stopped the tape and poked the rewind button, realizing its use would slow him down immensely. Frustrated by dwindling time and the irritating reality of the situation, he took the torch back in hand. It cleared the darkness in a ragged circle that left him longing for overhead lamps. It seemed a wonder that every man and woman of Barakhai had not gone blind.

As Collins walked, ears attuned for movement, vision glued to the uneven ground, he realized several things. First, he had no way of knowing whether or not the Barakhains saw clearly. He doubted they had the technology to create functional glasses. He also knew his own equipment had serious, previously unconsidered limitations. He could not remember the last time he had changed the batteries of the tape recorder, and a constant play and rewind cycle would run them down swiftly. The thought became an obsession. He needed to play the roars frequently enough to keep predators at bay yet not so constantly that he ran it out of power, slowed his pace to a frustrating crawl, or allowed the descendants of criminal carnivores to become accustomed to the sound.

Collins shuffled his feet, raising the torch to examine the walls of the second chamber. This one proved smaller, with only a single exit into an oblong cavern that seemed more like a corridor than a cave. He eased inside, then marked it with a "2." The closeness of the walls brought a sensation of tomblike enclosure that sent a shiver through his body. At the same time, he appreciated its narrowness. It left no space for anything to slip past and behind him, and he could easily and simultaneously explore both stone walls with his fingertips.

In this manner, Collins plunged deeper into the ancient caverns, pausing at intervals to play the recording of Prinivere's roar. Occasionally, he thought he heard a scrape or a scrabble, a hiss or a whisper bouncing from walls with impossibly complex acoustics. Torch after torch burned to a nub as an hour and a half slipped by without the need for Collins to enter any area twice. He had abandoned several openings in favor of others, six or seven to his count, leaving them marked and wondering if he had mistaken a better choice for a worse one. A few scattered bones littered the stony pathways, and Collins passed these without a second glance. He preferred not to waste time identifying any dead creature. Anything but fish were ultimately human, and none of these were fish. He had enough trouble noticing bones in a fish fillet on a plate six inches from his nose.

Needing a break, Collins sat on a crag to consider his plan, wedging the torch and flopping his backpack down beside him. He had no idea how far the caverns might span, but random wandering was beginning to seem pointless. He considered shouting for the dragons but worried about what else might choose to answer. Even if Quinton had trained them to come when called, she probably used names she had given them. He hoped Prinivere's roar would draw them out, if only from curiosity, yet he realized it might just as likely have the opposite effect. Raised by humans, the young dragons might find the sound as fearsome and terrifying as he did. So far, he had come upon nothing living, only the occasional sound of something unseen scuttling into the darkness.

Knowing time was not on his side, Collins sighed, took the recorder in hand, and hit the rewind button for what seemed like the hundredth time. He started to his feet, twisting to get his backpack.

The movement saved him. Something immense crashed into his shoulder instead of his throat, hurling him onto his stomach. Rocks stabbed his ribs and hip. Air exploded from his lungs. Momentum sent him flying across the cavern floor, rocks tearing and hammering his clothes and flesh. Claws sank into his back, and hot panting burned the back of his neck. Breathless, he found himself incapable of screaming, and agony destroyed all rational thought momentarily. Only one idea managed to wriggle through Collins' shock: *I'm going to die.*

Adrenaline pumped through Collins like acid, driving him to action. He gathered his hands and knees under him, attempting to crawl, but the thing remained with him, clamped to his back. Teeth closed over the rear of his head. Pain screamed through his scalp. He gasped in a series of ratcheting breaths. Warm blood trickled down his neck and spine. He eeled sideways, yawing violently, trying to dislodge a creature that seemed to weigh at least as much as he did. It rocked, keeping its balance with agile ease, though the wild motions did slow its assault. Every movement sent pain stabbing through Collins, but he dared not stop long enough to give the creature an easy shot at something vital.

Collins finally managed a scream, though he still harbored no hope that any creature of Barakhai would instinctively run from humans. He gave an abrupt twist that brought him halfway around and freed his arms for the battle. The teeth jarred loose, tearing away furrows of hair and scalp with a pain that brought tears to Collins' eyes. He flailed at the creature. His right fist struck something solid and furry. Still winched around the recorder, his left caught the creature a smashing blow across a whiskered cheek. The recorder shattered in his fist, pieces skittering through the cavern. The animal tumbled to the ground, and Collins surged to his feet, seeing it for the first time in the dim outer reaches of the lantern's glow. Tawny and cat-shaped, it launched its muscled frame at him again.

Cougar. Dizzy and slowed by his wounds, Collins threw himself sideways. *Puma, mountain lion.* The bulk of the creature crashed against his side, tossing him like flotsam in a gale. He scrabbled to regain his footing, desperate to find it before the cougar found him once more. He stumbled backward over a stalagmite, tripped, and fell. The unexpected motion foiled the graceful animal's attack again, and it went sailing over Collins. Shadows danced on the ceiling, and he found himself hemmed in by stone formations. He needed to act swiftly or die, and his mind raced, strangely clear. He had read more than his share of nature stories and preferred animal shows on public television to anything "prime time." He tried to recall any detail about cougars that might help him now.

Shadows. Collins glanced wildly around him, trying to locate the animal before it pounced again. *Shadows come from light.* It was not a cougar fact, but any animal would shy from fire. He dove for the source of the shadows, seizing the torch on the move. The cougar bounded after him, catching him a paw blow to the head that sent him skidding across the uneven ground, senses reeling. He let the force take him where it would, clutching the torch like a lifeline. Then, at last, memory surged to the fore. Men had hunted cougars to dangerously low numbers because of one fatal flaw: unlike other large cats, they never stood down dogs. Toy poodles had been known to tree the fiercest, most massive males. Once hunting dogs caught the scent of one of the now rare cats, the outcome was inevitable. Collins only hoped Barakhain cougars suffered from that same instinct.

As the beast flew toward him, Collins held his ground. He thrust the torch into its face, barking madly in his best imitation of Korfius.

With a yelp of pain and surprise, the cougar threw itself sideways, rolling, its fur alight. Turning on its heels, it screeched off into the deeper caverns.

The torch dropped from Collins' suddenly trembling fingers. His head buzzed, making coherent thought all but impossible. He dragged himself toward his backpack, seized it, then hauled it to his chest until it lay balled beneath him. Agony screamed through his whole body so that he found himself incapable of focusing on any one injury. Something pattered steadily to the stone. *Blood,* he realized, but it took another few beats to add, *my blood*. His consciousness swam, and he fought to anchor it with the terrifying knowledge that if he blacked out, he was cougar chow.

Staunch the bleeding. Collins did not need medical training to know that no first aid mattered more. Attuned to any sound that might herald the cougar's return, he pulled the tatters of his T-shirt tight across his back and head, knotting it over his chest and brow. The myriad abrasions and cuts over his ribs, abdomen, and limbs hurt but they did not require tending yet. His body could handle them. He tried to stand, instantly pummeled to the ground by vertigo. Still clutching the pack, he inched his way across the floor. Returning to Prinivere seemed the wisest course, though it would lose him all the ground he had attained. She could heal the wounds that hampered his every movement. Yet, Collins realized, he would have to find her first. Backtracking seemed at least as far as pushing onward, and he doubted she still waited for him at the entrance.

Collins lowered his head, driven to move but certain haste would only assure that he lost consciousness and, ultimately, lead to his death. Despair rushed down upon him. He was alive but gravely injured. His task had seemed nearly impossible before; now it had become even more so. But he also knew that the young dragons held the key to rescuing not only Zylas, but now himself as well. He had little choice but to push on and hope for the best.

Chapter 9

THE cart lurched toward Opernes Castle, drawn by a buckskin horse now disguised as a tea-brown, dusty mule. In the driver's seat, Ialin forced himself to grip the rope reins securely in both hands and concentrated on not fidgeting. He wore the face of Eshwyn the merchant, but he had known from the start that he could never pull off that deception for long. Aisa perched on his shoulder, and Vernon hid in a deep pocket, both as convinced as Collins that the plan was precisely as it seemed. The mind reading dragon had to know the extra layer Ialin had devised, but she feigned ignorance of his secret with the ease of long practice.

On the far side of the moat, a pair of male guards challenged from the parapets. "State your name and business."

Ialin met the gaze of one with trained steadiness and dutifully imitated the merchant's voice. He willed his body in place, winching his hands to white fists to keep from wringing them. So far, jettisoning his own nervous habits preoccupied him more than any attempt to pass for the other man. "Do not play games with me, Shirith." He continued to stare at the guard to his left. "Wittmore." He indicated the other with a tip of his head. "You know who I am."

Both guards smiled. Shirith spoke first, "Certainly we know you, Eshwyn, but not that rickety wreck you came in."

Ialin snorted, clenching and unclenching the muscles of his backside against the seat. It allowed him to give in to his need for constant movement without revealing it to the guards. "I lent the regular rig to my good-for-nothing brother. I didn't think I'd need it for a spell, but then I got a whole load of *vilegro*. It won't keep, and I wanted to give His Majesty first rights to it. I borrowed who and what I could to get it here." Ialin gestured at the old cart and Falima, who kept her head low in a mulish posture.

Silence followed.

"So," Ialin continued, "I'm irritable, annoyed, and tired. Are you going to let me in, or do I take my business elsewhere?" He had deliberately chosen an excellent product. Not only did the spoilage story work for explaining the mule cart in place of Eshwyn's finer ox-drawn wagon, the guards would anticipate the rare and delicious *gahiri* the castle cook would create from the *vilegro* seed.

"I'll get the drawbridge." Wittmore disappeared.

Ialin lowered his head, but not before he caught a glimpse of several faces peering at him over the parapets. The king had increased his outer wall guards and, probably, his patrols. Ialin hoped that meant shorting the inner defenses. Likely, no guard in human form was off duty, but that only supplied the castle with a few extra hands. No decree of the king could delay, abridge, or change the horse and dog times of his security forces.

Ialin dismounted from the cart as the drawbridge jerked downward, chains clanking and creaking. He caught Falima's halter as she tossed her head with a series of nervous snorts. The braid of rope tore at his callused palm. "Quiet," he reminded. "Be still. You're a mule, not a horse. A mule."

Falima quieted, though her hooves beat a wild, chaotic tattoo against the dirt.

Ialin gritted his teeth. Her behavior would give her away more surely than any noise. Mule vocalizations varied in their similarity to a horse's, but they tended toward a steady calmness that precluded panic. As the plank dropped to the ground in front of Ialin, he made a difficult decision he had considered on the trip. Falima's enormous switch-form turned her into a liability once inside the castle grounds. Aisa thought Falima could blend in with the guard forces, but Ialin had doubts. He preferred not to risk anyone unnecessarily. In her current form, Falima did not have the overlap to protest; and, though he knew he would catch trouble for it later, Ialin planned to take advantage of that weakness.

Ialin unbound Falima from the cart. He removed the various ropes, waving them into her face. "Yay, mule! Get on home with you!"

Startled, Falima reared. When she dropped back down, Ialin hissed into her ear. "Go on, Falima. Go somewhere safe. We'll meet up with you later." Seizing the traces, Ialin hauled the cart onto the drawbridge. Despite the light load, it was more difficult than he expected; he had to hurl all of his meager weight into the task. Not for the first time, he wished he were larger. Constant movement had granted him strength beyond his bulk, but only that of a normal-sized man.

The cart rumbled across the slats, boards squeaking. Aisa squawked and flapped, her wings kicking up a draft that stirred the water and dried the sweat on Ialin's neck. A wing beat slapped him in the face, flopping a greased clump of black hair into his eyes. He paused to brush it back into place. "Easy, Frida." He used the name of Eshwyn's wife to remind Aisa of her role. "Please don't make this any harder."

Aisa rumpled her feathers and hunkered down on Ialin's shoulder.

Once across the moat, Ialin met two more guards at the gate, one a willowy female, the other a compact male. He knew the man's name, Thelfori, but not the woman's. He nodded a greeting to both.

The woman studied him with clear curiosity. "Do you always leave one of your entourage behind?"

Ialin glanced over his shoulder, glad Falima had left his line of vision and not attempted to follow. The last time she had crossed this drawbridge, the hollow ring of her hooves against suspended wood had spooked her. "First time," he admitted. "She has another engagement, and she's just about ready to switch. I only paid her to come this far."

The guard just grunted, helping her companion pull open the heavy, ironbound gates.

Ialin hauled the cart into the gatehouse, trying not to look winded. The doors swung shut behind him, immersing him in darkness. He took the moment to flex every muscle. He felt locked in cramps from head to toe, tired of suppressing the natural and constant motion that kept him alive in hummingbird form. Then, the doors in front of him swung open, placing him back into the bright rush of sunlight and the judgment of a group of guards.

Now, Ialin could not wholly suppress his anxiety, nor did he believe he needed to do so. Even a regular to the court of King Terrin might find an increase in his guard accompaniment intimidating. He glanced around his escort, as if seeking solace in familiar faces. Though not as skilled at reading others' emotions as Zylas, Ialin did manage to pick out one soft-eyed woman who clearly sympathized. He smiled and winked at her, and her grin broadened.

A burly man held out his hands. "Let me take the cart, sir."

Ialin gave over his burden gladly. His companions lay safely on his person, for now. Aisa eyed the gathering, cocking her head this way and that to bring every guard within the scrutiny of at least one steel-blue eye. Vernon stayed still in his pocket, taking his cues from Ialin. For the mouse's sake, he tried to keep his muscles loose, his movements fine and smooth. If the guards examined his cargo closely, they would find lesser plants buried beneath a layer of *vilegro*. He hoped it would not come to that. Pawing through a merchant's wares was imprudent at best and potentially dangerous. To do it at the request of the king meant gravely insulting his guest. Without the monarch's consent, a guard risked charges of theft or treason.

The female guard who had returned Ialin's smile worked her way through the group to take his arm. He searched his memory for her name, without success. He smiled warmly and whispered, "Thanks."

"I thought you might prefer a familiar face." The guard steered Ialin toward the castle. "Your usual room, Eshwyn?"

Ialin nodded, knowing precisely which guestroom Eshwyn preferred, on the third floor in the south wing.

"Do you need to gather your personals?"

Ialin could have kicked himself. He should have anticipated that question, too. "We don't plan to stay long. Anything I need, I can send for."

"Very well." She gestured at her closest associates, and they gave Ialin more space. Some peeled away to various tasks, leaving a crew of five to lead him to the inner courtyard.

Ialin avoided speaking as much as possible, devoting the majority of his attention to maintaining his persona and not squirming. He tried to ignore all thoughts of Zylas. Worry already drove him to an extremely risky rescue. He could not afford to betray his intentions by exhibiting concern or need. So far, he appeared to have passed whatever tests the guards had thrown at him. The facade could only hold up so long, however. The renegades' information was as imperfect as the men and women who gathered it, and they could not be present for every miniscule interaction. At some point, he would need to properly recognize a stranger, would overlook an unanticipated fine detail that the real Eshwyn would never miss. Anyone who came to Opernes Castle now, in the hours before Zylas' execution, would have to weather suspicion and undergo intense scrutiny. Ialin wondered how long he could hold out.

They passed through another gatehouse, into the inner courtyard, and headed toward the castle. Unable to wholly suppress the fretfulness that assailed him even in the most familiar circumstances, Ialin turned every movement into something seemingly deliberate: a scratch, a readjustment, a gesture. When he had joined the renegades as a starry-eyed, idealistic youth, he had never expected any plan this crucial to fall squarely on his tiny shoulders. Zylas was the key to so much; without him, the renegades might fall apart without achieving the one goal that mattered: removing the Curse that had haunted Barakhai for centuries. Benton Collins had been right about one thing; they should never have risked Zylas on the previous mission. Like Prinivere, the rat/man should sit in some safe command center, changing quarters with every threat, concern, or whim.

That thought brought a smile to Ialin's lips. He could not imagine anything short of magic keeping Zylas from the rebel movement's front, and it raised a familiar paradox. That which made the albino such a charismatic key figure for their cause also placed him in positions of greatest peril. His many successes had left them all complacent. Luck, not omnipotence, had kept Zylas alive this long. Now, it seemed, he had run out of it.

Realizing he had come back to the very topic he had

vowed to avoid, Ialin turned his attention to the castle which was drawing ever closer. His entourage seemed unbothered by his long silence, even the woman who now unlinked her arm from his. Soon, they stood in front of the castle door, and Ialin's escort chatted briefly with the sentries. Those moved aside, and the massive door swung open to reveal the inner regions of Opernes Castle.

Ialin had never entered the massive edifice through the door before and never in human guise. He toed the line between gawking and giving enough of his mind to his surroundings to memorize them while still holding his constant drive to move at bay. He also kept his attention on the guards, watching for evidence of suspicion, anything that might suggest a need to switch to his second plan. He dared not rely on Collins, certain the blundering fool would foul up the rescue, just as he had his last mission, the one that ended in Zylas' capture. True, the Otherworlder had managed to bring them the crystal that enhanced Prinivere's fading magic, but he had nearly died in the process and had made innumerable mistakes along the way. *Including cannibalism.* Ialin still found the crime unforgivable and wondered how his friends managed to work so comfortably with a murderer. Other renegades had killed, when necessary, but they had never struck down innocents. The realization that Collins had slaughtered, butchered, and eaten a sweet elderly woman whose only crime was that she happened to have a rabbit switch-form sent a shudder through Ialin.

"Cold?" the female guard asked as she led Ialin up the spiraling staircase.

Though that was not the case, thanks to his racing metabolism, Ialin had no better explanation for his shivering. "A bit. That draft howling down the stairway bothers me every time I come. You'd think I'd have gotten used to it by now."

One of the men grumbled, "Never noticed it, myself."

"Really?" said a third, the only other woman. "It creeps into my bones, even when the hearth's going and it's warm air washing over me."

That started a casual discussion that Ialin appreciated, as it allowed him to fall back into silence. Slow plans frustrated him, especially with his switch time approaching. He would certainly find Zylas downstairs in the dungeon, yet he dared not even look in that direction yet. He allowed the group to usher him upward, past the kitchen/artisan level, past the dining hall/library level, and to the third landing. Ialin naturally turned south; but one of the guards opened the left-hand, northern door and gestured for him to enter the meeting room.

It was not standard procedure. Ialin swallowed his discomfort and forced a tense smile, concentrating on the need to hide his concern. Nothing this day had proceeded in its regular fashion, and that seemed to have more to do with the king's paranoia than any specific suspicions about him.

Ialin stepped around the guards to peek inside the small room, its only furniture a scarred wooden table surrounded by chairs. A colorful tapestry of patternless design filled most of one wall. Another wall supported a narrowing window that overlooked the courtyards, thin enough at its innermost dimension to thwart anything larger than an insect. From experience, Ialin knew he could wriggle through it in switch-form, and that gave him a guilty sense of security. If all else failed, at least he could escape, though it would mean abandoning his companions. A silver flagon of wine and three matching goblets sat on a lace napkin in the middle of the table. Two doors led out of opposite walls: the one he had entered by and another headed deeper into the castle to servant's quarters and more guest rooms.

Ialin froze on the lintel, uncertain and wondering if he faced another test. "Excuse me, but my 'usual quarters' are the other way." He made a motion toward the south door.

The familiar woman took Ialin's arm again and ushered him inside the meeting room with an apologetic look. "The chamberlain will be with you shortly."

The chamberlain? Ialin's heart skipped a beat, shaken by the idea of facing a chief officer in the king's household. Assuming she meant Jarvid, the chamberlain who oversaw the visiting merchants, Eshwyn had a close, long-term relationship with him. The renegade agents hidden among the servants managed only spotty information when it came to the specifics of conversations and personal interactions. Ialin would have to play things carefully and mostly by ear. He steeled his resolve, lifting his chin, and guessed at the best response. "Don't I even get a chance to settle in first?"

The woman laughed. "Don't you ever get tired of questioning the inscrutable motives of royals, Eshwyn?"

Ialin appreciated the reminder. It never hurt to remember that the upper echelons of the king's staff, and his family's personal assistants and aides, mostly consisted of trusted aunts, uncles, and cousins. Terrin relied on those few nonswitchers who could enter the rooms on the top two floors for everything from tidying up to strategizing. "I'm just hoping Jarvid gets tired of meeting with rumpled, exhausted, travel-filthy merchants after just this one time."

Ialin knew the actual business of trading and negotiation would occur in the courtroom, in the presence of nobles, litigants, diplomats, and whoever else had come to deal with the kingdom. Few were accorded the honor of meeting directly with any official before the proceedings. Likely, this was to be a friendly conference, only tangentially related to trading; and that realization only heightened Ialin's discomfort. Bartering he understood. He dreaded the thought of exchanging pleasantries with a stranger while feigning an extensive friendship.

The guard loosed another salvo of laughter. "I'll let him know you're here. Anything you want?"

Prinivere's mind reading would be nice. "No. Thank you." Eshwyn had a known penchant for gruff, sometimes crude, humor, so Ialin added sarcastically, "Who needs a warm bath or a nap on clean linens when he can sit in rock-hard, ass-pinching chairs?"

The woman raised her brows, but a few of the men smiled this time. They all exited, closing the door behind them.

For the first time, Ialin allowed himself to pace in a swift, short oval, dispelling some of the pent up energy he had held in check for too long. He glanced down at formal pantaloons that hid a carefully manufactured scar on his right ankle. Road dust had settled into the cuffs, further marring silks that already had a tear at the knee. It was the best garb he could find in Vernon's cottage, castoffs from some wealthy baron or merchant who could afford not to bother patching his clothing. Or, perhaps, a servant, tailor, or washerwoman had swiped the garment from a man with enough wealth not to notice one item missing, then donated it to the rebels' cause. It was even possible that someone of means had taken refuge with Vernon, leaving the silks in exchange for something less noticeable so that another could use them in future operations. Vernon had a kind heart that attracted strays and runaways of many stripes. His home had become a sanctuary, scouted by most of the *durithrin,* the wild folk. Fugitives had a way of disappearing once they reached Vernon, but even the constabularies rarely bothered him. They, or a loved one, might one day need his help.

When the door handle creaked, Ialin stiffened, pretending to stare out the window at the brightening sky and its vast array of puffy clouds etched against azure. Then, the door wrenched open to reveal Jarvid flanked by two elite guardsmen. The king's second cousin bore little resemblance to him. Aqua and white satin, tailored for the burly forms of the king and his brother, hung loose on Jarvid's slender frame. Unlike them, he wore no beard over his wide, dimpled chin. His cheekbones perched higher, and his cheeks were chapped and windburned. He had the same keen, brown eyes, however; and their classic wheaten ringlets fell around his ears, held in place with perfumed oil. He gave Ialin a friendly smile and made a gesture of greeting before the door had fully closed.

Ialin bowed, waiting for the other man to speak first. He knew little of the intricacies of court protocol but enough to treat a king's chamberlain with utmost respect. Caught off guard, Aisa squabbled to maintain her position on his shoulder.

"Good morn upon you, Eshwyn."

"Good morn upon you, too, sir," Ialin returned, completing his bow. Aisa grabbed his ear to steady herself. Sharp edges of rock-hard beak ground into sensitive flesh with an agony that made him gasp. For an instant, he thought she had bitten a chunk from his ear. Then she released her hold and the pain dropped to a dull throbbing.

"Sir?" Jarvid examined Ialin quizzically. "You know titles are unnecessary among old friends."

Ialin bit off a groan. The conversation had not even started, and he had already made his first mistake. He covered as best as he could. "Nothing else seems the same today. Last visit, Frida and I walked freely to the castle and crawled into a waiting bed. This time, we found ourselves surrounded like prisoners. Forgive me if I'm not sure exactly which protocols have changed."

Jarvid waved Ialin to a seat, grinning. "Ah, so you noticed our heightened security."

"Five guards close enough to look up my backside and tell me what I had for dinner?" Ialin accepted the proffered chair. "I noticed."

Jarvid huffed out a laugh and took the seat across from Ialin. The guards stationed themselves silently, still standing, at either hand.

Aisa reached over and, before Ialin could stop her, snipped off the top button of his shirt. He snatched for it as his collar flopped open, and she rewarded him with a sharp nip. Macaws found adornments difficult to resist, and discomfort seemed to have a negative affect on Aisa's overlap. Ialin swore, then turned an apologetic look toward the chamberlain. "I lose more buttons that way."

The chamberlain's smile had become a fixture. "I've seen you do the same to her, with more interesting results." He winked at the parrot, who ignored him, clutching the button in a claw while she gnawed it into glittering pieces.

"The security?" Ialin reminded.

Jarvid took the flagon and poured two mugs full. The wine smelled as heady and sweet as a flower bouquet. Ialin knew the taste would surpass anything he had ever tried, but he could not afford to put much alcohol into his slight figure. He needed every scrap of his wits about him. "We've captured the rebel leader. We know they'll attempt a rescue." The chamberlain slid a mug toward Ialin.

Ialin caught the handle, then released it quickly so as not to reveal his quivering hands. Vernon shifted in his pocket, and he quieted the mouse with a touch. "You know Frida and I are not for sale." He crinkled his face. "Especially to rebels."

"Of course." Jarvid took the first sip, which Ialin found reassuring. If someone had poisoned the wine, the royal would succumb as well. "But they have some sort of magic that changes faces. I'm afraid everyone is suspect. And we didn't expect you for another . . . half year."

Ialin raised his own mug to delay his response. He had to assume every royal utterance a test. He did not know exactly how long Eshwyn intended to go between visits to the castle. Usually, he came about four times per year, but that varied. Ialin had to decide if he needed to correct the chamberlain, without outthinking himself. He took a tiny sip of a honey-based wine that enticed him to have more, then lowered the mug with a contented sigh. "You've outdone yourself. This wine is good enough for the gods." In that moment, he decided to play the odds. "You meant quarter year, didn't you?"

"Quarter year, yes," Jarvid corrected. "What did I say?"

Aisa nibbled playfully at Ialin's cheek, then squawked out, "Half year."

The chamberlain stiffened, then the smile eased back onto his face. "Ah, yes. Thank you, Frida."

Ialin continued as if he had not noticed the sudden breaking of the bird's silence or the error clearly intended to test his identity, "Came upon an unexpected load of *vilegro*. Thought I'd bring it by before it gets unusable. If I'd known I'd come at a bad time, I'd have waited a few more days."

"Half a day would have been enough." The chamberlain sat back with his mug. "The rat will be dead at midday."

Terror flashed through Ialin. Before he could think to suppress it, his nostrils flared and his hands clenched in his lap. Aisa seized another death grip on his ear. Though glad for the distraction of the pain, Ialin swiftly found it unbearable. He grabbed the jagged, black beak, winching it open with thumb and forefinger to free his aching ear. "Damn it, Frida. That hurts!"

"I'm sorry." Aisa hunched into herself remorsefully, feathers ruffled and beak low.

"A hanging?" Ialin tried to keep his question matter-of-fact, though his voice broke a bit at the end.

"No." Jarvid studied his guest. "The king's Otherworld adviser came up with something more interesting that didn't require taking the rat outside where the traitors might manage a public and humiliating rescue." He lowered his voice conspiratorially. "Just between you and me . . ."

Ialin knew Eshwyn might interrupt with something sarcastic about the presence of the two guards making them four, but he did not wish to distract the chamberlain from what seemed like a crucial point.

". . . she scares me. She's always had a wicked streak, but

it's as wide as the Anale River since the fire damaged her and Prince Hardin. You know, she actually tried to talk His Majesty into letting her breed those dragons. Making more dragons. Deliberately. Can you believe such a thing?"

Ialin could scarcely believe his luck. Apparently, Eshwyn held high favor with Jarvid to have become privy to such secrets. He plastered a look of horror on his conjured features. "That's all Barakhai needs. A whole flock of enormous, carnivorous, magic-wielding monsters soaring through its skies." He shook his head. "You're right. The girl is mad." He tried to add casually, as a natural extension of the conversation. "But His Majesty is a wise man." The compliment came easily. Though the rebels struggled against his policies, especially his prejudices against magic and *Random* unions, they found the king himself reasonably just and intelligent most of the time. "Surely, he wouldn't let her do something so stupid."

"Of course not." The chamberlain took another sip of wine while the guards stirred restively. "He reinstated their executions, which should have happened years ago. Carrie went crazier than usual. It was a marvelous debate, though it was a foregone conclusion, of course. She did manage to talk him into letting her be the one who . . . ended their suffering." Jarvid dropped back into that secretive whisper. "The guards haven't had to perform a single execution in over a year. They just bind the condemned, place him on a cart, and turn him over to Carrie. I think she actually enjoys killing."

Ialin hunched into himself, hoping it was not a common trait among those of Carrie Quinton's world. He did not wholly trust Collins' judgment, but he did not believe the man would intentionally harm them. His blunders seemed more a result of ignorance and incompetence than cruelty. Ialin dropped his own head to his chin, and his volume fell to Jarvid's level. "So she put the dragons to death?"

Jarvid shrugged. "She must have. No sign of them since she led them into the mustier regions of the dungeon. The old torture area. As far as I know, no one's used those old devices for centuries, certainly not His Majesty, nor King Terrin's father."

Another hot wave of horror shot through Ialin. If he believed Jarvid, and the chamberlain's confidences seemed sincere, the royal family had had nothing to do with moving the dragons. Quinton had duped them just as she had the rebels, and only Prinivere's mind reading had rescued them from believing the same lie. *But how does one woman handle the care and feeding of dragons alone?* He hated the answer that seeped into his mind. *She's feeding them . . . the condemned.* Nausea flooded his gut, and acid crawled up his throat. *But how does she come and go safely through caverns filled with the descendants of carnivores to do it?* Ialin cleared his throat and swallowed painfully, forcing a return to the mindset of Eshwyn the merchant. *Is all this even true or just another test?* He looked up in time to see the chamberlain gesturing subtly to one of his guards.

Ialin gritted his teeth, clamping his fingers in his lap, hoping he had not made a serious miscalculation.

"So," Jarvid said carefully. "How did you know about the dragons? This is the first time I mentioned them to you."

"Indeed." Ialin scrambled to save his cover. "I thought it more polite to take the details from context rather than question your memory or your sanity." It was a bold move that might offend the chamberlain, but it seemed the best way out of a bad situation. Thus far, he had performed better than even he had expected. He had anticipated switching to his second plan long before now and worried that his and Aisa's switch-time might come upon them during an inopportune situation.

"Really?"

"Yes."

"Then you won't mind one more test, Eshwyn?"

Ialin folded his arms over his chest. "Actually, I'm tired and irritable and sick of the games. There's no law that says I have to offer the king my best wares first."

Jarvid chuckled, this time without amusement. "Of course not, but who else could afford to pay you what they're worth?"

Ialin could hardly argue the point. "Haven't I proved myself well enough yet?" He had little choice but to dissuade the chamberlain from any tests now, before he administered one. Ialin might manage to pass it; he had so far, but he dared not take the chance. His best gamble lay in pretending to take offense at treatment he considered unconscionably rude.

Jarvid ignored Ialin's protestations. "Did you bring what you promised the younger princess on your next visit?"

Ialin dodged the query, keeping the edge in his tone. "I brought only *vilegro*." He ran a hand down Aisa's back, a prearranged signal for her to start looking for an avenue of escape. If he distracted the guards, she might manage to evade them.

The chamberlain held Ialin's gaze. "Very well. Tell me what you promised her, then."

"That," the hummingbird/man replied stiffly, "is between me and Princess Lahtishah."

"Is it?"

"It is."

Jarvid's dark eyes glinted like diamonds. The guards' hands drifted toward their belts. "Then tell me, Eshwyn. What did I ask you to bring?"

The possibilities were endless. Only one answer seemed to provide better than the same miniscule odds. "Sir, you asked for . . . nothing."

"Is that your answer?"

Ialin read tension in every line of Jarvid's face. He hedged his bets. "If you asked for a specific item, I don't recall it."

"Even if your life depends on it?" The chamberlain made a gesture that sent one guard to the door and the other to wrap his fingers around his hilt. "Because . . . it does."

There was nothing more Ialin could say, nothing except a wild guess or a plea for his life. He shrugged one shoulder, Aisa rising and falling with the movement, and hoped she took the cue. The instant the door swung open, revealing all five of the guards who had brought Ialin there, Aisa swooped toward them.

Swords rasped from sheaths.

Concerned for Aisa's safety, Ialin scooped up his mug and hurled it at the clot of guardsmen in the doorway. Wine splashed the front rank, spoiling their aim, and the macaw wove through them in a blur of blue and gold. The mug caught one in the shoulder, staggering him into the woman who had earlier taken Ialin's arm. Both crashed to the floor, but the others split around them, two chasing after the retreating bird, the other two, including the elite guard who had opened the door, charging for Ialin.

Ialin remained in place, not bothering to run. He could never make it through the guards alive, and his death served no purpose. One of the chamberlain's elite guardians hurled himself at the still-seated guest. Ialin ducked under his wildly waving sword. The man crashed against him, sending the chair careening over backward. Ialin twisted with the fall, following the momentum in a light backward somersault to spare himself serious injury. He never made it to his feet. A guard's sword at his throat stopped him in an awkward crouch, and the elite guard's weight pinned his legs to the floor.

Ialin held out his hands in a gesture of surrender. "I won't fight; please don't hurt me." He kept his voice steady, revealing none of the cold squiggles of fear dancing through his chest. To sound defiant might goad them to attack, but helplessness panic was also known to arouse some dogs to go after prey. Jarvid's other bodyguard hauled the chamberlain out of harm's way. The guards who had fallen scrambled to their feet and moved to block both exits.

Jarvid stepped toward Ialin, to the obvious discomfort of his bodyguard. "Disarm yourself, rebel."

Ialin forced himself to remain calm and as still as his racing metabolism allowed. His successes of the last hour had made him believe the original plan might work, but he had already anticipated its failure. The assault on Opernes Castle was not yet lost. He glanced at the guards who held him in place. "Do I have permission to move?"

"They won't harm you," Jarvid promised. "So long as you cooperate."

The elite guard shifted his weight, freeing Ialin's legs, dragging some of the silk pantaloons with him as he moved. He stared at Ialin's ankles, looked at the chamberlain, then inclined his head toward the bared flesh between Ialin's cuffs and shoes.

Jarvid followed the gesture, then nodded in understanding.

Ialin knew they had found the crafted scar. *By the grace of all gods, let it fool them.* He rolled his eyes to the sword at his throat, pretending not to see the exchange.

The blade retreated slightly. With stiff, flighty movements, Ialin relieved himself of the utility knife he carried and tossed it to the floor. As he did so, he signaled Vernon with a touch to find a safer hiding place among the several layers of clothing he wore to pad his scrawny frame. The rest depended upon how thoroughly the guards searched him. If they simply patted him down, they would find nothing and believe him as large as he appeared. If they stripped him, the game would end here.

Jarvid's brown eyes met Ialin's again. Miraculously, they had softened. So far, he seemed to be convinced by Ialin's second, more mundane masquerade hidden beneath the first. The scar perfectly matched that of the bear/man, Draezon, well known to the royals since he had rescued a royal cousin, as a toddler, when she became hopelessly lost in a cold, dark forest. Bears were not usually liked or trusted. Of all the legal citizens of Barakhai, they were most likely to revert to cannibalism. Draezon had never done so, however, one of the few *durithrin* who learned social graces and interacted deliberately with the city folk. Once, he had blundered into a snare placed for a murderer. He had panicked in bear form, nearly severing his foot. The castle staff nursed him back to health, where he became a favorite of the children. The injury had left the familiar scar that Ialin had copied onto his ankle.

"Why, Draezon?" Jarvid asked softly.

Ialin thought he heard a hint of pain in the chamberlain's tone. He lowered his gaze, familiar with the bear/man's idiosyncrasies and comportment. They had worked together on several scouting projects for the rebels. "Y-you know . . . who I am?"

"Why would you turn against us? Against your liege? Against those who helped you in your time of greatest need?"

Ialin kept his head down, evading the chamberlain's gaze, as Draezon would. "I haven't turned against anyone." He balanced his explanation carefully. He needed to find the words that would keep him alive but still land him in the dungeon, nearer to Zylas. He had considered his backup operation as long and carefully as the original plan that his friends all knew about and assisted him with. If the royals discovered his true identity, they would kill him or, at best, place him in a container too small for his animal form to escape. A man who morphed into a bear could be safely kept in the regular prison, though its widely spaced bars would easily allow a hummingbird passage. "I never intended to hurt anyone, nor have I. I just wanted to make sure you didn't either."

Footsteps pounded up the stairway, and the two guards who had chased after Aisa returned, still panting from the chase. "She got away, sir," one announced.

Jarvid's teeth clamped together, and his breath escaped in a sharp hiss that corresponded perfectly with Ialin's relieved sigh.

Despite the simultaneity of the noises, the chamberlain heard. "Are you finding joy in our misfortune, Draezon?"

"No, sir." Ialin finally raised his head. "I'm finding joy in an innocent woman's fortune." Now, he met Jarvid's dark stare. "I'm willing to accept her punishment as well as my own."

The elite guard snorted. "You can only die once, traitor."

Jarvid raised a hand that silenced the guard. "I'll listen to Draezon."

Ialin resisted the urge to glare at the guard. The gentle bear/man would not act in such a petty fashion. "The parrot has little overlap and knew nothing of this mission. I took her with me only as a prop."

"And your mission?" Jarvid asked matter-of-factly.

Ialin shook his head. "I can't answer that."

The chamberlain's eyes narrowed.

Before he could speak, Ialin threw the man a crumb. "But I can tell you my reasons."

Jarvid took the bait, though he still looked dangerously perturbed. "Your reasons for turning traitor?"

"I don't see it that way. I see it as protecting my children."

"You're a *Regular*," Jarvid reminded the man he assumed was Draezon.

Though Ialin came of a *Random* union, he could not argue the point when it came to Draezon's background. "And my wife, too. My goose wife. Our children—"

"—are perfectly legal *Randoms*, sanctioned by the kingdom, who have done very well for themselves."

"And others." Ialin allowed a smile to cross his lips, trying to appear like a proud father. "A dog guard in Ashtar, awarded for courage. And a chipmunk who finds help for those in trouble in the most remote woodlands. The best children a father could have."

The smile returned to Jarvid's face, a careful echo. "Most fathers would say the same about their children."

"Perhaps." A full concession might diminish Ialin's point. "But your new law makes my children . . . criminal."

Jarvid shook his head, while the guards remained silently in place, attentive to every word of the exchange, to every movement of their prisoner. "The law isn't retroactive. It won't change the legitimacy of those already born. In fact, His Majesty delayed the institution of it to allow not only those inside their mothers to come into the world honestly but allowed several extra months for Random couples who wished to marry or to create another baby or litter before the ban was struck. I believe that more than fair, don't you?"

"Reasonable," Ialin gave where he could. "Which I always expect from His Majesty. "But had I lived at a later time, my love for Cellia would have been forever denied, my children would not exist. . . ."

Though Jarvid's expression revealed sympathy, his words did not show the same understanding. "Love denied is difficult, but fatal only to the weak of heart. Eventually, you would have found a bear to love and marry. I know it's hard to imagine others in the place of the children you have, but you would have loved your bear children as much as your current ones. *Lesariat* cats trade kittens all the time; it's the ones you raise, the ones who call you 'Poppa,' that you love, no matter where they come from or how they appear. Life would not be worse, I assure you. Only different."

Ialin considered his next approach. He could have discussed the flaws in the king's decree all day and appreciated the chance to get heard by a member of the royal family, a feat he could never have accomplished on his own. But he could feel the pressure of a switch to bird form that would come upon him too soon for long conversations.

Apparently interpreting Ialin's silence as skepticism, Jarvid continued, "Marriage and mating laws have limited the royal family much longer and more harshly than any others." He shrugged. "Some sacrifices are necessary for the good of Barakhai and her future. It's up to all of us to make them."

Ialin thought he detected a note of deeply engrained sorrow. Running only on instinct, he tried, "Like you, sir?"

Jarvid's eyes widened in clear surprise. "I've loved and lost," he admitted. "To marry a switcher would mean forever leaving a family that needs me."

Ialin knew that a formal, permanent union with a switcher would strip Jarvid of his royal status, yet he had little to lose by consorting with whomever he chose to in secret. A child born of any such liaison would assume the form of the mother forever and, therefore, be considered a *Regular*. To assure herself and her offspring special treatment, she would gladly claim not to remember a tryst that would seem to have occurred in animal form.

"What about the creatures denied *Regular* marriages who are now forbidden from *Random* ones as well?"

Jarvid's lids rose even further. "You mean . . . vermin?"

"Yes."

"You think we need more vermin?"

Having risked his life to rescue one such vermin while another lay hidden in the folds of his clothing, Ialin found an answer difficult. "I'm not sure that would harm anything. But even setting aside that part of the argument, snakes and mice spend half of their lives as people, too. Shouldn't they have a right to extra hands on the farm, offspring to try their patience and bring tears of joy to their eyes? My younglings are the source of my greatest joys and sorrows."

Jarvid retook his seat, though Ialin remained on the floor. He rubbed his naked, dimpled chin. "An interesting point, worth consideration. I could discuss that with the king's brother. Perhaps Prince Hardin and His Majesty would be willing to work out an arrangement with widows and orphans, those with unwanted or excessive offspring."

Stunned silent, Ialin remained in place. The enmity between royalty and rebels had gone on too long for meaningful dialogue. The king had long ago made it clear that he would jail or execute any rebel who dared set foot, claw, or wing on the castle grounds. Yet, the rebels might find an ally, albeit a harsh one, in the chamberlain for visiting merchants. Of course, the "compromise" fell far short of acceptable to any but the most conservative of the rebel forces. Most would settle for nothing less than complete freedom when it came to creating families and choosing mates, and Zylas would never consent to what now amounted to an absolute ban on mating for those animals considered undesirable.

Ialin had to agree. For now, the kingdom had chosen to breed out only vermin. How long before the prohibition spread to include others the royals found less desirable until whole groups of creatures disappeared from the world forever?

It was an argument Ialin did not have time to make, even if he believed it might prove fruitful. None of this mattered anyway if they managed to liberate the dragons and they could lift the Curse that had so long plagued the world of Barakhai. "Chamberlain Jarvid, I'm afraid I have nothing more to say."

Jarvid nodded as the guards studied him expectantly. Finally, he spoke the words that Ialin hated but needed to hear. "Take him to the dungeon. When court is finished, King Terrin will deal with him." He gave Ialin a pleading look. "I like you, Draezon. I hope you'll think things through and decide to talk willingly."

Ialin gave no reply as the guards of Opernes Castle led him away.

Chapter 10

COLLINS buzzed to bleary awareness without any memory of having fallen asleep. He ached all over. *Why?* A warm tongue massaged the flesh between the crudely bound tatters of his shirt. *Korfius,* his mind told him. He opened his eyes to fuzzy grayness. Dusty mucus glued his eyelashes together, and he raised a hand to wipe the mess away. At his movement, the animal stiffened with a high-pitched yelp that ill-suited a hound. Toenails scraped over Collins' already abraded back, and a puppy much smaller than Korfius skittered and tumbled into view. The world followed: a dirty, rocky dreariness that defined the inner reaches of a cave. Memory flooded back and, with it, panicky understanding. Before he could stop himself, Collins screamed.

The puppy scrambled into retreat, whip-tail tucked between its legs. It ran behind a boulder and disappeared from Collins' sight.

As the sound echoed gradually into silence, Collins cringed at his own stupidity. *A terrified shriek of distress. No, that won't attract more carnivores.* He turned his attention to his injuries. His back and scalp felt as if someone had slashed them repeatedly against a giant grater. Every breath reminded him of his bruised ribs, and his hip and head throbbed. He had suffered broken bones on his last visit to Barakhai and did not think he had any now, though his left arm sagged. He supposed he might have fractured his collarbone, dislocated his shoulder, or torn some tendons there.

A noise clicked through Collins' hearing, and he jerked his head toward it. The sudden movement sent vertigo crushing down on him and a lead weight of pain slamming through his head. Suddenly, he felt even less sure about his assessment; he might also have a skull fracture. That thought brought a trickle of fear. He could not forget his anatomy professor's warning that knocking someone out was not the benign process action/adventure movies would have viewers believe. If a man blacked out for longer than a minute, he might well have sustained a lethal injury. *I couldn't have been out long, or that damned cat would have eaten me by now.*

Collins raised his arm to consult his watch, only to find the puppy staring at him from behind the rock. Woolly with youth, it had a short, rounded snout, ears that stuck up in sharp triangles, and enormous brown eyes. Cowlike patches of black and white splattered its ribby body. *All Barakhain dogs are guards,* Collins reminded himself. *And only absolute carnivores live here.* He looked at the animal, trying to discern some feature that might reveal it as the equivalent of an African or Indian wild dog, but it looked more like a husky-or malamute-cross, perhaps three months old.

With slow, deliberate motions, Collins freed himself from his backpack and crouched.

The puppy watched him, head tipped sideways. It remained still, its back half hidden behind the boulder.

Collins' mind lurched through details he had already considered. *Any kind of* Random *breedings could have happened here through the centuries*. He fumbled in his pocket, freeing a dog biscuit which he held out toward the pup.

The dog's nose twitched. It did not otherwise move, continuing to study Collins.

Breaking the biscuit in half, Collins tossed one piece in a gentle arc. It fell to the uneven floor, sliding toward the puppy, who backpedaled farther behind the stone. Its nose wiggled again, and it craned its neck toward the offering. It raised a paw with obvious caution, then eased forward. Another wary step followed. It reached its muzzle as far forward as possible to sniff at the biscuit piece. It glanced at Collins one more time, seeming reassured by his stillness.

Finally, it scooped the biscuit into its jaws and crunched it down, lapping up every last crumb. It looked expectantly at Collins.

Smiling, Collins held out the rest of the biscuit. The dog trotted toward him, gait slowing as it drew nearer. It stopped just beyond his reach, sat, and waited.

Collins stretched out his arm as far as possible. The puppy snatched the biscuit from his hand, then retreated a few steps to eat it. While it did, Collins reached into his pocket again, drawing out a piece of jerky. He offered it to the dog.

This time, the puppy took the meat from Collins' hand, bolting it down without any visible chewing. Its oversized, underfurred tail waved wildly, overbalancing the puppy in a wobbly dance. As it worked down the food, Collins ran a hand along its head, scratching behind the fuzzy ears. In clear ecstasy, the puppy sat, tipping its head toward the man's touch. It sniffed Collins' fingers, then licked off the remaining grease and spices.

Collins looked up to find a full-sized version of the puppy watching quietly from the entryway. He swallowed hard, searching for the sword Ialin had insisted he bring. He had not thought to use it against the cougar; its assault had immediately separated him from his backpack and the blade thrust through the strap. He did not see the weapon and dared not make the necessary visual sweep to find it, which would require losing track of the full-grown dog. He groped blindly at his belt, but the knife had apparently also gone missing. Left with nothing but his wits, Collins debated whether to try to stare down the beast. The dominance maneuver might backfire if the dog chose to accept what amounted to a challenge.

Collins swallowed his terror. The dog might sense it, and that, too, could drive it to attack. Trying to appear in control, he casually reached back into the pocket for another stick of jerky. The puppy lunged for the treat; but, before its sharp little teeth closed around the jerky, Collins lobbed it toward the adult dog. The puppy skittered after the meat, nails scratching against stone, barking furiously.

Collins cringed. The sound might draw others. Or, he realized, it might drive some, like the cougar, away.

The adult walked toward the jerky as the puppy came

careening after it. The youngster missed, lost its footing, and crashed into the larger dog with a startled yelp. Seeming not to notice the collision, the adult hefted the meat in gentle jaws, bit off half, then dropped the rest. The puppy snapped up its share. The grown dog yapped out a single bark, paused, then barked twice more.

Collins stiffened at what sounded frighteningly like a signal. He knew canines of every sort hunted in packs.

As if to confirm his worst suspicions, movement rustled and rattled through the cavern, filled with the click of nails on stone, the swish of fur or fabric, and other small sounds he found harder to identify. His torch had burned out, so he reached with a measured, fluid motion into the backpack for another. A flick of a match set it aflame to reveal a grim semicircle of creatures hemming him against the rock formation. Humans of both genders interspersed with a surprising variety of animals, including a lioness, an orangutan, and a massive tortoise.

Collins nearly dropped the torch. He pressed his back against the stones, studying the crowd of creatures around him. Even at full strength, he could not fight all of them; the lion alone would do him in.

A lean, bearded man standing between the lioness and the tortoise cleared his throat. "You . . . understand . . . me?" He enunciated each word, as if addressing a deaf foreigner of dubious mental functioning, and he held Collins' sword in his hand.

Collins kept the torch in front of him, mind racing, trying to decide his best course of action. He could feign confusion but doubted anything good would come of that. They might speak freely in front of someone they believed didn't know what they were saying, but he would rather know his fate sooner and directly. "Every word," he responded.

Murmurs swept the human members of the group. Collins glanced around at them, realizing that what at first had seemed like a hundred was probably more like twelve. Besides the two dogs, the lioness, the ape, and the tortoise, he saw a bat dangling from the ceiling. Seven humans, four male and three female, closed the ranks. Though some sported well-defined muscles, they all appeared slender; and one woman looked as if she suffered from anorexia nervosa, a walking skeleton. Some wore tattered loincloths while others stood brazenly naked. They all had long hair, lank and uneven, though reasonably clean.

"Come with us," the speaker said.

Nodding, Collins secured his backpack and hefted it. The strap rubbed against an open wound, and he cringed. Getting fully to his feet proved harder. Dizziness assailed him in a rush of swirling spots and squiggles. He took an awkward step, uncertain of directions, not even sure about up and down. He struggled against gravity.

More incomprehensible whispers swept the group, and the animals stirred restlessly.

Collins held utterly still as his vision stabilized. Barely trusting himself to speak, he managed, "I'm hurt."

"Yes." The speaker revealed nothing with his tone. "Come."

Collins walked toward the bearded man, and the mixed group filled in the growing gap behind him. The circle tightened, though not enough to keep him from escaping under normal circumstances. The idea of running now incited a raw bubble of nausea. His balance would surely fail him.

The creatures nearest the speaker turned, glancing over their shoulders as they slid, in single file, through an opening Collins had not yet explored. He soon found himself in a small, rough-hewn cave filled with the obligatory stony growths on floor and ceiling. The bearded man led the way through one of that cavern's several exits and into a grotto. There, Collins saw an unusually large number of ledges shadowing a network of low, tunnellike openings and three larger entrances, including the jagged hole they had glided through. A stream wound along one edge, disappearing into a hole on the same side. Each entrance had a guard, one a man holding a pole, another a massive, grizzled wolf, the third a petite woman who looked as if she could not defend herself from her own shadow.

The man who had spoken gestured at a rocky prominence. Though free of slime or moss, it looked shiny with damp. Collins' aching body begged him to rest, but he dared take no chance of offending. "May I sit down, please?"

"Please do," said a voluptuous naked woman with the darkest skin and hair Collins had ever seen. She might have passed for an aboriginal African in his world except that she had threadlike lips, a long, narrow nose, and eyes that appeared more yellow than brown. Her inky hair fell in knotty straightness nearly to her knees, though it covered nothing women of his world would have considered significant for modesty.

Collins plopped heavily down on the ledge, feeling as if he had survived a journey through a wood chipper. He adjusted the crude bandage on his head and dropped the backpack beside him. "My name is Benton Collins," he said. "You can call me Ben."

"Ben," the original speaker repeated. The man held the sword awkwardly. Clearly, he knew or had surmised its purpose, but he had no experience with such a weapon. "Who are you, Ben?"

Collins thought he had already answered that question with his name. He tried to guess the reason for the question, what he would want to know were he the captor. But, first, he needed to figure out the purpose of this mismatched group; and his thoughts slogged through light-headedness and pain for an answer. "I'm from another world. One without switchers and switch-forms."

The way-too-skinny woman piped in, "Are you a royal?"

Collins bit his lower lip, uncertain of the consequences of answering with truth or various lies. He had no way of knowing whether this group held royalty in awed esteem or despised them for inflicting this life of anarchy and imprisonment upon them. The king's ancestors had literally visited the sins of the parents onto the sons and daughters; yet, the current king and his relatives were also innocent descendants. *Not that that simple, clearheaded and obvious reasoning prevents wars and resentment in my own world.* Preferring to die for honesty than deceit, Collins stuck with the truth. "My world ..." he recognized the fallacy of the statement he was about to make and amended it even as he spoke, "... at least my part of it, doesn't have royalty."

Glances circumnavigated the room. They seemed surprised by Collins' pronouncement, which made sense. Having lived under no other form of government, they might find it difficult to understand how others could. Even in his own world, Collins sometimes found it hard to see how communism had flourished and countries continued to accept monarchs, even if only as figureheads. On the other hand, he had loved science and math and suffered through subjects like history, geography, and social studies. He did not consider himself a stereotypical scientist who saw the whole world in black and white: provable theories versus ungrounded superstition. He had even dated a psychology student, albeit unsuccessfully.

The original speaker summed up the modicum of information they had gathered. "So you're not a royal, and yet you also have no switch-form."

"Correct." The snail's pace of the interview ground on Collins, who suddenly remembered the limitations on his time. He finally glanced at his watch. It read 11:08 A.M., to his horror. "Oh, my God! I've got to get moving." He would never have guessed how long he had lain unconscious, curled around his backpack, on the stones. The presence of this gang of switchers, including the dogs, must have kept the cougar from returning to finish him.

Humans and animals alike stared at Collins. Clearly, they believed his ability to go or stay depended wholly on them. And, Collins realized, they were essentially right. He could only attempt to prod them along.

Collins wrenched open his backpack. "Listen, you all seem nice enough, but the life of a man and a cause depend on me hauling ass out of here right now." He seized the Snickers bars and held them up. "Here. You'll like these." Even as he tossed them, Collins had a sudden wild thought. He had read that chocolate was poisonous to most of the animals people kept as pets. On the other hand, he had fed candy to his cat and hamster without any harmful effects that he knew of, and the animals he now faced spent half their lives as humans.

The puppy ran toward the bounty, but its father stopped it with a well-placed paw. The lioness sniffed one candy bar carefully, and a short, sinewy man who had not yet spoken hefted the other two. As he studied them, Collins remembered to add through his pounding headache, "Take the paper off first. The good stuff's inside."

Using his teeth, the man ripped the wrapper and sent it floating to the ground. He took a bite of the Snickers, and a smile lit his face. "This is . . . great!" He hefted it like a trophy. "Best food I've ever eaten." He handed the one he had tasted to the scrawny girl, who took a delicate nibble.

Her eyes widened. "Delicious."

The short man opened the other two candy bars and passed them around the group while Collins emptied his pockets of dog biscuits and jerky. "You can have all of these, too." No longer worrying about an attack, he went through his pack, emptying it of everything he could spare. Not only could those things work as bribes, but shedding them would lighten his load tremendously. "Here're some clothes. You look like you could use these." He left the selection of T-shirts, jeans, underwear, and socks on the ledge beside him. Finding the medicine bottle, Collins sorted through the Tums to find three Tylenols, which he forced down without water, using several hard swallows and all the saliva he could muster. He returned the bottle to his pack. The Bara-khain prisoners could probably use the medicine, too; but he did not want to take the time to explain it. He also kept his toiletries, the binoculars, keys, watch, and beeper but left the speaker wire he had used to lead Falima to the biology laboratory. He looked up at no one in particular. "Now, does any of that buy me the freedom to find the lost drag-ons?"

The prisoners in human form tore their gazes from the pile to glance at Collins, clearly bewildered. The short man who had opened the Snickers spoke first. "The lost what?"

"Dragons," Collins repeated dutifully, though he doubted that would prove enough. "Humongous scaly creatures with lots of sharp teeth."

"Like the one who attacked you?" the skinny woman tried.

Collins shook his head. "No. No. That's a large furry creature with sharp teeth. I'm talking about dragons. Big-ger. Just scales all over. Hairless wings." He glanced up to see two bats hanging upside down from a stalactite over his head and looked for the words to differentiate the dragons from them, without resorting to the word "scales" again. "Enormous creatures. Like alligators with wings, but bigger than elephants."

The humans traded glances, and Collins now realized that more had joined them. New animals had arrived as well, including an ocelot and a bobcat, who must have crept out from holes beneath the ledges. Some of the newcomers examined Collins' offerings, and a naked preteen girl began raking them into piles.

Collins stopped describing. Ultimately, it did not matter. "Look, if I can get those dragons out of this place, they can make magic that takes away that involuntary shape-changing . . . curse thingy."

Captivated either by Collins' words or his excitement, the group kept every eye focused directly upon him. No one spoke.

Collins delivered what he thought would prove the coup dc grâcc. "You can all walk out of this prison as casily as I walked in." He waited for applause or cheering, anything to show they understood the significance of his revelation.

Instead, they all looked at him curiously. The original speaker cleared his throat. "Prison?"

Skinny Girl added, "Walk out to where?"

The triumphant grin that had crept across Collins' face with his final pronouncement withered. "To—to the real world. The world beyond these inescapable caverns." Sudden realization hit him low in the gut. These switchers knew little or nothing of their history. To them, the entire planet began and ended at the barriers thwarting their escape. The river, with its life-giving water and the objects outsiders tossed into it, was probably a god to them.

"To your world?" the girl continued. "Where there're no switches or switch-forms. No royalty."

"No, no, no." Collins slapped the heel of his hand against the knot of torn T-shirt on his forehead, further worsening his headache. "You live in a small part of Barakhai. Out there, there's a whole . . ." He avoided the term "world" this time. ". . . a whole other place, more of Barakhai, with buildings and sunshine, towns and villages, where people don't worry that their neighbors might eat them. I come from somewhere else. Somewhere farther, separated from Barakhai by magic." He did not know what to name it, uncertain how the spell might translate English terms such as "The World" or "Earth," especially since he could not even say whether or not he had left the planet or the scientifically known universe. *With my luck, Earth would come out as Dirt.*

The human fraction of the group whispered among themselves, while the animals shifted from paw to paw.

Uncertain whether or not he had clarified things or muddled the situation even more, Collins tried to think it through. He believed he understood how such a strange bunch of creatures had come together. Likely, it had started with animals who tended to herd or pack and with human counterparts with an eye toward family and protection of those weaker, including their own offspring. Some of the stronger, less social creatures, like the cougar, preferred to spend most of their lives alone. Others might band solely for the purpose of hunting or procreation, such as pure in-bred packs of wolves or prides of lions. A group as mis-matched as the one that had discovered him had to have security and companionship in mind. Otherwise, the fiercest would already have devoured those most vulnerable. Amid the chaos of eternal imprisonment, at least this one civilized society had emerged, perhaps more. He had to play on their sense of community.

Collins felt utterly beaten. His head pounded, as prone to shatter as a glass-blown figurine. He ached in a million places, and the thought of dragging his tattered body one step farther made him cringe. Nevertheless, he gathered what little energy remained and declared, "I'm sorry I don't have time to explain any more. If I don't leave now, my mission will fail." It was not technically true. Even with Zylas gone, he could still complete the ultimate goal. "And a good man will die for nothing."

Collins tilted his chin, a defiant gesture that nearly cost him his consciousness. "I'm leaving. If you stop me, I will fight with every ounce of strength left in my body." *Yeah, that ought to last about a second.*

The tortoise started toward him, through a silence that admitted only the steady water-song of the stream. Enormous, paddlelike feet heaved the huge shell forward in a lumbering style that precluded speed. Collins clambered off the ledge to meet her, the simple gesture pounding him with exhaustion and dizziness. He hoped Ialin, Falima, Vernon, and Aisa fared better, because it seemed unlikely he would ever make it to the dragons. *In time.* The downward spiral of his thoughts quickened. *Oh, come on, Ben. Don't let hope turn you into a fool. If the dragons were here, some-one would certainly have seen them.*

Collins dropped to his haunches, and the tortoise practi-cally climbed into his lap to meet his gaze levelly. One an-cient, clay-colored eye met both of his, and the burden of its one foot on his thigh crushed him against stone. The tortoise had to weigh two or three hundred pounds. Uncertain of its purpose, or the best way to pet a reptile, he reached out a careful hand and set it gently on the animal's head. "Scaly," he murmured. "Scaly, like this."

The long, tortoise neck stretched from its domed shell. If Collins added even a vestigial tail, the creature had to measure a good four feet. He froze, uncertain how to react as the tortoise laid its beaked head upon his shoulder.

A redhead with a scarred face explained, "Mataia approves of you. She's the oldest and wisest of us, and we will help you."

Relieved, Collins gave the tortoise's neck a gentle hug, then scratched the scales on the top of her head. Though akin to stroking large-grained sandpaper, the gesture was the only one he could think of to express his appreciation. *She's human, too, stupid. Probably with great overlap.* "Thank you," Collins told Mataia. He looked past her enormous form to the humans and animals beyond, "And thank all of you, too. I'm not sure how you can help, but—" A possibility came to Collins even as he spoke the words. "Did any of you hear the sound I played on my recorder?"

The teenaged girl continued to sort through the food and clothing Collins had given them, and two boys who looked like they were about eight or nine years old came over to help her. The rest of the group continued to regard Collins in silence.

Realizing "recorder" might not have translated, Collins clarified, "I brought a sound with me. Until it broke, I used my little box thing to make it."

The black woman held up the smashed remains of the recorder, and Collins wondered where she had hidden it until that moment. He guessed someone had his knife as well.

"Yes, that's it! Did you hear it?"

Several of the humans, and even some of the animals, bobbed their heads. Mataia eased off of Collins' thigh, to his relief. His leg buzzed with a pins and needles sensation, and he cringed through the pain of returning circulation.

"Is that what you're looking for?" a middle-aged man in a loincloth asked, the only human in the gathering with gray in his hair. "The monsters who make that sound?"

"That's them!" Collins said, too excited to question the term "monsters."

The black woman made a decisive gesture. "Come with us, then." Her voice sounded inexplicably tired. "We'll take you there."

Once imprisoned, Ialin allowed his agitation free rein, pacing the confines of his dungeon cell relentlessly to work off a long-suppressed tide of nervous energy. He ceased caring about keeping up appearances. Even a usually composed bear could be expected to demonstrate discomfort when locked in a cage anticipating questioning and, possibly, execution.

As instructed, Vernon returned before Ialin's switch, though time would tell whether or not the mouse had located Zylas during his absence. It seemed long enough to the hummingbird/man for Vernon to have found an army of missing renegades, yet Ialin never trusted his own concept of time. Others tended to find him irritatingly impatient.

This time, Ialin did not heft the mouse, instead turning his back to his guard and pretending to lie down for a rest. The fuzzy gray rodent stood, planting his forepaws on Ialin's magically sculpted nose. The man kept his voice low. "At my switch time, you distract the guard." Though it required more words, Ialin dared not leave details to an animal who, like himself, had incomplete overlap. "Make something fall with a noise. Pick an object behind or beside him, so he doesn't look toward me."

The guard's voice boomed through the prison. "Did you say something, Draezon?"

Ialin twitched his nose until Vernon dropped to the floor. He glanced over his shoulder at the guard. "Just berating myself."

The guard chuckled. "For what you did or for getting caught?"

"I haven't decided yet."

The guard laughed harder. A tall, lanky man with unkempt brown hair, he would clearly transform into some lean, hungry-looking dog.

Ialin turned his head back and hissed at Vernon. The change would soon be upon him. "Go."

As Vernon scampered into the shadows, Ialin loosened

the layers of shirting that swaddled his slight frame. Becoming entangled would ruin his well-laid plan. A familiar tingle throbbed through his skin as he worked harder to shove down the cloth. *Hurry up, Vernon.* Ialin glued his gaze to the bars, solid iron with barely a spot of rust. The guards had clearly chosen a secure cell, afraid he might bend or damage the bars in bear form, just as he had hoped. He dared not become complacent, however. Many things had gone well with the previous plan, only to fail him when it mattered most. He could not count on anything going smoothly. A wave of warmth shunted through him, heralding the change. *Vernon!*

Falling metal crashed against the stone floor, followed by the sound of several more objects slamming and rolling. The guard spun, just as switch-form overtook Ialin. He felt himself shrinking, clothes flopping to the floor, beak sprouting. He sprang into the air, lacy green wings beating madly, all but invisible. His body a blur, he flitted through the bars and out into the main portion of the dungeon.

Ialin scanned a scattering of dented pans and chamber pots, and a small gray figure racing from the carnage. From the air, he followed Vernon, not bothering to watch the guard's reaction. In a few moments, the man would notice that his prisoner was missing and call for assistance. Ialin only hoped his sudden disappearance would confuse them, and the mystery would take significant time to piece together. Even if they figured it out immediately, he believed they would expect him to escape, not wend his way deeper into the dungeons.

Vernon led Ialin through a prison filled with empty cells, into a storage room where he disappeared beneath piled up junk. Ialin hovered, willing himself to stay focused. He had decent overlap; and, where excitement tended to unbalance others, it made him more alert and attentive. His beadlike eyes scanned the floor, seeking movement. At first, he saw no sign of his companion. Then, he caught a sudden flash of gray from his left eye. He barreled toward it, an abrupt, midair stop all that saved him from crashing into another door. Vernon disappeared through the crack beneath it.

Ialin dove. Leading with his slender beak, he followed the mouse's retreating form beneath the door and into a dusty room sparsely filled with furniture covered in tattered sheets. On top of one flat surface that appeared to represent a chest of drawers sat a cage barely large enough to contain his own miniscule form. A naked, pink tail protruded between the bars.

Vernon leaped to the dangling edge of sheet draped over the chest and scrambled upward. Ialin hovered over the cage, peering at its inhabitant through one eye. The white fur, the bright red eyes, now dulled by pain, the pink ears laid tight against the ratty head—he knew those features, if not their broken demeanor. Vernon had, indeed, brought him to Zylas.

"Zylas," Ialin buzzed to the only person other than Prinivere who could understand him in animal form.

The pink nose twitched, and the muzzle rose. "Ialin?"

As the mouse finished his climb, Zylas' ratty expression grew even more hopeful. "Vernon. Can you help me?"

In animal form, it never occurred to Ialin to lie to comfort his friend. "I don't know. I'll try." He fluttered to the lock, wings beating with furious ease. He had used his delicate beak many times to thwart the skill of locksmiths, but this one looked like nothing he had ever seen. It appeared brand new, its shiny, silver surface some strange amalgam of iron, and it had a black knob with figures that might represent foreign letters or numbers inscribed on it. He saw no hole in which to insert his beak. He pecked at the front, and his beak slammed against a substance as hard as glass yet like nothing he had ever encountered.

Ialin returned to Zylas' face. "The lock. It's weird."

Zylas clamped his muzzle tightly. His position in the cage did not allow him to view the lock, and he had no room to turn. "Carriequinton put it on there." His voice had a quaver to it that Ialin usually associated only with his own jerky movements. "It might come from her world. I think she spun it when she put it on."

Ialin went back to the lock, tapping the knob with his beak. It did move slightly. He continued experimenting, hoping to stumble upon the correct series of movements.

"She taunts me," Zylas was telling Vernon. "Wants to be here when I . . . change. Wants to watch me die."

Ialin paused to chirp out, nearly subvocally, "You're not going to die."

"You've got the lock?" Zylas asked hopefully.

"No," Ialin admitted. "But I'm not going to stop trying till I do." He drove that promise deep into his soul, working at the knob frantically while Zylas addressed Vernon.

"You watch for Carriequinton. If you see her, squeak loudly, then hide. Both of you, hide."

"All right," they promised in unison, then Ialin went back to work.

Chapter 11

BENTON Collins dragged through the carnivore caverns with an escort that included the lioness, the ocelot, the scrawny woman, and the bearded man who had first spoken to him. Exhausted from blood loss, assailed by a persistent headache scarcely alleviated by the Tylenol, fresh wounds throbbing, he staggered among the four with few verbal exchanges. They told him their names, but he retained only the last, Margast, and only because it reminded him of his ex-girlfriend, Marlys. At times, he discovered himself leaning heavily against the lioness' furry back. He always righted himself when he noticed it, glad she took no offense at his touch. One swipe of her enormous paw would send him tumbling, and he doubted he would ever regain his feet.

Collins staggered onward, though the reason seemed distant, and no strategy for handling the dragons once he found them came to mind. He was dimly aware that he would have to find a way to communicate with them, to convince them of the significance of following him back to the entrance where they could talk to Prinivere. She would likely have the words that he did not, the ones that might make them understand their role in rescuing every non-royal citizen of Barakhai. He hoped—and doubted—he could make it back to the cave opening with them. His body wanted only to lie down and surrender to sweet oblivion again, and the realization that a wandering carnivore might eat him barely overcame that desire. Inertia more than intent, the familiarity of forward movement surrounded by shapechangers, kept him going when even need failed.

Even though Collins glanced repeatedly at his watch, even though he had to force every step, time ticked by too fast for his liking. Every bone-weary step seemed to take a full minute, every one a beat closer to Zylas' death. *Please God, let Falima and the others be doing better than me.*

For over two switch times, two hours in Collins' world, Zylas listened to the click of Ialin's beak against the lock, his muttered buzzing indicating frustration. Though focused on this one task, Ialin's discomfort was gradually overcoming his overlap. With each failure, he became more birdlike and less human, which would impair his judgment when it came to perceiving the intricacies of the Otherworld lock. Driven to pace but confined to a quiver, Zylas concentrated on maintaining his own overlap. As his companions lost their humanity, he had to keep his as finely honed as possible. He shared Ialin's aggravation. If only he could turn around, he might find a way to aid them. He had explored the lock with his tail, knew its general feel and composition. He had yanked at the bar looping like an elongated semicircle through the matched tangs of the cage, but it seemed at least as solid and strong as the tangs themselves.

Cautiously, Zylas prodded Ialin, worried the humming-bird might become stuck on an untenable solution. "Try something different, my friend."

Ialin gave no reply but a tiny, bird grunt of assent.

Zylas' gaze swept the visible section of the room for the thousandth time. He could not see the trapdoor through which Carriequinton could descend at any moment. He only knew the scene in front of him: a wall thick with grime, including brown stains that could represent old blood as easily as dirt, the huge mirror the woman stared into obsessively, showing her as she used to look. Prinivere's illusion spell had fallen. With the return of Quinton's scars had come a grotesque anger she vented with taunts. She had spoken of destroying Zylas' friends, his family, everything he held dear. She described in detail the fate that awaited him, the shattering of his bones into shards that would tear his insides like swallowed knives, the mangling of every body part, the puddle of blood his compacted body would leave on the floor. Zylas had become resigned to the likelihood of his death, and the cruel agony of its execution, yet he preferred to avoid it. He had dedicated his life to a worthy cause and wished to see it through. At least, he knew others now believed in it as strongly as he did. His death would not end the quest to lift the Curse hanging so long over Barakhai. So many others had become as serious in their devotion as he. *So close. So damned close.* He shut his eyes. *If only I could have seen it through.*

The sounds of Ialin's beak ceased. "Hole back," he said at length.

Zylas froze, knowing the broken speech meant Ialin was becoming too birdlike to communicate effectively much longer. "What?"

"Hole back. Hole back!"

Vernon scurried to the lock. "There's a keyhole on the back."

"On the back?" Zylas' lids flicked open. "I'll hunch as much as possible. Get out of your way. See what you can do, Ialin."

To Zylas' relief, Ialin still understood enough to shift his attention to the new discovery. The lacy little wings beat wildly, stirring a gentle wind through Zylas' fur. The warmth of impending change swirled through his blood. By the reckoning of Collins' world, he had fifteen minutes. Zylas did not bother to warn his friends. They all measured in switch times, and reminding the hummingbird of his friend's looming death would only add to the plethora of nervous energy that assailed him at all times. Vernon's frequent trips to the storage room for honey and sugar had kept Ialin alive so far; but the more upset he got, the more energy the little bird/man expended. And Vernon would know about the coming change because he was also feeling those stirrings.

That last realization mobilized Zylas. Before he could emit a warning, however, Vernon squeaked first. "She's coming. Carriequinton's coming."

It's over. Zylas refused to dwell on his own approaching fate. "Vernon, run!"

"No!"

"Run, damn it! Get out of here." Worried the mouse's loyalty would serve no useful purpose, Zylas preyed on it.

"Do it for me, Vernon, as my last wish. The cause can't survive without both of us, and the lady needs to know what happened here."

With clear reluctance, Vernon turned tail and scurried back the way he had come. He had barely enough time till his change to get beyond the castle walls. Once there, he was safe. A royal patrol might find him, but only if they stumbled upon him before one of the hundreds of forest creatures in his employ did. Even then, the king's guards would have no right or reason to capture him.

Footsteps clomped on the stairs, Quinton's eternally angry tread. Beneath the noise, a close soft click touched Zylas' sensitive rat ears.

The lock? That reminded Zylas of his companion. "Ialin, fly!"

Too birdlike to reply in words, Ialin continued to tug at the lock.

"Fly! Fly!" Zylas squeaked frantically.

Quinton shouted, "Hey! Hey, you!" She charged toward the cage. "Get away from there, you damned bird." Her footsteps quickened as she raced toward them.

Ialin surged into the air in a sudden flurry of wings and feathers. He zipped forward.

Quinton made a leap for the hummingbird, tripped over something Zylas could not see, and tumbled to the floor amid a clatter of falling objects.

Go, Ialin! Go!

Ialin appeared suddenly in Zylas' vision, zipping at full speed toward the mirror.

What's he doing? With abrupt terror, Zylas understood. Nearly devoid of overlap, Ialin had mistaken the reflection for another room. Zylas had heard of young birds killing themselves by slamming into well-polished metal. If Ialin hit the mirror at his current speed, he would smash his skull and die before he was even aware of the impact. "Ialin, no! Swerve! Damn you, swerve!"

The warning came too late. At top speed, Ialin struck the mirror.

Zylas moaned out an unratlike noise, "No." He cringed, waiting for the terrible sound of impact that never came. Ialin passed through the mirror as if through an open door. *A portal! It's a magical portal!* As he stared, shaking his head, Zylas felt the prickle of the change passing in a wave through him. His time was running short, and the lock remained in place. Dismissing what he had just seen, he thrust his tail through the bars, wrapping it around the cold metal.

Quinton ran toward the mirror, swearing viciously. Her hair grew in strange patches amid the hectic swirl of scar tissue. As if in afterthought, she seized Zylas' cage. Thrown suddenly against the bars, Zylas clamped his claws against them, seeking grounding in a world gone mad. The index finger of Quinton's right hand came tantalizingly near his mouth, but it never occurred to him to bite. All of his concentration was directed at wrapping his tail around the padlock and desperately hoping he had not imagined the click.

Collins' escort stopped in front of an ironbound wooden door, and the incongruity of that one man-made entity in the middle of natural caverns took inordinately long to register. "What's this?" His voice emerged slurred, even to his own ears. Clearly, he had lost more blood than he had realized.

"It's a door," Margast said.

Does he think I've lost my mind? Pain and grinding fatigue made Collins irritable. "I can see it's a fucking door. Where's it go?"

The lioness whined.

The skinny girl shrugged. "We don't know. No one's managed to open it."

"Locked?" Collins examined the deteriorating structure. It looked as if a solid kick would shatter the soggy wood, leaving only rusted bands of iron on sagging hinges.

"I don't think so." Margast's blue gaze fell to the latch, where Collins saw no bolt or keyhole. "Touching it hurts, though, and it screams."

The description sounded familiar to Collins. *Warded.* The only similar magic he knew of kept switchers from the royal quarters. He hoped this worked the same way. Raising his arm, he reached for the latch. His watch slid on his wrist. Since 11:45, he had deliberately avoided glancing at it, superstitiously convinced that if he could not see the time passing, it remained the same. Now, as he readjusted the band, he accidentally read the time. *11:57* A.M. Tears burned Collins' eyes. *Good-bye, Zylas.*

Steeling for a ward that might work even against him, Collins reached for the latch. He would open that door no matter the difficulty, no matter the pain. But none came. The door swung open, its rusted hinges screaming, to reveal a room as craggy as the rest of the caverns. A padded wooden chair stood planted toward the middle, several feet from a huge dark pit in the center. Behind him, the animals and humans stared curiously. As Collins entered, Margast attempted to follow, then dropped back with a shrill cry of pain.

Suddenly, a flash of emerald zipped past, in the form of what appeared to be a large insect. *Ialin?* Before Collins could consider the possibility in more detail, Carrie Quinton charged into the cave, swinging her arms and swearing viciously, a small cage tucked beneath her right arm. A hairless, pink tail protruding through the bars worked frantically at a combination padlock that hung, unlatched, from the door. Before Collins' eyes, the rat's form blurred. *Zylas, it's Zylas.* Terror slammed him with a rush of adrenaline. *I'm about to watch him implode.* The idea galloped through his mind in half an instant. Faster than thought, he hurled himself across the room.

Quinton screamed, leaping from Collins' path. He wrenched the cage from her grip, twisting off the lock as momentum skidded him into an outcropping. He ignored the pain that impact flared through his injured hip and thrust his hand into the cage. By now, Zylas had become an incomprehensible glow. Seizing an unidentified body part, Collins tore the changing creature from the cage.

For a terrifying instant, it resisted. Then, Zylas flew free, body arcing through the air to land hard on the rocks. As he assumed man form, he continued sliding, out of control, toward the pit.

"No!" Once again, Collins found himself lurching to his friend's rescue.

"You bastard!" Quinton shouted. A heaved stone slammed into Collins' shoulder with a raw agony that would have stopped him in his tracks, had he not already sent himself airborne. His wits were nearly scattered, and his arm felt broken. He watched, helpless, as Zylas' pale form went over the edge of the pit, fingers scrabbling wildly at the edge.

That small attempt of Zylas' to save himself gained Collins

the seconds he needed. He managed to stop his own forward movement at the lip of the pit and grabbed blindly at his friend. By dumb luck, his fingers winched around one of Zylas' nakcd forearms. They both stared downward, dislodged pebbles toppling thirty feet to rain down on two enormous dark shapes below them. *The dragons!*

Collins lay still, focusing all his strength into supporting his dangling friend. All the exhaustion, all the suffering of the last few hours crashed back upon him at once. He closed his eyes as dizziness washed over him, hoping only that he could hold on long enough to regain some semblance of strength, that, somehow, he would find a way to bring them both safely out of danger.

Abruptly, Collins sensed a nearby presence. He whipped open his lids to find Quinton towering over him, her face hideous with scars, her mouth an asymmetrical sneer. "So, you found them. You found them all. What good does it do you?"

Collins' mind staggered through a tired coating of fuzz. He licked lips that had gone dry as sand. "Carrie. Help us."

"Why?"

So simple a question deserved an answer Collins could not find in the desert of his fading thoughts. He tried to summon back the natural body chemicals that had given him the ability to act so quickly to save Zylas. "Because the fall alone might kill us. Because, no matter how much you hate us, you don't want to become a murderer." Collins' arms ached, and his grip grew slippery on Zylas' forearm.

Quinton laughed. "I've already crossed that line, with people I didn't hate half so much as I do you." She drew right up to where he lay, prone, on the rocks, clutching Zylas. "You see, Ben," she spat out his name like a bite of bitter fruit, "dragons are natural carnivores. It didn't take long to teach them to eat Barakhai's undesirables, and King Terrin was glad to hand execution duties to me." She grinned with an inhuman wickedness. "He thinks I got rid of the dragons, too. But watch this." She called down into the darkness. "Dinnertime!"

The creatures in the pit surged like hungry crocodiles. It seemed to Collins that he could not catch a break. He wondered why none of this could have happened while at least one of the dragons held its human form.

Zylas was speaking quickly in a low voice that did not carry. It sounded to Collins like praying, an option that seemed like the only one left. But Collins still had one prospect—that Quinton had not fallen wholly into madness. "Carrie, please. Let's talk this out like civilized human beings."

"We're not," she hissed, "anymore."

"I am," Collins insisted. "And I believe, deep down, you are, too."

Carrie drew back her foot.

Aware he could not block a kick, Collins continued talking. "I'll do anything you want, Carrie. Anything. Just name it."

Carrie barely hesitated. "Marry me."

Collins despised the thought, but he would have promised more. "Done."

Quinton's boot crashed into the bandage on the back of Collins' head. His thoughts exploded. His grip on Zylas faltered. "Do you think I'd marry a jackass like you? I'd rather watch you die." She kicked him again.

Collins lay in a red fog of agony. He forced words through the pain. "Carrie, please. What . . . do . . . you . . . want?"

Quinton slammed the toe of her boot into Collins' groin. Cramps tore through his abdomen. Every muscle went limp. His hold on Zylas failed, and he watched the white blur of his friend's descent through eyes filled with tears. Quinton brought her face right up to Collins' and whispered in his ear. "I want . . . you both . . . to die." Then, she hammered both fists into the back of his claw-ravaged head.

Collins felt himself falling, twisted, and grabbed the only thing he could: Quinton's leg. He felt it give way. Then air surged around him, and he realized they were both tumbling in savage circles into the pit. Screeching, she embraced him like a lover, all semblance of righteous vengeance lost. They spun wildly for a moment. She was on the bottom when they hit rock-solid ground with enough force to drive all the breath from his lungs, too. Pain stabbed his chest, and he heard bones snap, most of them Quinton's. She lay still beneath him.

Suddenly, Collins felt hot breath puffing over him. Still gasping for air, he rolled to face a colossal mouth filled with dagger teeth. He only hoped he would die of suffocation before those massive canines skewered him.

Then air wheezed into Collins' lungs, bringing instinctive comfort even though it violated his wish.

Zylas spoke weakly, but his tone brooked no defiance. "Trinya, no! Bad girl! Bad girl!"

The massive teeth did not withdraw, but they did not impale Collins either. He willed himself to dodge but could not conjure up the strength even to save his own life. "Zylas," he gasped. "Zylas, she's listening."

Zylas did not respond. "Trinya ... remember ... me. Come on, girl, remember. Tell ... your friend ... to get his claws ... out of my ribs."

Collins did not know how long the albino had tried to speak with his daughter, but now he guessed that the low talk he had heard had more to do with attempts to communicate with her, rather than with begging some god to save him. He cringed at Zylas' plight. Dragon claws could stab all the way through a man. Collins remained silent. He had nothing to add to the situation, and the effort of speaking might steal what remained of his consciousness. *Don't give up, Zylas.*

Then, a strange and hesitant voice touched Collins' mind. *Papa?*

"That's right, Trinya. It's your Papa."

Papa?

"I've never stopped loving you, Trinya. I've been searching, and now I'm so happy I've found you."

Papa? The dragon seemed incapable of saying anything more. She retreated from Collins, to his vast relief.

The pit went silent, and Collins hoped Zylas had simply switched to mental communication. Cautiously, measuring each movement against vertigo, Collins slid off of Quinton. He winched his fist closed around a rock.

After a long silence, Zylas' voice startled Collins. "Carriequinton! Watch our backs. Where is she?"

Collins studied the woman lying still on the rocks. Her tortured features had gone lax, peaceful for the first time since he had met her. What little sanity she had maintained at that time had vanished, leaving a cruel and soulless shell. If she survived, she would need intensive inpatient therapy and strong medications; she would surely refuse both. He could not allow her to cause more suffering to herself, to Barakhai's innocents, to anyone else. He told his conscience that Quinton was already dead or, if not, she would never make it out of the pit. Then, without further thought, he slammed the stone down on her skull with all his remaining might.

Bone collapsed beneath the blow, and dark clotted blood barely oozed from the wound. Collins' gut pitched wildly, and he vomited. Wiping his mouth, he finally managed to speak, as if he had done nothing more than touch the pulse point at her neck. "She's dead."

Zylas loosed a relieved sigh. "Now," he said with frightening weakness. "Trinya, Artoth, get us out of here."

Though more worried about the dragons eating him than getting left behind, Benton Collins dragged himself up Trinya's side to settle against the V of musculature between her left wing and neck. His left arm barely functioned. His head throbbed, his body ached, and unconsciousness hovered, promising a reprieve to which he dared not surrender. He doubted the young dragons had experience serving as living helicopters, or that they had the maturity to understand complex commands or situations. His grip and balance might be the only things between him and a deadly fall.

"Are you secured?" Zylas called tiredly through the darkness. Despite his own ordeal and injuries, Zylas had the presence of mind to remain focused and in control.

For once, Collins resisted cracking a joke. "Safe and sound." He forced some courage of his own. "Don't forget Ialin."

"He's with me." Zylas paused.

Collins presumed the rat/man was communing with his daughter, so the next words surprised him.

"And he wants me to thank you for worrying over his welfare." Zylas added in deliberate English, "Told you he'd come around."

Collins mouthed a weary smile, though no one could see it. He had never truly believed Ialin would ever grow to like him, despite the albino's reassurances. "So how do we get out of this prison? Surely the dragons can't fly out of this pit, or they would have done so long ago. And how are we going to get them out of the caverns past the magical wards?"

"Just hold on tight, and don't let anything surprise you." Without further warning, Zylas disappeared beneath the slap of leathery wings against air. The dragon he had called Artoth rose from the pit, carrying the rat/man with him. A moment later, muscles shifted beneath Collins' buttocks, and Trinya sprang into awkward flight behind the other dragon.

Thrown sideways, Collins eased into a prone position, hugging the dragon's scales. They felt warm and dry against his skin, smoother than Prinivere's, but not slimy or slippery. A world of difference existed between Trinya's jerky movements and the old dragon's easy grace. He shifted his body weight in miniscule increments, seeking the safest, most comfortable position. Finally reasonably secure, he raised his head, only to find himself rocketing toward his own reflection in a large mirror.

Collins screamed, ducking behind his outstretched hands. Ignoring her passenger's consternation, the dragon flashed through the polished surface as if through open air. The universe seemed to hiccup, then Collins found himself hovering on Trinya's back in a storage room filled with large, unidentifiable shapes swathed in tattered bolts of cloth. Artoth stood on the floor, while a disheveled and limping Zylas struggled with the mirror. Ialin flittered wildly around him.

Suddenly, it all made sense. Quinton must have found the mirror in storage, discovered its ability to reflect her undamaged face, and kept it for her own. Given the king's ban on magic, she had hidden it in her wardrobe, eventually discovering its true purpose. And probably the dragons had remained in the pit because they didn't know they could escape. After all, they were mere babes in dragon years.

Trinya dropped to the ground beside Artoth, and the two nuzzled one another like old friends separated for days, not moments. They had clearly relied heavily on one another throughout their ordeal. "We're in the castle?" Collins guessed.

"The dungeon level." Zylas finally managed to heave the mirror onto Artoth's back. "Hold on tight, and try to look like you have control over your . . . mount." He settled onto the base of Artoth's neck, a leg dangling on either side.

Wondering how difficult Zylas found it to call his daughter a "mount," Collins scrambled to the same position on Trinya and found it far steadier than the one he previously held. It allowed him to balance more like the way he might on horseback, and he had the ability to clamp on tightly with his arms and knees, if necessary. He could even stay on upside down, though he hoped he would never have to test that theory.

The dragons walked across the floor, picking their way around the stacked furniture. Zylas reached across Artoth's neck to flip open the door onto another storage area. Unable to avoid the carefully piled provisions, the dragons bulled through crates, boxes, and bags with little attention to the carnage left in their wakes. Collins glanced to his left as Trinya's wing dislodged a bag of flour that immersed him in a billowing white cloud. Her tail sent a crate tumbling. It shattered, releasing a multicolored wash of buttons, ruffles, and lace. A shadow loomed over Collins, and he swiveled his head just in time to see a dangling cookpot headed for his face. He ducked, feeling it graze his dried, blood-and-sweat-plastered hair. Ahead of them, a door jerked open to reveal half a dozen startled guards and the familiar dungeon cells beyond them.

For a moment, no one did anything but stare.

Zylas broke the silence. "Move," he commanded the guards.

The guards shifted nervously, glancing at one another. Though they did not retreat, they showed no sign of attacking either.

Collins broke the stalemate with a pitiful roar, but the toddler dragon took the cue. Trinya mimicked him, the sound welling up from deep in her enormous diaphragm. Feeling her movement, Collins clamped his hands over his ears just in time. The roar belched out of her with the power of fire and brimstone, and terror crashed through Collins despite his foreknowledge of the power of a dragon's roar. The guards whirled and fled in a panicked scramble, opening the way for the dragons and their riders.

"Thank you," Zylas called after them as Collins managed a shaky laugh. He wondered if he could ever grow as accustomed to the sound as Zylas apparently had. Ialin fluttered up the steps, Artoth squeezing through the winding stairwell behind him.

Even with her wings tightly folded, Trinya struggled between the tightly packed banisters. At the ground level landing, they faced the open portcullis and the massive door to the inner courtyard.

Collins leaned toward the panel. "I'll get it."

Before he could snag the latch, Artoth's massive body slammed against the wood. The door shuddered wildly, and Collins scrambled out of the way. Again, the dragon crashed against it; and, this time, the wood shattered like a thin layer of ice. Wood shards sprayed the courtyard, people and animals ran screaming, and the dragon struggled into the air like a gangly, half-grown condor. Trinya flew after him, her wing beats slapping Collins with cold whirlwinds of air. Lying low, he clung to her neck and waited for one of the renegades' flying spies to find them and lead them to Prinivere.

Benton Collins awakened in a sudden rush of amazing clarity. His headache had disappeared, and the many injuries that had plagued him for the last hours he could remember seemed to have disappeared. He kept his eyes tightly closed, afraid that he would find himself back in Algary Hospital. He dreaded the barrage of questions that would certainly follow, the lies he would have to concoct to keep himself out of some mental institution, the even stranger looks the professors and other students would inflict upon him. *Oh. That Ben Collins.*

Gentle hands caressed his body, soothing the skin where they touched. He focused on this comfort, enjoying it as long as he dared, dodging the grilling that revealing his awakening might invoke.

You're up. The voice penetrated Collins' thoughts with a light sweetness that made it seem to float into his mind, bypassing his ears. Then, suddenly, he realized that was exactly what it had done. He was still in Barakhai.

Collins opened his eyes to another cave. Three massive dragon heads hovered over him, breath warm and sugary, their allspice dragon scent perfuming the air, their claws skipping lightly over his wounds. Zylas lay beside him, also prone, naked, and still in man form. Dirt peppered his snowy skin, and his pale blue eyes peeked out from fallen strands of white-blond hair. Prinivere instructed the younger two dragons in a wild barrage of mental communication that made little sense to Collins. The mirror portal stood against the wall at the farthest edge of Collins' vision.

Collins glanced at his watch, only to find spidery lines through the glass and a nonfunctioning display. Korfius trotted in frantic circles around them as a dog, which made it either before 3:00 P.M. or after 8:00 P.M.

Collins locked gazes with Zylas. "I see you got the portal."

"I suppose that's stealing," Zylas admitted, a red flush suffusing his cheeks. "But the king would only have destroyed it once he discovered—"

Collins cut off the explanation with a wave. "No justification necessary. I was just impressed that something so fragile made it here intact. I couldn't keep my eyes open long enough to bring us safely here, let alone an enormous, breakable knickknack."

Zylas tipped his head in a gesture that passed for a shrug. "You were hurt worse. And you're not a soldier." He grinned. "You got us through the worst of it. That roar of yours was inspired. How did you know she'd copy you?"

"Never met a toddler who didn't like to imitate loud noises." Collins smiled, hoping the dragons read his thoughts of appreciation through the confusion of their own conversation. He knew the others would already have thanked them, but he would do so personally when time allowed it. "Where's . . ." he started, preparing to ask about Falima. Then, not wanting to put one name above the others, he said instead, "the others?"

Zylas answered. "Ialin and Aisa are scouting, checking how our escape affected the castle. Apparently, King Terrin knew nothing about Carriequinton's sojourns in the caverns, nor that the dragons were still alive. Vernon's at home, where he's needed. Falima . . ." He swiveled his head. "Well, ask her yourself."

At that moment, Falima stepped into view. She wore a simple, plain dress that left him to imagine the exquisite curves that lay beneath it. Her sapphire eyes were swollen with tears and worry, her black hair wind-whipped to a snarl. She was the most beautiful woman in the world, and Collins found himself breathless.

Falima raised her brows. "You've got that hungry look again. And, this time, I'm not even naked."

Collins searched for his tongue, but it betrayed him, blurting out words he had not intended to say, "I love you, Falima."

She came toward him with natural grace. Her high cheekbones, golden skin, and spare lips became the very definition of perfection. She crouched to meet his gaze. "You said that already. Or did staring over the brink of death make you forget I love you, too?"

Now Collins wished he had saved the sentiment. There seemed no way to explain how his devotion had escalated to a heart-pounding fever complete with fireworks and the farthest reaches of heaven. "I've never loved anyone more."

Zylas cleared his throat, as if to remind the pair that they shared the room with others. "I'm devastated, Ben. I thought I was your one and only."

Collins barely heard him. "I want to be with you forever. Falima, I want you to marry me."

Falima slid between the two men and ruffled Collins' blood-matted hair. "Sweetie, there's still so much we don't know." She looked at the dragons hopefully. When she got no reply from Prinivere, she continued, "Can they lift the Curse? If they do, what becomes of us switchers?" She sighed heavily. "What if I'm a horse forever?"

Collins could not believe God would do that to him. He had finally found a woman he loved without conditions and a world that saw him as competent and capable, a place where he dared to become a hero, despite the risks. "Then I'll marry a horse. And love you just the same."

"You're an idiot," she said.

Collins agreed. "But at least I'd be *your* idiot."

Beyond Falima, Zylas rolled his eyes, shaking his head.

Prinivere finally joined the conversation. *Currently, the younglings don't switch forms. They'll stay dragons until their maturity level catches up with their human forms.*

Zylas sat up. "How long will that take?"

"Prinivere fell into silence for several moments, calculating. *I would guess about . . . three or four hundred.*

"Days?" Zylas supplied. "Weeks?"

"*Years.*"

"Wow." Zylas gave the exact same reply Collins would have. The albino would never see his daughter in her human form again, would never know how much she resembled himself or his beloved late wife. Still, he smiled, content. She had returned to him from the dead, and she remembered him.

Would you like to know my opinion?

Though Collins did not know which subject Prinivere meant to share her opinion on, he wanted to hear what she had to say on anything.

Falima nodded, and Zylas said, "Absolutely, my lady."

We don't yet have the ability to lift the Curse. The younglings need more experience, more maturity.

"How long?" Zylas spoke the words for all of them.

A century, at least. Longer if I'm not still here to help.

To Collins' surprise, no one objected to Prinivere's suggestion that she might not live long enough to assist in the project. The silence seemed awkward. It reminded him of how, at the end of every Christmas celebration, Great-Aunt Gertrude would say, "See you next year, God willing." They would always protest the possibility that she might not survive another year, even as her seventies became her eighties and old age finally claimed her. To say nothing felt like tacit condemnation, like giving death permission to remove her from the family.

Falima dropped her head.

Collins took her hand. "That doesn't change the way I feel about you. We'll deal with it."

"I can't go to your world."

"No," Collins confirmed.

"Do you love me enough to stay in mine?" Finally Falima raised her head to him, and Collins made certain to look right into her eyes.

"I do," he said without hesitation, without a trace of doubt. "But it's not really the life sentence you think it is. With Prinivere's help, I could go back occasionally, explain things to my parents, let them know I'm safe and happy." He smiled, squeezing her hand. "Bring back a Twinkie now and then."

Prinivere waited for them to finish before continuing. *There are modifications we can make now, until we can fully lift the Curse. We can create smaller magics that help switchers learn to control what they have: to increase the time* *spent in their preferred forms, to increase overlap, to allow those with strong overlap to control the switch itself so they can take whichever form they wish whenever they desire it.* *

Collins did not fully understand, but his companions bobbed their heads. "Are you saying you and the younglings could help Falima spend more time in human form? That you could give her enough overlap to understand me well even when she's a horse?"

"That's exactly what she's saying." Falima faced Collins and took his other hand. "And someone like Zylas, who has near-perfect overlap, could switch between rat form and human form at his own whim."

Collins looked at Zylas to determine how close Falima had come to the truth, only to find the albino standing utterly still, eyes wide, clearly considering the implications of her words.

Collins also found himself thinking about the possibilities. Controlled shapeshifting seemed more of a gift than a liability, even better than the royals' full-time humanity. *Cool!* He found himself wishing he had a switch-form. Collins considered another important detail, concerned for Korfius. "What happens to life span? To intelligence and memory?"

**I'm not sure.* Prinivere scratched behind one eye with a claw. *I can't remember if human and animal life spans differed much before the Curse. They both seemed pitifully short compared with mine.* She replaced her claw and fixed a craggy eye on Collins. *The intertwining of humans and animals has gone on so long in Barakhai, I don't think we can ever wholly separate what gets passed to future generations. And that's not a bad thing.* *

Collins had to agree. Mongrel dogs tended to live longer than the inbred species and to demonstrate higher intelligence. Carrie Quinton would have understood the details better than he could, but he suspected the genes of humans and animals in Barakhai probably had become inseparable.

Prinivere finished her point, *Lifting the Curse can't change history or "blood." I believe the natural life spans of all creatures of Barakhai will remain reasonably equal, in the realm of a hundred years, at least for the next several centuries. Longer for those with dragon blood.* * She glanced at

Zylas. *As to intelligence . . .* She flicked a claw. * . . . I think the same applies. It varies widely enough already.*

Collins had to agree.

Prinivere grinned and sent him a happy image of powder-blue sky speckled with clouds, filled with swooping dragon shadows.

Collins smiled at the joy the rescue he had assisted in brought to the old dragon as well as to the regular citizenry of Barakhai. Through Trinya and Artoth, a new generation of dragons might return to Barakhai as well.

And, if I might venture one more opinion, you should accept that proposal.

It took Collins inordinately long to figure out what Prinivere meant.

"Yes," Falima said, the word coming out of nowhere.

Collins blinked. "What?"

"Yes," Falima said. "I'll marry you."

Thank you, Collins thought in Prinivere's direction. Not long ago, he had believed himself too young for marriage, but now the idea filled him with an excitement that seemed eternal. He caught Falima into a gleeful embrace, and Korfius shoved in to shower the announcement with happy dog kisses.

Epilogue

IN Vernon's cottage in the middle of the Barakhai woodlands, Benton Collins slouched in a hard log chair
watching Korfius wrestle with the puppy he now knew as
Farrihn. The two rolled and yipped across the floor under
the watchful eye of the puppy's father, Ralthoroh, now in
a human form that little resembled the huge, pointy-eared
furball Collins had encountered in the carnivore caverns.
Falima explained the intricacies of furniture to the too-
skinny girl while Mataia, the tortoise, cruised around the
confines, exploring every object. Vernon ran a hand
through his tight black curls, studying a Wendy's fried potato pinched between his fingers. "What do you call these
things again?"

"French fries." Though Collins addressed Vernon, he
kept his gaze on Falima, thrilled by every confident movement, every casual toss of her ebony hair. "Though I'm not
sure why. They aren't any more French than Canadian bacon is Canadian." He added with sudden realization, "Or
even bacon."

Vernon's long silence finally drew Collins' attention. He
turned to find the enormous black man staring at him, thick
brows arched. "You do know you're speaking gibberish,
don't you?"

Collins could understand why none of his tangential jab-
bering would translate. "Yeah, I know. I've got to do something every once in a while to remind you I'm a foreigner."

"You mean in case your weird clothes and your weird food and the weird little devices you bring back with you aren't enough?"

"Exactly."

Vernon popped the fry into his mouth, chewing thoughtfully. Having exhausted his conversation with Collins for the moment, he addressed Falima. "I heard you got offered a guard position at the castle."

Falima raised her head, hands on the rope pulls of Vernon's dresser. Crouched beside her, Skinny Girl continued to examine the cupboard. "I'm not taking it."

The last Collins knew, his fiancée was still considering the offer. "Why not?"

Falima ruffled the other woman's tawny hair. "The cavern people need someone to help them adjust to civilization. I'd rather do that, at least for now." She turned back to the dresser. "Besides, if I'm going to preach that people no longer have to pursue careers prearranged by their animal form, I should set an example."

Though it bothered Collins that Falima had not consulted him before making her final decision, he found some solace in the realization that she had helped him make an equally difficult choice. "If we're not living on the castle grounds, I guess I can't take that job as adviser to the king." He shrugged. "The thought of following in Carrie Quinton's footsteps creeped me out anyway."

Falima rose and approached Collins, Skinny Girl following her every movement with worried eyes. "Sweetie, I can do my work anywhere. Just because I'm not a guard doesn't mean we can't live in Opernes Castle." She put her hands on the back of his chair and kissed the top of his head. "You don't have to walk the same path as Carriequinton just because you hold the same title."

Vernon added his piece, "Barakhai could really use someone like you to help keep the king on the moral path." He winked at Falima. "Besides, you could socialize with the new captain of security. I hear he's well qualified for the job, despite being . . . vermin."

Vermin? No way. Not—

Falima gasped, completing his thought aloud. "Zylas? Zylas is King Terrin's new captain of security?"

"Can you think of anyone better suited to fill the post?"

Collins doubted the king of Barakhai could find anyone as capable as the man who had dedicated his life to bringing together the most diverse people in the world, to gaining, winning, and keeping their loyalty and respect. That Zylas could speak every language, including those of animals, and mutated into a rat at will, would only sweeten the deal. Collins believed Terrin wise enough to understand the enormous asset he had obtained and that he could count on the rebels to support him so long as he followed the advice of his new captain. *A monarchy kept strong by alliances instead of magical physical advantage.* "Better suited than Zylas?" He shook his head with such vigor, it tousled his hair into knots. "Not on any world."